Victoria Line, Central Line

Silver Wedding

Maeve Binchy

Maeve Binchy was born in Co. Dublin and was educated at Holy Child Convent in Killiney and at UCD. After a spell as a teacher in various girls' schools, she joined the *Irish Times*. Her first novel, *Light a Penny Candle*, was published in 1982, and since then she has written more than a dozen novels and short story collections, each of them bestsellers. Several have been adapted for cinema and television, most notably *Circle of Friends* in 1995. She was awarded the Lifetime Achievement Award at the British Book Awards in 1999. She is married to the writer and broadcaster Gordon Snell.

By the same author

Circle of Friends
Copper Beech
Dublin 4
Echoes
Evening Class
Firefly Summer
Glass Lake
Light a Penny Candle
The Lilac Bus
Tara Road
Scarlet Feather

Victoria Line, Central Line

Maeve Binchy

First published by Arrow Books for WH Smith plc in 2001

This novel is a work of fiction. Names and characters are the product of the author's imagination and any resemblance to actual persons, living or dead, is entirely coincidental

Victoria Line Central Line first published in Great Britain in 1978 and 1980 by Quartet Books and Ward River Press Ltd as two volumes. They appeared together as part of a hardback edition entitled *London Transport*

Silver Wedding first published in Great Britain by Century in 1988

Arrow Books
The Random House Group Limited
20 Vauxhall Bridge Road, London SW1V 2SA

The Random House Group Limited Reg. No. 954009

WH Smith plc
Greenbridge Road, Swindon SN3 3LD

www.whsmith.co.uk

A CIP catalogue record for this book is available from the British Library

Papers used by WH Smith are natural, recyclable products made from wood grown in sustainable forests. The manufacturing processes conform to the environmental regulations of the country of origin

ISBN 0 09 943587 X

Printed and bound in Great Britain by
Cox & Wyman Ltd, Reading, Berkshire

CONTENTS

Victoria Line

Central Line

To Gordon with all my love

VICTORIA LINE

Tottenham Hale

Amy watched six taxis avoid her and go deliberately towards other people. Then she began to realise she was suffering from advanced paranoia and that she had better cut her losses and take the tube home. She was already so late and angry, that the lurching crowded journey couldn't make her much worse. And there was the danger that if she stood much longer on the side of the street being ignored by rush hour taxi drivers she might lose her small remaining ration of sanity. And she needed to hold on to what she had for tonight.

Tonight Ed's sister and her husband were coming to dinner. Tonight, for the first time, she would meet the Big Mama figure in Ed's American family, the one they all bowed to, the one Ed had practically written to for permission to marry Amy. At the time Amy had thought it funny; she had even suggested that her dental reports and photostats of her GCE certificates be sent to New York. But three years later, after a period of watching Ed write his monthly letter to his big sister Bella, she found it less funny. She was never shown these letters and in pique she had opened one before posting it. It was an infantile report on how their life had been progressing since last month: childish details about the floor covering they had bought for the kitchen, aspirations that Ed's salary would be reviewed and upped. Praise for a new dress that Amy had bought, minutiae about a picnic they had had with another couple. It had made Amy uneasy, because it had made Ed seem retarded. It was the kind of letter that a mother might expect from a small son who had gone off to summer camp, not something that a sister in far away America should need or want.

Ed had been euphoric about the visit. It had been planned for over three months. Bella and her husband Blair were coming to London for three days as part of a European tour. They would arrive in the morning; they did not want to be met, they preferred to recover from their jet lag alone in the privacy of a good hotel with a comfortable bedroom and bathroom. Fully refreshed, at seven p.m. they would come and see their beloved Ed and welcome their new sister Amy to the family. Next day there would be a tour to Windsor and an evening at the theatre, with a dinner for the four of them; and on the Saturday morning, Amy might kindly take her new sister Bella shopping, and point out the best places, introduce her to the heads of departments in the better stores. They would have a super girly lunch, and then Bella and Blair would fly out of their lives to Paris.

Normally, on any ordinary Thursday, Amy came home from Harley Street, where she worked as a doctor's receptionist, took off her shoes, put on her slippers, unpacked her shopping, organised a meal, lit the fire and then Ed would arrive home. Their evenings had begun to have a regular pattern. Ed came home tense and tired. Little by little, in front of the fire, he would unwind; little by little he relaxed his grip on the file of papers he had brought back from the office. He would have a sherry, his face would lose its lines; and then he would agree really that there was no point in trying to do too much work in the evening.

With a glass of wine, he would say that the Labourer was worthy of his Hire, and he would expand about people being entitled to their leisure. And afterwards, he would carve away happily at the table he was making, or watch television, or do the crossword with Amy; and she realised happily that she was essential to him, because only her kind of understanding could make him uncoil and regard his life as a happy, unworrying thing.

That was all before the threatened visit of Bella.

For three months now, he hadn't been able to relax. No matter how many blandishments and encouragements Amy put in his way, he seemed stressed and anxious. He was anxious on all fronts: Bella would think it strange that he hadn't moved out of sales into middle management before this; he must show Bella what the structure of the company was, he must prove to her that he had done as much home work and extra work as he could possibly do. Every night his briefcase bulged with sheets of incomprehensible figures. But this wasn't all. He couldn't even concentrate on the office work, he would jump up and spot some defect in the house.

'Heavens, Amy, that curtain rail is missing three hooks, can you fix it darling? Please.'

Sometimes he said: 'Before Bella comes', sometimes he didn't. He didn't even need to, really. Amy knew.

The phone mouthpiece was dirty, the bath-mat had got worn-looking, the window boxes needed repainting, the carving dish had one of its feet twisted the wrong way, the ice trays in the refrigerator were both cracked.

About a dozen times, Amy had reacted and explained that Bella was not coming on a mission of inspection; she hadn't flown the Atlantic to check the curtains, the telephone or the ice trays, she had come to see Ed. But his face just became more worried and he said that he would like things to be right.

So right was everything, that Amy was almost a nervous wreck. The house had been polished within an inch of its life. A magnificent casserole was waiting to be reheated, good wine had been chosen, the table had been set before she left the house that morning. If Bella were to go through the house with a fleet of police specially trained in house-searches, nothing damaging could be revealed. No hidden mounds of rubbish or unsorted paraphernalia in any cupboard. If Bella decided to pull back the sitting-room carpet and examine the underlay she would not be able to find fault.

Magazines and newspapers praising the excellence of this part of North London had been laid around strategically, so that Bella's gaze could be diverted to them should she disapprove of the suburb where Ed and Amy lived. They had even alerted one set of neighbours of the possibility that they might take Bella and Blair over for a drink if they wanted to say 'Hi' to some local people.

Amy had asked for the afternoon off, and she had spent it at the beautician's. She had suggested it herself and Ed's kind, worried face had lit up.

'It's not that you don't look lovely already, Amy,' he had said, afraid to offend her. 'It's just that . . . well, you know, I told Bella you were so groomed, and you know the photographs we send . . . well, we always send ones that make us look good.'

Bella was no oil painting, Amy often thought in rage. She was downright plain; she was tall and rather severe. Her clothes in the pictures that Ed had shown her – photographs taken some years back – had been simple and neat with no concession to fashion. Why, then, had Ed spent nights deliberating over Amy's wardrobe and planning what she should wear? Bella was a teacher, and Blair had some unspecified job in the same school, administration Ed thought, but he didn't really give it any time. None of the family gave Blair any time, he was good to Bella as a consort. He was mute and supportive. That was all that was needed. Bella's four younger brothers owed her everything. They would never have gone through school if she hadn't urged them; they wouldn't have got good jobs, and married suitable women without her wise influence; they would be nothings, hopeless orphans, rudderless, had not Bella persuaded the authorities to let her play Mama at the age of fifteen. Ed had only been five then, he couldn't even remember the mother and father who went into a lake in a drunken motor-accident.

Sometimes Amy wondered about the other sisters-in-law. Wasn't it odd that the sons had all gone so far afield from beloved Bella? There was a brother who had gone to California – that was about as far as you could get from New York State; and one was in Vancouver, and one in Mexico, and Ed was in London. Amy suspected that her three sisters-in-law and she would get along famously. She felt sure they were united in a common hatred of Bella and what she was doing to their men.

But no hint of this escaped in any of the family letters, all of which seemed to be full of Bella. When she had been in bed for three weeks with influenza, letters posted in San José, Vancouver and Mexico City had crashed on to the mat in Tottenham Hale giving the latest bulletins. The three brothers had written to Ed in terms of congratulation and encouragement once the visit of Bella to England had been announced. Bella's own letters were short and terse, and offered little news of her own life, only praise or enquiry about the life of the recipient. The more Amy thought about her, the more she became convinced that Bella was mad.

Now, beautifully coiffed, elegantly made-up, manicured, massaged at a cost which left her seething with rage, Amy stood on the platform waiting for the train to take her home to meet this monster. She got a couple of admiring looks which pleased her; a student pinched her bottom hard, which hurt her and annoyed her; but with confidence gained from parting with the huge sum of money to the beauty salon she said clearly and loudly, 'Please don't do that again,' and everybody looked at the student who went scarlet and got out at the next station. Two men congratulated her and she felt pleased that she was becoming mature.

She worked out that she would have two hours at home before the dreaded Bella arrived. That would be time to do the final fixing of the meal, have a bath and dress. Ed had taken the afternoon off and he was going to have arranged fresh flowers and done any last minute things.

'Won't she think it strange that you took time off work to do housework?' asked Amy.

'If she doesn't ask, we mightn't have to tell her,' he said, giggling like a schoolboy.

Amy told herself firmly that she was not a criminal, she hadn't kidnapped Ed, she had loved him and married him. She looked after him well by any standards, she encouraged him when he felt down but she didn't push him on to impossible heights. This appalling Bella couldn't fault her on her performance, surely? And if that was all true, which it undoubtedly was, then why did she feel so apprehensive? The train gave a great lurch which flung all those still standing into each other's arms. Carefully, they disentangled themselves, with little laughs and apologies; and it was a few moments before they realised that the train had actually stopped and they were not at a station.

'That's all we need,' said a florid-looking man with a briefcase. 'Told the wife I'd be home early, and now we're going to be stuck here all night.'

'Surely not?' asked a woman who looked tired and miserable. She was carrying a heavy bag of shopping. 'There'll be nobody to let the children in,' she added in a worried tone.

Amy began to realize the situation. Every minute here was a minute less in the elaborate count-down for Bella's arrival. If they were fifteen minutes delayed, then she might have to go without a bath. If they were half-an-hour delayed she might have to lose bath, and decorating the trifle. Her mind couldn't take in anything longer than half-an-hour's delay.

Very soon, a uniformed man came through the carriage assuring them that there was no danger, no crisis, but that there had been a fault which must be corrected, and that London Transport apologised infinitely but there would be a delay.

No, he didn't know how long the delay would be.

Yes, he could assure them that there would be no danger.

No, there was no possibility of another train running into them.

Yes, he understood that it was a great inconvenience.

No. There was no way of doing anything more quickly than it was already being done.

Yes, people would be electrocuted and die if they stepped out on to the rails.

'That would appear to be that,' said the florid man. He looked at Amy appreciatively. 'I suppose if we are to be marooned, I'm to be congratulated on finding such an elegant shipmate. I'm Gerald Brent by the way.'

'I'm Amy Baker,' said Amy smiling.

'Mrs Baker, would you care to have a drink with me?' said Gerald Brent. He took a bottle of wine out of his briefcase, a penknife with a corkscrew attachment, and the top of his vacuum flask.

Laughing, Amy accepted.

'I'll drink from the other side,' said Gerald.

The well-known patience and docility of Londoners was beginning to be evident around the compartment. People were settling down to read the *Standard* and the *News*; one man was even having a little sleep of sorts; the worried woman had taken out a woman's magazine and resigned herself.

'Wife's mother is coming to dinner,' said Gerald. 'Terrible old bat. I'm not sorry to miss her, really. Anyway, this wine is much too good for her. Have another drop.'

Amy took the refill and looked at him to see if he was joking.

'You don't really think we'll miss dinner, do you?' she asked.

'Bound to,' said Gerald. He explained what must have gone wrong on the line, how a safety mechanism had worked properly but it would mean that it now had to be rewound by hand. They would have to bring personnel into the tunnel to do this.

'Three or four hours, at least,' he said.

It just wasn't possible, that in the whole of London, one tube line should have a mechanical failure, and she should be on it. It was simply beyond belief that this should happen on this one day out of the thousand or so days she had been married to Ed. It was quite inconceivable that Bella, the big black shadow over all their lives, was going to become like a mushroom cloud of menace and disappointment ever more. Ed would never recover from it. The evening would be a shambles, he would run out into the street looking for her. He might believe that she had left him as some kind of protest about Bella. Amy felt a wave of nausea at the horror of her situation, her face whitened and she looked as if she was going to fall.

'Steady,' said Gerald. 'You mustn't rush that wine, it's very good, full bodied, rich. Here. Sit on this corner.' He moved her to the corner of someone's seat. A London mateyness had now begun to develop and people who would have travelled unspeaking for years became animated and friendly through shared disaster.

Amy told Gerald all about Bella: she told him about opening the letter, she told him that Bella had strong-armed all her brothers into a forced, humble, gratitude. As she told him, it became even clearer to her just how destructive Bella had been; and how in Vancouver, San José and Mexico City, as well as London, four normal men were working like nervous beavers to thank this woman for giving up her youth to rear them. While in fact, Amy realised suddenly, all that Bella had done was give full vent to normal maternal instincts, and got in return praise from authorities and social services. From four brothers she had got a slavish devotion.

Amy and Gerald finished the bottle of wine. Gerald muttered an occasional word of encouragement, and, whenever Amy began to panic at the thought of the ruined evening, he offered reassurance.

'Nonsense, of course he'll know where you are. They'll have it on the local news.'

'Heavens, girl, relax, he'll ring the station, they'll tell him.'

'Good God, woman, Bella doesn't expect you to get a pickaxe and hack your way out!'

He told her that his wife thought he drank too much, and that he did. He had once had an affair with his secretary, which his wife had never discovered, or he *thought* she'd never discovered; but he hadn't enjoyed the intrigue side of it, so he ended it, and his secretary called him a chauvinist bastard in front of three senior partners in the firm. It had been very distressing.

Coffee and sandwiches were brought in from the next station and a real party atmosphere began to develop. There was even a sing-song and by the time they did get out at ten p.m. to the flashing of photographers' light-bulbs and the attention of waiting crowds, Amy was quite unconcerned about Bella and the whole, ruined evening.

It was with a shock that she recognized Bella's features on the platform. Peering into the crowds emerging from the train she looked worried, and anxious for Amy's safety. Behind her were a worried Ed and a worried Blair.

'There she is,' cried Bella running forward, arms out. 'Amy, my little sister, are you all right? Are you hurt? Have you been looked after? My poor Amy, what an ordeal, what a catastrophe, for you!' She released her to let Ed hug her, and Blair hold her in a manful, silent grip.

Gerald watched the scene, and raised his hat before going on his way with a quizzical laugh.

Together the four of them went out of the station. Bella didn't look severe or plain, she looked aglow with interest and concern. She had telephoned the police four times, she had made sure that the train had been in no danger, she had taken first aid things to the station just in case. But now how wonderful, it had all ended happily and they were on the way back to Ed and Amy's lovely home. It had looked so really beautiful when she had arrived, those really cute window boxes, and my, how nice Amy sure kept everything, when she had to telephone she noticed just how fresh and dainty the whole house was. Well now, they could all go back and have that really delicious-looking dinner that she knew was there.

Blair smiled a great stalwart and supportive smile. And Ed looked like a child who got the candy; and Amy wondered why she could have resented Bella coming, she was so pleased that she was here. And even more pleased that she liked everything. Now, Amy would really go out of her way to give her a good shopping trip on the Saturday morning After all, the only important thing was to please Bella.

Seven Sisters

It was very odd that they should live in Seven Sisters, Pat thought for the hundredth time. It seemed too much of a coincidence that anyone who was giving a wife-swapping party, with uninhibited fun and carefree swinging for sophisticated couples, should just happen to live in a place with the group name of Seven Sisters. She had said so to Stuart as well.

'They have to live somewhere,' he said unhelpfully.

Pat had studied the *A to Z*.

'I don't really see why they call it Seven Sisters, it's more Hornsey really,' she complained.

'If they'd called it Hornsey you'd probably say that that was even more suggestive,' said Stuart mildly.

For two weeks before the party, Pat lived on a high level of anxiety. She examined her new set of underwear with a worried frown. It was red and black, the black bits were lace and, in one instance, a rosette. Again and again she tried them on in the bathroom and examined herself critically in the mirror. She looked so very white, and the dark colours made her look almost dead. She wondered whether this would fire all the men with lust, whether they would be driven insane by the combination of dead white skin, red silk and black lace, or whether one of the women would take her aside and advise her to use a fake tan lotion. The awful thing was that there was no one to ask. Even if she were to write to this appalling magazine where Stuart had first seen the article about wife-swapping and had replied to one of the box numbers, she still wouldn't get a reply in time.

Over and over she rehearsed what she would say: 'Hallo, *lovely* of you to ask us . . . what a super house.' No, she couldn't tell this terrifying harlot who owned the house in Seven Sisters that it was lovely of her to have invited Pat and Stuart, since Pat and Stuart had in their corrupt and pleasure-seeking way told the Seven Sisters lot that they wanted to come and take off their clothes to go to bed with a load of strangers. The more she reminded herself that this is what they had arranged to do, the more faint and foolish she felt.

Even though she tried to put it from her mind, she wondered if there would be time for any conversation before they got down to action. Would she find herself stark naked in a corner talking to some other naked housewife about the children's drama group or the new supermarket? Would Stuart stand naked laughing with new people about the tomatoes they grew in their allotment?

That was the kind of thing that happened at the ordinary parties they went to . . . tame little evenings where people kept their clothes on, and didn't mate with each other, and discussed how expensive the season tickets on the train had become, and how hard it was to find a doctor who could spend two minutes listening to you. Tame evenings, dull evenings. Getting in a rut, becoming old before their time, suburban even though they hadn't yet reached their middle-class suburbia, no excitement, nothing very different, nothing that made them gasp.

Two children, the national average, Stuart working in a bank . . .

God Almighty! – Suppose some of the bank's clients were at the party! It wasn't so ridiculous. People don't live beside their banks, some of them could easily live off the Seven Sisters Road. Had Stuart thought of that? She had better tell him, they could call it all off. It would be foolish to imperil his whole career . . . No. He must have thought of it. He was utterly set on going to this party now. He would only think she was groping around for some excuse.

. . . nice little flat, no garden unfortunately, but then they went to the allotment at weekends. Children very strong and happy, love their school. Debbie in the school play again this term, and Danny hoping to be picked for the third team. Lots of friends at school always running in and out of the neighbours' houses too and playing in the adventure playground at the end of the road. Not an earth-shaking life, but a happy one . . . even the school Principal had said the other day . . .

Sweet God! – Suppose the school ever got to hear of this! How utterly shaming for Debbie and Danny to be branded the children of perverts, sexual freaks. They might even be asked to leave lest their family shame might taint the other children. Relax. How could the school hear of it, unless other parents, or indeed some of the staff, were there being uninhibited and swinging in sophisticated adult fun? . . . Yes, of course, if anyone was there, a conspiracy of silence would have to be maintained.

. . . anyway the school Principal had said that he had enormous admiration for the parents of today, since they made so many sacrifices for their children and were so supportive and aware of all their needs. But he felt sure that this effort was repaid in a thousand ways by the fact that they lived in a peaceful community, far away from the wars and tensions and differences that rend other countries.

Stuart had said that people who went to these parties were normal, ordinary, good, respectable citizens like everyone else. He said that all they were doing was trying to push forward the frontiers of pleasure. They were trying to add to the delights of normal sexual love between a married couple . . . and be less selfish about it . . . by offering to share that love with other married couples. He had read, and he believed that there was a lot of truth in it, that this kind of generosity, this giving of your rights in your partner to other friends, was an act of love in itself. And, even more important in these treacherous days, it completely by-passed the need to be 'unfaithful' to the other partner – there would be no forbidden lovers, or illicit affairs. It would all be out in the open. It would be healthy and good.

Stuart talked about it with the enthusiasm he had when he first talked about his allotment. His eyes had that gleam that they once had when he had planned a life of self-sufficiency. The rest of London might starve, might poison itself with nuclear fall-out, but Stuart and Pat and Debbie and Danny would grow what they needed for survival on their little allotment, and, aha, who'd laugh then? Pat had asked mildly how Stuart would protect his runner beans and cabbages against twelve million starving Londoners, if they were the only family which had managed to be self-sufficient. Stuart had said it was a technicality.

The Saturday and Sunday gardening continued, it had lost its first flush of real excitement, but nowadays it brought them a gentle pleasure. Perhaps this would happen with wife-swapping too, Pat thought. Soon the heady excitement and flush of enthusiasm would pass, and they would settle into a weekly wife-swap happily and resignedly travelling to Seven Sisters, or Barking, or Rickmansworth, or Biggin Hill.

Stuart seemed so alarmingly calm about it all. This as much as anything disturbed Pat. She had asked him, did he think he should get new jockey-shorts.

'No, love, I've plenty up in the wardrobe,' he had said mystified.

'For the *party*,' she had hissed.

'Why should I need new jockey-shorts?' he had asked, as puzzled as if she had said he should buy a new transistor radio. 'I have nine pairs upstairs. I tell you, I have plenty.'

As the event drew nearer, Pat worried more about Stuart. Did he have no nerves, no feelings, that he could take it all so calmly . . . the fact that he had written to a box number and a woman with a voice like a circular saw had telephoned?

She had never given too much thought to their sex life. It had always seemed very pleasant and adequate, and she certainly didn't regard herself as frigid, not in the sense of the women's magazine articles on the topic. She couldn't remember saying that she had a headache, or that she didn't feel like it. There was, she supposed, a sort of sameness about it. But then, for heaven's sake, some things *are* the same. The taste of a bar of chocolate or a gin and lime is always the same. The sound of Beethoven's Fifth or Johnny Mathis is always the same. Why this great urge for something different?

Pat was hurt and puzzled. She had read about women who discovered that their meek and conventional husbands actually liked bondage or violent pornography . . . so perhaps she should feel relieved that Stuart had suggested only nice old middle-class wife swapping. Still, Pat felt aggrieved. If she were prepared to live for the rest of their days with their life as it was now, saving for the house, going on a caravan holiday once a year, and making love comfortably in the darkness and privacy of their own room twice a week, then it was somehow ungrateful of Stuart not to feel the same about it.

Pat had an appointment with the hairdresser on the afternoon of the Terrible Day.

'Going somewhere nice?' asked the hairdresser in her bright, routine way.

'Eer . . . yes,' said Pat.

'Oh, to a function is it?' asked the hairdresser.

'Um. No, no. Not a function. Private house. Old friends, and new friends. A party. An ordinary party,' Pat screamed defensively.

The hairdresser shrugged.

'Very nice, I'm sure,' she said huffily.

The baby-sitter arrived on time. Pat had hoped that she might ring and say she couldn't come. That would mean the end of this ludicrous outing across London to copulate with strangers. The only tingles of excitement she felt were the ones which ran through her brain asking her if she were certifiably insane.

Debbie and Danny barely looked up from the television.

'Goodnight, Mum. Goodnight, Dad. Come in and see us when you get back.'

Pat's eyes filled with tears.

'Stuart love . . .' she began.

'Goodnight, you lot.' Stuart said firmly.

She had assumed that they would take the car and was startled when Stuart said that it was much simpler than driving to take the tube.

'Only one change,' he said. And to Pat the words seemed sinister and fraught with meaning. She wondered if he was saying that they would only swap with one couple when they got there. She felt nausea rise in her throat. Suppose it were like a dance in the tennis club years ago, when nobody asked you to dance and you ended up grateful for some awful person who eventually did suggest a shuffle around the floor. Could this happen tonight? Suppose some appalling, foul couple rejected by everyone else nodded encouragingly at them? Would they have to say yes? Did the house rules say that there was no opting out?

'Yes, but wouldn't it be nice to have the car coming home?' she asked.

'Mightn't feel like driving on the way back,' said Stuart succinctly.

Worn out with pleasure? Exhausted? Asleep on some strange other wife's bosom? Going home with someone else? Staying with the awful woman in Seven Sisters? What could he mean, he mightn't feel like driving? The whole nightmare was now quite frightening. Why had she ever agreed to this wicked, and silly thing? Why had Stuart ever suggested it?

The tube came immediately, as trains always do when you are going to the dentist or a wife-swapping party. The stations flashed by. Stuart read the back of someone else's evening paper. Pat examined her face three times in her compact mirror.

'You look fine,' Stuart said to her when she got the compact out a fourth time.

'I suppose you're right. Anyway, it's not my face they'll be looking at,' she said resignedly.

'What? Oh. Oh yes,' said Stuart smiling supportively, and going back to reading the late football results.

'Do you think we'll take off our clothes immediately?' Pat asked wretchedly as they walked out of the station and towards the house.

'I don't know, I expect it depends on whether they have central heating,' Stuart said matter of factly.

Pat looked at him as if he were a total stranger.

'Did she give you any indication of how many people were going to be there?' Pat asked shrilly after another minute of walking. 'I mean, they're not very big houses. They can hardly have dozens.'

'No, she said just a few friends,' said Stuart. 'A few friends, she didn't say how many.'

'But we're not friends, we're sort of intruding on them in a way aren't we?' she begged. There were tears in her eyes. They were only one corner away from the house now. Right-turn that and they were in the road and there was no going back.

Stuart looked at her, moved by the tears he could hear in her voice.

'It'll be lovely, Pat dear. You'll love it. You're always a bit nervous at times like this.'

She looked at him, her eyes flashing.

'What do you mean at times like this? What "times like this" have there been before? When have we done anything remotely like this. It's the only time like this . . .' To her horror, she burst into tears.

Stuart looked very distressed. He tried to touch her, to put his arm around her, but Pat pushed him away.

'No, stop saying it's all right, and that I'll love it. I'll hate it. I'm not going. That's final.'

'Well why didn't you say this before? Why did you wait until we're nearly there?' Stuart asked, his innocent, round face looking both foolish and puzzled at the same time. 'I can't understand why you didn't say to me that you thought it wasn't on, then we'd never have set it all up. I thought you wanted to come too.'

Pat gave a snort into her tissues.

'You *said* it sounded an adventurous thing . . .' he said.

Pat coughed loudly.

'You *said* we'd try it once and if we didn't like it we'd have got it out of our system,' he went on.

Pat blew her nose.

'Why, love? Why have you changed your mind now? Just tell me. We'll do whatever you want to. We won't go if you really hate the idea. Just tell me.'

Pat looked at him through her red eyes. His face was indeed very round and innocent. She wondered that she had never noticed that before. He was simply another disappointed young bank clerk. Another man in a deadend job, with an average wife, a few drinks on a Saturday, two nice, but time-consuming and money-swallowing children, a car that needed a lot of money spent on it, or else needed to be replaced. They had a loan of a caravan each year, but he would never feel the sands of the West Indies or the Seychelles between his toes.

She began to speak and then stopped. She must be

very careful now. It was as if he had been a negative, and now somebody had shown her the developed print. She could see all the frustrations, the hours of commuting, the thickening of his waist. Those things were far from the James Bond or Wild West books he read for a half-hour before he went to sleep each night.

A surge of understanding went out from her. He just needed some excitement, something out of the ordinary, some proof that he wasn't a mouse, that he was going to do something daring in his life before he grew old and retired and walked with a stick and crumpled and died.

Quite calmly she looked at him and said:

'I'm jealous. That's it. That's the truth.'

'You're what?' he said.

'I don't want them, to have you, to see you. I don't want those girls to . . . you know, make free with you. I'd be very jealous. I love you. I don't want them loving you.'

'But Pat,' he said desperately. 'We've been through all this; it's got nothing to do with love. It's got to do with swapping. It's got to do with excitement, and frontiers . . . and not doing the same things always . . . till the end of our days.'

She had been right. She resolved that she would do everything her feeble imagination and some sex manuals could dream up if only they got home unscathed from Seven Sisters.

'You're too great,' she said hesitantly. They didn't use flowery endearments, they never paid each other extravagant compliments. It was hard to begin on a street in the middle of the evening in North London on the way to a wife-swapping orgy. But people have to begin somewhere.

'You're too . . . important. Too precious, and exciting. I love it when we . . . er . . . screw. I don't want other women to share it. It's my . . . er, pleasure.'

'Do you love it?' he asked innocently.

'Oh I do,' she closed her eyes, a sigh of genuine

pleasure that she might in fact be going to win escaped her, and it sounded like genuine desire.

'I didn't think you minded all that much one way or another,' he said.

'If you knew how I do,' she said. And then firmly, 'But I wouldn't feel at all the same if you let all these women crawl over you . . .'

She paused. It was a calculated risk. In fact she had given little thought to Stuart's part in the whole sorry business, she had been obsessed with her own role. But she thought that to say this would have been to confirm Stuart in thinking that he had married parochial, puritan riff-raff and that his excitement would be between the covers of books for the rest of his days.

'I often . . . er . . . get panicky in case some of the women who come into the bank might . . . er, proposition you,' she said.

Stuart looked at her.

'There's no need to worry like that. That's kind of paranoid that jealousy,' he said soothingly. 'I've always been faithful to you. Even this business tonight is *with* you.'

'I don't want to share you with them,' she said. 'I'm not going to. They've got lousy old husbands, awful fellows. I've got you. Why should I be so generous?'

He paused. He looked up the road, he looked down the road. Her eyes never left his face. Down the road won.

'Suppose we got a couple of kebabs . . .'

'And a bottle of wine.'

As they turned to go back to the station, a middle-aged couple stopped in a car to ask them where the Road was.

Pat asked them what number they wanted.

As she had suspected, it was number 17.

'Have fun,' she said as she gave them directions, and she and Stuart dissolved in laughter.

'They were a bit old,' said Stuart. 'Do you think it would have been very sordid and sort of pathetic?'

Pat wasn't going to let him think that.

'No there were probably fabulous birds there. Anyway, older ones are more passionate. She'd probably have had you pinned to the hearth rug the moment we got in the door.'

Under a street lamp, she thought his face looked a bit foolish. As if he had seen how tatty and grubby it might all have been. He was very gentle. In a great wave of affection she realised that indeed she would not have liked sharing him with anyone, and that an evening in bed with a bottle of wine, and a nice spicy donar kebab and all that black and red underwear might be the most exciting kind of thing that she had experienced for some time as well.

Women are so much more sensible about sex, she thought cheerfully as Stuart bought the tickets home. She had forgotten the weeks of anxiety, the endless examinations in the mirror, the ceaseless fears lest anyone should discover. Heady with relief she even allowed herself the indulgence of imagining what that elderly woman in the car might look like naked, and she smiled at Stuart who looked like a tiger now that his wife was too rabidly jealous to allow him to indulge in the wife-swapping party to which they had been invited. Horizons had been broadened without anyone having to do anything.

Finsbury Park

Vera hated to see television plays about poverty. She even disliked seeing working-class women, babies in their arms, hair in rollers, explaining some social problem to a concerned television reporter. It reminded her too much of her youth. In those shuffling, whiney women she could see her mother, cigarette always hanging from the corner of her mouth, cardigan held together with a safety pin, the door of the flat never closed since people were always coming in and out, the place smelling of clothes drying . . . clothes that had not been properly washed so it was really dirty clothes drying.

Vera hated to hear women laugh loudly, they reminded her of her mother and her elder sister, cackling away when things were at their worst, cheering each other up with bottles of ginger wine and announcing that they would be dead long enough. Vera never liked to think of anything that reminded her about life as it was lived before she was fifteen.

On her fifteenth birthday she was taken to the hospital with rheumatic fever, and during the long weeks there she got to know Miss Andrews, the gentle school teacher in the next bed who changed her life.

'Ask them to bring you lavender water not sweets.'

'Ask your school friends for hand cream not comics.'

'I'll choose some nice books for you from the library.'

'We'll tell the social worker you'd like a hairdo to cheer you up. . .'

The Vera who came out of hospital was slimmer and attractive looking. And she had changed inside too. Miss

Andrews had taught her a very important lesson – even awful things and unhappy times can have their uses, they can be a kind of apprenticeship. Vera must stay at school, she must pass some kind of exams even if school was hell and home was worse than hell.

She had closed her eyes to the dirt and depression around her. She had dreamed of the day she would live in a clean house with no frying pans encrusted with the remains of a thousand meals. She dreamed of having a room to herself where no noise and no shouting could be heard, where no younger sister with nits in her hair would bounce on her bed saying:

'It's half my room, you can't throw me out.'

'Don't leave too soon,' Miss Andrews had begged. 'Don't go until you are sure you can support yourself. It would be too depressing to have to return there. That would break your spirit.'

Vera found it difficult to remember the two years she stayed on in her mother's flat. She knew that her father must have come home from time to time . . . the period seemed to be punctuated with screaming and violence. She must have learned something at the school because she had managed to escape with some 'O' levels. And during those two years she must have formed the habit of visiting Miss Andrews once a week, some hundred calls must have been made to the quiet apartment with its piano, its dried flowers, its cabinets of china and its purring Persian cat.

As an apprenticeship it must have worked, but it was blotted out. By the time Vera had finished, she could type, she could take shorthand, she could spell. Miss Andrews had taught her to smile and to speak nicely. Not in actual lessons, but by example. Vera's voice was less shrill, her vowels less extreme, her reactions less speedy – so much so that her mother was totally unprepared for her flight from the tenement. It was done without fuss, without argument and without heed to the pleas.

'You'll come back often to see us, you'll come home every weekend,' begged her mother.

'Of course,' said Vera, and never did.

She sent her mother an envelope with a card and a pound in it three times a year, Christmas, birthday, and mother's day. No details of how she was or where she was. No plans about coming back for a visit. No enquiries about the rest of the family. They had no way of telling her, when Margaret died. And no way of appealing to her when Colin was lifted by the police. And when the pound had reduced to a fifth of its value she still sent it. Crisp and green, attached by a paper clip to a non-committal card of good wishes. Once her mother tore it up and threw it into the fire. But Vera was never to know that.

Miss Andrews had been too genteel, too ladylike to reveal to Vera what she later discovered to be a major truth in life – that money was the solution to almost every problem. If Miss Andrews had known this she hadn't thought of passing it on, and after Vera had cut her ties with the family she also stopped seeing Miss Andrews. To the teacher she sent more thoughtful cards, and sometimes a lace handkerchief or a little sachet for her drawer. She never said what she was doing or where she was, and soon, or at some time anyway, the lonely teacher put Vera out of her mind. There was a finality about her three-line notes . . . they said goodbye.

Throughout her first five years of freedom, which also meant five jobs and five different bed-sitters, Vera still regarded herself as in apprenticeship. There was no time for dalliances like every other girl she worked with seemed to have. There was no money to waste on silly things – the cinema, yes, sometimes, if it was the kind of film that might teach her something, about style, clothes, manners. Mainly British films, American style was too foreign, it might be outrageous, it might not even *be* style. Lunch hours spent in fashion stores, or in bookshops, reading but not buying the magazines; money, after the rent was paid, spent on evening classes in everything from Beginner's French to Grooming.

Suddenly she was twenty-three, and nicely spoken and well informed and living in an attractive bed-sitter. She had collected some pretty ornaments, not unlike those that Miss Andrews had in her glass-fronted cabinet. She knew extremely important things about not mixing styles in her decor. She had learned as if by rote some rules of elegant living and if she had ever given herself the opportunity to entertain anyone she was absolutely confident about how the table should be set and what wines to serve with each course.

She had never relaxed about her background, and was amazed that other girls, the kind she met at work, would talk so freely about the uncouth habits of their parents . . . and joke about the vulgarity of their backgrounds. Vera would never be drawn. Once or twice when people did press she said that it hurt her to talk about the past. And people assumed that there had been some tragedy or some unpleasantness and left it at that.

Because of her interest in china she got a job running the gift shop of a smart hotel and it was here that she met Joseph. Twenty years her senior, with his big anxious eyes and his worried face, he was the ideal catch, one of the giggling receptionists had told her. A lonely widower, no children, pots of money, so broken up after his wife's death that he had sold the house and moved into a hotel. He had been living in this hotel for three years. He was apparently looking for a wife, since hotel life had its drawbacks. Sometimes he called at her little shop to buy gifts for clients, always she advised him with charm and taste. He was very attracted to her. Soon he managed to find the courage to ask her out. Vera's own hesitation was genuine. In her effort to become her own version of a lady, she had given very little time to recognising that she was a woman. She knew little of men, and was very shy on their first few outings. This pleased Joseph more than anything else she could have done . . . In a matter of weeks he was telling her of his dream house, but his fears of being lonely in it if he bought it for himself alone. She agreed with him enthusiastically, she thought that a big place was bad if you were alone. That's why she only had a tiny bed-sitter.

Joseph wondered if he could come and call at her bed-sitter some time. Vera agreed and asked him for afternoon tea the following Saturday. The sunlight caught the beautiful china, and the gentle highlights in Vera's hair, and the shining wood of the one small table . . . and Joseph's eyes filled with tears. He started to apologise for being forty-five, and to excuse himself for his arrogance in supposing that a beautiful young girl could possibly . . . She let him babble on for some minutes and then just as he was about to retract everything he had said from sheer embarrassment, she laid a finger on his lips and said,

'Don't say any more, Joseph. I should love to see your dream house in Finsbury Park, and we'll make it the most wonderful palace in the world.'

She had heard dialogue a little like that in some old movie, and it seemed right for the occasion. It was indeed. Utterly right. The months passed in a flurry of inspecting the house, giving in her notice at the hotel, accepting a small marriage settlement from Joseph, a complete refusal on her part to have anything to do with her family, a quiet wedding, an undemanding honeymoon in the sunshine of the South of France and then Vera's apprenticeship ended and her life began.

The small scullery attached to the great kitchen in Finsbury Park became her headquarters. Here she sat and studied the plans, here she returned after great measuring trips around the rooms, here she studied fabrics, paint charts, samples of tiles, wood pieces. It was in this scullery that the catalogues began to mount up as she debated, and wondered and frowned, and pouted, and looked at the first ones again. Joseph began to fret after a few weeks.

'Is it proving too much for you, my little darling?' he asked anxiously. 'You know we can have a designer, and a consultant if you like. Someone who will take the donkey work from you.'

'Donkey work?' cried Vera in genuine amazement. 'But this is the best bit. This is what we want, to decide it ourselves, to have it perfect. To have a perfect house which we get for ourselves!' Her eyes looked almost wild with enthusiasm, so Joseph decided not to point out that they slept on a bed in a bedroom, and ate meals in the little scullery while a fourteen-room house awaited them. It was like a naked house waiting to be dressed.

It got dressed. Amazingly slowly. It took months for the painting, months for the curtains, the furniture to build up. Two years went by and it still looked as if they had just moved in. Joseph was deeply disappointed.

He worked hard all day as a company lawyer. He had thought that his life had taken a new and almost miraculous turn when the flower-like Vera had agreed to marry him. True, his evenings were less lonely than when he lived in the hotel. But they were a lot less comfortable. In the hotel he had room to rest, to relax, room to work. In the hotel he had excellent food. At home, in the future palace, he had no room. He lived from a box in their bedroom, since Vera would allow no furniture anywhere until it had been finally agreed and settled and each item took months. The cooking was negligible since they had to wait for all the equipment to be installed. Vera didn't seem interested in food, she didn't seem to think he needed it either. She rushed to greet him on his return each day with a peck on the cheek and a sheaf of leaflets and swathes of fabric.

'Oh there you are, my dear. Dearest, do you think this

flower is too large. I'm not quite certain, I'm almost certain but not quite.'

He began to try and guess what she wanted him to say, but knew that he had to give the pretence of ruminating over it, otherwise she would not be satisfied. Often, faint with tiredness and hunger after two hours of studying design, he wondered whether she might in fact be having some kind of nervous trouble that he hadn't noticed before. Then he would banish the thought guiltily, and tell himself that he was a selfish swine to expect his young wife to have a glass of scotch ready, a meal cooking and a lively interest in his day.

Sometimes he called at the hotel and ate before he came home. Vera never seemed to mind. Yes, of course she had plenty to eat, she made herself cups of soup and sandwiches she said vaguely.

Joseph's hope that they would have children was also doomed. It was a long time before he realised that Vera had been taking the contraceptive pill. All this time he had been hoping that she would tell him she had conceived.

'But darling we can't *think* of children in this beautiful house. I mean how could you have children with this wallpaper?' Her hands caressed the wallpaper almost sensuously.

'But not ever?' gasped Joseph shocked.

'Perhaps sometime,' Vera said distantly aware she might have gone a little too far.

Vera was twenty-eight, they had been five years married when he dared to say to her that the house was perfect. He had admired every single item, rearranged every piece of furniture with her and now he hoped that the endless business was over. To his increasing alarm he noted that she didn't seem too anxious to spoil the kitchen by cooking, and she didn't want to fade the colours in the sitting room by letting the light in. There was no comfortable fug in the study she had designed for him, because she begged him not to have the heating too high lest it blister the paint. His cigar smoking was done outside his own home.

That was the unhappiest year of Joseph's life, because he now realised that the completion of the house did not signal the start of a normal life together. Her attractive face was still bent over magazines and fabric charts. They had never entertained anyone. He had taken his mother, an elderly woman there once . . . for a drink before Sunday lunch. Vera said she couldn't possibly cook a huge Sunday roast if they were to show the kitchen at its best.

'But why do we have to show it, at its best?' he begged.

'Why spend all this time and money unless we want things at their best?' she answered.

He hoped that if he got her some regular help she might become more relaxed about it. Together they interviewed seventeen applicants, the wages he offered were high. Eventually she settled on a Filippino girl with as much interest in the house as she had herself. Together they cleaned and polished all day. Together Vera and the little Filippino washed woodwork, and held the fitments of glass lights in soft dusters rubbing gently till they shone. The little girl from Manilla saved every penny she earned, and drank packet soups with Vera all day to keep up her strength. At night she went to her own room, and watched a portable television. Vera had bought her this in order to keep her at home. She told Joseph that if Anna went out at night she would lose her energy for polishing.

Joseph suggested a cook as well, but Vera asked why did they want someone to mess the place up. She would however like a daily woman to do the heavy work so that Anna and she could be free to do the finer chores.

The cleaning woman came five days a week. She thought Vera was daft and told her so. Vera didn't even listen. She certainly didn't feel insulted.

'If you don't like the job and the money, I'll get someone else,' she said reasonably, without any offence in her voice.

The cleaning woman was called Mrs Murray, and she lived in a block of flats not at all unlike the ones where Vera had grown up. Sometimes Mrs Murray feeling a bit sorry for this poor madwoman she worked for, would tell tales of Life in the Buildings. Vera's face contorted with near spasms. She almost ran from the room if Mrs Murray began to evoke the life and sounds.

'Please, Mrs Murray, I beg you, go on with your work. I don't want to delay you. Another time.'

Behind her back Anna and Mrs Murray pointed to their own foreheads and shook their heads.

'I think she must have had nothing when she was young,' said Mrs Murray one day in a burst of confidence to Anna.

'I always think she very wealthy lady,' said Anna.

'Wouldn't you feel sorry for her old man?' Mrs Murray went on. 'He'd be better off down with us, coming in to a bit of a laugh and a good meat pie, and a block of ice cream with a glass of port after it, and his slippers. I think that's what he'd prefer, to tell you the God's honest truth.'

Anna gave it some thought.

'Yes, and when I think of my family back in Manilla . . . where there is little money . . . and little food and little furniture . . . but when the father comes in . . . all stops and there is smiling and welcoming and he is an important man.'

Mrs Murray nodded sagely.

Outside the door, where she had paused, not to eavesdrop but to polish the corner of a picture frame which had escaped them all, Vera stood and listened. Her body was flooded with a great pity for them. Two poor women, not much older than herself. One from a drunken Irish family, living now in slum conditions in a London council flat, one a poor Asiatic whose family and country were so wretched they had to export her to clean floors and send them back her wages.

And these two women pitied her. Vera gave a high-pitched little laugh at the wonderful way that nature allows people to bear their burdens so easily by considering themselves better off than others. Happily she moved from the door and knelt down to examine the ball and claw feet of the table which were known for their ability to trap dust.

Highbury & Islington

'I hope you'll like them all,' he said for the fourth time.

'Oh, I'm sure I will,' said Heather without looking up.

'I think you'll get on with them,' he said, anxiously biting his lip.

Heather raised her eyes from the magazine.

'I said I'm sure I will, funny face. Even if I don't it's not the end of the world. They don't have to live with me, I don't have to live with them.' Cheerfully she leaned over and kissed him on the nose. Then she took off her shoes, settled her feet in his lap and applied herself seriously to her magazine. A very colourful looking one with a lot of Sin and Passion and Frenzy in capital letters on the cover.

Adam hoped that she might have finished the magazine and, better still have thrown it away before they got home. He could see his mother's amazement – Frenzy and Sin magazines weren't forbidden at home, it was just that nobody would contemplate buying them. He could imagine his sister's sarcastic comments. Louise was always a little sardonic about strangers but he felt unhappily that Heather might give plenty of ammunition.

'A trifle bookish I see, your Heather?' Louise would shout as she retrieved the offending magazine. And, oh God, would Heather relax so thoroughly that she would actually sit in her stockinged feet as she was doing now?

Adam looked out of the train window, and fixed his face in what he hoped was a calm, pleasant expression while he tried to work out some of the more glaring problems which faced him at the weekend. He had explained to Heather that there could be no question of sharing a bed under his mother's roof. She had accepted it good-naturedly.

'No point in terrorising the poor old darling is there? I'll wait until they've all had their Ovaltine then I'll slip along to wherever you are.'

He had even managed to tell her that this would not do either. He painted a picture of a home with three women, Mother, Louise and old Elsie; this was the first time any guest had been invited to stay; there would be enormous excitement. There would be amazing scrutiny. Heather had sounded disbelieving but shrugged.

'Well, two nights' denial won't kill us.'

Adam had read a lot about love before he had met Heather. He knew only too well that love was often unreturned – as in the case of his loving Jane Fonda for a while. She had simply been unaware of his existence. And nearer home there had been a severe case of unreturned love when he had yearned for that stuck-up girl in the dramatic society. Of course, he too had been loved, by that mousey friend of Louise's; the quiet little girl with the irritating cough and nervous laugh. She had loved Adam for a bit and was always pretending that she had been given two theatre tickets and asking him would he like to come to plays with her. He hadn't loved her even a little bit.

Heather was his first experience of Real Love, and Adam frowned as he looked into people's houses from the train window. Real love often ran into problems, well, from Romeo and Juliet onwards. There were cases of families refusing to countenance young lovers. He didn't think this would happen at home. Mother and Louise wouldn't summon old Elsie from the kitchen and face him with an ultimatum. It would be very different and much harder to take . . . they would laugh at Heather, and ridicule his taste. In little ways they would call attention to her shortcomings; they would assume that she was a tasteless little dalliance on his part. They couldn't know that he loved her and wanted her more than he had ever wanted anything in his life.

He moved her feet slightly, she looked up and smiled at him over her torrid magazine.

'Dreaming?' she asked him affectionately.

'A bit,' he said and felt a wave of disloyalty flooding him. Love wasn't meant to be like this, it had nothing to do with trying to get two sets of people to make allowances, to change, to bend in order to accommodate each other. Love was meant to be straightforward. If things got in the way of love, then the Lover had to remove them, honestly and with integrity and dignity. The Lover wasn't meant to sit gnawing his fingers about the confrontation of those that he loved.

He had known Heather for a year and he had loved her for eight months, but this was the first time he had ever raised enough courage to take her home for a weekend. It hadn't been easy.

'But of course you can have a friend to stay, darling,' Mother had said. 'Who is he? Anyone we know?' Mother had an idea that she might know anyone of substance in London. Among the twelve million people Adam could meet, she felt sure that the one chosen to be a friend might be someone she knew.

'A girl. How dramatic!' screamed Louise pretending to be a Victorian Lady overcome with shock. Adam could have wrung her neck with pleasure. 'Is she a débutante? Do tell, do tell.'

Adam had explained that Heather had a bed-sitting-room in the same house in Islington. He did not go into the fact that for the past few months they actually shared the same bed-sitting-room so as to save rent. To the eager faces of Mother and Louise, and of Elsie who had come in from the kitchen at the noise of all the excitement, he announced that she really *was* just a friend, and that he would love to invite her for a weekend. He begged them not to ask people around for sherry on Sunday morning. He implored Elsie not to give the place a thorough spring clean before young Mr Adam's young lady came; he said that honestly Louise shouldn't save her supper party for the tennis club people until Heather arrived. Short of going on bended knees he couldn't have done more to ask for a quiet, normal weekend. It had, of course, been useless.

It was only natural that they should be so interested in his doings, Adam thought forgiving them, loving them for caring so much. Since Father died he was the only man in their life; Louise was too bookish, too brisk for men. Well, she was nineteen and had never shown any real interest in men. She worked in the local library, she never mentioned boyfriends. She couldn't have any secretly, could she? After all she lived at home. Every second weekend Adam arrived home to the Sussex town, and told them tales about his life in London. The work in the bank, his prospects. His squash games, his walks on the Heath. The little pub theatres he went to, his French classes preparing for big banking opportunities in the EEC.

He mentioned lots of friends by name, but never Heather. He said nothing about the discos they went to on the Saturdays he stayed in London. He thought Mother might find discos a bit, well, lower class, and Louise would ask in her penetrating voice: 'But why, Adam, why do people go to rooms with loud music and funny lights which eventually ruin their eyesight – I mean, do they enjoy it, Adam?' He told Elsie that he was learning a little bit more about cooking, but he didn't explain that it was Heather who taught him, Heather who said: 'I made the supper last night, you'll bloody do it tonight mate or I'll find myself a bloke who believes in equality.'

His worlds were so different that he had put off for as long as he could the date when they had to be brought together. Adam who sat down with a linen table napkin to tasteless, overcooked, plain food served from cracked china plates behind heavy net curtains . . . and Adam who sat on the bed with a great wooden bowl of highly spiced chili, a bottle of red wine on the floor, his arm around Heather as they laughed and watched television. In the summer evenings the window of their basement flat was often open for all to see . . . He could hardly believe they were the same person.

Heather had invited him to her home several times. Her stepfather had asked Adam for a loan of a pound on each occasion and Heather had cheerfully shouted at him not to be so daft. On one occasion Adam had secretly slipped the man a pound, hoping to buy his affection, but in fact it only worsened relations between them as Heather had said it would. Heather's mother was a hard-working Scot. She looked Adam up and down and said she hoped that he was a man who could hold down a day's work. Adam explained nervously that although he was still a lowly bank official he was indeed a regular worker and had great ambitions. Heather's mother said she approved of that because she herself had been unlucky in that she had married two wasters and two scroungers and two men who would drink the Thames Estuary dry if they got a chance. 'There were only two altogether, Mam,' Heather had said laughing. 'She always makes it sound as if there were six!'

Adam couldn't understand the casual bond that held the mother to her daughter. It wasn't love, it had nothing to do with duty. There was no need involved, it didn't seem to matter whether Heather went home for months or not. There were no recriminations, no interrogations. There didn't even seem to be a great deal of interest. Heather's mother could hardly remember the name of the department store where Heather worked. Adam marvelled at that: Mother and Louise and Elsie knew the name of every under-manager and a great many of the customers in his bank.

Heather had always seemed amused about his tales of home. But then, Adam wondered with mounting horror as the train was taking them ever nearer, had he told accurate tales? Had he let her know just how very formal Mother could be? Heather hadn't thought of taking a gift for the weekend, so Adam had bought a potted plant.

'You can give that to Mother,' he had said.

'Why? I don't know her. She'd think it was silly,' said Heather.

'No, first time meeting her, she'd think it was nice,' he insisted. 'It's what people do, honestly.'

'You didn't take a plant to my Mum,' she said reasonably.

Adam was furious. He hadn't taken a plant to Heather's mother because she lived forty minutes away on the tube, because they had gone there for tea one Saturday, because Heather had said that her mother hated airs and graces and he hadn't wanted to be considered a young dandy. Now it was being used against him.

He thought about the kind of weekend they could have had if they had stayed in London. The cinema tonight, perhaps, and a fish and chip supper. Saturday morning poking around antique shops and second-hand stalls. Drink a few pints with some of Heather's friends at lunchtime . . . the afternoon would pass in a haze of doing up the room they lived in, sweeping the leaves away from the basement gutters; they might carry on with that picture framing; they might go and drink a bottle of wine with other friends until they went to the disco; and instead he had this torture ahead.

The train stopped and his heart lurched; they couldn't be there yet. Surely there was another half-hour.

'Are we there?' Heather yawned and rooted for her

shoes. She hadn't a hint of nervousness or anxiety. She reached for his carefully chosen potted plant.

'Don't forget your geranium,' she said.

They hadn't arrived, but they had reached a situation which called for their having to change trains. That was how the guard put it.

'Has this one broken down?' Heather asked him.

'It is a situation where you have to change trains, Madam,' he said again.

'I'd love it if he was in charge of any crisis,' grumbled Heather getting out on to the platform. Her eyes lit on the Ladies Room. 'I'll take advantage of the change of train situation to have a relief of bladder situation,' she said happily and scampered off to the lavatory.

Adam stood glumly wondering why he thought everything that Heather said was funny and endearing at home in London and he thought it was coarse and offensive when he was starting to get into Mother's orbit. He leaned against a telephone box waiting for Heather to come back from the Ladies and for the next train to come and rescue them. On the opposite platform stood lucky people going to London. They would be there in time to go to a theatre perhaps, they might be salesmen coming home from some conference in Brighton. None of them had forty-eight hours of anxiety lying ahead of them as he did. None of them had to worry about Mother asking Heather, 'And what school were you at my dear?' and Louise asking Heather, 'You mean you actually sell things to the public? Heavens!', Elsie asking Heather, 'Would you like Earl Grey or English breakfast in the morning?' He winced and felt a real pain at the thought of it. And there was no way he could muzzle Heather and ask her to remain completely silent, so she was bound to talk about times when they had both been pissed and to let slip that they had smoked pot, and lived in the same room, and that her father had died in an alcoholics' home and her step-father was bankrupt . . .

Adam heaved a very deep sigh.

Love was turning out to be full of problems that the poets and the movie makers never spoke of.

Suddenly he thought he couldn't stand it. Not now, not yet. He wasn't ready to take the weekend now. Perhaps later when he and Heather were so sure of each other and of their happiness that a weekend like this wouldn't matter. Perhaps later when he didn't seem like a small boy wet behind the ears to the Mummy and the Sister and the Old Retainer . . . perhaps then Adam's Bohemian lifestyle and friends would be much more acceptable. Perhaps when he was more of a man.

He knew he had to act in the next minute if he was going to stop the disastrous visit. A quick phone call . . . he was most most dreadfully sorry but he had just come down with this dreadful flu, and Heather had sent her regrets and would so look forward to meeting Mother and Louise and everyone another time. Yes, yes he could do it now quickly. And to Heather? Well imagine how funny life is! He had just phoned home to explain that they were going to be late and, fancy, Mother had come down with this dreadful flu and had been trying to contact him, could they possibly put off the visit? Then he and Heather had only to cross the platform, jump on a London bound train. In an hour or two they would get off at their tube station, and, hand in hand, clutching their weekend bags and the geranium, they would go home . . . there would be no hurts, no confrontations. Love would remain separate and self-contained. He could be a loving son every second weekend until he was mature and manly enough not to care.

With one hand on his ear to cut out the noise of the trains he told the tale first to Elsie and, gritting his teeth trying to put out of his mind her tones of disappointment, he agreed to tell it all again to Mother.

'We had everything so nice,' Elsie said, 'We even had a

fire in Miss Heather's bedroom. Your mother had the chimney swept during the week.'

Mother was concerned about his imaginary flu, but he had the strangest feeling she didn't entirely believe him. She gave the merest of hints that she thought something more exciting and glittering had turned up for Adam and Heather.

'Don't go out to any parties or occasions now, if you have flu.'

There was something about the way his mother used the work 'occasions' that brought a prickle of tears to Adam's eyes. It was as moving as Elsie being disappointed not to see Miss Heather's pleasure at the fire in her bedroom. Mother thought that bank clerks and shop-girls were good worthy people in service industries . . . but she thought of her son Adam as being 'in banking' and she assumed that his nice friend Heather was a young lady who would indeed be invited to glittering functions.

'I'm sorry, Mother,' he said.

'Adam my dear, you can't help having influenza,' said Mother, and he could hear Louise in the background saying: 'Oh no, you don't mean after all this they're not coming. It's too bad.'

Fiercely he told himself that it was better this small hurt than two days of misunderstanding and misery. Then Heather came swinging easily along the platform.

'Any news on the train?' she asked.

He told her about his sudden call, his mother's flu, her deep regrets, he added that there had been a fire in her bedroom. Heather looked at him levelly.

'Yes, really, a fire in your bedroom, Mother had got the sweep to come in and do the chimney specially during the week,' he said, desperate that she should understand how much welcome had been prepared. After Elsie and Mother's pain he couldn't bear it if Heather were flippant.

'I see,' she said at last.

'So, we can just go back, back to London, we can cross the footbridge there,' he said reading the sign aloud.

'Yeah, that's right,' said Heather.

'And we're really only losing the cost of the ticket,' he said eagerly looking at her. 'That's all we're losing.'

'Sure Adam,' she said, but he knew from her voice that he was losing a great deal more. He had known that from Mother's voice too. For once in his life, Adam wondered if there were a danger that he might *never* grow up.

King's Cross

Eve looked around the office with a practical eye. There was a shabby and rather hastily put together steel shelving system for books and brochures. There were boxes of paper still on the floor. There was a dead plant on the window, and another plant with a Good Luck in Your New Job label dying slowly beside it. The venetian blind was black – there was so much clutter on the window ledge it looked like a major undertaking to try and free the blind. One of the telephones was actually hidden under a pile of literature on the desk. In the corner was a small, cheap and rather nasty-looking table . . . which would be Eve's if she were to take the job.

And that's what she was doing now, as she sat in the unappealing room . . . deciding if she would take the job of secretary to Sara Gray. Sara had rushed off to find somebody who knew about holidays and luncheon vouchers and overtime. She had never had a secretary before and had never thought of enquiring about these details before she interviewed Eve. She had pushed the hair out of her eyes and gone galloping off to personnel, which would undoubtedly think her very foolish. Eve sat calmly in the room waiting and deliberating, by the time Sara had bounded back with the information, Eve had already decided to take on Sara Gray. She looked like being the most challenging so far.

Sara heaved a great sigh of relief when she heard that Eve would stay and work with her. She had big kind brown eyes, the kind of eyes you often see shown close up in a movie or a television play to illustrate that someone is a trusting, vulnerable character and therefore likely to be hurt. She looked vague and bewildered, and snowed-under. She sounded as if she needed a personal manager rather than a secretary – and this is where Sara Gray had hit very lucky because that's what Eve was.

From the outset she was extraordinarily respectful to Sara. She never referred to her as anything but Miss Gray, she called her Miss Gray to her face despite a dozen expostulations from Sara.

'This is a friendly office,' Sara cried. 'I can't stand you not calling me by my name. It makes me look so snooty. We're all friends here.'

Eve had replied firmly that it was not a friendly office. It was a very cut-throat company indeed. Eve had asked Sara how many of the women secretaries called their male bosses by their first names. Sara couldn't work it out. Eve could. None of them. Sara agreed reluctantly that this might be so. Eve pressed home her point. Even the managers and assistant managers on Sara's level were not going to escape, they all called Sara by her first name because she was a woman, but she felt the need to call many of them Mr. After two days Sara decided that Eve must be heavily into Women's Lib.

'There's no need to fight any battles on my behalf, Eve,' she said cheerfully. 'Look at how far I've got, and I'm a woman. Nobody held me back just because I'm a downtrodden put-upon female. Did they? I've done very well here, and I get recognition for all I do.'

'Oh no, Miss Gray, you are quite wrong,' said Eve. 'You do not get recognition. You are the assistant promotions manager. Everyone knows that you are far better and brighter and work much harder than Mr Edwards. You should be the promotions manager not the assistant.'

Sara looked upset. 'I thought I could say I'd done rather well,' she said.

'Only what you deserve, Miss Gray,' said Eve who

seemed to have acquired a thorough familiarity with the huge travel agency and its tour operations in two days. 'You should have Mr Edwards' job. We all know that. You *must* have it. It's only fair.'

Sara looked at her, embarrassed.

'Gosh Eve, it's awfully nice of you, and don't think I don't appreciate it. You're amazingly loyal. But you really don't know the score here.'

'With great respect, Miss Gray, I think it's you who doesn't know the score,' said Eve calmly. 'It is absolutely possible for you to have Mr Edwards' job this time next year, I'll be very glad to help you towards that if you like. I have a little experience in this sort of thing.'

Sara stared at her, not knowing what to say.

'Miss Gray, I'm going for my lunch now, but can I suggest you do something while I'm gone? Can you telephone one or two of the people on the list of references I gave you? You will notice they are all women; I've never worked for men. Ask any one of them whether she thinks it's a good idea to trust me to help.Then perhaps you might add that you will keep all this very much in confidence . . .'

'Eve,' interrupted Sara, her good-natured face looking puzzled, 'Eve, honestly, this sounds like the mafia or something. I'm not into power struggles, and office back-stabbing . . . I'm just delighted to have someone as bright and helpful as you in the office . . . I don't want to start a war.'

'Who said anything about a war, Miss Gray? It's very subtle, and very gradual and – honestly the best thing is to telephone anyone on that list, it's there in the file marked Personal.'

'But won't they think it rather odd. I mean, I can't ring up and ask them what do they think of Eve trying to knock Mr Edwards sideways so that I can get his job.' Sara sounded very distressed.

'Miss Gray, I have worked in five jobs, for five women,

I chose them, they thought they chose me. At the very beginning I told them how a good assistant could help them get where they wanted. Not one of them believed me, I managed in a conversation like this to convince them to let me.'

'And . . . what happened?' asked Sara.

'Ask them, Miss Gray,' replied Eve, gathering her gloves and bag.

'They won't think I'm er . . .'

'No, all of them – except the first one, of course – rang someone else to check things out too.' Eve was gone.

Sara wondered.

You often heard of women becoming a bit strange, perhaps Eve was a bit odd. Far too young to be menopausal or anything, heavens Eve wasn't even thirty, but it did seem an odd sort of thing to suggest after two days.

Was there a wild possibility that she might have had a secret vendetta for years against Garry Edwards, the plausible head of promotions, who indeed did not deserve his job, his title, his salary or his influence, since all of these had been made possible only by Sara's devoted work?

Sara reached for the phone.

'Sure I know Eve,' said the pleasant American woman in the big banking group. 'You are so lucky, Sara, to have her. I offered her any money to stay but she wouldn't hear of it. She said her job was done. She acts a bit like Superman or the Lone Ranger, she comes in and solves a problem and then sort of zooms off. A really incredible woman.'

'Can I . . . er . . . ask you what problem she . . . er . . .' Sara felt very embarrassed.

'Sure. I wanted to be loans manager, they didn't take me seriously. Eve showed me how they would, and they did, and now I'm loans manager.'

'Heavens,' said Sara. 'It's a teeny bit like that here.'

'Well naturally it is, otherwise Eve wouldn't have picked you,' said the loans manager of a distant bank.

'And how did she . . . um . . . do it?' persisted Sara.

'Now this is where I become a little vague,' the pleasant voice said. 'It's simply impossible to explain. In my case there was a whole lot of stuff about my not getting to meet the right people in the bank. Eve noticed that, she got me to play golf.'

'*Golf?*' screamed Sara.

'I know, I know, I guess I shouldn't even have told you that much . . . listen, the point is that Eve can see with uncanny vision where women hold themselves back, and work within the system without playing the system properly so – she kinda points out where the system could work for us, and honestly honey, it worked for me, and it sure as hell worked for the woman who Eve worked on before me, she's practically running industry in this country nowadays. In her case it had something to do with having dinner parties at home.'

'What?' said Sara.

'I know, it sounded crazy to me too, and I got real uneasy, but aparently she needed to show people that she could sort of impress foreign contacts by having them to a meal with grace and style and all pizzazz in her country home. Eve sort of set it up for her with outside caterers and it worked a dream. You see, it's different for everyone.'

Sara was puzzled. She walked down to the local snack bar and bought a salami sandwich. She ate it thoughtfully on the road coming back to the building. In the lift she heard that Garry Edwards was going to a conference in the Seychelles next week. It was a conference for people who brought out travel brochures, a significant part of promotions for any travel firm. Sara had done all the imaginative travel brochures, Garry Edwards had okayed them. Yet he was going to the Seychelles and she was eating a tired salami sandwich. When she opened her office door Eve was sitting there typing.

'I'll do it,' she said. 'Whatever it is, play golf, give foolish dinner parties . . . I'll do it. I want his job. It's utterly unjust that he's going to that conference, it's the most unjust thing I've ever known.'

'He won't be going to it next year,' said Eve. 'Right, Miss Gray, I have a few points ready to discuss with you, shall we put this sign on the door?'

'What is it?' Sara asked fearfully.

'It merely says, "Engaged in Conference", I made it last night.' Eve produced a neat card which she then fixed on the outside of the office door.

'Why are we doing that?' whispered Sara.

'Because it is absolutely intolerable the way that people think they can come barging in here, taking advantage of your good nature and picking your brains, interrupting us and disturbing you from whatever you are doing. We need a couple of hours to plan the office design, and it's no harm to let them see immediately that you are going to regard your job as important. It may only be half the job they should have given you, but don't worry, you'll have the right job very soon.'

'Suppose that the really big brass come along, or Mr Edwards or you know, someone important.' Sara was still unsure.

'We are having a conference, about the redesign of your office.'

'But there isn't any money to redesign it . . . even if they'd let me.'

'Yes there is, I've been up to the requisition department, in fact they looked you up on the book, and wondered why you hadn't applied. Whenever you're ready Miss Gray, we can start.'

Together they worked out how the office should look. It was a big room, but it was in no way impressive; apart from the inferior furniture, its design was all wrong. Eve explained, that a separate cubicle should be built for her near the door. Eve should act as a kind of reception area for Sara, she should call through to announce visitors, even though it was only a distance of a few yards.

'They'll walk past and come straight on in,' said Sara.

'Not if I walk after them and ask can I help them. They won't do it twice, Miss Gray,' said Eve and Sara realised that most of them wouldn't even do it once.

The costing of the partition was not enormous, and it left a reasonable amount for the rest of the furnishings.

'We'll have the filing section in my part since you shouldn't really have to be looking things up yourself, Miss Gray, but it will of course be kept in a very meticulous way so you can always find anything.'

'What will I have in my part of the office then?' asked Sara humbly.

Eve stood up and walked around. 'I've been giving it a lot of thought, Miss Gray. You are really the ideas woman here. I'm sorry, I know it's jargon, but that's what you do for the promotions department. You thought up that whole idea about choosing a holiday from your stars in the zodiac and that worked, you thought of having a travel agents' conference in that railway station which suited them all since they had to come from all over the country and go back again by train. You thought up the scheme of having children write the section for children's holidays, so I think that this is what you should be doing really. Thinking. And let me handle the routine things, you know, the letters about "Can you trace what we did about Portugal two years ago?" If the filing system works properly then anyone will be able to do that for you. I'll set it up so that at least four-fifths of your incoming mail can be handled by any competent secretary. That should give you a great deal more time to do what you are really good at.'

Sara looked hopeful but not convinced.

'Me just sit in here with a chair?' She shook her head. 'I

don't think it's on Eve, I really don't. You know they'd think I'd gone mad.'

'I wasn't suggesting a chair. I was going to suggest a long narrow conference table. Something in nice wood, we could look at auctions or in an antique shop. And about six chairs. Then, for you a small writing desk. Again something from an old house possibly, with your telephone and your own big diary and notebook, a few periodicals and trade magazines or directories you need, that's all.'

'Eve, in God's name, what is the long conference table for. Eve, I am the assistant promotions manager, not the chairman of the board. I don't give conferences, call meetings, ask my superiors to come in here with the hope of blinding them about policy.'

'You should,' said Eve simply. 'Listen,' she went on. 'Remember that children writing the brochure idea? It was marvellous. I've been looking through the files, you got not one word of credit, no letter, no mention, no thanks even. I would not be at all surprised if you, Mr Edwards and I are the only people who know you thought it up, and the only reason I know is that I see entries in your diary about going to schools and talking to children and spending a lot of your free time working on it. Edwards got the praise, the thanks and the job, for not only that but for everything you did. Because you didn't do it right.'

'It worked, though,' said Sara defensively.

'Miss Gray, of course the idea worked, it was brilliant, I remember seeing those brochures long before I ever knew you, and I thought they were inspired. What I mean is that it didn't work for you, here within the company. Next time, I suggest you invite Mr Edwards and his boss and the marketing director and one or two others to drop in quite casually – don't dream of saying you are calling a meeting, just suggest that they might all like to come into your office one afternoon. And then, at a nice table where there is plenty of room and plenty of style, put forward your plans. That way they'll remember you.'

'Yes, I know, in theory you're right, Eve . . . but honestly, I'm not the type. I'm jolly old Sara Gray, with a nice, jolly, hopeless lover who comes and goes at home – and who is gone at the moment. And they all say to themselves, "poor Sara, not a bad old thing" – none of them would take me at a rosewood conference table for one minute Eve, they'd either corpse themselves laughing or else they'd think I was having a breakdown, they'd fire me. And you.'

Eve didn't look at all put out. 'I wasn't suggesting calling a conference tomorrow, I was suggesting having the furniture right. If you are someone who is valuable to the company for her ideas, you should have a space to think up these ideas, a platform to present them on, and the just recognition for them.'

'You're right,' Sara said suddenly. 'What else?'

'I think you should get into the habit of having Mr Edwards and others coming to this office, by appointment of course, rather than you rushing to theirs. It makes you more important. That's why we need the right furniture. Mr Edwards has an office like an aeroplane hangar, and very well laid out, I've inspected it. But yours could have a charm, it could become the place where ideas were discussed say on one particular evening a week, a Thursday, before people left. It would be relaxing, and pleasant, and *you* would be in control.'

As they talked on, it got darker outside, and they switched on the bright neon overhead light.

'That'll have to go for a start,' said Eve. 'It's far too harsh, there's no style, no warmth.'

A few times the door had been half-opened, but whenever people saw the two heads bent over the desk and lists, they muttered apologies and backed out.

'I never thought a notice would do that,' said Sara admiringly.

'Wait till we get things going properly, you'll be amazed.' said Eve.

Eve refused a drink, a girly chat and the offer of a share in a taxi. Instead she took out her notebook again.

'You should have an account with a taxi firm,' she said briskly. 'I'll set that up tomorrow, when I'm organising the flowers and your dress allowance.'

Sara stared at her in the windy, wet street as if Eve had gone completely mad.

'*What* are you organising . . .?' she began.

'Plants, flowers for the office, all the male senior executives have them, and they also get a special expense allowance for clothes because they have to travel, it being a travel company, and . . .'

'Eve, I'm not a senior executive, I can't have free flowers paid for by the office.'

'As assistant manager you are technically a senior executive. The other two assistant managers are elderly men who have been pushed upstairs, so if you equate your title with theirs then you can have flowers, nothing extravagant, about six nice flowering plants. I think we can choose them from a brochure, they'll arrive tomorrow.'

For the first time for a long time Sara sat back contentedly in her chair at home and didn't think about Geoff and wonder when his new obsession would end. Often she felt lonely and sad during his absences, so that she would hide from the feeling by having the television on or listening to music for long hours. But tonight she just sat calmly drinking her tea and looking into the fire. Eve's arrival meant that a lot of the tension in the office had been eased. It was like someone massaging your shoulders and taking away the stiffness – you didn't know how tense you had been until the massage was over – Eve was going to make things a lot better, and she was going to force Sara to take herself more seriously too. It was a bit exciting in a way.

Next morning was a Friday and Eve wanted to know whether Sara had any important plans and engagements for the weekend. Sara shrugged 'I was going to sort out those figures for Mr Edwards, you know the ones he wanted on the breakdown of age groups on the coach holidays. We need to know where to direct some of the coach tour promotions this year.'

'Oh, that's done.' said Eve. 'I did it this morning, I saw his note. I've two copies here for you to sign, one for Mr Edwards and I thought you should send one to the head of marketing, just to let him know that you are alive and well and working harder than Mr Edwards.'

'Isn't that a bit sneaky?' asked Sara looking like a doubtful schoolgirl.

'No, it's standard office procedure. Mr Edwards is the sneaky party, by not acknowledging your part in all the work that is being done.'

With a weekend free Sara agreed happily to go to look at second-hand furniture and office fittings. Eve had already organised the office partition, and it began with great hammering and activity after lunch.

'I suggest you go and check out a few new outfits for yourself, Miss Gray,' said Eve. 'You can't possibly work here with all this noise.'

'Could you come with me, I'm not exactly sure what I . . . ?'

'Certainly, Miss Gray, can you wait five minutes while I tell these gentlemen I shall be back in two hours to see how they are getting on?'

Eve managed to make three large men look as if they knew she was going to have them fired unless the partition was perfect. Then she went to the shop with Sara.

There was a brief objective discussion about what clothes Sara already possessed. Eve explained that she had only seen two tweed skirts and one black sweater in the three days she had been working there. Shamefacedly, Sara said she thought there were a couple of other sweaters and perhaps two more workable tweed skirts.

Eve seemed neither pleased nor put out; she was merely asking for information. In the store she suggested three outfits which could interchange and swap and make about a dozen between them. They cost so much that Sara had to sit down on the fitting-room chair.

'I took the liberty of getting you a credit card for your expenses, Miss Gray,' said Eve. 'I rushed it through, and what you are going to spend now is totally justifiable. You have to meet the public, you have to represent the company in places where the company may well be judged by the personal appearance of its representatives. What you are spending on these garments is half what Mr Edwards has spent in the last six months, and you have been entitled to expenses of this kind for over a year and never called on them.'

By Monday Sara could hardly recognise either herself or her new surroundings. On Eve's advice she had had an expensive hair-do; she wore the pink and grey wool outfit, put the pink cyclamens on her window sill, near the lovely old table with its matching half-dozen chairs which they had eventually found for half nothing since it was too big for most homes, and nobody except Eve would have thought of it as office furniture

Eve was living in her purpose-built annexe surrounded with files and ledgers. She had just begun to compile a folio of Sara's work so far with the company, a kind of illustrated *curriculum vitae* which would show her worth and catalogue her achievements. Nobody was more surprised than Sara by all she seemed to have done during her years in the company.

'I'm really quite good, you know,' she said happily.

'Miss Gray, you are very good indeed, otherwise I

wouldn't work with you,' said Eve solemnly, and Sara could detect no hint of humour or self-mockery in the tone.

Towards the end of the second week, Eve pronounced herself pleased with the office. She had bought an old coat-stand which ideally matched the table and chairs, and on this she urged Sara to hang her smart coat so that the whole place just looked as if it were an extension of her own creative personality. If anyone gasped with amazement at the changes in the room, Sara was to say that there was all this silly money up in requisitions for her to decorate the place, and she did hate modern ugly cubes of furniture so she had just chosen things she liked – which had in fact been cheaper. People were stunned, and jealous, and wondered why they hadn't thought of this too.

Remarks about her appearance Eve suggested should be parried slightly. No need to tell people that she now had regular twice weekly sessions with a beautician. Eve had booked her a course of twenty.

So on the second Friday of her employment Eve came into Sara's part of the office and said she thought that they were ready to begin.

'Begin?' cried Sara. 'I thought we'd finished.'

Eve gave one of her rare smiles. 'I meant begin your work, Miss Gray. I've been taking up a lot of your time with what I am sure you must have considered inessentials. Now I feel that you should concentrate totally on your work for promotions and let me look after everything else. I shall keep detailed records of all the routine work that I am doing. Each evening I'll leave you a progress report, too, of how I think we have been getting on in our various projects. These I think you should take home with you or else return to my personal file. We don't want them seen by anyone else.'

Sara nodded her thanks. Suddenly she felt overwhelmed with gratitude for this strange girl who was behaving not as a new secretary but as if she were an old family retainer blind with loyalty to the young Missie, or a kindergarten teacher filled with affection and hope for a young charge.

She felt almost unable to express any of this gratitude because Eve didn't seem to need it or even to like it.

'Are there any, er, major projects you see straight away?' she asked.

'I think you should look for an assistant, or a deputy, Miss Gray,' said Eve.

'*Eve*, you can't go, you can't leave me now!' cried Sara.

'Miss Gray, I am your secretary, not your assistant. I certainly shall not leave you for a year. I told you that. No, you need to train someone in to do your job when you are not here.'

'Not here?' Sara looked around her new office which she was beginning to love. 'Where will I be, why won't I be here?'

'Because you will be away on conferences, you will be travelling abroad to see the places the company is promoting, and of course, Miss Gray, you will be taking your own vacation, something you neglected to do last year I see.'

'Yes, but that'll only be a few weeks at most. Why do I need to have an assistant, a deputy? I mean it's like empire building.'

'You'll need to train an assistant to take over when you get Mr Edwards' job at the end of the year. One of the many reasons why women fail to get promotion is because management can say that there is nobody else to do their job on the present level of the ladder. I suggest you find a bright and very young, extremely young man.'

'But I can't do that. They'd know I was plotting to get Garry Edwards' job'.

Eve smiled. 'I'm glad you are calling Mr Edwards by his first name at last, Miss Gray. No, you need an assistant to do your work for you while you are away, of course.

Otherwise, if this whole office is seen to tick along nicely without you in your absence, people will wonder why your presence is so essential. If on the other hand, it turns into total chaos, they will blame you *in absentia*. So you need a harmless, enthusiastic, personable young man to sign letters which I will write and to postpone anything major until your return.'

'Eve, why do you have to go away in a year?' Sara said suddenly. 'Why can't you stay and together we'll take over the whole place. Honestly it's not impossible.'

'Oh, Miss Gray, there'd be no point in taking the place over. It's not what either of us want, is it?' asked Eve, accepting naturally that it would be perfectly feasible to takeover the largest travel company in Britain if she put her mind to it.

'You never tell me what you want,' Sara said, impressed by her own daring.

'I like to see women getting their work recognised. There's so much sheer injustice in the business world – I mean really unjust things are done to women. I find that very strange. Men who can be so kind to stray dogs, lost strangers, their own children, contribute generously to charities and yet continue appalling unfairness towards women at work.'

She stopped suddenly.

Sara said, 'Go on.'

'Nothing more,' Eve said firmly. 'You asked me what I wanted. I want to see that injustice recognised for what it is, and to see people fight it.'

'You should write about it, or make speeches,' said Sara. 'I never even saw it in my own case until you came. I do agree now that I've been shabbily treated and now I've got a bit of confidence to demand more. And that's only after ten days with you. Think what success you'd have if you were to go on a lecture tour or on television or something.'

Eve looked sad.

'No. That's just the whole trouble. It doesn't work that way, damn it. That's why it's going to take so long.'

Politely she extricated herself from further explanations, from any more conversation, from having a drink at a near-by pub with Sara. She had to go home now.

'You never tell me about your home,' said Sara.

'You never tell me about yours, Miss Gray, either,' said Eve.

'I would if I got a chance,' Sara said.

'Ah yes, but you and I would not get on so well if I knew about your worries and problems!'

Sara took it as a very faint warning. It meant that Eve didn't want to hear about Sara's problems and worries either. She sighed. It would have been very helpful if Eve could apply her amazing skills to Sara's disastrous relationship with Geoff. He had been gone now three weeks. No, it couldn't be three weeks. It was. She could hardly believe it. The last ten days had passed so quickly she had scarcely missed him. She was so stunned by this that she hadn't heard what Eve had said.

'I was only saying that I left your invitation for the supper party tomorrow night there on your desk,' Eve repeated as she gathered up her things. 'I hope you enjoy it. I heard that all senior executives were normally invited to meet the chairman and board members so I made sure your name was on the list. Nice chance to wear that black dress too, Miss Gray, I expect you're thinking.'

Sara's eyes were big with gratitude. As if by magic Eve seemed to have known that another lonely weekend was looming ahead. But she knew not to admit to any emotion.

'Great. I'll go in there and knock them dead. And on Monday we'll be ready to begin the campaign.'

'Excellent,' said Eve. 'I suggest you find out whether any of the board have young and hopefully stupid sons who might want to start in the business. As your assistant, you know. We need someone rather over-educated with no brains.'

'What are you going to do for the weekend?' asked Sara.

'This and that, Miss Gray. See you Monday,' said Eve.

Sara spent Saturday reading the company's reports which Eve had left thoughtfully on her desk. She took Eve's advice and wore the black dress to the party where Garry Edwards' surprise at seeing her was as exciting as any romantic flutter. 'I can see how people can become obsessed with all this infighting and competitiveness,' thought Sara.

She was charming to the chairman, she was respectful to Garry Edwards and risked calling him Garry once or twice: she caught him looking at her sideways several times. She was very pleasant to a middle-aged and lonely woman who was the wife of a noisy extrovert board member. The woman was so grateful that she positively unburdened her life story. Eve's face came like a quick flash across the conversation; Sara remembered how she had implied that people don't really want to be bogged down with personal life stories, particularly of a gloomy nature. She murmured her sympathy for the details and disclaimers of the woman's tale about neglect and being pushed into the background.

'All he cares about now is our son, he's coming down from Cambridge soon, with an Arts Degree: no plans, no interests.'

Eve would have been proud of her. She geared the conversation gently to her own office, to how she would be delighted to meet the boy – she even gave the woman her card with a little note scribbled on it. How amazing that she should suddenly find a need for those nice new cards which Eve had ordered for her and produced within days of her arrival. Garry Edwards came across at one stage to find out what she was up to; Sara steered the conversation away again.

'Where's that chap that you are seen with sometimes – and sometimes not?' asked Edwards, determined to wound.

'If he's not here, it must be one of the evenings I'm not seen with him,' said Sara cheerfully.

That night she went to sleep in her big double bed, hoping that Geoff would not come home. She had too much to think about.

The weeks went by, two more of them. She had already held three successful and supposedly impromptu gatherings in her office. Always she had included several people higher in the pecking order than Garry Edwards.

Everyone had thought it was a splendid idea to have the handsome young son of their important board member and his lonely wife in the department. He worked most of the time in the general promotions department and two afternoons a week he got what was described as a training from Sara. What it really was was an access to her files, permission to sit in her room as she worked out schemes with some of the other promotions executives, and he learned an almost overpowering respect for Miss Gray from Eve who stood up and expected him to do the same. Eve almost lowered her voice in awe when she spoke of anything Sara had done, and the well meaning, over-educated and not very bright Simon did the same.

Simply because Eve kept him under such an iron rule Simon did learn something. So much in fact that his parents were utterly delighted with him, and the head of marketing, who had opposed his appointment as the nepotism it undoubtedly was, had to admit that that young Miss Gray was able to do the most extraordinary things. He took to dropping in to her pleasant office occasionally, and once or twice that strange colourless secretary had told him very firmly that she couldn't be disturbed. When he implied that he was more important than whoever she could be talking to, the secretary had said very flatly that her instructions were to ask everyone to make appointments, or at least to telephone in advance if they intended to drop in. Since the head of marketing had been saying long and loud that too much socialising and twittering went on in his department in the name of work he could not be otherwise than pleased.

Geoff came back. His latest lady decided that she must go back to her husband and children. This she said was where her duty lay. She said it when all Geoff's money had run out. Geoff had shrugged and come back to Sara. Amazingly she wasn't at home. He let himself in one night with a bottle of champagne, a single rose and a long explanation, but there was nobody to receive any of these things so he just went to bed.

She wasn't there in the morning either. He checked her wardrobe, most of her sweaters and skirts seemed to be there. The place looked neater somehow, and there were no work files strewn about. She had a lot of much more expensive cosmetics in the bathroom too. He wondered what had been happening. He couldn't have been gone more than a month. She hadn't run out, surely? She couldn't have decided to end with him, surely? After all she hadn't changed the lock or anything. His key still opened her hall door.

He called her next morning, and a very cool voice that was not Sara's answered him. 'Miss Gray's office.'

'Oh we have gone up in the world,' giggled Geoff. Loyalty to Sara and building her up to her colleagues was never his strong suit.

'I beg your pardon?' said the voice.

'Listen, it's Geoff here, can I talk to Sara?'

'Can I know who wants to speak to Miss Gray please?' asked Eve.

'Hell, I've just told you. It's Geoff. Sara's chap, Geoff. Put me onto her will you, sweetheart.'

Eve answered very pleasantly. 'I'm afraid you must have the wrong number.'

Geoff sounded annoyed, 'Sara Gray's office, right?'

'Yes this is Miss Sara Gray's office, now will you kindly tell me who this is speaking?'

'Geoff. Geoff White, for Christ's sake, who is that?'

'I am Miss Gray's secretary. Mr White can you please tell me your business. You're taking up a lot of time.'

She didn't actually lie when Sara asked had Geoff phoned. She said that a totally inarticulate man had called but it could hardly have been Geoff. Sara had only paused momentarily to wonder. She had spent five days at a sales conference in Paris, and had told Eve excitedly how she had been asked to address the meeting twice about new brochure ideas. Mr Edwards – or that buffoon Garry as she was now calling him – looked positively yellow with rage. He had tried to make a pass at her which she had rejected with amazement and something akin to distaste. Eve was full of praise.

Next day Sara said: 'The inarticulate man must have been Geoff. His things were in the flat, but I couldn't bear to be woken at three a.m. with champagne and tears and all, so I bolted my door and didn't hear whether he called or not.'

Eve nodded in her cool way. She wanted to hear no more, not one word of Sara's private life. Yet she looked pleased. Things were going as hoped for. Sara was now too busy to worry about Geoff, and soon she would be too confident to accept his amazing behaviour which was already a legend in office gossip. The new Sara would either throw him out or make him behave in a civilised way. Very satisfactory.

The weeks passed again. By now it was already office gossip that Sara would shortly take over from Garry Edwards. People who hadn't rated her much before, were saying now that she had been holding back. Others said that she was always brilliant and that it was only a matter of time before it was recognised.

Garry Edwards blew it. He tried to drop Sara into great trouble for one of his own mistakes. Unlucky Garry Edwards that he had joined battle with Eve's filing system, the relevant documents were produced in a matter of minutes; quite obviously Sara had dealt with the problem, had recommended a correct course of action.

It was shortly after this that Eve asked Sara to come into her small cubicle and go over the filing system with her.

'Let's do a test,' Eve said. 'Suppose you had to find Press Comment on Senior Citizen Campaign, where would you look?' Sara checked first under 'publicity' then under 'Senior Citizens'. It took her five minutes.

'It's too long,' said Eve firmly. 'Perhaps you should have a look for something every day for the next month or so. Just to familiarise yourself.'

'You're going to leave me aren't you?' asked Sara.

'I think so,' said Eve.

'It's not the year, it's not even half a year,' Sara complained.

'But there's nothing left to do, Miss Gray. We get you a new efficient typist, we both explain to her and to Simon what the routine is, you'll be leaving shortly anyway for Mr Edwards' job, we'll just make sure that any changeover here goes smoothly.'

'Can't you come with me, upstairs?' Sara nodded in the direction of the promotions manager's office. 'Please.'

'No, you can do it better on your own really. And it's better for you.' She was like a swimming instructor encouraging a bright but apprehensive pupil.

'The office, Eve, how will I do up the office so that its like this . . . I mean I hate his furniture, I hate his style.'

'You choose, Miss Gray. A few months ago you wouldn't even have noticed his office or his style.'

'Eve, a few months ago you know very well nobody would have noticed me.'

'You underestimate yourself, Miss Gray. Shall I advertise for a secretary, I'd be happy to advise you on any points during any interview.'

'God, yes Eve,' Sara looked at her. 'I won't keep asking you but you know there's no problem about salary.'

Eve shook her head.

Sara put her face into a bright smile. 'In a few months I suppose I'll get a telephone call from some bewildered woman asking me do I know Eve and can I possibly recommend her insane notions.'

Eve looked solemn. 'Well, yes, if you don't mind. I should like your name as a reference.'

'And I'll say Miss whoever you are . . . Eve is not from this planet. Let her have her way with you and you'll be running your company in months.'

Eve stood up briskly. 'Yes, if you think it was all worth it.'

Sara put out her hand and held Eve's arm.

'I know you hate people prying but why, just why? You're far brighter than I am, than the woman in the bank, than the other woman – the one you told to have dinner parties. I mean, why don't *you* do it. Why don't you do it for *you*. You know better than any of us how to get on. It's like a kind of crusade for you but you stay in the background all the time. I don't know what you're at. What you want.'

Eve shrugged politely. 'I like to see you do well, Miss Gray, that's enough reward for me. You deserve it. You were being passed over. That wasn't just.'

Sara nodded. 'Now I promise, all the rest of the time you are here, I'll never ask again. Never. Just tell me. Why this way? If you feel there's discrimination against women there must be better ways to fight it.'

Eve leaned against the beautiful table and stroked it. 'If there are I can't find them. I simply know of no better way to fight it than from within. You have to use the system. I hate it but it's true.'

Sara didn't interrupt. She knew that if Eve was ever going to say anything it would be now. She let the pause last.

'How do you think I, as a feminist, like asking intelligent, sensitive women like you and like Bonnie Bernstein in the bank, and Marrion Smith in the ministry to dress properly? As if it mattered one goddamn whether you wore woad to the office . . . all three of you are worth more than any man I ever met in any kind of business. And I could say that for seven or eight other women, too. But women don't have a chance, they don't bloody know . . .'

Sara sat breathless.

'It's so *unjust*.' Eve stressed that word heavily. 'So totally unjust. A married man has a woman to look after his appearance and his clothes and his meals and his house, a woman does not. A single man has a fleet of secretaries, assistants, manicurists, lovers to look after him. A single woman is meant to cope. A man is admired for sleeping with people on his way up, a woman is considered a tramp if she does. A man . . .' She paused and pulled herself together, almost physically. 'Miss Gray, you must excuse me. I really don't think I should be taking up your time with all this. I do apologise. I feel ashamed of myself.'

The moment was gone, the spell was broken.

'I don't suppose you'll tell me why you feel like this? I mean was there some experience in your life, Eve, you are so young, too young to be bitter about things.'

Eve looked at her. 'No, of course I'm not bitter, I'm very constructive. I just try to get some justice for strong, good women who deserve it. When I've got it I move on. It's very satisfying. Slow but satisfying. Now, about this advertisement. I don't think we should phrase it "travel business'', it will attract the kind of woman who thinks in terms of cheap flights and free holidays.'

Sara played along. She owed Eve that much.

'Oh yes, of course. Let's word it now, and put it in whenever you want to. The later the better of course. You know I don't want you to leave here ever.'

'Thank you very much, Miss Gray. But I think really if you agreed I'll get it into tomorrow's papers.'

Sara looked up.

'So soon?'

'There's a lot to be done,' said Eve.

Euston

Elizabeth marvelled at the changes in Euston. She remembered the station much more clearly as the fairly gloomy and barracks-like place where she had gone with Mother and Father to meet Dara each year when she came over from Ireland on holiday. And here she was years later in the huge revamped place with its shops and its flashing lights and escalators waiting for Dara again. Dara who could well afford to fly but who decided that it would be more fun to retrace the old tracks and come on boat and train; Dara who had always made the holidays turn into technicolour for Elizabeth, the only child; Dara who was so quiet and gentle but somehow managed to make things cheerful in a house where there was little love; Dara who had been able to say things to Mother and Father even after one of their dreadful rows – something that would ease the atmosphere – while Elizabeth would sit mute and tight-lipped, afraid that by opening her mouth she would drive her parents further from each other than they already were.

Even after the divorce, when she and Dara were fifteen, there had been a visit. Mother and Elizabeth had waited in this very spot and when Dara got off the train and ran up to them, she had hugged Mother and said, 'You poor old thing, it must be desperately lonely and sort of low for you these days,' and Mother had hugged her back and cried. Mother crying in public and hugging Dara.

Elizabeth had felt her heart lift for the first time since

the divorce. Dara always had this gift of saying what people didn't say and it all worked perfectly.

During that particular visit Dara had suggested that she would like to see Father. Dara said she had a present for him from Ireland. Mother had pursed her lips and looked disapproving. Elizabeth had feared that everything was going to turn sour again. 'Aw, come on out of that,' Dara had said. 'Now for the rest of your life you can't be expecting that nobody except Elizabeth is going to want to be friends with both of you. It's not a battle for us.'

And because of Dara the visit to Father had been marvellous instead of stilted, and Dara had said 'Aw, come on out of that, of course you've got a new lady friend, why can't we meet her? It's silly to ask her to be out all day, or hidden away as if she were in disgrace.' So Father, delighted, had suggested that Julia join them for lunch, and it had been a memorable meal with wine and a sip of brandy afterwards, and Dara said that there was no purpose in carrying tales from one household back to another, it only made things worse on everyone . . . and with her carefree attitude she had brought some kind of happiness into that troubled summer also.

Dara lived in Ireland with an old grandmother, a housekeeper and a gardener. Her parents, who had been friends of Mother and Father in the old days, had been killed in a car crash and so now Dara's life was a matter of cycling to a local school each day, coming home and making sure her hands were nice and clean and that she came in to lunch or dinner when the gong sounded. She told her old grandmother little tales about what happened at school or with her friends, or during the holidays about what she had read. She seemed to lead an idyllic existence, wandering around the countryside exploring and reading in her large sunny bedroom which looked out on purple mountains. Once a year she came to spend two weeks in London, her annual treat.

The friendship lasted long after schooldays. Dara had trained as a nurse in an Irish hospital at the same time as Elizabeth was doing her training in London. They still holidayed in each others' homes, and as they became more adventurous they even went as far as Spain and Italy together. When Dara's grandmother died there was even talk of her coming to London to share a flat with Elizabeth but she said she would miss the purple mountains and the narrow roads, which she now drove along in her little car instead of pedalling on her creaking bike.

There was also a question of Dara marrying some doctor near-by. Elizabeth had become very excited about this and hoped the romance was going well.

'Do you think he's interested? Do you really think he's contemplating it?' she had asked Dara eagerly when she went to spend a spring week in the Irish countryside and had met the handsome doctor two or three times.

Dara had astonished her by saying: 'Oh, that's not the point. I mean it's easy enough to make him interested, it's just that I don't know yet if *I* want him or not. That's the only problem.'

Elizabeth had been mystified. She assumed in some vague way that Dara must be talking about sexual favours, but despite their years of friendship this was not an area that they discussed. The young doctor was dropped from conversation and from Dara's life, and always Elizabeth had a suspicion that Dara may have loved him a lot, but had failed to attract him. That her conversation had merely been bravado. Still, Dara seemed to have few regrets. She had transformed her grandmother's crumbling old house into an excellent old people's home. The housekeeper and the gardener lived there in style and comfort to work out their old age in payment for all they had given to the place. This gave Dara a very high reputation in the community. Many a young one who came into money might have been hoity-toity, but Miss Dara was different. A very kind young woman indeed. She employed a small staff, all of whom seemed to have been chosen on grounds of their pleasant personalities. It wasn't surprising that the place had a waiting list of several years. Dara kept a supervisory eye on the place but she still worked some hours in the local hospital and still took time to travel. People often wondered why she didn't marry. By the time she was thirty-five they assumed that she was a career woman. It couldn't be from lack of suitors or opportunities.

Elizabeth, too, wondered from time to time, why Dara had never married. But it had not been a serious worry. She assumed it was because of the gentle fulfilling pace that Dara's life always seemed to have been lived at. She had never been searching or seeking. She was always perfectly content with her lot. That's what had made her such a delightful companion. Perhaps these Irish men who must surely have fancied her had been too diffident, too unsure in their own minds about the whole concept of marriage to force Dara to change, to insist that barriers be broken down. Dara would have made a great wife and sailed through all the storms of matrimony, Elizabeth sighed as she waited at the station.

And there were many. Oh dear Lord, there were many. It was a simple fact that when you get married there are not enough hours in the day. Nothing more or less. There are not sufficient slots of time to be a wife, full of interest and concern, and dying to make love, and up to date with every aspect of Derek's work in research. To be a mother, wiping dirty faces, washing clothes, playing creative games, spotting incipient infections, participating meaningfully in the playgroup scheme, arranging baby-sitters that will get on well with the children. To be a worker, to put in thirty-eight hours a week in the nursing agency. To be a home maker, that awful American word which seemed to cover a full-time job polishing, shining, making curtains, cooking, entertaining, gardening.

Even if she slept only two hours a night, Elizabeth thought, it would be too much. There were not enough *hours*.

She needed the job, they both needed her to have the job. Derek's job was not well enough paid for the kind of lifestyle they wanted. Anyway, she liked the job. What she didn't like was the constant guilt, the foolish wearying feeling of being behind at everything. She hated taking the children's mending to work to try and do it in the crowded bus, but where else could she find that spare half-hour? She hated shopping at lunch hour, she hated having to rush and pick the children up from a neighbour's house and have them at home demanding her time and attention before she had time to unpack the groceries and have a shower. It would only take her half an hour, that extra half-hour would give her so much more freedom and energy, but it was impossible. Her bus passed the neighbour's house at five-thirty so it made sense to pick the children up there and walk the ten minutes home with them rather than coming back and having an extra twenty minutes added to the evening at the other end of a half-hour's peace at home. Or so Derek had said. Derek came home at seven, when the house was invariably a mess, the children and herself locked in some struggle about bed, toys, bath, supper. It had become so wildly unsatisfactory that Elizabeth was feeling severe strain, and because of her small medical knowledge she knew it was teetering near the edge of a breakdown.

She wrote it all out in a long letter to Dara, wondering whether she should just collapse and let it all take care of itself. Dara said she would come for a month. Elizabeth could spend a week in a nursing home, two weeks in a health farm and one week at home picking up the threads.

'I'll come at the beginning of February,' Dara had written. 'By March 1st you will be right as rain.'

It was as if a Messiah had announced an imminent coming. Elizabeth was happy already.

When Dara came bouncing up the ramp, her short brown hair ruffled and attractive, Elizabeth felt an almost physical pain of relief. Here was the one person who would make the household happy again. The great restorer of peace as she had been in Mother and Father's time, doing it over twenty years later for Elizabeth herself. She hugged her and clung to her with tears starting to flow.

Dara was obviously startled to see her friend in such poor shape. She put her hand professionally on Elizabeth's forehead.

'I see I'm just in time,' she said. She waved them into a taxi airily. 'You're in no shape to battle with the tube, silly,' she said. 'Anyway we can make our plan of campaign in comfort. Have you booked the nursing home?'

'Yes,' gulped Elizabeth. 'I think they must think I am not all there. It's very dear.'

'That's my wedding present to you, I never gave you a proper one,' said Dara. Elizabeth had a vague memory that Dara had given her some huge fluffy towels but she said nothing.

'Now, the health farm the next week.'

'Yes, yes. I booked it. I know you said to take it from Mother's legacy, I have. Do you think two weeks is too long?'

'No,' said Dara. 'Now Derek. Have you told him yet?'

'Well, yes and no,' said Elizabeth, her face becoming twisted in an effort to explain.

'That means no,' said Dara.

'He'd think I was silly, he'd think I was weak and self-indulgent.' Elizabeth began to stutter in her eagerness to defend Derek's attitude. 'You see, I've been so hopeless recently. So tired. And so complaining. I don't want to let him think he married a dud.'

'Tell him your doctor insisted on it,' said Dara. 'I'll back it up, and say in my professional opinion, which is true by the way, I never saw anyone so much on the verge of collapse. I'll run the house, mind the kids, give Derek his bowl of porridge now and then, and when you come back glowing and well you'll be as right as rain.'

That lovely expression, 'as right as rain', Elizabeth had used it a million times, without ever thinking about it She thought suddenly of the soft gentle rain in Ireland. She thought about the constancy of rain. She felt vastly cheered.

'I don't know why you came to meet me,' said Dara. 'I could easily have made my own way to the house, you know. It would have given you another couple of hours to yourself.'

'Oh we always meet you at Euston,' said Elizabeth, and Dara patted her hand affectionately.

The house was indeed in poor shape. Dara looked around with a practised eye. The children were sweet little three- and four-year-olds, Benny and Nell, but they had obviously worn Derek to a frazzle.

'What *do* they eat at this time darling?' he said in a harrassed tone to Elizabeth. 'They seem very restless. I've no idea what you would have given them.'

Dara gave Derek a peck, and vanished to her room. She returned in ten minutes dressed for work in a simple pinafore of green corduroy.

'You look very business-like,' said Derek with approval. Elizabeth felt even more foolish in her best silk suit, which she was hoping might escape the strains and dangers of Benny and Nell.

'Well, your wife is going to leave us together for three weeks, I'll tell you all about it later,' she said. 'So meanwhile, I suppose I'd better dress to please you.'

Already the tension was lifting.

Already the atmosphere was lighter.

Dara was working her familiar magic.

'Lie down, Elizabeth my love, I'll call you when the meal is ready. Do, there's a good girl,' said Dara.

And Elizabeth went up to her room, where she rested with a great sense of relief. Dara would explain it all to Derek. Dara would make him see that she wasn't a non-starter. Not a weakling. She closed her eyes. At peace for the first time for ages. It was nine o'clock when Dara came to waken her with a cup of consommé with sherry.

'This will liven you up,' she said.

Elizabeth drank it gratefully.

'What's happening? I must get up,' she said suddenly.

All her guilt came flooding back. The meat hadn't been unfrozen for the goulash, the dish-washing machine hadn't been emptied. Heavens. There might well be no clean linen. She had been asleep for two hours.

'It's under control,' said Dara. And indeed it was. Derek had been banished with a drink to the television, the children had been bathed and given cornflakes, the goulash had been designated tomorrow's dinner, while Dara's smoked salmon from Ireland had been carved and sliced and laid on beds of vegetables, the table had been polished and old mats with hunting prints had appeared. In the kitchen the soft whir of the washing machine meant that all the table linen as well as the children's clothes were purring around in a low suds detergent. Elizabeth sighed with pleasure. It was a delightful dinner, and Derek said to her tenderly that he felt very selfish for not having noticed her strain. All three of them made great plans for the week in the nursing home. They drank a toast to the joy of hospitalisation without any disease, or any terror of waiting for results. For the first time in months Elizabeth slept a long peaceful sleep.

Elizabeth went to the nursing home early in the morning. Derek drove her there before he went to work. Dara said she knew well the running of the house, and insisted that she could also replace Elizabeth at the nursing agency so that no extra cash would be lost. The real reason she wanted to do it was to ensure that nobody there could regard Elizabeth as a malingerer. Dara's nursing qualifications were even superior to Elizabeth's, there would be no problem.

And indeed there *were* no problems.

Dara realised quickly that a great deal of problems could be solved by buying food in bulk. So she made a master list and suggested that she and Derek buy this early on Saturday morning. She settled him with the children in a café and had the shopping ready to be collected from the supermarket door in forty minutes. Then she settled in to sit with the children while she sent Derek with a list to buy the week's drink and gardening requisites. 'That's a man's job,' she said when Derek demurred, and he felt very important.

On Sunday she arranged to have the neighbour's children for the day, mainly so that they would entertain Benny and Nell in the bedroom which she had made into a play room for them. But it also made the neighbour feel that she wasn't being taken for granted. It meant she could go to the pub and even have a leisurely lunch with her husband and a bit of slap and tickle. She agreed readily to hold on to Benny and Nell until whatever hour the family liked to collect them on work days. 'I think Derek should pick them up in his car. Their little legs get tired walking home,' said Dara. Derek wondered why nobody had ever thought of this.

She spent a half-hour each day in the garden, but always in places where it showed. The front looked weeded and cared for. Dara even organised funny winter window boxes which looked cheerier than anything else on the road.

When Derek arrived home with the children, she was there, cheerful, fire lighting, and drink in her hand. Derek relaxed while she bathed the toddlers, and together they read them funny stories while they had their supper and went to bed. Then Derek and Dara played chess or looked at television while she mended clothes. Dara told Derek funny tales of the people she nursed. She always made the people sound tender or witty or eccentric, never demanding or tiresome. He loved to hear of them. She was very interested to know where his research was going and why so much money was being given to the Americans while so little went to the British.

Each night they telephoned Elizabeth and listened to what she said. Sometimes she seemed very defensive, and self-justifying. 'You don't have to explain to us,' said Dara over and over. 'We know why you're run down. It's a killer running a job and a home.' Yet, Dara didn't look killed by it, she glowed with happiness, and the house seemed to turn on oiled hinges.

The day of Elizabeth's return was to be fêted, Dara decided. There would be a special celebration meal. Elizabeth was to come back at seven o'clock on a Friday.

'Be sure to take a taxi from the station, darling,' said Derek. He was beginning to believe that a small expense on taxis could save a lot of wear and tear and a lot of time.

Benny and Nell made a banner with 'Welcome Home Mummy' on it. There was to be a bottle of champagne and a cake. They all sat until nearly eight o'clock when Derek became worried and rang the health farm.

'Oh, she left here this afternoon,' the director said. 'She should be with you by now.'

The key turned in the lock and in from the wet sleet came Elizabeth dripping on the newly vacuumed floor.

'I took the tube, a taxi seemed such a waste. Then there were no buses,' she said.

There were cries of welcome, she looked less tired but very bedraggled from her long wait and walk in the rain. She gazed around the house admiringly, it looked very well kept somehow. There was much more peace than there had been three weeks ago when, weary and beaten, she had left it.

'I'll only have a very little piece of cake,' she said proudly. 'I've lost nearly a stone.' They all cooed over her, and Derek put his arm protectively around her shoulder and said he was delighted to have her back and her old self.

Dara tactfully went to bed early after dinner to leave them together. Derek began to tell Elizabeth about the new turn in his work but from habit her mind wandered, and she said she must think of tomorrow's lunch.

'It's done,' he said irritably.

'Done? How can it be done?' she asked mystified.

'Well it's Saturday tomorrow darling. We'll be going out shopping early, and then home to soup and sandwiches, like we do every Saturday.'

'Well, I'll make the sandwiches, if we're going to leave early,' said Elizabeth, a bit discomfited to hear him say 'like every Saturday', when there had only been three Saturdays.

'Oh, darling. They're made. We always have something on Friday night that can end up as sandwiches next day. Dara has mashed up the chicken with some mayonnaise I expect, and we'll get nice crusty bread tomorrow and that's lunch.' He said it with such confidence and sense of repeating the obvious that Elizabeth felt both amused and yet chilled. How very well the house had managed without her.

'It's a good idea this Saturday shopping then?' she asked timidly.

'Well, it makes sense doesn't it?' said Derek, making nothing of five years of her standing in line at delicatessens and greengrocers during lunch hours and carrying them home on crowded buses.

But the week was sheer pleasure. She went back to work and was oohed and aahed over by the other nurses and by her patients who all praised that nice Irish nurse who had been there during her illness.

Each evening when she got back the house seemed like

a welcoming palace; Dara had used the time to do a thorough spring clean and a reorganisation of the linen cupboard.

'Can you give me a list of all the things you buy on a Saturday?' Elizabeth asked humbly.

'Could you explain what exactly you do in the garden?' she begged.

'How are the clothes always clean when you are here?' she implored.

Dara always answered helpfully. She never implied that Elizabeth was an incompetent.

The day before she left Elizabeth said, 'I don't think I'm as right as rain.'

'You're nearly as right as rain,' said Dara as they sat in the sparkling kitchen and had a cup of tea. The children were gurgling happily in their bedroom-cum-playroom, and Derek was having a shower before his evening sherry and chat before dinner.

'What'll I do, Dara?' she asked.

'You *could* quit work, take a lodger to make up some of the dough.'

'No, no.'

'You could do extra hours for the agency and employ a home help.'

'No, no,' said Elizabeth.'

'Well, just keep sort of going I suppose,' said Dara. 'I mean it's not anyone's fault that you're not as right as rain. It's not Derek's fault, he's smashing, and the kids are lovely, and the work's fine, and that neighbour of yours is a real pal, if you take her kids on a Sunday she'll do anything for you. She loves her Sundays.'

'Don't go,' Elizabeth begged.

'Aw, come on Eliza,' Dara always called her that. For over twenty years it has been 'Come on Eliza'.

Eliza looked at her, hoping for a solution.

'Of course I've got to go. Take it easy, take it nice and easy. There aren't any problems at all you know.'

Elizabeth looked at her friend carefully. Dara had said that about Mother and Father. 'Aw, come on Eliza they're only having a bit of a barney with each other . . .' then they had got divorced.

'Aw, come on Eliza, it's not the end of the world, they're both nice happy people, don't make them into old miseries by your own attitude. Enjoy both of them.' Fine until Father had committed suicide and Mother had joined that funny religion of nutters leaving a small legacy to Elizabeth as a gesture towards sanity and family life.

'Aw, come on Eliza, everyone works and runs a home these days – why do you think you're going to be the one who won't manage?' she had said when Elizabeth had first complained of finding it all a little too much.

'Eliza, you'll be as right as rain,' she had said only four weeks ago. And Eliza wasn't.

It had always been the same, when Dara had left, Mother and Father had looked at her and each other, expecting something that Elizabeth wasn't able to give, and being disappointed with her, unreasonably disappointed, because she couldn't. She realised that everyone – Derek, Benny, Nell, that tiresome neighbour, the people at the agency – would all look expectantly at Elizabeth and wish that there was something there, something that Dara's presence had led them to believe was there.

She looked at her friend, and wondered for the first time why she hadn't had a duller friend, one against whom she could be measured and come out winning. Someone dull who would make her shine. Someone messy who would make her seem organised by comparison.

It had been a bad thing to have had Dara to stay. It had been a bad thing for twenty-six years, but she only realised it now, when she was as far as she ever was from being as right as rain.

Warren Street

Nan had had another god-awful day. Nobody seemed to use any under-arm deodorant any more. She had been wincing from whiffs of sweat all day, as people flung off their garments to try on her designs.

That maddening Mrs Fine had, of course, noticed the seam that wasn't exactly right; while that stupid, stupid woman – who apparently worked in some important position in an estate agents – had forgotten again what she wanted made out of the woollen material but was absolutely certain that it wasn't the poncho that Nan had cut out for her.

'Why would I have said a poncho, when I have one already?' she asked wide-eyed.

'That's what I asked you at the time,' hissed Nan.

But the thing that was making Nan's heart leaden was that she had had a row with Shirley.

Now nobody had rows with Shirley. She had a face so like the rising sun you expected rays to stick out from her head like in a child's drawing. If Nan had rowed with her, it had to have been Nan's fault and that was that.

Shirley had been coming to Nan for two years now, ordering maybe five garments a year. Nan remembered the first day she came she had been pressing her nose against the window rather wistfully, looking at a little bolero and skirt outfit on display. The skirt wouldn't have gone over Shirley's head, let alone made it to her waist.

Nan pulled back the curtain and waved her inside – she still wondered why she did it. Normally she never encouraged customers. She had enough enquiries she couldn't deal with, and this was obviously not a fashion-conscious girl whom it would be a pleasure to dress.

Shirley's great, happy face and bouncing, bulging body arrived in Nan's little shop.

'I think I have the wrong place,' she began. 'Lola who works with me and who's eight months pregnant said she got her smocks here, and I was wondering if you have any more smocks. I mean, they might fit me, even though I'm not pregnant.'

Nan had liked her cheerful face so much she'd encouraged her.

'Sit down. I'll go and see. I've very few things really – I mainly make clothes up for people you see.'

'Oh, are you a designer?' asked Shirley innocently.

She had touched on something very near to Nan's heart. She would have liked to think of herself as a designer and she had a flair for ideas and style. She sold things to classy boutiques from time to time. But something about Shirley's face made her answer, to her own surprise: 'No, more a dressmaker.'

'Oh, that's great,' Shirley had said. 'I thought that they'd disappeared. I wonder, would you be able to make me a smock . . . ?' She broke off, seeing a refusal beginning to form itself on Nan's face.

'Oh, please, please do!' she said. 'I can't find anything in the shops that doesn't have white collars or tiny, thoughtful, mum-to-be prints on it.'

'It's just that I'm very busy . . .' Nan began.

'It would be very easy to do,' said Shirley. 'You wouldn't have to put any shape in it, and you wouldn't have to waste time wondering if the fit was right.' She grinned encouragingly, and that did it. Nan couldn't bear her to go around the world as vulnerable as that, and indeed, as badly dressed in that hideous, diagonally-striped garment she had on.

'You win,' Nan had said, and they spent a happy

half-hour planning what Shirley would wear for the winter.

Away went the belted grey army issue-type coats – the only one that fitted Shirley – and on came a cape. Away, too, the men's warm sweaters and on with a rosy red dress and a warm pink one.

Nan also made her a multi-coloured evening dress, which had all the shades of the rainbow in it. It was, she thought, a pleasure to design a dress for Shirley. She was so grateful, so touched and happy when it was finished. Sometimes she would whirl around in it in front of the mirror, her fat little hands clasped excitedly like a child.

Shirely was one of the few clients who didn't seem to have a list of complaints and personal problems, which was another bonus. Nan thought of Mrs Fine, always running down her husband. Shirley never complained about men at all.

Miss Harris was always bitching about traffic or work, or how you couldn't get a taxi or a waiter who spoke English, or proper wholemeal bread. Shirley never seemed in the least upset by such deprivations.

In fact, Nan knew little of Shirley's life, except that she fancied her boss in an advertising agency. Or maybe she didn't – Shirley was always so jokey. The last garment she had made Shirley was a really lovely dress. Nan had spent hours on the very fine wool, with its embroidery, ruffs and frills, its soft blues and yellows. Shirley looked like an enormous, beautiful baby.

It was for some gala evening and Shirley had said: 'If he doesn't tear the clothes off me when he sees me like this, he never will.'

Nan worked on a system of appointments that meant you had to come and see her on the hour, and she only saw eight people a day. That way, she said, the job was manageable. People didn't stay longer than twenty minutes at the most. The rest of the hour Nan worked away with her quiet, little machinist burring on in the background.

She would never be rich, never be famous, but it was a living. She couldn't see a life where she would be finishing buttonholes at three a.m. for a show next day. Her own life and her own lover were far too precious for that. Colin and she had lived together happily for ages and often thought of getting married but they'd never actually got the details organised.

That's what they said. The truth was that Colin would have disappeared very sharply if Nan had suggested marriage. She didn't mind much; although sometimes she felt he had it all ways since they both worked. She did the housework and paid the rent; but then it was her place, and he did share the bills.

And he loved the fact that she worked downstairs. Sometimes if he had a day off he would come in and give her a rose in the workroom, and on one never-to-be-forgotten occasion he had asked the machinist to go for a walk, locked the door and made love to her there and then, to the accompaniment of Miss Harris pounding on the door.

One day Colin had seen Shirley leaving with a finished dress. 'Who on earth was the beach ball bouncing out a minute ago?' he asked. Shirley wasn't the usual mould of Nan's clients.

'That's our Shirl whom I talk about sometimes,' Nan said.

'You never told me she looked like a technicoloured Moby Dick,' said Colin. Nan was annoyed. True, Shirley was enormous; true, she was dressed extremely brightly – mainly at Nan's insistence. But because she had such a lovely face, she looked well in colourful clothes and Nan didn't like Colin's joke.

'That's a bit uncalled for, isn't it?' she said sharply. Colin was amazed.

'Sorry to tease her – let me hold out my hand for a

smack,' he mocked. 'Yes it was very uncalled for, teacher, nobody called for it at all.'

Nan retorted: 'It's cruel to laugh at somebody's shape.'

'Aw, come on, come on,' said Colin reasonably. 'You're always saying someone's like a car aerial or the Michelin Man or whatever. It was just a remark, just a joke.'

Nan forgave him. 'It's just that I feel, I don't know, a bit protective about her. She's so bloody nice compared with almost anyone who comes in here, and she's literally so soft – in every way. I just feel she'd melt into a little pool if she heard anyone making a remark like that about her, honestly.'

'She was halfway down the street before I opened my mouth,' said Colin.

'I know – I suppose I just hope that nobody says such things whether she hears them or not,' said Nan.

That conversation had been a few months ago, Nan reflected, as she sat, head in hands. Funny that it all came back to her now. She did remember exactly how protective she had felt, as if Shirley had been her favourite sister and their mother had entrusted Nan with the care of seeing that nobody ever laughed at the fat girl.

Nan could hardly believe that, not half an hour ago, Shirley had banged out of the door and shouted from the street that she would never come back. It was like a nightmare where people behave completely out of character.

Shirley had come along for a final fitting for the wedding outfit. Her best friend was getting married and Shirley and Nan had been through reams of ideas before setting on the emerald green dress and matching hat.

Nan had been delighted with it and Shirley's face was a picture of happiness as they both looked at the outfit in the mirror: the tall, slim, slightly wary-looking dressmaker in her elegant grey wool tunic and the short, mountainous client in her metres and metres of glittering emerald.

'You'll need green eye-shadow, not blue,' said Nan. 'I'll lend you some for the wedding if you like.' She looked around for her bag. 'Do you know, I was running out of some, and then I thought of you and this colour, so I asked Colin to get me some. He's in the trade, you know, so it's a little perk. I can't find the wretched thing anywhere.' As she hunted for the parcel which wasn't in her handbag after all, Nan felt a strange, unnatural, silence descend behind her.

'Is that it?' asked Shirley, holding up an envelope that was on a table. The envelope had writing on it. It said 'Green eye-shadow for burly Shirley.'

The two women looked at the inscription in silence for what must have been only four seconds or so, but seemed never-ending. Nan could think of only one thing to say.

When it was obvious that Shirley was going to say nothing either, she tried, but her voice only came out like a squeak. What she had been going to say was, 'I didn't write that', and that didn't seem a very helpful thing to say at that moment.

She thought she would kill Colin. She would physically hurt him and bruise him for this. She would never forgive him.

Shirley's face had turned pink. Her fat neck had gone pink too, which didn't go very well with the emerald.

'Is that what you call me: "Burly Shirley"? Well I suppose it has the advantage of rhyming,' she said. She was so hurt she was almost bleeding.

Nan found her words finally. 'Colin has rude, destructive nicknames for all my clients. It amuses him – it's childish, immature and senseless,' she snapped fiercely.

'How does he know I'm . . . burly? He's never met me,' said Shirley.

'Well, you see he makes up these nicknames without knowing who people are. You do see that it's not an insult and it's not a comment. He could have written anything.' Nan nearly laughed with relief. How marvellous to get out of it in this way. But Shirley was looking at her oddly.

'So I expect he just chose the word because it rhymes with your name. If you had been called Dotty he might have said Spotty.' Nan was very pleased with herself, at the unknown powers of invention that were suddenly welling up within her.

Shirley just looked.

'So now that's cleared up, why don't you take the eye-shadow and put a little on to see how it looks with the outfit?' urged Nan.

Shirley politely started to put it on, and Nan released her breath and foolishly didn't leave well, or nearly well, alone.

'I mean it's not as if anyone would deliberately make a joke about being fat to anyone, not that you are very fat or anything, but one wouldn't mention it even if you were.'

'Why not?' asked Shirley.

'Why? Well, you know why – it would be rude and hurtful to tell someone they were fat. Like saying they were ugly or . . . you know . . .'

'I didn't think being fat was on the same level as being ugly, did you?'

Desperately Nan tried to get back to the comparatively happy level they had just clawed their way to a few moments ago.

'No, of course I don't think being fat is the same as being ugly, but you know what I mean – nobody wants to be either if they can possibly avoid it.'

'I haven't hated being fat,' said Shirley. 'But I wouldn't like to think it was on a par with being ugly – something that would revolt people and make them want to turn away.'

'You're not very fat, Shirley,' Nan cried desperately.

'Oh but I am, I am very fat. I am very short and weigh sixteen stone, and no normal clothes will fit me. I am very, very fat, actually,' said Shirley.

'Yes, but you're not really fat; you're not fat like . . .' Nan's inventive streak gave out and she stopped.

'I'm the fattest person you know, right? Right. I thought it didn't matter so much because I sort of felt I had a pretty face.'

'Well, you do have a pretty face.'

'You gave me the courage to wear all these bright clothes instead of the blacks and browns . . .'

'You look lovely in . . .'

'And I didn't worry about looking a bit ridiculous; but you know, ridiculous was the worst I thought I ever looked. I didn't think it was ugly . . .'

'It isn't, you understood . . .'

'It's always disappointing when you discover that someone hasn't been sincere, and has just been having a bit of fun, that she's just been pitying you.'

'I don't pity you . . . I wasn't . . .'

'But thanks anyway, for the outfit.' Shirley started to leave. 'It's lovely and I'm really very grateful. But I won't take the eye-shadow, if you don't mind.'

'Shirley will you sit down . . . ?'

'The cheque is here – that *is* the right price, by the way? You're not doing it cheaply just for me, I hope.'

'Please, listen . . .'

'No, I'm off now. The life has gone out of it here, now that you pity me. I suppose it's just silly pride on my part, but I wouldn't enjoy it any more.'

'Shirley, let me say something. I regard you as my most valued customer. I know that sounds like something out of a book, but I mean it. I looked forward to your coming here. Compared with most of the others, you're a joy – like a friend, a breath of fresh air. I enjoyed the days that you'd been. Now don't make me go down on my knees. Don't be touchy . . .'

'You've always been very friendly and helpful . . .'

'Friendly . . . helpful . . . I regard you as some kind of

kid sister or daughter. I had a fight with Colin about you not three months ago, when he said you looked like Moby Dick with stripes or something.'

'Oh yes.'

'Oh God.'

Shirley had gone. The bang of the door nearly took the pictures off the walls.

'I'll miss her dreadfully,' thought Nan. 'She was the only one with any warmth or life. The rest are just bodies for the clothes.' To hell with it. She would telephone Lola, the friend who had sent Shirley to her in the first place.

'Listen, Lola, this sounds trivial, but you know that nice Shirley who worked with you . . .'

'Shirley Green? Yeah, what about her?'

'No, her name is Kent, Shirley Kent.'

'I know it used to be till she married Alan Green.'

'Married?'

'Nan, do you feel okay? You made her wedding dress for her, about a year ago.'

'She never told me she got married. Who's Alan Green? Her husband?'

'Well, he's my boss, and was hers. Nan, what is this?'

'Why do you think she didn't tell me she got married?'

'Nan, I haven't an idea in the whole wide world why she didnt' tell you. Is this what you rang up to ask me?'

'Well have a guess. Think why she mightn't have told me.'

'It might have been because you and Colin weren't getting married. She's very sensitive, old Shirl, and she wouldn't want to let you think she was pitying you or anything.'

'No, I suppose not.'

'Anyway, it was the most smashing wedding dress – all that ruffle stuff and all those lovely blues and lace embroidery. I thought it was the nicest thing you've ever made.'

Oxford Circus

Once she had decided to write the letter, Joy thought that it would be easy. She had never found it difficult to express herself. She found her big box of simple, expensive writing-paper and began with a flourish: 'Dear Linda . . .' and then she came to a sudden stop.

Joy didn't want to use any clichés about Linda being surprised to hear from her, she didn't want to begin by explaining who she was, since Linda knew. She had no wish to start by asking a favour since that would put her in a subservient role, and Joy wanted to have the upper hand in this whole business. She didn't want it to seem like girlish intrigue; both she and Linda were long past the age when schoolgirl plots held any allure.

Eventually she wrote a very short note indeed and regarded it with great pleasure before she put it into the envelope.

> Linda,
>
> I'm sure my name is familiar to you from the long distant past when Edward was both your friend and mine. There is something I would very much like to discuss with you, something that has little bearing on the past and certainly nothing to do with either nostalgia or recriminations! Perhaps if you are coming to London in the next few weeks, you could let me know and I can take you to lunch?
>
> Sincerely, Joy Martin.

Linda re-read the letter for the twentieth time. Everything, every single warning bell inside her told her to throw it away, to pretend she had never read it. Joy Martin must be mad to want to reopen all the hurts and deceptions and rivalries of ten years ago. They had never met, but she had read all Joy's passionate letters to Edward, she had sneaked a look at the photographs of Joy and Edward taken on their illicit weekends, the weekends when Edward had said he was visiting his elderly mother. Linda could feel her throat and chest constricting with the remembered humiliations and injustices of a previous decade. Throw it away, burn it. Don't bring it all back. It was destructive then, it can only be destructive again now.

Dear Joy,

How intriguing! I thought this kind of thing only happened in glorious old black and white movies. Yes, I do come to London fairly often and will most certainly take you up on your offer of lunch. Can we make it somewhere near Oxford Circus? That way it will leave me right in the middle of the shopping belt. Simply mystified to know what all this is about.

Regards, Linda Grey.

Joy breathed a great happy sigh. She had been so afraid of rejection. A whole week had passed without acknowledgement, and she had almost given up hoping for the Hampshire postmark. Her first hurdle had been cleared. She knew now that Linda Grey must feel exactly as she did about Edward. She had not been wrong. There had been a huge amount of caring, almost passion, in her love letters to him – those letters which Joy had sneaked from his wallet to read. There had been purpose and serious intent in her threats of suicide. No, her fear that Edward might have been forgotten in Linda's cosy Hampshire life was . . . unrealistic. Edward was never forgotten.

Linda came to London the night before this rendezvous. In her handbag she had Joy's card with the name of the restaurant: '. . . only a few minutes from Oxford Circus, as you requested.' She checked in at an inexpensive hotel and ordered a cup of tea to wash down her two sleeping pills. A night in London with the possibility of some showdown involving Edward on the morrow would keep her awake for hours, and she had no wish to arrive looking flustered. She had made appointments for hair and facials. She was going to buy herself some very expensive shoes and a handbag. Joy Martin could not sit elegantly and pity poor Linda who had lost Edward all those years ago. Still, she thought as her body began to relax with the mogadon. Still, Joy had lost him too. He had left Joy very shortly after he had left Linda.

She felt very guilty about Hugh. He had been concerned about her visit to London and wanted to come with her. No, she assured him, just a check-up. She really thought she needed the little break as much as the check-up. She begged him not to come. She would telephone him tomorrow and tell him that she felt perfect and that the doctor had confirmed it. He would be pleased and relieved. He would arrange to meet her at the station and take her out to dinner. He was so kind and good. She didn't know why she was making this ridiculous pilgrimage to dig up the hate-filled ghost of Edward.

Joy woke with a headache and a feeling that something was wrong. Oh God! This was the day. Linda Grey would be getting on her train somewhere in the countryside telling her mouse-like husband that she was going to look at some fabrics in Oxford Street, and was on her way panting with excitement at the very mention of Edward's name. She made herself a health drink in the blender and a cup of china tea. But the headache didn't lift so she took some pain-killers very much against her will. Joy liked to believe that she didn't need drugs. Drugs were for weak people. Today that belief didn't seem so clear. She also thought that only weak people stayed away from work when they felt a little below par. But today that wasn't a theory that she could substantiate. She telephoned her secretary. No, of course she wasn't seriously ill, just a little below par. Her secretary was alarmed. Crisply Joy gave instructions, meetings to be rearranged, appointments to be cancelled, letters to be written. She would be back tomorrow morning. Perhaps even this afternoon.

She felt alarmed that it was all taking so much out of her. She had planned it so very carefully. She had allowed no emotion, no waverings. It was now absolutely foolproof. Why did her stomach feel like water? Why did she think she couldn't face her job at all during the day. Full of annoyance she put on her smart sheepskin coat and set out for a long healthy walk in Hyde Park.

As she walked she saw people with their dogs. She would have liked to have a dog; she didn't disapprove of people having dogs in London if they gave them enough exercise. When all this business was over, Joy thought to herself, she might get a dog. A beautiful red setter, and she could walk him for hours in the park on a bright cold morning like this.

It was five to one and Linda was determined not to be early. She gave herself another admiring look in a window. Her hair was splendid. What a pity that nobody in the village at home could do that sort of thing with scissors and a comb. They really only liked you to have rollers and a half-hour under the dryer. Linda smiled at herself with her newly painted lips. She looked in no way like a woman of nearly forty. She supposed that Joy Martin probably spent days in beauticians. After all, she had a very glamorous job running an art gallery and an art dealing business. Linda had even seen her photograph once talking to a royal person. Facials and expensive handbags would be no treat for Joy.

She forced her feet to go slowly and only when she saw that she was a nice casual six minutes late did she allow herself to enter the restaurant, take two deep breaths and enquire about a table for two booked by Miss Martin.

'You look smashing,' said Joy warmly. 'Really glamorous. Much younger than you did years ago actually. I always think we improve in our thirties really instead of going off.'

'How on earth did you know what I used to look like?' asked Linda settling herself into the corner chair.

'Oh I used to look at the pictures of you in Edward's wallet. Now, will we have a gin or would you prefer a sherry?'

'A gin,' gulped Linda.

'What do you think of me? Have I aged or gone off do you think?'

'No, in fact you look very unsophisticated, sort of wind blown and young,' said Linda truthfully. 'I thought you'd be much more studied, obviously groomed, over made-up. A bit like me,' she giggled.

Joy laughed too. 'I expect you went to a beautician's just to impress me. I was so nervous at the thought of meeting you, I've been out walking all morning in the park. That's why I'm so windswept and rosy. Normally I'm never like this.'

Linda smiled, 'Isn't it funny?' she said. 'After all these years, and we both find it very anxious-making and . . . and well . . . disturbing.'

'Yes,' said Joy. 'That's exactly what it is. Disturbing.'

'Then why did you suggest it, I mean if it's going to make us both anxious and act out of character, what's the point?' Linda's face looked troubled.

Joy paused to order two gin and tonics and to tell the waiter that they would like a little time before they made up their minds about the lunch menu.

'Well,' she said, 'I had to. You see I want you to help

me. I want you and I together to murder Edward. Seriously. That's what I'm hoping you'll help me to do.'

Most of Linda's omelette aux fines herbes lay untouched. But Joy had managed to eat much of the wholewheat pizza. Linda had managed one sip of the dry white wine but it had tasted very sour. The longer Joy talked the more Linda realised that she was indeed perfectly serious.

'Well, it stands to reason that he's a man the world would be much better off without. We all agree about that. Well, Linda, be reasonable. There was my divorce. I haven't seen my son for nine and a half years because of Edward. If it hadn't been for Edward I would have a perfectly normal and happy relationship with my son who is now sixteen. As it is I am not allowed to visit him at school; everyone agrees it is less distressing for Anthony if his mother is kept away. Later when he's an adult I shall have some ridiculous "civilised" meeting with him, where we will have nothing to say. So that was one thing Edward destroyed.'

'But you were willing to divorce your husband, to leave everything for Edward. Wasn't it your fault too?'

'No it was not my fault,' Joy was calm and unemotional. 'I was twenty-eight and bored with marriage and a demanding child and Edward lied to me, used me, filled my head with nonsenses, betrayed me and then would not stop by me after I had done what he begged and implored me to do – leave home, leave my husband and child and run away with him. He laughed at me.'

Linda said: 'I didn't know that.'

'And look what he did to you. A nervous breakdown. A serious two-year depression. Two years out of your life because you believed him, and couldn't accept his betrayals, his double life, his endless pointless lies.'

Linda said: 'I didn't think you knew that.'

'There were people before us, Linda, there were people after us. Mine wasn't the only divorce he caused, yours wasn't the only nervous illness. And nobody has punished him. Nobody has said this man is evil and he must be stopped. He mustn't be allowed to roam the world destroying, destroying, turning good to bad and dark, turning simple things to twisted and frightening.' Joy's voice hadn't raised itself a decibel but there was something in it that was a little like a preacher, like some Southern Baptist in a movie describing Satan. It chilled Linda and forced her to speak.

'But it's all over Joy, it's all done. It's all finished. Other people are being silly and foolish nowadays, like you and I once were stupid. They're making mistakes now. Not us.'

Joy interrupted her. 'We were not silly, we made no mistakes, neither do his women of today. We all behaved normally as if Edward were normal. When we said things we meant them. When we told him tales they were true, when we made promises they were sincere.'

Once more her voice was uncomfortably like a preacher. In the busy crowded restaurant Linda felt frightened.

'But you don't seriously want to . . . er . . . get rid of him?'

'Oh yes,' said Joy.

'But why now? Why not years ago, when it hurt more?'

'It hurts just as much now,' said Joy.

'Oh, but it can't,' Linda cried sympathetically. 'Not now.'

'Not for myself,' said Joy. 'But now he has gone too far. Now he has done something he can't be forgiven for. He's taken my niece to live with him. She is, of course, utterly besotted with him. She's given up her job for him like you gave up yours, she's given up her fiancé like I gave up my marriage. She will shortly give up her sanity like you did, and her happiness like I did.'

Linda felt a little faint. The smart restaurant seemed somehow claustrophobic.

'Are you very concerned about your niece?' she asked, her voice coming from a long way away. She wanted to keep Joy talking. She didn't want to have to say anything herself.

'Yes, she lives with me. She's all I've got. I've had her since she was seventeen, three years. I thought that if, well if I did a good job looking after her, they might let me have Anthony back too. Anyway, I'm very attached to Barbara, I've told her everything, she's learning the trade in our company, she's studying art history as well. The one thing I couldn't foresee in a city of twelve million people was that she might meet Edward.'

'Does she know? Does he know?' Linda's voice was still weak: there was a coldness in Joy's tone now that terrified her.

'Barbara doesn't know. I've never seen any reason to tell her about my relationship with Edward. And Edward doesn't remember me.'

'What?'

'He came to the house, to my house last month to collect Barbara, she introduced him to me proudly. His eyes rested on me easily. He doesn't remember me, Linda. He has forgotten me.'

Linda was swept by sympathy for the woman ten years previously she would have like to have killed.

'He pretended. It was another ploy. He *can't* have forgotten you. Joy, don't get hurt over it, you know what he was like. He's just trying to wound you. Don't let him.'

'He had forgotten me, Linda. I am certain he has forgotten you too, and Susan or whoever came after us. I will not let him use Barbara. She took her things last week and has gone to him!'

'She's twenty years of age Joy, these days that's old enough . . '

'No day is anyone old enough for Edward, or cruel

enough,' said Joy. 'Oh, Barbara is sure she is doing the right thing:

"You know how it is, Auntie Joy.

"You were wild once they say, Auntie Joy.

"If you knew how he makes me need him, Auntie Joy."'

Linda looked across the table. 'Don't tell me what you want to do,' she said.

Joy reached for her hand. 'Please, please. It needs two. You know, you understand, you and I were the same age, we went through the same things. We know. No one else can do it.'

'Don't tell me. I don't want to hear,' said Linda.

'We need two. Nobody can ever connect you with it. You can come up to London for a day, just like today, to buy curtains or whatever. It's in two parts. You needn't even look at him I tell you. He'll be unconscious anyway. I shall have given him the tablets first.'

Linda stood up shakily. 'I beg you not to think about it any more. Do something, anything. Go away. Come and stay in the country with me. Just stop planning it.'

'It has been planned. It's all planned. You are to come to my house, I'll leave the key and the gun.'

'I won't listen,' said Linda. 'I can't listen. You don't want to kill him, you want him back. You don't give two damns about your niece. You want Edward. You want him dead if you can't have him. It gives you a wave of pleasure just thinking of his head on one side, dead. His mouth still, his eyes open but not seeing things, not darting . . .'

'How do you know? How can you know that it's like that?' Joy's eyes were bright.

'Because I planned to kill him ten years ago. Ten years ago when you went to live with him. I planned it, too. But I had to plan it on my own. I wasn't confident enough.'

'You what?' Joy looked at her in disbelief.

'I planned it all, I would tell him I needed to see him

once. I would assure him there would be no scenes, I would ask him to my flat but in fact I would have some friends there and when he came I would pretend that he had attacked me and that I was fighting him off in self-defence. In the mêlée a knife would be used.'

'Why didn't you do it?' asked Joy.

'Because of you. I knew that you would have known it was murder. You would know Edward didn't care enough for me to attack me. You could have had me convicted.'

'How far had you got?' whispered Joy.

'As far as organising the knife, the friends in my flat, and asking him to come and see me.'

'And what happened?'

'Oh when he called, I told him I had changed my mind, I didn't want to see him after all. He stayed for one drink, long enough to bewitch Alexandra, my friend.'

'Alex. Oh God! She was your friend?'

'So you saved me from doing it. Let me save you.'

Joy pulled herself together. It was almost a visible thing. First her spine straightened. Then her brow became unlined. A small smile came to her mouth.

'We are being very dramatic, aren't we?' she said in a brittle voice.

'Very,' agreed Linda politely.

'Shall we have coffee, or are you in a hurry to get on with your shopping?'

'Rather a hurry actually,' said Linda.

'So you're off back to Hampshire then and the peaceful life,' said Joy waving for the bill.

'Yes, nothing much to do,' said Linda.

'Very quiet and tranquil I expect,' Joy said producing her credit card for the waiter.

'Only excitement I get is reading the papers, seeing who's saying what and doing what. Reading about the things that happen in London, sudden deaths, scandal. You know the kind of thing.'

A small and almost genuine smile came to Joy's eyes.

'I see,' she said.

Linda left, pausing to ask the waiter if there was a phone she could use. She told Hugh that she was very pleased with her check-up and she might catch the earlier train home. He sounded very pleased. And, for the first time in a long time, his pleasure gave her pleasure too.

Green Park

They had both sworn that they would not dress up. They had assured each other that it would be ridiculous to try to compete with Jane after all these years and considering all the money she had. Very immature really to try on fine feathers and glad rags – like children dressing up and playing games. Yet when they met at the station they were almost unrecognisable from their usual selves.

Helen had bought a new hat with a jaunty feather, and Margaret had borrowed a little fur cape. Both of them wore smart shoes and their faces normally innocent of powder had definite evidence of rouge and even eye-shadow. After much mutual recrimination they agreed that they both looked delightful and settled themselves into the train to London with more excitement than two schoolgirls.

How extraordinary to be heading off for tea at the Ritz with Jane. Helen whispered that she would love to tell everybody in the railway compartment that this was where they were heading. Margaret said it would be more fun to let it fall casually in conversation afterwards: 'How nice you look today, Mrs Brown, what a sensible colour to wear, lots of people in the Ritz last week seemed to be wearing it.'

And of course they giggled all the more because, in spite of sending themselves up, they actually were a little nervous about going to somewhere as splendid as the Ritz. They were over-awed. The very mention of the Ritz made them nervous. It was for perfumed, furred people not people who had dabbed some of last Christmas's perfume behind the ears and borrowed a sister-in-law's well-worn Indian lamb.

In some way both Helen and Margaret feared they might be unmasked when they got there. And they giggled and joked all the more to stifle this fear.

None of their fear was directed towards Jane. Jane was one of their own. Jane had trained to be a children's nanny with them all those years ago. You don't forget the friends made during that kind of apprenticeship. It was far more binding than the services were for men. It was almost like having survived a shipwreck – the eighteen girls who survived that particular obstacle race in the school for nannies, which had long since closed down, had forged a friendship which would last for life. Some of them had gone to the Gulf states and they wrote regular newsletters saying how they were getting on. Some, like Helen and Margaret, had married and applied their nanny training to their own children; only Jane had become spectacular and famous. But because she was Jane from the nanny training school it didn't matter if she became head of the United Nations, Helen and Margaret would never be in awe of her.

They changed trains, twittering happily at Euston and took the underground to Green Park.

'Perhaps people think we are career women, dropping into the Ritz for a business conference,' whispered Helen.

'Or wealthy wives up for a day's shopping,' sighed Margaret.

Neither Margaret nor Helen were wealthy. Margaret was actually married to a vicar and lived in a draughty vicarage. She was so much the vicar's wife now that she felt quite guilty about wearing the Indian lamb in case any of her husband's parishioners saw her and wondered about her showiness. Helen, too, was far from wealthy. Jeff, her husband, had a flair for backing things that went wrong and that included horses. Yet never had a hint of envy been spoken or indeed felt by the two women about the wealthy friend they were en route to meet.

Jane was the mistress of a very eccentric and extraordinarily wealthy American industrialist. He had bought her many gifts, including a ranch and a small television station; she was one of the world's richest and best known kept women.

For the twentieth time Margaret wondered if Jane could possibly look as well as she appeared in the photographs, and for the twentieth time Helen said it was quite possible. If you didn't have to do anything each day except make yourself look well, then it was obvious you could look magnificent. Suppose each day when Margaret got up she didn't have to clean the vicarage, take her children to school, shop, cook, wash, go to coffee mornings, sales of work, cookery demonstrations and entertain the doctor, the curate, the headmaster – think how well she could look. Margaret had a very good bone structure, Helen agreed grudgingly, she could look very striking if only she had time to lavish on herself. Margaret felt a bit depressed by this; she knew that Helen meant it as a compliment but it left her feeling as if she were in fact a great mess because she didn't have this time, and that her good bone structure was wasted.

As they came up from Green Park tube station into the sunlight of Piccadilly the two women giggled again and reached for their powder compacts before they crossed the road to the Ritz.

'Aren't we silly?' tittered Helen. 'I mean we're forty years of age.'

'Yes, so is Jane of course,' said Margaret as if that was some kind of steadying fact. Something that would keep their feet on the ground.

Jane had been attractive twenty years ago, but she was a beauty now.

'You look ridiculous,' gasped Helen. 'Your face, your

whole face, it's the face of a twenty year old. You look better than when we were all teenagers.'

Jane gave a great laugh showing all her perfect teeth.

'Aw, for Christ's sake Helen, I bought this face, and bloody boring it was, I tell you. It's easy to have a face like that. Just give it to someone else to massage it and pummel it and file the teeth down and put caps on, no the face isn't any problem.'

Margaret felt that she wished the foyer of this overpowering hotel would open and gulp her into the basement area. She had never felt so foolish, in her ratty overdressed, over-done bit of Indian lamb.

'Come on, we'll go to the suite,' Jane said, an arm around each of their shoulders. She noticed how impressed Helen and Margaret were with the tea lounge and the pillars and the little arm chairs beside little tables where only the very confident could sit waiting casually for their friends. She knew they would love to sit in the public area and drink it all in with Jane herself there to protect them.

'We'll come back and do the grand tour later, but now we go and meet Charles.'

'Charles?' Both women said it together with the alarm that might be generated at a dorm feast if someone mentioned that the headmistress was on her way. It was obvious that neither of them had thought that the ordeal of meeting Charles was included in the invitation of tea.

'Oh yeah, the old bat wants to make sure I really am meeting two old chums from the college. He has a fear, you see, that I'll have hired two male go-go dancers from some show. I want him to get a look at you so that he can see you are the genuine article, not something I made up. Come on, we'll get it over with, and then we can settle down to cream cakes and tea and gins and tonics.'

Because Jane had shepherded them so expertly towards the lift, Margaret and Helen hadn't even had time to exchange a glance until they found themselves outside a door where two tall men stood.

'Are they bodyguards?' whispered Margaret.

'They speak English,' laughed Jane. 'I know they look like waxworks, but that's part of the qualifications. If you came in here with a machine-gun to kill Charles you wouldn't get far.'

They were nodded in by the unsmiling heavies at the door, and Charles was visible. He stood by the window looking out at the traffic below. A small, old, worried man. He looked a bit like her father-in-law, Helen thought suddenly. A fussy little man in an old people's home who didn't really care when she and Jeff went to see him, he only cared about what time it was, and was constantly checking his watch with clocks.

When Charles did give them his attention he had a wonderful smile. It was all over his face, even his nose and chin seemed to be smiling. Margaret and Helen stopped being nervous.

'I'm a foolish old gentleman,' he said in a Southern States drawl. 'I'm jes' so nervous of my Jane, I always want to see who she goes out with.'

'Heavens,' said Margaret.

'Well, I see, how nice,' stammered Helen.

'You ladies jes' must understand me. I guess you know how it is when you only live with someone, you aren't so sure, it's not the same binding thing as marriage,' he looked at them winningly, expecting some support.

Margaret found her vicar's wife's voice: 'Honestly, Mr . . . er . . . Charles . . . I'm not in any position to know what you're talking about. I don't know any couples who live together who are not married.'

She couldn't in a million years have said anything more suitable. Jane's mouth had a flicker of a smile and in two minutes Charles had taken his briefcase, his personal assistant, and his bodyguards and having made charming excuses he left for a meeting that had been delayed presumably until he had satisfied himself about Jane's activities and plans for the afternoon.

'Is the place bugged?' Helen whispered fearfully when he had gone. Her eyes were like big blue and white china plates.

Jane screamed with laughter: 'Darling Helen, no of course not. Hey, I'm really very sorry for putting all that on you both but you see the way he is.'

'Very jealous?' suggested Helen, still in a low voice.

'A little paranoid?' Margaret offered.

'No, dying actually,' said Jane flatly, and went to get a jewelled cigarette box. 'Yeah, he only has two months, poor old bat. He's half the size he was six months ago. They said well under a year, now it's getting quicker.'

She sounded as if she were talking about a tragedy in some distant land, a happening in a country where she had never been. Everyone is sad about far floods and droughts but they don't concern people like near ones do. Jane spoke of Charles as if he were a figure she had read about in a Sunday paper, not a man she had lived with for ten years. She seemed neither upset nor relieved by his terminal illness, it was just one of the many sad things that happen in life.

'I'm very sorry,' said Margaret conventionally.

'He doesn't look as if he had only a short time to live,' said Helen.

'I'm sure that if he's not going to get better it's all for the best that it should happen swiftly,' said Margaret being a vicar's wife again.

'Aw shit, that's not what I wanted to see you about,' said Jane. She looked at their shocked faces.

'Look, sorry, sorry for the language, and this, well, lack of feeling. I *am* sorry for the old bastard, he's been very brave, and he's very frightened, you know. But hell, Margaret, Helen, we are not fools. I mean, be straight. He's hardly the love of my life.'

There was a silence. Whatever they had expected from

afternoon tea with Jane in the Ritz, it certainly was not this.

Jane appealed to them: 'I thought that being in the nanny school was blood brothers, you know, for life? I thought that those of us who survived could say anything, anything and it wasn't misconstrued.'

Margaret said: 'Jane, of course you can say anything to me but remember we've all lived a life since we came out of nanny school. Mine has been very sheltered. I'm a vicar's wife for heaven's sake. What can be more sheltered than that? I ask you. It's the kind of thing people make jokes about, it's so well, so different from yours. Can you really expect me to take all this in my stride?'

'All what?' Jane wanted to know.

'Well your wealth, your lifestyle, the fact that your husband, your common-law husband is dying of cancer and you say awful words and . . .' Margaret looked genuinely distressed. Helen took up the explanation.

'You see, Jane, it's not that either Margaret or I are trying to be distant. It's just that we don't really live in the same world as you any more and I expect after a few minutes or an hour we'll all settle down and be the same as we used to be. It's just hard to expect us to act on your level.'

Jane walked around the room for a moment or two before she replied:

'I guess I was taking things a bit too much for granted. I guess I was reading too much into all that solidarity we had twenty years ago.'

She was silent, and looked perplexed. She looked young, beautiful and puzzled, the two matrons stared up at her from their sofa in disbelief. It was if they were watching a film of their youth where only Jane had stayed young. She used to look just like that when she was nineteen and thinking of a way to avoid detection by the nanny college principal.

'You needn't think the friendship isn't there,' said

Helen. 'In fact it is, enormously. I can tell Margaret things about my private life, my worries with Jeff and money. Susie was back from Kuwait and when we met she was telling us all about how she discovered she was lesbian and she could tell nobody.' Helen looked like a big innocent schoolgirl trying to join the senior girls by revealing secrets and showing herself to be mature.

'Oh I know, Susie wrote to me,' said Jane absently.

'I feel we've let you down, Jane,' said Margaret. 'I feel there was something you wanted us to do for you, and just by racing the wrong way at the outset we've made that impossible.'

Jane sat down.

'You were always very astute Margaret,' she said. 'There was indeed something I wanted to ask you. But now I don't know whether or not I can. You see I can only do it if I am utterly frank with you. I can't go through any charade with anyone from nanny college. There are rules I break in life but never that.' She looked at them.

'Of course,' said Helen.

'Naturally,' said Margaret.

'Well, you see, I wanted to stay in England until Charles kicks it. No, sorry, if we are going to be frank, I simply will not use words like "passes away", he's dying, he's riddled with cancer, he's not going to see Christmas. I don't wish him any more pain, I wish he were dead. Dead now.'

Their faces were sad, less shocked than before but still not understanding.

'So if we stay here till the end, I want Charles to see that I have friends, good decent normal friends like you two. I want to take him to your homes. He'll probably insult you and buy you new homes but we can get over that. I mean he'll buy you and David a new parsonage certainly Margaret, possibly the bishop's palace, and as for Jeff he'll either buy him a bookmaking business or he'll send him to a Harley Street specialist to have what he will consider compulsive gambling cured in some clinic at three hundred quid a day.'

There was a ghost of a smile passing over the faces of the two on the sofa.

'I wanted to ask your support in these last weeks. There's nobody else I could trust, and I've worked so goddamn hard for ten years I can't lose it all now.'

'What will you lose?' Margaret asked. 'You've already said you won't miss him. I don't see how our inviting him to our homes can help anything at all.'

'Don't you see?' Jane cried out. 'He is going mad, he has premature senility, he's paranoid. He thinks I'm unfaithful to him, he thinks I'm cheating on him. He's busy trying to dispossess me of everything.'

'He can't do that,' Helen gasped.

'You can't think that,' Margaret gasped at the same time.

'He can, he can do a lot of it, and I can and do think it because I know it,' said Jane.

In simple terms she told them a tale of stocks and companies, of the properties she owned absolutely which could not be repossessed, of the shares that had been bought back. The two women sat mutely listening to companies which were merged and stock transferred. They heard of the invalid wife whom Charles would never divorce because in his part of Georgia only cads and men who were not gentlemen divorced invalids. They heard of his suspicions, none of them founded on any truth, that Jane was in fact using his riches to buy herself young lovers.

'Even so, even if he does dispossess you,' said Helen, trying to find a word of consolation, 'You'll still be very rich.'

Margaret thought of the corridors upstairs in the vicarage which would never have a carpet on them because they could only afford to carpet to the top of the stairs.

'You'll still be young Jane, and wealthy compared to

almost everyone,' she said. 'I can't see how anything will be so terrible.'

'It's terrible to be denied over ninety per cent of what I could have had,' said Jane. 'If the old bat had stayed sane. That's why I want to try and recoup as much as I can. I can't chain him to his bed. The lawyers for his various trusts are slobbering with greed. They're helping him each bloody hour to get more away from me. My lawyers say it's an unequal struggle. They even want to be paid in advance in case I'm left with nothing at the end.'

She looked like a thwarted child.

'How would coming to visit us help?' Helen asked trembling at the thought of bodyguards and Charles and huge cars in her small terraced house.

'He'd see I was normal, came from some normal sinless background. He's heavily into sin now that he can't commit any any more. He'd see heavy respectability in your homes. We could act out a pantomime till he snuffs it.'

Margaret gave her a look of great distaste.

'You can't mean it, Jane.'

'I do.'

Helen looked at her as if she had been someone apologising for a drunken scene.

'You can't have been aware of what you were asking us to do. That's why you feel you can no longer ask it,' she said.

Jane slooked at them slowly.

'I'm asking you to join in a little deception with me, I'm telling you the whole score, I'm explaining why, and why I need it.'

'But Jane, it's so dishonest, it's so phoney, so high-powered,' said Margaret.

'I think it's only because you imagine it's *high-powered* you're asking me to drop it,' said Jane. 'We went in for a lot of things that were phoney and dishonest in the old days. No holds were barred when you two were landing your men but now that we're older and the stakes are higher, it's high-powered as well as dishonest, we can't do it.'

With a very swift movement she lifted a telephone and cancelled afternoon tea asking room service to make sure it was set for them downstairs instead.

'My guests will prefer to eat in the tea lounge instead,' she said crisply.

Her eyes were bright, she dismissed any further discussion of the matter, she shepherded them neatly downstairs, past another bodyguard at the door who plodded discreetly after them and eventually positioned himself in the hotel lobby where he could see them at all times.

As she poured tea, Jane insisted on hearing of all their happenings, and little by little the guard relaxed sufficiently for them to talk about their homes and lives. She told them, too, about some of the things she had done. Nothing relating to Charles and his short future or his pathetic paranoia.

She told how she had met a famous film star, and she described what it was like to have a beautician arrive every morning at seven a.m. and not to allow you to face the world until after nine. She ate no cream cakes but urged the others to finish the plate.

They parted at the door under the admiring glance of many people who thought Jane quite startlingly attractive, and under the watchful glance of the bodyguard who had instructions not to let Jane out of his sight. There were little kisses and assurances of further letters and visits and meetings, there were clasps and grins and pronouncements that it would all turn out fine in the end.

Helen and Margaret went down into the tube again. Green Park station looked less full of promise and giggles and a day out.

'Everything they say about money not bringing

happiness is true,' said Helen as she fumbled in her shabby purse for the coins for her ticket.

'You would have thought that with all that money and high life she would have been contented, but no, it's more, ever searching for more,' said Margaret.

They were very silent going home. It was unlike them to be silent. Such a long friendship meant that they could say things which others wouldn't broach. But even the apprenticeship in the nanny college and all that it involved was no help to them now.

Helen thought about how Jane had helped her to raise the money for her wedding to Jeff, when Jeff had lost the whole three hundred pounds on a horse. Jane had been efficient and practical and dishonest. She had sold tickets for a charity that did not exist. She delivered the money to Helen without a comment.

Margaret was thinking of the early days when she had fallen for Dave, the handsome divinity student. Jane had helped her then, so well had Jane helped her that David's fiancée had been dislodged. There was just a rumour here and tittle tattle there so that poor David thought that he had become engaged to a Jezebel. While the same process in reverse was worked about Margaret. A blameless innocent was how Margaret appeared.

In those days it had seemed the normal thing to do, to support your friends. After all, everyone knew that men were notoriously difficult and could cause all kinds of hurtful problems. They were always misunderstanding things. It was only right that friends should help each other when there was a problem of that sort. Those were their thoughts, but they didn't share them.

Victoria

Rose looked at the woman with the two cardboard cups of coffee. She had one of those good-natured faces that you always associate with good works. Rose had seen smiles like that selling jam at fêtes or bending over beds in hospitals or holding out collecting boxes hopefully.

And indeed the woman and the coffee headed for an old man wrapped up well in a thick overcoat even though the weather was warm, and the crowded coffee bar in Victoria Station was even warmer.

'I think we should drink it fairly quickly, Dad,' said the woman in a half-laughing way. 'I read somewhere that if you leave it for any length at all, the cardboard melts into the coffee and that's why it tastes so terrible.'

He drank it up obediently and he said it wasn't at all bad. He had a nice smile. Suddenly, and for no reason, he reminded Rose of her own father. The good-natured woman gave the old man a paper and his magnifying glass and told him not to worry about the time, she'd keep an eye on the clock and have them on the platform miles ahead of the departure time. Secure and happy he read the paper and the good-natured woman read her own. Rose thought they looked very nice and contented and felt cheered to see a good scene in a café instead of all those depressing, gloomy scenes you can see, like middle-aged couples staring into space and having nothing to say to each other.

She looked at the labels on their suitcases. They were heading for Amsterdam. The name of the hotel had been neatly typed. The suitcases had little wheels under them.

Rose felt this woman was one of the world's good and wise organisers. Nothing was left to chance, it would be a very well-planned little holiday.

The woman had a plain wedding ring on. She might be a widow. Her husband might have left her for someone outrageous and bad-natured. Her husband and four children might all be at home and this woman was just taking her father to Amsterdam because he had seemed in poor spirits. Rose made up a lot of explanations and finally decided that the woman's husband had been killed in an appalling accident which she had borne very bravely and she now worked for a local charity and that she and her father went on a holiday to a different European capital every year.

Had the snack bar been more comfortable she might have talked to them. They were not the kind of people to brush away a pleasant conversational opening. But it would have meant moving all her luggage nearer to them, it seemed a lot of fuss. Leave them alone. Let them read their papers, let the woman glance at the clock occasionally, and eventually let them leave. Quietly, without rushing, without fuss. Everything nearly stowed in the two bags on wheels. Slowly, sedately, they moved towards a train for the south coast. Rose was sorry to see them go. Four German students took their place. Young, strong and blond, spreading German and English coins out on the table and working out how much they could buy between them. They didn't seem so real.

There was something *reassuring* she thought about being able to go on a holiday with your father. It was like saying, thank you, it was like stating that it had all been worthwhile, all that business of his getting married years ago and begetting you and saving for your future and having hopes for you. It seemed a nice way of rounding things off to be able to take your father to see foreign cities because things had changed so much from his day. Nowadays, young people could manage these things as a matter of course; in your father's day it was still an adventure and a risk to go abroad.

She wondered what her father would say if she set up a trip for him. She wondered only briefly, because really she knew. He'd say, 'No, Rose, my dear, you're very thoughtful but you can't teach an old dog new tricks.'

And she would say that it wasn't a question of that. He wasn't an old dog. He was only barely sixty, and they weren't new tricks, since he used to go to Paris every year when he was a young man, and he and Mum had spent their honeymoon there.

Then he would say that he had such a lot of work to catch up on, so it would be impossible to get away, and if she pointed out that he didn't really have to catch up on anything, that he couldn't have to catch up on anything because he stayed so late at the bank each evening catching up anyway – well, then he would say that he had seen Europe at its best, when it was glorious, and perhaps he shouldn't go back now.

But he'd love to go back, he would love it. Rose knew that. He still had all the scrapbooks and pictures of Paris just before the war. She had grown up with those brown books, and sepia pictures, and menus and advertisements, and maps carefully plotted out, lines of dots and arrows to show which way they had walked to Montmartre and which way they had walked back. He couldn't speak French well, her father, but he knew a few phrases, and he liked the whole style of things French, and used to say they were a very civilised race.

The good-natured woman and her father were probably pulling out of the station by now. Perhaps they were pointing out things to each other as the train gathered speed. A wave of jealousy came over Rose. Why was this woman, an ordinary woman perhaps ten years older than Rose, maybe not even that, why was she able to talk to her father and tell him things and go places with him and type out labels and order meals and take pictures?

Why could she do all that and Rose's father wouldn't move from his deck-chair in the sun lounge when his three weeks' holiday period came up? And in his one week in the winter, he caught up on his reading.

Why had a nice, good, warm man like her father got nothing to do, and nowhere to go after all he had done for Rose and for everyone? Tears of rage on his behalf pricked Rose's eyes.

Rose remembered the first time she had been to Paris, and how Daddy had been so interested, and fascinated and dragging out the names of hotels in case she was stuck, and giving her hints on how to get to them. She had been so impatient at twenty, so intolerant, so embarrassed that he thought that things were all like they had been in his day. She had barely listened, she was anxious for his trip down the scrapbooks and up the maps to be over. She had been furious to have had to carry all his carefully transcribed notes. She had never looked at them while there. But that was twenty and perhaps everyone knows how restless everyone else is at twenty and hopefully forgives them a bit. Now at thirty she had been to Paris several times, and because she was much less restless she had found time to visit some of her father's old haunts – dull, merging into their own backgrounds – those that still existed – she was generous enough these days to have photographed them and he spent happy hours examining the new prints and comparing them with the old with clucks of amazement and shakings of the head that the old bakery had gone, or the tree-lined street was now an underpass with six lanes of traffic.

And when Mum was alive she too had looked at the cuttings and exclaimed a bit, and shown interest that was not a real interest. It was only the interest that came from wanting to make Daddy happy.

And after Mum died people had often brought up the subject to Daddy of his going away. Not too soon after the funeral of course, but months later when one of his old friends from other branches of the bank might call.

'You might think of taking a trip abroad again sometime,' they would say. 'Remember all those places you saw in France? No harm to have a look at them again. Nice little trip.' And Daddy would always smile a bit wistfully. He was so goddamn gentle and unpushy, thought Rose, with another prickle of tears. He didn't push at the bank which was why he wasn't a manager. He hadn't pushed at the neighbours when they built all around and almost over his nice garden, his pride and joy, which was why he was now overlooked by dozens of bed-sitters. He hadn't pushed Rose when Rose said she was going to marry Gus. If only Daddy had been more pushing then, it might have worked. Suppose Daddy had been strong and firm and said that Gus was what they called a bounder in his time and possibly a playboy in present times. Just suppose Daddy had said that. Might she have listened at all or would it have strengthened her resolve to marry the Bad Egg? Maybe those words from Daddy's lips might have brought her up short for a moment, enough to think. Enough to spare her the two years of sadness in marriage and the two more years organising the divorce.

But Daddy had said nothing. He had said that whatever she thought must be right. He had wished her well, and given them a wedding present for which he must have had to cash in an insurance policy. Gus had been barely appreciative. Gus had been bored with Daddy. Daddy had been unfailingly polite and gentle with Gus. With Gus long gone, Rose had gone back to live in Daddy's house. It was peaceful despite the blocks of bed-sitters. It was undemanding. Daddy kept his little study where he caught up on things, and he always washed saucepans after himself if he had made his own supper. They didn't often eat together. Rose had irregular hours as a traveller and Daddy was so used to reading at his supper, and he ate so early in the evening. If she stayed out at night there were no explanations and no questions. If she told him some of her adventures there was always his pleased interest.

Rose was going to Paris this morning. She had been asked to collect some samples of catalogues. It was a job that might take a week if she were to do it properly or a day if she took a taxi and the first fifty catalogues that caught her eye. She had told Daddy about it this morning. He was interested, and he took out his books to see again what direction the new airport was in, and which areas Rose's bus would pass as she came in to the city centre. He spent a happy half-hour on this, and Rose had looked with both affection and interest. It was ridiculous that he didn't go again. Why didn't he?

Suddenly she thought she knew. She realised it was all because he had nobody to go with. He was, in fact, a timid man. He was a man who said sorry when other people stepped on him, which is what the nicer half of the world does, but it's also sometimes an indication that people might be wary and uneasy about setting up a lonely journey, a strange pilgrimage of return. Rose thought of the good-natured woman and the man who must be ten or fifteen years older than Daddy, tonight they would be eating a meal in a Dutch restaurant. Tonight Daddy would be having his scrambled egg and dead-heading a few roses, while his daughter, Rose, would be yawning at a French restaurant trying not to look as if she were returning the smiles of an ageing lecher. *Why* wasn't Daddy going with her? It was her own stupid fault. All those years, seven of them since Mum had died, seven years, perhaps thirty trips abroad for her, not a mention of inviting Daddy. The woman with the good-natured countenance didn't live in ivory towers of selfishness like that.

Almost knocking over the table, she stumbled out and got a taxi home. He was actually in a cardigan in the garden scratching his head and sucking on his pipe and looking like a stage representation of someone's gentle, amiable father. He was alarmed to see her. He had to be reassured. But why had she changed her mind? Why did it not matter whether she went today or tomorrow? He was worried. Rose didn't do sudden things. Rose did measured things, like he did. Was she positive she was telling him the truth and that she hadn't felt sick or faint or worried?

They were not a father and daughter who hugged and kissed. Pats were more the style of their touching. Rose would pat him on the shoulder and say: 'I'm off now, Daddy,' or he would welcome her home clasping her hand and patting the other arm enthusiastically. His concern as he stood worried among his garden things was almost too much to bear.

'Come in and we'll have a cup of tea, Daddy,' she said, wanting a few moments bent over kettle, sink, tea caddy to right her eyes.

He was a shuffle behind her, anxiety and care in every step. Not wishing to be too inquisitive, not wanting, but plans changed meant bad news. He hated it.

'You're not *doing* anything really, Daddy, on your holidays, are you?' she said eventually, once she could fuss over tea things no longer. He was even more alarmed.

'Rose, my dear, do you have to go to hospital or anything? Rose, my dear, is something wrong? I'd much prefer it if you told me.' Gentle eyes, his lower lip fastened in by his teeth in worry. Oh what a strange father. Who else had never had a row with a father? Was there any other father in the world so willing to praise the good, rejoice in the cheerful, and to forget the bad and the painful?

'Nothing, Daddy, nothing. But I was thinking, it's silly my going to Paris on my own. Staying in a hotel and reading a book and you staying here reading a book or the paper. I was thinking wouldn't it be nice, if I left it until tomorrow and we *both* went. The same way, the way I go by train to Gatwick, or we could get the train to the coast and go by ferry.'

He looked at her, cup halfway to his mouth. He held it there.

'But why, Rose dear? Why do you suggest this?' His face had rarely seemed more troubled. It was as if she had asked him to leave the planet.

'Daddy, you often talk about Paris, you tell *me* about it. I tell *you* about it. Why don't we go together and tell each other about it when we come back?' She looked at him; he was so bewildered she wanted to shout at him, she wanted to finish her sentences through a loud speaker.

Why did he look so unwilling to join? He was being asked to play. Now don't let him hang back, slow to accept like a shy schoolboy who can't believe he has been picked for the team.

'Daddy, it would be nice. We could go out and have a meal and we could go up and walk to Montmartre by the same routes as you took in the Good Old Days. We could do the things you did when you were a wild teenager.'

He looked at her frightened, trapped. He was so desperately kind, he saw the need in her. He didn't know how he was going to fight her off. She knew that if she were to get him to come, she must stress that she really wanted it for her, more than for him.

'Daddy, I'm often very lonely when I go to Paris. Often at night particularly I remember that you used to tell me how all of you . . .'

She stopped. He looked like a hunted animal.

'Wouldn't you like to come?' she said in a much calmer voice.

'My dear Rose. *Some time,* I'd love to go to Paris, my dear, there's nothing in the world I'd like to do more than to come to Paris. But I can't go just like that. I can't drop everything and rush off to Paris, my dear. You know that.'

'Why not, Daddy?' she begged. She knew she was doing something dangerous, she was spelling out her own flightiness, her own whim of doubling back from the station, she was defining herself as less than level-headed.

She was challenging him, too. She was asking him to say why he couldn't come for a few days of shared foreign things. If he had no explanation, then he was telling her that he was just someone who said he wanted something but didn't reach for it. She could be changing the nature of his little dreams. How would he ever take out his pathetically detailed maps and scrap-books to pore once more with her over routes, and happenings if he had thrown away a chance to see them in three dimensions?

'You have nothing planned, Daddy. It's ideal. We can pack for you. I'll ask them next door to keep an eye on the house. We'll stop the milk and the newspaper and, Daddy, that's it. Tomorrow evening in Paris, tomorrow afternoon we'll be taking that route in together, the one we talked about for me this morning.'

'But Rose, all the things here, my dear, I can't just drop everything. You do see that.'

Twice now he had talked about all the things here that he had to drop. There was *nothing* to drop. What he would drop was pottering about scratching his head about leaf curl. Oh Daddy, don't you see that's all you'll drop? But if you don't see and I tell you, it means I'm telling you that your life is meaningless and futile and pottering. I will not tell *you*, who walked around the house cradling me when I was a crying baby, you who paid for elocution lessons so that I could speak well, you Daddy who paid for that wedding lunch that Gus thought was shabby, you Daddy who smiled and raised your champagne glass to me and said: 'Your mother would have loved this day. A daughter's wedding is a milestone.' I won't tell you that your life is nothing.

The good-natured woman and her father were probably at Folkestone or Dover or Newhaven when Rose said to her father that of course he was right, and it had just been a mad idea, but naturally they would plan it for later. Yes, they really must, and when she came back this time they would talk about it seriously, and possibly next summer.

'Or even when I retire,' said Rose's father, the colour coming back into his cheeks. 'When I retire I'll have lots of time to think about these things and plan them.'

'That's a good idea, Daddy,' said Rose. 'I think that's a very good idea. We should think of it for when you retire.'

He began to smile. Reprieve. Rescue. Hope.

'We won't make any definite plans, but we'll always have it there, as something we must talk about doing. Yes, much more sensible,' she said.

'Do you really mean that, Rose? I certainly think it's a good idea,' he said, anxiously raking her face for approval.

'Oh, honestly, Daddy. I think it makes *much* more sense,' she said, wondering why so many loving things had to be lies.

Pimlico

Olive sat in her little office making her weekly lists. First she balanced her books. It didn't take long. Her guests paid weekly and usually by banker's order. Her staff bills were the same every week. The laundry was always precisely the same – thirty-two sheets, thirty-two pillow-cases, thirty-two towels, seven large table-cloths, seven smaller teacloths. Olive had costed the business of getting a washing machine and a dryer and in the end decided that the effort, the space, and the uncertainly in case of breakdowns were simply not worth it. Her food bills were fairly unchanging too; she hadn't been twenty years in the hotel business for nothing. And other bills were simple as well, she transferred a regular amount weekly to meet the electricity, telephone, gas, rates and insurance demands when they arrived. Olive could never understand why other people got into such muddles about money.

Then she made her list of activities for the noticeboard. This involved going through the local papers, the brochures from musical societies and theatres, appeals from charitable organisations for support for jumble sales. When she had a good selection, she would pin them up on her cork board and remove those which had become out of date. She took care to include some items that none of her guests would dream of choosing like Wagner's Ring or a debate about philosophy. But she knew that they liked to be thought the kind of people who might want to patronise such things and it flattered them.

Then she would take out her loose-leaf file, the one she had divided into twelve sections, one for each guest, and in her neat small handwriting Olive would make some small entries under each name. It was here that she felt she could find the heart of her hotel, the memory, the nerve centre. Because Olive knew that the reason her twelve guests stayed with her, was not the great comfort, the food, the value, the style; it was simply because she knew all about them, she remembered their birthdays, their favourite films, their collar sizes, the names of their old homes or native villages. Olive could tell you quite easily the day that Hugh O'Connor had come to live there, all she had to do was open Hugh's section in the file. But it warmed him so much to hear her say: 'Oh, Hugh, don't I remember well the day you arrived, it was a Wednesday in November and you looked very tired.' Hugh would beam to think that he was so important that his arrival had seared itself into Olive's mind.

She never saw anything dishonest or devious about this. She thought it was in fact a common courtesy and a piece of good sense in what people nowadays called 'communications and relating'. In a way it was almost a form of social service. After all, if she was going to go and spend a half-hour with Annie Lynch on a Saturday afternoon, with Annie retired to her bedroom with what looked like the beginnings of a depression, then Olive thought how much more considerate to look up Annie's file and remember the little farm in Mayo and how it had to be sold when Daddy took to the drink, and how Annie's mother who was a walking saint had died and the boys were all married and the only sensible thing for Annie to do was to come and work in London. Olive had filed the kind of things that seemed to cheer Annie up, and would trot them out one by one. Yes, perhaps she should remember everything without writing it down, but really she lived such a busy life. It would be impossible to manage without her little Lists.

Nobody knew of Olive's filing system; they weren't even aware that she seemed to have a better than average memory. Each one of her guests simply marvelled at his or her own good fortune at having found a woman who ran such a comfortable place and who obviously understood them so well. Even the three Spaniards who had been with Olive for five years thought this too. They didn't question their money or their small living quarters, they just appreciated that she could remember their names and their friends' names and the village in the south of Spain where they went back once a year when Olive closed for her two-week break. She was determined that nobody would ever know and had even made preparations that after her death her executor should arrange to have her private records of her years in the hotel business destroyed unread. A solicitor had told her that such a request was perfectly in order.

She was only thirty years of age when she bought the small and then rather seedy hotel in Pimlico. Everyone had assured her that she was quite mad, and that if clever boys who knew about making money hadn't made a go of it, how could an innocent Irish girl with ten years' experience working in a seaside Irish boarding-house hope to do any better? But Olive was determined; she had saved since her teens for the dream of a hotel of her own, and when her uncle's legacy made it actually within her reach she acted at once. Her family in Ireland were outraged.

'There's more to it than meets the eye,' said her mother who foresaw gloomy summers without Olive's considerable help in the boarding-house.

'Maybe she'll find a fellow in London, she hasn't found one here,' said her sister cattily.

Olive's father was enthusiastic that she should try working in London for a little bit before actually committing herself to the buying of a hotel. He had worked there himself for ten years and found it a lonely place.

'When you've seen Piccadilly Circus and Buckingham Palace and you've said to yourself, this is me here sitting listening to Big Ben strike, well that's it. You've seen it then. It's time to come home. It's a scaldingly lonely place.'

As determined as any young woman about to enter religious life and take vows as a nun, Olive went ahead with her plans.

Ten years in a third rate boarding-house had given Olive more of an insight into the psychology of hotel work than any amount of professional courses. She saw the old and the lonely who could barely endure the sea winds and the bracing air and who hardly left the sun lounge during their two-week visit. She knew they came for company, and that the anticipation was much better than the holiday. She saw the couples with their children hoping that the two-weeks vacation would be a rest, a bit of peace, a time to get to know each other again, and she saw her mother disappointing them year after year by frowning at the children, complaining about noise and in general making the parents much more anxious than they would have been had they remained at home in the normal daily round. Oh, the number of times Olive would have loved to have been in charge, she knew what she would have done. She would have had a special room for the children with lino on the floor, a room where it didn't matter if they kicked the furniture or made a noise. She would have offered the guests a welcoming drink when they arrived instead of making an announcement about what time she expected them to be in.

But in the years of watching the visitors come and go, Olive gained what she thought was an insight into the returned emigrants, those who lived the greater part of their life in big English cities. What they seemed to appreciate so much when they came back was the smallness of the place, the fact that people saluted other people and knew all about them. These might have been the very things that they fled to London and Birmingham and Liverpool to avoid, but it certainly seemed to be something their souls cried out for now. Olive knew that when she had enough money she would run a place for Irish people in London, and she would make a small fortune. Not a big fortune, she didn't want that, just a little fortune. So that she could live in comfort, and could surround herself with nice furniture, nice pictures, so that she needn't worry about having two bars of the electric fire on. The kind of comfort which would mean she could have a bath twice a day, and take a taxi if it were raining.

And in her terraced house in Pimlico she built up the hotel of her dreams.

It had taken time. And a great deal of effort. For a year she lost money – heavy, frightening sums, even though she regarded it as an experiment. She advertised in local papers in boroughs where there were large Irish populations, she attracted lonely people, certainly, but not the ones she could help. Too many of her guests turned out to be working-on-the-Lump men who had forgotten their real names because they used so many in so many different jobs, men who appeared on no social welfare list, men who knew that if they got a bad dose of pneumonia or broke a leg that the other lads would pass a hat round for them, but there would be no pension, no insurance, no security.

They didn't stay long in Olive's little hotel, and she made them uneasy, asking where they were from and what they did.

'Sure the police wouldn't ask me that, Mam,' a man had replied to her once when she had asked some simple and she thought courteous question about his origins.

Then she had the con-men. The charmers, the people who were expecting money shortly, who cashed cheques, who told tales. It was an apprenticeship, she was learning. Soon she thought she was ready and she advertised again. By this time she had the hotel the way she wanted it. Not splendid, nothing overawing, but comfortable. There wasn't a hint of a boarding-house about it, no sauce bottles appeared with regularity on stained cloths. She arranged a weekly rate which included an evening meal, with no refund if the meal were not taken. She knew enough about her future clients to know that they were the kind of people who would like to be expected home at a quarter to seven. They could always go off out again afterwards.

She implied that those she was accepting were people of good manners and high standards. This was done very cunningly and without any hint of appearing restrictive. Whereas her mother would have said: 'I want no drink brought into the bedrooms', Olive said: 'I want you to consider this house very much as your home. I know you don't want to be in the kind of place where people have bottles in bedrooms.'

She chose the guests carefully. Sometimes after several interviews where she always gave them tea and managed to explain that it was simply a matter of having promised the place to somebody else who was to let her know by Thursday. It took her a year to build up to twelve and she sat back satisfied. They were right. They were the correct mix. They depended on her utterly, they needed her, and for the first time in her life she felt fulfilled. She felt she had got what other people got from teaching or nursing or maybe the priesthood. People who needed them, a little flock. She never included marriage and children in her list of fulfilling lifestyles. She had seen too many less than satisfactory marriages to be impressed by the state. And anyway she was too busy. You didn't run the perfect hotel without a lot of work.

There had been a question of marriage two years ago. A very nice man indeed. A Scot, quiet and industrious. She had met him at a hoteliers' trade fair, when she was examining a new system of keeping coffee hot. He had told her that it didn't really work, he had tried one in his own hotel and it had been wasteful. Their friendship got to a stage where her twelve guests were rustling and ruffled like birds in a coop fearing the intrusion of an outsider. Alec came to tea so often on Sundays that there were definite fears he might either join the establishment or else spirit Olive away. The ruffled feelings were balm to Olive, the ill-disguised anxiety among those men and women who paid her hefty sums of money to live with her was almost exhilarating. Olive kept them and Alec in suspense for some weeks and finally sent Alec away confused, wallowing in the luxuriating relief and happiness of the civil servants, bank clerks, book keepers, shop assistants and bus driver who were now her family.

She finished her list of entries in the ring file with the information that Judy O'Connor, the nice girl who worked in the chemist shop, had a brother who was a missionary and that he was coming back from Africa and through London on his way home to Ireland for Christmas. Olive thought it might be a nice occasion to have a mass in the hotel.

Well, why not? They were all Irish, they were all Catholic. Even the three little Spaniards, José, his wife Carmen and her sister Maria, they were Catholics, they would love a Mass in the dining-room. It would make it all much more like home. She must start putting it in Judy's mind soon. Olive was careful for people not to think that all the good ideas came from her. She let the guests think that it was their idea to strip their own beds on Monday mornings and leave all the dirty linen neatly ready for the laundrymen. The guests thought that they had suggested pooling fifty pence a week each to have wine with Sunday lunch.

Hugh O'Connor was absolutely certain that *he* had broken off his engagement to that rather forward hussy who had no morals and wanted to come in and share his room saying that it was perfectly all right since they were engaged. Annie never realised that it was Olive who suggested she should break her ties with Mayo, she thought she had done it herself. The guests thought that it had just come about that they all stayed in the hotel for Christmas, they saw nothing odd about it. Olive had carefully managed to distance herself from those who had been rash enough to go to relations or friends. They had felt lacking in some kind of spirit and had felt deeply jealous when they returned afterwards to hear about the wonderful turkey, and the presents and the carols by the Christmas tree and the Pope's Blessing in the morning and the Queen's speech in the afternoon – a combination of what was best about both cultures.

The last thing that Olive did on her List day was to write home. Her father was in hospital now, her mother almost crippled with arthritis. She sent them regular small contributions with pleasant cheering letters. She had no intention of returning home. They were nothing to her now. She had a real family, a family that needed her.

Vauxhall

On the first Sunday of the month Andrew's parents came to lunch. They arrived winter and summer at midday precisely . . . and every single time Andrew's father would rub his hands and ask his son how he felt about a spot of fresh air. In response Andrew would rub his own hands, pretend to consider it and then nod as if finding it a satisfactory idea.

'Back around two-fifteen – that all right dear?' he would call in to the kitchen where his mother and June were oohing and ahhing over some little gift of home-made tea cakes or tray cloths, then he and his father set off, rain or shine, for a twenty-minute walk to the pub, two and a half pints and a twenty-minute walk back home. Twelve times a year for fifteen years. That was thirty pints a year, a total of four hundred and fifty pints, but little communication shared with his father in the crowded pub which was always filled with jaded young people recovering from last night's swinging south-of-the-river party.

Then, looking at their watches anxiously in mock fear of great punishment, they left carefully at the time when last orders were being shouted and others were begging for that final injection to see them through the Sunday afternoon in Vauxhall. Andrew and his father walked back, more expansive about the roses in people's gardens, the value of property and the increase in hooliganism. When they let themselves into the flat, June and her mother-in-law would give little cries of mock relief, that the men hadn't disappeared for ever, that the lunch had not been spoiled and that they could all now sit down and have Sunday lunch.

At this point June or Andrew would go nervously to Cora's door and tap gently.

'Time for lunch, darling, Gran and Gramps are here.'

There was always a rising note at the end of the statement, questioning. It was as if they didn't know whether or not she would emerge. But she always did. Cora, their only daughter. Cora their tall fourteen-year-old only child.

The years had passed so inevitably, Andrew thought to himself that particular Sunday, as he felt the familiar relief surging through him when Cora came out, her long hair neatly held with a blue ribbon, her soft navy sweater coming well down over her jeans so that it actually looked some kind of formal attire. A huge smile for both grandparents, a kiss, an exclamation of pleasure over the joint – it was always lamb, beef or pork on a first Sunday but since Cora had been old enough to exclaim she had done so. Andrew looked at her with his constant bewilderment. How had he and June produced this lovely, blonde, distant creature? What went on in her head? What did she think of him really as she sat at his table and ate a Sunday roast with his wife and his parents? Would he ever know?

This Sunday was no different to any other. Mother had a hilarious tale about some new people who had moved into their road and had decided to invite all the neighbours in for drinks. The neighbours had disapproved strongly of such over-familiarity but had accepted, and everything had gone wrong – episode after episode of disaster from burst pipes, and clogged loos and stone cold cocktail sausages, to running out of sherry, were revealed to peals of laughters from June, grunts of recollection from father and a polite attention from Cora. To Andrew it seemed suddenly a cruel, heartless tale, unlike his mother's normal generosity, but then he remembered she often told little stories of the discomfiture of others. It made her own position more satisfactory.

June followed it with stories of the Residents' Association in the block of flats, and how they had forced the landlords to do up the entrance, and forced the council to improve the street lighting, and how they had forced the family in the top floor not to cook dishes which could be smelled all over the block.

Even though they often talked about the Residents' Association Andrew thought that today the chat seemed very militant; he got a momentary vision of all those old ladies and retired bank officials who seemed to be its inner circle, dressed up with arm bands and high boots. He smiled to himself.

Father was brought into the conversation by the two chatty women – his wife and daughter-in-law didn't want to monopolise the conversation: did he think that it was worth buying a cover for those plastic bags where people grew vegetables in cities, or should they be left to breathe, or would they look nice covered with attractive stones like a mini rockery or was there a danger that this might suffocate the tomatoes? To every one of these points Father gave his usual attention. His years of being a diplomatic clerk in chambers made him unwilling to come down too firmly on any side even in something as untendentious as this. He weighed everything happily and the audience listened respecfully.

It was a wet Sunday, which meant that they would not go for the little stroll down to the Albert Embankment, or the little walk to the park. When it rained they played Scrabble, looked at gardening catalogues, or Mother sometimes read an entire letter from Andrew's sister in New Zealand, full of people that none of them knew; but Mother would speculate happily and say: 'I think Vera is the one married to the Scottish chap, the couple they went camping with.' Then at four-thirty they had tea, and at five they were in their car, thanking and explaining that they had to go, because of the light in the winter and because of the traffic in the summer. Six times a year Andrew's father said to him: 'We'd better push off so's we can get home in the light, you know.' Six times a year: 'Have to leave now, otherwise we'll get into a hell of a mess with all the traffic building up.' Over fifteen years each phrase must have been said ninety times with an air of newness and discovery, and they had all nodded sagely. Since Cora had been old enough to nod she had always looked politely disappointed that they had to leave, but understanding as well.

'They were in very good form weren't they?' said June brightly as she pushed the tea trolley to the kitchen. Cora had disappeared to her room.

'Yes,' said Andrew getting the tea-cloth.

'Oh, will you? Thank you, love,' said June, even though Andrew had wiped the dishes after one hundred and eighty lunches and afternoon teas attended by his parents. There had always been a tradition that the lunch table was cleared and stacked neatly in the kitchen, not washed up at once.

'Andrew and I enjoy doing it later,' June always said.

'Next month is birthday month,' June said cheerfully. 'We'll have to think of what to get.'

By an odd coincidence all their birthdays fell in the same month, and this year his parents would both be seventy-five, he and June would be forty-five and Cora would be fifteen.

They had always celebrated it as a big family feast, one birthday cake for everyone, lots of presents and cards; and his mother and father always brought the cards that they had received from all their friends as well, and Cora had to say which of her school friends had given her a card.

'We've only got to hold out another fifteen years, and then we can have four generations,' Andrew said thoughtfully. 'Father and Mother could well make it to ninety don't you think?'

'What on earth do you mean?' June paused in the violent scrubbing of a difficult saucepan.

'Well, they're thirty years older than us, we're thirty years older than Cora . . .'

The same pang that always struck him when Cora was mentioned hit him sharply in the chest. He knew so little about her. Was it possible that this girl would soon be loved by a man, or desired by one?

He felt a chill at the thought. It wasn't a question of thinking her too young and innocent. In fact he had been pleased rather than distressed when he had seen one of her schoolfriends, an attractive boy, with his arm across Cora's shoulder one day walking from the bus. She had been carefully instructed in the Facts of Life by June with the help of an illustrated booklet. June had said that it was far more difficult than actually giving birth to her in the labour ward. Cora had read the pieces with interest and said; 'Oh, I see, thank you very much.'

June had tried to leave the door open for more discussion but it never came from Cora. So, from time to time she tried to add little helpful hints.

'You see, there's nothing *wrong* with feeling sexually attracted to someone. In fact it's all absolutely right if you see what I mean. The problem is that we start feeling these, um, feelings when we are rather too young to do anything about them. But they're not wrong or shameful you know.'

'Oh no,' Cora had agreed. 'I didn't think they were.'

'It's just that, economically, it would be silly for boys and girls to get married to each other and what not at thirteen and fourteen because they have no wages or money for a house, you do see?'

'Oh, yes, I see, it would be ridiculous,' Cora had said.

'I think she understood,' poor June had whispered. 'But she didn't sort of react or anything, so I can't be certain.'

Andrew knew exactly what she had meant.

Of course he was quite insane to think that because he and June had followed his parents so precisely in what they had done, Cora would do the same. She might even become part of a commune with lovers all over the house, he shuddered to himself. But then he dismissed that. It could involve a jollity, an intensity too, things that didn't characterise his cool, young daughter. An attractive young teenager, almost a young woman.

'I wonder,' he said tentatively, 'I wonder whether Cora should have her own party next month? You know, teenagers, records, dancing. She might like that. After all girls of fifteen seem grown up to each other these days.'

'A party? Here?' June was not aghast, but it was something that had never occurred to her. 'Do you think she'd like that?'

'Well, teenagers do,' said Andrew. 'Don't they?'

'And she has been to other people's birthday parties I suppose,' said June.

They looked at each other across the draining rack, their faces showing not so much shock that their daughter was turning into a young woman, but total confusion about what kind of young woman she might become. Neither of them knew.

'Shall I ask her, or will you?' asked June.

'I will if you like,' Andrew replied.

They finished the wiping and tidying in silence. Later on Cora would emerge from her room around seven and they would have a light supper. This was Cora's little job. She had been doing it now for about three years. Baked eggs, or sardines on toast, or cold meat and tomatoes if there had been a lot left over from the Sunday joint. She always prepared it quietly with no complaints, and washed up after it. She had been no trouble. Ever. Andrew wondered why he was defending her to himself. Nobody had attacked her.

This Sunday it was sardines. He joined her in the kitchen as she was cutting the crusts from the bread.

'Do you mind doing this Cora, would you prefer to be out with your friends?'

'No, of course I don't mind, Dad,' she smiled at him remote as a stranger who has done you a small service, like giving you more room in a bus or picking up a parcel you have dropped.

'Would you like your own party next month, when you're going to be fifteen?' he said straight out. 'With music and lights and beer for the boys and a kind of wine cup for the girls.'

She looked at him for a couple of seconds.

He tried to read what was on her face.

'Dad,' she began. He had never seen her at a loss before.

'Dad. No. I think I won't. It's very kind of you and Mum, but honestly.'

'But why, love? We'd like you to have a party, a real party for your friends. Perhaps it isn't beer and wine cups. You tell us, and we'll do it right.'

She looked wretched.

'Or you do it . . . you know we won't interfere, we'll be so much in the background we'll have faded into the wallpaper,' he laughed nervously.

With the knife she was using for the toast still in her hand she started to fasten up the buttons of his cardigan and unfasten them and fasten them again. She was as tall as he was, her hair fell over her face and she left it there.

'Dad, it's really very nice of you, but I've got everything I want. Honest. I don't want a party. Honestly.'

She seemed to feel that his buttons were now satisfactory and she moved back to the table.

He felt more hurt than he had ever felt and it must have shown in his face.

'We'd do it right, you know,' he said childishly.

'Of course you would, but there's no right way or wrong way. It's just not on Dad.'

'Other people have parties. You go to other people's

houses when their children have birthdays.'

'But it's such a waste, I mean, Dad, people do so much damage and they don't appreciate it, and the parents are always let down. Always. I don't know anyone who's had a party whose parents didn't get upset for about six months after it. I don't want it. Dad, not for you and Mum, you're not the type.'

'What type do we have to be to give parties that are good enough for your friends, Miss?' he said almost roaring with the pain of it.

'What do we have to do, hire a bloody disco on the King's Road, is that it?'

She had put down the knife, timidly she came over to him and went at his cardigan buttons again.

'I did them wrong,' she said. It took a great effort not to shy away from her, but he stood rigid, while she opened them and refastened them, the most intimate thing she had done since she was a toddler.

'It's not that I don't want my friends to meet you and Mum, that they won't think you're good enough – they won't see you, they won't know what you're like, they won't notice you. Can't you understand? I don't notice my friend's parents, I don't listen to them. I'm not thinking you're not good enough, Dad, you're too good to have your nice lounge all mucked up. You should be grateful to me, not all hurt.'

He felt numbed. His anger and hurt were gone but they hadn't been replaced by anything. Perhaps this is a breakthrough, he thought to himself. At least she acknowledges the possibility that I do have some feelings.

'Well, it's up to you, love,' he said. 'Your mother and I only want you to have what you want.'

She had arranged the sardines neatly, two on each piece of bread, head to tail, was putting the plates in to warm and turned on the grill.

'Honestly Dad, lunch here like always, you know, the cake and everything, that's what I'd like.'

'But it isn't much, Cora love, we'd like to do more for you, you know lunch with old fuddy duddies . . . a bit dull.'

'It's what people *do*, Dad, isn't it? I mean, you might want something different for you too when it's your birthday but that's not the point is it? I mean you don't go off and do what you want to do, you have a lunch and a cake here for Gramps and Gran. You always have, it's the way things *are*.'

He watched her put the sardines under the grill and start to make the coffee. Everything was ready on the tray. It was the way things were, it was what people did. He wondered what his old father might really like to do to celebrate being seventy-five.

Too old for a belly dancer, or a weekend in Paris probably. Father most possibly liked coming to the flat and having his walk, his two and a half pints, his lunch, his gifts, his doze over Scrabble, his tea and his drive home before the crowds. Andrew didn't know. Andrew didn't even know how he wanted to celebrate his own birthday. How did he want to spend the day? A slap-up lunch in a hotel? No. It would hurt June to think that she couldn't produce something as good as a hotel. Champagne on ice? No, he liked bitter. With a crowd of people his own age from the office and the golf club? No. It wasn't done in their set, he'd feel awkward. What he really liked was the family day, the feeling that it was everyone's birthday, and they had got through one more year, the five of them, with no disasters. That's what he really liked to do, or he supposed it was.

And if that was so for the man of seventy-five and the woman of seventy-five and the couple of forty-five, perhaps the young woman of fifteen felt the same. It was safe, it was the known thing.

It wasn't exciting, it wasn't imaginative but, by heavens, it was what people did. It was the way things were.

Stockwell

Mona had vomited when the news was given to her. It was the last thing she had expected would happen and she was very ashamed. She helped the doctor and his young aide to clean the carpet, brushing aside any of their cries that she leave it alone.

'I wouldn't hear of it. These things have to be done quickly. Have you any Borax? Good, and then I find a quick squirt with a soda syphon is good. I really am most frightfully sorry.'

The doctor finally got her to sit in a chair again. Gave her a glass of water, a pill and his hand.

'I didn't put it well. I probably gave you a far worse impression of the situation . . . you must excuse me, Mrs Lewis. I have been very crass.'

His hand tightened on hers and his kind brown eyes were filled with concern. Mora Lewis looked at him gratefully.

'Dr Barton, I can't thank you enough. You have been exactly what I needed in every way. You could not have been more supportive. It's not your fault that the diagnosis was so bad. You must realise that I am completely in your debt.'

The doctor took off his glasses and wiped his eyes. He looked at this handsome woman in front of him again and marvelled. He had told her that she had inoperable cancer of several glands. In response to her calm question, he said that he had been told it was a matter of months and probably not as many as six months. It was when he had added 'Before Christmas' that her stomach muscles had reacted even though her face had not.

How could he have been so heavy-handed, so thick-skinned, so leaden? Why did he have to mention Christmas to this glowing woman? Why remind her of the one most emotive date in the year and let her picture a family scene without her? He could have cut out his tongue.

But she encouraged him to talk calmly. She had talked calmly throughout their whole odd professional relationip. She had come to him four months previously saying that she was staying with friends in Stockwell and giving a local address. After her third visit, however, she explained that she really lived in a different part of London, it was just that she wanted a doctor far away from her friends, far away from people who might know her business. Mona Lewis lived in Hampstead and all her friends went to the same doctor. It wasn't that she didn't trust him, of course she did, but if what she suspected was wrong with her was indeed true, then she didn't want his pity, his sympathy, his concern, until she knew how she was going to cope with it.

It had seemed reasonable. He had referred her for all the tests, he had liked her breezy matter-of-fact ways. He had even had nice little chats with her which were rare for him to have with patients, since his was a largely immigrant practice and much of his work seemed to him to consist of trying to understand worried young Indian mothers who could not come to see him on any matter without the husband there to interpret and act as Chaperone. Mona Lewis with her light-hearted sense of mocking him was a special treat.

She had told him that her fingers were simply itching to re-pot the tired busy lizzies and ferns in his waiting-room. She had even bought him some plant food and left him a book on simple plant care which he had read to please her. even when she had gone for the biopsy she had remained cheerful. He had got her into a local hospital.

'Where do your family think you are this week?' he had asked, worried.

She had mentioned a husband and twin daughters of sixteen.

'I've told them I'm on a course.'

'Why?' he had asked gently. 'Why don't you tell your husband? He'd want to know.'

'Don't be ridiculous, Dr Barton, nobody would want to know that his wife was having a biopsy. Come now, that's not worthy of you.'

'Very well, let me put it another way. He would like to share these things with you, if they have to be undergone, he will want to be part of them.'

'I want to go through the first bit by myself,' she said. 'Later, later I'll talk to the others. Please let me do it this way.'

He hated having to give her the news, but there was no ethical way he could involve anyone else. He was, as she said, being supportive.

She finished her glass of water, examined the damp patch on the carpet and shook her head ruefully as if a favourite puppy, not herself, had made the mess.

'I am sorry again about that, Dr Barton, very shaming. Now, can I just settle up with you as usual, and then I'll leave you to the rest of your waiting room.'

She had established early on that she would like to be considered a private patient even though she always came in surgery hours, and she paid in cash. He hadn't liked the whole arrangement, and particularly as her diagnosis looked worse and worse. Today for the first time he was adamant about the money.

'Please, Mrs Lewis. Just pause and think about me as a human being, not just a doctor with a hand out for money from a private patient. I have given you distressing news today.'

She looked at him politely, her hand already on her wallet.

'It's quite bad enough for me to know that a charming and vital woman like you has a terminal disease and it is doubly hard to have to be the one who tells you this, can you please let me have the dignity of telling you and seeing you to a taxi or telephoning your husband, or calling a friend for you, without having to take your goddamn bank notes?'

She snapped her bag shut.

'Of course. And how considerate of you. I didn't pause to think. But no. I'd prefer to walk. I usually do walk around her, when I come to you. And take buses. I'd like to do that today. Please.'

As he shook her hand, and she assured him that she felt perfectly fine, he knew he was seeing her for the last time. She would not now come back to him. She didn't want to discuss remissions, radium treatment. She wanted to know nothing of drugs or palliatives. She implied that if anything were to be done, it might be done back in Hampstead.

'You have been exceptionally good to me. I know that professional people hate things to be irregular, and you have been wonderful at hiding your irritation that I didn't go through the more conventional channels.'

The doctor didn't know why he said it but it was uppermost in his mind so it just came out.

'People often try to . . . you know . . . beat it, get there first. It's not a good idea. They bungle it, and even if they don't . . . well . . . you know, nature does it in its own rotten way. It would be a pity to take your own life . . .'

'Oh no,' she smiled at him. 'No, I agree it would be a mess. Anyway, why would I go to all these measures to find out, if I were going to do something so feeble as take a bottle of pills and a bottle of vodka?'

'I'll keep feeding those plants in case you come back to

see me,' he grinned taking his tone from hers. She liked that.

'Of course I'll come back to see you,' she smiled. 'One day when you least expect it, when all the shoots need to be trimmed.'

He watched until she had turned the corner, then he pressed his buzzer and saw a malingering workman who claimed he had a bad back, and barked at him so fiercely that the man left in terror demanding to know when Dr Barton's relief doctor would be on duty.

Mona felt dangerously calm. It was a sunny July afternoon, and everything looked quite normal. Like it often looked in this strange part of London, less planted, less cared for than her own neighbourhood. Funny that she liked it so much. She was certain that Jerry would like it too, but it was something she would never share with him. What she had to do now was go through the whole sham of tests again. It seemed silly and wasteful, but this was how she had planned it. Tomorrow, tell Jerry that she felt below par, fix an immediate appointment with Franz, allow Franz to send her for tests at the clinic, follow through, slowly and remorselessly everything she had just done.

And at every step of the way now she could be clear-sighted and calm because there was going to be nothing hanging in the balance, no doubts, no waiting to know. Because she now knew the very worst she could behave with her customary calm. Reassuring everyone, allowing no panic, being utterly fatalistic. She even had a little sentence ready. 'Don't be silly, darling, it's not a question of knowing that I'm going to die, after all we all know we are going to. I just know *when* I'm going to die. That gives me the advantage over all of you.'

She was going to be perfectly frank with the girls also. There was no hiding and whispering and pretending as there had been when her own mother had died. Six months of confusion, and hope and counter hope, and bewilderment. Mona was going to be authoritative in death as she had been in everything in life. It was sad, it was obviously very regrettable since she was only forty-six. But to look on the bright side, she had had an excellent life, she would leave behind not a dependent, unsupported family, but a husband whose every comfort had been catered for, whose house ran smoothly and easily, two attractive sixteen-year-olds who had always been able to discuss their future plans with their mother and who would not cease to do so now. She would redouble her efforts to get Marigold into art school, and to direct Annabelle towards a career in social work. She would see that they both had advisors, separate ones, and contacts. She would also establish a proper social life for Jerry so that he wouldn't be left high and dry. If only she could persuade him to learn bridge. He had withstood it so long, and yet as a widower it would be his instant passport to people's houses. Nobody would say, we must have poor Jerry around, poor chap is utterly broken up since Mona's death, instead they would think more positively and say: 'We need a fourth for bridge. How about Jerry?'

Mona hated the thought of telling Sally, her dearest friend. Sally was so utterly sentimental and emotional, she could ruin everything by arriving around at their house with flowers and autumn bouquets saying that she wanted Mona to see one more bunch of dahlias or a last autumn crocus.

She had several plans also for the school where she taught. She would explain to the principal that a new teacher must be found for the autumn term, but she would ask if she could stay on as an advisor for the first two months or so, or until her strength gave out. She also felt she should like permission to discuss some aspects of death and facing it with the older girls, since they were unlikely to have the chance again of meeting someone who was going to face it as calmly as Mona was about to do.

And as for dear Jerry, she was going to try to explain to him how essential it was that he should marry again, lest he become eccentric and absent-minded and his whole lovely antique business fall apart. If she could find the right words to explain that posthumous jealousy cannot exist. She would be in a great sleep and nothing could hurt her or touch her. Mona realised that not everyone else felt as peaceful about facing death as she did, and she wondered whether she should give talks on the subject on the radio or to women's groups.

Thinking of women's groups reminded her of old Vera North, her mother's friend of many years, now bedridden and in a wheelchair. Mona usually went to see her once a month, but with all the tests and waiting and examinations she hadn't seen Vera for some time. I'll go today, she thought. It will give everyone an explanation of why I was out all day, and should my face look a bit gloomy in spite of myself then they'll think it was because of seeing Vera.

Vera called for tea, she had a faithful slave who had looked after her since childhood. Mona always admired the set up, they needed each other, Vera and the old retainer Annie. She didn't think it was shameful to have a maid, not if you were Vera, not if you were kind and considerate, and paid Annie a just wage.

'I've been busy,' she explained to Vera.

'I know,' Vera said. 'You look more cheerful now. You looked worried when I saw you last. Were you having a medical examination?'

'How on earth did you know?' asked Mona amazed.

'Is it a hysterectomy?' asked Vera.

'No, lymph glands,' said Mona before she realised.

'Poor Mona, you are so young, yet so courageous.' Vera did not look put out.

'I am brave, but by other people's standards, not my

own. I just feel that we should take the mythology out of cancer. I mean, people are afraid to mention its name. They call it silly names, they won't acknowledge it. Such huge strides have been made in, say, attitudes to mental illness, it seems strange that we cannot admit to cells going rogue which is all that cancer is.'

'I know, Mona,' said Vera gravely.

'So as a last gesture, as some kind of, I don't know, some kind of statement I suppose – I'm going to talk about it, I'm going to make it normal. Acceptable even.'

She smiled triumphantly at Vera. She just got a steady glance in return.

'You see since I *am* going to be gone by Christmas at least I know that there's some end to my courage, some defined end. It's not going to be all that hard . . . and it will make it so much easier for everyone else.'

'Do you think it will make it easier for other people?' Vera asked mildly.

'Well it stands to reason . . . if they see that I'm not terror stricken, if they see that if the one who has the bloody disease can accept it, then they will too. It will save so much time, it will cut through all that pretence, we needn't make all those absurd plans for holidays next year, when everyone knows that I won't be around next year . . .'

She was rather put out by Vera's refusal to be impressed, her unwillingness to admire such amazing bravery.

'They'll prefer to pretend. And they will definitely prefer you to pretend,' Vera said firmly.

'But that's nonsense. I'm doing it for them, I'm not going to have them go through what we went through with Mother. Vera, you must remember that, how dreadful it was.' Vera sat very still.

'How old were you when Clare died . . . seventeen, eighteen?'

'I was eighteen, Vera, and I won't put my family

through such an experience. We were constantly going to the Church and lighting candles in front of statues so that Mother's illness should turn out not to be serious. The word Cancer was simply not allowed to be mentioned, there was no honesty. All the things I would like to have said to my mother but never did because we were prevented from admitting it was goodbye by some confused code of keeping quiet. If mother even knew she was dying, which I doubt, none of us had a chance to ask her if she had any last things to discuss.'

'Oh she knew,' said Vera. 'She knew very well.'

'Did she talk to you about it?' Mona was startled.

'She began by wanting to talk to everyone, you are so like her it's uncanny. She wanted to face it . . . do all the things you want to do.'

'But *why* did she not do that?'

'It caused too much pain. Simply that,' Vera said. 'She saw after a couple of days that people couldn't take it. Your father for one: "Clare, stop this, there is hope, nothing is definite. I won't have you speaking as if you are a condemned woman".'

'And other people?'

'Just the same. Me too. I wouldn't look her in the eye and discuss the fact that her body was rotting, no, even though she wanted to laugh and tell me that it was nothing special, mine would rot too. I wanted to believe there was hope. I wanted not to see her getting thinner and comment that the disease was taking its toll. I wanted to say, "Yes you have lost a lot of weight and it does suit you". You see Mona, you're going to find the same thing. I know what I'm talking about.'

'But that was nearly thirty years ago,' Mona pleaded. 'Things have changed now. They must have.'

Vera touched her gently. 'Go and see if you like, and if they haven't changed, come back and talk to me.'

Mona looked at her stonily.

'I mean it, Mona, my brave young girl. Really I do. I

wasn't able to do it for your mother, and I don't want to do it for you. But if I couldn't face one generation being brave, if I let her go to her death with hypocritical exclamations of how well she looked, I won't do it a second time.'

Mona smiled at her and stood up to go.

'I mean it,' Vera said. 'Come back any time. And think before you bare it all to the others. You and your mother are unusual in this world, the rest of us aren't so strong.'

Mona kissed her goodbye. The first time she had done that.

'And I'll tell you more about Clare too . . . you'll like her,' said Vera.

'I'll come back anyway,' Mona said. 'You don't have to bribe me. And Vera, I'll try and tell the others, it would be very good if someone made a stand. Wouldn't it?'

'Clare wanted me to marry your father,' said Vera.

'I wish you had,' said Mona.

'Perhaps I'll marry Jerry instead,' said Vera with a tiny little laugh.

And Mona left quickly before she saw the tears that were going to come from it.

Brixton

The woman in personnel was about fifty and had a silly perm, all grey bubbles like an ageing Harpo Marx. Sandy looked at her without much hope.

'Well, of course, I can try and fix you with hostels or shelters organisation addresses, Miss Ring. But quite frankly I feel sure you would do better just to find accommodation for yourself.'

'How can I do that?' Sandy asked. It was so very different to the hospital where she had trained. There, the rules about where nurses had to live were still strictly enforced. There had been a list of approved lodgings and apartments, and only in these were the nurses permitted to stay.

'The nurses seem to play musical chairs with each other,' said the Harpo Marx personnel officer disapprovingly. 'You'll be very unlucky not to see about a dozen tattered notices on the board downstairs offering accommodation.'

'That sounds great,' Sandy said eagerly. 'And if I share with someone who works in the hospital, then I'll learn the ropes a bit more quickly.'

She got a watery and unenthusiastic smile. The personnel officer obviously found as little satisfaction in her job as she had found success with her hairdresser.

There were eight notices offering accommodation. Four were too expensive, two specified that the applicant must speak Spanish. That left two. One of them had a phone number, so Sandy dialled it at once. In her hand she had her *A to Z* so that she could identify where the place was.

'It's SW9,' the girl said.

'Clapham?' asked Sandy studying her map intently.

'More east of it,' the girl said.

'Near the tube?'

'Yeah, four minutes.'

'How many of you in the flat.?'

'Just me.'

'That's not a bad rent for a flat for two.'

'You ain't seen it, lady.'

'Shall I come over and look, and let you look at me?'

'Sure. Come now I'll make you tea.'

'That's very nice, I'm Sandy Ring.'

'That's funny. I'm Wilma Ring.'

'Hey, we might be cousins.'

'Yeah. Are you black?'

'Err . . . um . . . no. Are you?'

'Yeah, we most likely ain't cousins. See you for tea.'

It was certainly shabby, though nothing that paint and a new hall door could not have cured, Sandy thought to herself, but the street didn't have too much smart paint and new hall doors. There were three bicycles in the hall and a lot of very loud music came up from the basement.

What the hell, Sandy thought, I'm not going to be on nights for the first six months, and if I can't sleep after a day's hospital work because of a few bars of music I must be in bad shape. Wilma was standing at the door.

'Come in, cousin,' she called with a laugh. 'Have some nice English tea to get you over the culture shock of a walk through the Brixton West Indies.'

It was agreed in ten minutes. The room, the rent, the lifestyles.

'I don't have friends in, because I'm studying, see,' Wilma said. 'But I study in my own bedroom, so you can have people in so long as they don't shout through the walls. And if your guys don't eat all the food in the fridge and take all the hot water, they can stay all night.'

'What are you studying?' Sandy wanted to know. She didn't feel like telling Wilma yet that there would be no guys for a long time, not after the guy in Wales, the one she was running away from.

'Open University. I am reading for a university degree,' said Wilma. 'When you come back tonight, remember to get yourself a lamp and bulb for your room, there's only a centre light, it makes it even worse than it need be.'

'I can come back tonight?' Sandy said.

'I can't see why you should pay a hotel and pay me. You've only got one body and it can only sleep in one bed.'

For a few weeks they rarely saw each other. Wilma worked strange hours on the admission shifts, so that she could have appropriate time off for her studying and to watch the programmes on television. Sandy worked a day shift on the neuro-surgical ward. It was demanding and sometimes depressing. She often wished that Wilma were there to chat to when she got back. Bit by bit she got used to the area; they even joked with her in the corner store as she refused ackee and salt fish and other Jamaican treats.

'I only like the patties,' she said firmly.

'You wait till you go out to the island and have goat curry,' Nelson, the good-looking man who ran the shop, used to say to her. 'Then you never eat anything else.'

'I can't imagine going to Jamaica,' she said truthfully. 'It must be such a contrast between the rich tourists and the poverty of the people who live there.'

'What makes you think that?' Nelson wanted to know.

Sandy was about to say that if so many Jamaicans came to Britain to live in what she considered relative poverty, things must be in a very bad state back home. But she was unsure if that would be offensive, so instead she muttered vaguely about something she had seen on television.

'You don't take no notice of that Wilma,' Nelson had said. 'Wilma is a no-good communist, she is always finding something wrong with every society.'

The day she heard this new slant on her flat-mate, Sandy climbed the stairs and found Wilma at home. She had washed her hair and was sitting in an unaccustomed relaxed mood with her feet on the window box, a towel around her head and a beer in her hand.

'Come on, pretend we're in the sun-soaked Caribbean. There's a beer for you in the fridge,' she called to Sandy and they sat in the summer evening listening to the sounds from the street below, the planes overhead, the distant traffic, and the general hum of city noises.

'I hear you're a communist,' Sandy said lightly.

'That pretty boy Nelson has a big mouth an' no brain,' commented Wilma, unperturbed.

'I think he fancies you. He always mentions you,' probed Sandy.

'Yeah, he should fancy Margaret, the mother of his three children. She works sixteen hours a day for him. He should discuss her politics and her tits, not mine,' retorted Wilma, this time with more spirit.

'But *are* you a communist?' persisted Sandy. In a way she hoped Wilma was. It was quite outrageous enough to share with a Jamaican woman, that had them all whispering back in Wales, but a Jamaican communist, would be over the top.

'Of course not, dope,' said Wilma. 'Would I be lying here talking chicken shit to a silly little nurse like you, drinking beer, if I were a communist? No, I would be fighting the good fight somewhere and overturning things. Not planning to become rich and middle class and have a university degree.'

'I think you are mad to try and do all that studying,' said Sandy, stretching her tired muscles. 'It's bad enough doing what we do. I only want to sleep and look at telly when the day is over. Study! I couldn't even think of it.'

'I had always heard they were ambitious in Wales,' Wilma said.

'They may be. I'm not any more. Anyway, being a nurse isn't that far below being a teacher, you know, they rate about the same. And teachers don't get all that much more money. I don't know why you're killing yourself if all you'll do is teach in the end.'

'I'll do both,' said Wilma.

'How can you do both?' Sandy became suddenly irritated at the calm way this tall girl had everything planned. Even her short burst of leisure was carefully planned, hair shampooed, fresh air by the window, lounging in a robe, instead of sitting there, tired and hot, like Sandy was.

'I'll be a teacher during the day, and then some nights a week I'll do a night shift, and I can work full-time nursing in the long holidays. Teachers have vacations of three to four months, you know, when you add it all up. It is a ridiculous life . . . they get paid . . . I don't know.' She shook her turbanned head from side to side in amazement.

'My sister married a teacher in Wales. They don't get well paid I tell you, and he's knackered come the summer when the exams are over. You've got it wrong,' Sandy said. She didn't like to hear of people doing two jobs. She felt quite proud of herself, having managed to drag herself unwillingly from Wales, from a man who walked on her to a big strange city and find a job and a flat. She thought that Wilma was pushing it.

Wilma got them more beer.

'Ohh,' she sighed. 'Ohh, Sandy girl, if only you knew what my mother had to do for me, and what she and her sisters have had to do for all our family. I'll *never* stop getting degrees, every letter I have to my name is a shaft of sunlight for them. It's a reason to go on scrubbing floors, to go into offices and shops at five a.m. where the air is stale and the baskets are full of yesterday's sour milk cartons, but the letters after my name will make it worth while.'

'Oh, for heaven's sake, Wilma, you're far too intelligent to go along with that crap,' cried Sandy, annoyed now and tactful no longer. 'If you really wanted to help your mother, then you'd give her money, for God's sake. I mean, I send my mother money each week, not much, but a little, for her to get herself something nice, maybe a hair-do or a night at the bingo and a fish supper. My Dad keeps her very short.'

'Oh yes?' said Wilma.

'Yes, bloody yes. And that's what you should do instead of filling your poor Mam's head up with ideas and nonsense, and degrees and airy-fairy letters after your name. If you can't bear her being down on her knees then take her off them. You can send her ten quid a week – better, you can go and give it to her. She only lives an hour away. I can't understand why you don't go to see her more. My Mam lives hundreds of miles away, otherwise I'd go and take her out on a Saturday night for a bit of a laugh. That's what a daughter is for.'

Wilma sat up and looked at her.

'No, Sandy my little sister, that is *not* what a daughter is for. A daughter must never be for that. That means the system never ends. A daughter must be something better, something stronger, she must give hope and reason for what is being done. She must make some sense out of all the scrubbing, bring some logic to all that lavatory cleaning. Otherwise a daughter is just yourself again, on and on for ever.'

Sandy saw why Nelson thought that Wilma wanted to overturn society.

And because she thought of Nelson she mentioned him.

'But the other Jamaicans don't feel that way, Nelson

and those girls in the store for example, they have a laugh and they go to parties and they sing songs, and they say it's not too bad. Isn't that better for a mother, to see she has happy children?'

Wilma stood up and rested her hands on the window box. She looked as if she were about to make a speech to a crowd below but instead she spoke in a very gentle voice.

'My mother told me that before she came here she never knew that white women were poor too, when she saw poor white women in Britain she thought they had done something bad and were being punished. She came from a family where the women were strong.

'*Her* mother remembered being a Mammy and remembered having to lie down and let a white boss screw her. But that had all gone by my mother's time, she had five jobs, five different jobs to get her fare to England, and when she came here she had six jobs to make the money for us to come, but she didn't mind having six jobs because she lived in luxury. She had electricity, not kerosene, she had water in a tap, down the corridor but in a tap. She had a house where the food didn't melt, or rot, or go bad, she didn't have to buy expensive ice to keep food fresh for twenty-four hours. And one by one she sent for us. One by one we came.'

Her voice began to sound a little like a preacher's. Sandy could imagine her putting a few 'Yea, verrilys' into her conversation.

'You see, what was so wonderful was that we knew she would send for us. I was only nine when she went, only a child of nine when she got on the bus to Kingston that day, and I knew she would send for us one by one. That when I came first, part of her sending for Sadie and sending for Margaret and the others was that I should work hard at school. It was team work, it was solidarity like you've never known. If we had the homework done and our Mother's supper ready when she came in from one job, that gave her strength to go out to another. If she didn't have to worry about us, if we cleaned the house, then she could stay healthy, in her jobs and not fret. You have to scrub a lot of floors and get a lot of bonus and overtime to pay five airfares from Jamaica and for a home for them to live in.'

Wilma smiled seraphically.

'But we were a lucky family because it was the woman who came. No danger of the woman finding a fancy man and forgetting us like happened to some of the men who came. A woman with five children will not forget them. That Nelson you admire so much in the corner store, he has a wife and two children in Ocho Rios, as well as Margaret and the three children here. Nice for Nelson to be chatty and to have a laugh and a drink and a song. Very nice. My mother would spit on him. A disgrace to Jamaica, every song and every bit of a laugh which you said I should be having is a mockery.'

'But, Wilma, surely you can have both. I mean the pride in your doing well *and* a bit of a laugh, that's all I was suggesting. That's all I was saying, your Mam has to have some relaxation, some happiness.'

'I write to her and I tell her what I am studying, sometimes she looks at the television when the Open University programmes are on. She can't understand them, but that's her happiness.'

'What does she do on her time off?'

'She sleeps. And when she wakes to work again she remembers that her mother couldn't read but she can read and write, and she knows that even though she can read and write she will never have qualifications but I will have a university degree, and that sends a big surge of happiness right through her and she is glad that she didn't just sit and laugh with her mother while the chickens ran around the dusty yard, and that I did not sit and laugh with her, while we both went out to play bingo.'

'I see,' said Sandy, who didn't see at all.

'You don't see, because for you it has always been a possibility, a good life. You don't have to prove anything to your mother nor she to hers.'

'Oh I don't know. I've had more education, a better job, more freedom than she did.' Sandy didn't want anyone to think that there had been no progress. Life hadn't been a bed of roses in the small Welsh town.

Wilma sighed. Sandy was by far the nicest of the girls who had shared her flat, but she would leave, she would leave soon. Without a proper explanation. And Nelson would say that she left because she was too toffee-nosed for the area, and Old Johnny, the man from Barbados two floors down, would say that it was good riddance to that young whitey anyway, and only Wilman would know that it had nothing to do with colours of skin or area, or smells of curry or steel bands in the basement. It had everything to do with life being short and most people wanting to have a laugh and a good time.

CENTRAL LINE

Shepherd's Bush

People looked very weary, May thought, and shabbier than she had remembered Londoners to be. They reminded her a little of those news-reel pictures of crowds during the war or just after it, old raincoats, brave smiles, endless patience. But then this wasn't Regent Street where she had wandered up and down looking at shops on other visits to London, it wasn't the West End with lights all glittering and people getting out of taxis full of excitement and wafts of perfume. This was Shepherd's Bush where people lived. They had probably set out from here early this morning and fought similar crowds on the way to work. The women must have done their shopping in their lunch-hour because most of them were carrying plastic bags of food. It was a London different to the one you see as a tourist.

And she was here for a different reason, although she had once read a cynical article in a magazine which said that girls coming to London for abortions provided a significant part of the city's tourist revenue. It wasn't something you could classify under any terms as a holiday. When she filled in the card at the airport she had written 'Business' in the section where it said 'Purpose of journey'.

The pub where she was to meet Celia was near the tube station. She found it easily and settled herself in. A lot of the accents were Irish, workmen having a pint before they went home to their English wives and their television programmes. Not drunk tonight, it was only Monday, but obviously regulars. Maybe not so welcome as regulars on Friday or Saturday nights, when they would remember they were Irish and sing anti-British songs.

Celia wouldn't agree with her about that. Celia had rose-tinted views about the Irish in London, she thought they were all here from choice, not because there was no work for them at home. She hated stories about the restless Irish, or Irishmen on the lump in the building trade. She said people shouldn't make such a big thing about it all. People who came from much farther away settled in London, it was big enough to absorb everyone. Oh well, she wouldn't bring up the subject, there were enough things to disagree with Celia about . . . without searching for more.

Oh why of all people, of all the bloody people in the world, did she have to come to Celia? Why was there nobody else whom she could ask for advice? Celia would give it, she would give a lecture with every piece of information she imparted. She would deliver a speech with every cup of tea, she would be cool, practical and exactly the right person, if she weren't so much the wrong person. It was handing Celia a whole box of ammunition about Andy. From now on Celia could say that Andy was a rat, and May could no longer say she had no facts to go on.

Celia arrived. She was thinner, and looked a little tired. She smiled. Obviously the lectures weren't going to come in the pub. Celia always knew the right place for things. Pubs were for meaningless chats and bright, non-intense conversation. Home was for lectures.

'You're looking marvellous,' Celia said.

It couldn't be true. May looked at her reflection in a glass panel. You couldn't see the dark lines under her eyes there, but you could see the droop of her shoulders, she wasn't a person that could be described as looking marvellous. No, not even in a pub.

'I'm okay,' she said. 'But you've got very slim, how did you do it?'

'No bread, no cakes, no potatoes, no sweets,' said Celia in a business-like way. 'It's the old rule but it's the only rule. You deny yourself everything you want and you lose weight.'

'I know,' said May, absently rubbing her waistline.

'Oh I didn't meant *that*,' cried Celia horrified. 'I didn't mean that at all.'

May felt weary, she hadn't meant that either, she was patting her stomach because she had been putting on weight. The child that she was going to get rid of was still only a speck, it would cause no bulge. She had put on weight because she cooked for Andy three or four times a week in his flat. He was long and lean. He could eat for ever and he wouldn't put on weight. He didn't like eating alone so she ate with him. She reassured Celia that there was no offence and when Celia had gone, twittering with rage at herself, to the counter, May wondered whether she had explored every avenue before coming to Celia and Shepherd's Bush for help.

She had. There were no legal abortions in Dublin, and she did not know of anyone who had ever had an illegal one there. England and the ease of the system were less than an hour away by plane. She didn't want to try and get it on the National Health, she had the money, all she wanted was someone who would introduce her to a doctor, so that she could get it all over with quickly. She needed somebody who knew her, somebody who wouldn't abandon her if things went wrong, somebody who would lie for her, because a few lies would have to be told. May didn't have any other friends in London. There was a girl she had once met on a skiing holiday, but you couldn't impose on a holiday friendship in that way. She knew a man, a very nice, kind man who had stayed in the hotel where she worked and had often begged her to come and stay with him and his wife. But she couldn't go to stay with them for the first time in this predicament, it would be ridiculous. It had to be Celia.

It might be easier if Celia had loved somebody so much that everything else was unimportant. But stop, that wasn't fair. Celia loved that dreary, boring, selfish Martin. She loved him so much that she believed one day he was going to get things organised and make a home for them. Everyone else knew that Martin was the worst possible bet for any punter, a Mammy's boy, who had everything he wanted now, including a visit every two months from Celia, home from London, smartly-dressed, undemanding, saving away for a day that would never come. So Celia did understand something about the nature of love. She never talked about it. People as brisk as Celia don't talk about things like unbrisk attitudes in men, or hurt feelings or broken hearts. Not when it refers to themselves, but they are very good at pointing out the foolish attitudes of others.

Celia was back with the drinks.

'We'll finish them up quickly,' she said.

Why could she never, never take her ease over anything? Things always had to be finished up quickly. It was warm and anonymous in the pub. They could go back to Celia's flat, which May felt sure wouldn't have even a comfortable chair in it, and talk in a business-like way about the rights and wrongs of abortion, the procedure, the money, and how it shouldn't be spent on something so hopeless and destructive. And about Andy. Why wouldn't May tell him? He had a right to know. The child was half his, and even if he didn't want it he should pay for the abortion. He had plenty of money, he was a hotel manager. May had hardly any, she was a hotel receptionist. May could see it all coming, she dreaded it. She wanted to stay in this warm place until closing-time, and to fall asleep, and wake up there two days later.

Celia made walking-along-the-road conversation on the way to her flat. This road used to be very quiet and full of retired people, now it was all flats and bed-sitters.

That road was nice, but noisy, too much through-traffic. The houses in the road over there were going for thirty-five thousand, which was ridiculous, but then you had to remember it was fairly central and they did have little gardens. Finally they were there. A big Victorian house, a clean, polished hall, and three flights of stairs. The flat was much bigger than May expected, and it had a sort of divan on which she sat down immediately and put up her legs, while Celia fussed about a bit, opening a bottle of wine and putting a dish of four small lamb chops into the oven. May braced herself for the lecture.

It wasn't a lecture, it was an information-sheet. She was so relieved that she could feel herself relaxing, and filled up her wineglass again.

'I've arranged with Doctor Harris that you can call to see him tomorrow morning at 11. I told him no lies, just a little less than the truth. I said you were staying with me. If he thinks that means you are staying permanently, that's his mistake not mine. I mentioned that your problem was . . . what it is. I asked him when he thought it would be . . . em . . . done. He said Wednesday or Thursday, but it would all depend. He didn't seem shocked or anything; it's like tonsillitis to him, I suppose. Anyway he was very calm about it. I think you'll find he's a kind person and it won't be upsetting . . . that part of it.'

May was dumbfounded. Where were the accusations, the I-told-you-so sighs, the hope that now, finally, she would finish with Andy? Where was the slight moralistic bit, the heavy wondering whether or not it might be murder? For the first time in the eleven days since she had confirmed she was pregnant, May began to hope that there would be some normality in the world again.

'Will it embarrass you, all this?' she asked. 'I mean, do you feel it will change your relationship with him?'

'In London a doctor isn't an old family friend like at home, May. He's someone you go to, or I've gone to anyway, when I've had to have my ears syringed, needed antibiotics for flu last year, and a medical certificate for the time I sprained my ankle and couldn't go to work. He hardly knows me except as a name on his register. He's nice though, and he doesn't rush you in and out. He's Jewish and small and worried-looking.'

Celia moved around the flat, changing into comfortable sitting-about clothes, looking up what was on television, explaining to May that she must sleep in her room and that she, Celia, would use the divan.

No, honestly, it would be easier that way, she wasn't being nice, it would be much easier. A girl friend rang and they arranged to play squash together at the weekend. A wrong number rang; A West Indian from the flat downstairs knocked on the door to say he would be having a party on Saturday night and to apologise in advance for any noise. If they liked to bring a bottle of something, they could call in themselves. Celia served dinner. They looked at television for an hour, then went to bed.

May thought what a strange empty life Celia led here far from home, miles from Martin, no real friends, no life at all. Then she thought that Celia might possibly regard her life too as sad, working in a second-rate hotel for five years, having an affair with its manager for three years. A hopeless affair because the manager's wife and four children were a bigger stumbling-block than Martin's mother could ever be. She felt tired and comfortable, and in Celia's funny, characterless bedroom she drifted off and dreamed that Andy had discovered where she was and what she was about to do, and had flown over during the night to tell her that they would get married next morning, and live in England and forget the hotel, the family and what anyone would say.

Tuesday morning. Celia was gone. Dr Harris's address was neatly written on the pad by the phone with instructions how to get there. Also Celia's phone number at work, and a message that May never believed she would hear from Celia. 'Good luck.'

He was small, and Jewish, and worried and kind. His examination was painless and unembarrassing. He confirmed what she knew already. He wrote down dates, and asked general questions about her health. May wondered whether he had a family, there were no pictures of wife or children in the surgery. But then there were none in Andy's office, either. Perhaps his wife was called Rebecca and she too worried because her husband worked so hard, they might have two children, a boy who was a gifted musician, and a girl who wanted to get married to a Christian. Maybe they all walked along these leafy roads on Saturdays to synagogue and Rebecca cooked all those things like gefilte fish and bagels.

With a start, May told herself to stop dreaming about him. It was a habit she had got into recently, fancying lives for everyone she met, however briefly. She usually gave them happy lives with a bit of problem-to-be-solved thrown in. She wondered what a psychiatrist would make of that. As she was coming back to real life, Dr Harris was saying that if he was going to refer her for a termination he must know why she could not have the baby. He pointed out that she was healthy, and strong, and young. She should have no difficulty with pregnancy or birth. Were there emotional reasons? Yes, it would kill her parents, she wouldn't be able to look after the baby, she didn't want to look after one on her own either, it wouldn't be fair on her or the baby.

'And the father?' Dr Harris asked.

'Is my boss, is heavily married, already has four babies of his own. It would break up his marriage which he doesn't want to do . . . yet. No, the father wouldn't want me to have it either.'

'Has he said that?' asked Dr Harris as if he already knew the answer.

'I haven't told him, I can't tell him, I won't tell him,' said May.

Dr Harris sighed. He asked a few more questions; he made a telephone call; he wrote out an address. It was a posh address near Harley Street.

'This is Mr White. A well-known surgeon. These are his consulting-rooms, I have made an appointment for you at 2.30 this afternoon. I understand from your friend Miss . . .' He searched his mind and his desk for Celia's name and then gave up. 'I understand anyway that you are not living here, and don't want to try and pretend that you are, so that you want the termination done privately. That's just as well, because it would be difficult to get it done on the National Health. There are many cases that would have to come before you.'

'Oh I have the money,' said May, patting her handbag. She felt nervous but relieved at the same time. Almost exhilarated. It was working, the whole thing was actually moving. God bless Celia.

'It will be around £180 to £200, and in cash, you know that?'

'Yes, it's all here, but why should a well-known surgeon have to be paid in cash, Dr Harris? You know it makes it look a bit illegal and sort of underhand, doesn't it?'

Dr Harris smiled a tired smile. 'You ask me why he has to be paid in cash. Because he says so. Why he says so, I don't know. Maybe it's because some of his clients don't feel too like paying him after the event. It's not like plastic surgery or a broken leg, where they can see the results. In a termination you see no results. Maybe people don't pay so easily then. Maybe also Mr White doesn't have a warm relationship with his Income Tax people. I don't know.'

'Do I owe you anything?' May asked, putting on her coat.

'No, my dear, nothing.' He smiled and showed her to the door.

'It feels wrong. I'm used to paying a doctor at home or they send bills,' she said.

'Send me a picture postcard of your nice country sometime,' he said. 'When my wife was alive she and I spent several happy holidays there before all this business started.' He waved a hand to take in the course of Anglo-Irish politics and difficulties over the last ten years.

May blinked a bit hard and thanked him. She took a taxi which was passing his door and went to Oxford Street. She wanted to see what was in the shops because she was going to pretend that she had spent £200 on clothes and then they had all been lost or stolen. She hadn't yet worked out the details of this deception, which seemed unimportant compared to all the rest that had to be gone through. But she would need to know what was in the shops so that she could say what she was meant to have bought.

Imagining that she had this kind of money to spend, she examined jackets, skirts, sweaters, and the loveliest boots she had ever seen. If only she didn't have to throw this money away, she could have these things. It was her savings over ten months, she put by £30 a month with difficulty. Would Andy have liked her in the boots? She didn't know. He never said much about the way she looked. He saw her mostly in uniform when she could steal time to go to the flat he had for himself in the hotel. On the evenings when he was meant to be working late, and she was in fact cooking for him, she usually wore a dressing-gown, a long velvet one. Perhaps she might have bought a dressing-gown. She examined some, beautiful Indian silks, and a Japanese satin one in pink covered with little black butterflies. Yes, she would tell him she had bought that, he would like the sound of it, and be sorry it had been stolen.

She had a cup of coffee in one of the big shops and watched the other shoppers resting between bouts of buying. She wondered, did any of them look at her, and if so, would they know in a million years that her shopping money would remain in her purse until it was handed over to a Mr White so that he could abort Andy's baby? Why did she use words like that, why did she say things to hurt herself, she must have a very deep-seated sense of guilt. Perhaps, she thought to herself with a bit of humour, she should save another couple of hundred pounds and come over for a few sessions with a Harley Street shrink. That should set her right.

It wasn't a long walk to Mr White's rooms, it wasn't a pleasant welcome. A kind of girl that May had before only seen in the pages of fashion magazines, bored, disdainful, elegant, reluctantly admitted her.

'Oh yes, Dr Harris's patient,' she said, as if May should have come in some tradesman's entrance. She felt furious, and inferior, and sat with her hands in small tight balls, and her eyes unseeing in the waiting-room.

Mr White looked like a caricature of a diplomat. He had elegant grey hair, elegant manicured hands. He moved very gracefully, he talked in practised, concerned clichés, he knew how to put people at their ease, and despite herself, and while still disliking him, May felt safe.

Another examination, another confirmation, more checking of dates. Good, good, she had come in plenty of time, sensible girl. No reasons she would like to discuss about whether this was the right course of action? No? Oh well, grown-up lady, must make up her own mind. Absolutely certain then? Fine, fine. A look at a big leather-bound book on his desk, a look at a small notebook. Leather-bound for the tax people, small notebook for himself, thought May viciously. Splendid, splendid. Tomorrow morning then, not a problem in the world, once she was sure, then he knew this was the best, and wisest thing. Very sad the people who dithered.

May could never imagine this man having dithered

in his life. She was asked to see Vanessa on the way out. She knew that the girl would be called something like Vanessa.

Vanessa yawned and took £194 from her. She seemed to have difficulty in finding the six pounds in change. May wondered wildly whether this was meant to be a tip. If so, she would wait for a year until Vanessa found the change. With the notes came a discreet printed card advertising a nursing home on the other side of London.

'Before nine, fasting, just the usual overnight things,' said Vanessa helpfully.

'Tomorrow morning?' checked May.

'Well yes, naturally. You'll be out at eight the following morning. They'll arrange everything like taxis. They have super food,' she added as an afterthought.

'They'd need to have for this money,' said May spiritedly.

'You're not just paying for the food,' said Vanessa wisely.

It was still raining. She rang Celia from a public phonebox. Everything was organised, she told her. Would Celia like to come and have a meal somewhere, and maybe they could go on to a theatre?

Celia was sorry, she had to work late, and she had already bought liver and bacon for supper. Could she meet May at home around nine? There was a great quiz show on telly, it would be a shame to miss it.

May went to a hairdresser and spent four times what she would have spent at home on a hair-do.

She went to a cinema and saw a film which looked as if it were going to be about a lot of sophisticated witty French people on a yacht and turned out to be about a sophisticated witty French girl who fell in love with the deck-hand on the yacht and when she purposely got pregnant, in order that he would marry her, he laughed at her and the witty sophisticated girl threw herself overboard. Great choice that, May said glumly, as she dived into the underground to go back to the smell of liver frying.

Celia asked little about the arrangements for the morning, only practical things like the address so that she could work out how long it would take to get there.

'Would you like me to come and see you?' she asked. 'I expect when it's all over, all finished you know, they'd let you have visitors. I could come after work.'

She emphasised the word 'could' very slightly. May immediately felt mutinous. She would love Celia to come, but not if it was going to be a duty, something she felt she had to do, against her principles, her inclinations.

'No, don't do that,' she said in a falsely bright voice. 'They have telly in the rooms apparently, and anyway, it's not as if I were going to be there for more than twenty-four hours.'

Celia looked relieved. She worked out taxi times and locations and turned on the quiz show.

In the half light May looked at her. She was unbending, Celia was. She would survive everything, even the fact that Martin would never marry her. Christ, the whole thing was a mess. Why did people start life with such hopes, and as early as their mid-twenties become beaten and accepting of things. Was the rest of life going to be like this?

She didn't sleep so well, and it was a relief when Celia shouted that it was seven o'clock.

Wednesday. An ordinary Wednesday for the taxi-driver, who shouted some kind of amiable conversation at her. She missed most of it, because of the noise of the engine, and didn't bother to answer him half the time except with a grunt.

The place had creeper on the walls. It was a big house, with a small garden, and an attractive brass handle on the door. The nurse who opened it was Irish. She checked May's name on a list. Thank God it was O'Connor, there were a million O'Connors. Supose she had had an unusual name, she'd have been found out immediately.

The bedroom was big and bright. Two beds, flowery covers, nice furniture. A magazine rack, a bookshelf. A television, a bathroom.

The Irish nurse offered her a hanger from the wardrobe for her coat as if this was a pleasant family hotel of great class and comfort. May felt frightened for the first time. She longed to sit down on one of the beds and cry, and for the nurse to put her arm around her and give her a cigarette and say that it would be all right. She hated being so alone.

The nurse was distant.

'The other lady will be in shortly. Her name is Miss Adams. She just went downstairs to say goodbye to her friend. If there's anything you'd like, please ring.'

She was gone, and May paced the room like a captured animal. Was she to undress? It was ridiculous to go to bed. You only went to bed in the day-time if you were ill. She was well, perfectly well.

Miss Adams burst in the door. She was a chubby, pretty girl about twenty-three. She was Australian, and her name was Hell, short for Helen.

'Come on, bedtime,' she said, and they both put on their nightdresses and got into beds facing each other. May had never felt so silly in her whole life.

'Are you sure we're meant to do this?' she asked.

'Positive,' Helen announced. 'I was here last year. They'll be in with the screens for modesty, the examination, and the pre-med. They go mad if you're not in bed. Of course that stupid Paddy of a nurse didn't tell you, they expect you to be inspired.'

Hell was right. In five minutes, the nurse and Mr White came in. A younger nurse carried a screen. Hell was examined first, then May, for blood pressure and temperature, and that kind of thing. Mr White was charming.

He called her Miss O'Connor, as if he had known her all his life.

He patted her shoulder and told her she didn't have anything to worry about. The Irish nurse gave her an unsmiling injection which was going to make her drowsy. It didn't immediately.

Hell was doing her nails.

'You were really here last year?' asked May in disbelief.

'Yeah, there's nothing to it. I'll be back at work tomorrow.'

'Why didn't you take the Pill?' May asked.

'Why didn't you?' countered Hell.

'Well, I did for a bit, but I thought it was making me fat, and then anyway, you know, I thought I'd escaped for so long before I started the Pill that it would be all right. I was wrong.'

'I know.' Hell was sympathetic. 'I can't take it. I've got varicose veins already and I don't really understand all those things they give you in the Family Planning clinics, jellies, and rubber things, and diaphragms. It's worse than working out income tax. Anyway, you never have time to set up a scene like that before going to bed with someone, do you? It's like preparing for a battle.'

May laughed.

'It's going to be fine, love,' said Hell. 'Look, I know, I've been here before. Some of my friends have had it done four or five times. I promise you, it's only the people who don't know who worry. This afternoon you'll wonder what you were thinking about to look so white. Now if it had been terrible, would I be here again?'

'But your varicose veins?' said May, feeling a little sleepy.

'Go to sleep, kid,' said Hell. 'We'll have a chat when it's all over.'

Then she was getting onto a trolley, half-asleep, and going down corridors with lovely prints on the walls to a room with a lot of light, and transferring onto another table. She felt as if she could sleep for ever and she hadn't even had the anaesthetic yet. Mr White stood there in a coat brighter than his name. Someone was dressing him up the way they do in films.

She thought about Andy. 'I love you,' she said suddenly.

'Of course you do,' said Mr White, coming over and patting her kindly without a trace of embarrassment.

Then she was being moved again, she thought they hadn't got her right on the operating table, but it wasn't that, it was back into her own bed and more sleep.

There was a tinkle of china. Hell called over from the window.

'Come on, they've brought us some nice soup. Broth they call it.'

May blinked.

'Come on, May. I was done after you and I'm wide awake. Now didn't I tell you there was nothing to it?'

May sat up. No pain, no tearing feeling in her insides. No sickness.

'Are you sure they did me?' she asked.

They both laughed.

They had what the nursing-home called a light lunch. Then they got a menu so that they could choose dinner.

'There are some things that England does really well, and this is one of them,' Hell said approvingly, trying to decide between the delights that were offered. 'They even give us a small carafe of wine. If you want more you have to pay for it. But they kind of disapprove of us getting pissed.'

Hell's friend Charlie was coming in at six when he finished work. Would May be having a friend too, she wondered? No. Celia wouldn't come.

'I don't mean Celia,' said Hell. 'I mean the bloke.'

'He doesn't know, he's in Dublin, and he's married,' said May.

'Well, Charlie's married, but he bloody knows, and he'd know if he were on the moon.'

'It's different.'

'No, it's not different. It's the same for everyone, there are rules, you're a fool to break them. Didn't he pay for it either, this guy?'

'No. I told you he doesn't know.'

'Aren't you noble,' said Hell scornfully. 'Aren't you a real Lady Galahad. Just visiting London for a day or two, darling, just going to see a few friends, see you soon. Love you darling. Is that it?'

'We don't go in for so many darlings as that in Dublin,' said May.

'You don't go in for much common sense either. What will you gain, what will he gain, what will anyone gain? You come home penniless, a bit lonely. He doesn't know what the hell you've been doing, he isn't extra-sensitive and loving and grateful because he doesn't have anything to be grateful about as far as he's concerned.'

'I couldn't tell him. I couldn't. I couldn't ask him for £200 and say what it was for. That wasn't in the bargain, that was never part of the deal.'

May was almost tearful, mainly from jealousy she thought. She couldn't bear Hell's Charlie to come in, while her Andy was going home to his wife because there would be nobody to cook him something exciting and go to bed with him in his little manager's flat.

'When you go back, tell him. That's my advice,' said Hell. 'Tell him you didn't want to worry him, you did it all on your own because the responsibility was yours since you didn't take the Pill. That's unless you think he'd have wanted it?'

'No, he wouldn't have wanted it.'

'Well then, that's what you do. Don't ask him for the money straight out, just let him know you're broke. He'll react some way then. It's silly not to tell them at all. My sister did that with her bloke back in Melbourne. She never told him at all, and she got upset because he didn't know the sacrifice she had made, and every time she bought a drink or paid for a cinema ticket she got resentful of him. All for no reason, because he didn't bloody know.'

'I might,' said May, but she knew she wouldn't.

Charlie came in. He was great fun, very fond of Hell, wanting to be sure she was okay, and no problems. He brought a bottle of wine which they shared, and he told them funny stories about what had happened at the office. He was in advertising. He arranged to meet Hell for lunch next day and joked his way out of the room.

'He's a lovely man,' said May.

'Old Charlie's smashing,' agreed Hell. He had gone back home to entertain his wife and six dinner guests. His wife was a marvellous hostess apparently. They were always having dinner parties.

'Do you think he'll ever leave her?' asked May.

'He'd be out of his brains if he did,' said Hell cheerfully.

May was thoughtful. Maybe everyone would be out of their brains if they left good, comfortable, happy home set-ups for whatever the other woman imagined she could offer. She wished she could be as happy as Hell.

'Tell me about your fellow,' Hell said kindly.

May did, the whole long tale. It was great to have somebody to listen, somebody who didn't say she was on a collision course, somebody who didn't purse up lips like Celia, someone who said, 'Go on, what did you do then?'

'He sounds like a great guy,' said Hell, and May smiled happily.

They exchanged addresses, and Hell promised that if ever she came to Ireland she wouldn't ring up the hotel and say, 'Can I talk to May, the girl I had the abortion with last winter?' and they finished Charlie's wine, and went to sleep.

The beds were stripped early next morning when the final examination had been done, and both were pronounced perfect and ready to leave. May wondered fancifully how many strange life stories the room must have seen.

'Do people come here for other reasons apart from . . . er, terminations?' she asked the disapproving Irish nurse.

'Oh certainly they do, you couldn't work here otherwise,' said the nurse. 'It would be like a death factory, wouldn't it?'

That puts me in my place, thought May, wondering why she hadn't the courage to say that she was only visiting the home, she didn't earn her living from it.

She let herself into Celia's gloomy flat. It had become gloomy again like the way she had imagined it before she saw it. The warmth of her first night there was gone. She looked around and wondered why Celia had no pictures, no books, no souvenirs.

There was a note on the telephone pad.

'I didn't ring or anything, because I forgot to ask if you had given your real name, and I wouldn't know who to ask for. Hope you feel well again. I'll be getting some chicken pieces so we can have supper together around 8. Ring me if you need me. C.'

May thought for a bit. She went out and bought Celia a casserole dish, a nice one made of cast-iron. It would be useful for all those little high-protein, low-calorie dinners Celia cooked. She also bought a bunch of flowers, but could find no vase when she came back and had to use a big glass instead. She left a note thanking her for the hospitality, warm enough to sound properly grateful, and a genuinely warm remark about how glad she was that she had been able to do it all through nice Dr Harris. She said nothing about the time in the nursing-home. Celia would prefer not to know. May just said that she was fine, and thought she would go back to Dublin tonight. She rang the airline and booked a plane.

Should she ring Celia and tell her to get only one chicken piece. No, damn Celia, she wasn't going to ring her. She had a fridge, hadn't she?

The plane didn't leave until the early afternoon. For a wild moment she thought of joining Hell and Charlie in the pub where they were meeting, but dismissed the idea. She must now make a list of what clothes she was meant to have bought and work out a story about how they had disappeared. Nothing that would make Andy get in touch with police or airlines to find them for her. It was going to be quite hard, but she'd have to give Andy some explanation of what she'd been doing, wouldn't she? And he would want to know why she had spent all that money. Or would he? Did he even know she had all that money? She couldn't remember telling him. He wasn't very interested in her little savings, they talked more about his investments. And she must remember that if he was busy or cross tonight or tomorrow she wasn't to take it out on him. Like Hell had said, there wasn't any point in her expecting a bit of cossetting when he didn't even know she needed it.

How sad and lonely it would be to live like Celia, to be so suspicious of men, to think so ill of Andy. Celia always said he was selfish and just took what he could get. That was typical of Celia, she understood nothing. Hell had understood more, in a couple of hours, than Celia had in three years. Hell knew what it was like to love someone.

But May didn't think Hell had got it right about telling Andy all about the abortion. Andy might be against that kind of thing. He was very moral in his own way, was Andy.

Holland Park

Everyone hated Malcolm and Melissa out in Greece last summer. They pretended they thought they were marvellous, but deep down we really hated them. They were too perfect, too bright, intelligent, witty and aware. They never monopolised conversations in the taverna, they never seemed to impose their will on anyone else, but somehow we all ended up doing what they wanted to do. They didn't seem lovey-dovey with each other, but they had a companionship which drove us all to a frenzy of rage.

I nearly fainted when I got a note from them six months later. I thought they were the kind of people who wrote down addresses as a matter of courtesy, and you never heard from them again.

'I hate trying to recreate summer madness,' wrote Melissa. 'So I won't gather everyone from the Hellenic scene, but Malcolm and I would be thrilled if you could come to supper on the 20th. Around eightish, very informal and everything. We've been so long out of touch that I don't know if there's anyone I should ask you to bring along; if so, of course the invitation is for two. Give me a ring sometime so that I'll know how many strands of spaghetti to put in the pot. It will be super to see you again.'

I felt that deep down she knew there was nobody she should ask me to bring along. She wouldn't need to hire a private detective for that, Melissa would know. The wild notion of hiring someone splendid from an escort agency came and went. In three artless questions Melissa would find out where he was from, and think it was a marvellous fun thing to have done.

I didn't believe her about the spaghetti, either. It would be something that looked effortless but would be magnificent and unusual at the same time. Perhaps a perfect Greek meal for nostalgia, where she would have made all the hard things like pitta and humus and fetta herself, and laugh away the idea that it was difficult. Or it would be a dinner around a mahogany table with lots of cut-glass decanters, and a Swiss darling to serve it and wash up.

But if I didn't go, Alice would kill me, and Alice and I often had a laugh over the perfection of Malcolm and Melissa. She said I had made them up, and that the people in the photos were in fact models who had been hired by the Greek Tourist Board to make the place look more glamorous. Their names had passed into our private shorthand. Alice would describe a restaurant as a 'Malcolm and Melissa sort of place', meaning that it was perfect, understated and somehow irritating at the same time. I would say that I had handled a situation in a 'Malcolm and Melissa way', meaning that I had scored without seeming to have done so at all.

So I rang the number and Melissa was delighted to hear from me. Yes, didn't Greece all seem like a dream nowadays, and wouldn't it be foolish to go to the same place next year in case it wasn't as good, and no, they hadn't really decided where to go next year, but Malcolm had seen this advertisement about a yacht party which wanted a few more people to make up the numbers, and it might be fun, but one never knew and one was a bit trapped on a yacht if it was all terrible. And super that I could come on the 20th, and then with the voice politely questioning, would I be bringing anyone else?

In one swift moment I made a decision. 'Well, if it's not going to make it too many I would like to bring this friend of mine, Alice,' I said, and felt a roaring in my ears as I said it, Melissa was equal to anything.

'Of course, of course, that's lovely, we look forward to meeting her. See you both about eightish then. It's not far from the tube, but maybe you want to get a bus, I'm not sure . . .'

'Alice has a car,' I said proudly.

'Oh, better still. Tell her there's no problem about parking, we have a bit of waste land around the steps. It makes life heavenly in London not to have to worry about friends parking.'

Alice was delighted. She said she hoped they wouldn't turn out to have terrible feet of clay and that we would have to find new names for them. I was suddenly taken with a great desire to impress her with them, and an equal hope that they would find her as funny and witty as I did. Alice can be eccentric at times, she can go into deep silences. We giggled a lot about what we'd wear. Alice said that we should go in full evening dress, with capes, and embroidered handbags, and cigarette-holders, but I said that would be ridiculous.

'It would make her uneasy,' said Alice with an evil face.

'But she's not horrible, she's nice. She's asked us to dinner, she'll be very nice,' I pleaded.

'I thought you couldn't stand her,' said Alice, disappointed.

'It's hard to explain. She doesn't mean any harm, she just does everything too well.' I felt immediately that I was taking the myth away from Malcolm and Melissa and wished I'd never thought of asking Alice.

Between then and the 20th, Alice thought that we should go in boiler suits, in tennis gear, dressed as Greek peasants, and at one stage that we should dress up as nuns and tell her that this was what we were in real life. With difficulty I managed to persuade her that we were not to look on the evening as some kind of search-and-destroy mission, and Alice reluctantly agreed.

I don't really know why we had allowed the beautiful couple to become so much part of our fantasy life. It wasn't as if we had nothing else to think about. Alice was a solicitor with a busy practice consisting mainly of battered wives, worried one-parent families faced with eviction, and a large vocal section of the female population who felt that they had been discriminated against in their jobs. She had an unsatisfactory love-life going on with one of the partners in the firm, usually when his wife was in hospital, which didn't make her feel at all guilty, she saw it more as a kind of service that she was offering. I work in a theatre writing publicity-handouts and arranging newspaper interviews for the stars, and in my own way I meet plenty of glittering people. I sort of love a hopeless man who is a good writer but a bad person to love, since he loves too many people, but it doesn't break my heart.

I don't suppose that deep down Alice and I want to live in a big house in Holland Park, and be very beautiful and charming, and have a worthy job like Melissa raising money for a good cause, and be married to a very bright, sunny-looking man like Malcolm, who runs a left wing bookshop that somehow has made him a great deal of money. I don't *suppose* we could have been directly envious. More indirectly irritated, I would have thought.

I was very irritated with myself on the night of the 20th because I changed five times before Alice came to collect me. The black sweater and skirt looked too severe, the gingham dress mutton dressed as lamb, the yellow too garish, the pink too virginal. I settled for a tapestry skirt and a cheap cotton top.

'Christ, you look like a suite of furniture,' said Alice when she arrived.

'Do I? Is it terrible?' I asked, anxious as a sixteen-year-old before a first dance.

'No, of course it isn't,' said Alice. 'It's fine, it's just a bit sort of a sofa-coverish if you know what I mean. Let's hope it clashes with her décor.'

Tears of rage in my eyes, I rushed into the bedroom and put on the severe black again. Safe, is what magazines call black. Safe I would be.

Alice was very contrite.

'I'm sorry, I really am. I don't know why I said that, it looked fine. I've never given two minutes' thought to clothes, you know that. Oh for God's sake wear it, please. Take off the mourning gear and put on what you were wearing.'

'Does this look like mourning then?' I asked, riddled with anxiety.

'Give me a drink,' said Alice firmly. 'In ten years of knowing each other we have never had to waste three minutes talking about clothes. Why are we doing it tonight?'

I poured her a large Scotch and one for me, and put on a jockey necklace which took the severe look away from the black. Alice said it looked smashing.

Alice told me about a client whose husband had put Vim in her tin of tooth powder and she had tried to convince herself that he still wasn't too bad. I told Alice about an ageing actress who was opening next week in a play, and nobody, not even the man I half love, would do an interview with her for any paper because they said, quite rightly, that she was an old bore. We had another Scotch to reflect on all that.

I told Alice about the man I half loved having asked me to go to Paris with him next weekend, and Alice said I should tell him to get stuffed, unless, of course, he was going to pay for the trip, in which case I must bring a whole lot of different judgements to bear. She said she was going to withdraw part of her own services from her unsatisfactory partner, because the last night they had spent together had been a perusal of *The Home Doctor* to try and identify the nature of his wife's illness. I said I thought his wife's illness might be deeply rooted in drink, and Alice said I could be right but it wasn't the kind of thing you said to someone's husband. Talking about drink reminded us to have another and then we grudgingly agreed it was time to go.

There were four cars in what Melissa had described as a bit of waste land, an elegantly paved semi-circular courtyard in front of the twelve steps up to the door. Alice commented that they were all this year's models, and none of them cost a penny under three thousand. She parked her battered 1969 Volkswagen in the middle, where it looked like a small child between a group of elegant adults.

Malcolm opened the door, glass in hand. He was so pleased to see us that I wondered how he had lived six months without the experience. Oh come on, I told myself, that's being unfair, if he wasn't nice and welcoming I would have more complaints. The whole place looked like the film set for a trendy frothy movie on gracious modern living. Melissa rushed out in a tapestry skirt, and I nearly cried with relief that I hadn't worn mine. Melissa is shaped like a pencil rather than a sofa; the contrast would have been mind-blowing.

We were wafted into a sitting-room, and wafted is the word. Nobody said 'come this way' or 'let me introduce you' but somehow there we were with drinks in our hands, sitting between other people, whose names had been said clearly, a Melissa would never mutter. The drinks were good and strong, a Malcolm would never be mean. Low in the background a record-player had some nostalgic songs from the Sixties, the time when we had all been young and impressionable, none of your classical music, nor your songs of the moment. Malcolm and Melissa couldn't be obvious if they tried.

And it was like being back in Andrea's Taverna again.

Everyone felt more witty and relaxed because Malcolm and Melissa were there, sort of in charge of things without appearing to be. They sat and chatted, they didn't fuss, they never tried to drag anyone into the conversation or to force some grounds of common interest. Just because we were all there together under their roof . . . that was enough.

And it seemed to be enough for everyone. A great glow came over the group in the sunset, and the glow deepened when a huge plate of spaghetti was served. It was spaghetti, damn her. But not the kind that you and I would ever make. Melissa seemed to be out of the room only three minutes, and I knew it takes at least eight to cook the pasta. But there it was, excellent, mountainous, with garlic bread, fresh and garlicky, not the kind that breaks your teeth on the outside and then is soggy within. The salad was like an exotic still-life, it had everything in it except lettuce. People moved as if in a dance to the table. There were no cries of praise and screams of disclaimer from the hostess. Why then should I have been so resentful of it all?

Alice seemed to be loving every minute of her evening, she had already fought with Malcolm about the kind of women's literature he sold, but it was a happy fight where she listened to the points he was making and answered them. If she didn't like someone she wouldn't bother to do this. She had been talking to Melissa about some famous woman whom they both knew through work, and they were giggling about the famous woman's shortcomings. Alice was forgetting her role, she was breaking the rules. She had come to understand more about the Melissa and Malcolm people so that we could laugh at them. Instead, she looked in grave danger of getting on with them.

I barely heard what someone called Keith was saying to me about my theatre. I realised with a great shock that I was jealous. Jealous that Alice was having such a nice time, and impressing Melissa and Malcolm just because she was obviously not trying to.

This shock was to physical that a piece of something exotic, avocado maybe, anyway something that shouldn't be in a salad, got stuck in my throat. No amount of clearing and hurrumphing could get rid of it and I stood up in a slight panic.

Alice grasped at once.

'Relax and it will go down,' she called. 'Just force your limbs to relax, and your throat will stop constricting. No, don't bang her, there's no need.'

She spoke with such confidence that I tried to make my hands and knees feel heavy, and miracles it worked.

'That's a good technique,' said Malcolm admiringly, when I had been patted down and, scarlet with rage, assured everyone I was fine.

'It's very unscientific,' said the doctor amongst us, who would have liked the chance to slit my throat and remove the object to cries of admiration.

'It worked,' said Alice simply.

The choking had gone away but not the reason for it. Why did I suddenly feel so possessive about Alice, so hurt when she hadn't liked my dress, so jealous and envious that she was accepted here on her own terms and not as my friend? It was ridiculous. Sometimes I didn't hear from Alice for a couple of weeks; we weren't soul mates over everything, just long-standing friends.

'. . . have you had this flat in the City long?' asked Keith politely.

'Oh that's not my flat, that's Alice's,' I said. Alice was always unusual. She had thought that since the City would be deserted at weekends, the time she wanted a bit of peace, that's where she should live. And of course it worked. Not a dog barked, not a child cried, not a car revved up when Alice was sleeping till noon on a Sunday.

'No, I live in Fulham,' I said, thinking how dull and predictable it sounded.

'Oh I thought . . .' Keith didn't say what he thought but he didn't ask about my flat in Fulham.

Malcolm was saying that Alice and I should think about the yachting holiday. Keith and Rosemary were thinking about it, weren't they? They were, and it would be great fun if we went as a six, then we could sort of take over in case the other people were ghastly.

'It sounds great,' I said dishonestly and politely. 'Yes, you must tell me more about it.'

'Weren't you meant to be going on holiday with old Thing?' said Alice practically.

'That was very vague,' I snapped. 'The weekend in Paris was definite but the holiday . . . nothing was fixed. Anyway weren't you meant to be going to a cottage with your Thing . . . ?'

Everyone looked at me, it was as if I had belched loudly or taken off my blouse unexpectedly. They were waiting for me to finish and in a well-bred way rather hoping that I wouldn't. Their eyes were like shouts of encouragement.

'You said that if his wife was put away for another couple of weeks you might go to their very unsocialistic second home? Didn't you?'

Alice laughed, everyone else looked stunned.

Melissa spooned out huge helpings of a ten thousand calorie ice-cream with no appearance of having noticed a social gaffe.

'Well, when the two of you make up your minds, do tell us,' she said. 'It would be great fun, and we have to let these guys know by the end of the month, apparently. They sound very nice actually. Jeremy and Jacky they're called, he makes jewellery and Jacky is an artist. They've lots of other friends going too, a couple of girls who work with Jeremy and their boy friends, I think. It's just Jeremy and Jacky who are . . . who are organising it all.'

Like a flash I saw it. Melissa thought Alice and I were lesbians. She was being her usual tolerant liberated self over it all. If you like people, what they do in bed is none of your business. HOW could she be so crass as to think that about Alice and myself? My face burned with rage. Slowly like heavy flowers falling off a tree came all the reasons. I was dressed so severely, I had asked could I bring a woman not a man to her party, I had been manless in Greece when she met me the first time, I had just put on this appalling show of spitely spiteful dikey jealousy about Alice's relationship with a man. Oh God. Oh God.

I knew little or nothing about lesbians. Except that they were different. I never was friendly with anyone who was one. I knew they didn't wear bowler hats, but I thought that they did go in for this aggressive sort of picking on one another in public. Oh God.

Alice was talking away about the boat with interest. How much would it cost? Who decided where and when they would stop? Did Jeremy and Jacky sound madly camp and would they drive everyone mad looking for sprigs of tarragon in case the pot au feu was ruined?

Everyone was laughing, and Malcolm was being liberated and tolerant and left-wing.

'Come on Alice, nothing wrong with tarragon, nothing wrong with fussing about food, we all fuss about something. Anyway, they didn't say anything to make us think that they would fuss about food, stop typecasting.'

He said it in a knowing way. I felt with a sick dread that he could have gone on and said, 'After all, I don't typecast you and expect you to wear a hairnet and military jacket.'

I looked at Alice, her thin white face all lit up laughing. Of course I felt strongly about her, she was my friend. She was very important to me, I didn't need to act with Alice. I resented the way the awful man with his alcoholic wife treated her, but was never jealous of him because

Alice didn't really give her mind to him. And as for giving anything else . . . well I suppose they made a lot of love together but so did I and the unsatisfactory journalist. I didn't want Alice in that way. I mean that was madness, we wouldn't even know what to do. We would laugh ourselves silly.

Kiss Alice?

Run and lay my head on Alice's breast?

Have Alice stroke my hair?

That's what people who were in love did. We didn't do that.

Did Alice need me? Yes, of course she did. She often told me that I was the only bit of sanity in her life, that I was safe. I had known her for ten years, hardly anyone else she knew nowadays went back that far.

Malcolm filled my coffee cup.

'Do persuade her to come with us,' he said gently to me. 'She's marvellous really, and I know you'd both enjoy yourselves.'

I looked at him like a wild animal. I saw us fitting into their lives, another splendid liberal concept, slightly racy, perfectly acceptable. 'We went on holiday with that super gay couple, most marvellous company, terribly entertaining.' Which of us would he refer to as the He? Would there be awful things like leaving us alone together, or nodding tolerantly over our little rows?

The evening and not only the evening stretched ahead in horror. Alice had been laying into the wine, would she be able to drive? If not, oh God, would they offer us a double bed in some spare room in this mansion? Would they suggest a taxi home to Fulham since my place was nearer? Would they speculate afterwards why we kept two separate establishments in the first place?

Worse, would I ever be able to laugh with Alice about it or was it too important? I might disgust her, alarm her, turn her against me. I might unleash all kinds of love that she had for me deep down, and how would I handle that?

Of course I love Alice, I just didn't realise it. But what lover, what poor unfortunate lover in the history of the whole damn thing, ever had the tragedy of Coming Out in Malcolm and Melissa's lovely home in Holland Park?

Notting Hill Gate

Everyone knew that Daphne's friend Mike was a shit and to give us our due most of us said so. But she laughed and said we were full of rubbish. She agreed, still laughing, to take the address of the battered wife place, just in case, then we gave her a lovely fur jacket that Mike wouldn't be able to share, and she left us and married him. We never saw her again. But we had to find a new secretary.

Nowadays nobody thinks any more that you meet a lot of interesting people on a newspaper, so you don't have breathless, over-educated, anxious-to-please Oxford graduates rushing around doing all the dirty work willingly as well as all the ordinary work efficiently. Nowadays you have temps earning a fortune, but with no security, and no plans and no interest in what they're doing. My woolly, right-minded, left-thinking views thought that this was unfair on the girls . . . they had no career structure, no dignity, and the agencies made all the money. But then from time to time my wrong-minded right-wing views made me wonder what the country was coming to when you couldn't get a girl who could spell, read, take orders and be grateful for a good job. It was a month of temps before Rita came.

Rita was big and black and tough about luncheon-vouchers, and wanted us to buy her a season ticket on the tube. She walked not like other people walk . . . she rolled along as if she had wheels in her shoes. She had a lot of low-cut purple or green blouses and she wore a series of desperately tight orange or yellow skirts. Marian, who deals with readers' letter, said she thought that Rita's skirts must rip open every evening after the strain of the day, and she would throw them away.

She looked slow and lazy, and as if she was thinking of something else almost all the time, but she was far better than anyone we had had up until then. You didn't have to tell Rita twice that there were ten hopeless people who kept coming into the office with ideas for stories, and that none of the ideas were ever any use. Rita just nodded vaguely, but she knew how to deal with them. She would write down what they said, type it out and put it in a file. The people would go away satisfied that things were underway, and Rita had all the ideas neatly put in the H file, under Hopeless.

After three weeks, we realised two things, firstly that Rita was still there, that she hadn't walked out at 11 a.m. one day like the other temps were in the habit of doing, and secondly that she didn't need to be watched and advised all the time. Martin, the features editor, asked her if she would like a permanent job, and Rita looked as if she had been offered a potato crisp at a bus-stop, and said she might as well. But only if he would pay for a monthly ticket on the underground for her.

Rita lived in Notting Hill but that's all she said. This was a change too, because normally whoever sat in the desk seemed to unburden themselves of a long and complicated life history. There was nothing about Daphne's Mike that we didn't know, his deprived childhood, his poor relationship with Daphne's mother, his disastrous early marriage . . . even Daphne's black eyes were explained away by some incredible misunderstanding, some terrible mistake for which Mike was now heart-broken. All the useless temps had told us tales about their flats being too far out, or their fellows thinking they owned them, or distant boyfriends in Cumbria or on sheep-stations in Australia who wanted them to throw up the job and come home and marry them. Rita never told us anything.

'Do you live in a flat or with your family?' Marian asked her once.

'Why?' asked Rita.

'Oh well I just wondered,' said Marian a bit confused.

'Oh that's all right,' said Rita quite happily, but didn't answer the question.

She used her luncheon-vouchers to buy a huge sandwich and a carton of milk, and she ate it quietly reading a trashy magazine, or at least one that was marginally more trashy than our own features pages. Because she was so uncommunicative, I suppose we were more interested in her. She got the odd phone call, and I found myself listening to her side of the conversation with all the attention of a village postmistress. She would speak in her slow flat tone, smiling only rarely, and seemed to be agreeing with whoever was on the other end about some course of action.

Once she said, 'He's a bad bastard I tell you, he used to be a friend of my husband . . . get out of it if you can.' Full of secret information I told Marian and the others that Rita had a husband. Martin said he had always supposed she did; nothing about Rita would suggest she was a lonely girl who went home to an empty bed, she was too sexy. We had long arguments about his attitudes, like that only sexy women had husbands and that all single women went home to empty beds . . . but it was an old and well worn line of argument. I was more interested that he thought Rita sexy. I thought she was overblown, and fat, and very gaudily dressed, but assumed that West Indians might like brighter colours than we would because of all their bright sunlight back home. Sexy. No.

I was waiting one night in a pub for my sister who's always late and I had forgotten to bring anything to read. So I looked around hopefully in case anyone had abandoned an evening paper. There was one on the floor near a very good-looking blond lad and I went over to pick it up. He put his foot on it immediately.

'That's mine,' he said.

He was very drunk. When someone's very drunk you don't make an issue about nicking their evening paper. I apologised and said I thought it was one that someone had finished with. He looked at me coldly and forgave me. Irritated, I went back to my seat and wished that my sister could for once in her life turn up at something approaching the time arranged. The blond boy now stumbled over to my table and in exaggerated gestures began to present me the paper. He managed to knock my gin and tonic over my skirt and the contents of the ashtray on top of that. I could have killed him I was so annoyed, but before I had time to do anything, a big shadow fell on the whole scene. It was of all people Rita.

She didn't seem embarrassed, surprised, or apologetic. She said, 'You drunken bum,' pulled him away back to a distant seat, ordered me another gin and tonic, brought a cloth, and a lot of paper napkins, all in what looked like slow movements, but they only took a minute or two all the same.

I was so surprised to see her that I forgot about the disgusting mess seeping into my best cream-coloured linen skirt. What was even more amazing, she offered no explanation. I'd have said I was sorry about my friend, or made some nervous joke about it being a small world. Rita just said, 'Hot water, and if that doesn't work, dry cleaning tomorrow, I suppose.' She said it in exactly the same way she'd say, 'We can try the usual photographer for the fashion pictures, and if he's busy get the agency ones I suppose.' With no involvement at all.

Hot water didn't work very well, the whole skirt now looked appalling. When my sister Trudy came in, I was in such a temper that it frightened her.

'You can wear a coat,' she said trying to placate me.

'I haven't got a bloody coat,' I said. 'It's the middle of bloody summer. My coat's at home on the other side of London, isn't it?'

Rita asked with the mild concern of a bystander and not the sense of responsibility of someone whose drunken boyfriend had just ruined an expensive skirt:

'Do you want something to wear? I'll give you something.'

Trudy thought she was an innocent concerned bystander and started to gush that it would be perfectly all right thank you . . .

Rita said, 'I live upstairs, you can come up and choose what you'd like.'

Now this was too good to miss. Firstly I had discovered that Rita had a white boyfriend who looked like a Greek God, that he was as drunk as a maggot, and that Rita lived over a pub. Now I was going to see her place . . . this would be a great dossier for the office.

'Thanks, Rita,' I said ungraciously, and left Trudy open-mouthed behind me.

As we went out the pub door and almost immediately through another, I wondered, Was I mad? Rita's clothes would go around me four times. How could she or I think that any skirt of hers would fit me?

She opened the door of a cheaply furnished, but neat and bright, apartment. Two small and very pigtailed girls sat on a big cushion looking at a big colour telly.

'This is Miss that I work with,' said Rita.

'Hallo Miss,' they chorused, and went back to looking at bionic things on the screen.

We walked into a bedroom also very neat and bright, and Rita opened a cupboard. She took out what looked like two yards of material with a ribbon around the top.

'It's a wrap-around skirt, it fits any size,' she said. I got out of the dirty dishcloth I was wearing, and wrapped it around, and tied the ribbon. It looked fine.

'Thank you very much indeed, Rita,' I said, trying at the same time to take in every detail for the telling tomorrow in the pub, while Rita would be sitting at her desk. There were big prints on the wall, Chinese girls, and horses with flying manes. The bed had a beautiful patchwork quilt, it looked as if it could sleep four people comfortably.

'Are those your little girls?' I asked, a question brought on indirectly by the bed I suppose.

'They're Martie and Anna, they live here,' said Rita.

I realised immediately she hadn't told me whether they were her daughters, her sisters, her nieces, or her friends. And I also realised that I wasn't going to ask any more.

'You can leave the other skirt,' said Rita and then, for the very first time volunteering some information, she added, 'Andrew has quite enough money to pay to have it dry-cleaned, and I'll bring it into the office for you on Friday.'

Oh, so he was called Andrew, the young beautiful boy, and he had plenty of money, oh ho. I was learning something anyway. I didn't dare to ask her whether he was her boyfriend. It wasn't that Rita was superior or distant, but she drew a shutter down like someone slamming a door, and didn't find it rude or impolite. It left you feeling rude and impolite instead.

I thanked her for the skirt. Martie and Anna said 'Goodbye Miss' without removing their eyes from the screen. Somehow *they* seemed so much at ease with the goings-on that it made me very annoyed with myself for feeling diffident because this was a black house and I was a white woman. Who creates these barriers anyway, I argued with myself, and, taking a deep breath, said to Rita on the stairs:

'Why do they wear their hair in those tight little pigtails? They'd be much prettier if their hair was loose.'

'Maybe,' Rita shrugged, as if I had asked her why she didn't move the coffee percolator to another table in the office to give herself more room. 'Yeah maybe,' she agreed.

'Do you like them with their hair all tied up like that?' I asked courageously.

'Oh it has nothing to do with me,' she said, and we were out on the street and into the pub again.

Trudy had a face like thunder when I came back but she greeted Rita pleasantly enough, and asked her if she would like to join us.

Rita shook her head. 'This drunken baby has to be taken to bed,' she said enigmatically, and she frog-marched the handsome Andrew out the door without a good-bye. I ran to the window to see whether she was taking him up to her own flat, but they had gone too quickly. There was no way of knowing whether they had gone in her door or turned the corner, and I didn't really want to run out into the street to check.

Trudy wasn't very interested in my speculation.

'I don't suppose I should have been so surprised to see her,' I reflected. 'I knew she lived in Notting Hill. This is a very black area around here too, I suppose.'

'Quite a few white people live here as well,' said Trudy acidly, and I forgot that she had just paid what seemed like an enormous sum of money for a very small, very twee house around the corner.

The others were interested at lunch-time the next day. They wanted to know what Andrew looked like.

'Like that actor who plays the part of Henry in that serial,' I said, meaning an actor whose dizzying looks had sent people of all ages into some kind of wistful speculation as to what a future with him might be like.

'You mean Andy Sparks,' said Marian, and with a thud I realised it *was* Andy Sparks. It was just that his face seemed so contorted, and he hadn't worn the boyish eager look nor the boyish eager anorak he always wore in the serial.

'My God, it was definitely him,' I said. By this time the others were losing interest, they thought I had gone into fantasy. Large lumbering black Rita, who read rubbishy magazines, who never seemed interested in anything, not even herself . . . she could never have been the petite amie of Andy Sparks.

'We did a feature on him about three weeks ago,' said Martin. 'No, it can't have been the same guy, you only think so because they had the same name.'

'You did say Rita was sexy,' I pointed out, trying to bolster up my claim that she might be so sexy that she could have been seen with the superstar of the moment.

'Not *that* sexy,' said Martin, and they began to talk about other things.

'Don't tell her I told you,' I said. I felt it was important that Rita shouldn't think I had been blabbing about her. It was as if I had gone into her territory by being in that pub, and I shouldn't be carrying back tales from it.

I looked up the back pages surreptitiously. It *was* the same guy. He had looked unhappy and drawn compared to the pictures we used of him, but it was the same Andrew.

On Friday Rita handed me a parcel and an envelope. The parcel was my skirt, which she said the cleaners had made a lovely balls of. They were sorry but with a stain like that it was owner's risk only, and she had alas agreed to owner's risk. They were, she said, the best cleaners around. I looked at the docket and saw she was right. I also saw the name on the docket. It said 'A. Sparks'. She took the docket away and gave me the envelope. It was a gift-token for almost exactly what the skirt had cost, and it was from the shop where I had in fact bought it. Not a big chain-store but a boutique.

'I can't take it,' I said.

'You might as well, he can afford it.' She shrugged.

'But if it had been a stranger, not a . . . er . . . well someone you knew, then I wouldn't have got it replaced,' I stammered.

'That's your good luck, then,' said Rita and went back

to her desk. She hadn't even left me the docket so that I could show the others I was right about the name.

At lunchtime I invited Rita out with me.

'I thought you were having lunch with that woman who wrote the book about flowers,' she said, neither interested nor bored, just stating a fact.

'She rang and cancelled,' I said.

'I didn't put her through to you,' said Rita.

'No, well I rang her on the direct line actually,' I said, furious to have my gesture of taking her out to lunch made into an issue. 'I didn't feel like talking to her.'

'And you feel like talking to me?' asked Rita with one of her rare smiles.

'I'd like to buy you a nice lunch and relax with you and thank you for going to all that trouble over my skirt,' I snapped. It sounded the most ungracious invitation to lunch ever given.

Even if I had been down on my knees with roses I don't think Rita would have reacted differently.

'Thanks very much, but I don't think I will. I don't like long boozy lunches, I have too much work to do in the afternoons here anyway.'

'For Christ's sake it doesn't have to be long and boozy, and though you may not have noticed it, I work here in the afternoons myself,' I said like a spoiled child.

'Okay then,' she said, took up her shoulder bag, and with no coat to cover her fat bouncing bottom and half-exposed large black breasts, she rolled down the corridor with me, into the lift and out into the street.

I chose a fairly posh place, I wasn't going to have her say I went to less expensive places with her than with the journalists or people I interviewed.

She looked at the menu as if it were a list of cuttings we needed her to get from the library. I asked her if she would like pâté and said that they made it very well here.

'Sure,' she said.

I could see it was going to be hard going.

We ordered one glass of wine each, she seemed to accept that too as if it were extra dictation. The few starts I made were doomed. When I asked her whether she found the work interesting in the office, she said it was fine. Better than where she had worked before? Oh yes she supposed so. Where had that been? Hadn't I seen it on her application? She'd been with a lot of firms as a temp. I was driven to talk about the traffic in London, the refuge of all who run out of conversation.

Just then a bird-brained rival of mine on another newspaper came over. Normally I would have walked under buses to avoid her. Today she seemed like a rescue ship sent to a desert island.

She sat down, had a glass of wine, wouldn't eat because of some new diet, wouldn't take her coat off because she was in a hurry, and looked at Rita with interest. I introduced them just name by name without saying where either worked.

'I expect you're being interviewed,' the bird-brain, highly-paid writer said to Rita. Rita shrugged. She wasn't embarrassed, she wasn't waiting for me to give her a lead. She shrugged because she couldn't be bothered to say anything.

At least now I didn't have to do all the talking. Rita and I heard how hard life was, how long it took to get anywhere these days because of the traffic, how hopeless hairdressers were, how they never listened to what you wanted done, how silly the new summer clothes were, how shoes didn't last three months, how selfish show-biz people were making big productions out of being interviewed, instead of being so grateful for all the free publicity. Then her eyes brightened.

'I'm doing Andy Sparks,' she said. 'Yes I know, your lot had him last week, but he's promised to tell me all about his private life. I'm taking him to dinner in a little club I've just joined, so that people won't keep coming over to disturb us. He's meant to be absolutely as dumb as anything, only intelligent when he gets lines to read. Anyway we'll see, we can't go far wrong if he tells a bit about the loves of his life, I only hope it won't be religion or his mother or a collie dog or something.'

Rita sat half-listening as she had been doing all along. I started to say about three different things and got a coughing fit. Finally it dawned on the world's most confident bad writer that she was losing her audience so she excused herself on the grounds that she wanted to go and get herself smartened up at the hairdresser, just in case this beautiful man by some lovely chance wasn't in love with his mother or the man who directed the series.

'Do people usually talk about him like that?' I asked Rita.

'About who?' she said.

'About Andy Sparks,' I said relentlessly.

'Oh, I suppose they do,' she said uncaringly. 'I mean he's quite famous really, isn't he? In everyone's homes every night – as they say.'

'Did you know him before he was a star?' I asked.

'No, I only got to know him a couple of years ago,' she said.

'Are you fond of each other?' I asked, again amazed at my bravery.

'Why?' she said.

'Well, I thought that he seemed very dependent on you the other night.'

'Oh, he was just pissed the other night,' she said.

There was a silence.

'Look,' I said. 'I don't want to talk about him if you don't. I just thought it was interesting, there you are knowing him very well while we just had to do bits and pieces about him to make up that feature. I suppose I wonder why you didn't say anything.'

'And have my picture in the paper you mean? Like Andy Sparks and the girl he can't have . . . that sort of thing.'

'No, of course we wouldn't have done anything like . . .'

'Of course you would,' she said flatly. 'You work on a newspaper.'

'There might have been a bit of pressure yes, but in the end it would have been up to you. Come on, Rita, you work with us, you're part of our team, we wouldn't rat on you that way.'

'Maybe,' she said.

'But why can't he have you . . . ?' I went on. 'You said Andy Sparks and the girl he can't have.'

'Oh well, I'm married to someone else,' she said.

'I see,' I said, though I didn't.

Another silence.

'And does he want to marry you, Andy, I mean?'

'Oh yes, I think Andrew would like to, but I don't think he really knows what he wants.'

'Do you not want to leave your husband?' I asked, remembering suddenly that there had been no sign of a man around that little flat.

'He's inside, served four years of fifteen, he'll probably have to do two more anyway.'

'Oh God, I'm sorry I asked.'

'No you're not, if you hadn't asked you wouldn't know. You want to know, it's partly you yourself, it's partly your job. You all like to know things.'

It was the longest speech I'd heard her make. I didn't know what to say.

She went on.

'Listen, I'm not coming back to the office. I don't want to go back now, because everyone already knows I know him. Oh yes they do, you told them, but you told them not to mention it, I'm not a fool. I can't bear offices where everyone knows everything about everyone else, that's why I stayed so long with you lot . . . you didn't talk too much about your own lives, and you didn't pry into mine. I thought you'd like me being fairly buttoned up

. . . but no, it's all of you who've been doing the prying . . .'

'I understand what you mean, Rita, honestly I do. The girls who did your job before were always so boring about their boyfriends and their life's history . . . but seriously I understand if . . .'

She looked at me.

'You understand nothing if I may say so. You don't understand the first little thing. And because it isn't clear to you at once, you turn it all into a little mystery and have to solve it. You don't understand why Andrew fancies me, you don't understand why I wait for a husband to come out of prison, you don't understand whether those kids Martie and Anna are mine or not.'

'It's none of my business,' I said, distressed and unable to cope with the articulate and very, very angry Rita. 'I can't say anything right now.'

Rita calmed down. Her eyes didn't flash, but they were not back to the dead dull look they normally held.

'Well, I could tell you a few things which would give you information, but you still wouldn't *understand*. Martie and Anna aren't my girls, they're Nat's. Nat is my husband. Nat is in gaol because he beat Myrtle to death. Myrtle was my best friend. Myrtle always loved Nat. Nat never loved Myrtle but he had two children by her. Even after he married me, he would see Myrtle. I knew, I didn't mind, that's the way Nat was. I knew it at the time, I know it now. Myrtle found this other fella, he wanted to marry her, take the kids and all he would. Myrtle told Nat, Nat said no, he didn't want another man raising his kids. Myrtle asked me what she should do. I said I thought she should marry the other fella, but then my advice was prejudiced.

'Myrtle said I was right, and she told Nat. They had a great row. Nat he lost his temper and he beat Myrtle and he beat her, and she died. I telephoned the police and they came, and they took him, and he got fifteen years and I look after Anna and Martie.'

She paused and took a drink of her wine, and though I didn't understand I could approach an understanding of how strong she must have been, must still be.

'And you won't understand either why Andrew wants me to go away with him. He just needs me. I don't know whether he loves me or not, or whether he knows what love is, but he needs me, because I . . . well I'm what he needs. And he doesn't understand either, he can't understand that Nat don't mind me seeing him. He knows that Nat has a lot of friends who tell him or his friends what's going on. But Nat doesn't mind me going about with a white man, a white actor from the television. Nat thinks that's just company for me. Now can you understand any of that at all?'

At the end of the week when the bird-brain's story appeared it was pretty tame stuff. She did have an angle that Andy Sparks had some mystery woman in his life, someone he leaned on, someone he needed, but was not prepared to discuss.

Rita came around that day to collect some things she'd left in the drawer of her desk, and to pick up her salary. She came at lunch-time when there was nobody there, except her replacement, who was full of chat and said that she had told Rita all about her fiancé being mean with money. She asked Rita if she thought that was a bad omen. Rita had said that she couldn't care less.

'Odd sort of woman, I thought,' said the replacement. 'Very untidy, sort of trampishly dressed really. Funny that she wasn't more pleasant. Black people are usually happy-looking, I always think.'

Queensway

Pat wished that she didn't have such a lively imagination when she was reading the advertisements. When she saw something like 'Third girl wanted for quiet flat. Own room, with central heating' she had dark fears that it might be a witches' coven looking for new recruits. Why mention that the flat was quiet? Could central heating be some code for bonfires? But she couldn't afford a flat of her own, and she didn't know anyone who wanted to share, so it was either this or stay for ever in the small hotel which was eating into her savings.

She dreaded going for the interview, which was why she kept putting off answering any of the offers. What would they ask her? Would they give her a test to see whether she was an interesting conversationalist? Might they want to know all about her family background? Did they ask things like her attitude towards promiscuity, or spiritualism, or the monarchy? Or would it be a very factual grilling, like could she prove that she wouldn't leave a ring around the bath or use the phone without paying for her calls?

There were about twenty women working in the bank, why did none of them want to share, she complained to herself. At least she knew something about them, that they were normal during the daytime anyway. But no, they were all well-established in London, married to men who wouldn't do the shopping, or living with blokes who wouldn't wash their own socks, or sharing flats with girls who wouldn't clean up the kitchen after them. There was no place in any of their lives for Pat.

Three months was all she was going to allow herself in the hotel, three months to get over the break-up of her home, to calm herself down about Auntie Delia being taken away to hospital and not recognising anyone ever again. It was better, the doctors said, that Pat should go right away, because Auntie Delia really didn't know who she was any more, and would never know. She wasn't unhappy, she was just, well there were many technical terms for it, but she was in a world of her own.

If you have worked in a bank in Leicester, you can usually get a job working in a bank in London. But if you've lived with Auntie Delia, funny, eccentric, fanciful, generous, undemanding, for years and years, it's not so easy to find a new home.

'What should I ask them?' she begged the small, tough Terry who knew everything, and who had no fears about anything in this life. 'I'll feel so stupid not knowing the kind of questions that they'll expect *me* to ask.'

Terry thought it was so simple that it hardly needed to be stated.

'Money, housework and privacy, are the only things girls fight about in flats,' she said knowledgeably.

'Find out exactly what your rent covers, make sure there aren't any hidden rates to be paid later, ask how they work the food – does everyone have their own shelf in the fridge, or do they take it in turns buying basics? If you are all going to have a week each in charge of the food, get a list of what people buy and how much they spend. Stupid to have you buying gorgeous fresh-ground coffee or expensive tea, when they only get instant and tea bags.'

'And what should I ask about the housework?' Pat wondered.

'Do they have a Hoover, if so who uses it and when? It would be awful if they were all manic house cleaners, washing down paintwork every day. And examine the place carefully, they might be so careless that the place is full of mice and rats.'

Privacy meant that Pat was to inquire what arrangements they had about the sitting-room: did people book it if they were going to ask anyone in, or did everyone eat, play, watch telly together, or did people entertain in their own bedrooms?

So, armed with all this intelligence, she dialled the 'Third Girl wanted, lovely flat, near park, own room, friendly atmosphere' advertisement. Auntie Delia would have snorted at the ad, and said that they sounded like a bunch of dikes to her. Pat still couldn't believe that Auntie Delia didn't snort and say outrageous things any more.

The girl who answered the phone sounded a little breathless.

'I can't really talk now, the boss is like a devil today, he says I shouldn't have given this number. Can I have your number and I'll phone you back later when he leaves the office? It's a super flat, we wouldn't want to leave it in a million years, it's just that Nadia went off to Washington and we can't afford it just for two.'

Pat didn't like the sound of it. It seemed a bit fast and trendy. She didn't like people who said 'super' in that upward inflection, she didn't like the thought of people suddenly dashing off to Washington, it was too racy. And she thought the name Nadia was affected. Still, she might use them as a rehearsal. There was no law saying you had to take the first flat you saw.

The breathless girl rang back ten minutes later. 'He's gone out for an hour,' she confided. 'So I'm going to make use of it, ringing all the people back. I thought I'd start with you because you work in a bank, you might get us all an overdraft.'

Pat took this little pleasantry poorly, but still you had to practise flat-getting somewhere, and she arranged to call at eight o'clock. She made a list of questions, and she promised herself that she would take everything in, so that she would go better equipped to the next and more serious interview.

It was an old building, and there were a lot of stairs but no lift. Perhaps they all became permanently breathless from climbing those stairs. Feeling foolish to be feeling nervous, Pat rang the bell. It had a strange echoing chime, not a buzz. It would have, thought Pat. Nadias, and Washingtons, and Supers, naturally they'd have to have a bell that pealed, rather than one which buzzed.

Joy wasn't at all breathless now that she was home. She wore a long housecoat, and she smelled of some very, very expensive perfume. She was welcoming, she remembered Pat's name, she apologised for the stairs but said that you got used to them after a month or so. There were eighty-three steps, counting the flat bits between floors, and they did encourage you not to be forgetful about things like keys.

Pat stared around the hall. It was literally covered in pictures and ornaments, and there were rugs on the walls as well. At one end there were a couple of flower baskets hanging and at the other a carved hall-stand full of dried flowers.

'It's far too nice to sit inside,' said Joy, and for a wild moment Pat thought that they would have to go down all the stairs again before she had even seen the flat.

'Come into Marigold's room, and we'll have a drink on the balcony.'

Marigold! thought Pat. Yes, it would have to be Marigold.

A big room, like one of those film-sets for an Anna Neagle movie, with little writing-desks, and a piano with photographs on top. There were flowers here too, and looped lacey curtains leading out to a balcony. There in a wheelchair sat Marigold. The most beautiful woman that Pat had ever seen. She had eyes so blue that they didn't really seem to be part of a human body. She could have played any number of parts as a ravishing visitor from Mars. She had so much curly hair, long, shiny and curly, that it looked like a wig for a heroine, but you knew it wasn't a wig. She smiled at Pat, as if all her life she had been waiting to meet her.

'I wish Joy would tell people I live in a wheelchair,' she said, waving at Pat to get her to sit down. She poured some white wine into a beautiful cut crystal glass and handed it to her. 'I honestly think it's so unfair to let people climb all those stairs and then face them with what they think will be a nursing job instead of a home.'

'Well I don't, I never, you mustn't . . .' stammered Pat.

'Rubbish,' said Joy casually. 'If I said you were in a wheelchair nobody would ever come at all. Anyone who has come, wants to move in, so I'm right and you're wrong.'

'Have you had many applicants?' asked Pat.

'Five, no six including the lady with the cats,' said Joy.

Pat's list had gone out of her head, and she had no intention of taking it from her handbag. They sat and talked about flowers, and how wonderful that in a city the size of London people still had a respect for their parks, and rarely stole plants or cut blooms for themselves from the common display. They talked on about the patchwork quilt that Marigold had made, how difficult it was to spot woodworm in some furniture, and how a dishonest dealer could treat it with something temporary and then it all came out only when you had the thing bought and installed. They had more wine, and said how nice it was to have an oasis like a balcony in a city of ten million or whatever it was, and wondered how did people live who didn't have a view over a park.

'We must have a little supper,' Marigold said. 'Pat must be starving.'

No protests were heeded, a quick move of her wrist, and the wheelchair was moving through the pots and shrubs of the balcony, the flowers and little writing bureaux of the bedroom, the bric-à-brac of the hall, and they were in a big pine kitchen. Barely had Joy laid the table for three before Marigold had made and cooked a cheese soufflé, a salad had been already prepared, and there was garlic bread, baking slowly in the oven. Pat felt guilty but hungry, and strangely happy. It was the first evening meal anywhere that seemed like home since they had taken Auntie Delia away.

She felt it would be crass to ask how much did people pay and who bought the groceries, and what kind of cleaning would the third girl be expected to do. Neither Marigold nor Joy seemed to think such things should be discussed, so they talked about plays they had seen, or in Marigold's case books she had read, and it was as if they were just three friends having a nice dinner at home instead of people trying to organise a business deal.

At eleven o'clock Pat realised by the deep chiming of a clock that she had been there three hours. She would have to make a move. Never had she felt socially so ill at ease. She wondered what she should say to bring the visit to an end and the subject of why she was there at all into the open. She knew quite a lot about them. Marigold had polio and never left the flat. Joy worked in a solicitor's office as a clerk, but next year was going to go into apprenticeship there and become a solicitor too. Marigold seemed to have some money of her own, and did the housework and the cooking. They had met some years ago when Marigold had put an ad in the paper. Marigold had found the flat.

Nadia was mentioned, a little. There were references to Nadia's room and Nadia's clock, which was the big one that chimed, and some chat about the time they had made the curry for Nadia's dinner-party and everyone had gone on fire from it.

Resolutely Pat stood up and said that her little hotel closed at midnight and she had better get back, as they didn't have a night-porter.

'Well, when shall we expect you?' asked Marigold.

Pat, who hadn't even been shown her room, hadn't been informed about how much rent, what kind of lifestyle was to be expected, was stunned.

'What about the five other people, and the lady with the cats?' she asked desperately.

'Oh no,' said Marigold.

'No indeed,' said Joy.

'Well, can I think about it?' Pat asked, trying to buy time. 'I don't know whether I could afford to live here, and you mightn't like my friends, and we haven't really sorted anything out.'

Marigold looked like an old trusted friend who has suddenly and unexpectedly been rebuffed.

'Of course you must decide for yourself, and perhaps you have somewhere else in mind. We are terrible, Joy, not to give Pat details of rent and things. We're simply hopeless.'

'The rent is £20, and we usually spend about £10 a week each on food, and flowers and wine,' said Joy.

That was expensive, but not for what you got. You got a magnificent home, you got lovely meals, you got two very bright nice women to live with.

Pat heard her own voice saying, 'Fine. Yes, if you think I'd fit in here with you, that's fine. Can I come at the weekend?'

That night she wondered what she had done. Next morning she wondered whether she had been insane.

'I don't know,' said tough little Terry. 'If the food's as good as all that, if the one in the wheelchair does all the work, if the place is like something out of *Home and Garden*, I think you're laughing. If you don't like it you can always move out.'

'I didn't even look at my bedroom.' said Pat with a wail.

'They'll hardly give you a coal-hole,' said Terry practically.

Joy rang her breathlessly that day.

'It's super that you're coming. Marigold's so pleased. She asked me to tell you that there's plenty of room in your bed-sitting-room for anything you want to bring, so don't worry about space. Any pictures or furniture you like.'

Pat wondered why Marigold didn't ring herself. She was at home, she didn't have to avoid a spying boss. Pat also wondered whether this was a polite way of telling her that there were four walls and nothing else in her room.

On Saturday she arrived with two students who ran a flat-moving service, They carried up her little tables, her rocking-chair, and her suitcases. They had cluttered up her hotel bedroom ridiculously, and she wondered whether there would be any more room for them where she was going. As they all puffed up the eighty-three steps, Pat felt very foolish indeed.

Joy let them in, with little cries of excitement. They paraded through the bedecked hall to a huge sunny room, which had recesses for cupboards, a big bed and a washbasin. Compared to the rest of the flat it looked like an empty warehouse.

Joy fussed along behind them. 'Marigold said we should empty it so that you wouldn't feel restricted. But there's lots of furniture available. There are curtains and shelves for these,' she waved at the recesses. 'Marigold thought you might want your own things.'

Pat paid the students, and sat down in the warehouse. Even her rocking-chair looked lost. When she unpacked it wouldn't be much better. Auntie Delia's things would look lovely here. All those monstrous vases, even that beaded curtain. Maybe she should send for them. They were all in the little house in Leicester. They would be hers when Auntie Delia died. Strictly speaking they were hers already, since she had rented the house out just to get money to pay for her poor Aunt in the nursing-home.

The rent covered the fees. The tenants didn't like all the overcrowding from the furniture but Pat had insisted the house should remain untouched since Auntie Delia *could* get better one day and *might* come home. She felt slightly disloyal thinking about taking Auntie Delia's treasures, but surely she couldn't live in a barn like this, while Auntie Delia lived in a world of her own, and the tenants lived in a house that they thought vastly over-stuffed with things they didn't like.

It was morning coffee time, so she gathered from the smell of fresh coffee coming from the kitchen. She was right, they assembled on the balcony, and had coffee from lovely china cups.

'I'll be sending to Leicester for my real furniture this week,' she said.

'We'll be dying to see it,' said Marigold, her china-blue eyes lighting up with excitement.

'And I must give you some money and everything,' blurted out Pat. 'I'm not much good at this you know, not having shared a flat before.'

'Oh, Joy will look after that,' said Marigold. 'She's so good with money, working in that office, where there's a lot of accountancy. She should have been a solicitor from the start you know, it's so silly to have waited until she's twenty-seven before starting her indentures.'

'I'd never have done it at all if it weren't for you,' said Joy gratefully. 'I'd still be working on there and taking my money each week.'

'It would have been pointless,' said Marigold. Her blue eyes looked out over the park, where people who weren't in wheelchairs jumped and played and ran about.

Pat sighed happily. It was so peaceful here and she had the whole week-end before facing the bank again. Nobody ever told you how easy it was to find a flat.

'Would you like me to do any shopping or anything?' she asked helpfully.

'Joy does that on Friday nights, we're very well

organised', smiled Marigold. 'We have a small deep freeze as well. It helps a great deal.'

While the rest of London sweated and fussed and shopped and dragged themselves through traffic jams or in crowded trains to the seaside, Joy and Marigold and Pat sat peacefully reading, listening to music, or chatting. By Monday Pat felt she had been on a rest-cure. She and Joy had done a lot of the washing-up, and preparing of things, rougher jobs like peeling potatoes and cutting up meat, and taking out rubbish.

Joy was friendly and eager to do everything, Marigold was gentle, serene and calm. Pat began to think that she couldn't have found two more perfect flat-mates.

On Sunday night she telephoned the people in Leicester and asked them to arrange to have seventeen pieces of furniture, some huge, some tiny, collected and delivered to London.

Nobody had telephoned the flat, nobody had gone out. Pat wondered what happened if you invited a friend in for supper. Would they all eat as a foursome? She saw no other way.

She gave Joy £80, and asked what to do about the tenner for food.

'I'll spend £20 this week, and you spend it next week,' said Joy cheerfully.

Pat wondered where Marigold's tenner came into it but said nothing. Why upset things? Things are not always so peaceful in life, it's silly to question just for the sake of questioning.

On Tuesday she rang Joy at work to say that she was going to the theatre so would not be home for dinner.

'Oh.' Joy sounded upset.

'But that's all right, isn't it?' asked Pat. 'Marigold won't start to cook until we get home anyway, so it's not a question of letting her know in advance. I'd ring her at home but I . . . well, I just thought I'd ring you.'

'Oh yes, it's better to ring me,' said Joy. 'No, no

problems. I'll pop home at lunch-time and tell her, it's not far. Don't worry.'

It all seemed very odd to Pat, but she put it out of her mind.

On Thursday her furniture arrived. Marigold was delighted with it. She whirled around in the wheelchair, stroking this and patting that.

'Lovely inlay,' she said.

'We must strip this down,' she said.

'What a magnificent curtain. Wouldn't it look lovely on the balcony?' she said.

So of course Pat, flattered and pleased, hung Auntie Delia's bead curtain up on the balcony, where indeed it looked lovely.

That night she asked if they ever heard from Nadia how she was enjoying Washington.

'No, we've not heard,' said Marigold.

'Nadia doesn't write many letters,' said Joy.

'What did she do, I mean what job had she?' asked Pat. Her slight jealousy of Nadia had disappeared, now she had only curiosity.

'She worked in an antique shop,' said Joy.

'Managed an antique shop,' said Marigold.

'Well, she worked there first,' laughed Joy. 'but Marigold told her she knew much more than anyone in it, and gave her confidence, so she ended up managing it for Mr Solomons.'

'She knew twice as much as Mr Solomons from the start,' said Marigold.

'Anyway Mr Solomons fancied her enormously, so that it didn't hurt,' said Joy with a giggle.

'Did she fancy him?' asked Pat with interest.

'Not until Marigold told her to have some intelligence and fancy him,' giggled Joy again.

'Oh,' said Pat.

Marigold seemed to think some clarification was called for.

'It always strikes me as silly to go to bed with half-drunk people, who forget it, or who feel embarrassed by it, or who do it so often that it's meaningless, and then refuse to go to bed with someone like Mr Solomons who would appreciate it, would remember it with affection, and would advance Nadia because of it. It just seems a foolish sort of thing to have a principle about.'

Put that way, thought Pat, it was unanswerable.

'But she left him all the same?' she probed.

'Oh no, she didn't leave Mr Solomons,' said Joy laughing. 'Mr Solomons left her. He had a heart attack and went to live in the country, so she managed his place for him, and took a share in the profits.'

'And had a very nice cut and first refusal on everything they stocked,' said Marigold, stroking the little mahogany cabinet beside her, almost sensuously.

'So why Washington?' asked Pat.

'She's running a little antique shop in Georgetown now,' said Marigold distantly. 'Very different kind of stuff, I'm sure.'

'She got sort of unsettled, and took the first job she heard of,' said Joy artlessly.

'Some silly business with a chap who used to restore paintings, very silly really,' said Marigold. And the conversation about Nadia stopped there. It was as clear a break as if 'End of Episode One' had been written in fire in the air.

Out of sheer curiosity, Pat stopped in Solomon's antique shop. There was no elderly owner type about, so she supposed that the good proprietor's heart could not yet have recovered from Nadia's exertions.

She asked how much they would give her for Aunt Delia's inlaid cabinet if she were to sell it. She described it very carefully.

'About five hundred pounds,' said the young man. 'Depends on what condition it's in, of course, but not less I'd say.'

That was odd. Marigold had said it was pretty but without value. Marigold said she should take great care of it because it might be worth fifty pounds. Imagine Marigold now knowing how much it was worth. A flaw in the lovely, graceful, all-knowing Marigold. A flaw no less.

'Is Nadia still here?' she asked on impulse.

'No, why, you a friend of hers?' the man asked.

'No,' said Pat. 'I just know people who know her.'

'Oh, she left here a few weeks ago. Kevin would know where she is.' He pointed out a young and very attractive, bearded, bending figure, who was examining the frame of a picture.

'It doesn't matter really,' said Pat hastily, thinking this might be the silly young man of Marigold's description.

'Hey, Kevin, this lady's a friend of Nad's.'

Kevin stood up. He was very handsome in a definitely shabby, ungroomed way. Pat could see that his nails, his unwashed hair wouldn't have fitted into the elegant furniture back in the flat.

'I was just looking around, and I remembered that this is where the girl who lived in the flat where I've just moved in used to work . . .' said Pat apologetically.

'Have you moved in there?' asked Kevin flatly.

'Yes, a few days ago.'

'Have you moved all your stuff in?' he asked.

'Well yes, yes I have,' Pat's voice trailed away. She felt unreasonably frightened.

'Did she tell you it's worth buttons, peanuts?'

'No,' said Pat defensively. 'Marigold said it's very nice furniture and I must take care of it. Why, anyway?'

'Will you tell her you've been in here?' he asked very unemotionally.

'I might, I might not. Why do you ask?' said Pat. She was definitely frightened now, which was ridiculous. She also knew that she would never admit to Marigold that she had nosed around Nadia's old place of employment and nosed out Nadia's silly young man.

'I don't think you will,' he said. 'Nadia never told her anything towards the end, she was absolutely terrified of her. So was I. It's her eyes, they're not human.'

'They're just too blue,' said Pat. 'She can't help that.'

'No, but she can help a lot of things. Do you know that she hasn't polio at all?'

'I don't believe you,' said Pat, feeling her legs getting weak.

'No, she hasn't, that's why none of them ring her at home. She goes out, you know, when everyone's at work.'

'Don't be ridiculous.'

'No, I saw her several times running down the stairs, and taking a taxi. I took a photograph of her once to prove it to Nadia, but she said it was trick photography.'

'But she's paralysed,' said Pat.

'So she says. It's nice being paralysed if you get everyone else to do all the work, pay all the bills, and live in fear of you.'

'Don't you think that someone would have to be mad to pretend to have polio, just to get out of carrying out the rubbish?'

'Marigold is mad, very mad,' he said.

Pat sat down on a reproduction sofa.

'Didn't you guess?' he asked.

'I don't believe it,' said Pat.

'Nadia doesn't to this day,' said Kevin.

'Is that why she went to Washington?' asked Pat.

'She's not in Washington, she's back in my flat. In Clapham,' he said. 'She told them she was going to the States, that was the only reason that Marigold let her go.'

'You mean she has no job, and just lives in your flat because she's afraid of Marigold?' Pat said. 'I don't believe a word of it.'

'Go down there and see,' he said. 'She'll be sitting

there complaining about the noise, and saying how little light there is, and how cramped the place seems to be. She doesn't even bother to get dressed properly, she hangs about all day complaining. That's what Marigold has done to her.'

'Does she want to be back in the flat?'

'She wants it so much I think she's becoming as mad as Marigold. "It was so peaceful. We were so gracious. We had such lovely music, not the neighbours' trannies." That's all she says, day in, day out.'

'Why did she leave it if she liked it so much?' asked Pat, almost afraid to hear the answer. Everything Nadia said about the flat was so true, there might be some truth in Kevin's whole terrible tale.

'She left it because I told her that she had given all her lovely furniture to this woman, that she had turned herself into a prostitute for her, that she had cut off her whole life for her, that she was working to support her. I told her to examine all these statements and if she thought they were true to move out. So she did and they were and she moved. But not without tissues of lies of course about Washington, which that nice silly Joy believes but Marigold saw through at once. Marigold didn't mind anyway, she had loads of stuff, hundreds of pounds worth, from Nad over the years, and she'll always get other slaves.'

'But Joy's normal.'

'She used to be, when she had a bit of a life of her own, and boyfriends, and big plates of spaghetti with the girls from work. She should have been married years ago and have three nice fat children by now, instead of trying to become a solicitor and earn more money for that Marigold.'

'You're very bitter about her.'

'I'm bleeding obsessed with her, that's what I am. She's ruined Nadia totally, she's turned Joy into a zombie, there was another one there too, I can't remember her name, but she had to go out to bloody Africa as a missionary or something to get over it all. Having left some very nice lamps and some very good old cut glass thank you.'

Pat's heart missed something of its regular movement. She remembered admiring the lamps, and Marigold had said they were from a dear friend who went to Africa and didn't need them.

It was the end of her lunch-hour. She walked out without saying anything. She knew where to find him if she needed to know any more. He would take her home to meet Nadia if she wanted confirmation of it all. She was a free, grown-up woman, nobody could keep her there against her will.

On the way back to the bank she passed an expensive flower shop. It had unusual little potted plants. One of them was very, very blue. It had a long name but Marigold would know it anyway. It would look lovely on the balcony table. It would be so peaceful there this evening after work. It was like a dream world really. It would be such a misery trying to get everything out of the flat now that she had just got it in. Anyway, why should she? Kevin was just a silly young man. Jealous obviously because Nadia had been so happy in the flat. Anyone would be happy in that flat, it was so very, very peaceful, you didn't need anyone else or anything else in the world.

Lancaster Gate

It was funny the way things turned out. If she hadn't made that huge scene, and cried, and nearly choked herself crying, and admitted all kinds of weaknesses, she wouldn't be here now. She would be back in the flat, cleaning the cooker, polishing the furniture, ironing his shirts, so that he would think it was wonderful to have all these home comforts and value her more.

She would have gone to the cinema maybe, but maybe not. Films were so full of other people's relationships, and she kept identifying, and saying 'If I behaved more like her, would he value me more?', or wondering why some screen woman could be so calm when everything was collapsing around her. Lisa could never be calm. She could pretend at calmness very successfully, but deep down it was churn, churn, churn. Sometimes she was surprised that he couldn't hear her heart sort of hitting against her bones, she could hear it thudding as well as feel it from inside, she could actually hear the wuff wuff sound it made. But fortunately he never managed to hear it, and she could always fool him into thinking she was relaxed and at ease. Sometimes the nights that had started with her heart thudding very seriously had turned out to be their best nights, because she acted out the calm role so well. Lisa had often thought how extraordinarily easy it was to fool someone you loved and who loved you.

Or who sort of loved you. But no, no, don't start that, don't start analysing, worrying, your heart will begin the booming thing again, and you've got nothing to boom about. Here in London, staying in a big posh hotel, signing the room-service dockets with his name, putting the Mrs bit in casually as if you had been doing it for years and it was now second nature. She wondered how long it took married people to forget their single names. Brides were always giggling about it. She supposed it would take about three weeks, about the same time as it took you to remember each January that the year had changed and that you must write a different date.

And it was what they called a glorious day on the weather forecast, very flowery indeed for the Met Office, but that was the word the man had used, and she had run to the window to see if he was right, and he was. There were railings across the road and people were putting up pictures, and postcards, and souvenirs, to sell to the passing tourists. And they seemed to be shouting to each other and laughing. They must know each other from meeting every week-end here, and they didn't sound like rivals or enemies. They didn't look as if they'd mind if a passing tourist bought from one rather than another. They were unpacking little canvas stools as well, and some of them had flasks. They were old and young. Lisa thought it was a funny kind of life. She wouldn't be able for it, her old anxiety would show. People wouldn't buy from her because she would have an anxious face wanting them to buy, and the more they passed her by because of her anxious face the more anxious it would become. But then that was the same kind of vicious circle that everyone kept getting caught in. It was like the whole problem with Him. If she felt unsure of him and thought that he was losing interest in her, she became strained and worried and not the carefree girl he had once fancied, and so he *did* start to lose interest, and because she could see this happening she became more strained and worried, and he lost more interest.

But stop, stop. Not today, today is glorious. It has been defined as such by the weatherman on the radio, than whom there must be surely no saner, soberer judge. And today you don't need to act at being relaxed, you are. He's there in the bathroom shaving, he's happy, he's glad you're here. You've made love a half an hour ago, he liked it, he's humming to himself. You make him happy or happier than he'd be if you weren't here. You're fine really. Remember that. He didn't have to take you with him to London for the conference, now did he? He couldn't have been planning something else, something awful like meeting someone else, if he took you so readily.

Lisa smiled happily, thinking of how readily he had agreed to take her with him. She hadn't meant to ask at all. She had packed his case yesterday morning . . . was it only yesterday? Friday, it must have been. She had been polishing his shoes.

'You don't need to do that,' he had said, a bit embarrassed.

'I was doing my own,' she had lied.

'They're suede, funny face,' he had said, laughing.

What was it? It couldn't have been funny face, he called her that a lot, it was meaningless as an endearment, it wasn't even special. He called his daughter funny face on the phone . . . often. He called his secretary funny face. Once she had been holding for him on the phone, and she could hear his voice clearly as he crossed the office. 'Get me a cup of coffee, funny face,' he had said. 'I've got a bugger of a day.' It was probably because he knew she wore suede shoes. Idiotic, it couldn't have been that. Put badly it was really madness. What was it then? Why did two tears fall down onto the shining leather shoes in her hand? She could have hit herself with rage. It wasn't as if she knew it was going to happen. You always sort of know when you're going to cry but not this time. It was automatic, as if someone had tinkered about with her tear-ducts when she wasn't looking. And once started there was no stopping. She dropped the shoes and said a hundred times that she was sorry, she didn't know what was wrong. She tried to laugh through this appalling shower of tears, and that made her worse. She would sort of catch her breath and cough, and then it would get worse, and there were actual whoops coming out of her at one stage.

He was astounded. He thought he was to blame.

'What did I say, what have I done?' he had said over and over. 'You knew I was going away today, you *knew*,' he had repeated. He felt cornered, he felt she was blaming him. She couldn't even stop this terrible heaving to assure him that of course she knew, and that today wasn't any worse than any other day. He looked very wounded.

'The conference starts on Monday. I want to get into top form for it, I don't want to arrive exhausted. I want to be there and rested, and to have made my own tour of the hotel. I don't want to be thought of as your typical Northern hick who arrives all impressed by everything. It's important, Lisa. You said you understood.'

The use of her name maybe. She stopped for a moment. She actually had breath to speak. But instead of saying what she meant to, something like *of course* she understood, she heard her own voice betraying her, ratting on her. She actually said, '*Why* do you have to go away? We could have had this week-end together, just the two of us. Nobody would have known we were here, it would have been lovely.'

When the words were said, she decided that she had now lost everything, that the whole hard uphill race had been lost. She didn't know to whom she had lost, but she had lost. He couldn't stand people who begged, people who made demands. He had told her that was why he had left his wife, why the great love of his life (which had not been his marriage) had ended, because these women made demands. They wanted more of him than he could give, they saw something wonderful in a forced intimacy, they thought that the phrase 'just the two of us' was safe and reassuring. He thought it was threatening and claustrophobic.

And because Lisa had thought that she had lost him, she abandoned herself to the tide. It was a great luxury, like getting into a warm bath when you're tired and cold. She had said all the unsayable things, the whines, the moans, the loneliness, how hard it had all been on her. How she had given him, if not the best years, then all the fun hours of her life, and for what? Nobody could know they lived together. Nobody could see them out together. It was clandestine and anxious-making, and leading nowhere, and she, Lisa, who was free, was abandoning every other man, every other chance of happiness, and for what? For someone who didn't give two damns about her. Well all right, it was all right. She kept repeating the words 'all right' as if they were a magic charm. She had no idea what she meant by them, but they were safer and less final than saying something even more hackneyed like 'it's all over'.

He hadn't seemed relieved that it was all over or all right or whatever she meant; he hadn't seemed distressed, either. He looked interested, like he would have been interested in a farmer telling him about spraying crops, or a newsvendor explaining what margin of profit there was in selling papers. He sounded as if he might like to hear more.

'Come with me then,' he said.

He had never taken her anywhere before, it was too dangerous. He had always said that in his position he couldn't afford anyone to point at him about anything. Times were too tricky, things were too rough. He couldn't mean it now, he was just saying it to placate her, he knew she'd refuse for his sake. It was another ploy, another bluff. He had once explained to her why he won so much at poker. She had realised even then that the same rules that he used at the card-table he used everywhere.

As suddenly as he had asked her she accepted.

'Fine,' she said. 'I will. Where shall I meet you?'

No back-tracking, no well-perhaps-not-this-time. He was on as well, that was one of the rules of the game. If you offer, you must follow through.

'Nowhere near the office, too likely to be seen. Take a bus to the big petrol station on the London road. I'll meet you there at . . . ten past four.'

'Right,' she said. He kissed her and said it would be great, he'd like showing her London.

'You hardly know it any better than I do,' she said.

No tears, no joy, no excitement, no gratitude. He looked at her approvingly. It was almost as if he thought she had gained a few housepoints. She had faked grief, she had got him to take her to London. Well done Lisa. He said jauntily that he wouldn't wait a minute after a quarter past four, and she said equally lightly that that was fine, and he left, suitcase in his hand, and she heard the car starting as he went off to work and to talk to the office funny face.

Lisa had felt light-headed, like the time she once went out in a speedboat, and nothing had been real. She sat down to steady herself. She must make a list. Obviously she wouldn't go to work. So what excuse this time? She didn't know how long she'd stay with him in London. The conference lasted four days, Monday to Thursday. She'd have to invent something that would take a week. Quick, she'd have to telephone in the next few minutes and alert the Head's secretary, before Assembly began and someone started looking for her. A death. Exactly, a death in London. Better than flu, a woman's disease, or a heavy cold. She dialled, she spoke, she waved her hands around in the air as she told the weary Miss Weston, the Head's tame dog, that an aunt, her nearest relative, was dying. She even got a bit sad about it as she filled in the form and details of this mythical aunt. No, there simply was nobody else, nobody at all, she had to go. She'd ring from London next week to tell them what was happening. She knew how terrible it would be trying to find a substitute at this late stage, but she had heard only just now, this minute, and she was going to London this afternoon. 'At ten past four,' she said meaninglessly but to make it more real in her own mind. Miss Weston said she would tell the Head, and implied that the job of telling the Head was far worse than saying good-bye to a favourite aunt. Miss Weston was never very good with small chat anyway.

Now, on with the list. Lisa had to get a smart case, she only had an old grip, not suitable at all, and what else? Take money out of the bank, get her hair done, ring her brother to make sure he didn't call her at school. He hadn't telephoned her for four months, but there was always the chance. Her brother was in his usual bad humour.

'You got me away from my scrambled eggs, they'll be all hard. Oh all right. No, of course I wouldn't telephone you, why should I? Oh very well. I don't know what you think you're doing. Have you read about the unemployment in this country? Where do you think you're going to get another job if you're fired? Sometimes I think you've no sense of responsibility. No, of course I won't say anything to anybody, but Lisa, I wish you'd tell me what you're up to. I was saying to Angela the other night that you are so secretive and you just ring me out of the blue to say the oddest kind of things. No, why the hell should I wish you a good time? I'm not able to run out on everything and everybody and dash off to London on some whim. Good-bye now, good-bye.'

No other friends to alert really. Funny after all the years of living in the same town. But she'd see Maggie at lunch and she'd tell her, and they'd have a bit of a giggle, and then Maggie would say, 'Make sure he pays for you, I think he's mean,' and Lisa would defend him to the hilt, he wasn't mean, he was careful with money, and that's how he got where he was and had all the things he had. She admired him for it.

It was a rush but it was a great day. There had been a few valleys. Maggie said she had heard that his wife was expecting another baby. Lisa said that it couldn't be true, he hadn't even seen his wife for six months. Maggie said it took nine months to produce a baby and this one was nearly ready to be produced. Lisa said it was all ridiculous, he'd have told her, and Maggie said sure, and anybody would tell you it didn't have to be *his* baby just because it was hers, and Lisa brightened. She darkened a bit at the bank when she tried to take out £60 from her deposit account and the clerk told her she had only £50 in it. She was sure there was over £200, but of course things like avocados were more expensive than the things she ate when she lived alone, and she did buy lots of little things for the flat.

She bought him a Johnny Cash cassette that they could play in the car, the kind of music he liked. It was a new one, they assured her. She was there at 3.30 and by four o'clock she knew every car accessory that they make these days. She bought a chamois so that the assistant wouldn't think she was loitering with intent. At five past four she got a horrible feeling that he might have been joking. She really should have rung him to make sure he meant it, but that would have looked humble and she didn't want that. Suppose she saw his car flying past. Suppose just suppose he did stop there for petrol and saw her, and hadn't meant to take her. That wouldn't be merely humble, it would be pathetic. Lisa shook herself, physically, like a dog trying to get rid of drops of rain, but she was trying to get rid of these hauntings and fancies. She seemed to have them these days the way people got mosquito bites, or dandruff. And then she saw him pulling in and looking around for her.

And the four hours, well it had been like a dream sequence in a movie. Or rather, like one of those sequences where they show you people making a long journey across America, and they cut from shots of the car on one motorway to another, lights from petrol stations and hotels flash on and off, signposts to cities pass by – and they were in London, and they hadn't talked much, just sat beside each other listening to both sides of the Johnny Cash over and over, and Lisa never asked where they'd be staying or how they'd hide from all the people from his company who were bound to be at the hotel, or what day she was going to be sent home. She didn't want to break the magic.

And when they came to London he looked a bit helpless because he didn't know which way to go, and he turned right once when there was no right turn and a taximan shouted at him, and Lisa was secretly delighted because he looked vulnerable then, and like a little boy, and she wanted to hug him to take the shame away, but she made no move, and finally after an hour of going backward and forward he found the hotel and suddenly he was his old self again. Because the world of hotels is pretty much the same everywhere, it's just London traffic that can throw you.

She had wondered what to do about a wedding-ring. He had never bought her any kind of ring, and she hadn't liked to get one this morning when she was shopping . . . well, in case he thought she was being small-townish about it all. Perhaps people didn't wear rings when checking in, perhaps it was more sophisticated not to. She had worn gloves anyway, it seemed a good way of avoiding doing the wrong thing.

The foyer was huge and impersonal, but full of people and shops, and newspaper-kiosks and theatre booking-stands. It was very different from the hotel that she and Bill had stayed in when mother was ill, and had suddenly been taken into hospital in London. That time they stayed in a small hotel near the station, and the woman who ran it asked them for the money in advance, and Bill had said they would have to sleep in the same room to save paying for two. And the woman who ran the hotel had turned out to be nice and kind when she discovered that their mother was dying, and had made tea for Lisa, and had told her how her own mother had died.

And it was different from the hotel that they had all stayed in when mother and father and Bill and herself had come to London for a week one October as a treat. That had been owned by a friend of father's, a North Countryman, and father said they wouldn't be robbed there like they would everywhere else. And it had been a vaguely unsatisfactory holiday for no reason that any of them ever understood and none of them ever dared say. Just a lot less than they all had hoped for probably.

But here in Lancaster Gate it was a different world and a different life, and he looked pleased that she was there and that was all that mattered. She smiled at him as the porter took their cases. She had bought one very like his, and got a cosy warm feeling in the lift because the cases looked like matching luggage, the kind of thing they might have been given as a wedding-present if they had been a normal couple.

And he must have ordered a room with a double-bed specially because she saw from the brochure she had been looking at in the lobby that most of the rooms had twin beds. And he gave her a kiss when the porter had gone, and said, 'There's nothing like a life of sin. Let's ring for a gin-and-tonic and let's go to bed.'

And they did, and then they went out to a restaurant where the Italian waiter asked them if they were married and Lisa said 'No' very quickly so that he wouldn't think she was trying to pretend in any way (except to the hotel) that she *was* his wife, and the waiter said he thought not, they looked too happy and too much in love. And Lisa's heart which hadn't pounded or thudded since that morning went into a little cotton-wool ball of happiness.

So it was indeed funny the way things turned out, she

thought again. Instead of losing out by behaving like a weak wife-type, clinging, dependent, she was being patted on the back and taken on a nice happy trip to London. There was a knock at the door and she leaped off the bed to answer it, thinking it was breakfast. It wasn't, it was a bowl of fruit and some flowers with a Compliments card. She gave the boy twenty pence and hoped that it was enough. He came out of the bathroom, all clean and young-looking, a towel around his waist. He was as excited as a child and nearly as excited as she was.

'Who's it from, who's it from?' she begged.

He tried to look casual. 'I always arrange little surprises like this for you,' he said, teasing her, and they opened the card.

It was from the President of the Company, an American gesture, he said, to make the employees feel they are part of a happy family, to make them pull harder because they think they are being looked after. He was very pleased, even though he wouldn't show it.

'Must have taken a secretary a long time to write out all these personal cards,' he said, not wishing her to think that he thought the President had written it.

'Still,' said Lisa. 'They did go to the trouble.'

She reached out for the card, and her heart became a big ball of putty and sank down in her body. It was addressed to 'Mr and Mrs' and hoped that they would both enjoy their stay.

'Is it . . . is it to tell you that they *know* you've brought a woman with you?' she asked fearfully.

He looked unconcerned. Not at all, the secretary had probably found out from the hotel which delegates had checked in with their wives and put Mr and Mrs on those cards. Just administration. He was putting on the cufflinks she had given him and he gave her a kiss on the nose.

She felt that the day was a bit less glorious and immediately felt very angry with herself for feeling that way. What had happened? Nothing. She was a cheat and a tramp, and a mistress, and illegally registered in the hotel as the 'Mrs' she wasn't. But that was all rubbish. The first night she had gone to bed with him she had rid her mind of all those labels, they didn't count in anybody's mind except the fevered minds of a long-gone generation. Why was a silly card upsetting her?

The breakfast arrived and they sat by the window reading the two newspapers that had been sent up as well. She touched his hand when she poured him more coffee. He smiled, and she hoped in a beaten sort of way that it was going to be fairly glorious anyway.

'What shall we do?' he said.

'I'd like to look at the pictures and things they're hanging up on the railings down there. Maybe I might buy a couple of things.'

'It's bound to be rubbish,' he said, not disagreeably, but as one who knew about such things.

'All the same, it would be nice to stroll around and then maybe go for a walk in the park,' she said.

'Perhaps we should move further away from the hotel,' he said. He was right, of course. It would have been idiocy to have hidden it for seventeen months back home, where such things were hard to hide, and then blow it in a city of ten million people, just by parading around in front of people who were bound to know him, and to know that she oughtn't to be there. Lisa agreed quickly.

'We can go anywhere else,' he said helpfully.

'We could get the underground to St Paul's and have a look at that,' she said eagerly, to show that she didn't mind being a second-best woman, a person who had to be hidden rather than paraded.

'Yes, we could do that,' he said.

'Or walk up to Oxford Street maybe, and look at the shops.'

'They'll be a bit crowded, Saturday morning,' he said.

She felt the familiar terror, the well-known realisation that she was losing his interest came flooding over her. You counter that with brilliant acting, she told herself smartly. You don't give in, you don't allow yourself to look beaten or sulky. You act.

'Listen my love, I'm doing all the suggesting, I don't mind *what* we do. It's a glorious day, even the man on the wireless said so. I'll do whatever you'd like, or anyway I'll discuss it.'

She smiled the bright bird-like smile that she felt must look so phoney. She always thought she must look like a model in an advertisement on telly who has suddenly been told she must act.

But no, as always, he responded as he would have done to a normal remark.

'Well, I'll tell you what I'd *like* to do,' he said.

'Yes?' Mask set, eyebrows raised, mouth in inquiring smile.

'It sounds a bit odd but, well, I've arranged to have one of these executive health check-ups. You know, we were talking about them. They have them on Saturday mornings. Do everything: heart, blood pressure, X-rays, blood tests, the lot. It makes more sense than spending hours and days at home.

'They have them on Saturdays so that executives can go without telling anyone at work what they're up to. When I thought I was going to be here by myself, I booked one for today, and sent a deposit. I could cancel it but you . . . you know, it seems a pity. It would set my mind at rest.'

The fluttering fear that was never too far from her heart came back and buzzed at her, it even got into her eyes.

'Stop looking worried, funny face,' he said, laughing. 'Nothing happens to me, it's because I do things like this that I'm so healthy. They won't find anything wrong. It's just wise to have it done at forty-five, that's all.'

She was ten years younger and a hundred times slower

in every way, in thinking, in walking, in making up her mind, in knowing what to say.

'Are you sure you don't have any pains or anything?' she faltered.

He was sure, and he was quite willing to cancel it. It was just that they didn't have anything like this at home, and you know that once you went for any kind of check-up back there, everyone knew about it, and they all had you buried before you came out of the doctor's surgery. Still, it did seem a pity to waste the nice morning, and she had been saying only yesterday that they didn't have much time together, just the two of them. Perhaps he would ring and cancel it.

She knew she was being manipulated when she insisted that he go. She knew he used the phrase 'just the two of us' in heavy inverted commas. She knew that he had never intended to back out of it for a minute. Anyway she thought it was a good idea for him to have the check-up. So it was on with the act.

No, nonsense, she would be very happy to stroll around herself. She'd meet him afterwards. She'd go down and look at those pictures that he didn't want to see. It was ideal really, they could each do what they wanted, and then meet for lunch.

He didn't know whether it would be over by lunch-time. But she thought that this was the point, that the check-up only took a couple of hours. Yes, well he hoped so but maybe they had better not make a firm arrangement for lunch just in case.

Oh act, act. Fine, that suited her too. After she had looked at the paintings on the railings, she'd have a quick look at Oxford Street, and then take the tube to St Paul's. She hadn't been there since she was a child, she'd love to see it again. Don't cling, don't cling, you mustn't appear dependent. Choose some very late time and he'll suggest earlier. He'll like you for saying you can manage alone, you'll like it if he says he wants you earlier. Don't ruin it, don't balls up the glorious day.

'Why don't we say six o'clock here!' Bright, light tone, utterly non-clinging, utterly ridiculous as a suggestion. His examination couldn't possibly take from eleven in the morning until six at night.

'That sounds about right,' he said, and the day went dark, but the voice stayed bright, and there were no give-away signs as she bounced cheerfully out the door.

The lobby looked less glittering and glamorous and Londonish. It looked big and full of people who trusted other people or didn't give a damn about other people. She looked at the house-phones on the wall. Should she ring up and just say 'Love you'? They did that to each other, or they used to a lot in the beginning. No, it was silly, there was nothing to be gained and it might irritate him. Why risk it?

She wound her way across the road, jumping this way and that to avoid the traffic, because it looked too far to walk to the pedestrian crossing, and anyway she was anxious to get to the other side. It reminded her of Paris, and all those thousands of water-colours of Notre-Dame, all of them exactly the same and all of them different prices, or so it seemed.

There was a young man with very red hair and a very white face looking at her.

'Scarf, lady?' he asked hopefully.

'I want to look at everything before I buy,' she said happily.

'Surprising more of you Northerners aren't killed if that's the way you cross roads up there,' he said good-naturedly.

He meant it nicely. It was to keep her chatting, she knew that. She also thought that he fancied the look of her, which was nice. She felt it was so long now since anyone had fancied her that she wouldn't know how to react. But somehow his marking her out as a Northerner annoyed her, she was irritated, even though she knew it was said in friendship. Did she sound provincial, did she look provincial, crossing the road like that?

Suddenly she thought with a violence that made her nearly keel over, that there was a great possibility that he thought she was provincial too. That could be the reason why he wasn't prepared to make any public announcement of their being together. Not announcement, she didn't really want as much as that, she wanted . . . a bit of openness. It was bloody obvious now that she thought of it. Living with someone, having it off with someone, having an affair, all this was accepted now . . . by everyone.

She stood there, not even seeing the blur of Towers of London, Trafalgar Squares, and Beefeaters that waved like flags from the scarf-rack. She could only see her herself years ago at supper-time, listening to her mother talking about people who gave themselves airs. Her mother had wanted Lisa always to remember that she came from good stock. They could hold their heads up with any of them, they were as good as anyone for miles around, they had nothing hidden away that could never be dragged out. Lisa and Bill never knew what brought on these kind of statements, they had never even known what she was talking about. Suddenly Lisa knew. It was the reassurance game, it was trying to say 'it's all right'.

Lisa felt like shouting it out aloud this very moment. She had an urge to tell the boy with the red hair that her father had been a local government official, that her mother had been a nurse, that her mother's father had owned a chemist's shop. She wanted to say it in a voice so clear and loud that he would hear it, before he left for his check-up, so that he would realise how lucky he was to have got a girl from such good stock, who was so willing to play along in a shabby game with him. That it was against her training, her background, her . . . well her kind of people. She wanted him to know, without having to spell it out, that she was better than he was, better in the way that older people valued things, that she had come from respectable people. His father had worked in the Potteries, that much she knew and only that.

Of course he had married into money, and why shouldn't he, a bright boy like him? Any family would have been delighted to have him as a son-in-law. Would her own family have liked him? Yes, her father would have admired him, her mother would have been a bit boringly embarrassing about stock, but she would have accepted him. However, she'd have liked him to know, if only there were some way of telling him indirectly, that her family wouldn't have fallen over themselves in gratitude . . . that he'd have had to make an effort to be accepted.

Lisa's head cleared and she looked at the boy again.

'I don't feel very well,' she said, feeling she owed him some explanation of why she was standing there looking at him wildly.

'Do you want to sit down, darling?' he asked kindly, and pushed out a stool for her. He looked a bit worried and even embarrassed. His customer had turned out to be a nutcase. That's what he must be thinking, Lisa told herself miserably.

He gave her a cup of very sweet coffee from his little orange flask. Over the rim of the cup she looked up at the hotel. Was there any chance that he would be looking out the window and would see her sitting down, drinking coffee there? Would he be worried, would he rush down to know if she felt faint? What would she say if he did? But as the hot sweet coffee went down inside her chest, Lisa had another feeling too. No, he wouldn't be looking out the window, straining for a view of her crossing the road. *She* did that kind of thing, he didn't. She was the one who would look hopefully out the window of the flat at home to see him turning the corner in the evenings. If she was the late one home, he was always reading or looking at television. He never stood at windows. He wouldn't be looking down.

'I feel much better, thank you ever so much,' she said to the red-haired boy.

'You still look a bit shaky, love,' he said.

'Could I sit here for a little bit?' asked Lisa, more to please him really than because she wanted to. She thought he would like to feel he was doing her a service. She was right, he was delighted. He moved the stool back against the railings and lit her a cigarette, while he talked to two Americans and sold them a wall-hanging with Big Ben on it.

'When they get home they'll probably have forgotten what city Big Ben is in,' he said. He didn't think much of Americans, he told her. Scandinavians were educated people, Americans weren't. He asked her if she was going to be in London for long.

'My husband is going to Harley Street for a check-up today,' she said cosily. 'It may depend on what he's told. But I think we'll be here a week.'

She wondered whether she was going mad, actually mad, at the age of 35. It did happen to people, they started telling the most fantastic, unreal tales and nobody noticed for a while, then they had to go and have treatment.

'Harley Street today, a Saturday?' said the red-haired boy cheerfully. 'Meeting some bird more likely. You won't find any doctors in Harley Street today. You'd better keep an eye on your old man, my darling, he's with some blonde.'

He smiled a big cockney grin, full of quickness and good humour. He liked most people he met, this boy did. He didn't particularly fancy her probably, he was like this with old dears of a hundred and with fellows as well.

'It's possible,' she said. 'Quite possible.'

The red-haired boy looked alarmed. She must look as if

she were going mad again; he must be regretting his little pleasantry.

'He'd be mad if he was,' he said. 'Lovely woman like you, no blonde could be any better. No, he'd need his head examined he would, if he told you he was going to a doctor and went off to hold hands in a park with a blonde.'

His face had a kind of transparency about it. It was watery somehow, with pale eyes set far apart from each other. It was a very simple face. It wouldn't disguise things, and look differently to the way it was feeling. It wasn't the kind of face that could smile and tell you that its health needed a check-up if it wasn't true. That face could never become troubled and talk about its marriage having been a sad sort of thing, better not spoken of, if in fact his wife were pregnant and it were planning to try and get the marriage revved up again.

'Are you married?' she asked him.

'No darling, never met a lady that was worthy of me,' he said.

'Neither am I,' she said.

She didn't care what he thought. She tried not to look at the flicker of puzzlement and irritation that came over his white, transparent face. It was because of his face that she had decided to tell him the truth, even though it would have been better in the short encounter between them if she hadn't.

She got up, folded the stool together, and placed it very precisely beside the railings.

'I really do feel a lot better, thank you. I might come back and buy something from you later on,' she said.

'You do that, my darling,' he said, relieved that she was going. She felt that even here she had stayed too long, talked too much, revealed a dependence. Was she ever going to be able to stop?

There was an opening into the park and she walked in. The grass was yellowish, there hadn't been any rain for a long time. A series of glorious days probably. She looked at the people. No delegates to the conference, nobody from back home had arrived yet; there was no danger of being seen by anyone. And even though he was careful about his health, it was funny that he hadn't said anything about the check-up before. And why had they got a 'Mr and Mrs' card with the fruit and flowers? He must have said all along that he was bringing his wife with him. And the room had already had a double-bed in it, before he had planned for her to accompany him. And what kind of fool did he think she was to believe he was having an executive check-up all bloody day? Or did he care what she thought? Was it just a case of it being more comfortable to have an undemanding fool of a woman who paid her own way and wasn't any extra trouble than not to have one, or to leave her at home sulking?

She strolled around idly, noticing that everyone in the park seemed to be with other people. There were groups of girls, and there were families, and there were a lot of pregnant women walking with that proud waddle they develop, hands folded oddly over the bulk in front, managing to look frail as well as huge, so that husbands had protective arms around shoulders.

And she wondered, did he have his real wife in London for the week-end, and was he in fact going to go back to her, and was it she who was pregnant or someone else? Maggie would say anything to get her nice friend Lisa out of this thing. Or did he have some other girl, who also had to be fobbed off with lies and hurried telephone calls? She knew how real his excuses could sound. She wondered whether any other woman in the whole world would have gone to live with a man who was not divorced and who went home every six months to see his daughter, but aparently didn't talk to his wife except about business matters.

She wondered if it was worth going back to the hotel to pick up the case. She thought not, really. It had cost £12 and that was a pity, but what was £12 compared to other things she had spent? She had her handbag with her and her money, there weren't many clothes at the hotel. She hadn't brought much with her in order not to appear too eager, not to look as if she was assuming that she was staying for the whole week.

She didn't make any plans about what was his and what was hers in the flat. She'd sort that out tomorrow or the day after when she got back, and she'd take what she felt like taking. She wouldn't take lots out of viciousness, or too little out of martyrdom.

She didn't even start fussing and worrying about what stations the trains went from and how to get there, or what times they were at, and how much they cost. She didn't even know whether she would go in to work on Monday and say her aunt hadn't died in London after all. It was strange, but she didn't even seem to be imagining how he would react when he came back at six o'clock and she didn't turn up. Would he contact the police? Would it embarrass him with the hotel and with everybody? Would he think she was dead? It didn't matter.

She always thought that things ended suddenly, that people had a big row, or they parted with clenched teeth and noble smiles like they did in old movies. And she stood still beside a seat which had a lot of old people sitting on it, and she took some deep breaths one after another as if she was testing to see how her heart was feeling, whether it was thudding, or if it was surrounded by that awful, horrible, empty feeling of fear like it so often was, when she thought he was angry or bored with her. And funnily it didn't seem to be in a bad state at all.

She wished she had someone to tell, someone who would congratulate her, someone who would be interested. If mother was alive . . . no, of course she couldn't have told mother about it, what was she dreaming about? Mother had been interested certainly, but you didn't tell mother about having affairs, that wasn't something people from our stock did, people who were busy holding their heads up with the best of them. And father, he might have liked the story if it had been about someone else. He used to listen to her tales about other people, and say, 'Fancy, aren't folk strange?' Maggie would treat it lightly, and probably come out with new stories about him, things she hadn't liked to tell Lisa at the time. And there was nobody in the staffroom she could tell, and Bill, well Bill and Angela would just have one of their worried conversations about her. She really had very few friends.

And that was the one cloud on her new freedom, she realised. That's what she'd miss, having him for a friend. In a few ways and some of the time, he had at least been a friend.

Marble Arch

These days she felt that the flower sellers, the men with piles of things that had fallen off lorries, the policemen and the road-sweepers were her friends. She felt they were all part of some kind of club, the only remaining English people in a sea of foreigners. It was a racist kind of thought perhaps, she said to herself, because if you started noticing how many people there were who smelled of garlic, or who wore face-veils, or head-dresses, then the next step might be to wish they weren't there. It would be better not to notice differences at all, to think that everything which walked on two feet was a fellow human.

Anyway she had no right to be anything but grateful to all the tourists. She reminded herself of this as an Arab thrust a piece of paper at her with an address down the Edgware Road on it, and she pointed him in the right direction. He was going to a chemist's shop, she noticed. She wondered whether it was for a prescription or to buy boxes of soaps and talcums. Without the Arabs her own business would have folded long ago. She sold hand-made handbags in a shop within a shop. They were quite expensive. Young Londoners didn't have the money young Kuwaitis did.

Sophie unlocked her little shop and started to hang up the bags. She then got a stool and sat out in the morning sunlight waiting for custom. It was much more expensive to have a street frontage, but it trebled business. She was glad she had such a good head for business. She really needed it because nobody around her seemed to understand the first principles of earning a living. She frowned with the beginning of a headache, and moved out of the sun. It had been a very late night.

It hadn't been night when she finally got to bed, it had been four o'clock in the morning. Eddie had brushed the hair out of his eyes and half-raised himself on an elbow as she left, but he was now back in a deep innocent sleep again and here she was sitting with a headache, trying to trap the tourists who came to Marble Arch, trying to keep awake and make a living for Eddie and herself.

She never thought of herself as earning a living for both of them. That wasn't the way the words or the ideas fell together. Only sometimes, when she had a headache or when they had talked long and without direction during the night, did she think wistfully how nice it would be if he was the one who got up in the mornings, and she was the one who could raise herself on an elbow and say 'Good-bye love, take it easy'. But that wasn't really considering an alternative, it was only thinking about things that would never be, like the way you sometimes imagined what it would be like to be a seagull when you saw one swooping backwards and forwards over a harbour.

Sophie thought a bit about last night's discussion. It hadn't been any different from the ones that had gone before, just longer. Eddie's dark brown eyes and their long black lashes looked dull with the pain of the world. They had lost all the flash and brilliance they had when he wasn't talking about the cruelty of the world. Dead they sat on his face as he spoke on bitterly about the producers who were pansies, the agents who were fairies, the script-editors who promised the moon, the misguided advice of friends who said, 'Well, why don't you just *go* to Framlingham or Fraserburgh or some ridiculous place and see what happens?'

Eddie wasn't going to just go anywhere. At thirty-seven he was too old now to just go to a stupid group of over-excited students or experimentalists and help them out with their productions. He had been in acting too long, learned too much, was too professional to give in, to sell the past. What had all these years been for if he was going to give in now? What would his love for Sophie mean if he was to allow that painted Jeffrey to feel him up and take him to that queers' pub as a possession, just in order that Eddie could get a part? No, life was cruel, and rotten, and the good people always lost out, and it was a plot, and you couldn't fight the system hoping to win, but at least you could try.

Sophie had never seen life as being cruel and rotten before she met Eddie, but she had always seen it as fairly difficult and tiring. She thought if you worked hard you made money, and then you had leisure time and you enjoyed that. If you were very lucky indeed you worked at something that wasn't awful, and then you enjoyed both work and leisure. She thought it must be very strange and sad to work in a world where there seemed to be steaming clouds of sexual desire and frustration, mostly homosexual, and that this was governing who got jobs and who played where and who succeeded or who failed.

It was so different to her own world. She had managed to leave the very dull, very depressing place where they had trained her how to sell cosmetics so well that she firmly believed she could sell lip-gloss to men with beards. She had always wanted to be in business for herself but with no capital it looked impossible. Her father hadn't wanted her to leave the cosmetic people. He thought she should thank her lucky stars day and night for the good luck she had got in life. Her father had never had much luck, there were more weeks when he collected money from welfare than from an employer. Her mother had worked regularly and quietly in a restaurant. She said that her one ambition was that Sophie should never have a job which meant walking and standing, and dealing with dirty plates and difficult customers. She was happy when Sophie was selling nice, fresh, good-smelling oils and paints for people's faces. She was worried when she seemed to become a person of no account sitting in a little stall shouting her wares to the public.

Sophie sighed, thinking how little everyone around her knew about business. If she had been her father, she would have kept a steady job; if she had been her mother, she would have demanded to be a cashier in that restaurant, where she could have sat in a little glass box near the door, rather than get varicose veins by walking and standing; if she were Eddie, she *would* take any acting job anywhere if she wanted to act, or more probably she would decide that if acting didn't want her among its ranks, she would take some other job and act in her spare time. Really she had made very little impression on anyone, with her own business-like attitudes. Nobody realised that it wasn't easy to be organised and disciplined, and to make money. It took a lot of time, and worry, and ate into all those hours you could be sitting around and enjoying yourself. Nobody ever got drawn into her little belief that people might be here on earth to work hard. Nobody but Peggy. Peggy was her one success.

Peggy had been a mess, and Sophie thought she would always be one, but she was so warm and friendly, that you looked through all this bamboo curtain of rubbish and saw a lovely, big, responsive soul inside. Peggy had been to the same school, had done the same useless meaningless course in 'Business administration'. Well, hardly done it, Peggy had barely attended a class there. She had been in chip-shops and coffee-shops, and places with plastic table tops where people ate ice-creams and drank fizzy drinks instead of learning Business administration or delivering bundles of dresses from the wholesale house to the retail which was what they were being paid for.

Peggy had a year of liberty, then came the storm. Her mother couldn't understand why she wasn't fitted for a wonderful job, some high business post. Gradually the tales of the chip-shops emerged, and Peggy left home under the darkest cloud you could find, a cloud of ingratitude.

Sophie had seen her from time to time. Usually she came to borrow a few pounds. More often than not Sophie got them back. Sometimes she came to grumble. This man had let her down, that man hadn't told her he was married, the other man had been perfectly nice for a fortnight and then it turned out that all he wanted was to beat her and for her to beat him. She worked in Woollies for a while and was sacked for stealing. She thought that this was unfair. Sophie thought it was also pretty unfair to steal from Woollies, and Peggy only grudgingly agreed.

She worked for a while in one of the coffee-shops of her youth. Sophie always had coffee there just to have a chat. Sometimes she thought it mightn't be such a good idea. Peggy looked weary, and dirty, and beaten, she seemed to resent Sophie's smart looks, essential for her trade, and her smart little car essential for bringing her trade from door to door.

But still Peggy didn't have anyone else, and when she was arrested the first time and charged with being drunk and disorderly, Sophie was the one she sent for. She sent for Sophie when she was in hospital, too, suffering, they told her, from malnutrition. Sophie came when she was charged with soliciting, and when she was finally sent to prison on her third charge, it was Sophie who waited for her three weeks later in the little car and drove her back home.

When Peggy immediately retrieved a bottle of barley-wine that she had hidden in the hallway of the depressing house where she lived, Sophie decided she had had enough. Quite enough. There they were sitting in this filthy room, and she was refusing a glass of cloudy, muddy-looking drink with the excuse that it was a bit early in the day. Her old friend Peggy had become a prostitute, a thief, and a near-alcoholic.

The years of dragging herself up and away and onwards were looking useless, if she could be dragged down again so quickly by Peggy. She lost her temper, and said all this and more.

'I'm not just dumping you, because I've become all up-in-the-air,' she shouted eventually. 'Stop telling me that I have ideas about myself. I've no ideas for God's sake, I just work bloody hard, and it isn't easy and everyone around me seems afraid of work or . . . or sneers at it and at me. So now I'm telling you I'm sick of it, sick, sick, sick. I have no more pity for you. I haven't any more words, any more "Poor things" to say to you. You can go whatever bloody way you like, I don't care if I never hear about you again, because every time I hear from you you want something, money, help, someone to take you home from gaol. If you don't want something at the beginning, you end up wanting something. You drain me, and make me feel weak and feel nothing. So to hell with you Peggy, to hell with you, I'm sick of you.'

And then it was Sophie not Peggy who cried. Peggy was amazed. Not upset, just amazed.

The great cool Sophie was sitting there crying, the calm Sophie had shouted. The mask had slipped. Peggy was transfixed. Instead of the list of excuses, explanations, and life's miseries that normally fell out unasked for, she heard herself say quite calmly:

'What would you like me to do?'

'I'd like you to look after yourself for a change and not rely on me to look after you. I'd like you to do something quite extraordinary for you, that's go out and earn a bloody living like most people in the world.'

Sophie gathered up her bag and her car keys and banged out of the dirty room in the depressing house, and went off and sold cream that took lines from under your eyes to women who ran small dress shops. In and out of her car she got, dragging display literature, explaining that people who bought dresses would like to have unlined faces to wear with them. She went on and on until the last late-closing shop had closed, then returned to her flat and worked on reports until midnight and went to sleep.

Next day Peggy was at her door. A tidier Peggy, not drunk, not hungover, not pleading.

'Can I come with you on your rounds?' she asked simply.

Sophie was tired. 'Yes, if you don't talk,' she said, and the day was much like any other, except for the vaguely comforting feeling of Peggy sitting silently beside her. They hardly spoke a word to each other until lunch-time. Then Sophie offered her a drink.

'I'll have a coffee,' said Peggy.

During the coffee Peggy had asked intelligent questions about the kind of stores, shops and boutiques they had been visiting. She wanted to know how much credit they got. Since Peggy couldn't have had a pound note to her name, Sophie wondered at the drift of the conversation. Surely Peggy couldn't see herself as a shop-owner, even if she were going to pull herself together? But anything was better than the kind of thing Peggy normally talked about, so Sophie answered her sensibly. Sophie was also relieved that no malice seemed to be directed towards her for yesterday's outburst.

Peggy came silently in the car with Sophie for about a week, except for the day she had to go and see a probation officer or social worker. She didn't have any tales to tell about these visits, no theories about how women in such jobs were sadists. Sophie began to feel quite optimistic about her, but didn't want to rock any boat by saying it was a useless way to spend your days, sitting in someone else's car. Perhaps Peggy was just desperately lonely, she thought.

Then Peggy came up with her suggestion. She wondered, would these women in the shops buy handmade bags?

Sophie's first thought was that Peggy was planning to steal the bags, but no, she said, she had learned a bit of leather work once, and it turned out she was quite good at it. Would Sophie like to come and see some of it that evening?

The dirty and untidy bedroom was still untidy, but not with clothes, make-up and empty barley-wine bottles. This time it was with bits of leather and cord. Sophie stood transfixed.

Because the bags in all sorts of shapes and sizes were beautiful.

Some of them were soft pinks and blues, others were bold blacks and whites. They were made on a patchwork system, because Peggy had only enough money for scraps, she said. She looked shyly at Sophie, and blushed with pleasure at the evident delight and surprise she saw.

'I was wondering, could I earn a living selling them?' asked Peggy as timidly as a child. Sophie's heart was so full of pride and delight and resolution that she hardly trusted herself to speak. This must be the way teachers feel, or nurses when their patients get better, she thought; and they sat down and made plans for Peggy's new career.

Things moved very quickly after that; the only problem was that Peggy couldn't keep up with the demand. One boutique took a dozen, and rang up three days later for three dozen more. Sophie spent a whole Sunday with Peggy working out what they should do. If she were to get someone else to help her, they would have to halve the money. They had already seen the huge mark-up that shopkeepers put on the bags. It was time to define them as 'luxury items', as 'specialist work'. They got labels made with 'handcrafted by Peggy Anderson' on them, and they charged three times the price. They got it. And Peggy was in business.

So great was the business that Sophie decided she would abandon cosmetics for it, and that is why she was sitting in her little stall near Marble Arch. Not all the bags were Peggy's, no one person could keep up with that demand. But she sold six of Peggy's a week, and she paid Peggy ten pounds a bag, everyone was happy.

Now that Sophie had time off from the endless reports, and shop calls, and fights about commission that had made up her working life, she was able to have a social life. This was something she hadn't seen much of in the hard years of the cosmetic world. But it wasn't hard to find. There was George, silly, dull, kind George who wanted to marry her six weeks after he met her, and who took her to tennis parties and to drink outside Hooray Henry bars, where everyone talked about the last or the next tennis party, and what car everyone else was driving.

And then there was Michael, who was kind and dull too. And Fred who was far from dull, but also very selfish and made no bones about telling her that he would like a wife doing something a little more classy than working as a hawker on Oxford Street. And suddenly one night there was Eddie. At the theatre on a summer evening, when Fred had gone to get the drinks and they had started talking about the play, Eddie had asked if she was an actress, and on impulse she had told him exactly where her little shop was, hoping he would call there. He did, and they drifted into friendship, and an affair that became a real love affair, and then it seemed only right that Eddie should live with her, and now she couldn't live without Eddie.

It was for Eddie that she got up early in the mornings

because bills were bigger for two. It was for Eddie that she begged Peggy to make more bags, since the Peggy Andersons were the sure-fire sellers. It was for Eddie that she closed the shop for an hour and went off to the Berwick Street market to buy each night's dinner.

People told her that she had become nicer since she met Eddie. Her tired mother, whose veins were like knots of rope nowadays, and her sad-eyed father, both said she was more cheerful these days, but they put it down to her feckless life among the traders rather than to any love or warmth that had been added. They still thought her foolish to have thrown up her chances of real money.

Peggy said she looked marvellous, better than the days when she used to wear all the make-up she was selling. Love was great, said Peggy gloomily, for those lucky enough to find it. But Peggy didn't seem to like Eddie. She thought he was lazy and that he took too much from Sophie.

'I don't trust him,' she had said once. 'He's one of the takers. I should know, I used to be one. He'll take all you can give, and then one day he'll decide you are nagging, or not enough fun, or not sexy enough, and he'll go and take from someone else.'

Sophie had just laughed. 'Nothing worse than a reformed drunk for telling you the evils of having a glass of sherry.'

Peggy simply shrugged. 'Don't say I didn't warn you,' she said, and went back to her leather cutting. She worked now about ten hours a day. Whenever Sophie called, she was either bent over minute pieces of leather or she was out. Looking for pieces from her various outlets, she said, or having a walk to clear her head. Sophie was amazed that she could change lifestyles so simply but Peggy said that she mustn't be naive. Occasionally she visited Mr Shipton in the afternoons, he had a couch in his office, and Mr Shipton was very nice about giving Peggy pieces of leather and suede from his factory, so Peggy was very nice to him from time to time on his office couch.

Sophie found that sad and a bit disgusting, but Peggy said rubbish, it was glorious compared to picking people up in the streets, and how else could she afford all the material, so Sophie tried to put it out of her mind.

But today her mind was troubled as she sat and smiled at the tourists and made the odd sale. She felt very restless and anxious for something to change. It wasn't just the heat and the headache, it was as if she had been getting ready for this feeling. Systematically she ticked off all the good things about the way she lived. She had Eddie, beautiful tender Eddie, with his big dark eyes that made her feel weak just thinking about them, like girls were meant to go weak at the knees over pop stars. Eddie was so moody and marvellous that you never knew what to expect when you got home in the evenings. But that's what made the evenings when he had bought her a huge bunch of lilac, and was waiting in his black dressing-gown to take her straight to bed . . . so magic. It quite paid for the other evenings when he wasn't in, and came in sulkily slamming the door, because yet another fairy casting-director had wanted his body, not his acting.

The only time they talked about the future was about Eddie's future. There had been that time he nearly got a part in a show going to the States, and Sophie had become so excited and said she must get Peggy working overtime to make enough bags so that she could sell them there. Eddie had been firm that she mustn't leave her place in Marble Arch, and that it would only be a couple of months' separation. She had loved him for being so solicitous about her work.

At school they used to have a teacher who always made them 'count their blessings'. Sophie remembered that it had been a hard thing to do in those days when she wanted to look like a model, and live in a house with a swimming pool. Nowadays it wasn't really all that much easier. Blessings should be accepted, not counted. So she had Eddie, so she had her health, apart from the odd bad headache. So she had a way of earning a living that she enjoyed. At the age of twenty-seven she was in business for herself, few other women could boast that. Even if Peggy became unreliable again, she still had plenty of other people who made bags. What could be wrong with her?

A couple stopped and picked up one of Peggy's bags. They examined the label and gave funny little cries of recognition.

'That's the girl we met at the theatre yesterday,' said the woman. 'Peggy Anderson, she said she made bags, these are lovely.'

'Do you know Peggy?' asked Sophie with interest. Peggy never mentioned anyone at all except the awful man whom she met on the couch now and then.

'Yes,' said the man, who seemed a nice chatty kind of fellow, but to Sophie's practised eye, a chatty fellow who would be nice to meet and who would buy nothing. 'We went to this lunch-time play yesterday, and got talking to a girl in the wine-bar, she was waiting for her fellow to turn up. Very good-looking girl, lovely red hair.'

'They are awfully dear,' said the woman sadly. 'But they are lovely. Are there any others of hers a bit cheaper?'

'What was the play?' asked Sophie suddenly, knowing somehow that they were going to say *The Table-lighter*, a silly little play which Eddie had seen yesterday. He had said it was a silly little play because he hadn't got a part in it. He had also said he had gone to it with Garry, a friend of his who was an agent, a useless agent. Peggy must have gone with Eddie, she didn't know anyone else, but why had neither of them mentioned it?

'It was *The Table-lighter*,' said the woman. 'This Peggy says she usually goes out at lunch-time, it takes her mind off work, and her chap is an actor, very good-looking fellow. He was late because he had been seeing someone about a job, I think.'

'It's a small world,' said the man.

'It is indeed,' agreed the woman.

'Oh very small,' said Sophie. 'Did they seem very close, Peggy and this actor? I just ask because I used to be rather worried about her, you know, she didn't seem to have much social life . . . I was wondering whether this might be something, well, you know, serious . . .'

Her heart was pounding, and she felt strangely outside herself as she asked the question. How great it was to be so cool and calm and not to panic, when the world was falling down. This is what she must have been expecting all morning.

'I don't think so, do you?' said the woman to her husband. 'Not a real thing going, they just seemed to be great friends laughing and joking without a care in the world. It's incredible to think that he's an actor and she's a leather worker like this. They didn't seem to have a care in the world.'

The nice man put the bag down. £20 was too much even for the work of someone he had met.

'That's right, I felt that too, sort of carefree. But then you know there are people who can be like that, and something sort of looks after them. It's like as if there were a big smiling God who says, "Go on Peggy and Eddie, amuse yourselves, I'll look after you".'

They couldn't know as they looked at the steely green eyes of the little girl in the bag shop that they were looking into the face of a big smiling God, who didn't know how to stop smiling.

Bond Street

The light was very bright when Margaret came out of the station. Everything seemed to dazzle her. Even the daffodils on sale in big baskets seemed too harsh a yellow. People's spring clothes seemed too loud, and the buses must have been re-sprayed recently. Surely they were never so aggressively red before? Or was it because there were so many of them in Oxford Street?

She was a little tired, she often felt tired before she began a shopping spree, it was tension she supposed Nobody liked shopping, places were too crowded, assistants not at all helpful, so many foreigners who didn't even attempt to speak English properly. Shopping was hardly something you did for fun. But then Margaret did shopping slightly differently from most people. She didn't actully pay for the goods she brought home. Her tensions and frustrations came not from trying to catch the eye of a shop assistant, but from avoiding it.

She made a list, like any conventional shopper would do. She took a shopping bag, she always carried enough money to pay for these listed items, but rarely if ever broke into it. She paused and window-shopped. She had coffee when her feet were tired, she got into little chats with other resting shoppers. In the evening she would go home again, sighing a little on the underground until someone would stand and give her a seat. Margaret had shopped in London like this once a month for nine years. Never in those nine years had she come into contact with a store detective, a security man, or anyone remotely suspicious of her.

Blinking slightly in the sunlight, she looked at her list.

Red towels.

Knives.

Tights.

Remnants.

Pendant.

Giant cup.

Table-lighter.

Jacket.

A lot of them could be 'bought' in Selfridges, but she wanted a jacket from Marks, and she had seen a nice table-lighter in a small souvenir-type shop on her last visit. She might go down to Liberty's for the remnants. She made sure that her wallet with the eighty-four pounds in it was safely zipped into the pocket inside her coat. You couldn't be too careful these days, with teams of pickpockets coming to London from abroad. She straightened her shoulders and went off to buy towels.

She had painted the bathroom last week. Harry had been delighted with it. He said it looked really cheerful with all that white and the window-frame red. He was going to buy a nice cheerful red-and-white bath-mat, he promised.

'And I'll get some red towels, when I'm doing my shopping,' Margaret had said.

'Aren't towels a bit dear?' Harry had wondered with a frown coming over his big kind face.

'Not if you shop around, they would be if you bought the first good ones you saw,' said Margaret.

'I don't know what I'd do without you, you're a great little shopper,' Harry had beamed, and Margaret felt safe when she saw his frown disappear. She felt very frightened when Harry worried, he looked so old.

The towels were easy. You pick up a big one, a middle-size one and two small ones, you take them out under the light to examine them properly, so that you have separated them from the big piles where they are stacked.

Then moving slowly, and concentrating on them carefully, looking neither left nor right, you move farther and farther away from their original place. Put down your shopping bag and examine the corners of the towels to see that they are properly finished, drop the smaller ones into the bag on the ground, never looking around, that's the secret, then in a business-like way fold the big one into a small manageable size and put it in on top of the others, walking with the bag held out in front of you towards the desk where it says PAY HERE. Anyone watching you would think you are taking the items to pay for them, people at PAY HERE never watch anything at all. You then ask the PAY HERE people where curtains are, and if, suppose, by some terrible chance you are stopped . . . then you say, 'I went straight to the Pay place, and I got so absorbed in the curtains that I simply forgot.'

Margaret didn't know what would happen if she were caught. She assumed she would be able to talk herself out of it, if there were only one item in her bag, which was why she worked on the time-consuming principle of taking only one thing, and then checking it in as a parcel or in a left-luggage locker. *That's* what made shopping so tiring for her, all the endless walking backwards and forwards to luggage lockers, but it seemed only sensible. The day she was lazy was certainly the day she would be caught.

No problem either with the knives. Nice steak knives with wooden handles, Harry would love these. She would say she had found them in the attic, that they were a present for an anniversary, a present which must have got tidied away. They would laugh together over their good fortune in having found them.

The tights were a luxury for herself. She still had good legs and she hated the kind of stockings that looked cheap and hairy. Every month she collected four or five pairs of nice sheer tights, sometimes in what they called 'the new fashion shades'. She never mentioned these to Harry. He would occasionally say, 'You've got better legs than half these women on the television,' and she would smile happily.

The remnants were for dressmaking. She wasn't very good at it, but anyone could sew a pillow-case or a cushion cover, and it made Harry feel happy and comfortable, looking over at his wife sewing away contentedly while they watched television. She took enough to make a table-cloth too. That would only need a hem around it and Harry would never look at the edges, just at the nice bright colour on the table at breakfast, and he might say, 'Imagine you made that cloth yourself. I don't know how other fellows manage with their wives, I really don't.'

The pendant was a present for their son Jerry, who was away in the North at university. It would be his birthday next week. Jerry was a worry to her, he often looked at her very hard without saying anything.

'What are you thinking about?' she'd ask.

'Nothing, Mum,' came the invariable reply, but she felt that he was staring at her, and pitying her somehow and worrying about her. She didn't like that at all.

Once she had sent him a cashmere sweater for his birthday and he had rung up not so much to thank her as to protest.

'They cost a fortune, Mum, however did you afford it? They cost half what Dad earns in a week.'

Margaret realised she had gone too far.

'I bought it in an Oxfam shop,' she said, pretending to confess to a little economy, but her heart was pounding with fear.

'But it's new, it's all wrapped up in cellophane,' argued Jerry.

'Someone gave it away, a present they didn't want.'

'They must have been mad,' grumbled Jerry, still suspicious. From then on, it had to be gifts that nobody could put a real price on. The pendant would have cost about £7 had she paid for it, but she hadn't of course because she had asked the nice young man to show her some earrings and put the pendant in her pocket as he went to get an earring tray.

She and Harry had seen a television play the other night where the husband had his tea out of a huge china cup. Harry had smiled and said wasn't it lovely.

'I've seen those in the shops,' said Margaret. 'Would you like one?'

'No, it's only silly, they cost a fortune and maybe my tea would get cold in it. It just looked nice, that's all.'

Margaret said she had a half-memory of seeing them in a sale where they cost about fifty pence.

'Oh well then,' Harry had said and went back to looking at the television.

The one Margaret took would have cost her seven pounds fifty pence, but when she was showing it to Harry tonight she would leave out the seven pounds. She thought it was a great deal of money to pay for one cup and saucer. Sometimes she felt aggrieved if the items she took were very expensive. She liked the best, but she liked things to be good value.

The table-lighter was a present for Harry's brother and his wife, who were having a twenty-fifth anniversary party next week. Harry's brother Martin never approved of Margaret, something Harry wouldn't and couldn't see in a million years. The families met rarely. A cursory visit around Christmas time, another in the summer. Martin's wife never had a cigarette out of her mouth, she never wore stockings, her hair was a mess, she had a loud laugh. Margaret was glad not to see too much of her. But she was always charming when they came to the house, and laughed insincere little peals when Martin said to his brother, 'Well, she has you rightly tamed, Harry, never thought I'd see the day when you'd be out planting vegetables and filling window-boxes.'

'Harry's marvellous at gardening, he grows a great deal of what we eat,' Margaret would say loyally.

'That's how you must be able to afford this place,' Martin had once said, looking around at lamps, ornaments, vases, and linen tray-cloths, all carried home from Margaret's monthly shopping trips.

'I don't know how you afford this style, I really don't.'

Martin had been far from helpful over that bad business years ago. Far from standing up for her and trying to keep up a good name for them, he had encouraged Harry in all that silliness.

'Never thought you had it in you,' he laughed coarsely, when Margaret had called a family conference to deal with the situation. 'A young lassie too, well that beats everything.' Martin's sluttish wife had let the cigarette ash fall down her stained cardigan with excitement. Old Harry, and a young girl from the factory, and a baby on the way. Excitements like that didn't come very often.

Margaret wondered whether the table-lighter was too good for them. After all they would have humiliated her, set her adrift if they had their way. Why should she get them anything? But still, it was all part of the scheme, the plan, the whole elaborate complicated business that made her victory assured. She had to be the perfect sister-in-law as well as the perfect wife. Only a perfect sister-in-law, herself a non-smoker, would be so thoughtful as to give something like a table-lighter. So quietly it went into the bag. Later she would get a really cheap box for it, they would assume it had a cost a couple of quid instead of twenty. They would be surprised it worked so well. Part of Margaret's good taste.

It would be a dull evening at their anniversary. Their children were loud too, and drank beer from cans. The lazy wife would make a small attempt at food, but it might only be sandwiches and trifle. There would be a lot of drink of course. And sometime in the evening Martin would nudge Harry and ask him were there any more little girls that he could pass on to his old brother, and Harry would look sheepish and silly and hope that Margaret hadn't heard.

Martin would love Margaret to have her come-uppance even at this late stage. He couldn't believe how well she had managed that business years ago. Looking back on it, Margaret herself often wondered how she had been able to cope with it.

There was Harry, all shuffling and foolish, and not able to look at anyone. There was this girl, small, fat, very fat now that she was five months pregnant. There was her father, a bit older than Harry, and even more shuffling, and everyone shouting about money, and rights and duties, and doing the proper thing, and not letting anyone get away with anything. Until Margaret had spoken.

'The only decision we have to make is this,' she had said. 'If Harry accepts that he is the father of this child, then he must marry the lady as soon as possible and give the child a name and a home. I will take our son and this house, and whatever it costs for both of us to live here. Harry must provide for two families, he will have no access to my home. I'm sure with overtime, he'll earn enough to keep us all.'

Her voice sounded so calm that everyone stopped shouting, and listened. Martin and his wife had been invited especially to give more support, but they sat open-mouthed through it all.

'If Harry thinks that he is only one of several people who might be the baby's father, then he should give the lady some money towards the upkeep of the child – a small lump sum, to thank her for his pleasure, and to acknowledge some limited degree of responsibility.'

The room was silent.

'And what about you Margaret?' asked Harry. 'What will you do?'

'If you leave our home, and go with this lady to some

room, I will never see you, nor allow you to see Jerry as long as I live. If you fail in your payments, I will get a court order against you. I have to look after *my* child, just as this lady has to look after hers. If you decide that you cannot be the sole person to be named as father, and you pay this lady a sum of money, to be agreed between you and her and her father, then when everybody has gone, I will make your supper as usual, and I will live here with you, never mentioning this whole incident again, unless you want to.'

'You'd forgive me?' stumbled Harry.

'It's not a question of forgiving, there's nothing to forgive, it's the bargain we made when we got married. I give you a comfortable home, and you give me your presence and loyalty, and support me. There's nothing unusual about it at all.'

And she had gone out into the kitchen to put some flowers in water, while their voices came from the sitting-room, and then they all left. Nobody came in to say goodbye or to tell her what had happened.

There had been no sound from the sitting-room, and she didn't know whether Harry had left with them. The five minutes were like five hours, the clock ticked, and the water tank burbled, loudly menacingly. But she wouldn't run in to see was he there, had he stayed, had she won.

She tore the stems of the flowers to little green rags as she waited. She knew this was some kind of test. It was too long, he must have gone. If she had lost, what would she do with the house. There was no point in scraping and saving to make it nice, just for a ten-year-old boy, and herself. If she had won, she would really keep her promise, she would make it a wonderful home for him, for them. Even if she had to steal, she thought, she wouldn't back-track on her word.

Then the door of the kitchen opened, and Harry, red-eyed, came in.

'I'm giving her £50,' he said.

'That seems very fair,' said Margaret.

She never asked why, or whether he had loved the girl, or whether she was a marvellous lay, or how and when they had met. She kept her bargain, and the next time she had gone to Oxford Street, she started bringing home little treats for Harry and herself. Her reward was his guilty devoted smile, his belief that he had married a Wonderwoman and nearly lost her through his own stupidity. That made her feel very good.

There was only the jacket left now; everything else, including her coat, was in the left-luggage office. She had a scarf and a brooch in her handbag. That was how she had got the jacket four years ago, the nice lilac one, that Harry had said made her look so young. This time she wanted black velvet.

She took one from the rail, and with one movement removed the price tag, throwing it behind the radiator, and pinned her own brooch on the lapel. The jacket was on her in a flash, with her scarf knotted under its collar. In seconds she had taken a different jacket out to hold it up to the light.

'It's nice,' she said to the sales girl.

'Nice cheerful red,' said the girl.

'And they wear very well,' said Margaret. 'I've had this one for quite a while, I was wondering should I get it in another colour.'

'It's a good idea to buy a couple if they suit you,' said the girl.

'But,' said Margaret, 'I think it's a bit extravagant of me really. I'll just go and do the rest of the shopping and if I've anything left over I'll come back later.'

'That's a good idea,' said the girl politely.

And she walked out into the afternoon sunlight to collect all the shopping from the left-luggage, and go home to Harry.

Oxford Circus

My heart sank when Frankie got a job in the BBC. Up to now all the disasters in her life had been reasonably contained among her ever-dwindling circle of friends. But if she were in reach of a microphone she might easily broadcast them to the nation. They might even become national incidents. Because Frankie was rarely out of trouble. I think it was only because I was such a boss, that I was a friend of hers at all. I liked the self-importance of rescuing her. I liked her undying gratitude and useless promises to be more careful the next time.

Clive didn't like Frankie, which was unusual because Clive liked almost everyone. He said she was brainless. Yet she had a far better degree than any of us. He said she liked getting into trouble, but he hadn't seen the tears pouring down her face as she sat in the police-station wrongly accused of starting a fight in a restaurant and causing a breach of the peace. Frankie hadn't started the fight, she had tried to stop somebody else's. Clive said she was vain. That couldn't be right either. Would somebody who was vain turn up at a dinner party in filthy painting clothes, because she had become so involved in doing up a neighbour's child's playroom that she had forgotten to look at her watch and just ran out to catch a taxi the way she was?

Frankie had recently disentangled herself from a particularly horrible man, who owned a restaurant and a bad temper, and who had beaten Frankie very badly on three separate occasions. The day she said she was leaving him, he had taken some of her best clothes and burned them in his incinerator.

She had taken nothing from the horrible man except a few bruises and a series of misunderstood memories. That was another fault of Frankie's, she never learned from anything. If she were to fall down and pass out six nights in succession because she had drunk too much, she never considered for one moment that there was an element of cause and effect. She just regarded each falling-down as a terrible happening to be deeply regretted. There would be other restaurant-owners who would throw all her clothes into the incinerator. I just hoped there wouldn't be many of them in the BBC.

'I want a reduction in the licence fee,' was all Clive said when I told him that Frankie was going to work at Broadcasting House. 'The thought of that woman's voice coming at me from the radio is enough to make me take sick-leave.'

Clive can be very silly once he has a bee in his bonnet about something, so I took no notice except to say that she would be doing research, not actually speaking on the air.

'That's a mercy,' said Clive. 'But the number of apologies for whatever she has researched for some unfortunates will be legion.'

For once we were having a quiet night at home, and I had cooked a dinner. Usually neither of us have much time, what with Clive giving evening classes and me taking them. For once we decided not to study but to stick photos into an album, and we had them all out on the floor when the doorbell rang. In London that's unusual. We hadn't invited anyone, and nobody selling bibles or double-glazing would ever climb the stairs to our flat, however great the commission in this world or the next.

It was Frankie.

'I'm not going to stay a minute, I'll leave the door open so that I won't even be tempted,' she said, blocking the door open with her handbag and creating such a draught that all the photos blew out of their little piles.

'Close the bloody door,' said Clive and I knew the evening was ruined.

'I just wanted to borrow one sweater, and one skirt. Until lunchtime tomorrow only. To go to work in, the job starts tomorrow you see, and because Bernard burned all my things I've got nothing to wear except this dress, which I don't think would be suitable for the Beeb.'

It was a lovely dress, cut to the navel, with rhinestones all around the bit of bosom it had. It would be unusual in the BBC but might just hasten on the disaster that was bound to befall Frankie. I said cheerfully that I would go and see what I could find.

Frankie sat on the floor, falling out of her rhinestones and oohing and aahing at the pictures.

'My God, didn't we all look foul at your wedding?' she shouted, and even through the bedroom door I could feel Clive bristling.

Then.

'Clive, that's not you. I don't believe it. With all the curls and the little toy horse sitting on a stool. It's beautiful.' She positively gurgled over the picture. I had begged him once with tears in my eyes not to throw it out, and had won only by such a small margin that I had always kept it hidden in the bottom of the drawer. I took it out to gurgle a bit myself over, privately.

I rushed out of the bedroom carrying my only good skirt and a new blouse which I had not yet worn.

'Would these do?' I said hurriedly.

Frankie was so far into the photos now that nothing would have got her out of them.

'Look at that picture of you and me and Gerry!' she exclaimed happily. 'Do you remember that night you went out with him and I had to pretend to your mother that you stayed with me? It was awful, I kept getting so confused about what I was meant to have been doing, or what we were meant to have been doing, that I'm sure I gave the game away.'

Oh she had, she had, then and now, but that was Frankie, so innocent, and hopeless. Always.

'I believe you have joined the BBC,' said Clive in a heavy overdone effort to save me embarrassment. It was as if he had flashed a notice saying let us change this unsavoury subject of my wife's past. I hated him for it.

Even Frankie must have sensed some tension, because she sort of gathered up her limbs, and breathed a few dizzy remarks about hoping she'd cope with her first day as a new girl, and snatched my clothes and ran.

Clive had put away the photos. The one of him with curls he had torn into eight pieces, and thrown into the basket. He said he had remembered he had a lot of study to catch up on. I went to bed in a sulk, couldn't sleep, so got up and did the ironing. Clive said I was behaving like a martyr, that I was only ironing to make him feel guilty. No, I said, harassed working wives love ironing, it keeps them sane, they use it as therapy in mental hospitals, everyone knows that. He said I was becoming as childish as my friend Frankie, and even more immature. I said his shirts were now a size too small for him, or a half size anyway, why else would all the top buttons be loose?

Oh it was a lovely evening.

Frankie rang me at work, nobody except Frankie ever rings me at work. The Principal hates it, and he's right, you can hear the whole form screaming while you're out of the classroom. I've told Frankie this again and again, but she never remembers. She wanted to meet me at six o'clock to give me back my clothes.

'I don't need them at once,' I said, furious to have brought the Principal's wrath down on me again for nothing.

'But I want you to have a little drink, just two little drinks in the BBC Club,' she said beseechingly.

There was no time to chat. I could hear a noise like a

tank division coming from my classroom. Anyway I'd always wanted to go into the BBC Club, that's what did it.

'Yes,' I shouted. 'Where is it?'

'Get off at Oxford Circus, and walk in a straight line,' she said. 'I'll have your clothes in a nice plastic bag ready for you.'

I hoped that she'd remember to get some replacements for herself. I could only too easily see her sitting there in her bra and pants drinking a pink gin.

The real reason I gave in so easily was that I wanted to avoid meeting Clive. We had parted in a mutual sulk that morning and I didn't look forward to apologising or waiting for him to. It would do him good not to see me waiting there anyway. We usually had a beer and a sandwich from the fridge at about six, before he went out to teach a lot of foolish self-advancing housewives all about economics, and before I went to learn Italian. I was doing a degree in Italian so that I could teach it in a school where the children were older, and more appreciative, and didn't scream like deprived railway engines.

Two little drinks at six o'clock, and the chance of seeing some personalities . . . it was a great idea.

The BBC Club was huge, and had two separate entrances, each with a porter's desk where you had to show an identity card before being let in.

'Perhaps your friend has signed you in,' said a porter kindly, examining the visitors' book. My friend hadn't. There was no passport to personalities for me at all. I felt very sad.

I waited on a chiar, feeling foolish, for about half an hour until Frankie arrived, breathless. She was desperately sorry but she'd been to the shops, it was late closing, and she'd got herself something to wear instead of my skirt and blouse.

She had indeed. It was an outfit of skin-tight black velvet pants and a sort of a big red handkerchief tied under her bosom. It looked great, but it didn't look like the kind of thing she could wear the next day at work. I had grave doubts whether it was even the kind of thing she should wear in this club.

We were about to sweep in when the porter asked for her card.

'But I work in the BBC,' said Frankie proudly.

'I'm afraid you have to be a member of the club though,' he said kindly.

Frankie was like a toddler whose ice-cream had been snatched away. I thought she was going to cry.

'We can go to a pub,' I said.

'I don't want to go to a pub, I want to go in here, it's where all the BBC people go,' said Frankie in a five-year-old voice.

At that moment a couple of men were waiting for the porter to finish so that they could go in, and they were amused by Frankie's predicament. They asked her what programme she worked on, and good-naturedly signed us both in, looking at Frankie's outfit appreciatively.

We were in. It was a big room, hot and smoke-filled, and crowded with people. I couldn't see anyone I had ever seen on television, and I wasn't near enough to people to hear any famous voices from radio either. I was a bit disappointed.

Frankie had wriggled up to the bar and got us drinks. There was nowhere to sit, nowhere to lean even, so we stood in the middle of a crowded room, like people at a party where we knew no one. I didn't like it at all.

'I have a purpose in coming here,' hissed Frankie, looking left and right in case anyone was listening.

'Oh my God,' I said.

'No, listen, you're always getting frightened over nothing. I think you don't go out enough, you and Clive. I mean poring over old baby pictures every night, it's not natural.'

'We won't be doing that again for a while,' I said darkly.

Frankie didn't notice any nuance in my tone. She was far more interested in her purpose.

'I'm here for a special reason,' she said again. Anyone who knew Frankie even slightly could see that trouble lay ahead. I who had known her since school felt weighed down with doom.

'You see there's this guy, my boss on the programme. He's absolutely great, very dynamic, people just do anything he says, and he was saying today that he thought I was getting on very well for someone who had just come in. I really did, you know. I used my initiative and brought many more files than they asked for, and we found a whole new line to go on . . .'

'Go on about the guy,' I said resignedly.

'Well, he said that what I needed was someone to sort of talk me into the programme, let me know the feel of the place, what they were at, where they were going, and what they wanted to do. And he said that I should try to live and breathe the programme constantly, thinking up new ideas, new ways of dealing with them, that's what makes a programme great he says. Martin says.'

'So?' I said.

'So I thought I should start doing it straight away,' beamed Frankie.

'Are we going to look for people from the programme and start living it and breathing it?' I asked in disbelief.

'No . . . not exactly. You see the one to tell me is this boss man, Martin. He really IS the programme. I thought I'd meet him here and get to know him, off-duty.'

'But if you're going to meet him, why am I here?' I said, hurt.

The two little drinks didn't seem such a good idea now I thought Frankie was going to dash off and leave me at any moment with over half an hour to kill before going to my Italian class.

But that wasn't it, there was more.

'No, he's much too important for me just to turn up

here and strike up a chat with him about the programme. That would be very forward. It's more complicated than that.'

I sighed.

'Some of the others were telling me that he has this utter dragon of a wife, a real Tartar woman, who won't let him out of her sight. She works in the Beeb, too, but in another department and she won't let him have any fun. She comes in here every night and stares across the room at him with awful eyes; then at seven o'clock she marches him home for dinner like a school boy.'

I automatically looked at the clock as if to count the minutes before this ritual took place.

'You've only got half an hour,' I said jokingly.

Frankie was utterly serious.

'I know, that's why I have to find her. I must strike up a friendship with her as soon as possible, so that she'll realise she has nothing to worry about, that I'm not after her husband. If she and I became friends then it would all be fine.'

I looked at Frankie, in her flame-coloured top and her tight, tight pants, her hair falling over her face like someone who had just got out of bed and was waiting, slightly tousled, for the next lover. I didn't think her mission was going to be possible. But there's no use explaining some things to Frankie so I offered to get another drink, and plunged into a sea of bodies around the bar.

When I came back Frankie was gone, or I thought she was, but she had only gone out to make a phone-call.

'I have to identify her first,' she said. At that moment someone was paged over the loudspeaker.

'That's her,' giggled Frankie.

'Where?' I scanned the room.

'We'll see. I went out to a public phone-box and rang her asking to speak to her. We'll just have to see who goes out.'

Like schoolchildren, we watched the door. Eventually a small blonde disappeared through it.

'That couldn't be his wife, not monsterish enough,' said Frankie firmly.

'Did they tell you he hasn't slept with her for years, but he can't leave her because of the children or her health?' I asked sourly. I was feeling very annoyed with this childishness, and hated being part of it. I also wondered whether Clive was worried about me. Maybe I should have rung him.

The small blonde came back, shrugging her shoulders at her friends. 'Nobody there apparently,' she said. 'The phone was dead.'

'It is her,' said Frankie in amazement.

'Now Frankie,' I begged. 'Don't go up to that woman and start one of your explanations, you know how people misunderstand your way of talking. It's always happening if you think about it. Why do you have to do it today? Let it go for a day or two. Please, Frankie?'

It was, of course, useless. I hadn't even finished speaking when Frankie had bounded over to the blonde's side.

I was too embarrassed to do anything except stare into my drink, and wish I were a million miles away, or about three miles away, at home with Clive, the row over, forgiven, forgotten, the two of us sitting there listening to records, laughing over it all, and making great plans about how we would see the world eventually. It all seemed so safe, and so much what I wanted compared to standing in this awful place with terrible things going on a few feet away.

I hardly dared look over for fear of what was happening. The small blonde woman was hauntingly familiar. Was she on a telly programme? Was she a film star? How did I know her face so well? Frankie had said something about her being a producer, you don't see producers' faces.

I knew it, I knew it, I was summoned over and introduced. Everyone seemed to be quite happy and relaxed, they always do with Frankie . . . initially.

'Is it your first day in the BBC too?' asked the blonde kindly.

'No, I'm not here, I mean I'm only here because Frankie asked me to have a drink with her after work. I'm just going off to my Italian lesson,' I said, wondering why did I always sound like someone who had never learned English but was trying to pick it up as I went along.

'I'm a teacher actually, in a dreary old school, nothing bright and glittery like this,' I said, wondering why I said it. I preferred the school a million times with its familiarity and chalk and noise to this strange place where you might be standing next to a news-reader and anything could happen.

The blonde seemed nice. Frankie had obviously told her some cock-and-bull story about being lonely and nervous in her job and wanting to get to know colleagues in the Corportation. This had endeared her to all of them. They said that it was only too rare that people admitted to knowing nobody, most people went around and knew nobody for ages because of this English trait of reticence.

One of the men bought us a drink, we were part of a group.

Frankie was making a great effort to convince the blonde that she was a serious, steady person interested only in her job.

'I'm not at all like my teacher friend, always flitting around,' she said. I didn't think anyone could have believed her. There was I in a jumper and skirt, while Frankie looked as if she was about to do a gypsy dance, and strip in the middle of it. They couldn't have believed her, could they? But it was important for Frankie's purpose that they did, so I went along with it.

'Yes, Frankie is always trying to get me to settle down. I couldn't give two pins for my work, just the holidays and the hours are all I could care about. Frankie likes to live and breathe her job, she puts in endless hours of overtime, silly I call it.'

Frankie smiled, the blonde frowned at me.

'You shouldn't stay in teaching, if you don't like it, it's bad for you and the children. I really do think it's a vocation, half my family are teachers, and the other half used to be. Those of us that didn't do it well got out,' she said.

Inside I agreed with her, but I had to go on, no use in being converted too easily. I'd never see this woman again, and she wouldn't judge Frankie by her hopeless, feckless friend, surely. I'd better make myself a really bad case, whom Frankie was trying to reform.

'Oh I don't know, it's a job the same as any other. Worse paid than a lot, but then you can always read the paper when the kids are doing a test, and our Head is a bit soft about things like doctors' certs. If I want to earn a few quid, real money I mean, in some other job, I just don't turn up for a few days. I get paid just the same.'

Never in my life had I done anything of the sort. One teacher had once, and we were all appalled and shocked. The Principal was a kind man who thought I was a bit flighty sometimes, but only because I did play with the children so much, even after school. His only real grievance was that my classes were too exuberant.

'I'm always trying to make her grow up, to tell her the joys of living and breathing her work,' said Frankie in a good-goody voice.

'Is it seven?' said the blonde. 'Damn it, I was having a lot of fun. Martin will be around in front of the building in his car, I must run.' She gave Frankie a warm good-bye, and wished her well, hoped to see her again. Barely glancing at me, she said she hoped I'd find a happier job soon.

'I'm really sorry to run,' she said to the others. 'It's just that we have to be home to change, we're going out tonight. My brother's having a little dinner.'

It was only as I saw her side-face on, that I realised why she was so familiar. She was like a twin of my Principal. My nice kind idealistic headmaster, who had, now that I remembered it, a sister who used to be a teacher but who was now a senior producer in the BBC.

Tottenham Court Road

A lot of the books seemed to be about lesbians, which wasn't what she wanted, however uninhibited and daring they might be according to the jacket descriptions, and then there were a sizeable number for gay men, with pictures of very beautiful muscled men on the covers, but this again wouldn't be any help. In horrified fascination she saw the section where Alsatian dogs and horses seemed to be people's partners, and about five shelves where people weren't naked at all but clad from head to toe in black leather and brandishing whips.

What she wanted and couldn't find was a book that would tell her how to be an enormous success as a woman in bed with a man. They didn't have any books for twenty-nine-year-old virgins. Such things weren't meant to exist . . . they were an embarrassment to society.

Oh the world was full of books telling twelve-year-olds not to be afraid of menstruation, and telling eight-year-olds about little eggs growing inside mummy's tummy, and assuring seventeen-year-olds that they would go neither blind nor mad from masturbation but that it wasn't as good as a healthy, meaningful, one-to-one sexual relationship. Julia was worn out reading helpful letters to people who complained of being frigid, advising them to relax and to be loving and to specify what they wanted. Who would tell her what she should want, and how to do it at her age without making an utter fool of herself? Twelve, even ten years ago, she could have put herself at the mercy of her seducer, virginity would have been an honour then, something to be treated with respect and awe and tenderness. Nowadays she couldn't possibly tell any would-be seducer that this had never happened before. If it weren't so sad, it would be laughable.

There were no men in raincoats in the shop, no sinister figures with moustaches and sun-glasses salivating over pictures in filthy books. In fact Julia found it very hard to find a book to salivate over herself. They all seemed to be wrapped in cellophane. She wondered how you knew what to buy. There was no way she was going to ask for assistance either from that man who looked as if he should have been a head-gardener in a stately home or from the tired, ageing woman at the cash-desk. She would have to hope that the blurbs, and the overwritten sentences about the material being uncensored, and straight from Scandinavia, would put her on the right trail.

The worst bit was over really, the walking into the shop and settling down with the browsers. She wore a head-scarf, which she normally didn't do, in some mad wish to look different, to put on a different personality for this reckless, sinful venture. She had given herself two hours to look for the right book, or maybe books. She had five pounds in her handbag. If it worked it would be an investment well made, and perhaps there was an additional gain, in courage. She would never have believed herself capable of setting off deliberately and examining the outside of pornographic bookshops. She had finally settled on the one which looked as if it had the biggest selection. Really, you could get used to anything, Julia decided. She had now stopped worrying about what the other people in the shop thought about her, and was no longer afraid that they were all going to jump on her and rape her because she had shown herself mad for it by going into a sex shop anyway.

She moved unhappily from the Oral Love section to a

small specialist area called Domination. Mainly women in thigh-high boots with evil smiles, and men cowering behind sofas. Disconsolately she leafed through one of the magazines which was open – they had to leave something for you to browse through in those kind of shops – and saw sadly that it was Party Games, and that you would need colouring pencils to work out whose limb belonged to whom.

It was very depressing not to be able to find what she wanted when she had got herself as far as this. Julia had thought that the hard part would be making the decision to find the shop, and going in, and perhaps even understanding the terminology of the book without anyone to practise with, like you could with Yoga or wrestling. She didn't know that her specific requirement would be uncatered for. And it wasn't as if it was easy to know where to go either. She had thought that Soho was the right area to hunt, but fortunately she had been able to ask people at work in a jokey way where they bought sexy magazines, and a knowing guy had said anywhere on Charing Cross Road, in the small places. Much better than Soho, because not priced for tourists. 'Get out at Tottenham Court Road tube station, and you'll be fine then, Julia,' he had said, and the others in the travel-agency had laughed. Because you just didn't associate Julia with poking around in a porn shop. She looked too clean and wholesome and well brought-up.

But they probably assumed that she had at least some kind of sex life, Julia thought in a troubled way. She didn't talk about having one, true, but then neither did anyone else. They were fairly sophisticated there, or even distant about things like that. Katy was married, and Daphne was divorced, and Lorna wasn't married but seemed to have a regular chap called Clive who was mentioned casually in dispatches. They probably thought that Julia met people at week-ends, and maybe went to bed with them. If they knew she didn't, and hadn't, they would have been mildly embarrassed and sorry for her rather than shocked. It was that kind of office.

But her two friends Milly and Paula would have been shocked, and horrified. They were heavily into going to bed with people. Milly regularly with the same, very unavailable man, whom she said she didn't love, but was irresistibly drawn to, and Paula with somebody new and hopeful-sounding every couple of weeks. Julia invented the odd holiday sexual happening, and would feel very trapped when Paul would ask, 'But was he good? I mean, you know, did he *satisfy* you?' Julia would say that some had and some hadn't and this kept Paula happy, and reflective about the differing abilities of men in this field.

Everyone plays games, even with friends, and Julia felt that she would have been breaking all the rules of the game if she had suddenly confessed that she had not known the experience and would they please tell her what it was like from start to finish. Paula and Milly would assume that she was having an early menopause, an unexpected nervous breakdown or had developed unhealthy voyeuristic tendencies that she wanted to indulge. They would never actually believe that such a thing could be true.

And really it was only too easy. Julia had been adamant about not going to bed with Joe, her first and long-lasting boyfriend. She was full of the kind of thought that said in letters of fire that you lost them if you gave into them. She had this firm belief that if she and Joe made love outside marriage he would never trust her again, and that he would assume she would be lifting her skirts for all and sundry. She didn't know from where she got this expression 'lifting her skirts', it was coarse and unlikely and had nothing to do with love. She must have heard her aunt use it about some serving-girl. Her aunt was like that.

Joe had gone to university and found a nice girl there.

When he told Julia that their unofficial engagement had now better be forgotten, Julia had asked in a pained way, 'Does she . . . er . . . sleep with you?' and Joe had laughed lightly and said that there wasn't much chance of actually sleeping with someone at university but they did make love of course.

So Julia, who was now twenty, decided that there must be other standards than her own, but for the next five years the only people who offered her the initiation rights were drunken people, or people who had been stood up or let down by some other girl, and who were using her as a substitute. And suddenly the years were passing, and she never knew what it was like to have the earth move, or to hear wild cries of ecstasy mingling with her own, and she felt frowningly that this was bad news . . . Still, there had been so much else to think about, borrowing the money, setting up a different kind of travel agency to anyone else's in a different kind of partnership, going abroad three times a year to investigate things like they all did, and there was getting a flat and doing it up, and keeping her aunt and her father happy by visiting them regularly with lots of cheery stories and bright dismissals of all their ills and complaints. And there was going to the theatre, and meeting Paula and Milly in each other's flats for great meals with lots of wine, and really it was hard to know how the years went by without going to bed with people.

But now it was important. Julia had met a very nice man indeed. He was in publishing and she had met him one evening last year when she was touring the night-clubs of a foreign resort with a notebook, writing down details of atmosphere for next season's brochure. Michael had been sitting in one of the clubs and had seen what she was doing. He offered her a bit of advice about excluding it, because the drinks were too dear and the floor-show was too touristy. Together they roamed several other clubs and at the end of a long night he suggested she come back to his room for a drink. Julia was about to agree when she suddenly realised with a horrible shock that she literally didn't know how to do it. There she was, twenty-eight years old, and she didn't know whether she was meant to lie down on the bed naked and wait for him to do everything, or if she should undress him, or if she should move up and down when it was happening or round and round, and it was all very well to say that she'd learn in time, but who could learn in two minutes what they should have been learning over the last ten years?

Lightly she said no, and refused for the rest of the week also, on the grounds that she didn't go in for holiday things. This sounded, she hoped, as if she went in for real-life things very seriously, and Michael seemed to think that this was reasonable enough. He didn't live in London, but he came to see her for half a dozen week-ends, and for three of those she pretended she had someone staying in the flat and couldn't ask him to stay. Then twice she said she had too much work to do, and didn't want to ask him back. Finally, the last time, she had asked him to the flat for a meal, and when she was getting the usual excuses ready he had held her hand very gently.

'We get on well together,' he had said.

'Sure, very well,' she admitted, almost grudgingly.

'Then why do you close me out?' he asked. He had been so gentle and understanding that if she had said at that very moment what was worrying her she knew it would have been all right. Why couldn't she? Because she felt foolish. She felt that she was grown-up and intelligent in every way except this. She couldn't bear the vulnerability, it would show. She was even afraid that the whole thing might be messy and might hurt her. Because she was such an ancient virgin, it might be impossible to pierce her virginity. Think how appalling that would be.

She had bought time.

'The next time you come to London you can stay here for the whole week-end,' she said. 'I'd like that. It's just that, well, I'm not ready for it now, and I don't think people who are grown-up and equal should have to make excuses to each other, do you?'

He had agreed, and they had talked of other things, and he had his hand on her neck as they talked, and occasionally he kissed her and told her she was very dear to him. And deep down she thought that it would be possible to lose her virginity before he came back in a few weeks, and it would all be fine from then on.

It's harder than you think to find somebody to sleep with you, in a limited time, and for a limited time and with no strings, and with no build-up. Julia went to a party and behaved outrageously with a businessman who was in London for a few days, having what he said was a whale of a time. She even managed to get him home to her flat. Staring at herself in the bathroom mirror, she wondered whether it could ever have been so terrible for anyone as it was going to be for her. He was very silly and he kept laughing at his own jokes, and he was rather drunk. His idea of romance was to plunge his hand unexpectedly and painfully down the front of her dress. But Julia thought, brushing her gritted teeth in order to be nice and inoffensive for the beautiful act, it was better to learn on someone awful.

When she went back to the sitting-room, he was asleep on the sofa, and no amount of cooing or even shouting could revive him. Eventually she took off his shoes, threw a rug over him, and went in bed in a rage. Next morning she had to make him breakfast, assure him that his wife wouldn't be hurt in any way, and kind of hint that it had all been rather wonderful. She went to the office in a rage also.

In the next ten days she got two more men back to her flat. One was a friend of Lorna's and Clive's who told her eighteen times about his wife having upped and left with a teenager. She promised him consolation and a shoulder, even a whole body, to cry on. First though, there was the story of the wife, over and over, what he had done wrong, what he hadn't done wrong, how he couldn't blame her, how he'd like to throttle her, how he hoped she'd be happy, how he hoped she'd rot in hell. When it was bed-time and Julia got herself into and out of the state of self-pity and self-disgust about making love to such an unlovable man, he said that he would like to lie beside her all night, but that they couldn't make love as he hadn't been able to do that for a long time now. It was quite normal. Apparently the doctor had told him that thousands of men had the same problem.

The other possible bed-mate had been a really loud vulgar friend of Paula's who showed a marginal interest in Julia one night in a pub. Immediately she returned his interest a hundredfold. Since he had been making passes at her unsuccessfully for a couple of years, he was delighted. On the way home he told her what a splendid stud he was, that he wished one could get references for that sort of thing, that he loved women, big women, little women, young women, all women. Julia was nearly in a state of collapse by the time the taxi turned into her street.

'Do you like virgins?' she inquired hopefully.

He did, he loved them, he was very good with them. He hadn't had one for ages now, but he did like virgins.

It was half-way through the drink before deflowering that Julia remembered an article she had read the previous Sunday about veneral disease. It would be just her luck to wait twenty-nine years and then do it for the first time with someone who was riddled with syphilis, and then pass it on the next week to the only man she had ever really wanted. Suddenly she went all funny and said that she couldn't go to bed with him because she thought she had sprained her back. The remark sounded even more stupid than she could have believed possible.

'Let me do all the work,' he had said.

Julia had no idea what he was talking about, but was sure she would catch some disease if she allowed herself to find out. She shooed him out into the night, and decided it would have to be a bookshop.

She had told the girls in the travel agency that she was going to the Family Planning Association, so she would take a long lunch-hour. She had in fact been on the Pill for a month so that she was now protected. All she needed was someone, anyone, who would tell her how not to make an utter fool of herself and drive Michael away next Friday night. It was Tuesday now, for God's sake, she really didn't have any time to lose. She had suffered so many humiliations already, it didn't seem too much to ask the man who looked like a head-gardener for some advice.

'I wonder if you could tell me, do they publish any books, sort of manuals of instruction really, on how to make love . . . in an ordinary sort of way?'

'I beg your pardon?' said the gardener, and for one wild moment Julia wondered whether he in fact worked in some other shop, and she had done something unpardonable. No, of course he worked here, she had seen him directing people towards the shelves of their choice.

'Well, I was looking for something . . . to give to my niece,' she said triumphantly. 'She's . . . er, getting married soon, and I don't think she knows exactly what will be expected of her.'

The gardener looked concerned on behalf of the niece but didn't see how he could help.

'Couldn't you tell her yourself, madam?' he asked politely, but puzzled.

'Oh I have, I have,' Julia said. 'But only basic things really, and she wants to be sort of tigerish if you know what I mean. She feels she's going to lose out by not knowing the techniques that a man expects. She wants more than just clinical information, it's the response she's keen to learn really.'

'I don't expect her husband will want anybody to teach her that except himself,' said the gardener, a trifly hypocritically and pompously Julia thought. What was he doing running a porn shop, if these were his views? Oh well, I've got as far as this, she thought in despair, I might as well wade on.

'You see she's in an unfortunate position. This chap she's marrying, he's been around a lot, and my . . . niece more or less pretended that she had too, so she's going to feel very foolish when he discovers that she hasn't. I said I'd try and find a book that would tell her what to do.'

The gardener still looked mystified by it all. Oh why couldn't he understand, why couldn't he just say that there was such a book and sell it to her?

'But I don't see what she can learn from a book, madam,' he droned on, trying to be helpful. 'If I might suggest something, you'd be better off spending the money on a couple of bottles of wine, and sitting down with her and giving her the benefit of your own experience. If it's hard to talk about things like that, a drink often helps. She'd thank you much more for that than for just a book.'

Julia was now desperate, and desperate people say desperate things.

'I *can't* tell her anything,' she hissed in a low voice. 'I don't know anything. I'm a nun.'

'*A nun?*' bayed the gardener in horror.

'Well yes, we don't wear nuns' clothes these days, we work out in the world. You see, it all changed after that council in Rome, you hardly ever see nuns as nuns so to speak these days. Half the people walking around might be nuns.'

She wasn't even a Catholic, she knew only the vaguest things about nuns, but she was banking that a man who ran a porn shop might know less.

She was wrong.

'Well I never,' he said. 'My sister is a nun too. But she wears dark clothes, and a short veil like a scarf since Vatican Two.' He looked stunned at Julia's poncho cape and green trousers, at her sunglasses pushed back over the top of her scarf, and at her long, painted fingernails.

'I suppose that you Sisters must be getting more and more worldly all the time,' he said with deference.

'Well, it's so we'll look more normal at work,' Julia explained. 'Not to frighten off the other people, and make them think we are too holy or anything.'

'And do you teach, Sister, or do you work in a hospital?' he asked with awe.

'A travel agency,' said Julia before she could help herself.

'Why do nuns do that?' he asked with interest.

'It's mainly to help send people out on the Missions,' Julia replied, beginning to sweat, but thinking that in fact, it mightn't be a bad side-line for their own agency. If she ever survived this ordeal she would suggest it to the others.

'So now you see why I need that book for . . . my niece,' she went on briskly, and hoping to give the air of a worldly, business-like nun.

'Well, I really don't like to suggest anything, Sister,' he said fearfully.

'Nonsense,' Julia said. 'You must learn to accept us as we are, women working in the world, like other women. It's just that we've given up sex . . . or never taken it up,' she finished lamely.

'Perhaps a bigger store might have one of these books on preparing for marriage . . . by a woman doctor,' he said, trying to get out of it.

'I've been through those, nothing tigerish enough for my niece,' said Julia.

'Tigerish.' He thought for a while. 'We're out of tigerish books, Sister,' he said firmly.

'What would you suggest?' she begged.

'I don't think the fellow's going to mind at all, he'll like showing her around, if you'll forgive the expression.'

'But she's quite old, my niece. I mean she's in her mid-twenties, he'll expect her to know tigerish things.'

'Oh no, he won't, Sister. I'd go off and set her mind at rest about that. I mean it's not as if she was nearly thirty or something, he won't expect anything.'

Julia walked sadly out of the shop. The man who looked like a gardener rushed and opened the door for her.

'It was a pleasure to meet you, Sister,' he said. 'I hope we'll have the pleasure of seeing you here again . . . but perhaps not, of course. I'm sorry. And I'm sorry for suggesting all that stuff about the bottles of wine and the bit of chat. I mean I wasn't to know you were a nun, Sister.'

On the way back to Tottenham Court Road tube station she saw an off-licence. The gardener was probably right, maybe two bottles of wine would work better than a book. Maybe she could pretend to get drunk on Friday and see what happened, maybe she could make Michael a little bit drunk and watch what he did.

For the first time since the whole terrible problem had begun to obsess her, Julia saw a ray of hope. Perhaps it mightn't be as awful as she thought it was going to be. He was hardly going to get out of bed, put on all his clothes and say, 'You have deceived me.' It was laughable, really, and that was another thing. She and Michael did laugh together about a lot of things, they might even be able to laugh one day about the thought of a nun in cape and trousers running a travel agency for missionaries and visiting porn shops in her lunch hour.

Well, it was either believe that, or ask the good-looking Italian boy who was struggling with his map trying to find Oxford Street, whether he'd like to rent a hotel-room for the afternoon with her. And, really, Julia thought that for a twenty-nine-year-old virgin, she had coped with quite enough that day.

Holborn

Rita sat down to make a list of all the things she needed to do. Now that she had been such a fool as to agree to the whole ridiculous idea she might as well try and get through it as painlessly as possible.

She wrote LIST at the top of a piece of paper and stared at it in rage. Why had she agreed to meet them? Normally she was so quick and firm at getting out of things she didn't want to do, but his voice had disarmed her.

Ken had rung up last night and said he was in London, he and his new wife, they were still on their honeymoon, wouldn't it be nice if they and Rita and . . . er . . . Jeremy, was it, could get together for a civilised meal? It wasn't Jeremy, it was Jeffrey, he must have known. She knew that his wife was called Daisy, people didn't forget names, he must have done it on purpose.

She said hold a minute and she'd see if Jeffrey had planned anything. It was meant to be her excuse, she was going to come back to the phone and tell some lie.

'Right, of course,' Ken had said pleasantly. 'I hope he hasn't. It's our first time in London, and we'd love a bit of advice from a native.'

Jeffrey had said why not, it would be nice to meet them, he'd love to give them a bit of advice, he'd tell them about boat trips to Greenwich and he'd mark their card. He was full of enthusiasm. The fact that she had spent a whole year living with Ken didn't seem to disturb him in the least. What was past was past; they had both agreed that it was silly to brood.

She had come back to the phone and said it would be

fine, where should they meet? Ken didn't know London at all, so he said he'd make his way to wherever she said. He wondered if they could make it straight after work or early evening anyway, because they'd want an early night.

'You haven't changed,' giggled Rita, with a small pang of jealousy that he still wanted to be between the sheets with his bird well before midnight.

'Oh, it's not that,' Ken said casually. 'It's just that we . . . well, Daisy gets tired easily. She's rather frail you know, we don't like too many late nights.'

So Daisy had turned out to be frail, had she? Marvellous, bloody marvellous, thought Rita. She was cunning to be frail, old Daisy. It meant she didn't have to go on all those wearying walks with Ken that Rita had endured, climbing hard sides of hills instead of easy ones, packing endless pairs of woollen socks for week-ends because you never knew when the next bout of walking fever would come on. How wise to be frail. Rita went back to her list-making.

Hair, she wrote. Yes, she'd take time off at lunch, an extra half an hour, and get her hair done. Silly to try a totally new style in case it didn't work, but she did need a cut and a conditioning treatment some time, so why not today? She decided that as soon as the hairdresser's opened she would ring round and get a lunch-time appointment.

She had another cup of coffee to celebrate that decision being made. Jeffrey was still asleep. Most of the world was still asleep. It was only 6 a.m., but Rita couldn't sleep.

Clothes, she wrote. They had arranged to meet at Holborn station of all places; it was the only possible meeting-point she could think of that was near Jeffrey's work, her work, and that Ken would be able to find. Ken really did sound bewildered by the size of London, not at all like the confident man she had known in Wales. Yes, clothes. She would wear her new skirt, the long patchwork one, and she would get a very simple sweater to go with it, in a matching colour, green maybe, or dark brown. She needed a new sweater anyway, it wasn't a question of buying anything specially for the occasion, that would be idiotic. What did she want to impress Ken for now? All that business was long over. She had ended it, she had left and come to London, she wasn't hoping he'd still fancy her. No, she needed a new sweater. Why not get it today? The shops in the Strand opened at nine o'clock, and she needn't be at work until half-past.

Photos, she wrote. She had a small pocket album of pictures of their wedding last year, it would be nice to show them to Ken. He would be interested, he would even recognise some of the people, her sister, her friends from Cardiff. And anyway, Rita thought, I look great in those pictures. After three months on a diet, naturally I look great. Why not let the frail Daisy have a look at me when I was two stone less than I am now? If they were still on their honeymoon, they wouldn't have wedding pictures yet, so she could be one up.

Handbag. Her own was a bit tattered, it didn't really go with the patchwork skirt, it didn't go with anything. She definitely needed one. At least twice last week she had been on the point of buying one. It had nothing to do with the fact that Daisy would probably have a frail little trousseau handbag with her either. No, she must get a handbag today.

She would borrow Lilly's cape. Lilly had a lovely black cape of fine wool with braid on the edge, which would be ideal over the outfit she was planning to wear. She must telephone Lilly at 8.30 a.m., before she left home, so that she could bring it to work with her. She had borrowed the cape twice already for parties and had lent Lilly her pendant in return. It was a gold pendant that Ken had given her. She still hadn't decided whether she would wear it tonight. Probably not.

It was still too early to talk to people, Rita grumbled to herself. She wished that people woke up sooner. Not that she could say much to Jeffrey, he would be busy getting out his guide-books to London, and his list of pubs that served Real Ale. He was so very confident of her, it would never cross his mind that she was excited about seeing Ken again, and that she was sleepless with worrying about how to present herself in a good light. Jeffrey would laugh tolerantly and say how like a woman. Jeffrey had a good comforting line in clichés when he wanted. Rita often thought he used them like warriors used armour to avoid having to meet any real thoughts head-on. Jeffrey was always pretty predictable.

Now that's one thing he wasn't. He was tiresomely unpredictable, you never knew what was going to happen. She hadn't liked it at the time and she didn't like it now, but that was the real reason she had got up so early. For all his protestations about having an early night, Ken might easily be persuaded to come back to the flat for just one drink. Jeffrey loved people to come back and so normally did she, but if Ken was going to see her home she wanted to look at it with an eagle eye herself first.

Coffee-cup in hand, Rita walked through the sitting-room. Ken would laugh at the coffee-table, not out loud but he would laugh. They used to use the word 'coffee-table' as an adjective to describe things and people they didn't like.

But what *did* you put things on, Rita complained to herself in irritation, if you didn't have a table of some sort? She just wished it didn't look so much like the kind of thing that held posh magazines and books nobody read. Well, she could cover it in things, ashtrays, knitting even. But God, how she and Ken had laughed at people who spent their time knitting. She hadn't known then that it was quite a peaceful thing to do while you watched television or listened to records. No, it might be pushing it to leave out her knitting, even though she was halfway through another great sweater for herself, and they only took her a week these days.

When she lived with Ken they had stripped down furniture and thought that the modern reproduction stuff was so ugly that it made you want to cry. She had no stripped-down pine in her sitting-room now; in fact, quite a few little desks and corner cupboards of the type they used to laugh at. Rita shook herself and reasoned that she could hardly refurnish the whole flat before 10 p.m. that night for a man who might not even see it, and for one whom she no longer loved. Yes, she knew that she didn't love him, but she wanted to think that he still loved and admired her. Having it both ways certainly, why not? A lot of people had things both ways.

Jeffrey, for example, had things both ways. He had his freedom to go racing, she never interfered with that, and he had his home to come back to. He had her as a kind of modern practical stepmother to his two sons who came to tea every Saturday. She never bothered doing the place up for them, she never wanted to impress them with tales that they could tell their mother when they got home. Funny that she never put on any show for these two silent big-eyed children, so that they could observe and note and tell their strange, silent, big-eyed mother, Jeffrey's first and foolishly ill-considered wife.

In fact she had met Heather on a few occasions and talked to her exactly like she would have talked to a client in the beauty-salon. She regarded Heather as somebody you made conversation with, it didn't grow naturally. A lot of the women she beautified were like that, they wanted nothing about you, nothing about them, but lots of cheery stuff on the weather, the price of shoes, the traffic jams and the wisdom of taking a holiday early in the season. Rita was very good at it. Heather had been easy.

So perhaps Ken and the dreaded Daisy would be easy

too. But she could never in a million years talk like that to Ken, she used to imitate salon-chat to him when they were living together, and sometimes he and she would make up a joke salon-conversation with each other . . . the kind of one where both sides were eager to find some harmless incontroversial middle-ground to speak about. If Ken caught a hint of that in her conversation tonight . . . an accidental little suspicion of it . . . she would die. Yes, she couldn't bear him to think she had gone over to the other side, to the enemy.

It was time to ring Lilly. Lilly grumbled and said it was raining and she was going to be taking her dry-cleaning anyway, but of course agreed. 'I love a bit of excitement over people's past,' said Lilly. 'You've always been so uneventful, happy, safe, married, never trying to pick up clients' husbands like we have. I'm glad there's a bit of drama here.'

Drama indeed! It could hardly be described as that. Much more a middle-class acquisitive wish to show off, Rita thought sadly, as she woke Jeffrey and handed him a cup of tea, because of some feeling that she was being disloyal to him by all this concentration on Ken. Jeffrey was pleased and touched, he looked very boyish and tousled sitting up in bed, drinking his tea as if it had been the most generous gift anyone had ever given him. Somehow this irritated Rita, and she said she was late and ran out of the flat.

She spent half an hour and almost a whole week's salary in a department store before she went into the salon. The sweater was far too dear and so were the handbag and the ear-rings that she felt she needed as well. They were all items she would have defined as luxury and out of her reach. She felt a low gloom come down on her after the initial exhilaration. A lot of eyebrow plucking, contour-massaging, skin-peeling and salon-chat went into earning that much money. She tried to tell herself that she needed a couple of nice things, but she felt guilty. The kind of people who bought handbags and sweaters at that price were usually debs or wives of tycoons. There would be problems at the end of the month when they came to do the hire-purchase repayments, but perhaps she could borrow something before then.

Lilly handed over the cape. They sympathised with each other again and again about working in the only beauty-salon in London that didn't incorporate a hairdresser's, and the day's work began. Between clients they had a giggle about how funny it would be if the dreadful Daisy came in to have a face-lift or something, and how Lilly would deliberately sabotage her.

Since she was already so much in debt Rita thought that it would be a pity to spoil the whole appearance by forgoing the hairdo, so that took care of the best part of a tenner and a half-hour over her lunch-hour. The afternoon seemed very long. Lilly wanted to know all about Daisy, but Rita didn't know very much apart from her newly-discovered frailty. She had been a nurse in the hospital where Ken ended up after one of his falls from a cliff, and had met Ken shortly after Rita left Wales. Rita had heard surprisingly little about her from the couple of friends she still had in Cardiff. She was said to be 'very sensible' and 'very good for Ken', two remarks which Rita always assumed were in the nature of mild insults.

'Well, whatever she's like, she can't look as well as you do tonight,' said Lilly loyally and admiringly, when the salon finally closed and Rita dressed herself up.

'I don't really care,' Rita said. 'But I'd like him to have a bit of a pang about me. It's only natural, isn't it?'

Lilly agreed it was totally the right attitude, and asked if she could sort of pass by the station too, so that she could have a look at them all meeting.

Rita didn't want that at all. It seemed too stagey. 'That's not fair,' complained Lilly. 'I've lent you my cape,

I've been excited about it all day. I want to have a look. I won't say a word, I won't pretend I know you.'

'Jeffrey will recognise you,' said Rita.

'No, I'll keep my head down. Oh go on, you can't stop me anyway. It's a public street, everyone has a right to be there.'

Very reluctantly Rita agreed, and they set off about thirty yards apart from each other.

It was a mild evening, and the lights of the shops were competing with the sunset as the girls walked towards the station. On evenings like this Rita felt that she had made London her own, she lost the impersonal side of it. It was like any big town, you had your own little quarters, the place where you lived, the place where you worked, the place where you shopped. It was a matter of breaking down a huge city and making it manageable.

Lilly was ahead. She stopped to buy a newspaper, and looked up the cinema times. This was her ruse, her cover for why she was hanging about. Rita saw Jeffrey there, looking at his watch. This irritated her too, because he was early, at least five minutes early, and there he was already fussing about the time. She could see no sign of Ken and his frail bride.

Just as she reached Jeffrey, who began to make delighted sounds at the way she looked, she saw Lilly talking to a woman with a walking-stick. They seemed to be greeting each other as old friends. Rita squinted. No, she didn't know the woman, and by her appearance she was hardly a client from the salon. You had to have a certain kind of chic and a certain kind of money before you could come in and have your face slapped by Rita or Lilly. Then, with a shock that nearly knocked her down, she saw that the woman was introducing Lilly to Ken. There he was, all smiles and grins and eager handshakes, the kind of overeagerness that meant he was shy. My God, that woman couldn't be Daisy. She was years older than everyone, she could be Ken's mother. There had to be a mistake. Daisy was around the corner, this was some dreadful old woman who knew everyone, Ken, Lilly, half of London perhaps. Wave after wave of sickness passed over Rita, she actually thought she was going to faint. Jeffrey was talking away:

'. . . really smashing, and you bought ear-rings too. They do suit you. Love, you look like a magazine cover, that's what you look like.'

'That's Ken,' Rita rapped out, pointing.

'And he's talking to Lilly,' beamed Jeffrey. 'Isn't that a coincidence?'

He started moving over in great bounds with his hand held out and Rita followed on legs that seemed too weak to carry her. She kept well away from the edge of the pavement, the slightest stumble she felt might push her out under the traffic.

'Ken!' she said. 'And Lilly! Now who says London isn't a village?'

'This is Daisy, Rita,' said Ken in the voice of a child coming home from school with his first prize.

Rita looked at her. She was forty, she couldn't have been a day less. She had stringy hair pushed behind her ears, and she lent on a stick. She had a great big smile, like someone's elderly and kindly invalid aunt.

'You're just the way I imagined,' beamed Daisy, and with her free hand clutched Rita's shoulder and gave her a sort of clumsy hug. She gave Jeffrey a hug too. Jeffrey looked as if all his birthdays had come at once. A little world of good-natured nice people had all gathered together, he was as happy as a king.

Lilly was like someone with shellshock.

'Rita told me that she was meeting friends tonight, but . . . well, isn't it absolutely extraordinary.'

'How do you know each other?' snapped Rita in a bark. She was just recovering from the hug. She hated women who embraced you, and particularly women who embraced you from the awkward position of leaning on a stick.

'Peggy's an old . . . Peggy's a family friend . . .' stammered Lilly.

'I used to nurse with Lilly's mother,' said Daisy. 'And when Lilly was a child I used to come to the house and scrounge Sunday lunch. Your mother was so good to us, Lilly. We young nurses never had a penny in those days and there was always a huge meal there. It was really like home.'

Ken couldn't go to bed with this woman, Ken couldn't be on honeymoon with her. She wasn't frail, she was a cripple. What had he been thinking of? He must have had some kind of nervous breakdown? Why was she called Peggy and Daisy, and why was she standing there leaning on her stick in her shabby jacket and skirt smiling all around her and looking so horribly *old*?

'Let's all go and sit down,' said Jeffrey happily. 'There's a pub near here or we can go straight to the restaurant. Lilly, you'll come with us. Shall I get a taxi?' He was so excited by it all that Rita could have hit him hard with her new handbag.

'Oh no, I can't, I have to, I mean I'm going,' said Lilly, who, to give her some credit, thought Rita, looked wretched about it all. She didn't want to come and witness the shambles of an evening that it was going to be.

'Nonsense,' said everyone at once including Rita, and suddenly there was a taxi and the five of them were in it, four of them chattering like birds in a box, Rita trying to calm down her mind which seemed to be trying to get out of her forehead.

Why had nobody mentioned to her, even in passing, that this Daisy was an old woman? Very sensible, very good for Ken, what did they mean? Ken was fifteen years younger than her, at least. That might have merited a brief remark when Daisy's name came up. Rita looked at her. She was laughing and saying how exciting it was to be in London, and that she had already seen a man who read the television news, and an actor, and thought she had seen a woman MP, but Ken said it wasn't her after all.

'Why does Lilly call you Peggy?' asked Rita suddenly.

Daisy had an explanation for that too. Daisy had been her family name, like a nickname. When she was younger and worried about what people thought of her, she thought it was a silly name to have. So in the hospital she had pretended she was called Peggy. She had two identities now, the people she knew from those four years in the training hospital, who still called her Peggy, and her real name, which she had taken up again when she got a bit of sense, and decided not to upset her parents any more than she need by rejecting the name they had given her.

They got to the restaurant. Everyone fussed about Daisy. The taximan helped her out of the cab.

'Did you have a fall, my girl?' he asked her kindly.

Girl! Rita nearly laughed aloud.

'No, it's arthritis,' said Daisy. 'It's normally not nearly as bad as this. I feel such a fool with the stick, I'm always tripping people up with it. Most of the time I don't need it at all, it's just this week it's bad. I couldn't have timed it better, a wedding and a honeymoon and a stick, wouldn't you know?' The taximan was delighted with her. So was the waiter in the restaurant. He found her a chair with arms to sit on. Quite naturally, as if she had been the one who invited them all there, Daisy started arranging where they should sit.

'Rita, sit there by Ken, you have so much to say to him after all these years, and I'll take Jeffrey and Lilly here to tell me all about London.'

There was no fuss. They were seated. Rita raised her eyes to Ken.

'It's great to see you,' she lied straight at him.

'You look lovely, like a model,' he said truthfully, straight back at her.

'I feel overdressed and stupid,' she said, with honesty and feeling.

'You were always lovely to look at,' he said. 'But I think you've got even better-looking.' His voice had a simple quality about it, like the way he used to say that mountains were beautiful, or that some piece of wood they had been scraping and stripping all week-end looked perfect. Just objective, happy admiration.

'Jeffrey's in insurance, isn't he?' said Ken after Rita had just stared at her plate for a bit.

'Oh yes, he's with a company but he does a bit of free-lancing as well.'

'Perhaps we could get a bit of advice from him. We've got a small house. Do you remember Rodney Row? It's one of those.'

They used to laugh at Rodney Row and say they were doll's houses for doll people.

'I'm sure he'd be glad to give you any tips,' she said. 'Jeffrey loves helping people he knows, and not just to make a commission, you know.'

'Oh no I wouldn't think that, but of course we'd be very happy to do anything through him if it would help. I mean if there was any value to him out of it,' said Ken.

'I don't think he'd like to make money out of friends.'

'No, perhaps it's better not to mix work and pleasure,' said Ken agreeably, looking at the menu.

Pleasure. Pleasure. Had she remembered it all wrong? Was it she, not Ken, who was going mad? Perhaps he had always been the man who was destined to marry some ageing nurse with a walking-stick? Those wild months of freedom and abandon, and being sure with each other because together it was easy to reject other people's pretensions and nonsenses . . . had all that been real, or was it just in her head?

The others were laughing loudly. Daisy had said something endearing to the waiter, and he had brought her a rose. She put it behind her ear, in the middle of that lank greasy hair, and smiled a big smile with a lot of yellow teeth.

'Isn't this all great, Ken?' she laughed at him down the table.

Rita wouldn't let it go, there had to be something. There must have been something there, she couldn't have got it all so wrong, her memories of what they had. If they had nothing it would be like some kind of surgery, something would have been taken out of her.

'Look at those four over there,' she said desperately indicating a table where two middle-aged couples sat eating and making occasional little forays of conversation. 'Looks like a real salon-talk set-up, don't you think?'

Oh please, please, let him fall back into it, let us both start like we did in the old days. He might say 'One thing about the Italians is they know how to cook food' and she would say 'Isn't it funny the way all Italian restaurants seem to be run by families?' and he would say 'And they always seem to be so good-humoured, it must be coming from all that sun' and together they would laugh about how people could and did talk in clichés from birth to death. Please, please, let him remember salon-talk.

Ken looked obediently at the four eaters.

'They don't seem to be having a good time, is that what you mean?' he asked.

'Yes,' said Rita flatly.

'I often think that people in restaurants must look over at other tables and envy them,' he said. 'They must wish they were part of a good scene like this.' He beamed down the table at Lilly and Daisy and Jeffrey and raised his glass to his travesty of a wife, and Rita wondered with a sharp pain whether she was going to be wrong about everything else as well. Had she never got anything right?

Chancery Lane

Dear Mr Lewis.

I'm sure you will think this very, very odd and you will spend the rest of your life refusing to talk to strange women at parties in case something of the sort should happen again. We met very briefly at the Barry's last week. You mentioned you were a barrister and I mentioned the Lord knows what because I was up to my eyebrows in gin. I was the one who was wearing a blue dress and what started out as a feather boa, but sort of moulted during the night. Anyway, your only mistake was to let me know where you worked, and my mistakes that night were legion.

I know nobody else at all in the legal world and I wonder if you could tell me where to look. In books people open yellow pages and suddenly find exactly the right kind of lawyer for themselves, but I've been looking in the windows of various solicitors' offices and they don't seem to be the kind of thing I want. They're full of files and girls typing. You seemed to have a lot of style that night, and you might know where to direct me.

I want to sue somebody for a breach of promise. I want to take him for everything he's got. I want a great deal of publicity and attention drawn to the case and photographs of me leaving the court to appear in the newspapers. What I would really like is to see all the letters involved published in the papers, and I want to be helped through the crowds by policemen.

But what I don't know is how to begin. Do I serve something on him, or send him a writ or a notice to prosecute? I feel sure the whole thing will gather its own momentum once it starts. It's the beginning bit that has me worried. If you could write back as soon as possible and tell me where to start, I should be for ever grateful.

I feel it would be unprofessional to offer you a fee for this service, but since it's a matter of using your knowledge and experience for my benefit, I should be very happy to offer you some of mine in return. You may remember that I am a tap-dancing teacher (I probably gave several exhibitions to the whole room that night). So, if ever you want a lesson, I'd be delighted to give you one.

Yours sincerely,
Jilly Twilly.

Dear Tom,

Thanks belatedly for a wonderful party last week. I don't know what you put in those drinks but it took me days to get over it all. I enjoyed meeting all your friends. There was a woman with the impossible name of Jilly Twilly, I think, but perhaps I got it wrong. She wore a blue dress and a feather boa of sorts. I seem to have taken her cigarette-lighter by mistake, and I was wondering if you could let me have her address so that I could return it. She seemed a lively sort of girl, have you known her long?

Once more, thanks for a great party.

John Lewis.

Dear John,

Glad you enjoyed the party. Yes, I gather her name is Jilly Twilly, unlikely as it sounds. I don't know her at all. She came with that banker guy, who is a friend of Freddy's so he might know. Pretty spectacular dance she did, wasn't it? The women were all a bit sour about it, but I thought she was great.

Greetings to all in chambers.

Tom.

Dear Ms Twilly,

Thank you for your letter. Unfortunately you have approached the wrong person. Barristers are in fact briefed by solicitors in cases of this kind. So what you must do if you have a legal problem is to consult your family solicitor. If his firm does not handle the kind of litigation you have in mind, perhaps he may recommend a firm who will be able to help you.

I enjoyed meeting you at the party, and do indeed remember you very well. You seemed a very cheerful and happy person, and I might point out that these breach of promise actions are rarely satisfactory. They are never pleasant things for anyone, and I cannot believe that you would actually crave the attendant publicity.

I urge you to be circumspect about this for your own sake, but please do not regard this as legal advice, which it certainly is not.

I wish you success in whatever you are about to do, but with the reservation that I think you are unwise to be about to do it at all.

Kind wishes,

John Lewis.

Dear Mr Lewis,

Thank you very much for your letter. I knew I could rely on you to help me, and despite all those stuffy phrases you used I can see you will act for me. I understand completely that you have to write things like that for your files. Now, this is the bones of the story. Charlie, who is the villain of the whole scene and probably of many other scenes as well, is a very wealthy and stuffy banker, and he asked me to marry him several times. I gave it some thought and though I knew there would be problems, I said yes. He bought me an engagement ring and we were going to get married next June.

Because you are my lawyer and can't divulge anything I tell you, I will tell you privately that I had a lot of doubts about it all. But I'm not getting any younger, I haven't been in so many shows recently, and I teach dancing when I'm not in shows. I thought it would be fairly peaceful to get married and not to worry about paying the rent and all that. So Charlie and I made a bargain. I was to behave nicely in front of his friends, and he was to behave unstuffily in front of mine. It worked fine, a bit gruesome at some of those bank things. Merchant bankers en masse are horrific and Charlie did his best with my friends. I wasn't going to let him down in his career and he wasn't going to interfere in mine. If I got a dancing part, so long as I wasn't naked, I could take it.

And it was all fine until Tom Barry's party, and when I woke up Charlie wasn't there, he had left a note and taken my engagement ring, the rat. He said . . . oh well I'll make a photostat of the note, we'll probably need it as evidence. I'll also write out his address and you could get things going from your end.

I suppose it will be all right to pay you from the proceeds. I don't have any spare cash just now.

Warm wishes,

Jilly Twilly.

Photostat of note:

Jilly,

Now I've finally had enough. Your behaviour tonight is something that I would like obliterated from my mind. I do not want to see you again. I've kept my part of the bargain, you have failed utterly in yours.

Perhaps it is as well we discovered this before we were married. I am too angry to thank you for the undoubtedly good parts of our relationship because I cannot recall any of them.

I have reclaimed my ring. You may keep the watch.

Charles.

Dear Ms Twilly,

You have utterly misunderstood my letter. I really cannot act for you in any way in your projected action against Mr Benson. As an acquaintance, may I take the liberty of reminding you once again of how unwise you would be to start any such proceedings? You are an attractive young woman, you seem from my short meeting with you to be well able to handle a life which does not contain Mr Benson. My serious and considered advice to you, not as a lawyer but as a fellow guest at a party, is to forget it all and continue to live your own life without bitterness. And certainly without contemplating a litigation that is unlikely to bring you any satisfaction whatsoever.

Yours sincerely,
John Lewis.

Dear John,

Stop telling me what to do with my life, it *is* my life. If I want to sue I'll sue. Please have the papers ready or I will have to sue you for malpractice. You have wasted quite a lot of time already. I am enclosing a copy of the letter where Charlie mentions my marrying him. It will probably be exhibit A at the trial.

Kind wishes and hurry up,

Jilly.

Darling Jilly,

You must know that the bank can't put any money into the ridiculous venture you suggest. I didn't come to

America to meet show-biz people and interest them in your little troupe of dancers. I know that it must be disheartening for you not to get any backing, but in six months' time we will be married and you won't need to bother your pretty little head or your pretty little feet about a career. I love you, Jilly, but I wish you wouldn't keep telephoning the bank here on reverse charges, because I am only here for a conference and it looks badly to get several calls a day, all about something which we haven't the slightest intention of doing.

Look after yourself if you can,

Charles.

Dear Ms Twilly,

These Chambers will have no further correspondence with you about any legal matters whatsoever. Kindly go through the correct channels, and approach a solicitor who will if necessary brief counsel for you.

Yours faithfully,

John Lewis.

Dear John,

What have I done? Why is this kind of thing always happening to me? I thought we got on so well that night at Tom Barry's party. Did I tell you by the way that Charlie was quite wrong? Tom Barry was not one of his friends, he was a mutual new friend that we had met with Freddie who was one of Charlie's friends. So I didn't break any bargain by behaving badly.

I just thought that the publicity of a big breach of promise case might give me some chance of being noticed. People would hear of me, I'd get more jobs. You see without Charlie or my ring or anything I have so little money, and I was only trying to claw at life with both hands.

It's fine for you, you are a wealthy, settled barrister. What would you do if you were a fast-fading, poor little dancer betrayed by everyone. I'm nearly 26, my best years of dancing are probably over.

It was my one chance of hitting back at life, I thought I should grab it. Anyway, I'm sorry, I seem to have upset you. Goodbye.

Jilly.

Dear Jilly,

My letter may have seemed harsh. I do indeed see what you mean about grabbing at life, and I admire your pluck, believe me I do. What you need is not so much a court action, it's much more a good friend to advise you about your career and to cheer you up. I don't think you should get involved with anyone like Charlie, your worlds are too different. I only vaguely remember him from the party at Tom Barry's but I think he was a little buttoned up.

You need somebody younger than Charlie Benson.

Perhaps you and I might meet for a meal one evening and discuss it all, totally as friends and in no way in a client-lawyer relationship. If you would like this please let me know.

Cordially,

John.

Dear Monica,

I'm afraid I won't be able to make the week-end after all. Rather an important case has come up and I can't leave London just now. I know you will be disappointed, still we did agree that I should do everything possible to advance my career, so that is what I'm doing. I hope the week-end goes awfully well, looking forward to seeing you soon.

Love,
John.

Dear John,

I was sorry about the week-end. Daddy and Mummy were sorry you were kept in London. Daddy kept saying that all work and no play . . . you know the way Daddy does.

I came to London last Tuesday. You weren't in Chambers and you weren't in your flat, even though I phoned you there lots of times up to midnight. Maybe Daddy is right and although we all want to advance your career, perhaps it is a question of all work and no play.

Love anyway darling,

Monica.

Darling John,

How can I thank you for the lovely, lovely week-end. I always wanted to go to Paris and it really cheered me up. It was such a relief to be able to talk to someone so understanding. I'm afraid you must have spent a fortune but I did enjoy myself.

See you next week-end,

love Jilly.

Dear Monica,

I must say I thought your phone-call to the office today was hysterical and ill-timed. I was in consultation and it was very embarrassing to have to discuss my private life in front of others. I do not know where and why you have got this absurd notion that we had an understanding about getting married. From my side certainly we have no such thing. I always regarded you as a good friend, and will continue to do so unless prevented by another phone-call like today's.

You may check your letters from me to see whether any such 'understanding' was mentioned. I think you will find that nowhere do I mention marriage. I find this an embarrassing topic so will now close.

John.

Dear Tom,

I appreciate your intentions in writing to me with what you consider a justifiable warning. I realise you did this from no purposes of self-interest.

Still, I have to thank you for your intention and tell you that your remarks were not well-received. Ms Twilly and I are to be married shortly, and I regard your information that she has had seven breach of promise actions settled out of court as utterly preposterous. In fact I know for a certainty that the lady is quite incapable of beginning a breach of promise action, so your friend's sources cannot be as accurate as he or you may think.

Under other circumstances I would have invited you to our wedding but, as things are, I think I can thank you for having had the party where I was fortunate enough to meet my future bride and wish you well in the future.

Sincerely,
John Lewis.

Silver Wedding

Maeve Binchy

WH S

For Gordon Snell
my dear love and best friend.

CONTENTS

1
Anna

Anna knew that he was doing his best to be interested. She could read his face so well. This was the same look she saw on his face when older actors would come up and join them in the club and tell old tales about people long gone. Joe tried to be interested then too, it was a welcoming, courteous, earnest look. Hoping that it passed as genuine interest, hoping that the conversation wouldn't last too long.

'I'm sorry, I'm going on a bit,' she apologized. She pulled a funny face at him as she sat at the other end of the bed dressed only in one of his shirts, the Sunday papers and a breakfast tray between them.

Joe smiled back, a real smile this time.

'No, it's nice that you're so het up about it, it's good to care about families.'

He meant it, she knew, in his heart he thought it was a Good Thing to care about families, like rescuing kittens from trees and beautiful sunsets and big collie dogs. In principle Joe was in favour of caring about families. But he didn't care at all about his own. He wouldn't have known how many years his parents were married. He probably didn't know how long he had been married himself. Something like a silver anniversary would not trouble Joe Ashe.

Anna looked at him with the familiar feeling of tenderness and fear. Tender and protective – he looked so lovely lying there against the big pillows, his fair hair falling over his face, his thin brown shoulders so relaxed and easy. Fearful in case she would lose him, in case he would move on gently, effortlessly, out of her life, as he had moved into it.

Joe Ashe never fought with people, he told Anna with his big boyish smile, life was much too short for fights. And it was true.

When he was passed over for a part, when he got a bad review, there was the shrug – Well, so it could have been different but let's not make a production out of it.

Like his marriage to Janet – It was over, so why go on pretending? He just packed a small bag and left.

Anna feared that one day in this very room he would pack a small bag and leave again. She would rail and plead as Janet had done and it would be no use. Janet had even come around and offered Anna money to go away. She wept about how happy she had been with Joe. She showed pictures of the two small sons. It would all be fine again if only Anna would go away.

'But he didn't leave you to come to me, he had been in a flat by himself for a year before he even met me,' Anna had explained.

'Yes, and all that time I thought he would come back.'

Anna hated to remember Janet's tear-stained face, and how she had made tea for her, and hated even more to think that her own face would be stained with tears like this one day, and as unexpectedly as it had all happened to Janet. She gave a little shiver as she looked at the handsome easy boy in her bed. Because even if he was twenty-eight years of age he was still a boy. A gentle cruel boy.

'What are you thinking?' he asked.

She didn't tell him. She never told him how much she thought about him and dreaded the day he would leave.

'I was thinking it's about time they did another film version of *Romeo and Juliet*, you're so handsome it would be unfair on the world not to get a chance to look at you,' she said laughingly.

He reached out and put the breakfast tray on the floor. The Sunday papers slid after it.

'Come here to me,' said Joe. 'My mind was running on the same lines entirely, entirely at all, at all as you Irish say.'

'What a superb imitation,' Anna said drily, but snuggling up to him all the same. 'It's no wonder that you're the best actor in the whole wide world and renowned all over the globe for your great command of accents.'

She lay in his arms and didn't tell him about how worried she was about this silver wedding. She had seen from his face that she had already been going on about it far too long.

In a million years Joe would not understand what it meant in their family. Mother's and Father's twenty-fifth anniversary. They celebrated everything in the Doyle household. There were albums of memories, boxes chronicling past celebrations. On the wall of the sitting room at home there was a gallery of Major Celebrations. The wedding day itself, the three Christenings. There was Grannie O'Hagan's sixtieth birthday, there was Grandpa Doyle's visit to London with all of them standing beside a sentry outside Buckingham Palace, a solemn young sentry in a busby who seemed to realize the importance of Grandpa Doyle's visit.

There were the three First Communions, and the three Confirmations; there was a small sporting section, Brendan's school team the year he had been on the Seniors. There was an even smaller academic section, one graduation portrait of Anna herself, very studied and posed, holding her certificate as if it were a ton weight.

Mother and Father always joked about the wall and said it was the most valuable collection in the world. What did they want with Old Masters and famous paintings, hadn't they got something much more valuable, a living wall telling the world what their life was all about?

Anna had winced whenever they said that to people who came in. She winced now lying in Joe's arms.

'Are you shuddering at me or is that passion?' he asked.

'Unbridled passion,' she said, wondering was it normal to lie beside the most attractive man in London and think not of him but of the sitting room wall back in the family home.

The family home would have to be decorated for the silver wedding. There would be a lot of cardboard bells and silver ribbon. There would be flowers sprayed with a silver paint. They would have a tape of the 'Anniversary Waltz' on the player. There would be window sills full of cards, there might indeed be so many that it would call for an arrangement of streamers with the cards attached as they had for Christmas. The cake would have traditional decorations, the invitations would have silver edges. Inviting people to what? That was what was buzzing around Anna's head. As a family this was something they should organize for their parents. Anna and her sister Helen and her brother Brendan.

But it really meant Anna.

She would have to do it all.

Anna turned towards Joe and kissed him. She would not think about the anniversary any more now. She would think about it tomorrow when she was being paid to stand in a bookshop.

She wouldn't think of it at this moment when there were far better things to think about.

'That's more like it, I thought you'd gone to sleep on me,' Joe Ashe said, and held her very close to him.

Anna Doyle worked in Books for People, a small bookshop much patronized by authors and publishers and all kinds of media. They never tired of saying that this was a bookshop with character, not like the big chains which were utterly without soul. Secretly Anna did not altogether agree.

Too many times during her working day she had to refuse people who came in with perfectly normal requests for the latest bestseller, for a train timetable, for a book on freezer cookery. Always she had to direct them to a different shop. Anna felt that a bookshop worthy of the name should in fact stock such things instead of relying for its custom on a heavy psychology section, a detailed travel list, and poetry, sociology and contemporary satire.

It wasn't as if they were even proper specialists. She had intended to leave a year ago, but that was just when she met Joe. And when Joe had come to stay it happened to coincide with Joe not having any work.

Joe did a little here and there, and he was never broke. There was always enough to buy Anna a lovely Indian scarf, or a beautiful paper flower or find the most glorious wild mushrooms in a Soho delicatessen.

There was never any money for paying the rent or for the television, or the phone or the electricity. It would have been foolish of Anna to have left a steady job without having a better one lined up for herself. She stayed in Books for People, even though she hated the name, believing that most of the buyers of books *were* people anyway. The others who worked there were all perfectly pleasant, she never saw any of them outside work but there were occasional book signings, poetry evenings and even a cheese and wine evening in aid of a small nearby theatre. That was when she had met Joe Ashe.

Anna was at work early on Monday morning. If she wanted time to think or to write letters then to be in before the others was the only hope. There were only four of them who worked there: they each had a key. She switched off the burglar alarm, picked up the carton of milk, and the mail from the mat. It was all circulars and handbills. The postman had not arrived yet. As Anna put on the electric kettle to make coffee, she caught sight of herself in the small mirror that was stuck to the wall. Her eyes looked large and anxious, she thought. Anna stroked her face thoughtfully. She looked pale and there were definitely shadows under the big brown eyes. Her hair was tied up with a bright pink ribbon matching exactly her pink tee-shirt. She must put on a little make-up, she thought, or she would frighten the others.

She wished she had gone ahead and got her hair cut that time. It had been so strange, she had made an appointment in a posh place where some of the Royal Family went to have their hair done. One of the girls who worked there as a stylist came in to the bookshop and they had got talking. The girl said she would give Anna a discount. But the night she met Joe at the benefit evening for the theatre he had told her that her thick dark hair was beautiful the way it was.

He had asked her, as he so often did still, 'What are you thinking?' And in those very early times she told him the truth. That she was thinking about having her hair cut the following day.

'Don't even consider it,' Joe had said, and then suggested that they go to have a Greek meal and discuss this thing properly.

They had sat together in the warm spring night and he had told her about his acting and she had told him about her family. How she lived in a flat because she had thought she was becoming too dependent on her family, too drawn into everything they did. She went home of course on Sundays, and one other evening in the week. Joe had looked at her enthralled. He had never known a life where adults kept going back to the nest.

In days she was visiting his flat, days later he was visiting hers because it was more comfortable. He told Anna briefly and matter-of-factly about Janet and the two little boys. Anna told Joe about the college lecturer she had loved rather unwisely during her final years, resulting in a third-class degree and in a great sense of loss.

Joe was surprised that she had told him about the college lecturer. There was no hassle about shared property, shared children. He had only told her about Janet because he was still married to her. Anna had wanted to tell everything, Joe hadn't really wanted to hear.

It was only logical that he should come to live with her. He didn't suggest it, and for a while she wondered what she would say if she were invited to take up residence in his flat. It would be so hard to tell Mother and Father. But after one long lovely weekend, she decided to ask Joe would he not move in properly to her small ground-floor flat in Shepherd's Bush?

'Well I will, if that's what you'd like,' Joe had said, pleased but not surprised, willing but not over-grateful. He had gone back to his own place, done a deal about the rent and with two grip bags and a leather jacket over his arm he had come to live with Anna Doyle.

Anna Doyle, who had to keep his arrival very secret indeed from her mother and father who lived in Pinner and in a world where daughters did not let married men come to spend an evening let alone a lifetime.

He had been with her since that April Monday a year ago. And now it was May 1985 and by a series of complicated manoeuvres Anna had managed to keep the worlds of Pinner and Shepherd's Bush satisfactorily apart while flitting from one to another with an ever-increasing sense of guilt.

Joe's mother was fifty-six but looked years younger. She worked at the food counter of a bar where lots of actors gathered, and they saw her maybe two or three times a week. She was vague and friendly, giving them a wave as if they were just good customers. She hadn't known for about six months that they lived together. Joe simply hadn't bothered to tell her. When she heard she said, 'That's nice, dear,' to Anna in exactly the same tone as she would have spoken to a total stranger who had asked for a slice of the veal and ham pie.

Anna had wanted her to come around to the flat.

'What for?' Joe had asked in honest surprise.

Next time she was in the pub Anna went to the counter and asked Joe's mother herself.

'Would you like to come round and see us in the flat?'

'What for?' she had asked with interest.

Anna was determined. 'I don't know, a drink maybe.'

'Lord, dear, I never drink, seen enough of it in this place to turn you right against it, I tell you.'

'Well, just to see your son,' Anna went on.

'I see him in here, don't I? He's a grown-up now, love, he doesn't want to be looking at his old mum, day in day out.'

Anna had watched them since with a fascination that was half horror and half envy. They were just two people who lived in the same city, and who made easy casual conversation when they met.

They never talked of other members of the family. Nothing about Joe's sister who had been in a rehabilitation centre on account of drugs, nor the eldest brother who was a mercenary soldier of some sort in Africa, nor the youngest brother who worked in television as a cameraman.

She never asked about her grandchildren. Joe had told Anna that Janet did take them to see her sometimes, and occasionally he had taken the boys to a park nearby where his mother lived and she had come along for a little while. He never took them to her home.

'I think she has a bloke there, a young fellow, she doesn't want a lot of grandchildren trailing in to her.' To Joe it was simple and clear.

To Anna it was like something from another planet.

In Pinner if there were grandchildren they would have been the central pivot of the home, as the children had been for nearly a quarter of a century. Anna sighed again as she thought of the celebrations that lay ahead and how she would have to face up to them, as she had to face up to so many things on her own.

It was no use sitting in an empty bookshop with a coffee and a grievance that Joe wasn't as other men, supportive and willing to share these kinds of things with her. She had known there would be nothing like that from the first evening together.

What she had to do now was work out how the silver wedding could be organized in October in a way that wouldn't drive everyone mad.

Helen would be no use, that was for certain. She would send an illuminated card signed by all the sisters, she would invite Mother and Father to a special folk Mass with the Community, she would get the day off and come out to Pinner in her drab grey jumper and skirt, her hair dull and lifeless and the big cross on a chain around her neck constantly in her hand. Helen didn't even look like a nun, she looked like someone a bit dopey and badly dressed retreating behind the big crucifix. And in many ways that's what she was. Helen would turn up all right if everything was organized, and in her canvas bag she would take back any uneaten food because one nun loved gingerbread and another had a weakness for anything with salmon in it.

With a sense of despair Anna could see into the future months ahead with her younger sister Helen, a member of a religious community in South London, picking her way through the food like a scavenger and filling a biscuit tin with foil-wrapped titbits.

But at least Helen would be there. Would Brendan come at all? That was the real worry, and the one she had been trying to avoid thinking about. If Brendan Doyle did not get the train and boat and then the train again and make it to Pinner for his parents' twenty-fifth wedding anniversary they might as well call the whole thing off now. The disgrace would never be disguised, the emptiness would never be forgotten.

An incomplete family picture on the wall.

They would probably lie and say that he was in Ireland and couldn't be spared from the farm, the harvest or the shearing or whatever people did on farms in October.

But Anna knew with sickening clarity that it would be a paper-thin excuse. The Best Man and the Bridesmaid would know there had been a coldness, and the neighbours would know, and the priests would know.

And the shine would be taken off the silver.

How to get him back, that was the problem. Or was it? What to get him back for? Perhaps that was a bigger problem.

Brendan had always been so quiet when he was a schoolboy. Who would have known that he felt this strange longing to go away from the family to such a remote place? Anna had been so shocked the day he told them. Utterly straightforward and with no care about what it would do to the rest of the family.

'I'm not going back to school in September, it's no use trying to persuade me. I'll never get any exams, and I don't need them. I'm going to Vincent. In Ireland. I'll go as soon as I can leave.'

They had railed and beseeched. With no success. This is what he was going to do.

'But why are you doing this to us?' Mother had cried.

'I'm not doing anything to you.' Brendan had been mild. 'I'm doing it for me, it's not going to cost you any money. It's the farm where Father grew up, I thought you'd be pleased.'

'Don't think he'll make the farm over to you automatically,' Father had spluttered. 'That old recluse could just as well leave it to the missions. You could easily find you've put in all that graft for nothing.'

'Father, I'm not thinking of inheritances and wills and people dying, I'm thinking of how I'd like to spend my days. I was happy there and Vincent could do with another pair of hands.'

'Well if he does isn't it a wonder that he never married and provided himself with a few pairs of hands of his own around the place without asking strangers in to him?'

'Hardly a stranger, Father,' Brendan had said, 'I am his own flesh and blood, his brother's child.'

It had been a nightmare.

And the communication since had been minimal, cards at Christmas and on birthdays. Perhaps anniversaries. Anna couldn't remember. Anniversaries. How was she going to assemble the cast for this one?

The Bridesmaid, as they always called her, was Maureen Barry. She was Mother's best friend. They had been at school together back in Ireland. Maureen had never married, she was the same age as Mother, forty-six, though she looked younger. She had two dress shops in Dublin – she refused to call them boutiques. Perhaps Anna could talk to Maureen and see what would be best. But a warning bell went off loudly in her head. Mother was a great one for not letting things go outside the family.

There had always been secrets from Maureen.

Like the time that Father had lost his job. It couldn't be told.

Like the time that Helen ran away when she was fourteen. That was never breathed to Maureen. Mother had said that nothing mattered in the end, everything could be sorted out just so long as family matters weren't aired abroad, and neighbours and friends weren't told all of the Doyle business. It seemed to be a very effective and soothing cure when things went wrong, so the family had always stuck to it.

You would think that Anna should ring Maureen Barry now and ask her as Mother's oldest friend what was best to do about Brendan and about the anniversary in general.

But Mother would curl up and die if she thought there was the remotest possibility of any member of the family revealing a secret outside it. And the coldness with Brendan was a big secret.

There were no family members who could be asked to act as intermediaries.

So what kind of party? The day was a Saturday, it could be a lunch. There were a lot of hotels around Pinner, Harrow, Northwood, and restaurants and places used to doing functions like this. Perhaps a hotel would be best.

It would be formal for one thing, the banqueting manager would advise about toasts and cakes and photographs.

There wouldn't have to be weeks of intensive cleaning of the family home and manicuring the front garden.

But a lifetime as the eldest of the Doyles had taught Anna that a hotel would not be right. There were all those dismissive remarks about hotels in the past, destructive and critical remarks about this family who couldn't be bothered to have the thing in their own home, or the other family who would be quite glad to invite you to a common hotel, an impersonal place, but wouldn't let you over their own doorstep, thank you very much.

It would have to be home, the invitation would have to say in silver lettering that the guest was being invited to Salthill, 26 Rosemary Drive, Pinner. Salthill had been a seaside resort over in the West of Ireland where Mother and Maureen Barry used to go when they were young, it had been lovely, they said. Father had never been there, he said there was little time for long family holidays when he was a boy making his way in Ireland.

Wearily Anna made the list; it would be this size if there wasn't an Irish contingent, and that size if there were. It could be this size if there was to be a sit-down meal, that size if it were a buffet. This size if it were just drinks and snacks, that size if it were a proper meal.

And who would pay for it?

Very often the children did, she knew that.

But Helen had taken a vow of poverty and had nothing. Brendan, even if he did come which wasn't likely, was working for an agricultural worker's wages. Anna had very little money to spend on such a party.

She had very little money indeed. By dint of hard saving, no lunches and a few wise buys at Oxfam she had saved £132. It was in the building society hoping to become £200 and then when Joe had £200 they were going to Greece together. Joe had £11 at the moment so he had a longer way to go as regards saving. But he was sure to get a part soon. His agent had said there were a lot of things coming up. He'd be working any day now.

Anna hoped that he would, she really and truly did.

If he got something good, something where they recognized him properly, something steady, then everything else could fall into place. Not just the Greek holiday but everything. He could arrange a settlement for his sons, give Janet something that would make her feel independent, he could begin the divorce proceedings. Then Anna could risk leaving Books for People and go to a bigger shop, she would easily get promotion in a large bookshop, a graduate, experienced in the trade already. They would love her.

The time had gone by in thought, and soon the keys were turning in the door and the others arriving. Soon the door was open to the public. Planning was over, yet again.

At lunch time Anna made up her mind, she would go out to Pinner that evening and ask her parents straight out how they would like to celebrate the day. It seemed less celebratory than telling them that it was all in hand. But to try and do that was nonsense really, and she could still get it wrong. She would ask them straight out.

She rang them to say she would be coming over. Her mother was pleased.

'That's good, Anna, we haven't seen you for ages and ages, I was just saying to Daddy I hope Anna's all right, and there's nothing wrong.'

Anna gritted her teeth.

'Why would there be anything wrong?'

'Well it's just been so long, and we don't know what you do.'

'Mother, it's been eight days. I was with you last weekend.'

'Yes, but we don't know how you are getting on . . .'

'I ring you almost every day, you *know* how I'm getting on and what I do, get up in Shepherd's Bush and get the tube in here, and then I go home again. That is what I do, Mother, like a great many million people in London do.' Her voice rose in rage at her mother's attitude.

The reply was surprisingly mild. 'Why are you shouting at me, Anna my dear child? I only said I was delighted you were coming over this evening, your father will be overjoyed. Will we have a little steak and mushrooms? That's what we'll have as a celebration to welcome you back. Yes, I'll run down to the butcher's this afternoon, and get it . . . That's simply great you're going to come back. I can't wait to tell your father, I'll give him a ring at work now and tell him.'

'Don't . . . Mother, just . . . well I mean . . .'

'Of course I'll tell him, give him pleasure, something to look forward to.'

When she hung up, Anna stood motionless, hand on the receiver, and thought about the one time she had brought Joe to lunch at Salthill, 26 Rosemary Drive. She had invited him as 'a friend' and had spent the entire journey making him promise not to reveal that he was (a) living with her, and (b) married to someone else.

'Which is the more dangerous one to let slip?' Joe had asked, grinning.

'They're both equally dangerous,' she had said with such seriousness that he had leaned over and kissed her on the nose in the train in front of everyone.

It had been all right as a visit, Anna had thought, Mother and Father had inquired politely about Joe's acting career and whether he knew famous actors and actresses.

In the kitchen Mother had asked was he by way of being a boyfriend?

Just a friend, Anna had insisted.

On the way home she asked Joe what he had made of them.

'Very nice but very tense people,' he had said.

Tense? Mother and Father. She had never thought of them as tense. But in a way it was true.

And Joe didn't know what they were like when there was no outsider there, Mother wondering why Helen hadn't been there on two occasions during the week when they had telephoned her convent. Father striding around the garden snapping the heads off flowers and saying that boy was so restless and idle that he could only end up with the job of village idiot sucking straws on a small farm, it was hard to know why he had to go back to the one village in Ireland where they were known, and live with the one man in Ireland who could be guaranteed to give the worst impression of the Doyles and all their activities, his own brother, Brendan's Uncle Vincent. Just to inherit that miserable farm.

Joe had seen none of this side of things and yet he still thought her parents tense.

She had pursued it. Why? How did it show itself?

But Joe didn't want to be drawn.

'It's like this,' he had said to her, smiling to take any hurt out of his words. 'Some people just live that kind of life where this can be said and that can't be said, and people think what can be told and what can't. It's a way of going on where everything is a pretence, an act . . . Now that doesn't bother me if people want to live like that. It's not my way, but people make up a lot of rules and live by them . . .'

'We're not like that!' She was stung.

'I'm not criticizing you, my love! I'm just telling you what I see . . . I see Hare Krishnas shaving their heads and dancing and waving bells. I see you and your family acting things out just like they do. I don't let the Hare Krishnas get up my nose, I won't let your old man and old lady either. Right?' He had grinned at her winningly.

She had grinned back with a hollow empty feeling inside her and resolved not to go on about home any more.

The day came to an end. One of the nicer publishing reps was there as the shop closed. He asked her to come and have a drink.

'I'm going to darkest Pinner,' Anna said. 'I'd better set out now.'

'I'm driving that way, why don't we have a drink en route?' he said.

'Nobody's driving to Pinner,' she laughed.

'Oh, how do you know I don't have a mistress out that way, or am hoping to acquire one?' he teased.

'We wouldn't discuss such things in Rosemary Drive,' Anna said, mock primly.

'Come on, get in, the car's on a double yellow line,' he laughed.

He was Ken Green, she had talked to him a lot at the bookshop. They had both started work the same day, it had been a common bond.

He was going to leave his company and join a bigger one, so was she; neither of them had done it.

'Do you think we're just cowards?' she asked him as he negotiated the rush-hour traffic.

'No, there are always reasons. What's holding you back, these moral folk in Rosemary Drive?'

'How do you know they're moral folk?' she said, surprised.

'You just told me there'd be no talk of mistresses in your house,' Ken said.

'Too true, they'd be very disappointed to know that I was one myself,' Anna said.

'So would I.' Ken seemed serious.

'Oh, come on out of that,' she laughed at him. 'It's always easy to pay compliments to someone you know is tied up, much safer. If I told you I was free and on the rampage you'd run a hundred miles from me instead of offering me a drink.'

'Absolutely wrong. I left your bookshop to the last specially, I was thinking all day how nice it would be to see you. Don't you accuse me of being faint-hearted, hey?'

She patted his knee companionably. 'No. I misjudged you.' She sighed deeply. It was easy to talk to Ken, she didn't have to watch what she said. Like she would when she got to Salthill in Rosemary Drive. Like she would when she got back to Joe later on.

'Was that a sigh of pleasure?' he asked.

With Joe or with Mother or Father she would have said yes.

'Weariness: I get tired of all the lies,' she said. 'Very tired.'

'But you're a big girl now, surely you don't have to tell lies about your life and the way you live it.'

Anna nodded her head glumly. 'I do, truly I do.'

'Maybe you only think you do.'

'No, I do. Like the telephone. I've told them at home that my phone has been taken out, so that they won't ring me. That's because there's a message on the answerphone saying "This is Joe Ashe's number". He has to have it, you see, because he's an actor and they can't be out of touch.'

'Of course,' Ken said.

'So naturally I don't want my mother ringing and hearing a man's voice. And I don't want my father asking what's this young man doing in *my* flat.'

'True, he might well ask that, and why he hadn't a machine of his own and number of his own,' Ken said sternly.

'So I have to be careful about not mentioning things like paying the phone bill, I have to remember I'm not meant to *be* on the phone. That's just one of the nine million lies.'

'Well, is it all right at the other end, of the line, I mean you don't have to lie to this actor chap?' Ken seemed anxious to know.

'Lie? No, not at all, what would I have to lie about?'

'I don't know, you said all the lies you had to tell everywhere. I thought maybe he was a jealous macho fellow, you couldn't tell him you went for a drink with me. That's if we ever get anywhere near a drink.' Ken looked ruefully at the tailbacks.

'Oh no, you don't understand, Joe would be glad to think I went for a drink with a friend. It's just . . .' Her voice trailed away. What was it just? It was just that there was an endless utterly endless need to pretend. Pretend she was having a good time in the odd club place where they went. Pretend she understood this casual relationship with his mother, his wife, his children. Pretend she liked these fringe theatres where he played small parts. Pretend she enjoyed lovemaking every time. Pretend she didn't care about this heavy family business ahead of her.

'I don't lie to Joe,' she said as if she were speaking to herself. 'I just act a bit.'

There was a silence in the car.

'Well, he *is* an actor, I suppose,' Ken said, trying to revive the conversation a little.

That wasn't it. The actor didn't act at all, he never pretended to please anyone else. It was the actor's girlfriend who did all the acting. How odd that she had never thought of it that way before.

They sat and talked easily when they eventually found a pub.

'Do you want to ring your people to say you've been delayed?' Ken suggested.

She looked at him, surprised that he should be so thoughtful.

'Well, if they've bought steak and everything . . .' he said.

Mother was touched. 'That was nice of you dear, Father was beginning to look out for you. He said he'd walk down to the station.'

'No, I'm getting a lift.'

'Is it that Joe? Joe Ashe the actor?'

'No, no, Mother, Ken Green, a friend from work.'

'I don't think I got enough steak . . .'

'He's not coming to supper, he's just driving me there.'

'Well, ask him in, won't you? We love to meet your friends. Your father and I often wish you brought friends back here more often. That all of you did over the years.' Her voice sounded wistful, as if she were looking at her wall of pictures and not getting a proper charge from them.

'I'll ask him in for a moment then,' Anna said.

'Could you bear it?' she asked Ken.

'I'd like it. I can be a beard.'

'What on earth is that?'

'Don't you read your gossip magazines? It's someone who distracts attention from your real love. If they get to meet upright fellows like me they won't get the wind of evil sensual actor lovers who have their answering machines tied to your phone.'

'Oh shut up,' she laughed. It was easy laughter, not forced.

They had another drink. She told Ken Green about the anniversary. She told him briefly that her sister was a nun, her brother had dropped out and gone to work on the farm of her father's eldest brother Vincent, a small run-down place on Ireland's west coast. Feeling a little lighter and easier already, she told him that this was why she was having supper with her parents. For the first time in a long while she was going to come right out in the open, ask them what they wanted, tell them the limitations. Explain the problems.

'Don't go too heavily on the limitations and problems, if they're like you say, dwell more on the celebratory side,' he advised.

'Did your parents have a silver wedding?'

'Two years ago,' Ken said.

'Was it great?' she asked.

'Not really.'

'Oh.'

'When I know you better I'll tell you all about it,' he said.

'I thought we knew each other well now?' Anna was disappointed.

'No. I need more than one drink to tell the details of my whole life.'

Anna felt unreasonably annoyed that she had told him all about Joe Ashe and about how he had to be kept a secret at home.

'I think I talk too much,' she said contritely.

'No, you're just a nicer person. I'm rather buttoned up,' Ken said. 'Come on, drink that back and we'll head for the Saltmines.'

'The what?'

'Isn't that what you said your house was called?'

Anna laughed and hit him with her handbag. He made her feel normal again. The way she had felt a long time ago when it was great to be part of the Doyle family, instead of walking through a minefield which is what it was like these days.

Mother was waiting on the step.

'I came out in case you had any difficulty parking,' she explained.

'Thanks, but it seemed to be quite clear . . . we were lucky.' Ken spoke easily.

'We haven't heard much about you, so this is a nice surprise.' Her mother's eyes were bright, too bright.

'Yes, it's a surprise for me too. I don't know Anna very well, we just talk when I go to the bookshop. I invited her for a drink this evening and as it was one of her evenings for coming to Pinner it seemed like a good chance of a drive and a chat.'

Ken Green was a salesman, Anna remembered. He earned his living selling books, getting bigger orders than booksellers wanted to give, forcing them to do window displays, encouraging them to take large cardboard presentation packs. Naturally he would be able to sell himself as well.

Her father liked him too.

Ken managed to ask the right questions, not the wrong ones. He asked easily what line of business Mr Doyle was in. Her father's usual mulish defensive look came on his face. His voice took on the familiar pitch he had when he spoke of work, and rationalization.

Most people shuffled and sort of sympathized, mixed with jollying Desmond Doyle along when he began the tale of woe, the company that had been going along very nicely thank you until in the cause of rationalization a lot of jobs, perfectly sound secure jobs, went. Desmond Doyle's job had got changed, he told Ken Green. Changed utterly. It wasn't the same breed of men in business these days.

Anna felt weary. It was always the same, Father's version of the story. The truth was that Father had been sacked over what Mother called a personality conflict. But it was a secret. A great secret nobody was to know. At school it was never to be mentioned. Anna's first great habits of secrecy must have begun then, she realized. Perhaps that was when the secrecy all began. Because a year later Father was employed again by the same firm. And that was never explained either.

Ken Green didn't mutter agreement about the world in general and the ways of businessmen in particular.

'How did you manage to survive the rationalization? Were you in some essential post?'

Anna's hand flew to her mouth. No one had been as direct as this before in this household. Anna's mother looked with alarmed glances from one face to another. There was a short pause.

'I didn't survive it; as it happens,' Desmond Doyle said. 'I was out for a year. But they brought me back, when there was a change of personnel along the line, when some personality differences had been ironed out.'

Anna's hand remained at her mouth. This was the first time that Father had *ever* acknowledged that he had been a year unemployed. She was almost afraid to see how her mother had taken it.

Ken was nodding in agreement. 'That often happens, it's something like putting all the pieces into a paper bag and shaking a few of them back on to the board. Though the pieces aren't always put back in the right holes?' He smiled encouragingly.

Anna looked at Ken Green as if she had never seen him before. What was he doing, sitting in this room interrogating her father about forbidden subjects? Was there the remotest possibility that Mother and Father would think she had discussed private business with him?

Mercifully, Father hadn't taken it at all badly; he was busy explaining to Ken that people had indeed been relocated into the wrong positions. He himself who should have Operations Manager was in fact Special Projects.

Special Projects meant as little or as much as anyone wanted it to mean. It was a non-job.

'Still, that leaves it up to you to make what you will of it, that's the thing with non-jobs. I have one, Anna has one, and we try in our different ways to make something of them.'

'I have *not* a non-job!' Anna cried.

'It could be called that, couldn't it? There's no real ceiling, no proper ranking or way of getting recognition, you make it a good job because you're interested in publishing, you read the catalogues, you understand why books appear and who buys them. You could stand filing your nails like that colleague of yours with the purple hair.'

Anna's mother giggled nervously.

'Of course you're right when you're young, Ken, people have chances to make something of their job, but not when they're old . . .'

'So you were all right, then.' Ken was bland.

'Come now, don't be flattering me . . .'

'I wasn't.' Ken's face showed that nothing was further from his intentions. 'But you can't be more than forty-six, can you, forty-six or forty-seven?'

Anna fumed at her own stupidity, inviting this lout home.

'That's right, forty-seven next birthday,' Father was saying.

'Well, that's never old, is it? Not *old* like fifty-eight or sixty-two.'

'Deirdre, can we make that steak stretch to four pieces? This young fellow's doing me good, he has to stay for supper.'

Anna's face burned. If he said yes she would never forgive him.

'No, thank you, Mr Doyle, no, I mean it Mrs Dóyle. I'm sure it would be lovely but not tonight. Thanks again. I'll just finish my drink and let you get on with your evening.'

'But it would be no trouble and we'd like to . . .'

'Not tonight, Anna wants to talk to you, I know.'

'Well, I'm sure if it's anything . . .' Anna's mother looked wildly from her daughter to this personable young man with the dark hair and dark brown eyes. Surely Anna couldn't have come home with some announcement about him. Was the message written in her face. . . ?

Ken put her out of her misery. 'No, it's got nothing to do with me. It's a family thing, she wants to talk about your silver wedding anniversary and how you're going to celebrate it.'

Desmond Doyle was disappointed that Ken was definitely leaving. 'Oh, that's not for months,' he said.

'Anyway, whenever it is, the main thing is that you discuss it and do what you both want, and I know that's what Anna came home to talk to you about, so I'll leave you to it.'

He was gone, there had been handshakes all round and a quick grip of Anna's arm with his other hand.

They watched him pull out into the road and he tooted his horn very gently, just an acknowledgement.

The three Doyles stood almost wordless on the doorstep of Salthill, number 26 Rosemary Drive.

Anna faced them. 'I just told him casually that we were going to make plans, I don't know why he made such a big thing out of it.'

She got the feeling that neither of her parents was listening to her.

'That wasn't the only reason I came back. I came anyway to see you both.'

Still a silence.

'And I know you won't believe it but I just said that to him because . . . well, because I had to say something.'

'He's a very pleasant young man,' Desmond Doyle said.

'Good-looking too. Smartly turned out,' Deirdre Doyle added.

A wave of resentment washed over Anna. They were already comparing him favourably to Joe Ashe, Joe whom she loved with her body and soul.

'Yes,' she said in a dull voice.

'You haven't talked much about him before,' her mother said.

'I know, Mother, so you told him two seconds after you met him.'

'Don't be insolent to your mother,' Desmond Doyle said automatically.

'I'm twenty-three years of age, for Christ's sake, I'm not insolent like a child,' Anna stormed.

'I can't think what you're so upset about,' her mother said. 'We have a lovely supper for you, we ask a civil question, pass a remark about how nice your friend is, and get our heads bitten off.'

'I'm sorry.' This was the old Anna.

'Well, that's all right, you're tired after a long day. Maybe the little drinks on top of all that driving didn't agree with you.'

Anna clenched her fists silently.

They had walked back into the house and stood, an uneasy threesome, in the sitting room. They were beside the wall of family pictures.

'So what do you think we should do, eat now?' Mother looked from one to the other helplessly.

'Your mother went down to the shops especially when she heard you were coming tonight,' Father said.

For a mad moment she wished that Ken Green hadn't left after all, that he was here to drive a wedge through this woolly mass of conversation, this circular kind of talk that went nowhere. It just rose and fell, causing guilt, creating tension, and then was finally patted down.

If Ken were still here he might have said: 'Let's leave the meal for half an hour and talk about what you would really like to do for your anniversary.' Yes, those had been his very words. He hadn't said anything about what should be done or what might be expected, or what was the right way to go about it. He had said as he was leaving that Anna would want to talk to her parents about what they would both like for this day.

Like. That was a breakthrough in this family.

On an impulse she used exactly the words she thought Ken Green would say.

Startled, they sat down and looked at her expectantly.

'It's your day, it's not ours. What would *you* like best?'

'Well, really . . .' her mother began, at a loss. 'Well, it's not up to us.'

'If you all want to mark it, that would be very gratifying of course . . .' her father said.

Anna looked at them in disbelief. Did they really think that it wasn't up to them? Could they possibly live in a wonderland where they thought that life was a matter of all their children deciding to mark the occasion together? Did they not realize that in this family everything was acting . . . and that one by one the actors were slipping off the stage – Helen to her convent, Brendan to his remote rocky farm in the West of Ireland. Only Anna who lived two rail journeys away was even remotely around.

A great wave of despair came over her. She knew she must not lose her temper, that the whole visit would have been useless if it ended in a row. She could hear Joe asking her mildly why on earth she took such long wearying journeys on herself if it only ended up making them all tense and unhappy.

Joe had life worked out all right.

She felt an ache, a physical ache to be with him, and to sit on the floor by his chair while he stroked her hair.

She hadn't known it was possible to love somebody so intensely, and as she looked at the troubled man and woman sitting obediently on the sofa in front of her she wondered, had they ever known any fraction of this kind of love? You never could think of your parents expressing love, it was gross beyond imagining to think of them coupling and loving like real people did . . . like she and Joe did. But Anna knew that everyone felt that about their parents.

'Listen,' she said, 'I have to make a phone call. I want you to stop worrying about dinner for a moment, and just talk to each other about what you'd really like, then I'll start organizing it. Right?' Her eyes felt suspiciously bright, maybe the little drinks hadn't agreed with her.

She went to the phone. She would find an excuse to talk to Joe, nothing heavy, just to hear his voice would make her feel fine again. She would tell him that she'd be home a little earlier than she thought, would she get a Chinese takeaway, or a pizza or just a tub of ice cream? She wouldn't tell him now or later how bleakly depressing her old home was, how sad and low her parents made her feel, how frustrated and furious. Joe Ashe wanted to hear none of this.

She dialled her own number.

The phone was answered immediately, he must have been in the bedroom. It was a girl's voice.

Anna held the phone away from her ear like people often do in movies to show disbelief and confusion. She was aware she was doing this.

'Hallo?' the girl said again.

'What number is that?' Anna asked.

'Hang on, the phone's on the floor, I can't read it. Wait a sec.' The girl sounded good-natured. And young.

Anna stood there paralysed. In the flat in Shepherds Bush, the phone was indeed on the floor. To answer it you had to lean out of bed.

She didn't want the girl to struggle any more, she knew the number.

'Is Joe there?' she asked. 'Joe Ashe?'

'No, sorry, he went out for cigarettes, he'll be back in a few minutes.'

Why hadn't he put the answering machine on, Anna asked herself, *why* had he not automatically turned the switch, like he did always when leaving the flat? In case his agent rang. In case the call that would mean recognition came. Now the call that meant discovery had come instead.

She leaned against the wall of the house where she had grown up. She needed something to give her support.

The girl didn't like silences. 'Are you still there? Do you want to ring him back or is he to ring you or what?'

'Um . . . I'm not sure.' Anna fought for time.

If she got off the phone now, he would never know that she had found out. Things would be the same as they were, nothing would have changed. Suppose she said wrong number, or it doesn't matter, or I'll call again, the girl would shrug, hang up and maybe might not even mention to Joe that someone had called and rung off. Anna would never ask, she wouldn't disturb what they had.

But what had they? They had a man who would bring a girl to her bed, to *her* bed as soon as she was out of the house. Why try to preserve that? Because she loved him and if she didn't preserve it there would be a big screaming emptiness and she would miss him so much she would die.

Suppose she said she'd hold on, and then confront him? Would he be contrite? Would he explain that it was a fellow actress and they were just learning their lines?

Or would he say it was over? And then the emptiness and ache would begin.

The girl was anxious not to lose the call in case it might be a job for Joe.

'Hang on, I'll write down your name if you like, won't be a jiff, just let me get up, should be up anyway . . . Let's see, there's some kind of a desk over here by the window, no it's a dressing table . . . but there's an eyebrow pencil or something. Right, what's the name?'

Anna felt the bile bitter in her throat. In her bed, lying under the beautiful expensive bedspread she had bought last Christmas was a naked girl who was now going to carry the phone across to the simple table where Anna's make-up stood.

'Does the phone stretch all right?' Anna heard herself asking.

The girl laughed. 'Yes it does, actually.'

'Good. Well, put it down for a moment on the chair, the pink chair, and reach up on to the mantelpiece, good, and you'll find a spiral-backed pad with a pencil attached by a string.'

'Hey?' The girl was surprised but not uneasy.

Anna continued, 'Good, put back the eye pencil, it's kohl anyway, it wouldn't write well. Now just put down for Joe: "Anna rang. Anna Doyle. No message." '

'Sure he can't ring you back?' A hint of anxiety had crept into the voice of yet another woman who was going to spend weeks, months, even years of her life trying to please Joe Ashe, say the right thing, not risk losing him.

'No, no, I'm with my parents at the moment. In fact I'll be staying here the night. Could you tell him that?'

'Does he know where to find you?'

'Yes, but there's no need to ring me, I'll catch up on him another time.'

When she had hung up she stood holding on to the table for support. She remembered telling them that the hall was the very worst place to have a telephone. It was cold, it was too public, it was uncomfortable. Now she blessed them for having taken no notice of her.

She stood for a few moments but her thoughts would not be gathered, they ran and scurried like mice around her head. Finally when she thought she had at least recovered the power of speech she went back into the room where her mother and father sat. They who had never known the kind of love she knew nor the kind of hurt. She said that if it wouldn't put them out she'd like to stay the night, then they'd have all the time in the world to discuss the plans.

'You don't have to ask can you stay the night in your own home,' her mother said, pleased and fussing. 'I'll put a hot-water bottle in the bed just in case, the rooms are all there for you, not that any of you ever come and stay in them.'

'Well, I'd love to tonight.' Anna's smile was nailed firmly on her face.

They had got to the actual numbers that should be invited when Joe rang. She went to the phone calmly.

'She's gone,' he said.

'Has she?' Her voice was detached.

'Yes. It wasn't important.'

'No. No.'

'No need for you to stay over and make a big scene and meaning of life confrontation.'

'Oh no, none of that.'

He was nonplussed.

'So what are you going to do?' he asked.

'Stay here, as I told your friend.'

'But not for ever?'

'Of course not, just tonight.'

'Then tomorrow night after work . . . you'll be home?'

'Yes indeed, and you'll be packed.'

'Anna, don't be so dramatic.'

'Absolutely not, calmness itself. Stay there tonight of course, no, for heaven's sake there's no need to go immediately. Just tomorrow evening. Right?'

'Stop this, Anna, I love you, you love me, I'm not lying to you.'

'And neither am I to you, Joe, about tomorrow night. Truly.'

She hung up.

When he called back ten minutes later, she answered the phone herself.

'Please don't be tiresome, Joe. That's a great word of yours . . . tiresome. You hate when people press you on things and ask you about things that concern them, tiresome you call it. Maybe I'm learning from you.'

'We have to talk . . .'

'Tomorrow after work. After *my* work that is, you don't have any work, do you? We can talk then for a bit like about where I'm to send your mail, and there won't be any answering machine messages so you'd better set something else up.'

'But . . .'

'I won't come to the phone again, you'll have to talk to my father, and you always said he was a nice bloke with nothing to say . . .'

She went back to the discussion. She saw that her mother and father were wondering about the phone calls.

'Sorry for the interruptions, I've been having a row with Joe Ashe, my boyfriend. It's very antisocial to bring it into this house, if he rings again I won't talk to him.'

'Is it serious, the row?' her mother asked hopefully.

'Yes, Mother, you'll be glad to know it's fairly serious as rows go. Possibly final. Now let's see what people should have to eat.'

And as she told them about a very nice woman called Philippa who ran a catering business, Anna Doyle's mind was far away. Her mind was back in the days when things had been new and exciting and when her life was filled to every corner by the presence of Joe.

It would be hard to fill up all those parts again.

She said that they could ask for sample menus and decide what they wanted. They would write to everyone in very good time, individual letters, personal letters with the invitation, that would mean it was special.

'It is special, isn't it? Twenty-five years married?' She looked from one to the other hoping for reassurance. The cosy claustrophobic sense of family that the Doyles had managed to create around them. To her surprise and regret it didn't seem to be there tonight. Mother and Father looked uncertain about whether a quarter of a century of marriage had been a good thing. This was the one time in her life that Anna needed some sense that things were permanent, that even if her own world was shifting the rest of civilization was on fairly solid ground.

But maybe she was only reading her own situation into it all, like those poets who believed in the pathetic fallacy, who thought that nature changed to suit their moods, and that skies were grey when *they* were grey.

'We'll make it a marvellous occasion,' she told her father and mother. 'It's going to be even better than your wedding day, because we're all here to help celebrate it.'

She was rewarded with two smiles and she realized it would at least be a project for the great yawning frighteningly empty summer that lay ahead of her.

2
Brendan

Brendan Doyle went to the calendar to look up the date that Christy Moore was coming to sing in the town twenty miles away. It was some time next week, and he thought he'd go in to hear him.

He had written it down on the big kitchen calendar the day he had heard it billed on the radio. To his surprise, he realized that today was his birthday. It came as a shock to think it was already eleven o'clock in the morning and he hadn't realized that it was his birthday. In the olden days he would have known it was his birthday weeks in advance.

'Only three weeks to Brendan's birthday,' his mother would chirrup to anyone who might listen.

He had hated it when he was very young, all the fuss about birthdays. The celebrations. The girls had loved it of course, wearing smart frocks. There were never any outsiders there; Brendan couldn't remember having a real party, one with other children and crackers and games, just the family all dressed up and crackers and jelly with whipped cream and hundreds and thousands on it. There would be presents from all the others, wrapped properly, with little tags, and birthday cards as well which would all be arranged on the mantelpiece. Then there would be a photograph of The Birthday Boy all on his own, maybe wearing a paper hat. And then one with the rest of the family. These would be kept in the album, and brought out triumphantly when any guests arrived. The first of the birthdays, Brendan, wasn't he getting so big? And then this was Helen's birthday, and then Anna's. Look. And people looked and praised Mother. She was marvellous they said, marvellous to do all that for them, go to so much trouble.

His mother never knew how he hated it. How he had hated the singing, and seeing her clapping her hands and running for the camera during the 'For He's a Jolly Good Fellow'.

He wished they could just sit down and get on with it instead of all these antics and actions. As if they were all on stage.

And all the secrecy too. Don't tell Auntie Maureen about the new sofa. Why? We don't want her to think that it's new. Why don't we want her to think that? We just don't want them saying we put a lot of store by it, that's all. But it's gorgeous, isn't it? Yes, but we don't want them to say that we think it's something special, when Auntie Maureen asks about it just say "Oh the sofa, it's all right'," as if you weren't impressed. *You* know.

Brendan didn't know, he had never known. They always seemed to be hiding something from somebody. From the neighbours, from people at school, from people in the parish, from Maureen Barry, Mother's great friend, from Frank Quigley who worked with Father, who was meant to be the greatest friend of the family. And specially from everyone back in Ireland. Don't tell this to Grannie O'Hagan, and never let a word of that be said in front of Grandpa Doyle.

It was quite simple to live by Mother's and Father's rules if you understood that nothing was to be said outside the family.

Brendan thought that there was very little of importance said within the family either.

He remembered his birthday the year that Father had lost his job. There had been *huge* secrecy at that stage of their lives. Father used to leave the house in the mornings at the usual time and come back again as if things were normal. What was it all for, Brendan had wondered then and wondered still.

And here in Vincent's farm, the smallholding on the side of a hill where his father had grown up, he felt even more remote from the man than he had done when he lived in Rosemary Drive pretending that he was bright at school, pretending that he was going to get A levels and go to university. When all the time he knew he was going to come back here to this stony place where nothing was expected and nothing claimed to be what it was not.

He had never been *Uncle* Vincent, even though he was the oldest of Father's brothers, he was Vincent from the start. A tall stooped man, much lined and weatherbeaten. He never spoke until he had something to speak about. There was no small talk in the small house on the side of the hill, the house where Father had grown up one of six children. They must have been very poor then. Father didn't speak of it or those times. Vincent didn't speak of any times. Although a television aerial waved from almost every small farm in the countryside hereabouts, Vincent Doyle saw no need of one. And the radio he had was small and crackly. He listened to the half-past six news every evening, and the farm report that went before it. He sometimes came across some kind of documentary on the Irish in Australia, or some account of the armies of Napoleon coming to the West of Ireland. Brendan never knew how he tracked these features down. He didn't buy a daily newspaper nor any guide to look up what was on. And he wasn't a regular enough listener to know what was being broadcast when.

He wasn't a hermit, a recluse or an eccentric. Vincent always wore suits. He had never come to terms with a world of jackets and trousers. He bought a new suit every three years, and the current one was moved down a grade, so that one day it would have been the good suit for going to Mass and the day after a new purchase it would have been relegated to a different league. It could be worn when he went to tend the sheep, and even when lifting them in and out of his trailer.

Brendan Doyle had loved this place that strange summer when they had come for the visit. Everyone had been very tense all the way over on the boat and train, and there were so many things to remember. Remember not to talk about sitting up all night on the way to Holyhead. Remember not to talk about the crowds sitting on their luggage or people would know they had gone steerage. Remember not to say that they had waited for ages on a cold platform. There were to be no complaints, it was all to have been fun. That was the message that Mother kept repeating over and over during the endless journey. Father had said almost the opposite, he had told them not to go blowing and boasting to their Uncle Vincent about all the comforts they had in London. Brendan remembered asking a direct question; he had felt slightly sick before he asked it, as if he knew it wasn't the thing to say.

'Well – which are we? Are we rich like we're pretending to Grannie O'Hagan, or are we poor like we're pretending to Uncle Vincent and Grandpa Doyle?'

There had been a great pause.

Horrified, his parents had looked at each other.

'Pretend!' they had cried almost with one voice. There was no pretending, they protested. They had been advising the children not to gabble off things that would irritate their elders or bore them. That was all.

And Brendan remembered the first time he saw the farm. They had spent three days with Grannie O'Hagan in Dublin and then a long tiring train journey. Mother and Father seemed upset by the way things had gone in Dublin. At least the children had behaved properly, there had been no unneccessary blabbering. Brendan remembered looking out the window at the small fields of Ireland. Helen had been in disgrace for some horseplay at the station, the main evil of it was that it had been done in the presence of Grannie O'Hagan. Anna was very quiet and stuck in a book. Mother and Father talked in low voices over and over.

Nothing had prepared him for the sight of the small stone house, and the yard with the bits of broken machinery in it. At the door stood his grandfather, old and stooped, and wearing shabby old clothes, a torn jacket and no collar on his shirt. Beside him was Uncle Vincent, a taller and younger version but wearing a suit that looked as if it were respectable.

'You're welcome to your own place,' Grandpa Doyle had said. 'This is the land you children came from, it's a grand thing to have you back from all those red buses and crowds of people to walk your own soil again.'

Grandpa Doyle had been to London once on a visit. Brendan knew that because of the pictures, the one on the wall taken outside Buckingham Palace, and the many in the albums. He couldn't really remember the visit. Now as he looked at these two men standing in front of the house he felt an odd sense of having come home. Like those children's stories he used to read when an adventure was coming to an end and they were coming out of the forest. He was afraid to speak in case it would ruin it.

They had stayed a week there that time. Grandpa Doyle had been frail, and hadn't walked very much further than his front door. But Vincent had taken them all over the place. Sometimes in the old car with its bockety trailer; the trailer had not changed since that first visit. Sometimes Vincent couldn't be bothered to untackle it from the car even though there might be no need to transport a sheep, and it rattled along comfortingly behind them.

Vincent used to go off to see his sheep twice a day. Sheep had a bad habit of falling over on their backs and lying there, legs heaving in the air; you have to right them, put them the right way up.

Anna had asked was it only Uncle Vincent's sheep that did this or was it all sheep? She didn't want to speak about it when she got back to London in case it was just a habit of the Doyles' sheep. Vincent had given her a funny look but had said quite agreeably that no harm could come from admitting that sheep fell over, it was a fairly common occurrence in the breed, even in England.

Then Vincent would stop and mend walls; sheep were forever crashing through the little stone walls and dislodging bits of them, he explained. Yes, he confirmed to Anna before she had to ask, this too was a general failing in them as a species.

In the town he brought them into a bar with high stools and bought them lemonade. None of them had ever been in a public house before. Helen asked for a pint of stout but didn't get it. Vincent hadn't minded. It was the barman who had said she was too young.

Even way back then, Brendan had noticed that Vincent had never bothered to explain to people who they were;

he didn't fuss and introduce them as his brother's children, explain that they were over here for a week's visit, that in real life they lived in a lovely leafy suburb of North London called Pinner, and that they played tennis at weekends in the summer. Mother and Father would have managed to tell all that to almost anyone. Vincent just went on the way he always did, talking little, replying slowly and effortlessly when he was asked a question.

Brendan got the feeling that he'd prefer *not* to be asked too many questions. Sometimes, even on that holiday, he and Vincent had walked miles together with hardly a word exchanged. It was extraordinarily restful.

He hated it when the week was over.

'Maybe we'll come back again,' he had said to Vincent as they left.

'Maybe.' Vincent hadn't sounded sure.

'Why do you think we might not?' They were leaning on a gate to the small vegetable area. There were a few drills of potatoes there and easy things like cabbage and carrots and parsnips. Things that wouldn't kill you looking after them, Vincent had explained.

'Ah, there was a lot of talk about you all coming back here, but I think it came to nothing. Not after they saw the place.'

Brendan's heart skipped.

'Coming back . . . for more than a holiday do you mean?'

'Wasn't that what it was all about?'

'Was it?'

He had seen his uncle's eyes looking at him kindly.

'Yerra, don't worry yourself, Brendan boy, just live your life the best you can, and then one day you can go off and be where people won't be getting at you.'

'When would that day be?'

'You'll know when it arrives,' Vincent had said without taking his eyes away from the few rows of potatoes.

And indeed Brendan *had* known when the day arrived.

Things changed when they went back home to London after that visit. For one thing Father got his job back, and they didn't have to pretend any more that he had a job when he hadn't. And there had been all kinds of terrible rows with Helen. She kept saying that she didn't want to be left in the house alone. She would interrogate them all each day about what time they were going out and coming back, and even if there seemed to be five minutes of unaccounted-for time, she would arrange to go and meet Brendan when school finished.

He had tried to ask her what it was all about, but she had shrugged and said she just hated being by herself.

Not that there was ever much fear of that in Rosemary Drive. Brendan would have loved some time on his own instead of all the chit-chat at mealtimes, and getting the table ready and discussing what they ate and what they would eat at the next meal. He couldn't understand why Helen didn't welcome any chance of peace with open arms.

Perhaps that was why she had gone to be a nun in the end. For peace. Or was it because she still felt the need to be with people, and she thought the numbers were dropping at Rosemary Drive, with Anna moving out to her flat and Brendan a permanent resident in Ireland?

It was strange to have lived for so long with this family, and lived so closely during weeks, months, years of endless conversation and still to know them so little.

Brendan had decided to go back to that stone cottage on the day that his school ran a careers exhibition. There were stands and stalls giving information about careers in computing, in retailing, in the telephone service, in London Transport, in banking, in the armed forces. He wandered disconsolately from one to another.

Grandpa Doyle had died since that family visit when he welcomed them to the soil they came from. They had not gone home for the funeral. It wasn't really *home*, Mother had said, and Grandpa would have been the first to have agreed. Uncle Vincent wouldn't expect it, and there were no neighbours who would think it peculiar and talk poorly of them for not going. There had been a special Mass said for the repose of his soul in their parish church and everyone they knew from the parish sympathized.

The headmaster said that a decision about how to spend the years of one's life was a very major decision; it wasn't like choosing what cinema to go to or what football team to support. And suddenly like a vision Brendan realized that he had to get away from this, he had to escape the constant discussions and whether this was the right decision or the wrong one, and how he must tell people he was a management trainee rather than a shopworker or whatever new set of pretences would appear. He knew with the greatest clarity that he had ever possessed that he would go back to Vincent's place and work there.

Salthill, 26 Rosemary Drive, was not a house that you walked out of without explanations. But Brendan realized that these would be the very last explanations he would ever have to give. He would regard it as an ordeal by fire and water, he would grit his teeth and go through it.

It had been worse than he could ever have imagined. Anna and Helen had wept, and pleaded and begged him not to go away. His mother had wept too and asked what she had done to deserve this; his father had wanted to know whether Vincent had put him up to this.

'Vincent doesn't even know,' Brendan had said.

Nothing would dissuade him. Brendan hadn't known that he possessed such strength. For four days the battle went on.

His mother would come and sit on his bed with cups of drinking chocolate. 'All boys go through a period like this, a time of wanting to be on their own, to be away from the family apron strings. I've suggested to your father that you go on a little holiday over to Vincent, maybe that will get it all out of your system.'

Brendan had refused. It would have been dishonest. Because once he went he would not come back.

His father made overtures too. 'Listen, boy, perhaps I was a bit harsh the other night saying you were only going to try and inherit that heap of old stones, I didn't mean that to sound so blunt. But you know the way it will look. You can see how people will look at it.'

Brendan couldn't, not then, not now.

But he would never forget the look on Vincent's face when he arrived up the road.

He had walked all the way from the town. Vincent was standing with the old dog, Shep, at the kitchen door. He shaded his eyes from the evening light as Brendan got nearer, and he could make out the shape in the sunset.

'Well now,' he said.

Brendan had said nothing. He had carried a small grip bag with him, all his possessions for a new life.

'It's yourself,' Vincent had said. 'Come on in.'

At no time that evening did he ask why Brendan had come or how long he was staying. He never inquired whether they knew his whereabouts back in London, or if the visit had official approval.

Vincent's view was that all this would emerge as time went by, and slowly over the weeks and months it did.

Days came and went. There was never a harsh word between the two Doyles, uncle and nephew. In fact there were very few words at all. When Brendan thought he might go to a dance nearby, Vincent said he thought that would be a great thing altogether. He had never been great shakes at the dancing himself but he heard that it was great exercise. He went to the tin on the dresser where the money was and handed Brendan forty pounds to kit himself out.

From time to time Brendan helped himself from the tin. He had asked in the beginning, but Vincent had put a stop to that, saying the money was there for the both of them, and to take what he needed.

Things had been getting expensive, and from time to time Brendan went and did an evening's work in a bar for an extra few pounds to add to the till. If Vincent knew about it he never acknowledged it, either to protest or to praise.

Brendan grinned to himself, thinking how differently things would have been run back in Rosemary Drive.

He didn't miss them; he wondered could he ever have loved them, even a little bit? And if he hadn't loved them did that make him unnatural? Everything he read had love in it, and all the films were about love, and anything you heard of in the papers seemed to be done for love or because someone loved and that love wasn't returned. Maybe he was an odd man out, not loving.

Vincent must have been like that too, that's why he never wrote letters or talked to people intensely. That's why he liked this life here in the hills and among the stony roads and peaceful skies.

It was a bit unnatural, Brendan told himself, to become twenty-two all by yourself, without acknowledging it to another soul. If he told Vincent, his uncle would look at him thoughtfully and say 'Is that a fact?' He would offer no congratulations nor suggest a celebratory pint.

Vincent was out walking the land. He would be back in by lunch. They would have that bacon cold, and plenty of tomatoes. They would eat hot potatoes with it because a dinner in the middle of the day without a few big floury potatoes would be no use to anyone. They never ate mutton or lamb. It wasn't out of a sense of delicacy to the sheep that were their living, it was that they had no big freezer like some of their neighbours who would kill a sheep each season. And they couldn't bear to pay the prices in the butcher's shop for animals that they had sold for a greatly smaller sum than would warrant such a cost by the time they got to the butcher's cold store.

Johnny Riordan the postman drove up in his little van.

'There's a rake of letters for you, Brendan, it must be your birthday,' he said cheerfully.

'Yes it is.' Brendan had grown as taciturn as his uncle.

'Good man, will you buy us a pint later?'

'I might do that.'

The card from his father was one with a funny cat on it. Quite unsuitable from an estranged father. The word 'Father' was written neatly. No love, no best wishes. Well, that was all right. He sent an automatic card to Father with just 'Brendan' on it each year too.

Mother's was more flowery, and said she could hardly believe she had such a grown-up son, and wondered whether he had any girlfriends and would they ever see him married.

Helen's card was full of peace and blessings. She wrote a note about the Sisters and the hostel they were going to open and the funds that were needed and how two of the Sisters were going to play the guitar busking at Piccadilly station and how the community was very divided about this and whether it was the right way to go. Helen always wrote with a cast of thousands assuming he knew all these people and remembered their names and cared about their doings. At the end she wrote, 'Please take Anna's letter seriously.'

He had opened them in the right order. He opened Anna's slowly. Perhaps it was going to tell him some bad news, Father had cancer, or Mother was going to have an operation? His face curled into a look of scorn when he saw all the business about the anniversary. Nothing had changed, simply nothing, they had got trapped in a time warp, stuck in a world of tinsel-covered cards, meaningless rituals. He felt even more annoyed about the whole thing because of Sister Helen's pious instruction to take Anna's letter seriously. Talk about passing the buck.

He felt edgy and restless as he always did when drawn into family affairs. He got up and went outside. He would walk up the hills a bit. There was a wall he wanted to look at. It might need a bit more work than just rearranging the stones like they did so often.

He came across Vincent with a sheep that had got stuck in the gate. The animal was frightened and kicking and pulling so that it was almost impossible to release her.

'You came at a good time,' Vincent said, and together they eased the anxious sheep out. She bleated frantically and looked at them with her silly face.

'What's wrong with her at all, is she hurt?' Brendan asked.

'No. Not a scratch on her.'

'Then what's all that caterwauling out of her?'

Vincent looked long at the distressed sheep. 'That's the one that lay on its lamb. Crushed the little thing to death,' he said.

'Stupid thicko sheep,' Brendan said. 'Sits on her own perfectly good lamb, then gets stuck in a gate, that's what gives sheep a bad name.'

The ewe looked at him trustingly and gave a great baaa into the air.

'She doesn't know I'm insulting her,' Brendan said.

'Divil a bit she'd care. She's looking for the lamb.'

'Doesn't she know she suffocated it?'

'Not at all. How would she know that?' Vincent said.

Companionably the two men walked back towards the house to make their lunch.

Vincent's eyes fell on the envelopes and cards.

'Well now, it's your birthday,' he said. 'Imagine that.'

'Yes.' Brendan sounded grumpy.

His uncle looked at him for a while.

'It's good of them to remember you, it would be scant remembering you'd get if you had to rely on me.'

'I don't worry about remembering . . . not that sort.' He was still bad-tempered as he washed the potatoes at the sink and put them into the big saucepan of water.

'Will I put them up on the mantelpiece for you?'

Vincent had never said anything like that.

'No, no. I wouldn't like that.'

'All right so.' His uncle collected them neatly and left them in a little pile. He saw Anna's long typed letter but made no comment. During the meal he waited for the boy to speak.

'Anna has this notion I should go over to England and play games for some silver wedding celebrations. *Silver*,' he scoffed at the word.

'That's how many?' Vincent asked.

'Twenty-five glorious years.'

'Are they that long married? Lord Lord.'

'You weren't at the wedding yourself?'

'God Brendan, what would take me to a wedding, I ask you?'

'They want me to go over. I'm not going next or near it.'

'Well, we all do what we want to do.'

Brendan thought about that for a long time.

'I suppose we do in the end,' he said.

They lit their cigarettes to smoke while they drank their big mugs of tea.

'And they don't want me there, I'd only be an embarrassment. Mother would have to be explaining me to people, and why I didn't do this or look like that, and Father would be quizzing me, asking me questions.'

'Well, you said you weren't going so what's the worry about it?'

'It's not till October,' Brendan said.

'October, is that a fact?' Vincent looked puzzled.

'I know, isn't it just like them to be setting it all up now?'

They left it for a while but his face was troubled, and his uncle knew he would speak of it again.

'In a way, of course, once in a few years isn't much to go over. In a way of looking at it, it mightn't be much to give them.'

'It's your own decision, lad.'

'You wouldn't point me one way or the other, I suppose?'

'Indeed I would not.'

'It might be too expensive for us to afford the fare.' Brendan looked up at the biscuit tin, maybe this was an out.

'There's always the money for the fare, you know that.'

He did know it. He had just been hoping that they could use it as an excuse. Even to themselves.

'And I would only be one of a crowd, if I were to go it would be better to go on my own some time.'

'Whatever you say yourself.'

Outside they heard a bleating. The sheep with the foolish face, the one that had suffocated her lamb was still looking for it. She had come towards the house hoping that it might have strayed in there. Vincent and Brendan looked out the kitchen window. The sheep still called out.

'She'd have been a hopeless mother to it even if it had lived,' Brendan said.

'She doesn't know that, she's just living by some kind of instinct. She'd like to see it for a bit. To know that it's all right, sort of.'

It was one of the longest speeches his uncle had ever made. He looked at his uncle and reached out to touch him. He put his arm gently around the older man's shoulder, feeling moved to the heart by the kindness and generosity of spirit.

'I'll go off into the town now, Vincent,' he said, taking his arm away. 'I'll write a couple of letters maybe and maybe work pulling a few pints tonight.'

'There's enough in the biscuit tin,' Vincent said gently.

'There is, I know. I know.'

He went out into the yard and passed the lonely ewe still calling for her lost lamb and started up the old car to drive to the town. He would go back for their silver anniversary. It was only a little time out of this life. The life he wanted. He could give a little time to show them he was all right and that he was part of the family.

3
Helen

The old man looked at Helen hopefully. He saw a girl in her twenties with a grey jumper and skirt. Her hair was tied back in a black ribbon but it looked as if any moment it might all escape and fall wild and curly around her shoulders. She had dark blue restless eyes and freckles on her nose. She carried a black plastic shopping bag which she was swinging backwards and forwards.

'Miss,' said the old drunk, 'can you do me a favour?'

Helen stopped at once, as he had known she would. There were passers-by who went on passing by and those who stopped. Years of observation had taught him to tell one sort from the other.

'Of course, what can I do?' she asked him.

He almost stepped back. Her smile was too ready, too willing. Usually people muttered that they didn't have change or that they were in a hurry. Even if they did seem about to help a wino they didn't show such eagerness.

'I don't want any money,' he said.

'Of course not,' Helen said as if it was the last thing that a man with a coat tied with string and an empty ginger-wine bottle in his hand would want.

'I just want you to go in there and get me another bottle. The bastards say they won't serve me. They say I'm not to come into the shop. Now if I were to give you two pounds into your hand, then you could go in and get it for me.'

From his grizzled face with its wild hair above and its stubble below his small sharp eyes shone with the brilliance of the plan.

Helen bit her lower lip and looked at him hard.

He was from Ireland of course, they all were, or else Scotland. The Welsh drunks seemed to stay in their valleys, and the English didn't get drunk in such numbers or so publicly. It was a mystery.

'I think you've had enough.'

'How would you know whether I've had enough or not? That's not what we were debating. That, as it happens, was not the point at issue.'

Helen was moved, he spoke so well, he had such phrases . . . the point at issue. How could a man who spoke like that have let himself go so far and turn into an outcast?'

Immediately she felt guilty about the thought. That was the way Grandmother O'Hagan would talk. And Helen would immediately disagree with her. Here she was at twenty-one thinking almost the same thing.

'It's not good for you,' she said, and added spiritedly, 'I said I'd do you a favour, it's not a favour giving you more alcohol, it's a downright disservice.'

The drunk liked such niceties and definitions, he was ready to parry with her.

'But there is no question of your *giving* me alcohol, my dear lady,' he said triumphantly. 'That was never part of our agreement. You are to act as my agent in purchasing the alcohol.' He beamed at his victory.

'No, it's only going to kill you.'

'I can easily get it elsewhere. I have two pounds and I will get it elsewhere. What we are now discussing is your word given and then broken. You said you would do me a favour, now you say you will not.'

Helen stormed into the small grocery-cum-off-licence.

'A bottle of cider,' she asked, eyes flashing.

'What kind?'

'I don't know. Any kind. That one.' She pointed to a fancy bottle. Outside, the drunk knocked on the window and shook his head of shaggy hair, trying to point to a different brand.

'You're not buying it for that wino?' asked the young man.

'No, it's for myself,' Helen said guiltily and obviously falsely. The drunk man was pointing feverishly at some brand.

'Listen, don't give it to him, lady . . . I beg you.'

'Are you going to sell me this bottle of cider or are you not?' Helen could be authoritative in short bursts.

'Two pounds eighty,' the man said. Helen slapped the money, *her* money, down on the counter, and in an equally bad temper the bottle was shoved into a plastic bag for her.

'Now,' Helen said. 'Did I or did I not do what you asked me?'

'You did not, that's only rat's piss, that stuff, fancy bottles for the carriage trade. I'm not drinking that.'

'Well don't then.' There were tears starting in her eyes.

'And what's more I'm not spending my good money on it.'

'Have it as a present.' She was weary.

'Oh high and mighty, Lady Muck,' he said. He had a good quarter of it drunk from the neck by this stage. He was holding it still by its plastic carrier bag.

Helen didn't like the look of his face, the man was working himself up into some kind of temper, or even fit. She looked at him alarmed, and saw a huge amount of the despised cider vanishing down his throat.

'The urine of rodents,' he shouted. 'Bottled by these creeps of shopkeepers and dignified with the name of alcohol.'

He banged on the window again loudly. 'Come out, you cheat and rogue, come out here and justify this garbage.'

There were vegetable boxes piled neatly with apples and oranges, with potatoes loose and mushrooms in baskets. The man with the near-empty cider bottle began to turn them over on to the street systematically.

The staff ran from the shop; two of them held him, another went for the law.

'Thank you very much,' said the boy who had served Helen. 'That was a very nice day's work.'

'You wouldn't bloody listen to me,' shouted the man, who had foam flecks at the side of his mouth by now.

'Her sort don't listen to anyone, mate,' said the irate shopkeeper who was trying to immobilize him.

Helen moved from the scene awkwardly. She walked away almost sideways as if she were trying not to turn her back on the chaos and distress she had created. But then this happened so often.

It was always happening, Helen found, everywhere she went.

Back in the convent she wouldn't say anything to Sister Brigid about it. It would be so easily misunderstood. The sisters wouldn't grasp that it would all have happened anyway. The man might have got even more violent and upset if nobody had bought him the drink. He might have broken the window or hurt someone. But Helen wouldn't tell the upsetting tale. Brigid would be bound to look at her sadly and wonder why trouble seemed to follow Helen Doyle wherever she went.

It might even put further away the day when they would allow Helen to take her vows and become a member of the Community rather than just a hanger-on. How much did she have to prove? Why did Sister Brigid keep putting off the time when Helen should be considered seriously as one of their Community? She worked as hard as any of them, she had been with them for three years and still there was this feeling that it was somehow a passing whim.

Even the most minor and accidental events made them see Helen as unstable in some way. It was terribly unfair and she wouldn't add to the long list by telling them about the confusion she was walking away from. Somehow it would be seen as her fault.

Instead she would think about the silver wedding celebrations and what she could do best to help.

Well obviously she hadn't any money or anything so there could be nothing expected from her on that score. And as well as the vow of poverty that she had taken – or to be more honest was trying to take – she was a bit unworldly these days, she had left the mainstream of everyday life. And even if she did go out to work each day, as all the Sisters did, she didn't see the side of life that Mother and Anna would be concentrating on, the more material end of things. And she wouldn't be any good rounding up neighbours and friends. Perhaps she could see whether they might have a special Mass or Liturgy . . . But Helen was doubtful whether the old priest in the parish church where the Doyles went was going to be well up on the modern liturgy of renewal.

Better leave it to Anna who had plenty of time for all that sort of thing. Anna got so tetchy often when Helen did things to help, it was often better to do nothing, to say in a calm voice, Yes Anna, No Anna, Three Bags Full Anna. This is what Brigid would suggest. Brigid was very big on the calm voice. Or on Helen's developing it. It often sounded like blandness, and even hypocrisy to Helen, but Brigid said that it was what the world in general seemed to want. And there were times when Helen thought gloomily that she might be right.

Certainly Mother always wanted things underplayed and understated, and in most cases not mentioned at all. Mother would like not so much calm as silence. Perhaps Mother might be pleased if Helen had been born deaf and dumb.

By this stage she had arrived at St Martin's, the house where the Sisters lived. Brigid never called it the Convent, even though that is what it was. Brigid called it just St Martin's, or home. She didn't criticize Helen Doyle for using a more formal and official word to describe the red-brick house where eleven women lived and went about their daily business as social workers in various London agencies.

Nessa was working with young mothers, most of them under sixteen, and trying to teach them some kind of mothering skills. Nessa had a child herself a long time ago, she had brought the baby up on her own but the child had died when it was three. Helen couldn't remember whether it was a boy or a girl. The other Sisters didn't talk about it much. But it did give Nessa the edge when it came to looking after children. Brigid usually worked in the day centre for vagrants. Serving them lunches, trying to organize baths and delousing. Sister Maureen worked with the group that were rehabilitating ex-prisoners. The days were gone when these kinds of nuns just polished the big tables in the parlour in the hopes of a visit from a bishop. They went out to do God's work and found plenty of opportunity to do it in the streets of London.

Helen had moved from one area to another since she had come to join St Martin's. She would like to have worked with Sister Brigid running the day centre. What she would really have liked is if Brigid would let her run it on her own, and just call in from time to time to see how things were getting along. This way Helen felt she would be really useful and special, and that once seen in a position of calm control over the wellbeing of so many people, she would have no difficulty in proving her readiness to be a full member of the Community.

She realized that Obedience was very much part of it, and like Poverty and Chastity this was no problem to her, Helen believed. She didn't want to be laying down the law and making rules, she would obey any rule. She didn't want money for jewels or yachts, she laughed at the very notion of such things. And Chastity. Yes she was very sure she wanted that in a highly positive way. Her one experience of the reverse side of that coin was quite enough to reassure her on this particular score.

She had worked in the kitchen, done her turn as a skivvy. She was never sure why Brigid hadn't liked her using that term. Skivvy. She had not been able to understand that people used that word quite respectably nowadays, as a sort of a joke. Debs said they were skivvying for a while before going skiing, it meant minding someone's house. Australians over here for a year often got jobs in bars, in restaurants, or as skivvies. It wasn't an insulting term.

Helen sighed, thinking of all the gulfs in understanding there were everywhere. She let herself in the door of St Martin's. It was Sister Joan's month for running the house, as Brigid liked it called. Joan called out from the kitchen as she heard her come in.

'Just in time, Helen, I'll take the stuff from you now. You couldn't have timed it better, as it happened.'

With a lurch Helen remembered the reason she had taken the large black plastic carrier bag that had been swinging emptily beside her on her journey home. She had meant to come by the market and buy cheaply what the sellers hadn't got rid of during the day. She had forgotten it once, and that was why she had been heading towards the grocery and off-licence where she had assisted her compatriot to destroy his liver even faster than he was already doing. She had been given three pounds to buy the vegetables. She had spent it on cider for an alcoholic.

'Sit down, Helen. It's not the end of the world,' said Joan, who didn't know the details of the story but recognized the substance and knew there would be no vegetables for the casserole.

'Sit down, Helen, stop crying. I'll put on a cup of tea for you just as soon as I've scrubbed some of those potatoes. We'll have jacket potatoes with a little bit of cheese. It will be just as nice.'

Nessa was tired; it had been a particularly bad day.

An eighteen-year-old mother had sat whimpering in a corner while her fate was being discussed by social workers and a woman police officer. Her baby would live, thanks to Nessa, but what kind of life?

The mother had not turned up at the centre for two days running and Nessa became worried. The door to the block of flats always swung open and as Nessa went in she almost fell over Simon crawling along the filthy corridor. Beer cans and bottles were strewn everywhere, the place smelled of urine, there were dangers every few feet, broken bicycles, crates with sharp corners. Simon was crawling earnestly towards the open door. In a minute he would have been on the street where no car or motor bicycle would have expected a child to crawl. He would have been dead.

As it was he was alive, the sores from his stinking nappies being treated. Anti-tetanus injections were being given against the germs he must have encountered, and his bruised eye was pronounced mercifully intact.

His mother hadn't beaten him, of this Nessa was sure, but she was too feeble-minded to look after him. He would be in care when he came out of hospital. A lifetime of care lay ahead of him. But care with a capital C.

Nessa was not in the mood for Helen's tears and explanations. She cut her very short.

'So you forgot the vegetables again. So what, Helen? Let's have a little peace. That's what would be really nice.'

Helen broke off mid-sentence. 'I was only taking it all on myself, I didn't want you to blame Sister Joan.'

'Oh for God's sake, Helen, who in their right mind would blame Sister Joan or any Sister? Cut it out, will you?'

It was the sharpest remark that had ever been made in St Martin's House, a place of peace and consideration.

Sister Joan and Sister Maureen looked shocked at Nessa with her white tired face going up the stairs.

Helen looked at all three of them and burst into tears again.

Sister Brigid never seemed to be aware of any little atmosphere. It was one of her characteristics. Sometimes Helen thought it was a weakness, a rare insensitivity in an otherwise remarkable character. Other times she wondered whether it might in fact be a blessing and something that Sister Brigid cultivated purposely.

There was no mention made of Helen's red eyes and blotchy face as they sat, heads bent, waiting for Sister Brigid to say the simple blessing over their food. Nobody acknowledged that Nessa looked white and drawn, though they were solicitous about passing her things and smiling at her a little more often than they smiled at the rest of the table. Eleven women including Brigid, the quiet Mother Superior who never used that title. She had been very stern with Helen for calling her Reverend Mother.

'But isn't that what you are?' Helen had been startled.

'We are sisters here, it's a community, this is our home, it's not an institution with ranks and rules and pecking orders.'

It had been hard to grasp at first, but after three years Helen felt that she had surely earned her place. Biting her lip she looked at the ten women chattering around the simple meal. Made more simple still by the fact of her forgetting the vegetables.

They talked easily about the work they had done during the day, the practicalities, the funny things, the optimisms, the chance of more help here, of fighting the cuts there.

Brigid had said that they must not bring their problems to the supper table or even home to the house, otherwise St Martin's would be weighed down by the collective grief and anxiety of these workers in the sad end of society. They would become so depressed if they were to dwell every night on the amount of misery and pain they had seen in their different worlds that it would be counter productive. People needed escape, time out, retreat. They didn't have the luxury of going *on* retreat like the nuns of a previous generation, but neither did they have the demands and responsibilities that many trained social workers who were married women or men had. There were no children needing time, love and attention, there were no social demands nor the intensity of one-to-one relationships. Brigid told them often that small communities of nuns like theirs were ideally situated to serve the many and apparently increasing needs around them in London. The only thing they had to fear was too great an introspection or a depth of worry which might render their help less effective because it was becoming self-important.

Helen looked around at their faces: apart from Nessa who was still looking frail the others were like women who had few cares. You would not know from listening to them that some of them had spent the day in magistrates' courts, in police stations, in welfare centres or in squats and run-down council estates, or like herself in a clothing centre.

She was pleased that they laughed when she told them about the bag lady who had come in to get a coat that morning. Helen's job was to arrange the sorting, the dry-cleaning and mending of clothes that came in to the bureau. A generous dry-cleaning firm let them use the big machine free at off-peak hours if they ensured that paying customers didn't realize they were sharing with hand-me-downs for tramps.

The woman had been very insistent. 'Nothing in green, I've always found green an unlucky colour, Sister. No, red's a bit flashy, in my day only a certain kind of woman wore red. A nice mauve, a lilac shade. No? Well, safer to settle for a brown then. Not what you'd call cheerful for spring. But still.' A heavy sigh. Helen Doyle was a good mimic, she caught the woman perfectly, all the others could see her as clearly as if they had been there.

'You should be on the stage, Helen,' said Joan admiringly.

'Maybe she will one day,' said Maureen innocently.

Helen's face clouded. 'But how can I? I'll be here. Why don't any of you believe I'm going to stay? I've joined as much as you'll let me.' The lip was trembling. Dangerously.

Sister Brigid intervened. 'What did she look like in the brown coat, Helen?' she asked firmly. The warning was plain.

With an effort Helen pulled herself back to the story. The woman had asked for a scarf too, something toning she said, as if she had been in the accessories department of a fashion store.

'I found her a hat in the end, a yellow hat with a brown feather in it, and I gave her a yellow brooch I was wearing myself. I said it sort of brought the whole colour scheme together. She nodded like the Queen Mother and was very gracious about it, then she picked up her four bags of rubbish and went back to the Embankment.'

'Good, Helen.' Sister Brigid was approving. 'If you can make it seem like a fashion store with a bit of choice then you're doing it exactly right, that woman would never have taken what she thought was charity. Well done.'

The others all smiled too, and Nessa's smile was particularly broad.

'There's no one like Helen for these old misfits,' Nessa said, as if to make up for her earlier outburst. 'You always get on to the wave length so well.'

'It's probably that I'm there already,' Helen said. 'You know, about taking one to know one and all that.'

'You'd never be a bag lady, Helen,' Brigid said affectionately. 'You'd lose the bags.' The laughter around the supper table in St Martin's was warm and good-natured.

Helen felt very much at peace and very much at home.

She thought she heard Nessa get up in the middle of the night and go downstairs. It was an old house full of creaks and sounds. They could each recognize the others' steps and coughs. Like a family.

Helen was about to get up and follow her down to the kitchen for cocoa and a chat. But she hesitated. Brigid had often said that when people were upset the last thing they needed was someone to arrive in on top of them offering tea and sympathy. Helen had listened without agreeing. It was what she always wanted. There hadn't been any of it at home. Daddy too tired, Mother too anxious, Anna too busy, Brendan too withdrawn. It was why she had found this other family. They always had time to sympathize. It was what their work was all about. Listening.

Surely she should go down now and listen to Nessa, and maybe tell her all about the drunk today and how upsetting it had been. But maybe not. As Helen was deciding she heard Sister Brigid's light step go down the stairs.

She crept to the landing to hear what they were talking about.

Strangely it was all about the garden, and what they should plant. Shrubs would be nice to sit and look out on, Brigid said.

'When do you ever sit down?' Nessa spoke in a tone that was both scolding and admiring.

'I do sit down, lots of times. It's like that thing we got to charge the batteries for the radio, it puts new energy into me, into all of us.'

'You never seem tired, Brigid.'

'I feel it, I tell you. I'm getting old anyway, I'll be forty soon.'

Nessa laughed aloud. 'Don't be ridiculous, you're only thirty-four.'

'Well, forty is the next milestone; I don't mind, it's just that I don't have as much energy as I used to. Who'll do the garden, Nessa? I'm too full of aches and pains. You can't be spared from the children.'

'After today I think I could be spared only too easily. I don't have any judgement . . .'

'Shush, shush . . . Who will we ask to do it? It's hard work, you know, trying to make that little patch look like something restful and peaceful.'

'Helen maybe?' Nessa sounded doubtful.

Helen on the landing felt a dull red come up her neck and to her face.

'Oh, she'd do it certainly, and she'd be full of imagination . . .' Sister Brigid sounded doubtful too. 'The only thing is . . .'

Nessa came in immediately. 'The only thing is she'd lose interest halfway through after we'd bought all the plants, and they'd die. Is that what you mean?'

Helen felt a wave of fury come over her.

'No, it's just that I don't like her to think that we're shunting her to do something that isn't really . . . our work, you know.'

'But it's *all* our work, isn't it?' Nessa sounded surprised.

'Yes, you know that, I know that, Helen doesn't. Anyway we'll see. Come on, Nessa, if us old ones are to be any use to this Community we'd better get a few hours of sleep a night.' She was laughing, Sister Brigid had a lovely warm laugh that included you and wrapped you up.

'Thank you, Brigid.'

'I did nothing, said nothing.'

'It's the way you do it, say it.' Nessa was obviously feeling better now.

Helen slipped back into her room and stood for a long time with her back to the door.

So they thought she wouldn't finish things? She'd show them, by heavens would she show them.

She'd dig that garden single-handed, she'd build a magic garden where they could all sit and think and be at peace and they would realize that Sister Helen more than any of them knew that anything done for the Community was as important as any other thing. Then they would have to let her take her vows. And she would be completely part of their world. And safe. Safe from everything else.

Like everything Helen had touched, the building of the garden had its highs and lows. Helen found three boys who said they were anxious to help the Sisters in their great work building a refuge and they'd be happy to join in with a bit of the heavy work. They brought spades and shovels and Sister Joan said it was beyond the mind's understanding how much tea they wanted, how they couldn't have this butter on their bread, or marge, it had to be a particular spread. And they wondered was there a little something going at lunch time. Sister Joan said nervously that the nuns all had their meal in the evening, but fearing that the volunteer workforce would abandon everything, she ran out and bought provisions.

After three days Sister Brigid thanked them and said that there could be no further imposition on their kindness.

The lads had begun to enjoy the good food and overpowering gratitude of the nuns and didn't really want to leave at all.

They left the place in a possibly greater mess; earth had been turned over certainly, but no pattern or plan had emerged.

But Helen soldiered on, she dug until she had blisters, she spent her scant off-time in bookshops reading the sections of gardening books that concentrated on 'Starting Out'.

She learned the differences between one kind of soil and another.

She told the Sisters amazing things each evening about the sexuality of growing things.

'They never told us a word about this at school,' she said indignantly. 'It's the kind of thing you should know, about everything being male and female even in the garden, for heaven's sake, and going mad to propagate.'

'Let's hope it all does propagate after your hard work,' Brigid said. 'You really are great, Helen, I don't know where you find the energy.'

Helen flushed with pleasure. And she was able to remember those words of praise too a little later when the problem of the bedding plants came up. The nice woman who said she really admired the Sisters even though she wasn't a Roman Catholic herself and disagreed with the Pope about everything, brought them some lovely plants as a gift. Red-faced with exertion from planting them, Helen assured the others that evening they were very very lucky. It would have cost a fortune if they had to buy all these, nobody knew how expensive things were in garden centres.

She had barely finished talking when the news came that the plants had all been dug up from a park and a nearby hotel. The repercussions were endless. The explanations from every side seemed unsatisfactory. Helen said she had to protect her sources and wouldn't give them the name of the benefactor. But in mid conversation she mentioned to the young policewoman that Mrs Harris couldn't possibly have taken them deliberately, she wasn't that kind of person, and that was enough for the two constables to identify exactly who she was talking about. Mrs Harris had been in trouble before. A latter-day Robin Hood was how she was known down at the station, taking clothes from one washing-line, ironing them and presenting them as gifts to another home.

Only Helen could have got herself involved with Mrs Harris, the other nuns sighed. Only Helen could have got them all involved, was Brigid's view, but she didn't say anything at the time.

Helen realized that the garden couldn't be considered her full-time work. And even when she had reassured the Community that she was taking on no further assistance from gargantuan eaters of meals or compulsive plant thiefs she felt she should take on more than just a horticultural role. She was determined to play her part as fully as possible. She said she would do half the skivvy work, leaving Sister Joan or Sister Maureen free for a half day to do something else.

It worked. Or it sort of worked.

They all got used to the fact that Helen might not have scrubbed the table or taken in their washing when it started to rain. They knew that she would never know when they were running out of soap or cornflakes. That she wouldn't really rinse out and hang the dishcloths up to dry. But she was there, eager and willing to help.

And she did answer the phone and more or less coped when people came to call.

Which is why she was there when Renata Quigley came to see the Sister in charge.

Renata. Tall and dark, somewhere in her mid-thirties. Married for fifteen years to Frank Quigley.

What on earth could she want, and how had she tracked Helen down to St Martin's? Helen felt her heart race and she could almost hear it thumping in her ears. At the same time there was a sense of ice-cold water in the base of her stomach.

She hadn't seen Renata since the wedding, but she had seen pictures of her of course, in magazines and in the trade papers Daddy had brought home. Mrs Frank Quigley, the former Miss Renata Palazzo, exchanging a joke or enjoying herself at the races or presenting a prize to the apprentice of the year or walking among the high and mighty at some charity function.

She was very much more beautiful than Helen had thought, she had skin that Mother would have called sallow but looked olive-like and beautiful with her huge dark eyes and her dark shiny hair with its expensive cut. She wore her scarf very artistically caught in a brooch and draped as if it were part of her green and gold dress. She carried a small leather handbag in green and gold squares.

Her face was troubled and her long thin hands with their dark red nails were twisting round the little patchwork bag.

'Can I please speak to the Sister in charge?' she asked Helen.

Helen looked at her, open-mouthed. Renata Quigley didn't recognize her. Suddenly the memory of an old movie came back to her, and some beautiful actress looking straight at the camera and saying, 'Nobody looks at the face of a nun.' It was the kind of thing that would drive Sister Brigid mad. Helen had never forgotten it. Until this moment she had never realized how true it was. There was Renata Quigley on her doorstep looking straight into her eyes and she didn't recognize Helen, the daughter of Deirdre and Desmond Doyle, her husband's friends.

Helen who had caused so much trouble that time.

But perhaps she had never known. With another shock Helen realized that Renata might have been told nothing at the time.

While all this was going through her mind, Helen stood at the door, a girl in a grey jumper and skirt, with a cross around her neck, her hair tied back with a black ribbon, her face perhaps covered in grime from the garden where she had been when she heard the doorbell.

Perhaps she didn't even look like a nun.

It was obvious that Renata didn't connect her with the child she had known in Rosemary Drive, Pinner, when she had come to call.

'I'm sorry, there's nobody here but me,' Helen said, recovering slightly.

'Are you one of the Community?' Renata looked doubtful.

'Yes, well yes. I'm here in St Martin's, part of the house, one of the Sisters.' It was straining the truth but Helen was not going to let Renata Quigley go until she knew why she had come here in the first place.

'It's a little complicated, Sister,' Renata said nervously.

Helen's smile nearly split her face in half.

'Well, come on in and sit down and tell me, that's what we're here for,' she said.

And she stood back and held the door open while Frank Quigley's wife walked into St Martin's. Into Helen's home.

That face, that dark lean face with the high cheekbones. Helen Doyle knew it so well. She remembered well her mother saying with some satisfaction that it would run to fat all the same in the end, mark her words, all the middle-aged Italian women you saw with several chins, they too had been lean girls with long, perfectly formed faces. It was in their diets, in their lifestyles, in the amount of olive oil they managed to put away.

When she was a child Helen had been irritated with her mother for all this kind of niggling. What did it matter? Why was Mother so anxious to criticize, to find fault?

But later, later Helen was to look at pictures of the face and wish that her own were like it, that she had hollows and soft golden skin instead of round cheeks and freckles. She would have killed to get that dark heavy hair she saw in the photographs, and wear those loop earrings, which made Helen look like a tinker running away from an encampment, but made Renata Palazzo Quigley look glamorous as an exotic princess from a far land.

'I came here because I heard that there is a Sister Brigid . . . I thought perhaps . . .' She faltered.

'I suppose you could say I'm Sister Brigid's deputy,' Helen said. In ways it could be true. She *was* in charge of the house when they were all out, that could be considered being a deputy. 'I'll be glad to do what I can.'

Helen fought back the other thoughts in her mind. She simply closed a door on Renata's picture in a silver frame on a small table with a long white cloth reaching to the floor. She closed another door on Frank Quigley, her father's friend, with tears in his eyes. She tried to think only of this moment. A woman had come to St Martin's for help in some way, and Sister Brigid was out. Helen was in charge.

'It's just that you're very young . . .' Renata was doubtful.

Helen was reassuring. She had her hand on the kettle and paused to look at Renata.

'No, no, I'm much more experienced than you think.'

She felt a little light-headed. Could she really be saying these words to Frank Quigley's wife?

It had been impossible in Rosemary Drive that time when Father had lost his job. Helen thought back on it and it flashed in front of her as if she were watching a video on that machine that she had got for St Martin's once because the company had *assured* her it was free for a month and there would be no obligation. It had all been very difficult, the business about the video, like everything.

But nothing was as frightening as the time her father had left Palazzo. There was a council of war every night and Mother had warned them that they must tell nobody.

'But why?' Helen had begged. She couldn't bear her sister and brother to accept that this was the way things should be from now on. 'Why does it have to be a secret? It's not Daddy's fault that they changed the place. He can get another job. Daddy can get *any* job.'

She remembered still how Mother had snapped at her.

'Your father doesn't want *any* job, he wants his job at Palazzo back. And he will have it back soon, so in the meantime nothing is to be said. Do you hear me, Helen? Outside this house not one word is to be said. Everyone is to think that your father is going to work as usual in Palazzo.'

'But how will he earn money?' Helen had asked.

It was a reasonable question. To this day she didn't regret it, like she sometimes regretted the things she had said, the offers she had made, the questions she had asked.

Anna had said nothing, for an easy life she had explained.

Brendan had said nothing because nothing was what Brendan always said.

But Helen couldn't say nothing.

She was sixteen years old, grown up, in her last year at school. She would not stay on and do A levels like Anna. Even though she felt she was twice as bright as Anna in many ways. No, Helen was going to see the world, try her hand at this and that, get on-the-job experience.

She was so full of life, at sixteen some people thought she was years younger, a big schoolgirl. Other people thought she was years older, a lively student going on twenty.

Frank Quigley had no idea how old she was the afternoon she went to see him in his office.

The dragon woman Miss Clarke had protected him as she always had. Helen wondered could she possibly be there still? It was years ago. Surely she had given up hoping that Mr Quigley was going to look into her eyes and say that she was beautiful without her glasses?

Helen had left her school blazer downstairs with the doorman, and had opened the top buttons of her school shirt in order to look more grown up. The dragon woman had eventually let her in. There were very few who could withstand Helen when she was in full flow. Explanation came hard upon explanation, and all the time she was moving towards his office. Before the dragon realized it, Helen was in.

She was flushed and excited.

Frank Quigley had looked up, surprised.

'Well, well, Helen Doyle. You're not meant to be here, I'm sure.'

'I know.' She laughed easily.

'You should be at school, not bursting into people's offices.'

'I do a lot of things I shouldn't do.'

She had sat on the corner of his desk swinging her legs, shoulders hunched up. He looked at her with interest. Helen knew she had been right to come here, the silence of Rosemary Drive was no way to handle things. There had to be confrontation.

'What can I do for you?' He had a mock gallantry. He was quite handsome in a way, dark with curly hair. Old of course, as old as her father, even. But different.

'I suppose you could take me to lunch,' she said. It was the kind of thing people said in films and in plays on telly. It worked for them, perhaps it would for her too. She gave him a smile much braver and more confident than she felt inside.

'Lunch?' He laughed in a short bark. 'Lord, Helen, I don't know what kind of lifestyles you think we live down here . . .' He broke off, looking at her disappointed face. 'Aw hell, I've not had lunch out for years.'

'I never had,' Helen said simply.

That did it.

They went to an Italian restaurant which was almost dark like night and there were candles on the table.

Every time Helen tried to bring up the subject of her father he skirted around it. She knew that in those television series about big business they always came to the point at the coffee stage.

There was no coffee. There was a Zambucca. A liquorice-tasting liqueur. With a little coffee bean in it and the waiter set it alight. Helen had never seen anything so marvellous.

'It's like a grown-up's birthday cake,' she said delightedly.

'You're fairly grown up for seventeen,' Frank said. 'Or is it older?'

This was to her advantage, if he thought she was older than sixteen he would listen better. Take her more seriously.

'Almost eighteen,' she lied.

'You've been around, despite the schoolgirl get-up,' he said.

'I've been around,' Helen said.

The more travelled he thought she was, the more he would listen when the time came to talk.

The time didn't come to talk.

He had been affectionate and admiring and had patted her cheek and even held her face up to the candlelight to see if there was any telltale ring of red wine around her mouth before she went back to school.

'I'm not going back to school,' Helen said very definitely. She looked Frank Quigley straight in the eye. 'You know that, and I know that.'

'I certainly hoped it,' he said, and his voice sounded a bit throaty. Something about the way he stroked her cheek and lifted her hair made it difficult to talk about her father's job, Helen had felt it would somehow be wrong to bring the subject up when he was being so attentive. She was relieved when he suggested they go back to his place so that they could talk properly.

'Do you mean the office?' She was doubtful. The dragon would keep interrupting.

'I don't mean the office,' he said very steadily, looking at her. 'You know that and I know that.'

'I certainly hoped it,' she said, echoing his words.

The apartment block was very luxurious. Mother had always said she could not understand why Frank Quigley hadn't bought himself a proper house now that he was a married man. But then he probably had expectations of the big white house with the wrought-iron gates and the large well-kept gardens. The house of the Palazzos.

But Mother couldn't have known how splendid the flat was. Flat wasn't the word for it, really. It was on two floors, there was a lovely staircase leading up to a floor which had a big balcony with chairs and a table outside, the balcony ran along the whole length of the place, past the sitting room and the bedroom.

They went out the sitting room door to look at the view from the balcony. And Helen's heart lurched with a sudden realization as they left the balcony to return indoors through the bedroom.

Her hand went to her throat in an automatic gesture of fright. 'Your wife. . . ?' she said.

Long long afterwards when she played it back in her mind, she thought of all the things she could have said, should have said, might have said. How had it been that the only thing which *did* come to her to say was something that could obviously be taken to mean that she was willing and enthusiastic, but just afraid of discovery?

'Renata isn't here, Helen,' Frank Quigley said softly. 'You know that and I know that, just as we both knew you weren't going back to school.'

She had heard that it wasn't healthy to try to blot something out of your memory, to try to pretend that it had never happened. Helen didn't care whether it was healthy or not, for a long time she tried to forget that afternoon.

The moment of no return, the look of bewilderment and anger when she had shied away from him first.

The urgency, and the pain, the sheer hurt and stabbing and fear that he was so out of control that he might do literally anything and kill her. The way he rolled away and groaned, not like that first groan but with shame and then with fury.

'You told me, you said you'd been around,' he said with his head in his hands as he sat on one side of the bed, white, naked and ridiculous-looking.

She lay on the other beside the silver-framed photograph of the lean olive-faced Renata. Silent and disapproving-looking beside her marriage bed. As if she had always known what might happen there one day.

Helen had lain there and looked at the picture of Our Lady, it was the one you saw everywhere called Madonna of the Wayside. At least Our Lady hadn't had to go through all this to get our Lord. It had been done miraculously. Helen looked at the picture because that meant she didn't have to look at her father's friend Frank Quigley who was crying into his hands. And it meant she didn't have to look at the white sheets which were stained with blood and she didn't have to think about how badly he had injured her and if she would have to go to a doctor. Or if she might be pregnant.

She didn't know how long it was before she made a move to the bathroom and cleaned herself up. She didn't seem to have been very badly injured, the bleeding had stopped.

She dressed herself carefully and dusted herself with Renata's talcum powder which wasn't in a tin like ordinary powder, it was in a big glass bowl with a pink swansdown puff.

When she came out, Frank was dressed. And white-faced.

'The bed. . . ?' she began.

'Forget the bloody bed . . .'

'I could . . .'

'You've done enough,' he snapped.

Helen's eyes filled with tears. 'I've done enough? What did I do, I came to talk to you about my father and why he'd been sacked, it was you, you who did all this . . .' With her hand she waved in the direction of the bed.

His face was contrite. 'Your father. You did this to try and get Desmond back his piffling little job. Jesus Christ, you'd whore around to get your father a penny-farthing nothing place in a supermarket.'

'It is not a nothing job.' Helen's face burned with anger. 'He was a very important person there, and now, now he's been sacked and Mother says we are not to tell anyone, neighbours, relatives, anyone, and he goes off each morning pretending he's going to work . . .'

Frank looked at her in disbelief.

'Yes he does, and I just wanted to have lunch with you and tell you straight out how bad it was and you'd understand because you were Dad's friend way back at school in the Brothers when you used to climb over stone walls . . . he told me . . . and you're doing so well there and married to the boss's daughter and everything . . . And *that's* all I wanted, I didn't whore around, I've never slept with anyone in my life and I didn't mean to sleep with you, I wasn't to know you'd fall in love with me and all this would happen, and now you say it's all my fault.' She burst into tears.

He put his arms around her and held her close to him. 'Christ, you're only a child, what have I done? Christ Almighty what did I do?'

She sobbed against his jacket for a bit.

He held her away from him and his eyes were full of tears.

'I'll never be able to make amends. Literally there's nothing I can do to tell you how sorry I am. I'd never . . . never if I hadn't thought . . . I was so sure that . . . but that doesn't matter now. What matters is you.'

Helen wondered had he always loved her or was it only now. People could fall in love so easily.

'We'll have to forget this,' she said. She knew that a woman had to take the lead in such matters. Men would dither and give in to temptation. Anyway there was no temptation for Helen, if this was what it was like then the rest of the world could have it as far as she was concerned.

'It happened, it can't be forgotten. I'll do anything to make it up to you.'

'Yes, but we can't keep on seeing each other, it wouldn't be fair.' She looked over at the picture of Renata.

She thought he looked puzzled. 'No, of course,' he said.

'And we won't tell anyone, either of us.' She was girlishly eager about this.

'Lord no, nobody at all,' he said, looking highly relieved.

'And my father?' She spoke without guile, she spoke as Helen always spoke, eager to get over the meaning and burden of what she wanted to say, heedless of timing or other people's feelings.

She saw a look of pain cross Frank Quigley's face.

'Your father will get a job. He told me that he didn't need one, that he was looking about, that he had plenty of offers.' Frank's voice was cold. 'He will be reinstated in

Palazzo. Not overnight, I have to talk to Carlo, these things have to be done tactfully. They can take a little time.'

Helen nodded vigorously.

'And you, Helen. Will you be all right, will you forgive me?'

'Of course. It was a misunderstanding.' Her voice sounded eager, as if she too wanted to be let off a hook.

'That's what it was, Helen, and Helen listen to me, please. The only thing I can tell you is that it won't always be like this . . . it will be lovely and happy . . .' He was straining to try to tell her that this gross happening would not be the pattern for the rest of the lovemaking in her life.

He might as well have been talking to the wall.

'Are you sure I couldn't do anything about the sheets, like a launderette or anything?'

'No.'

'But what will you say?'

'Please, Helen, please.' His face was pained.

'Will I go now, Frank?'

He looked unable to cope.

'I'll drive you . . .' His voice trailed away. His face showed that he didn't know where he was to drive her.

'No, it's all right, I can get the bus. I know where I am, I'll just get the bus home and say . . . say I don't feel well.' Helen gave a little giggle. 'It's true in a way. But listen, Frank, I don't have the bus fare, could I ask you . . .'

She couldn't understand why Frank Quigley had tears pouring down his face when he handed her the coins and closed her hand over them.

'Will you be all right?' He was begging to be reassured. He was not ready for what she told him.

'Frank.' Helen gave a little laugh. 'I'm not a child, for heaven's sake, I was sixteen last week. I'm a grown-up. I'll find my way home on the bus.'

She left then because she couldn't bear the look on his face.

Of course he had to stay away from the house in case he wasn't able to control himself when he saw her. That's what she told herself.

She never remembered him coming to Rosemary Drive again after that. There had always been some excuse, he was on a conference, he was abroad, he and Renata were going to see some of her relations in Italy. He was terribly sorry, it was such bad timing. Mother said he was getting above himself, still wasn't it great that they never had to go to him cap in hand to ask him to reinstate his old friend in Palazzo's? At least that idea had come straight from Mr Palazzo himself, who had realized that this was no way to treat valued managerial staff.

Helen never knew whether her father realized that it was Frank. It was hard to talk to her father, he had built a little shell around himself almost for fear of being hurt, like Mother's shell for fear of letting themselves down somehow.

She had found those last school terms endless, the world had changed since that strange afternoon. She was always frightened of being misunderstood. She had started to scream one day when the singing master at school asked her to come into the storeroom and help him carry down the sheet music to the school hall. The man hadn't touched her but she had this sudden claustrophobic fear that he would think she was encouraging him somehow, and that he would begin this hurtful business and then blame her. As things turned out he *did* blame her very much indeed and had said that she was a neurotic hysterical fool, a troublemaker, and if she were the last female on earth he wouldn't touch her with a barge-pole.

The Principal of the school seemed to agree with him and asked Helen sharply why she had begun to scream if she agreed that there had been no question of an attack or even an advance.

Helen had said glumly that she didn't know. She had felt that she was in some kind of situation she couldn't handle and that unless she *did* scream something else would happen and it would all be too late and too complicated.

'Has anything of this sort happened to you before?' The Principal was not entirely sympathetic. Helen Doyle had always been a difficult pupil, gushy, anxious to please, always creating waves of trouble around her.

Helen had said no, unconvincingly.

The Principal had sighed. 'Well, you can be certain that it will keep happening to you, Helen. It's your personality. This sort of thing will turn up in your life over and over again, situations that you can't handle. That is unless you pull yourself together and take control of your own actions.'

She sounded so final it was as if she were passing a life sentence.

Helen had been dazed at the unfairness of it all.

It was then that she decided to be a nun.

And now, years later, she was almost a nun. Well, she would be a nun if Sister Brigid had not been so adamant about telling her that she was only using the convent as a crutch, that she was using it as a place to hide and that those days were over in religious life.

Helen felt safe in St Martin's. And even as she made a mug of coffee and sat down to join the beautiful Renata Palazzo Quigley whose face had looked at her from a silver frame on that frightening day . . . she felt safe. Safe from the memories and the fear of that time.

'Tell me what you want and I'll see if there's anything we can do,' she said with the big smile that made everyone love Helen. When they met her first.

'It's very simple,' Renata said. 'We want a baby.'

It was very simple. And very sad. Helen hugged her mug of coffee to her and listened. Frank was too old at forty-six. Too old. How ridiculous, but adoption societies wouldn't consider him. Also he had a poor medical history, some heart trouble, nothing very serious, due to stress at work, and all businessmen had this in today's world. Natural mothers and fathers were allowed to bring a child into the world into any kind of appalling conditions, tenements, places of vice, nobody stopped them and said that they couldn't have any children. But for adoption everything had to be over-perfect.

Renata had heard that sometimes, if she were only to meet the right person, there must be occasions where a child could be given to a good loving home, to a father and mother who would love the little boy or girl as their own. There surely were cases when this happened.

There was a look of longing in her eyes.

Helen patted the hand of the woman who had once looked at her from the silver frame.

She had told Renata that they would meet again in a week when she would have made some inquiries. She thought it wiser not to consult Sister Brigid for the moment. Sister Brigid being an authority figure had to keep so well within the limits of the law . . . Better just let Helen inquire a little. All right? All right.

She told nobody. They said she looked feverish and excited, and Helen entertained the Community with tales of how she made her garden grow.

'Anyone call?' Brigid asked.

'No. Not anyone really, you know, usual callers.' Helen avoided her eye. It was the first time she had told a direct lie in St Martin's. It didn't feel good but it was for the best in the end.

If she could do this one thing, if she could do what she hoped she might be able to do, then even at the age of twenty-one her whole life would have been worth living.

It was Nessa's turn to do the kitchen for half a day. Nessa was the one woman at St Martin's who found Helen almost impossible to get on with. Normally when they worked together Helen stayed out of Nessa's way. But this time she positively hung around her neck.

'What happens when the children are born to really hopeless mothers, Nessa? Don't you wish you could give them to proper homes from the start?'

'What I wish isn't important, I don't rule the world.' Nessa was short, she was scrubbing the kitchen floor and Helen kept standing in her way.

'But wouldn't a child be much better off?'

'Mind, Helen, please. I've just washed there.'

'And you always have to register the births, no matter what kind of mother?'

'What do you mean?'

'I mean do you have to go to the town hall or the registry office or whatever and sort of say who the child is?'

'No, I don't always.'

'Oh, why not?'

'Because I'm usually not the one who does it, it depends. It depends. Helen, do you think that if you're not going to do any work you could move out of the kitchen so that I could clean it?'

'And no babies end up without being registered?'

'How could they?'

'I don't know.' Helen was disappointed. She had thought there might be long twilight times when nobody knew who or what the baby was. She hadn't understood how the Welfare State at least checked its citizens in and out of the world.

'And foundlings, babies in phone boxes, in churches, where do they end up?'

Nessa looked up in alarm. 'God, Helen, don't tell me you found one?'

'No, worse luck,' Helen said. 'But if I did would I have to register it?'

'No, Helen, of course not, if *you* found a baby you could keep the baby and dress him or her up when you remembered, and feed the child when it occurred to you, or when there was nothing else marginally more interesting to do.'

'Why are you so horrible to me, Nessa?' Helen asked.

'Because I am basically pretty horrible.'

'You can't be, you're a nun. And you're not horrible to the others.'

'Ah, that's true. The real thing about being horrible is that it's selective.'

'And why did you select me?' Helen didn't seem put out or hurt, she was interested. Actually interested.

Nessa was full of guilt.

'Oh, for heaven's sake, I'm just short-tempered, I hate doing this bloody floor, and you're so young and carefree and get everything you want. I'm sorry, Helen, forgive me, I'm always asking you to forgive me. Really I am.'

'I know.' Helen was thoughtful. 'People often are, I seem to bring out the worst in them somehow.'

Sister Nessa looked after her uneasily as Helen wandered back into the garden. There was something more than usual on her scattered brain and it was weighing very heavily.

Helen rang Renata Quigley. Same address, same apartment, same bed presumably. She said that she was still inquiring but that it wasn't as easy as people thought.

'I never thought it was easy,' sighed Renata. 'But somehow it does make all the going out to functions and to this celebration and that celebration a little easier if I think that somebody as kind as you, Sister, is looking out for me.'

With a thrill of shock that went right through her body Helen Doyle realized that she would meet Frank and Renata Quigley at her parents' silver wedding party.

Frank Quigley had been the best man back in those days when he and Father were about equal.

Before everything had changed.

The garden was finished and more or less ran itself. Sister Joan loved being in the clothing centre, and she was quick with a needle, so that she could do an alteration on the spot, move the buttons on a jacket for an old man, praise him, admire him, say that the fit made all the difference in the world. Let him think it was custom tailored.

There was no real work for Helen, no real place.

Once more she asked Brigid about taking her vows.

'It's very harsh to keep me on the outside, seriously I have been here for so long, you *can't* say it's a passing fancy any more now, can you?' She begged and implored.

'You're running, Helen,' Brigid said. 'I told you that from the word go. This is not like a convent in the films, a place in a forest where people went to find peace, it's a working house. You have to have found peace already to bring it here.'

'But I've found it now,' Helen implored.

'No, you're afraid of engaging with real people, that's why you're with us.'

'You're all more real than anyone else. Honestly I've never met any group I like so much.'

'That's not the whole story. We shelter you from something. We can't go on doing that, it's not our role. If it's men, if it's sex, if it's the cut and thrust of the business world . . . we all have had to face it and cope with it. You're still hiding from something.'

'I suppose it is sex a bit.'

'Well, you don't have to keep indulging in it,' Brigid laughed. 'Go back out into the world, Helen, I beg you, for a couple of years. Stay in touch with us and then if you still feel this is your home, come back and we'll look at it all again. I really do think you should go. For your own good.'

'Are you asking me to leave. Truly?'

'I'm suggesting it, but do you see what I mean about this not being like the real world? If this was a real place, I'd be telling you to go or promoting you. It's too protective here for you, I feel it in my bones.'

'Let me stay for a little while. Please.'

'Stay until after your parents' twenty-fifth wedding anniversary,' Brigid said unexpectedly. 'That seems to be preying on your mind for some reason. And then after that we'll see.'

Helen went away from Sister Brigid's little workroom, more wretched than she had been for a long time.

She looked so sad that Sister Nessa asked did she want to come and help with the young mothers. This was the first time the invitation had ever been made.

Helen went along, for once silent and without prattle.

'Don't be disapproving or anything, will you Helen?' Nessa asked nervously. 'We're not meant to be passing judgement, just helping them cope.'

'Sure,' Helen said.

She sat listless as any of the girls who were on low-dosage anti-depressants or who lived in fear of a pimp who had wanted them to have an abortion. Nessa looked at her from time to time with concern. But Helen was quiet and obedient. She did everything she was asked to do. She was useful too in a way. She went out to the flats of those who had not turned up, Nessa had always been nervous since the incident of the little Simon who had crawled out of his flat almost into the mainstream of rush-hour traffic.

In the late afternoon Nessa asked Helen to go and find Yvonne, who was eight months pregnant with her second child. Her eldest, a beautiful girl with Jamaican eyes like her father long gone, and a Scottish accent like her mother who gave birth to her at sixteen, was waiting at the door.

'Mummy's gaen do wee wee,' she said helpfully.

'That's great,' Helen said, and brought the toddler back into the house.

From the bathroom came the groans and the cries of Yvonne.

Suddenly Helen found courage.

'You're better in your bedroom,' she said suddenly to the chubby child and moved a chest of drawers to make sure the child couldn't get out.

Then she went to cope with what she thought was a miscarriage in the lavatory.

But in the middle of the blood, the screams and the definite smell of rum all around the place, Helen heard a small cry.

The baby was alive.

Yvonne remembered nothing of it all. She had been so drunk that the day passed in a terrible blur.

They told her she had lost the child, that she had flushed it down the lavatory.

The ambulance men had been tender and gentle as they lifted her on to the stretcher, they had looked around the place and even down the lavatory bowl in confusion.

'They told us she was near to her time, she couldn't have got rid of a full-term foetus, surely.'

But Helen, the cool-eyed girl who said she was a voluntary welfare worker at the mother and child centre, and that she lived with the Sisters in St Martin's, assured them that she had not been able to get in to the flat and had heard continuous flushing of the chain and then found the place covered in blood.

The small round three-year-old seemed to back her up, saying that her mother had been long time wee wee and that Helen had been long time at the door.

Nessa, ashen-faced and trying not to let herself believe that this would never have happened if she had sent anyone else but Helen, agreed that Helen had been gone ages and ages and could get no reply. Helen had made a call to Nessa saying that there were problems but that she knew she would get in if she could persuade the child to open the door. She had called from a nearby shop where she had stopped to buy a bottle of milk for herself because she felt faint thinking of what might be inside.

That night, with Yvonne in her hospital bed, with Yvonne's three-year-old lodged temporarily in a local orphanage until the care order could be signed, Helen told Brigid she felt restless and she would like to go out for a walk.

'You *are* restless tonight,' Brigid said absently. 'You've been out to the garden a half a dozen times.'

'I wanted to make sure it was all right,' Helen said.

Carefully she picked up the little bundle, the boy who would inherit the Palazzo millions, and took him in her arms. She had him wrapped carefully in a towel and in one of her own nighties. She had a soft blue rug, which used to lie folded on the back of her chair, wrapped well around him.

She slipped out the back gate of St Martin's and walked until her legs were tired. Then in a shop where nobody would recognize her and mention to one of the sisters that they had seen one of the Community carrying a baby, she found a phone and telephoned Renata.

'I have it,' she said triumphantly down the phone.

'Who is this, you have what?'

'Renata, it's Sister Helen from St Martin's, I have your baby.'

'No, no, it's not possible.'

'Yes, but I must give him to you now, tonight, now this minute.'

'It's a little boy, you got us a little boy?'

'Yes. He's very very young, he's only one day old.'

Renata's voice was a screech. 'But no, one day, he will die, I cannot know what to do for a child of one day . . .'

'I don't know either, but I bought him a bottle of milk, he seems to be taking it off my finger,' Helen said simply.

'Where are you?'

'I'm in London of course, about two miles from the convent. Renata, have you any money?'

'What kind of money?' She sounded worried.

'Enough to pay for a taxi.'

'Yes, yes.'

'So will I come to your flat. And give him to you. No one must know.'

'Yes, I don't know, perhaps I should wait till . . . I don't know what to do.'

'I went to great trouble to get him for you.' Helen sounded tired.

'Oh I know, Sister, I'm so foolish, it's just that it's so quick and he is so very little.'

'I'm sure you'll learn, you can always ring someone and ask them. Will I get a taxi now, it might cost pounds?'

'Yes, come now.'

'And Frank's not there is he?'

'Frank, how did you know my husband is Frank?'

'You told me,' Helen said, biting her lip.

'I suppose I must have. I don't know what to say.'

The taxi man said that this wasn't where he wanted to go. He was on his way home. South London is what he wanted. Not miles out to Wembley.

He saw the tears beginning to form.

'Get in before I change my mind,' he said. 'Anyway, at least you've had it, let's look on the bright side, I could have ended up delivering it.'

'That's true,' Helen said, and the taxi driver looked at her anxiously, wondering would he get his fare when he got to Wembley.

She recited the address of the apartment block as if by rote and asked the driver to wait. The lady of the house would be down in a moment and would pay him.

He told the other cab drivers afterwards that he had spotted her as trouble the very moment he saw her. The moment that her eyes had filled with tears when he said perfectly normally of an evening that he wanted to go south of the river rather than up to this neck of the woods in Wembley. Anyway, he said, it all seemed to have happened at once, the lady came down and was carrying a purse with money. Classy she was and foreign, she took one look at the baby and she started to scream.

'He's got blood on him, he's not properly formed, no, no, I didn't want this! This is a baby that still is not ready to be a baby. No, no.'

She backed away from the girl in the grey skirt and jumper with her hand up to her mouth and at that moment a fellow in a Rover came along and leaped out, he took one look at what was happening and he shook the foreign woman till her head near as anything fell off, then he took the child and seemed to recognize the girl in the grey. He kept saying 'Oh my God' too, as if she were something from outer space.

Then there was a bundle of notes stuffed in the taxi man's window, four times the fare out to bloody Wembley. So he had to go and he never knew what it was all about and how it ended.

It ended badly. As everything Helen Doyle had ever touched seemed to end.

She had refused to go into the flat, crying too now, louder than Renata, but neither of the women cried as much as the bewildered hungry baby that had been born in a lavatory that morning.

Sister Brigid was summoned eventually to make some sense out of the whole scene. She came with Nessa, white-faced but calm.

Nessa saw to the baby and Brigid listened to the hysterical explanations.

The Italian woman was saying that she had intended only to inquire if any mother wanted to give her baby privately for adoption, she hadn't asked anyone to take one for her.

The tall Irish businessman was pleading for Helen, saying that she had done it for the best as she had always done everything for the best, but the world was never able to perceive it that way. He sounded tender towards her and yet terrified of her as well.

He knew her parents, he explained. Desmond Doyle had been one of his oldest friends.

'She is the daughter of those Doyles?' Shock was being piled on shock for Renata.

'Yes, she can't have known it was us.'

There was something in the way the man spoke. There was something that sounded a warning. Brigid looked from one stricken face to another to try and read the signals.

Helen was opening her mouth. 'But I *did* know, I *did* know, it's only because it *was* Frank that I'd do this, I'd never have taken a baby, and told all those lies. If it hadn't been Frank I'd not have risked the baby's life. I felt I owed it to him, after all, after everything . . .'

Brigid had worked with people for all her adult life. Mainly people who were in some kind of distress. She didn't know what was going to be said now but she felt it was crucial that whatever it was, Helen should not say it. Helen was in mid-flight, through the tears and the gulps the story was coming out.

'I never meant it to be like this, but they could have given it such a good life, so much money, and Frank's too old to adopt a child, and she said he had been having heart attacks . . .'

'You told her that?' Frank snapped at his wife.

'I thought she was a nun miles away, how did I know she was bloody Doyle's daughter?'

Helen was oblivious. 'I wanted to make amends, to make up for everything. To try and put things right. After all, my life worked out all right and I got everything I wanted, but Frank didn't, he had no children and he had heart attacks, he was punished . . . I wanted to try and even it out.'

Renata was looking from one to another now in confusion. Out in the other room Sister Nessa had quietened the baby and Helen was gathering breath again.

'You work with Mr Doyle still?' Brigid asked quickly.

'Yes, and he helped my father when he was sacked, he asked Mr Palazzo to give him back his job . . .'

Brigid saw an avenue of escape. She stood up as she spoke.

'So Helen with her usual impetuous nature decided to thank you for this by getting you a child when it was not going to be easy through the proper channels. Isn't that right?'

Frank Quigley looked into the grey eyes of Sister Brigid, competent, unemotional, strong. Irish perhaps a generation ago, but now with a London accent. She reminded him of bright men he met in business.

'That's it. Exactly, Sister.'

Helen hadn't stopped crying. Brigid felt she might not have stopped speaking either. With what seemed like a deliberate effort she put her arm around the girl's shoulder.

'Let's take you home, Helen, back to St Martin's. That's the best thing now.'

'Will I drive you?' Frank asked.

'No, but if you could get us a mini-cab or a taxi, Mr Quigley.'

At this moment Nessa came in; the baby was asleep. They would take him to the hospital, the one they knew, and where they were known. He would be looked after.

'It seems a pity in a way, Sister.' Frank looked at Sister Brigid, and she looked back. The glance was a long one.

It was a pity in many ways. They could give the boy everything, including more love than he would ever know from Yvonne.

'Yes, but if we do this, everything breaks down. Every single thing.'

He felt she was tempted.

'Not everything, just one little bit of form-filling. The mother thinks he is dead.'

'Please,' Renata said. 'Please, Sister.'

'I'm not God, I'm not even Solomon,' said Brigid.

They knew it was hard for her, and they drew together, the handsome couple. Helen watched them with a look of pain in her face.

The porter had been asked to hail a taxi, and the unlikely foursome walked to the lift, Helen tearful and supported by Sister Brigid, red-haired Sister Nessa carrying the tiny baby wrapped in its blue rug.

Renata stretched out her hand to touch Helen's arm.

'Thank you, Sister Helen, I know you meant kindly for me,' she said.

'Sister Helen has a great big heart,' Brigid said.

'Thank you,' Frank said at the door. He did not look at Helen, he looked instead admiringly into the grey eyes of Brigid.

'There are countries where it is all legal. If you like, some day you can ask me and I will tell you what I know,' she said.

'Goodbye, Frank,' Helen said.

'Thank you, Helen. Sister Brigid is right, you have a great big heart.' He touched her cheek.

In the taxi they were silent, until Helen said, 'You called me Sister Helen, does this mean I can stay?'

'It means we won't ask you to go yet. But maybe now that you have faced some things you haven't faced before, it mightn't be as necessary to hide as it once was. Perhaps you will be able to make your life somewhere else. Travel the world, even.'

This time Helen didn't think that Sister Brigid was asking her to leave. She felt better than she had felt for a long time.

She looked at Sister Nessa holding the tiny boy close to her breast.

'Isn't it sad that you can't keep the baby, Nessa,' Helen said with a rush of generous spirit. 'To make up for the one you had that died. It could be a kind of substitute, couldn't it? A consolation.'

She didn't even notice the two women glance at each other and then look out the windows on each side of the taxi.

4
Desmond

Of course the corner shop was more expensive than the supermarket but then it *was* on the corner, that's what you were paying for. And the fact that it stayed open so late at night.

Desmond liked calling in there. There was a mad magical feel about the place and the way Suresh Patel was able to pack in so many goods on his shelves . . . and in such a way that they didn't all come tumbling down. Desmond often said that Mr Patel must have a secret. Over in the big supermarket chain Palazzo Foods where Desmond worked, the principle was totally different. You had to give maximum space so that the customer could walk around and choose and best of all be persuaded by something that had not been on the original shopping list. Mr Patel's business was the other end of the market. They came in because they had run out of sugar or they hadn't bought anything for the supper and the shop they intended to go to had been closed. They came for the evening paper and a tin of beans sometimes. Mr Patel said that you'd be surprised how many people must be going home to a lonely evening. He often felt better off standing in his shop talking to whoever came and went.

Desmond's wife Deirdre said she had nothing against Mr Patel personally, he was extremely polite and respectful always, but everything was that little bit dearer there. The place was a mixem gatherem, a bit like those hucksters' shops you didn't go into years ago at home in case things mightn't be quite . . . well, fresh.

And she never knew why Desmond would stop and buy an earlier edition of the paper in the corner shop when he could have got one nearer work and had the pleasure of reading it on the way home.

Desmond found it hard to explain. There was something solid about the little place. It didn't depend on the fluctuations of far-away suppliers and huge multinationals. If Mr Patel noticed a customer asking for something he gave it a lot of thought. Like the time Desmond had asked for red-currant jelly.

'Is it a jam or a condiment?' Mr Patel had asked with interest.

'I think it can be either.' Desmond had been equally interested in the definition. Between them they decided that once it had been bought, it would be placed on a shelf with the mustards, the chutneys and the little green jars of mint sauce.

'Soon I will know exactly the tastes and temperaments of a fine British suburb, I will know enough to write a book, Mr Doyle.'

'I think you know that already, Mr Patel.'

'I am only starting, Mr Doyle, but it is all so interesting. You know the saying they have in your country about all human life is here . . . that's what I feel.'

'All human life is in my job too but I don't welcome it as much as you do.' Desmond smiled ruefully.

'Ah, that's because your job is so much more important than mine.'

Deirdre Doyle would have agreed with him, Mr Patel was right to look with respect at a man like Desmond who though well under fifty was Special Projects Manager at Palazzo. Palazzo was a name like Sainsbury's or Waitrose. Well not quite like them, but in certain areas it was just as well thought of and back home in Ireland where nobody knew any of the others anyway, a Palazzo sounded much grander.

The Patels didn't live in Rosemary Drive, naturally they lived somewhere else, somewhere more suitable for Indian and Pakistani people, Deirdre said, when anyone brought the subject up.

Desmond knew that in fact Suresh Patel, his wife, his two children and his brother lived in the tiny storerooms behind the small shop. Mrs Patel could speak no English and the brother was fat and looked as if he had some illness. He used to sit there and smile perfectly pleasantly but he spoke little and did not seem to be any help in the running of the corner shop.

For some reason that he never totally understood Desmond never mentioned that the Patel family lived there. That their two children, immaculate in school uniform and wearing blazers and spectacles, came out each morning from this tiny place. Desmond felt that somehow it demeaned the Patels to be thought to live in such a small place, and somewhere in his subconscious he felt that Deirdre might think it demeaned the neighbourhood to have Pakistanis actually living there rather than just trading.

The shop was busy in the early morning, people buying papers, bars of chocolate, orange drinks and plastic-wrapped sandwiches. The stuff that kept the commuters more or less alive on their journeys to work. The oil that ran the machinery of British industry.

Not that Desmond felt too cheery about his own part in British industry. He was on his way to work at the big headquarters of Palazzo Foods, the supermarket chain which was now ninth largest in Britain. Desmond had begun to work for it back in 1959 when it was simply called Prince. That was the year he and Frank Quigley had left Mayo and come to London by train, boat and train to make their fortune. They arrived during the heatwave that went on month after month, they thought they had come to paradise.

As Desmond took his regular morning journey down Rosemary Drive into Wood Road and on to the bus stop at the corner he often looked back on those days when things were simpler and when he and Frank worked behind the counters in the two Prince Stores. One day they might be slicing bacon, another day dressing windows. Every day they met the customers and they knew everyone who worked in the shop.

It was Frank who had seen that this was a company where they could rise and rise, it was no stopgap job. Prince Foods were breaking new ground, they were getting bigger, soon they would expand and Frank would be a manager in one branch and Desmond in another if they played their cards right. Frank played his cards magnificently. Desmond had always been slower to see the opportunities. But he saw how everything was changing and saw sadly that the higher he rose, dragged, pulled and cajoled by his friend Frank, the further he got from the people, which was what he had liked about it all in the first place.

Desmond Doyle had been a thin wiry young man then with a thick shock of fair brown hair. His children had often teased him about the old photograph, saying that he looked a proper teddy boy, but their mother wouldn't allow that at all. That was the way all young men of style looked then, she would say firmly. He looked different now, combing his hair in a way where it might look as if it was covering his head, and wearing shirts that had a neck size far wider than he wore that first summer when he had only been able to buy two shirts as his entire wardrobe and there was always one hanging on the back of a chair drying.

He supposed that many people looked back on the old days as good days even though they had been practically penniless days. He certainly did.

He could never understand why people liked the Palazzo Building so much. It was a perfect example of Art Deco, they said, a thirties masterpiece. Desmond always thought it looked like one of those big brutalist buildings you saw in documentaries about Eastern Europe. It was a square menacing-looking place, he thought, it was strange that there was a preservation order on it and articles in magazines talking about its perfect proportions.

Frank had been instrumental in getting that building for Palazzo, it was then the disused headquarters of a motor group that had gone bankrupt. Nobody else had seen its potential, but Frank Quigley who knew everything said that they had to have storage space for stock, they had to have a depot and maintenance centre for their vans and they had to have some kind of central offices. Why not combine them all behind this splendid facade?

A facade is what it was. Wonderful stairways and reception rooms on the ground floor. But upstairs a warren of prefabricated and jerry-built offices and partitions.

Accounts had been modernized and gone on line in computers, so that was housed in a modern extension at the back. But there was a strange limbo land on the third floor, a place where there were names on doors and people often bursting in saying, 'Oh, sorry'. There were vague storage areas where panelling that hadn't worked or plastic display units that hadn't fitted were left pending decisions.

There in the heart of this hidden chaos, the unacceptable face of Palazzo, lay Desmond Doyle's workplace. The Special Projects Department. Officially it was the nerve centre of new ideas, plans, concepts and illuminations that would wipe the competition off the map. In reality it was the place where Desmond worked and drew his month's salary and kept his managerial title because he was the boyhood friend of Frank Quigley. Because they went back a long way and because they had set out on the same day over a quarter of a century ago.

Frank Quigley the quiet but powerful Managing Director, the man who had seen the way to jump and jumped with the Italians when it came to takeover time. The man who had married the boss's daughter. It was thanks to Frank that Desmond walked up to the third floor of Palazzo and opened the door of his office with heavy heart.

The Special Projects Department was coming under scrutiny. There had been definite rumours that a big investigation was upcoming. Desmond Doyle felt the familiar knot of sour bile in his stomach and the panic beginning to grip his chest. What did it mean this time? An accusation that the section wasn't pulling its weight, a demand for exact quantifying of how much the last in-store presentations had realized, and the projected figures likely from the children's promotional exercises.

The antacid tablets seemed to do no good any more, he was eating them like sweets. He was weary of the confrontations and the need to seem bright. Once that business of looking bright and being on top of things had been the be-all and end-all of his day. Not any more. At an age which the rest of the world persisted in thinking of as young, Desmond Doyle felt an old, old man. Forty-six going on ninety. That's what he would have answered truthfully if anyone had asked him caringly about his age.

His office, blessedly free from the photographs that covered the walls in his home, had a pale print of a Connemara countryside. It looked somehow more mauve, blue and elegant than he remembered it, but Deirdre said it was the very spirit of the West of Ireland and he should hang it there so that it could be a conversation piece. He could talk about it to visitors, tell them this was the place he came from. Those were his roots.

Poor Deirdre, thinking that was the kind of conversation that took place in his box-like cubicle of an office. He was lucky to have walls that were not that rough glass or Perspex, he was lucky to have a desk, a telephone and two filing cabinets. The luxury of chats about roots based on over-pastelized views of County Mayo was not anything he had known. Or would ever know.

He no longer felt that the words stuck with cardboard lettering on his door were important . . . there had been no Special Projects in the old days, it was only a made-up word. There had been real jobs like Stores Development Manager, or Operations Manager. Merchandising Manager. These were what the business was about. Special Projects meant nothing to Desmond Doyle because he knew that in his case it was nothing. In other countries it was a real job, he knew that from reading the retail magazines. In Palazzo Foods it meant only a pat on the back.

Desmond remembered way back reading an advertisement which said 'A title on the door means a Bigelow on the floor'. A Bigelow was some kind of a carpet. It was a lovely innocent advertisement trying to drive young executives mad for status. He had told Deirdre about it once but she had missed the point. Why shouldn't he have a carpet too, she had asked. Perhaps they could get some off-cut of carpet themselves and fit it over the weekend, then it would look important and nobody would have to go to war over it and risk a confrontation they might lose. Wearily at that time he had settled for a small rug, which he kept under his desk so that nobody could see it but assured Deirdre that it gave the place class and superiority.

Desmond wouldn't lose his job in Palazzo even if the whole Special Projects Department was deemed to be useless, a criminal waste of time. It was hardly a department anyway, he had that young pup who was meant to be a trainee and the very occasional services of Marigold, a big Australian girl with a mouthful of teeth and a mane of hair who was on what she called OE, Overseas Experience, and had worked in a funeral parlour, as a dentist's receptionist and in the office of an amusement park, all to get an idea of what the world was like before she went home and married a millionaire from Perth, which was her goal.

She was a handsome friendly girl who would sit on Desmond's desk companionably asking if he had any correspondence or memos to type. She thought typing was the golden key to unlocking the world. 'Tell your girls to learn to type, Dizzy,' Marigold told him often. She never accepted that one of his girls was a BA graduate working in a bookshop and the other was a sort of worker nun. Neither of them would take Marigold's golden key to the world.

If Special Projects was wound up Marigold would be sympathetic, she would tell Dizzy that Quigley was a sod and what's more he always tried to pinch her bum. She'd offer to buy him a beer and tell him he was too good for Palazzo and should look around for something better. The young pup of a trainee would hardly notice, he would go and pick his nose in some other part of the store. The pup's father was an important supplier, he would be kept on no matter what happened.

As would Desmond himself. He had been let go once. Never again. Frank Quigley would see to that. His job or a form of it was his for life. He had almost fourteen years more with Palazzo. The company had a retirement at sixty policy. In fact it was less than fourteen years, it was now only thirteen and a bit. They would find something for him to do in that time.

Desmond Doyle would not find himself explaining his existence and justifying his role to his old friend Frank.

No, if there was anything unpleasant like that ahead you could be sure that Frank would have pressing business in the furthest part of the land, or a meeting that was so important it could not be rearranged. Desmond would have to talk to Carlo Palazzo himself. The father-in-law, but in no ways a Godfather figure.

Carlo was a man who thought about his family and his soft leather jackets, he had always wanted to be in the fashion business and now with the profit he was making from Palazzo he could have his showrooms and his life's dream. Carlo Palazzo, a mild-looking Italian whose accent seemed to become more pronounced with every year he spent in North London, made none of the day-to-day decisions about his supermarket empire, he left the running of all that to the bright Mr Quigley who he was sharp enough to spot many years ago as the type of hungry young Irishman who could run it. And who could marry Carlo's daughter too.

There were no children yet and Desmond knew that this was a great sadness, but he kept hoping. Even though it seemed increasingly unlikely with every year that went by, fifteen years of marriage and Renata now well into her thirties.

Carlo was an optimist about his grandchildren. But he was a practical man about his profits and if it were he who would conduct the investigation, Desmond sighed, there would be no emotional confidences today, only harsh facts, and even harsher questions. What has Special Projects added to the sum of Palazzo's profit in the last six months? Just list the achievements please, Desmond. Yes?

Desmond drew his pad nearer to him to get the sorry list together. It wasn't that he had no ideas, he was bursting with ideas, but somehow they got lost in this welter of departments and other pressures and needs.

Like the time he suggested they have a bakery on their own premises. That had been a long time ago and very much ahead of its time. Desmond had not been adventurous enough, he had suggested only that they make brown bread and scones. But his reasoning had been so sound it had been taken over on a larger scale than he had ever dreamed. He had said that the smell of freshly cooked bread was very attractive when a customer came in the door, it was the living guarantee that it was absolutely made that day. The fact they could see it being cooked in hygienic conditions spoke volumes for the general hygiene of the rest of the store as well.

But somehow it had gone from him, it was never the Desmond Doyle idea, or the Special Projects suggestion, it had become part of Merchandising, and then a separate section called Bakery started and there were articles and photographs in all the papers about the baps and the twists and the yeast breads they made. Palazzo bread had become a legend.

Desmond didn't waste too many tears over it, an idea was only an idea, once you gave it to other people then it was no longer yours. In terms of seeing it through it didn't really matter whether you got credit for it or not, it was out of your hands. But if you *had* got credit of course, if you had the reputation of being Mister Ideas in the company then life would have a different colour to it during the working day. There would be a bigger office, a proper name on the door and even one of those carpets. Mr Palazzo would ask him to call him Carlo and invite Desmond and Deirdre to their big summer parties in the large white house that had a swimming pool and a big barbecue. And he would beg Deirdre to try on a soft blue leather jacket that had just come in from Milan and exclaim that it looked so well on her she must have it. As a gift, as a token of the esteem in which they held her husband. The ideas man in Palazzo.

The list was looking scrappy. Marigold came in saying she had a raging hangover which had not been improved in the canteen where she had gone to get some cold orange juice to dilute the miniature of vodka. In the canteen Marigold had heard that Mr Carlo was on the warpath, there had been a less than lovely session with his accountants, and he wasn't going to get enough pocket money to play with those dishcloth rags of leather jackets. So he was about to reorganize everyone. Stupid little wop greaseball, Marigold said, if he was back in Australia he'd be man enough to get the hell out into whatever turned him on like these pathetic frocks and coats rather than pretending he knew how to run a business which everyone knew was run by that gangster Frank Quigley.

Desmond was touched by the partisan nature of Marigold's response.

'Sit down there now and stop exciting yourself, you'll only make your head worse,' he said sympathetically.

Marigold looked at him, her eyes pink and puffy but full of concern.

'Jesus Dizzy, you're too good for this shower,' she said.

'Shush, shush. I'm going past the cold store, will I get you some ice for that? A cure's no good without ice.'

'No wonder you'll never run the bloody place, you're a human being,' said Marigold with her head in her hands.

Marigold had only been with Palazzo six months, she said it was nearly time for her to move on already. She had been thinking of a hotel next, or a job as receptionist in a Knightsbridge hairdressing salon where you might see members of the Royal Family coming in.

Greatly revived by her chilled vodka and orange which she had tried to pursuade Desmond to share without any success, she put her mind to dredging up some details of work done in the section during the period she had worked there.

'Jesus, we must have done *something*, Dizzy!' she said, her face frowning with concentration. 'I mean you were never coming in here every day and looking at that picture of the pale blue outback in Ireland all day, were you?'

'I wasn't, I don't think I was, there always seemed to be things to do but they were other people's things, you see.' Desmond sounded apologetic. 'So they don't count as being from here. It's not going to look very impressive.'

'Where will they send you? If they wind it up?'

'This is one of the smallest offices, they might leave me here, reporting to someone else, you know. Same place, same job, different line of responsibility.'

'They'd never give you the heave-ho?'

He reassured her. 'No, no, Marigold, don't worry about that. No.'

She smiled at him roguishly. 'You mean you know where the bodies are buried?'

'In a way,' he said.

He spoke so softly and sadly Marigold let it go.

'I'll go out and see what I can gather from the letters I typed for you anyway,' she said.

It was more or less as Desmond had thought it would be. Carlo sat in the small office not even remotely impressed by the efforts Marigold made calling him Mr Doyle and talking about people on the telephone and saying he was in conference. Marigold had even been to borrow two china cups and saucers for the coffee rather than use the two scarlet mugs with D and ? on them which were usually brought into play.

Carlo Palazzo spoke about the need to redeploy, to continue to expand, to experiment, never to stand still. He spoke about the competition. He talked about inflation, recession, about industrial unrest and about the difficulty of parking cars. In short, he brought in almost every common topic of gloom to support his reluctant decision that the department *as such* should be fused with other departments and its work, important and useful of course as it was, might best be served by being redeployed.

When he came round to using the word redeployed for the second time Desmond felt that it was like going to the cinema and recognizing the part where you had come in.

He felt a great weariness. A realization that this would happen again and again in the next thirteen and a half years. Until possibly the decision might be that he should work in the car park, that would be the best redeploying.

Desmond's head felt heavy, he wondered how best to explain it to Deirdre that evening. He knew there would be no diminution of salary, he knew there would be no public announcement. Only the title would have gone. He was down to essentials now.

'And do you think I should continue in whatever new deployment is agreed from this room, this office?' he asked.

Carlo Palazzo spread out his big hands. If it were up to him, then of course.

'But it's not, Mr Palazzo?'

It wasn't, it appeared, it was reorganization and taking down some partitions and having an open flow, and a lot more light, and a change in some of the stocktaking.

Desmond waited patiently. He knew that it would be told, and no amount of hurrying tactics would work.

He let his eyes wander to the picture with its unlikely blue skies and its soft grassy slopes. Mayo had never been like that. There had been very big white skies and stony walls and small brown fields. The picture was chocolate-box stuff.

Carlo Palazzo was coming to the point.

The point was definitely upcoming, Desmond thought to himself. He felt the familiar acid taste coming from his stomach to his mouth. Please let there be some kind of office. Something which need never have to be explained. Some part of the building where there would be a person, a person like Marigold who would answer the telephone to Deirdre. Someone who would say 'Hold on and I'll put you through' when his wife rang and asked as she always did to speak to Mr Doyle Special Projects Manager, please. With an upward inflection on the please.

Please let there be some word 'manager' somewhere along the line, and let Deirdre not have to spend the rest of her life phoning a business who would not know who he was, let alone where he was.

'So we thought it best if your work was to be in a roving capacity,' Carlo Palazzo said.

'Not roving, Mr Palazzo,' said Desmond Doyle. 'Please, not roving.'

The Italian looked at him with concern.

'I assure you, Desmond, that the work will be just as important, more important in many ways, and as you know there is no question of changing the salary structure, that will remain with the usual emoluments . . .'

'Any kind of base. Anything at all.' Desmond felt the sweat on his forehead. God Almighty, he was beginning to beg. Why could he not have talked it straight through with Frank Quigley?

He and Frank, who had played on the stony hills of Mayo together, who had never seen a West of Ireland sky like the one in the picture, they knew the same language. Why had the barriers of years meant that he couldn't say to Frank straight out that he must have an office even if it was a doorway leading nowhere? It wasn't much after all these years to give Deirdre, the belief that her husband was of managerial stuff in a large and important retailing organization.

There was a time when he and Frank had been able to talk about anything, anything at all. Like how Frank's father drank away a fortune of compensation in three weeks buying large measures for the whole town. Like how much Desmond wanted to escape from the farm and the silent brothers and sisters who seemed happy to stalk the barren land after the scrawny difficult sheep.

They had told each other of their first conquests with girls when they had come here, two ignorant young paddies in the fifties, they had shared everything from the day they had gone to work for Prince Stores. But then a hunger had taken Frank over, and it must have been about that time that the close friendship died.

And Frank had gone for ever up, for ever and ever, he ran everything now. But the Palazzos had bought out Prince Stores and made it their own. It was known that Carlo Palazzo had never made a decision larger than what sauce he would have on his pasta without consulting Frank Quigley. So it was Frank who was dooming his old pal Desmond to be on a roving basis.

Did Frank not remember Deirdre, did he not know how hard this was going to be for him?

Frank came so rarely to Rosemary Drive these days. But still, every time they met each other it was as if the old days were still the same. They banged each other on the shoulders and laughed, and since Desmond never made anything of being on such a low rung of a ladder they had joined so long ago, Frank equally never made any reference to his own high position. Only at the marriage to Renata Palazzo had the real gulf between them become apparent.

Nobody else from Desmond's level was at the wedding, everyone was many degrees above.

Deirdre had hated that wedding. She had been looking forward to it for months and even believed that she and Renata Palazzo would somehow become great friends. It had always been so unlikely that Desmond had never taken her seriously. Renata was years younger than they were, she was from a different world. Deirdre persisted in thinking of her as an Italian immigrant of her own age who would be shy and needing some kind of sisterly advice.

Desmond would never forget how Deirdre's smile had faded at the wedding when the bright yellow dress and coat made in matching man-made fibre came up against the pure silks and the furs of the other women. She who had left the house so cheerily that morning had been sinking into the background even during the church service when an Italian opera singer was getting through 'Panis Angelicus' for the newlyweds. By the time they had arrived at the marquee and joined the line of guests waiting to be received she was tugging at her dress and his arm.

It had been a black day for her and her hurt had darkened the day for Desmond too.

But none of it had been Frank Quigley's fault. Frank's smile never lessened, not ever in the years since then.

You could always go to Frank. You didn't have to say things in so many words. You could use code.

Where in the name of God was Frank today, this new black day when Carlo Palazzo was telling Desmond Doyle that he would have no office, no door, no telephone on a desk possibly?

Should he ask whether he could shortcut the whole thing for them by putting on one of the beige coats that the men who swept the shops put on, and getting down to work immediately with his bucket and pail and cleaning cloth, wiping the vegetable racks just after the doors closed? Would it perhaps be easier than waiting for half a dozen further slides? But then anger filled him too, he wasn't a stupid man, he wasn't a fool who could be passed over like this. He could feel his face working in a way that was beyond his control. To his horror he saw something like pity in the older man's face.

'Desmond, my friend, please,' Carlo began uncertainly.

'I'm all right.' Desmond stood up behind his small desk. He would have strode across to the window so that the telltale tears in his eyes could subside. But his office wasn't one for striding, he would have had to squeeze past the filing cabinet and possibly knock over the small table or ask Mr Palazzo to move his chair. It was too confined a place for grand gestures. Of course, come next week there would be no place for any gestures at all.

'I know that you are all right. I just don't want you to understand me wrongly. Sometimes even after all these years in this country I can't make myself clear . . . you know.'

'No, you make yourself very clear, Mr Palazzo, clearer than I do, and English is meant to be my native tongue.'

'But perhaps I have offended you in something I said. Can I try to say it again? You are so valued here, you have been here so long and your experience is so necessary . . . it is just that circumstances change and there is an ebb and flow . . . everything is being . . . what word will I use . . . ?'

'Redeployed,' said Desmond flatly.

'Redeployed.' Carlo Palazzo seized it and ran with it, not knowing he had already used it twice. His smile was broad. As if this word somehow rescued things.

He saw from Desmond's face that it didn't.

'Tell me, Desmond, what would you like best? No, it's not an insulting remark, not a trick question . . . I ask you what would you like best in work, what way would be the best way for things to work out for you today? Suppose it were possible for you to stay here, would that be your dream, your wish?'

The man was asking seriously, it wasn't a game of going forwards and back. Carlo wanted to know.

'I don't suppose it would be my dream, no. Not to stay in this room as Special Projects Manager.'

'So.' Carlo looked for some silver lining desperately. 'So why then is it so bad to leave it? What other place would have been your dream?'

Demond leaned on the corner of the filing cabinet. Marigold had decorated the place a little with a few borrowed plants which she must have grabbed from the carpeted offices. Desmond hoped she hadn't actually taken any of Carlo's own greenery. He smiled a little to himself at the thought, and his boss smiled back, looking up eagerly from the chair in front of the desk.

Carlo had a big kind face. He didn't look shifty, he was the kind of Italian who always played the kind uncle or indeed the loving grandfather in a film.

It was Carlo's dream to be a grandfather many times over, to have a lot of little grandsons with half-Irish and half-Italian names running in and out of that huge white house. Children to leave his share of Palazzo to. Did Desmond dream of grandchildren too? He didn't know. What a dull man he must be not to know his own dream when he was asked it by this big straightforward man.

'It's so long since I allowed myself to have a dream I suppose I've forgotten what it was,' he said truthfully.

'I never forgot mine, I wanted to go to Milano to work with the fashion,' said Carlo. 'I want to have the finest craftsmen and stitchers and designers all together and to have my own factory with the name Carlo Palazzo.'

'You have your own name over your work,' Desmond said.

'Yes, but it is not what I wanted, not what I had hoped, I only have a little time in what I would have loved. My father he told me I must go into the food business, with my brothers, with my uncles, not playing with clothes like a ladies' dressmaker, he said.'

'Fathers don't understand,' Desmond said simply.

'Your father . . . did he not understand perhaps?'

'No, my father neither understood nor didn't understand, if you know what I mean. He was always an old man. When I was ten, he was old, and it wasn't just that I *thought* it, he looks it in every picture. He only understood sheep and hillsides and silence. But he never stopped me, he said I was right to go.'

'Then how do you mean fathers never understand?'

'I didn't understand. I did all this for my son. I wanted him to have as good an education as possible, I didn't understand when he left.'

'Where did he go?'

It had never been admitted outside Rosemary Drive. Never beyond the walls.

'He ran away, he ran back to the sheep and the stones and the silence.'

'Well, you let him go.' Carlo didn't seem shocked that Desmond's son had run off uneducated to the back of beyond.

'But not with a good grace.' Desmond sighed.

Carlo was still puzzled. 'So did you want a life of high education?'

For some reason the small eager face of Suresh Patel flashed into Desmond's mind, his dark eyes feverish with the wish to heap degrees and diplomas on his family.

'No, not a high education. Just a place, I suppose, a place that was mine.'

Carlo looked around the featureless office, which he probably remembered as being even more featureless over the previous months without its injection of borrowed plants.

'This place? It feels so important?'

Desmond had somehow come to the end of the road.

'To be honest, Mr Palazzo, I don't know. I'm not a man of very strong opinions. I never was. I have ideas, that's why I suppose Frank and you thought I'd be good here. But they are personal ideas, not corporate ones, and I'm inclined to get a bit lost whenever there's redeployment and the like. But I'll manage. I'll manage. I've always managed before.'

He didn't sound frightened now or self-pitying. Just resigned and practical. Carlo Palazzo was relieved that the mood, whatever it had been, had passed.

'It's not going to happen overnight, it will be in two to three weeks, and in many ways it will give you more freedom, more time to think about what you really want.'

'Maybe it will.'

'And there *will* be a title of manager, it hasn't been quite worked out yet but when Frank gets back I'm sure. . .'

'Oh, I'm sure he will,' Desmond agreed readily.

'So . . .' Once more Carlo spread his hands out.

This time he was rewarded with a half smile and Desmond stretched his own hand out as if to shake on something that had been agreed between two men of like mind.

Carlo paused as if something had struck him.

'Your wife? She is well?'

'Oh yes, Deirdre's fine, thank you Mr Palazzo, blooming.'

'Perhaps she might care to come some evening to have . . . to have a meal in our house with us, the family, you know, Frank and Renata and everything. . . You were all such friends in the old days . . . before any of this . . . that's true, yes.'

'That is very kind of you Mr Palazzo.' Desmond Doyle spoke in the voice of a man who knew that no such invitation would be issued.

'That will be good, we will enjoy that.' Carlo Palazzo spoke in exactly the same voice.

Marigold held the door open for the great chief Mr Palazzo. He looked at her with a vague and pleasant smile.

'Thank you, thank you . . . um.'

'I'm Marigold,' she said, trying to iron out her Australian accent. 'I'm lucky enough to work for Mr Doyle. There have been several important calls, Mr Doyle, I told them that you were in conference.'

Desmond nodded gravely, and waited until the footsteps were gone for Marigold to hiss at him, 'Well, what happened?'

'Oh Marigold,' he said wearily.

'Don't "Oh Marigold" me, didn't I make you look good? Didn't you hear me? Bet he thinks a lot more of you now. Saying I was lucky to be working for you.'

'I expect he thinks you're sleeping with me,' Desmond said.

'I wouldn't half mind.'

'You're possibly the nicest girl in the world.'

'What about your wife?' Marigold asked.

'Oh, I don't think she'd like you to sleep with me, not at all.'

'I mean isn't she the nicest girl in the world, or wasn't she once or what?'

'She's very nice, very nice indeed.' He spoke objectively.

'So no chance for me then.' Marigold was trying to jolly him along.

'Palazzo's not the worst. That's a great Irish expression for you, to say a man is not the worst, it's grudging praise.'

'He didn't give you the bum's rush then?' Marigold's face lit up.

'No, he gave me the bum's rush all right.'

'Aw, shit. When? Where?'

'Soon, a week or two when Frank gets back.'

'Frank's not away,' Marigold said furiously.

'No, but you know, we say he's away.'

'And where are they sending you?'

'Here and there, roving apparently.'

'Is there any good in it, any good at all?' Her eyes were tender, her big handsome face concerned, and she bit her lip at the unfairness of it all.

He couldn't bear her sympathy.

'Oh, it's all right, Marigold, there's plenty of good in it. I don't see this as anything we should fight them on the beaches for, do you . . . ?'

He looked around the office and made a theatrical gesture with his arms.

'But roving?' She seemed upset, he had to reassure her.

'It's more interesting than sitting here and seeing nothing at the end of it. I'll roam up and see you from time to time, you'd brighten my day.'

'Did they say why?'

'Redeployment of resources.'

'Redeployment of balls,' Marigold said.

'Maybe, but what's the point?'

'You didn't *do* anything, they shouldn't take your job away.'

'That could be it, perhaps I really *didn't* do anything.'

'No, you know what I mean, you're a manager for God's sake, you've been here years.'

'There's still going to be a manager's title, of whatever sort . . . We don't know yet, we'll know later . . .'

'Later, like when Frank gets back.'

'Shush, shush.'

'I thought you two were meant to be such friends.'

'We were, we are. Now please, Marigold, don't *you* start.'

She saw, sharp and quick, Marigold, and impulsively she said it.

'You mean you're going to have all this with your wife tonight, is that it?'

'In a way, yes.'

'Well, consider me a bit of a dry run.'

'No. Thank you, I know you mean well.'

She saw the tears in his eyes.

'I mean very well, and I'll tell you this: if your wife doesn't understand that you're one of the best . . .'

'She does, she does.'

'Then I'll have to go round to your house and tell her she's got one beaut guy and I'll knock her head off if she doesn't know it.'

'No, Deirdre will understand, I'll have had time to think about it, explain it properly and put it in perspective.'

'If I were you I wouldn't spend any time rehearsing, ring her up, take her out to lunch, go on, find a nice place with tablecloths and buy a bottle of grog, tell her about it straight, there's no perspective.'

'Everyone does things they want to in the end, Marigold,' he said firmly.

'And some people, Dizzy, do nothing at all,' she said.

He looked stricken.

Impulsively she flung her arms around him. He felt her sobbing in his arms.

'I'm such a loudmouth,' she was saying.

'Hush, hush.' Her hair smelled lovely, like apple blossom.

'I was trying to cheer you up, and look at what I ended up saying.'

Her voice was becoming more normal. Gently he released her and held her from him, looking admiringly at the lovely Australian, the same age perhaps as his own Anna or a little older. The daughter of some man out on the other side of the world who had no idea of the kind of jobs this girl was doing and how she entered into them with all her heart. He said nothing, just looked at her until she sniffed herself to some kind of calm.

'Great if the old greaseball had come back and found us in a clinch, would have confirmed everything he suspected.'

'He'd have been jealous,' said Desmond gallantly.

'He would in a pig's eye, Dizzy,' she said.

'I'm going out, I think,' Desmond said.

'I'll tell them you're practising roving if they ask,' she said, almost grinning.

'Don't tell them anything,' he said.

That was what he always said.

He phoned Frank from a call box near one of the entrance gates.

'I'm not sure if Mr Quigley's available, can I say who wants him?'

Long pause. Obviously a consultation.

'No, I'm very sorry Mr Doyle, Mr Quigley's away on business, was this not told to you? I believe Mr Palazzo's secretary was to let you know . . .'

'Sure, I just wondered was he back.' Desmond was mild.

'No, no.' The voice was firm, as if speaking to a toddler who hadn't quite understood.

'If he calls in tell him that . . . tell him.'

'Yes, Mr Doyle?'

'Tell him nothing. Say Desmond Doyle rang to say nothing, like he's been saying all his life.'

'I don't think I quite . . .'

'You heard me. But I'll say it again.' Desmond said the words again and felt some satisfaction at the sound of them. He wondered was he perhaps going mad.

It was the middle of the morning and there was a strange sense of freedom about walking out through the big Palazzo gates. Like a child being sent home from school with some kind of sickness.

He remembered at the Brothers years ago how he and Frank had mitched off for the day. Nobody knew that word over here, skived is what they called it. They had told the Head Brother that they had inhaled a bag of chemicals in the schoolyard and that their eyes were red and they were choking. They managed to persuade him that the cure would be fresh air.

Desmond could still recall thirty-five years later that freedom, as they ran and skipped over the hills, liberated in every way from the small classroom.

One of the things they had found lacking then was any way of finding people to play with. Everyone else was sitting resentfully in the classroom. They had felt the lack of a gang and had gone home earlier than they would have thought likely.

It was somehow the same today. There was nobody that Desmond could ask to come and play. Nobody to buy a bottle of grog for as Marigold had suggested. Even if he were to take the train in to Baker Street and go to Anna's bookshop she might not be free. And she would be alarmed, it was so out of character. His only son who had been lucky enough to recognize some kind of freedom and run for it was far far away. His other daughter away in her convent would not understand the need that he had to talk, the great urgency to define himself somehow.

It was a poor totting up of twenty-six years in this land that he could think of no other person in the whole of London that he could telephone and ask to meet him. Desmond Doyle had never thought of himself as a jet-setter but he had thought of Deirdre and himself as people with friends, people who had a circle. *Of course* they were. They were going to have a silver wedding anniversary shortly and their problem was not looking for people, it was trying to cut down on numbers.

What did he mean that he had no friends, they had dozens of friends. But that was it. *They* had friends. He and Deirdre had friends and the problem had nothing to do with redeployment or managerial titles, the trouble was a promise made and a promise broken.

He had sworn to her that night so many years ago that he would rise in the business, he would be a name for the O'Hagan family in Ireland to take seriously. He had said that Deirdre would never go out to work. Her mother had never gone out to work, and none of Deirdre's friends who married back in 1960 would have expected to go and look for a job. Ireland had changed since then, had become more like England. Mrs O'Hagan's nose, which seemed to turn up very easily, would not turn today if a young woman went on for further education or took any kind of work to help build a family home.

But those were black days long ago, and the O'Hagan scorn had been hard to bear. And Desmond knew that his promise was given under no duress. He had held Deirdre's small hand and on the night they were about to tell her parents the news, he had begged her to trust him. He remembered his words.

'I always wanted to be in buying and selling, I know it's not the thing to tell your family but even when the tinkers came to town I loved it, there was an excitement about it, about the way they put out their scarves and bright glittering combs on the ground, I knew what it was about.'

Deirdre had smiled at him confidently, knowing he would never bring up anything as alien as tinkers in the O'Hagan household.

'I want *you*,' he had said, 'I want it more than anything in the world and when a man has a dream there's nothing he cannot conquer. I'll conquer the retail business in England. They'll be glad they didn't lose you to a doctor or a lawyer. The day will come when they'll be so glad they settled for a merchant prince.'

And Deirdre had looked at him trustingly as she had always looked ever since.

He supposed that she was still his dream, but why had she not come to his mind when Mr Palazzo had asked him?

Desmond found himself walking the well-trodden path towards home. His feet had taken him on automatic pilot to the bus stop. At this time of day there were no crowds, no queues, how pleasant to be able to travel like this instead of incessant rush hours.

Suppose he *did* ring Deirdre, he knew she was at home, she was working over that infernal silver wedding list again. Surely she would appreciate his honesty and directness?

She loved him in a sort of way, didn't she? Like he loved her. And he did love her. She had changed of course like everyone changed, but it would be ludicrous to expect her to be the fluffy blonde desirable young Deirdre O'Hagan who had filled his thoughts and his heart so urgently. Why wasn't she the dream? She was connected with the dream in a way. The dream was to make good his promise. But he couldn't have told that to Carlo Palazzo in a million years, not even if he had been able to articulate it, which he hadn't. Not until this moment when the bus was approaching.

Desmond hesitated. Should he let the bus go, find a telephone and invite his own wife out to lunch and tell her his own real thoughts? In the hope that they could somehow share them the way they had shared every little heartbeat during that time when they stood strong against the might of the O'Hagans about their marriage.

'Are you getting on or are you not?' the conductor asked him, not unreasonably. Desmond had been standing holding the rail. He remembered Marigold saying to him, 'Some people, Dizzy, do nothing at all.' But he was nearly on the bus.

'I'm getting on,' he said. And his face was so mild and inoffensive that the tired young bus conductor who also wanted a different and a better life abused him no further.

He sorted it out for Deirdre as he walked towards Rosemary Drive, little phrases, little reasoning steps. There would be more scope in a roving managerial position, he would get to know the workings of the company at first hand rather than being tucked away in his own little eyrie. He would explain that Frank had been called away, he would mention that the exact wording was not firmed up but the magic word Manager would be included. He would not mention the Palazzo invitation to supper because he knew it would not materialize.

He felt no bitterness towards Frank for avoiding the confrontation. Nor indeed for initiating the move. Frank was probably right, the functions of Special Projects had indeed been taken over.

Frank at far remove might even be giving him a chance to find a better niche. He wished he could summon up more enthusiasm for this niche, whatever it might be.

It would confuse Deirdre to see him arriving home unexpectedly for lunch. She would fuss and say over and over that he should have warned her. The importance of his news would be lost in a welter of worries about there being nothing at hand.

Desmond decided that he would go into the corner shop, and tell Mr Patel that yet again he had provided a service. They sold pizzas there, not very good ones, wrapped in rather too much plastic and with the wrong ratio of base and topping. Still that might do. Or he might get a tin of soup and some crusty French bread. He didn't remember whether Mr Patel sold chicken pieces, that might be nice.

There were no customers in the shop, but more unusually there was nobody sitting at the till. On the few occasions when Suresh Patel did not sit there himself as if at a throne, still able to advise and direct his tiny empire, there was always another occupant. His silent wife, wordless in English but able to ring up the prices she read on the little labels. Sometimes it was the young owlish son or the pert little daughter. Mr Patel's brother didn't seem capable of manning the family business.

Desmond moved past the central aisle and saw with that lurching feeling of recognition that a raid was in progress.

There was that slow-motion sense of things not being real. Desmond felt as he looked at the two boys in their leather jackets beating the fat brother of Suresh Patel that this was like an action replay when watching a football match.

Desmond felt the old bile, but this time it was a sharper feeling. He thought he was going to choke.

He took two steps backward. He would run out and raise the alarm, he would run around the corner to the street where there would be more people passing by. *And*, if he was honest, where there would be less chance of the two muggers catching him calling for help.

But before he could go any further he heard the voice of Suresh Patel calling to the boys with the bars.

'I beg of you, I beg of you, he is simple in the head, he does not know anything about any safe. There *is* no safe. There is money in the night deposit. Please do not hit my brother again.'

Desmond saw with another shock that he could feel physically in his own stomach that Mr Patel's arm hung at an odd angle. As if it had already been beaten. And already broken.

Even if Marigold had not said to him sadly that there were some people who never did anything at all, he would have done what he did. Desmond Doyle, the man so mild that he had to be moved from an office lest he take root, so meek that he made a young Australian beauty cry over his future, knew suddenly what he had to do.

He lifted the stack of trays which had held the bread delivered that morning and he brought it suddenly down on the neck of the first leather jacket. The boy, who could hardly have been as old as his own son Brendan, fell with a thud to the floor. The other one looked at him wild-eyed. Desmond pushed him, jabbing him with the trays, and manoeuvred him towards the back rooms, the living quarters of the whole family.

'Is your wife in there?' he shouted.

'No, Mr Doyle.' Suresh Patel looked up from the floor like people look up in films when rescuers arrive.

The brother who didn't know where the safe was smiled as if his heart was going to burst.

On and on Desmond pushed and prodded, his strength flooding to him. Behind him he heard voices come into the shop. Real customers.

'Get the police immediately, and an ambulance,' called Desmond Doyle. 'There's been a raid. Go quickly, any private house will let you phone.'

They ran, the two young men delighted to be on the safe end of a heroics job, and Desmond pushed a cabinet up against the door to the room where he had cornered the bewildered boy in the leather jacket.

'Can he get out that way?' he asked.

'No. We have had bars on the window and everything, you know in case something like this . . .'

'Are you all right?' Desmond knelt on the floor.

'Yes. Yes. Did you kill him?' He nodded towards the boy on the floor who was regaining consciousness and starting to groan.

Desmond had taken his iron bar away from him, and stood prepared to deal another blow, but the boy was not able to move.

'No, he's not dead. But he'll go to gaol, by God he'll go to gaol,' said Desmond.

'Perhaps not, but it doesn't matter.' The shopkeeper tried to get himself to his feet. He looked weak and frightened.

'What matters then?' Desmond wanted to know.

'Well, I have to know who will run this shop for me – you see my brother, how he is, you know how my wife cannot speak, I must not ask the children to desist from school, they will miss their places and their examinations . . .'

Far away Desmond heard a siren, the two heroes were bursting back in saying the Law was on the way.

'Don't worry about that,' Desmond said gently to the man on the floor. 'That will all be organized.'

'But how, how?'

'Have you any relations, cousins, in businesses like this?'

'Yes, but they cannot leave their own places. Each place, it has to make its own way.'

'Yes I know, but when we get you to hospital, will you be able to give me their names? I can get in touch with them.'

'It is no use, Mr Doyle, they will not have the time . . . they must work each in their own.'

His face was troubled and his big dark eyes filled with tears. 'We are finished now. It's very simple to see,' he said.

'No, Mr Patel. I will run the shop for you. You must just tell them that you trust me and that it's not any kind of trick.'

'You cannot do that, Mr Doyle, you have a big position in Palazzo Foods, you only say this to make me feel good.'

'No, it is the truth. I will look after your shop until you come back from hospital. We will have to close it today of course, put up a notice, but by tomorrow lunch time I will have it working again.'

'I cannot thank you . . .' Desmond's eyes also filled with tears. He saw that the man trusted him utterly, Suresh Patel saw Desmond Doyle as a great manager who could do what he willed.

The ambulance men were gentle. They said he had very likely broken a rib as well as an arm.

'It might be some time, Mr Doyle,' said Suresh Patel from the stretcher.

'There's all the time in the world.'

'Let me tell you where the safe is.'

'Not now, later, I'll come to see you in the hospital.'

'But your wife, your family, they will not let you do this.'

'They will understand.'

'And afterwards?'

'Afterwards will be different. Don't think about it.'

The policemen were getting younger, they looked younger than the villains. One of them was definitely younger than Desmond's son Brendan.

'Who is in charge here?' the young policeman asked with a voice that had not yet gained the confidence it would have in a few short years.

'I am,' said Desmond. 'I'm Desmond Doyle of 26 Rosemary Drive and I'm going to look after these premises until Mr Patel comes back from hospital.'

5

Father Hurley

Nobody except his sister called Father James Hurley Jimbo, it would have been unthinkable. A man in his sixties with silver hair and a handsome head. He had the bearing of a bishop, and a lot of people thought he looked much more bishoplike than many of those who held the office. Tall and straight, he would have worn the robes well, and even better the cardinal's red. But Rome didn't go on appearances, and Father Hurley's name had never been brought to any corridors of power.

It was impossible to find anyone who would speak a word against him. His parishioners in several County Dublin districts had loved him. He was able it seemed to move just fast enough with the changes that came to the Church after the Vatican Council, but not too fast. He could murmur calming things that soothed the most conservative and yet he seemed to go far along the road that allowed the laity to have a say. He wasn't exactly all things to all of his flock but he certainly avoided irritating them.

And in a Dublin where anti-clericalism among the younger liberals was becoming rife, this was no mean feat.

He was not a television priest, he had never been seen on the screen debating any issue. He was not the kind of man who would officiate at the marriage of known atheists having a church wedding just for the show, but neither was he the old-fashioned curate who went to Cheltenham in March with a pocket full of fivers, or cheered on the dogs at a coursing match as they followed the hare. Father Hurley was a travelled educated soft-spoken man. People often said that he looked like an academic. This was high praise. And he was amused that it was sometimes regarded as even higher praise when he was described as looking not like a priest but more like a vicar!

James Hurley seemed to have moved quietly from parish to parish without either an upward or a downward movement. There did not seem to be the sense of advancement that such a well-spoken thoughtful man might have been led to expect, but it was rumoured that he never sought any promotion. You couldn't say he was unworldly, not Father Hurley who liked fine wines and was known to enjoy pheasant and to relish lobster.

But he always seemed totally contented with his lot, even when they had sent him to a working-class parish where he was in charge of fourteen youth clubs and eleven football teams instead of the drawing rooms and the visits to private nursing homes of his previous position.

He had been at school at one of the better Catholic schools in England, not that he ever talked about it. His family had been wealthy people and it was rumoured that he was brought up on a big estate in the country. But none of this ever came from the man himself, he would laugh easily and say that nobody in Ireland should try to shake their family trees for fear of what might fall down. He had a sister who lived in the country with her husband, a country solicitor of substance, and their only son. Father Hurley did speak of this boy, his nephew, with great affection. Gregory was the only part of Father Hurley's private life where he ever volunteered information.

Otherwise he was just a very good and interested listener to other people's stories. Which is why people thought he was such a good conversationalist. He talked only about them.

In the various presbyteries where Father Hurley's life had taken him there were pictures of his mother and father, now dead, in old-fashioned oval frames. There was a family picture taken at Gregory's first Communion, and another one of Gregory's Conferring. A handsome boy with his hand lightly laid on his parchment scroll and his eyes smiling through the camera as if he knew much more than any other graduate who was posing for stiff formal photographs that day but took it all very casually.

For the people who told Father Hurley their own life stories, their worries and their tittle-tattle, Gregory was an ideal conversation piece, they could ask for him, and hear an enthusiastic response, enough to look polite, then they could return to their own tales again. They didn't notice that after a certain date the stories about Gregory never originated with Father Hurley and that his replies were vaguer and less informed than they had been once. He was far too diplomatic to let that be seen. That was another thing people said, he would have been very good at the Department of Foreign Affairs, or a consul or an ambassador even.

When James Hurley was a boy his mother had died and he had always thought of Laura as being a combination of mother, sister and best friend. Laura was five years older than he was, she had been seventeen when left in charge of a big crumbling house, a small crumbling brother and a remote and withdrawn father who didn't give any of himself to his children any more than he had given of himself to his wife or the estate he had inherited.

Father James Hurley knew all that now, but then he had lived in a childlike fear of offending his stern cold father still further. Laura could have gone away to university, he always thought, if it had not been for her little brother. Instead she stayed at home and took a secretarial course in the nearby town.

She worked in the local grocery which was eventually taken over by a bigger firm, then she worked in the local bakery which merged with three nearby bakeries and her secretarial job there was over. She worked as the doctor's receptionist and during her time there he was taken off the medical register for professional misconduct. Laura used to tell her little brother Jimbo that she seemed to have a fairly unlucky effect and a dead hand on those she went to work for. Her little brother Jimbo used to suggest she came to work in his school in the hope that she would close it down.

She encouraged him in his Vocation, she took long walks in the country roads with him, and together they sat on mossy banks and on the stile between the fields and talked above the love of God the way others might have talked about sport or the cinema.

Laura Hurley had knelt with tears in her eyes to receive her brother's first blessing after he had said his First Mass.

Their father had died by this stage, remote and uninvolved to the end. James had become a priest; he might have become a soldier or a jockey, it would have been on the same level of interest for his father.

While away at the seminary James had often worried about Laura. She lived in the gate lodge of what had been their home. The Big House was not really big in terms of the landed estates thereabouts but it had been substantial. But Laura felt no sense of having come down in the world, living in the cottage where once people lived rent free if they opened and closed the gates after the Hurley family. Laura had always said cheerfully that it was much easier to keep a small place than a big one, and since their father had gone first to a nursing home and then to his eternal reward she was alone, so it didn't make sense to run the Big House. When it was sold there were so many debts that had gathered from James being a student, from father being a patient in a private nursing home, that the place had been thoroughly mortgaged. There was little in the bank, there was no dowry for Miss Laura Hurley, faithful sister and dutiful daughter.

Laura never thought like that. She was happy, she walked her two big collie dogs, read her books in the evening by her small fire, and went to work by day for the local solicitors. She said laughingly that she hadn't managed to close them down like she had done to every other business she worked for but she had managed to change them utterly.

Like changing the confirmed bachelor status of young Mr Black. The Mr Black who had once been the most eligible man in the county. At the age of forty he looked at Laura Hurley aged thirty-four and a lot of his iron-hard resolve about staying single, uninvolved and free began to chip away.

Then the letter arrived: 'Dearest Jimbo, you'll never believe it but Alan Black and I are going to get married. We would very much like it if you could perform the ceremony for us. Since we're not in the first flush of youth to put it mildly we won't make an exhibition of ourselves here with everyone coming to stare. We would like to come to Dublin and be married in your parish if that's possible. Dearest Jimbo, I never knew I could feel so happy. And so safe and as if things were meant to turn out like this. I don't deserve it, I really don't.'

Father Hurley always remembered that letter from his sister, he could see it, the words almost tumbling over each other on the small cream writing paper. He remembered the way his eyes had watered with a feeling of pleasure that things really did seem to have some point if this kind woman had found someone generous and good to share her life with her. He couldn't remember Alan Black except that he had been very handsome and rather dashing-looking in the past.

Father James Hurley felt that at twenty-nine he was a man of the world. And in a strange way he felt protective of his older sister as he joined her hand with Alan Black's at the wedding ceremony. He hoped this man with the dark eyes and dark hair just greying at the temples would be good to Laura and understand her generosity and how she had never sought anything for herself.

Several times he found himself looking at them and with a hope that was more than a wish, it was a silent prayer, he willed his sister to have a good relationship with this tall handsome man. Laura's face was open and honest, but even on this her wedding day nobody could call her beautiful, her hair was pulled back and tied with a large cream-coloured ribbon which matched the colour of her suit. The ribbon was large enough to be considered a hat or head covering for church. She had a dusting of face powder and a smile that warmed the small congregation to the heart. But she was not a beautiful woman. Young Father Hurley hoped that the attentions of the handsome solicitor would not wander.

Years later he marvelled at his own callow approach and wondered how he could ever have thought himself any use in advising men and women in their lives on their road to God. In a changing world there never was and never had been anything more strong and constant than the love

Alan Black had shown to his bride. From the day that they had come to see him, back suntanned and laughing from their honeymoon in Spain, he should have realized that his own judgements based on appearances and vanity were superficial. Why should Alan Black, a bright intelligent man, not be able to see the great worth, goodness and love in Laura Hurley? After all James Hurley had always seen it himself, why should he think it would pass Mr Black the solicitor by?

And as the years went on he used to go to stay with them. They had done up the little gate lodge and built on extra rooms. There was a new study out at one side of the house filled with books from ceiling to floor, they lit a fire there in the evenings and often the three of them sat in big chairs reading. It was the most peaceful happy place he had ever been.

Sometimes Laura would look up from the chair where she lay curled up and smile at him.

'Isn't this the life, Jimbo?' she'd say.

Other days when he visited she might walk with him through the fields and over the stiles and hedges and ditches they had once owned.

'Did we ever think it would turn out so well, Jimbo?' she said often, ruffling the hair of her young brother who would never be the great Father Hurley to her.

And then they told him they were building a similar long low room at the other side of the house. It was going to be a nursery playroom. They would never call it the nursery, they said, they would call it the child's room whatever his or her name was. Nursery was only a baby name. The name was Gregory, Father James held the baby in his arm for the Baptism. A beautiful child with the long dark eyelashes of his father. Gregory Black.

He was their only child; Laura said they would like to have had a brother or sister for him but it was not to be. They made sure he had plenty of other children to play with. He turned out to be the dream child that every doting uncle hopes for.

He would run from the window seat of his own big low room when he saw the car approaching.

'It's Uncle Jim,' he would shout and the old collie dogs would bark and leap and Laura would rush from the kitchen.

When Alan got back from work the smile was broad and the delight obvious. They loved to see him come for a couple of days mid week. They loved the way he got on so well with their son.

Gregory wanted to be a priest of course, when he was around ten. It was a far better life than working in his father's office, he told them all seriously. As a priest you had to do nothing at all, and people paid you money for saying Masses that you'd be saying anyway, and you could get up on a pulpit and tell them all what to do or else they'd go to hell. Sensing a delighted if half-shocked audience, Gregory went on eagerly. It was the best job in the world. And you could refuse to forgive anyone in Confession if you didn't like them and then they'd go to hell, it would be great.

They came to Dublin to see him too and James Hurley never tired of talking about this warm bright boy. Gregory wanted to know everything, to meet everyone. He could charm crabbed old parish priests and difficult women parishioners who were always quick to fancy slights.

'I think you would be good as a priest actually,' his uncle said to him laughingly one day when Gregory was fifteen. 'An awful lot of it is public relations and getting along with people, you're very good at that.'

'It makes sense,' Gregory said.

Father Hurley looked at him sharply. Yes of course it made sense to present an amiable face towards people rather than a pompous one, of course it was the wise thing to do to take the path that would not bring the wrath of authority around your ears. But fancy knowing that at fifteen. They were growing up a lot faster these days.

When Gregory got his place in UCD he was studying Law, that made sense too, he said. He had to study something and Law was as good a training as anything else, meanwhile it kept his father, grandfather and uncle happy to think another Black was going to come into the business.

'And is that what you are going to do?' Father Hurley was surprised. Gregory seemed to him to be too bright, too lively to settle in the small town. There wouldn't be enough to hold his sharp eyes that moved restlessly from face to face, from scene to scene.

'I haven't really thought it out, Uncle Jim. It's what my mother and father would like certainly, and since I don't know yet it makes sense to let them assume that it's what I'll do.'

Again there was a slight chill in the words. The boy had not said he was lying to his family, he had said that since nothing in this world was definite why cross your bridges before you came to them? Father James Hurley told himself that once or twice when he was saying his Evening Office and when the memory of Gregory's words troubled him. He began to think that he was becoming a foolish fusspot. It was ridiculous to read danger into the practical plans of a modern young man.

Gregory graduated well and was photographed on his own and with his father, mother and uncle.

His father was now white-haired, still a handsome man. He was sixty-three now, forty-two years older than his boy. Alan Black had always said that it didn't matter whether you were eighteen years older than your son or forty-eight years older, you were still a different generation. But that in his case it had been everything and more than he had hoped, the boy had never wanted a motorbike, hadn't taken drugs or brought hordes of undesirables back to the home. He had been a model son.

His mother Laura looked well on the Conferring day. She didn't twitter like other mothers did about having produced a son who could write Bachelor of Civil Law after his name and who would shortly be admitted to the Incorporated Law Society as a solicitor as well. Laura wore a bright pink scarf at the neck of her smart navy suit. She had spent what she considered a great deal of money on a haircut, and her grey hair looked elegant and well shaped. She did not look fifty-six years of age but she did look the picture of happiness. As the crowds milled around the university campus she grasped her brother by the arm.

'I almost feel that I've been too lucky, Jimbo,' she said, her face serious. 'Why should God have given me all this happiness when He doesn't give it to everyone else?'

Father Hurley, who certainly did not look his fifty-one years either, begged her to believe that God's love was there for everyone, it was a matter of how they received it. Laura had always been an angel to everyone, it was just and good that she should be given happiness in this life as well as in the next.

He meant it, every single word. His eye fell on a woman with a tired face and a son in a wheelchair. They had come to watch a daughter be conferred. There was no man with them.

Perhaps she too had been an angel, Father James Hurley thought. But it was too complicated to work out why God hadn't dealt her a better hand in this life. He would not think about it now.

They had lunch in one of the best hotels. People at several tables seemed to know Father Hurley, he introduced his family with pride, the well-dressed sister and brother-in-law. The bright handsome young man.

A Mrs O'Hagan and a Mrs Barry, two ladies treating themselves to a little outing, seemed very pleased to meet the nephew of whom they had heard so much. Father Hurley wished they wouldn't go on about how often and how glowingly he had mentioned the young man. It made him feel somehow that he had no other topic of conversation.

Gregory was able to take it utterly in his stride. As they sat down at their own table he grinned conspiratorially at his uncle.

'Talk about me being good at public relations, you're the genius, just feed them a little bit of harmless family information from time to time and they think they know all about you. You're cute as a fox, Uncle Jim.'

It was rescue from being thought to be the gossipy over-fond uncle, certainly, but it did seem to classify him as something else. Something a bit shallow.

Gregory Black decided that he would practise law in Dublin for a few years in order to get experience. Make all his mistakes on strangers rather than his father's clients, he said. Even his old grandfather now in his late eighties and long retired from the firm thought this was a good idea, and his uncle who had no children of his own. His parents accepted it with a good grace.

'It would be ridiculous to keep him down in a backwater after he's been so long on his own in Dublin,' Laura told her brother. 'And any way he says he'll come down and see us a lot.'

'Does he just think that or will he really?' Father Hurley asked.

'Oh he will, the only thing that made it difficult for him when he was a student was all the train and bus travel. Now he'll have a car it will be different.'

'A car of his own?'

'Yes, it's Alan's promise. If he got a good degree a car of his own!' She was bursting with pride.

And Gregory's gratitude was enormous. He embraced them all with pleasure. His father, gruff with delight, said that of course in time Gregory would change this model and trade it in for another smarter kind. But for the moment . . . perhaps . . .

Gregory said he would drive it until it was worn out. Father James Hurley felt his heart fill up with relief and pleasure that this dark eager young man should know how much love and need encircled him, and respond to it so well.

His parents went back happily to the country, his uncle went happily back to the presbytery and the boy was free to do what he wanted with his life, with a brand-new car to help him on the way.

And Gregory did indeed visit home, he drove smartly in the entrance of the gate lodge and fondled the ears of the collie dogs, children and even grandchildren of the original collies that his mother had loved so much. He would talk to his father about the law and to his mother about his social life in Dublin.

He seemed to have lots of friends – men and women, Laura told her brother eagerly – they went to each other's houses and they even cooked meals for each other. Sometimes she baked a steak and kidney pie for him to take up to his flat, she always gave him bread and slices of good country ham, and bacon, and pounds of butter. Once or twice James Hurley wondered what did she think they sold in shops around the bedsitterland where his nephew lived, but he didn't ever say anything. His sister loved the feeling that she was still looking after the big handsome son she had produced. Why disturb that good warm feeling? To use his nephew's own words, 'it wouldn't make sense'.

He hardly ever coincided with Gregory back down home because the priest was never free at weekends, Saturdays were busy with Confessions and house calls, Sundays with the parish Masses, the sick calls and the evening Benediction. But when he did get back himself mid week for an overnight now and then he was pleased to see that the pleasure of the visits totally outweighed what might be considered the selfish attitudes of their only son.

Laura talked delightedly of how Gregory had this big red laundry bag she had made him and often he just ran into the kitchen and stuffed all the contents into her washing machine.

She said this proudly as if it had taken some effort. She mentioned not at all that it was she who took them out and hung them up to dry, she who ironed and folded the shirts and had an entire laundry ready packed on the back seat of his car for his return journey.

Alan talked about how Gregory loved coming to have Saturday dinner with them in the golf club, how he appreciated the good wines and nice food that were served there.

Father Hurley wondered why Gregory hadn't on some occasions at least put his mother and father into the car they had bought him and driven them to one of the hotels nearby to treat them to a dinner.

But as usual it made no sense to bring up something so negative. And he remembered with some guilt that he had never thought of treating his sister in the old days. He had a vow of poverty perhaps on his side, but there were things he hadn't thought of then. Maybe it was the same in all young men.

And Gregory was great company. He could talk a lot without saying anything, something that could be a compliment or an insult. In Gregory's case it was something to be admired, praised and enjoyed.

Sometimes Gregory went swimming with his uncle out in Sandycove at the Forty Foot, the men's bathing place. Sometimes he called in to have a drink in the presbytery, where he would raise the nice crystal Waterford glass to the evening light and admire the golden whiskey reflecting in the midst of all the little twinkling shapes of glass.

'Great thing this ascetic life,' Gregory would say, laughing.

You couldn't take offence at him, and it would only be a very churlish person who would notice that he never brought a bottle of whiskey with him to add to the store, ascetic or not.

Father Hurley was totally unprepared for a visit from Gregory in the middle of the night.

'I'm in a bit of trouble, Jim,' he said straight away.

No Uncle, no sorry for getting you out of bed at three a.m.

Father Hurley managed to shoo the elderly parish priest and the equally elderly housekeeper back to their respective quarters. 'It's an emergency, I'll deal with it,' he soothed them. By the time he got into the sitting room he saw that Gregory had helped himself to a large drink. The boy's eyes were too bright, he had sweat on his brow, he looked as if he had already had plenty to drink.

'What happened?'

'A bloody bicycle swerved out at me, no proper light, no reflecting clothes, nothing. Bloody fools, they should be prosecuted, they should have special lanes for them like they do on the continent.'

'What happened?' The priest repeated the words.

'I don't know.' Gregory looked very young.

'Well is he all right, was he hurt?'

'I didn't stop.'

Father Hurley stood up. His legs weren't steady enough to hold him. He sat down again.

'But was he injured, did he fall? Mother of God, Gregory, you never left him there on the side of the road?'

'I had to, Uncle Jim. I was over the limit. Way over the limit.'

'Where is he, where did it happen?'

Gregory told him, a stretch of dark road on the outskirts of Dublin.

'What took you up there?' the priest asked. It was irrelevant but he didn't feel he yet had the strength to stand up and go to the phone to let the guards and the ambulance know there had been an accident.

'I thought it was safer to come back that way, less chance of being stopped. You know, breathalyzed.' Gregory looked up, like the way he had looked up when he had forgotten to take one of the dogs for a walk, or hadn't closed a gate up in a far field.

But this time a cyclist lay on the road in the dark.

'Please tell me, Gregory, tell me what you think happened.'

'I don't know. Jesus, I don't know, I felt the bike.' He stopped. His face was blank.

'And then . . .'

'I don't know, Uncle Jim. I'm frightened.'

'So am I,' said James Hurley.

He picked up the phone.

'Don't, don't!' screamed his nephew. 'For God's sake you'll ruin me.'

James Hurley had dialled the guards.

'Shut up, Gregory,' he said. 'I'm not giving them your name, I'm sending them to the accident, then I'll go myself.'

'You can't . . . you can't . . .'

'Goodnight Sergeant, it's Father Hurley from the presbytery here, I've had a message, a very urgent one, there's been an accident . . .' He gave the road and the area. He thought the time was in the last half hour or so. He looked over at Gregory, the boy nodded miserably.

'Yes, it seems it was a hit and run.'

The words had a disgusting finality about them. This time Gregory didn't even lift his head.

'No, Sergeant, I can't tell you any more. I'm sorry, it was reported to me in the nature of confession. That's all I can say. I'm going out there now to see what happened to the unfortunate . . .

'No, it was just confessed to me, I know nothing about any car or who the person was.'

Father Hurley went for his coat. He caught a sight of his nephew's face and the relief that flooded it.

Gregory looked up at him gratefully.

'I never thought of that, but of course it makes sense, you *can't* really tell because of the seal of Confession.'

'It wasn't Confession, I could tell but I'm not going to.'

'You couldn't break the sacred . . .'

'Shut your face . . .'

This was a different uncle than he had ever seen before.

He took a small bag with him in case he would have to administer the last sacrament to a seriously injured victim on the side of a dark road outside Dublin.

'What will I do?'

'You will walk home. And you will go to bed.'

'And the car?'

'I will deal with the car. Get home and out of my sight.'

The cyclist was a young woman. She was according to the student card in her wallet a Ms Jane Morrissey. She was aged nineteen. She was dead.

The guards said that it was always the same no matter how often they saw it, a dead body on the side of the road when some bastard had not stopped, it was terrible. One of them took off his hat and wiped his forehead, the other lit a cigarette. They exchanged glances over the priest, a pleasant soft-spoken man in his fifties. He prayed over the dead girl and he sobbed as if he were a child.

He did it all for Laura, he told himself afterwards in the sleepless nights, because he couldn't drop off and be in a deep dreamless unconscious state for seven and eight hours a night any more. He had changed it to Confession because if it hadn't been then he would have had to report his sister's only boy as a hit-and-run driver. Even within the sacrament of Confession he should still have urged the boy to confess and admit.

In real life things weren't like an old black and white movie with Montgomery Clift playing the tortured priest in an agony of indecision. Today a priest would insist that if a penitent wanted absolution he must face up to the responsibility of his actions, he must make his restitution.

But James Hurley had thought of Laura.

This was a way to save her. It was a way to tell that weak son of hers that he was regarding the matter as one between sinner and Confessor. It hadn't a leg to stand on in civil or canon law.

He lied to the Garda Sergeant, he said it had been a hysterical call from someone trying to confess, that he had no idea who the driver was. He lied to the parish priest about the caller in the night, he said it was a man looking for alms.

He lied to his sister when she asked him why he couldn't come down soon and see them again. He said there was a lot on in the parish. The truth was that he couldn't look them in the eyes. He couldn't listen while they told him some new tale of Gregory's excellence.

He had driven Gregory's car to a service station on the other side of Dublin in a place where nobody had known him. He had lied to the garage owner, said that he had driven the parish priest's car and hit a gate. The garage man loved to hear that a priest could do wrong too, he knocked out the dent and he gave it a thorough going over.

'The parish priest will think you kept it in great nick now,' he said, glad to be in on some kind of a game.

'How much do I owe you?'

'Ah, go on Father, there's nothing in it, say a few Masses for me, and my old mother, she's not been well.'

'I don't say Masses in exchange for repairs.' The priest had turned white with fury. 'In God's name man will you tell me how much it cost?'

Frightened, the garage owner stumbled out an amount.

Father Hurley recovered and put his hand on the man's arm, 'Please forgive me, I'm desperately sorry for losing control and shouting at you like that. I've been under a bit of strain but that's no excuse. Can you know how sorry I am?'

Relief flooded the man's face. 'Sure, Father, there's nothing like giving a car a bit of a tip against an old gate for putting the heart across you, and specially in the case of a respectable clergyman like yourself. Think nothing of it, it wasn't even as if there was any harm done.'

Father Hurley remembered the white face of Jane Morrissey aged nineteen, student of Sociology with the side of her head covered in rapidly drying blood. He felt faint for a moment.

He knew his life would never be the same again. He knew he had entered a different kind of world now, a world of lies.

He had placed the keys of the car in an envelope and left them through the letter box of Gregory's flat. He had parked the car in the car port and walked back to the presbytery.

He read in the evening papers about the accident, he listened to the appeal for witnesses on Radio Eireann.

He played a game of draughts with the old parish priest with his mind a million miles away.

'You're a good man, James,' said the old priest. 'You don't let me win like the others do. You're a very good man.'

Father Hurley's eyes filled with tears. 'No I'm not, Canon, I'm a very weak man, a foolish, vain and weak man.'

'Ah, we're all foolish, weak and vain,' said the parish priest. 'But given all that, there's goodness in some of us as well and there certainly is in you.'

But those frightening days were long over now, and still sleep didn't come. He had established an uneasy and formal relationship again with his nephew.

Gregory had phoned at once to thank him for the car.

Father James Hurley had said calmly down the phone, 'I'm afraid he isn't here.'

'But that *is* you speaking, Uncle Jim.' Gregory was puzzled.

'I've told so many lies, Gregory, what's one more?' His voice sounded tired.

'*Please*. Please, Uncle Jim, don't talk like that. Is there anyone there listening to you, you know?'

'I've no idea.'

'Can I come and see you?'

'No.'

'Tomorrow?'

'No. Stay away from me, Gregory. Far far away.'

'But I can't do that, not for ever. I don't want to for one thing, and what about Mother and Father for another thing? It would look . . . well, you know how it would look.'

'I don't think they'd guess in a million years. I think you're safe. They would believe better of you. To them it will be just a small paragraph in the papers, another sad thing that happened in Dublin . . .'

'No I mean about us . . . if we're not going to be speaking.'

'I suppose we'll speak again. Give me time. Give me time.'

Gregory couldn't get through to him, not for weeks. If he turned up at the presbytery his uncle apologized but said he was rushing out on a sick call. If he telephoned it was the same.

Eventually he chose the one place where he knew he could get the undivided attention of the man who was running away from him.

In the Confession box the little partition slid back. Father Hurley's handsome head could be seen leaning on his hand, not looking straight at the penitent, but looking forward and slightly down. In a listening position.

'Yes, my child?' he began comfortingly.

'Bless me Father for I have sinned,' Gregory began the ritual. His voice was too familiar not to be recognized. The priest looked up suddenly in alarm.

'Good God, have you decided to make a mockery of the sacraments as well?' he whispered in a low voice.

'You won't listen to me anywhere else, I have to come here to tell you how sorry I am.'

'It's not me you have to tell.'

'But it is, I've told God already through another priest, I have decided to give a certain amount each month out of my salary to a charity to try and make up, I know it won't. I've given up drink. God, Uncle Jim, what more can I do? Please tell me. I can't bring her back to life, I couldn't have even then.'

'Gregory, Gregory.' There were tears in Father Hurley's eyes.

'But what is the use, Uncle Jim, what good will be served if you don't speak to me, and you don't come back home because you don't want to speak about me? I mean if I had been killed that night too, it would all have been different, you'd have been locked in with my mother and father. So shouldn't we be glad I'm alive anyway even if that poor girl was killed in an accident?'

'By a hit-and-run drunken driver.'

'I know, I've accepted it.'

'But not the punishment for it.'

'But what *good* would it do? Really and truly. It would break Mother's heart and disgrace Father, and humiliate you, and suppose it all came out now, now weeks later, it would look so much worse. We can't relive that whole night. I would if I could . . .'

'Very well.'

'What?'

'Just very well. We will be friends.'

'Ah, I knew you'd find it in your heart.'

'Good, well you were right, I've found it in my heart, now can you allow someone else in to make their peace with God?'

'Thank you, Uncle Jim. And Uncle Jim . . .'

The priest said nothing.

'Will you come and have lunch in my flat some time? Maybe Saturday. No liquor but a couple of my friends. Please?'

'Yes.'

'Thank you again.'

He went to the boy's flat. He met two young men and a girl. They were pleasant easygoing company. They drank wine with their lunch and argued genially about whether the Church still ruled everything in Ireland. Father Hurley was practised in this kind of conversation, most of his friends' children took this line. He was bland and unfailingly courteous, he saw the point of view on this hand, on the other hand and on yet further hands. He had a soothing murmur, an ability to appear to lose a point in order to let the opposition concede a point too.

He watched Gregory carefully. Only mineral water went into his glass. Perhaps the boy was shaken and was trying to start a new life. Perhaps James Hurley really should find it in his heart to try to forgive the boy even if he couldn't forgive himself. He smiled at his nephew and got a warm smile back.

They all helped to clear the table out to the small smart kitchen.

'Hey Greg, what's this bottle of vodka doing, if you've given up the jar?' asked one of his friends.

'Oh, that's from the days before, take it with you.' Gregory spoke easily.

Father Hurley wondered whether his own soul had become somehow poisoned because he had a suspicion that his nephew's eyes were somehow too bright for a boy on plain water, perhaps he had been topping it up with vodka out in the kitchen. The other drink was kept on a sideboard.

But if this was the way he was going to think all the time then there was no point in having any relationship with his nephew at all. He put it firmly from his mind. Into that store of other things he was simply refusing to think about these days.

He went to see Laura and Alan during the week. They were delighted to hear about the presence of the girl at the Saturday lunch party, they thought she might be a current girlfriend.

'She didn't seem to be relating to him specially.' Father Hurley felt like an old lady gossiping at a tea party.

'She's been around for a while,' Laura said happily. 'I think this may be the one all right.'

It had been a strange visit, everything his sister and his brother-in-law said seemed to grate on him.

They told him he was lucky to have certainties. Sometimes in the law there were grey areas.

He smiled grimly as if there were no grey areas in his line of work.

They said how lucky they were with Gregory, the son of a friend of theirs had joined Sinn Fein, first as a legal adviser, then as an active campaigner and then as a fully fledged member of the Provisional IRA.

'At least he had some ideals, however misplaced and mad,' Father Hurley said.

'Jimbo you must be mad, there's no ideals in that lot,' Laura cried.

And as always he smiled self-deprecatingly. There was no way he was going to explain to them that he thought any cause was better than the weak-minded cause of saving your own skin which their son had done. With his connivance.

He looked uneasy and unhappy; Alan Black in his diplomatic way changed the subject.

'Tell us, are you officiating at any nice society weddings these days? We love to feel near the high and mighty of the land through you, Jim.'

No, Father Hurley told them that young people always had some friend of their own to marry them nowadays, they didn't go for old family friends of the parents these days. No, not a posh wedding coming up. A silver wedding though, he said brightly, and in England no less.

They were interested as they always were in everything he did. He explained he had married this couple way back in 1960 – it didn't seem like a quarter of a century ago but that was apparently what it was! The daughters and son of this couple wanted him to attend, they had said it would be meaningless if he didn't have some kind of ceremony for them all.

Laura and Alan thought that it was only right that this couple whoever they were would want Father Hurley again.

'I didn't know them very well,' he said, almost as if talking to himself. 'I know Deirdre's mother Mrs O'Hagan slightly, and I knew Mrs Barry, the mother of the bridesmaid Maureen Barry. But I didn't know the young man at all.'

'You never mentioned them.' Laura was drawing him out.

'Well no, I suppose I marry a lot of people. Some I never see again. I always get a Christmas card from Deirdre mind you, I used not to remember exactly who they were, Desmond and Deirdre Doyle and family . . .' He sighed heavily.

'Did you not like them?' Laura asked. 'It doesn't matter telling us, we don't know them, we won't ever meet them.'

'No, they were perfectly nice, I *did* like them as it happened. I suppose I didn't think they were well suited, that they'd stay together . . .' He gave a little laugh to lighten the mood. 'But there you go, I was wrong. They've been together now for twenty-five years and it don't seem a day too much.'

'They must like each other.' Laura was thoughtful. 'Otherwise they wouldn't want you round and have a big do and everything. Will there be a renewing of vows?'

'I don't know, it was their daughter who wrote to me.'

He relapsed into silence, but silence in the big book-lined room of Alan and Laura Black was never anything to worry about.

He thought about that wedding, the year that Gregory was born. He remembered how Deirdre O'Hagan had come into his sacristy saying that she had heard from her mother that he was going on a six-month secondment to London. It was partly a study assignment and partly in case he might want to join the Irish chaplaincy scheme in Britain. There were so few English Vocations, and so many of the Catholic flock were Irish or second-generation Irish who preferred a priest from their own tribe.

Deirdre O'Hagan had seemed distressed and tense. She wanted to know could he organize a marriage for her in the next month or so.

It had all the hallmarks of a shotgun marriage but she would not be drawn into any conversation about the reasons for the speed.

He had asked mildly that she should consider having the ceremony in Dublin but she had been adamant. Her fiancé's people were from the West.

But surely Dublin was nearer to the West of Ireland than London was?

Deirdre O'Hagan whom he had remembered as the pretty giggling university student daughter of Kevin and Eileen O'Hagan who were supportive and well-off parishioners seemed to have developed a will of steel. She was marrying in London, she said it would be a kindness to her family to involve a curate whom they knew and liked, but of course if he wasn't able to she would make other arrangements.

Father Hurley had tried at the time, he thought looking back on it, to involve the girl in some questioning of the suddenness of her decision. He had said that one shouldn't go into matrimony too hastily and for all the wrong reasons.

He had obviously sounded stuffy and inquisitive, for he remembered her voice clear as a bell and cold, very cold.

'Well Father, if one was to take your own attitude to matrimony one would never marry at all and one would suddenly find that the whole human race had died out.'

Despite this poor start the wedding had been perfectly pleasant. The boy's people were simple small farmers from the West, they didn't field a very large contingent. The O'Hagans were there in force. A nice man, Kevin, quiet and thoughtful. He had died some years back but Eileen was still going strong.

The bridesmaid had been that handsome young woman Maureen Barry, who ran the smart dress shops nowadays. He had seen her only the other day when he had said the Requiem Mass for her mother. He wondered would she go across to London for this ceremony. He wondered would he. He sighed again.

'You're not in good form, Jimbo.' Laura was concerned.

'I'd love to be an old settled priest, you know, totally certain about everything, no doubts at all.'

'You'd be unbearable if you were,' she said affectionately.

Alan looked up from his book. 'I know what you mean, it would be easier if there was just one law and you had to administer it, abide by it. It's all this awful business of trying to judge each case on its merits that confuses things.'

James Hurley looked at his brother-in-law sharply but the solicitor had no hidden meaning, no insight about his son and the trouble he had caused. He was thinking in terms of the district court and a justice being lenient here and strict there according to what he knew of the person before him.

'You'd end up like the Nazis if you couldn't make your own decisions,' Laura consoled him.

'Sometimes they're not right, though.' His face was still troubled.

'You'd never do anything unless you thought it was right at the time.'

'And afterwards? What happens afterwards?'

Laura and Alan exchanged glances. Jim was never like this.

Alan spoke eventually. 'Well at least it's not like a hanging judge in the old days. You didn't actually sentence anyone to death.' It was meant to be reassuring. It didn't really work.

'No. No not to death.'

'Will we take the dogs for a walk?' Laura said.

They walked, the brother and sister, sprightly and strong through the fields that they had walked since they were children.

'If I could help?' she said tentatively.

'No, Laura, I'm a weak man to be letting you see my black side.'

'You're my young brother for all that you're a grand important priest.'

'I'm not grand and important. I never got a parish, I never wanted one. I don't want to take charge.'

'Why should you, then? People don't have to.'

'There are some things they have to take charge of.'

She knew he would talk no more about it, and his brow seemed to clear as they walked home in the fading light.

He knew after that afternoon that if the whole terrible business was to have any value whatsoever he must cease these self-indulgent moods. What was the point of saving them worry on one score only to cause it on another? So, they had been spared from knowing that their son had killed a cyclist while drunk and had failed to stop, that had been peace of mind. Why take that peace away from them again by letting them think that he was cracking up and heading for serious nervous trouble?

In the months that followed he hardened his heart to the doubts and he fought the sense of betrayal when he sat with the only family he ever had or would ever know. He began to laugh easily at his nephew's jokes, and managed not to wince at some of Gregory's more insensitive remarks. The priest told himself over and over that to expect a fallible human being to be perfect was to go against the revealed word of God.

He took pleasure in the simple joy that Gregory Black's parents got from their son. He reminded himself that in all his years of parish work he had never come across a family where there was such peace and genuine accord. Perhaps the price for this might never have to be paid in their lifetime.

He forced his smile not to falter when he saw Gregory helping himself liberally to the gins before dinner, the wines with and the whiskies after. The non-drinking resolution had not lasted very long. Neither had the girlfriend.

'She's too determined, Uncle Jim.' He had laughed as he drove Father Hurley across the country rather too fast for the priest's liking. 'You know everything is an absolute with her. No grey area.'

'It's admirable in its way,' Father Hurley said.

'It's intolerable, nobody can be that sure, that definite.'

'Did you love her do you think?'

'I could have I suppose, but not with all this black and white, honesty or dishonesty, you're either a saint or devil. That's not the way it is in the real world.'

Father Hurley looked at the handsome profile of his sister's son. The boy had forgotten the girl he had killed. The ambiguity and hypocrisy of that night had literally been put out of his mind. He was driving his uncle because Father Hurley's car was out of action, and Gregory had wanted to come down mid week, wanted to talk to his father about a loan. There was something coming up, he had heard a piece of information, the kind of chance that only comes once in a lifetime. Something he really shouldn't know, but if he invested now. Boy!

Father Hurley felt sick that he should be allowed to receive this confidence. But then what was he except another grey-area person? Someone prepared to lie when it made sense. It was a strange visit. Gregory's father seemed apologetic about not being able to raise the money that Gregory needed and a little mystified that he wasn't being told exactly what it was needed for.

Gregory's smile didn't falter but he said he would drive out to be on his own for a while near the lake.

Laura said after he had left that it was very sensible of him to go and work out his annoyance sitting looking at the lake. She said that she wished Alan had just given him the damn money, it would all be his after their time, why couldn't he have it now?

By ten thirty he hadn't come back.

Father Hurley knew he was in the pub, the roadhouse out on the lake drive. He said he'd fancy a walk himself, it was a nice night. It was a three-mile walk. He found his nephew in the bar being refused a drink.

'Come on, I'll drive you home,' he said in what he hoped didn't sound a tone likely to anger his very drunk young nephew.

When they got to the car Gregory pushed him away.

'I'm perfectly able to drive.' His voice was steely.

James Hurley had a choice once the boy was behind the wheel – go with him or let him go on his own.

He opened the passenger door.

The corners were legion and the surfaces were not good.

'I beg you, take it slowly, you don't know what's coming round the corner, there's no way we can see the lights.'

'Don't beg me,' Gregory said, his eyes on the road. 'I hate people who whine and beg.'

'Then I ask you . . .'

They were on top of the donkey and cart before they saw it. The frightened animal ahead reared and was emptying the two old men and their belongings on to the road.

'Jesus Christ.'

Helpless they watched as the donkey, roaring in pain, dragged the cart over the body of one old man and started to slip down the bank towards the lake.

Father Hurley was running towards the cart where two children were screaming.

'You're all right, we're here, we're here,' he called.

Behind him he felt the breath of his nephew.

'You were driving, Uncle Jim, in the name of Christ I beg you.'

The priest didn't stop. He had caught the first little tinker child in his arms and pulled her to safety, then the second, and with all the strength in his body he pulled at the braying donkey too.

'Listen, I beseech you. Think about it, it makes sense. They'll hit me with everything, they can't put a finger on you.'

It was as if Father Hurley hadn't heard him, he had children and cart up to the road where the two dazed old men sat. One was holding his head in his hands and blood was coming through his fingers.

In the moonlight Gregory's face was white with terror.

'They're tinkers, Uncle Jim, they're not meant to be out here without any signs or warning or lights . . . nobody could blame you . . . they heard you saying you were driving me home.'

Father James Hurley knelt beside the old man and forced him to take his hands away so that he could see the wound.

'It's all right my friend, it's all right, when somebody comes we'll get you to the hospital, it'll only be a stitch or two.'

'What are you going to do, Uncle Jim?'

'Oh Gregory.'

The priest looked up with tears in his eyes at the only son of the two people who would realize tonight that perhaps life wasn't meant to be all that good on this earth, and that some people had been too lucky.

6
Maureen

The one thing Maureen's mother would have insisted on had she been alive was that the funeral be done right. Maureen knew exactly what that meant. It meant that there be sufficient notice in the paper for everyone to attend, that there be a judicious invitation back to the house, not everyone but the right people. Both on the day she was brought to the church and on the following day after the burial itself.

Maureen arranged it meticulously, a last homage to the mother who had given her everything and had made her what she was.

She wore a magnificently cut black coat and asked a hairdresser to come to the house so that she would look immaculately groomed in front of all the people who turned up at the church. Maureen did not consider this vanity, she considered that she was carrying out to the letter her mother's last wishes: that Sophie Barry go to her rest mourned publicly by her exquisite and devoted daughter Maureen, successful businesswoman, person of standing in Dublin.

Her mother would have approved too of the drinks and canapés served in the big drawing room, and the way that Maureen moved among the guests pale but calm, introducing here and thanking there, and always being able to remember if it was a wreath, a mass card or a letter of sympathy that had to be acknowledged.

She had nodded in total agreement to all who told her that her mother was a wonderful woman, because this was only the truth. She nodded that it was better her mother didn't have a long illness, she deplored the fact that sixty-eight was too young to die, she was pleased that so many people told her that her mother had been so proud of her only daughter.

'She never talked about anything else.'

'She had a scrapbook of all your achievements.'

'She said that you were more than a daughter, you were her friend.'

Soothing words, gentle touches, graceful gestures. Just as Mother would have liked it. Nobody got drunk and became boisterous but there was the kind of buzz about the whole proceedings that Mother would have thought the mark of a successful gathering. Several times Maureen had found herself planning to talk to her mother about it afterwards.

But then people often said that this was the case. Particularly when you had been close. And there were few mothers and daughters as close as Sophie Barry and her only child Maureen.

Possibly it was because Sophie was a widow and Maureen had been left fatherless for so many years. Possibly because they looked so alike, people read more into their togetherness than there was. Sophie had only become grey late in her fifties, and when she did it was a steel-dark grey as shiny and glamorous as had been the raven-black hair. She had been a size twelve up to the last day and said that she would die rather than wear one of those tent-like creations that so many women seem to sink into after a certain age.

Sophie's good looks and harsh standards did not always endear her to the more easygoing in her circle. But she had what she wanted from them, their total admiration all of her days.

And Maureen would make sure that it would continue in terms of whatever needed to be done now. The house would not be sold with unseemly haste, the mortuary cards would be simple and black-edged, with some tasteful prayer that could be sent as a memento to Protestant friends too. Not something dripping with indulgence-gaining imprecations, no photograph. Mother would say that's what maids did. Maureen would know better than to insult her memory.

Friends had offered to help her go through her mother's things, it can be upsetting they said, it's often easier if an outsider comes to help. Everything can be divided into categories much less emotionally. But Maureen smiled and thanked them, assuring them that this was something she would like to do herself. She didn't particularly want to go through things alone, but Mother would never have let a stranger look at private papers in a million years.

Father Hurley who had known them for years offered to help. He said it was often a lonely business and he would be happy even to sit with her as company. He had meant well, and Mother had always liked him, she said he was a credit to the Church, nicely spoken, very cultured, knew everyone who was anyone; high praise from Mother. But still Mother would not have let him become involved in her private papers. A gentle moving sermon yes, exactly the right kind of priest for this parish, but he couldn't be involved in anything personal. That would be for Maureen alone.

Walter would want to help of course. But it was out of the question, Walter had been kept at arm's length during the whole proceedings. Maureen had no intention of marrying him, or of being seen to rely on him. Why then should he be allowed to be present at all the funeral ceremonies as her right-hand man? This would be giving a false impression to all those old biddies, friends of her mother, women who had nothing left to talk about in their own lives and speculated instead about each other's children. Maureen, unmarried at forty-six, must have given them many good years of chat and supposition, she thought with a grim pleasure.

Kind courteous Walter, who was thought to be suitable for her because he too was unmarried, of a good family and had a good practice at the Bar. Maureen knew that if she wanted to she could marry Walter. He didn't love her, and she felt nothing even remotely like love for him. But Walter was the kind of man who wouldn't have expected love at this stage in life. Once when he was a younger man, perhaps an unsuitable dalliance or two, maybe even a real affair that didn't work out.

Walter had his male bonding in the Law Library, he had a busy social life. People always wanted an extra man.

Mother had liked Walter but Mother was far too intelligent to push her towards him. Anyway Mother would have been the last to use the argument about insuring against a lonely old age. Look at her own years as a woman without a man. Her life had been very full.

Once Maureen had made it clear that she had no thoughts about Walter as a life partner her mother had never pushed the notion again. There had been no talk of including Walter in a bridge party, a theatre outing, or in the party made up to go to the Aga Khan Cup at the Horse Show.

Walter was kind, courteous, and could indeed after several glasses of good claret be a little emotional. Sometimes he talked of lonely roads, and sacrificing all else on the altar of one's career. But Maureen would laugh at him affectionately and ask him to consider what on earth she and he had sacrificed. They had lovely apartments, good cars, hosts of friends and freedom to go where they liked. In Maureen's case to London and New York buying clothes, in Walter's to the West of Ireland fishing.

In a Dublin which more and more would have accepted such a state they were not lovers. It had been suggested one evening and rejected, with charm and elegance on each side, and broached once more in case the first refusal had been only a matter of form. But they remained two attractive single people whose eyes often met resignedly over a table, as yet again a hostess had brought them together as an inspired idea for a dinner party.

It was ironic that of all the men who had wandered into Maureen's life the only one that Mother would have considered suitable was the one who came too late, who came along when Maureen knew she didn't want to change her ways. If she had met Walter, a young earnest barrister in his twenties when she had been struggling to establish the shops, she might well have settled for him. So many of her friends had settled for men who they could not possibly have loved in any real sense. These were not great loves, the wedding ceremonies that Maureen had attended all through the 1960s, they were alliances, refuges, compromises, arrangements. Deirdre O'Hagan, who defied everyone and married her first love in that long summer when they had all been in London, that might have been real love. Maureen was never sure. Even though she had been Deirdre's bridesmaid, and they had slept in the same room the night before the wedding, she had not been certain that Deirdre ached for Desmond Doyle and cried out to be with him. As she herself had cried out to be with Frank Quigley.

It was a strange friendship, hers with Deirdre, their mothers wanted them to be friends so desperately that they gave in at the age of fourteen and agreed to go to the same tennis parties, and later the same hops and rugby-club social evenings on Saturday nights.

By the time they got to UCD they were in fact friends of a sort. And they each knew that their salvation lay with the other. If Maureen said she was going anywhere with Deirdre, then Mother would relax. It was the same in the O'Hagan household, Deirdre could always use Sophie Barry's daughter Maureen as an excuse.

That was why they had been able to go off to London together that summer. The summer they should have been at home working for their degrees. The summer they met Desmond Doyle and Frank Quigley on the boat to Holyhead.

Maureen wondered what Frank Quigley would say if he knew that Mother had died. She didn't know how he talked these days, whether his accent had changed, if he spoke as a lot of Irishmen living twenty-five years in London spoke, with two distinct strands in their voices and telltale words of both cultures coming in at the wrong place.

She had read about him; who hadn't read about Frank Quigley? He was profiled always amongst the Irish who had done well in Britain. Sometimes she saw pictures of him with that sullen-looking young Italian he had married to advance himself still further in the hierarchy of Palazzo.

Frank might be so suave of course nowadays that he would write an elegant note of sympathy on a gilt-edged card. He might be so down to earth and still such a rough diamond that he would say she should have died a quarter of a century earlier.

One thing Maureen knew was that Frank Quigley would not have forgotten her mother, any more than he would have forgotten Maureen.

This was not arrogance on her part, believing that her first love would remember her with the same intensity as she remembered him, when she allowed him into her mind at all. She knew it was true. Still it was irrelevant; he might hear about it from Desmond and Deirdre, but it was hard to say whether they all remained friends still.

Admittedly Desmond still worked in Palazzo, but despite Mrs O'Hagan's great reports of her son-in-law's managerial promotions from time to time, Maureen had the feeling that Desmond had stuck somehow low on a scale, and that all the patronage and friendship from his old friend Frank couldn't pull him any higher.

The day of sorting through Mother's things could not be put off for ever. Maureen decided to go on the Sunday following the funeral. It would not take long if she put her mind to it and did not allow herself to become emotionally upset by everything she touched.

Already she had wept over her mother's glasses in their spectacle case which had been given to her in the hospital. Somehow it seemed sadder than anything else to see the sign of Mother's frail fading eyesight, handed to her in a useless little case. Maureen, usually so decisive, hadn't known what to do with them. They were still there zipped into a side compartment of her handbag. Mother would not have been so soft-hearted. She would have been cool and practical as she had been about everything.

They had only fought once, a long time ago, and it had not been about Frank Quigley nor about any man. Mother hadn't thought that the clothing business looked all right, or sounded respectable enough.

Maureen had blazed her anger, what the hell did it matter how things looked or sounded? It was how they were, what they were about that was important. Mother had smiled a cool infuriating smile. Maureen had stormed out. Up to the North of Ireland first where she got a thorough grounding in retail dress sense from two sisters who ran a smart clothes shop and were pleased and flattered to see the dark handsome young university graduate from Dublin come up to learn all they could teach her. Then she went to London.

It was then that she realized how she had never been really close to Deirdre, they had met rarely while she was there. Deirdre had been tied up with two babies at that stage, and Maureen had been going to trade fairs and exhibitions, and learning what to look for. Maureen told Deirdre nothing of her coldness with her mother for fear that it would go straight back to the O'Hagan household, and presumably Deirdre had secrets, worries and problems that she didn't tell Maureen either.

And anyway the coldness didn't last. It had never been an out-and-out hostility, there were always postcards, and short letters and brief phone calls. So that mother could tell Eileen O'Hagan how well Maureen was doing here, there and everywhere. So that appearances could be kept up. Appearances had been very important to Mother. Maureen determined that she would honour this to the very end, far beyond the grave.

Maureen Barry lived in one of the earlier apartment blocks that had been built in Dublin. She lived ten minutes by foot and two minutes by car from the big house where she was born and where her mother had lived all her life. It had been Mother's home, and Father had married in. For the short married life that they had. He had died abroad when Maureen was six, forty years ago this year.

It would be his anniversary shortly, in three weeks; how strange to think that she would attend the Mass they always had said for the repose of his soul totally on her own. Normally she and Mother went together, for as long as she could remember. Always at eight o'clock in the morning. Mother had said that it was discourteous to involve others in your own personal mourning and memorials. But Mother had always told people afterwards that they had been to the Mass.

The living arrangements were yet one more way in which the relationship between the two women was widely praised. Many another mother would have clung to her daughter and kept her in the family home as long as possible, not noticing or caring about the normal wish of the young to leave the nest. Many a less dutiful daughter might have wanted to go away to another city. To London perhaps or even Paris. Maureen was successful in the fashion world. To have two shops with her own name on them by the time she was forty was no mean achievement. And such smart shops too. She moved from one to another with ease, each had a good manageress who was allowed freedom to run the day-to-day business. It had left Maureen free to buy, to choose, to decide to lunch with the fashionable women whose taste she monitored and even formed. She went to London four times a year and to New York once every spring. She had a standing that her mother would never have believed possible in those bad days, the bad time when they had not seen eye to eye. It hadn't lasted long, and every relationship was allowed to have some valley periods, Maureen told herself. Anyway, she didn't want to think about those days now, not so soon after Mother's death.

It had indeed been so sensible to live apart but near. They saw each other almost every day. Never in all the years since she moved into her apartment did Maureen open her front door and find her mother unannounced on her step. Mother wouldn't dream of calling to a young woman who might be entertaining someone, and wish to do so privately.

It was different about Maureen going back to her old home. No such strictures applied there. Maureen was welcome to call at any time, but Mother managed to let her know that at the end of a bridge party was a particularly suitable time to drop in for a sherry, because everyone could have the chance to admire both the elegant daughter and the evidence of her consideration and devotion to her mother.

On the Sunday she walked to the house where she would never again see her mother walking lightly down the hall to open the door, viewed through the multi-coloured stained glass of the hall-door panels. It felt strange to go to the empty house, because by now there would be no kind friends and relatives staying around as support. Mother's great friend Mrs O'Hagan, Deirdre's mother, had been very pressing and begged Maureen to come and see them, to drop in for supper, to use the O'Hagan house just like she had her old home.

It had been kind, but not the right thing. Maureen wasn't a little girl, she was a middle-aged woman for heaven's sake. It was not appropriate for Mrs O'Hagan to invite her up to the house as she had done thirty years ago when she and Mother had decided that Deirdre and Maureen should be friends.

Mother had always set a lot of store on what Eileen O'Hagan thought about this and that. Eileen and Kevin were her greatest friends. They had always invited Mother to join them at the theatre or the races. They had never to Maureen's recollection tried to find a suitable second husband for her. Or perhaps they had. She would not have known.

As she walked through the sunny streets towards her old home Maureen wondered what life would have been like if Mother had married again. Would a stepfather have encouraged her or fought her when she wanted to take up her career in what she had called the fashion industry and her mother had said was common drapery and glorified salesgirl work?

Would Mother have been coquettish with men years ago? After all Maureen herself did not feel old and past sexual encounters at the age of forty-six, so why should she assume that her mother had? But it was something that never came into their lives.

They talked a lot about Maureen's young men, and how they had all somehow failed to measure up. But they had never talked about any man for Mother.

She let herself into the house and shivered slightly because there was no little fire lit in what Mother had always called the morning room. Maureen plugged in the electric fire and looked around.

Two weeks ago on a Sunday she had come here to find Mother looking white and anxious. She had this pain, possibly indigestion but . . . Maureen had acted quickly, she helped her mother gently to the car and drove calmly to the hospital. No point in disturbing the doctor, calling him away from his Sunday breakfast she had said to Mother, let's go to the outpatients' department, to Casualty. They were there the whole time in a hospital, they would set her mind at rest.

Mother, looking more and more anxious, agreed with her, and even at this stage Maureen had noticed with sinking heart that her mother's careful speech sounded slurred, the words were running together.

They were seen at once, and within an hour Maureen was waiting outside the intensive care to be told the news that her mother was having a massive stroke. One that she might very well not recover from.

Mother recovered, but not her faculties of speech; her eyes, bright and burning, seemed to beg for an end to this indignity.

She could press once for yes and twice for no on Maureen's arm. Maureen had spoken to her alone.

'Are you afraid, Mother?'

No.

'You do believe that you'll get better, don't you?'

No.

'I want you to believe that, you must. No, sorry: of course you can't answer that. I mean, don't you want to get better?'

No.

'But surely for me, Mother, for all your friends, *we* want you to get better. God, how do I say something that you can answer? Do you know that I love you? Very very much?'

Yes, and a lessening of the strain in the eyes.

'And do you know that you are the best mother that anyone could have?'

Yes.

Then she had been tired and not long after that she had slipped into unconsciousness.

They had been right, the friends who had stood in this room, Mother's morning room that got the early light, when they had nodded and said Sophie Barry could not have lived the dependent life of an invalid. It was better that she had been taken quickly away from pain and indignity.

Could it really only have been two weeks since that Sunday morning? It felt like ten years in so many ways.

Maureen unfolded the black plastic sacks. She knew that a great deal of Mother's things could indeed be thrown away, there was no one to gasp and wonder over old mementos of cavalry balls years ago, or programmes of long-forgotten concerts signed with some illegible squiggle. No grandchildren to ooh and aah over worlds gone by. And Maureen in her own busy life would not look at them, a lot of things would go.

She sat at the small writing desk: an antique. She might take it for the hallway of her own flat. It was such an impractical thing dating from a time when ladies only penned little notes or invitation cards. It had nothing to do with today's world. Mrs O'Hagan had been surprised that Maureen was going to remain in her flat. She was sure that Sophie would have wanted her own home to continue in the family. But Maureen was adamant. She lived a life too full to involve cleaning a house with as many nooks and crannies as this. Her own space was custom-made for her, wall-long closets for her clothes, a study with proper filing cabinets as a mini-office, a big room where she could entertain, its kitchen in full view of the dining table so that she could talk to her guests as she served them their dinner.

No, it would be a backwards move to come home to this house. Mother knew that too.

First she went through the finances. She was surprised how fiddly and disorganized Mother had become lately. It was sad to see little notes Mother had written to herself: a reminder here, a query there. It would have been so easy for Maureen to have set up an uncomplicated system like her own, five minutes would have done it, a letter to the bank asking them to pay so much each month to electricity, gas, insurance fund . . . It would have cut out all these final demands and letters of bewilderment. Mother must have appeared much more in control than she was.

Then there was an endless correspondence with a stockbroker. Like everyone of her generation, Mother had believed that wealth was measured in stocks and shares. Only the broker's letters were to be found: Mother had kept no copies of her own side of the correspondence. It was a sorry tale of confusion and disappointment.

Maureen felt weary and sad as she finished the series of responses to what had obviously been querulous demands for information and explanations why shares that everyone knew were excellent seemed to have vanished into nothingness. Briskly Maureen wrote a letter to the broker explaining that her mother had died and asking him to send her details of the nature of the portfolio as it stood now. She wished that she had involved herself more but with Mother there was such a dignity, there was a boundary you didn't cross.

Maureen kept all the letters she had written in her slim briefcase, she would photocopy them later, back at her own apartment. Mr White who had been Mother's solicitor had already congratulated her on her efficiency; he wished that many more young women could be as organized but then of course she hadn't built herself a big business without having a good financial brain and a sense of administration. He had shown her Mother's will, a simple document leaving everything to her beloved daughter Mary Catherine (Maureen) Barry with gratitude for all her years of devoted love and care. The will had been made in 1962. Just after the reconciliation. After Mother had accepted that Maureen was not going to abandon her idea of how she would live her life. Since the day that Sophie Barry had written down her gratitude for the devoted love and care, twenty-three more years of it had been given. Surely she would never have believed that for over two decades Maureen would remain single and remain her close friend.

It was taking more time than she had thought, and she felt a strange sense of loss, different entirely to the grieving at the funeral. It was as if she had lost her idea of Mother as someone almost perfect. This nest of confusion stuffed into the drawers of a lovely writing desk spoke of a peevish old woman, confused and irritable. Not the calm beautiful Sophie Barry who until two weeks ago had sat like a queen in her throne room in this her morning room with its tasteful furnishings. Maureen didn't like discovering this side of her mother.

She had made herself a cup of coffee to give her more energy for the task and reached out resolutely for the next big bulky envelope. She remembered the way Mother used to say, 'Maureen my child, if a thing is worth doing, it's worth doing properly.' That used to apply to anything from cleansing her face twice a day with Mother's special cream and then splashing it with rosewater, to going back and having six more tennis lessons so that she would look that much better at the summer parties. Well if Mother could see her now, something Maureen doubted, she would certainly agree that the devoted daughter was doing the job properly.

She was totally unprepared for the papers she found in the envelope marked Solicitor. She thought it might be some more foostering dealings about shares or pensions, but these were letters from a completely different solicitor, and they were dated forty years ago. There were a series of legal documents, all signed in 1945. And they showed that Maureen's father Bernard James Barry had not died of a virus when he was in Northern Rhodesia just after the war. Sophie Barry's husband had deserted her forty years ago. He had left his wife and child and gone to live with another woman in Bulawayo in what was then Southern Rhodesia.

Maureen realized that for all she knew she might have a father still alive, a man of seventy years, living in Bulawayo, Zimbabwe. That she might even have stepbrothers and sisters, men and women not much younger than herself. The woman described as his 'common law wife' was called Flora Jones and had come from Birmingham in England. Wildly Maureen thought that Mother would have said that Flora was a maid's name.

She wasn't in the habit of pouring herself a stiff drink in the middle of a Sunday morning. Maureen Barry, disciplined in this as in everything else, realized the perils of drinking alone. She had seen too many of her friends lapse into it, at the end of a long hard day with no one to relax with. She had learned this from Mother as she had learned everything. Mother said that widows could slip into tippling if they didn't exercise some control. Widows, what did Mother mean, acting out a lie for forty years? What kind of closeness was it that meant she couldn't tell her only daughter the biggest event of her life? What manner of woman could perpetuate a myth about a man who had to be buried abroad?

With another ripple of shock running through her like the continuous waves after an earthquake, Maureen realized that her mother who had been a sane woman had gone out every May and had a Mass said for the repose of the soul of Bernard James Barry, a man who must have been alive for some if not all of the time that she was doing this.

There was whiskey in a decanter. Maureen smelled it, it reminded her of when she had a toothache years and years ago and Mother would put a whiskey-flavoured piece of cotton wool on the gum to numb the pain. Mother had loved her so much.

Maureen poured out a large measure of neat whiskey, drank it, and burst into tears.

It was a measure of the lonely life she led, she realized, that she had no one to tell. There was no bosom pal to ring up, no house where she could run around and share this staggering news. Like her mother, she had kept aloof from intimacies. There was no man she had let close enough to her thoughts to confide in. Her work colleagues knew nothing of her private life. Her mother's friends . . . oh yes . . . they would be interested. My, my, would she get a hearing at O'Hagans' if she were to turn up with the news.

Flora. Flora Jones. It was like a name from a musical comedy. And now presenting Miss Flora Jones, the Carmen Miranda of our town. There had been letters about divorce, and copies of letters from Mother's solicitor repeating over and over, that not only was there no divorce in Ireland, and that his client was a staunch Roman Catholic, but that this was not the matter at issue, the question at issue apparently had been money. Maureen leafed still unbelieving through the documents . . . kept meticulously in order – this was a younger firmer Mother, more in control forty years ago, wounded and enraged and determined she was going to get the last penny from the man who had betrayed her. A sum had been paid over. A sum which in today's money would have been considered staggering. The solicitor of Bernard James Barry in Bulawayo wrote to the solicitor of Mrs Sophie Barry in Dublin that his client was willing to realize most of his assets in order to provide for his wife and eldest daughter. His client Mr Barry had now, as was already known to Mrs Barry, a second daughter by Miss Flora Jones, a daughter whose birth he was most anxious to legitimize.

Mother's letter of reply to that had been extraordinary, it was written exactly as Mother spoke. Maureen could hear her voice as she read the words. She could literally hear Mother's voice, slow, measured, articulate, a younger stronger voice than of late.

'. . . while you will understand that there can never be any question of a divorce since it is against the rules of the Church to which we both belong, I cannot legislate for you and your actions in a foreign land. I am writing this letter without the approval of the solicitors but I think you will understand its general drift. I have accepted your settlement for Maureen and myself, I shall pursue you in no court, nor under any jurisdiction. You shall be totally free from me if and only if you never return to Ireland. I shall announce your death. Today is April 15th. If you return this letter to me with your promise that you will never come back to Ireland again, then I will say that you died abroad of a virus on May 15th.

'If this promise is ever broken or if you try to get in touch with Maureen in any way even after she is legally an adult, I can assure you that you will be made to regret it to the end of your days . . .'

It was the way Mother spoke to a tradesman who had offended her in some way, or to a handyman who had not done a job to her satisfaction.

He had accepted her terms, the man in Bulawayo, the man Maureen had thought was dead for forty years. He had returned the letter, as ordered to do. Attached to it by a small pearl-topped pin was a postcard. A brown sepia picture of mountains and savannah.

The words on the postcard said, 'I died of a virus on May 15th 1945.'

Maureen put her head down on her mother's desk and cried as if her heart would break into little pieces.

She didn't feel the time passing. And when she looked at the clock, the way the hands were placed seemed meaningless. It said a quarter past two or ten past three. It was bright so it must be daytime.

She had come to the house at ten o'clock, she must have been in this semi-trance for over two hours.

She walked around feeling the blood beginning to flow again in her veins. If anyone had looked in the window of the morning room they would have seen a tall dark young woman, looking considerably less than her forty-six years, apparently hugging herself around the waist of her smart navy and pink wool dress.

In fact Maureen was holding in each hand the elbow of the opposite arm, in a physical attempt to hold herself together after this shock.

She felt a rage against her mother, not just because this man had been ordered summarily out of her life, and threatened not to contact his own flesh and blood. But she felt a burning anger that if her mother had kept this secret so successfully for so long, why on earth had she not destroyed the evidence?

If Maureen had never found these papers, she would never have known. She would have been happier, more safe and sure in the world she had built for herself.

Why had her mother been so casual and cruel? She must have known that Maureen would find the evidence some day.

But of course Mother knew that Maureen would not betray her. Maureen would keep up appearances to the end.

Like hell she would. Like bloody hell.

It came to her suddenly that she could do anything she liked about this whole farcical bargain. She had entered into no melodramatic promises about mythical deaths. She had entered into no promise not to contact him for fear of some awful punishment.

By God, she was going to find him, or Flora, or her half-sister.

Please, please may they be alive. Please may she find her father from this welter of documents. The latest being in 1950, confirming a final transfer of assets.

Please God may he still be alive. Seventy wasn't that old.

She began to work with the kind of controlled furious energy that she had not known since the night before her first big high-fashion sale when they were up almost all night in the stockrooms marking clothes down, and recataloguing and estimating the takings of the following day.

This time she approached her mother's belongings with different categories in mind. She found two boxes which she filled with early photographs and memorabilia of herself when a child.

If she did find this man, if he was a man with any heart he would want to know what she looked like at her first Communion, in her hockey outfit, dressed for her first dance.

Items which would have been carefully cut up and destroyed were now filed in boxes and labelled 'keepsakes'.

She sorted and arranged and tidied until she was ready to drop. Then she tied up the bags which were real rubbish, folded the clothes and other items which were to go to the Vincent de Paul, and ordered a taxi to take back the boxes of keepsakes to her own flat.

There wasn't a drawer now that hadn't been emptied and dusted out. Much of the ordinary kitchen equipment would go to Mrs O'Neill who had come to clean for Mother over the years. Jimmy Hayes who did the garden could have the lawnmower and any of the gardening tools he wanted. Maureen also wrote him a letter asking him to take for his own use any plants that he particularly liked, and to have them removed quickly. She had decided now that the house would go on the market as soon as possible.

She laid her hand on the small writing desk. The one she had been going to take for the entrance hall of her own apartment. She patted it and said, 'No'. She didn't want it now. She wanted nothing from here.

The taxi man helped her in with the boxes. Because he was curious she told him that she had been clearing away her mother's effects. He was very sympathetic.

'Isn't it a pity now that you didn't have anyone to help you do a job like that?' he said.

That's what people often said to her in different forms, like wasn't it a wonder that a fine girl like herself had never married and settled down.

'Oh my father would have done everything but he was away, far away,' she said.

She had mentioned her father. She didn't care about the surprised look that the taxi driver gave her, or how odd it was to have a father far away when a mother had died.

She felt that by mentioning him she was making him be alive.

She had a long, long bath and felt better but ravenously hungry. She telephoned Walter.

'I'm being very selfish, and literally using you, so feel free to say no, but are there any nice restaurants open on a Sunday night? I'd love to go out for a meal.'

Walter said nothing could suit him better, he had been doing a particularly tedious kind of Opinion where there seemed to be no solution or a thousand solutions, and one was as hard as the other. He would love to escape from it.

Together they sat and ordered good food and wine by candlelight.

'You look a little feverish,' Walter said with concern.

'I've a lot on my mind.'

'I know, it must have been very distressing today,' he said.

Her eyes seemed to dance at him across the table. She had never looked more beautiful, he thought.

'I know it's not the time, but then there never is any really good time, but perhaps you might think of . . .'

'Yes?'

'Well, should we go on a holiday together, somewhere we would both like, Austria you once said you would like to visit?'

'There's no fishing in Austria, Walter.' She smiled at him.

'There are probably no fashion trade fairs either, but we could manage for two weeks couldn't we?'

'No, Walter, we'd drive each other mad.'

'We could leave each other alone.'

'Can't we do that better living apart?' She gave him a very bright smile.

'There's something on your mind.' He looked hurt and troubled.

'Yes, there is, and I can't tell you now. But please remember tonight and that I wanted to tell you something. I will soon.'

'When?'

'I don't know. Soon.'

'Is it another man? I know that sounds very corny but you have that kind of look about you.'

'No, it's not another man. Not in that sense. I'll tell you, I've never lied to you, and when I do tell, you'll realize.'

'Now I can't wait,' he said.

'I know, neither can I, I wish people worked on Sundays, why does the world close down on Sundays?'

'You and I work on Sundays,' Walter complained.

'Yes, but offices all over the world don't, damn them.'

He knew it wasn't worth asking any more, he would hear nothing. He leaned over and patted her hand.

'I suppose I must love you to let you get away with all of this performance.'

'Oh will you go away to hell, Walter, of course you don't love me, not even in the slightest, but you're a great friend, and I'm sure, though I don't intend to find out, that you're a smashing lay as well.'

The waiter's arrival just at that moment, in time to hear Maureen's extravagant compliment, prevented Walter from saying anything in reply.

She slept a little but not much. She was out of her bed, showered and dressed, by six a.m. The time difference would be three hours. She would start telephoning International Inquiries, and giving the out-of-date numbers, hoping that it would not be too long a haul. She had almost weakened enough to ask Walter if there were international directories of solicitors worldwide that she could study down at the Four Courts, but no, she must give him no details, no hints; later she would tell him. He deserved that. She hadn't decided what she would tell everyone else, when she found her father; if she found him.

It was not as difficult as she had feared. It was probably twenty times as expensive in terms of telephone calls, but she didn't care.

The firm no longer existed in Bulawayo, helpful operators got her listings of other solicitors, finally she found that the original company had moved to South Africa. She found herself talking to people in cities she had never even thought about even if she had acknowledged their names ... Bloemfontein, Ladysmith, Kimberley, Queenstown.

She found one of the names that had signed one of the letters in Pretoria. Maureen Barry was crisp.

She explained that her mother had died and that it was her last wish that she Maureen should contact her late father: to whom should she now make the inquiries?

It wasn't a file that would have been kept open for forty years, the man told her.

'But you haven't thrown it away. Lawyers don't throw anything away.'

'Can't you inquire at your end?'

'I have, they know nothing, the firm has changed, they say, and it's true that all the documents were handed back to my mother at her request. I have to try at your end.'

He sounded a nice man despite his accent and the way he said *rilly* instead of really and tried to work out what was the best way to go in the *ind* instead of the end.

'I fully realize that this is professional work, to research on my behalf, I am totally prepared to pay a professional fee for your time and expertise,' Maureen said. 'Would you like me to approach you through solicitors here to put it on a more formal basis?'

'No, it seems to me that you are a person who could be dealt with in her own right.'

She could hear him smiling from across the world, a man whom she'd never met in a country she would never visit (nor would any of her friends) on account of its policies. Mother had been heard to say once she felt very sorry for those whites having to give up all their privileges and nice homes. But it hadn't gone down well. Mother hadn't been a fool, she didn't go that route again.

He said he would call her shortly.

'I wonder have you any idea how shortly I hope it's going to be.'

'I think so,' he said in his curious clipped accent. 'If I had just lost one parent and had the hope of finding another I would know that there was a lot of urgency involved.'

She didn't know how she got through the Tuesday and the Wednesday. He phoned her, the man from Pretoria, on Wednesday at 8 a.m. with an address of a solicitor's firm in London.

'Is he dead or alive?' she asked, her hand at her throat waiting for the reply.

'They didn't tell me, truly they didn't tell me.' He sounded regretful.

'But these people will know?' she begged.

'These people will be able to get a message to whoever is concerned.'

'Did they hint?'

'Yes. They hinted.'

'What?'

'That he was alive. That you would be talking to the principal involved.'

'I'll never be able to thank you,' she said.

'You don't know yet whether you have anything to thank me for or not.'

'But I'll tell you. I'll ring you back.'

'Write to me, you've spent enough on telephone calls. Or better come out and see me.'

'I don't think I'll do that, would you be any use to me? What class of an age of a person are you at all?'

'Stop putting on that accent. I am sixty-three, a widower, with a beautiful home in Pretoria.'

'God bless you,' she said.

'I hope he's alive and good to you,' said the stranger from South Africa.

She had to wait an hour and a half before she could talk to the man in the London firm of solicitors.

'I don't know why you're talking to me,' he said in a slightly peeved tone.

'I don't know either,' Maureen confessed. 'But the original agreement was that my father and I should not get in touch during my mother's lifetime. I know it sounds like something from Hans Christian Andersen but this is the way it happened. Can you listen for two minutes, only two? I can explain it quickly, I'm used to business conversations.'

The English solicitor understood. He said he would be in touch.

Maureen began to have far greater faith in the speed of the law than she ever had before. Walter would tell her about delays and adjournments, she knew herself the endless palaver about contracts with suppliers. But suddenly in the middle of the most important event of her whole life she had met two law firms who seemed to understand her urgency. To sense her impatience and respond to it. On Thursday night she checked the answering machine in her flat but there was nothing except a kindly invitation from Mother's friend Mrs O'Hagan to drop in any evening for a sherry just as you did with your own poor mother. And there was a message from Walter who was going to the West of Ireland at the weekend, there would be lots of lovely walks and gorgeous food, he said, as well as fishing. And there needn't even *be* any fishing if Maureen would care to join him.

She smiled. He was a good friend.

There were two clicks where people had hung up without leaving a message. She felt restless, and then annoyed with herself. How could she expect these people to act so swiftly? And suppose her father *was* alive and in England, which was the way it looked now . . . perhaps he didn't want to get in touch, or he did and Flora didn't want him to, or his daughter. She suddenly realized that there might have been other children.

She paced the apartment, walking the length of her long living room, arms hugging each other. She couldn't remember when she had last been like this, unable to settle to anything.

The phone when it rang made her jump and the voice was hesitant.

'Maureen Barry. Is that Maureen Barry?'

'Yes.' She spoke half words, half breath.

'Maureen, it's Bernie,' the voice said. And there was a silence, as if he was waiting desperately to know what she would say.

She was able to say nothing. No words would come out.

'Maureen, they told me you had been trying to get in touch, if that's not so . . .' He was almost ready to ring off.

'Are you my father?' she whispered.

'I'm an old man now, but I was your father,' he said.

'Then you still are.' She forced a lightness into her voice. It had been the right thing to do, she heard him laugh a little.

'I rang before,' he said. 'But it was one of those machines, you sounded so formal I had to ring off without saying anything.'

'I know, people should be hanged for that,' she said. Again it was right, he was relaxing.

'But I rang again just to hear your voice and think: This is Maureen speaking, actually the sound of her voice.'

'And did you like the sound of it?'

'Not as much as now when it's a real conversation. Is it a real conversation?'

'Yes, yes it is.'

There was a silence, but it wasn't a heavy one, it was as if they were both settling into the strange ritual of talking to each other.

'Would you like to meet me?' she asked.

'There's nothing I would like more. But would you be able to come to England to find me? I'm a bit feeble now, I couldn't come to Ireland to see you.'

'That's no problem. I'll come as soon as you like.'

'It won't be the Bernie you used to know.'

She understood he wanted her to call him Bernie, not Father. Mother had always referred to him as poor Bernard.

'I never knew you anyway Bernie, and you only knew me for a short time, it will be no shock to either of us. I'm freewheeling down to fifty, a middle-aged woman.'

'Stop, stop.'

'No, it's true, I'm not actually grey because I have such a regular relationship with a hairdresser . . .' She felt she was burbling on.

'And Sophie . . . she told you . . . before she . . .' He was hesitant.

'She died two weeks ago . . . Bernie . . . it was a stroke, it was quick and she wouldn't have recovered, it was all for the best . . .'

'And you . . .?'

'I'm fine. But what about seeing you, where will I come, and Flora, and your family?'

'Flora is dead. She died shortly after we left Rhodesia.'

'I'm sorry.'

'Yes, she was a wonderful woman.'

'And children?' Maureen felt this was an extraordinary conversation. It sounded so normal, so run of the mill, yet she was talking to her own father, a man she had thought was forty years dead until four days ago.

'There's just Catherine. She's in the States.'

Maureen was pleased somehow.

'What's she doing there, is she working, is she married?'

'No, she's neither, she's gone with this rock musician, she's been with him eight years now. She sort of goes along wherever he is to make a type of home for him, she says, it's all she ever wanted. She's happy.'

'She's lucky then,' Maureen said almost without thinking.

'Yes she is, isn't she? Because she's not hurting anyone. People say she's a loser but I don't think that, I think she's winning if she has what she wants without hurting anyone else.'

'When can I come and see you, Bernie?' she asked.

'Oh the sooner the better, the soonest the very best,' he said.

'Where are you?'

'Would you believe Ascot?' he said.

'I'll come tomorrow,' she said.

Before she left she went through her post quickly. Hardly anything to do with work came to her apartment, all business mail was addressed to her main shop. There were a couple of bills, circulars and a letter that looked like an invitation. It was from Anna Doyle, the eldest of Deirdre O'Hagan's children, a formal invitation to a silver wedding for their parents and a note saying that she apologized for the ludicrously early notice but she wanted to make sure that the key figures were able to come. Perhaps Maureen could let them know.

Maureen looked at it almost without seeing it. A silver wedding seemed such a small milestone compared to what she was about to embark on herself. She wouldn't think now about whether she would go or not.

It was a very comfortable guest Home, Bernard James Barry had left the colonies in style, Maureen realized. She had hired a car at Heathrow and driven to the address he had given her.

She had taken the precaution of telephoning the Home herself to inquire whether her arrival would not put too much strain on her father, who said he had bad rheumatoid arthritis and was recovering from a mild heart attack.

She had been told that he was in the best of health and was already eager for her to arrive.

He was dressed in a blazer with some colourful crest, he had a carefully tied cravat, he looked the perfect gentleman lightly tanned, a lot of thick grey hair, a cane and a slow walk, but in every way the kind of man her mother would love to have entertained back in Dublin. He had a smile that would break your heart.

'I have the Egon Ronay guide, Maureen,' he said after she had kissed him. 'I thought we should go out and have a proper lunch to celebrate.'

'You're a man after my own heart, Bernie,' she said.

And he was a man after her own heart. There were no apologies, no excuses. In life there were only just so many chances for happiness, he didn't regret his daughter Catherine taking hers, he didn't blame Sophie for seeking happiness through status, it was just that he couldn't stick with it himself.

He had known all about Maureen, he had never lost contact, not until Kevin O'Hagan died. He had written to Kevin at his club and asked him for news of his little girl. He showed Maureen a scrapbook he had made, cuttings from the newspapers about Maureen's shops, photographs cut from society magazines about Maureen at this dance or that reception. Photos too of Maureen with Deirdre O'Hagan, including one showing her in bridesmaid's outfit.

'They're having a silver wedding would you believe this year.' Maureen winced at the picture of the very inelegant 1960 wedding outfits. How could they have known so little then, had she only developed a clothes sense much later?'

Mr O'Hagan had written regularly, it was only when his letter was returned from the club with a note that Maureen's father had heard of his friend's death. He had been instructed to leave no evidence of the correspondence in his house, part of the deal had been that Bernard Barry be mourned as a dead man.

They talked easily, old friends with a lot in common, it seemed.

'Did you have any great love that you didn't follow?' he asked as he sipped his brandy. At seventy he felt entitled to a little luxury like this, he said.

'Not really, not a great love.' She was uncertain.

'But something that could have been a great love.'

'I thought so at the time, but I was wrong, it would never have worked. It would have held us both back, we were too different, it would have been unthinkable in many ways.' Maureen knew that her voice sounded like her mother's as she said this.

She found it easy to tell this man about Frank Quigley, about how she had loved him so much when she was twenty she thought that her whole body and soul would explode. She found it not at all difficult to use such words, although she had never even articulated them before.

She told how she had done everything but sleep with Frank that summer, and the reason she held back was not the usual fear of pregnancy that had held every other girl back, but simply she knew that she must not get more involved than she already was as he would never fit into her life.

'And was this something you believed or was it something Sophie told you?' His voice was gentle, without accusation.

'Oh I believed it, I believed it utterly. I thought there were two types of people, us and them. And Frank was definitely them. So was Desmond Doyle but somehow Deirdre O'Hagan managed to get away with it. I remember at the wedding we were all pretending Desmond's people came from some estate in the West instead of a cabin on the side of a hill.'

'She didn't get away with it entirely,' Maureen's father said.

'You mean Mr O'Hagan wrote to you about that?'

'Yes, a bit. I suppose I was someone he could talk to who wasn't involved, who never would be.'

Maureen told how Frank Quigley had come to Dublin uninvited for her Conferring day. How he had stood at the back of the hall and made whooping sounds and shouted as she went to receive her parchment.

He had called to the house afterwards. It had been terrible.

'Did Sophie order him away?'

'No, you know Mother, well maybe you don't but she wouldn't do that, she killed him with kindness, she was charm itself . . . "Oh and tell me Frank, would my late husband and I have met your people when we were in Westport" . . . you know the kind of thing.'

'I do.' He looked sad.

'And Frank somehow behaved worse and worse, everything she did seemed to make him more bolshie and thick and badly behaved. He took out his comb during supper and combed his hair, you know, looking at himself in that bit of mirror in the sideboard. Oh and he stirred his coffee as if he were going to go through the bottom of the cup. I could have killed him, and I could have killed myself for caring.'

'And what did your mother say?'

'Oh, something like "Have you enough sugar, Frank? Or perhaps you would have preferred tea?" You know, terribly polite, not a hint that anything was out of place unless you knew.'

'And afterwards?'

'Afterwards, she just laughed. She said he was very nice and laughed.'

There was a silence.

'But I went along with it,' Maureen said earnestly. 'I can't say she threw him out, she didn't, she never denied him the house, she even inquired about him from time to time with that little laugh, it was as if somehow by mistake we had invited poor Jimmy Hayes who did the garden in for supper. And I went along with it, because I agreed with her, I went along with her way of thinking.'

'And did you regret it?'

'Not at once, he was so foul-mouthed and called me all the snobby bitches under the sky, he almost proved Mother's point, my point. He said he'd show me, that he would be received in the highest houses in the land, and that one day my crabbed old mother and I would regret that we hadn't welcomed him to our poxy house. That's the way he spoke.'

'Out of hurt.' Her father was sympathetic.

'Yes, yes of course. And of course he *did* become a merchant prince and Deirdre O'Hagan married his equally ignorant and non-acceptable best friend . . . so he was right. His day did come.'

'And is he happy?'

'I don't know, I think not. But maybe he's like a lark in the spring. I don't know.'

'You're lovely, Maureen . . .' her father said suddenly.

'No I'm not, I'm very stupid, was very stupid for too long. It wouldn't have hurt anybody to use your phrase, it wouldn't have hurt anybody at all for me to say to Mother when I was twenty-one that I was off with Frank Quigley, pedigree or no pedigree.'

'Maybe you didn't want to hurt her, after all I had abandoned her, you didn't want it to happen to her twice.'

'Ah, but I didn't know you'd abandoned her, I thought you got an awful virus and died.'

'I'm sorry.' He looked contrite.

'I'm delighted, you old devil,' she said. 'Nothing has given me as much happiness in my whole life.'

'Come on out of that, an old man, ready for a wheelchair.'

'Will you come and live with me in Dublin?' she asked.

'No, no, my dearest Maureen, I won't.'

'You don't need to be in a home, you're as fit as a fiddle. I can see you well looked after, not in Mother's house, we'll get somewhere together. Some place bigger than my flat.'

'No, I promised Sophie.'

'But she's dead now, you kept your promise while she was alive.'

His eyes were sad.

'No, there is a kind of honour about a thing like this, they'd reassess her, you know, they'd go over everything she said, it would be degrading her afterwards. You know what I mean.'

'I do, but you're being too honourable in a sense, she

didn't give you the chance to stay in contact with your own daughter, she didn't give me that chance, she didn't play really fair with us. I thought you were dead until a few days ago.'

'But at least she told you in the end,' said Bernard Barry, his face happy.

'What?'

'Well at least she told you that she wanted you to find me. I heard that from the solicitors. When she knew she was dying she wanted you to have the chance to meet me again.'

Maureen bit her lip. Yes, that was what she had said at the outset, when she was making those early inquiries to Bulawayo.

She looked closely at her father's face.

'I must say I was touched and pleased at that. I thought she was implacable. Kevin O'Hagan told me that there was an anniversary Mass for me every year.'

'I know,' Maureen agreed, 'it's coming up again shortly.'

'So she did something she needn't have done, I owe it to her not to go back and disturb her memory. Anyway, child, I don't know anyone there any more, not since Kevin died, and I'd only be an object of curiosity to them all. No, I'll stay here, I like it, and you'll come and see me from time to time, and your sister Catherine and her young man will come, I'll be in clover.'

Her eyes filled with tears. She would never tell him that Mother hadn't sent her to find him, she would let him think something good as he sat in the sunset thinking he was in clover.

'I'll find lots of excuses to come and see you then, maybe I'll open a shop in Ascot here or in Windsor. I mean it.'

'Of course you do, and won't you be coming over for Kevin's daughter's silver wedding? Won't that be another excuse?'

'I mightn't go to that. Frank Quigley was the best man, you know, it's meant to be a kind of a reunion of everyone who was there, dredging up all the past memories and everything.'

'Isn't that all the more reason to go?' asked Bernie Barry, the man with the tan and the twinkle in his eye who fell in love on a business trip forty years ago and had the courage to follow his star.

7
Frank

He never knew why everyone made such a fuss about travelling, Frank loved to get into his car and head off a hundred miles or more along motorways past signposts. He felt free and as if there was a sense of adventure about it all. Even if it was only a catering exhibition that he had been to a dozen times before he enjoyed it. And why wouldn't he? As he often reminded himself, not everyone else on the motorways had a Rover, this year's model, with fitted stereo and radio filling the sleek comfortable world with music. Or whenever he wanted it with *Italian for Businessmen*. Nobody in Palazzo Foods knew that Frank Quigley could understand every single word of Italian spoken in his presence. He never let a flicker of the eye acknowledge that he had understood what might be being said. Even when it was about him. Particularly when it was about him.

Sometimes Frank thought that his father-in-law Carlo Palazzo might have a suspicion, but if he had he kept it to himself. And he would have admired Frank all the more for it. He had let Frank know a long time ago that they had been watching him and grooming him, and that he would never have got to first base with the boss's daughter unless Carlo Palazzo and his brother had wanted it that way.

Frank had known this already, it came as no surprise that a wealthy girl like Renata would be heavily protected by her father and uncles from fortune hunters. He knew that he was suitable because he didn't need to marry the Palazzo Princess to rise in the company. He didn't even need Palazzo, Frank Quigley would have been able to walk into any business in Britain. He had no initials after his name, he had never finished his formal schooling. He didn't need any of it. He had the flair and the ability to work long hard days and nights. They had known all that fifteen years ago when they let him take Renata out to dinner. They knew he would lay no untoward hand on the dark shy heiress to the Palazzo fortunes until they were wed. And the Palazzos knew that if ever he were to be the teeniest little bit unfaithful to his wife it would be something anonymous and discreet and far from home. There would be no hint of scandal.

Frank sighed about the unwritten rules. He had sailed a little near the wind on one or two occasions but nothing he couldn't handle. Until now. Now the situation was very different, and he needed every moment alone that he could seize in order to work out what to do. If it were business, if it were only business . . . ah, then he would know exactly what to do. But Joy East was not business. Not when she was in her yellow tee-shirt and nothing else, walking confidently around her house proud and sure of herself. And sure of him, as he lay there admiringly afternoon after long sunny afternoon smiling at her mane of streaked brown and gold hair, her perfect teeth, her long tanned legs.

Joy East the designer who had got Palazzo into the smart magazines, who had raised their image from the tatty to the stylish, as Frank Quigley had raised their sales and their progress from the mass of small so-called supermarkets to the very front rank. Joy East who had told him the first night they had looked at each other with non-professional eyes that they would be the ideal match. Neither wanted to change their lifestyle, neither was in any position to force the other to do so. Joy wanted her independence and freedom, Frank wanted to remain in his marriage with the boss's daughter. Who better to suit each other than two people with everything to lose by being silly and everything to gain by enjoying each other's company discreetly? She had told him this partly in words, partly by her look and partly by the way she had leaned across the restaurant table and kissed him full on the lips.

'I checked first,' she had said, laughing. 'There's nobody in the place except tourists.'

It had been exciting then, it had continued to be exciting. Frank had rarely met women like Joy. The finer and indeed the main points of the women's movement had passed him by, this new independence seemed to him very exotic. Joy East was proud of her single state, she had almost married, she told him, a very lucky escape when she was twenty-three but she had called it off days before the wedding. Her father had been furious and they still had to pay a huge whack of the wedding reception cost, and the cake, and the limousines. Not to mention all the talk and the fuss. Everyone would have preferred her to get married just to save all the embarrassment. And the man? Oh, lucky escape for him too, Joy thought, laughing and thinking about him not at all.

She lived in a small house on the corner of a road which had been not at all fashionable when she found it but which day by day was seeing the removal vans of ever smarter neighbours. Her white-walled garden was private and had vines on the walls. Her long comfortable living room could fit sixty comfortably at one of her parties. Joy gave wonderful parties and often said that it was terribly easy to flatter and please people by asking them for two hours' drinks and canapés to your house.

And they loved her in Palazzo for doing it. So generous of Miss East, the board always said, above and beyond what Miss East needed to do for them. It bought her further goodwill. Their admiration was unstinting. Joy East could invite clients, press people, foreign contacts and local dignitaries into her house with such ease. She hired caterers and then contract cleaners afterwards. Joy told Frank that it was no trouble, in fact it was positively useful. She had her house cleaned once a month professionally, she had a freezer full of hors d'oeuvres. She always cleared away her ornaments and valuables before any gathering. You never knew if strangers might be light-fingered, much better to leave out forty big blue glass bowls as ashtrays. They had cost £1 each in some warehouse. She had another forty in a cardboard box in the garage. On a high shelf over the small sports car.

Frank Quigley the handsome Managing Director of Palazzo and Joy East the Design Consultant who had been in charge of Palazzo's image from its Art Deco building to its smart carrier bags had been having an affair for three years and they could both say with certainty that nobody knew about it. They were not fooling themselves like so many other lovers in the world who believed that they were invisible. They knew that nobody else had the slightest suspicion. Because they had been very careful and they had lived by a set of rules.

They never telephoned each other except on legitimate business for the company. And Joy made no telephone calls to the Quigley apartment about anything at all. Once the affair had got under way Renata was never brought to Joy East's house whatever the social occasion. Frank Quigley felt that it would be undignified for his wife to be entertained in a house where he himself had been entertained so many afternoons a week in a very different sense of the word. Frank would not let his wife lay her fur coat across the wide bed where he and Joy had spent so many hours. Even though he swore to himself that Renata would never learn of the relationship, he still felt that he owed it to her not to betray her by pretending to be an equal guest in a house which was in reality so much his home. He didn't think about any other kind of betrayal because Frank had always believed that his strongest quality was an ability to compartmentalize his life. He had always been able to do this. He never thought of his violent drunken father and his weak forgiving mother . . . not once he had left them to live in London. But when he had returned to visit them and his brothers and sisters who had never left the small town in the West of Ireland he brought no tales and even no thoughts of his London life back with him. He had managed to come back if not exactly shabby at least unkempt. None of them would have guessed at his lifestyle in the business world and the social life of retailing. He had bought Renata a shapeless tweed coat for her one-off regulation visit there and had told her they should play down the comfort they enjoyed back in Wembley. Renata had understood very quickly, she had gone almost wordlessly to help in the kitchen with the women while Frank had talked to his brothers, and offered a little investment here and buying into something there . . . all of them polite ways of giving money without being seen to do so. During the four days he had spent in the place where he had grown up, his leather briefcase and hand-made shoes were locked in the boot of the hired car with Renata's silk scarves and jewellery roll.

Frank had said that you diminished everything by trailing one life and one set of memories with you. Better far to live whatever life you were living at the moment to the full with no connecting links.

So a wife could not be brought unawares to the house of a mistress.

Similarly when the Quigleys entertained as they always did at Christmas Miss East would be said to be out of town. They met on common ground all right, like at his father-in-law's, but the conversation was always about work. Frank was literally able to divorce himself from the other side of their life together and talk guiltlessly about plans and projects. He got none of the sense of illicit excitement that he knew others felt about an extra-marital affair. He knew that Joy felt the same. She must have felt the same. After all it was she who had laid down the ground rules.

Joy had been to the forefront in saying they would have no sense of over-responsibility to each other. She was not going to suffer the agonies of the typical Other Woman, she had assured him. There would be no image of poor Joy sitting alone with a sandwich on Christmas Day listening to 'Jingle Bells' on the radio. No, she was thirty when she met him and she had lived ten years more or less alone. She had a hundred places to go for Christmas, and would spend no time feeling abandoned. They would take the time they could have without destroying either their careers or their plans for the future. She was free as the air to go where she pleased without consulting him. If a trip to the States came up she would take it, and he could find other ways of filling those afternoon hours until she returned.

It had been idyllic . . . yes, a real afternoon idyll over three years. In summertime they often sat and drank cold white wine and peeled each other pears and peaches in the warm walled garden. In winter, they sat on the thick rich carpet beside the fire and watched pictures in the flames. At no time did they ever say what a pity that they couldn't get away together for a week, for a holiday or for a lifetime. Renata's name was never mentioned between them. Nor was David, the name of the man in the advertising agency who had great hopes of the lovely Joy East and sent her large bouquets of flowers. Sometimes she went out with him at weekends but so great was the sense of independence between Frank and Joy that Frank never asked whether they slept together or if David's attentions were in any way a threat to his own position. He assumed that David had been kept at arm's length with a convincing story about work and not wishing to get involved.

Frank had listened to the stories of colleagues, men who had as they put it had a little fun, played around a bit, thought they had a good thing going. Always and in every case there had been some disastrous turnabout of events. And it was invariably obvious and predictable to the outsider but never to the man involved. Frank examined his own relationship with Joy as minutely as he would have examined a contract or a proposition put to him in his office. If there were any flaws, then he couldn't see them. Not until the Christmas party at Palazzo last year, which was when the trouble had begun. And even then it had been small and insignificant. At first.

It was all very clearly etched on his mind. Supermarkets found it hard to have Christmas parties like other firms did since they were literally serving the public all hours. But Frank was ever mindful of the importance of some kind of ceremony and group loyalty, particularly at a festive time.

Frank had persuaded Carlo to have the party on the Sunday before Christmas each year, it would be a lunchtime party with Carlo as Santa Claus for the kiddies. Wives and children all came, there were small gifts for everyone and paper hats, and because it was a family day out the usual office party nonsense didn't happen with young secretaries being sick behind the filing cabinets and older managers making fools of themselves doing a striptease.

Renata had always loved it and was very good with the children, organizing games, and paper streamers. Every year for as long as he could remember Frank's father-in-law had looked fondly at his daughter and said that she was so wonderful with the bambinos, wasn't it a pity that there were no bambinos of their own. Every year Frank had shrugged and said that the ways of the Lord were strange.

'It's not for lack of loving,' he would say regularly, and Carlo would nod gravely and suggest that perhaps Frank should eat more steaks, a lot of red meat never did a man any harm. Every year with patience and a smile fixed easily on his face. It was a small price to pay, it was not intended as humiliation, it wasn't received as such. Frank took it as an old man's affectionate and perhaps tactlessly expressed regret. It was one of the few areas where he humoured Carlo Palazzo. In business they spoke as equals, always.

But last Christmas the party had been different. Joy East was usually in charge of decorating the big warehouse where they had the festivities. Not the actual work of pinning crepe up on the walls and laying out the trestles with the sausage rolls and mince pies of course, but with organizing a colour scheme, providing huge paper ornaments, or giant sunflowers as she had done one year. Arranging someone to make mighty bells out of silver paper. Seeing to it that a big green baize-covered table full of gifts be arranged for Santa Claus Carlo and that the photographer from the local and sometimes even national papers be present. Together Frank and Joy had organized a huge Christmas calendar that would have the name of every employee on it. It cost practically nothing to print and yet everyone who worked in Palazzo took it home proudly to keep for the next year. It sometimes changed their mind if they were thinking of leaving. It was hard to leave a place where you were so highly thought of as family that they put your name among the names of board members and senior managers on the calendar.

Last Christmas Joy said she was going to be away in the time before the party. There was this packaging fair she really had to go to. It was important, she needed new ideas.

'But that's on every year at this time and you don't go,' Frank had complained.

'Are you telling me what I can do and can't do?' Her voice had been steely.

'Of course not. It's just that it's become such a tradition . . . your ideas for the Christmas party . . . always. Long before you and I . . . always.'

'And you thought that it would always be so . . . long after you and I?'

'What is this, Joy? If you're trying to say something say it.' He had been brusque to cover his shock.

'Oh I'm never trying to say anything, I assure you. I really assure you of that. Either I say it or I don't say it, there's no question of trying to say anything.'

He had looked at her sharply, her voice had sounded slurred when she was repeating the word 'assure'. It was unthinkable that Joy East had been drinking, drinking in the middle of the day. He put the suspicion out of his mind.

'That's good then,' he had said with false joviality, 'because I'm the same. If I want to say something I say it, we're two of a kind, Joy.'

She had smiled at him oddly, he thought.

When she returned from the packaging fair they met as had been arranged at her house. One of the many things that made it all so safe was that Joy really did work from home with a small bright studio filled with light, and Frank did have legitimate reason to call on her. But even better her house was very near the offices of the firm of accountants they used as tax advisers. Frank had even more legitimate reason to visit them regularly. If his car was ever seen in the area he was well covered.

Joy said she hadn't done much at the packaging fair, it was Mickey Mouse stuff.

'Then why did you go?' Frank had asked, irritated.

He had been responsible for finding other people to take over Joy's work preparing the hall for the party and nobody had anything like her flair.

'For a change, for a rest, for some time off,' she had said, considering her words.

'Jesus, I never think a trade fair is a rest,' he had said.

'It is if you hardly leave your room in the hotel.'

'And what did you do in your room in the hotel that was so important?' His voice was cold.

'I never said it was important. Now did I?'

'No.'

'It wasn't at all important what I did in my room, I read the catalogues, I had room service, I had a lot of nice cold white wine. Oh, and I had a nice Scotsman, head of a stationery firm. But nothing at all important.'

Frank's face had gone white but he was still in control. 'Is this meant to hurt me?' he asked.

'But how could it, we're two of a kind, you've often said it. You have your life with your wife, I have my life with the odd ship that passes in the night. Nothing hurtful there.'

They were lying in her bed. Frank reached out for a cigarette from the slim case on the bedside table.

'I usually prefer you not to smoke here, it does sort of linger in the curtains,' Joy said.

'I usually don't need to smoke here, but the things you're saying sort of linger in my mind and make me anxious,' he said, lighting up.

'Ah, it is all a game, isn't it?' Joy said perfectly amicably. 'I thought about this a long time while I was away. What you and I have is not love, not one of those great passions that make people do foolish things . . . it's just a game. Like tennis, one person serves, the other returns it . . .'

'It's much more than a game . . .' he began.

'Or like chess.' Joy was dreamy now. 'One person makes a crafty move and then the other responds to it with something even craftier.'

'You know very well what we have, there's no point in finding fancy words for it. We love each other . . . but we have set limits to this love, you and I. And we admire each other and we're happy together.'

'It's a game,' she repeated.

'Well, people who go out to play a game of golf or squash or chess together are friends, Joy, for God's sake, you don't decide to spend a day with someone you don't like. Use this example if it gives you pleasure, keep saying game game game. But it doesn't mean anything. It doesn't change anything. We're just the same. You and I.'

'Oh you *are* playing it well.' She laughed admiringly. 'Trying to diffuse it all, asking no questions about whether there really was a Scotsman or not. I think you'd be a very dangerous adversary in a game.'

He put out his cigarette and reached for her again, he held her close to him and spoke into her long shiny hair with its stripes of gold among the brown and its smell of lemony shampoo.

'Well so would you . . . a terrifying adversary. Isn't it just as well that we're the best of friends and the best of lovers and not enemies at all?'

But he had spoken more cheerfully than he felt, and her body had not been responsive to him. She had a half smile that was disturbing and had nothing at all to do with any pleasure which she might or might not have been feeling.

At the party Joy was dressed in a dazzling navy and white dress. The gleaming white collar was cut low into her cleavage revealing a lot of breast and expensive lace-trimmed brassiere. Her hair seemed to shine out like gold and copper. She looked ten years younger than thirty-three, she looked like a young beautiful girl on the prowl. Frank watched her with alarm as she moved through the crowds of Palazzo employees. This time there was no doubt about it, she had been drinking. And well before she arrived at the party.

Frank felt a cold knot of nervousness in his stomach. Joy sober he could cope with easily, but she was an unknown quantity drunk. His father's terrible and unpredictable rages flashed before him suddenly. He remembered the time that the entire dinner had been thrown into the fire in a fit of temper . . . nearly forty years ago but as clear as yesterday. And what had always stuck in Frank's mind was that his father had not intended to do it, he had wanted to eat his dinner as he told them over and over all night. It had given Frank a fear of drunks, he drank very little himself and he scanned his, managers and sales force for signs of the bottle. It was the feeling that you couldn't rely on someone who was so dangerous. They would probably be all right but you couldn't be sure. He looked at the flashing smile and the low neckline of Joy East as she cruised around the room ever refilling her glass at the trestle tables, and he felt not at all sure that the day would end all right.

Her first target was Carlo, struggling offstage into his Santa outfit.

'Wonderful, Mr Palazzo,' she said. 'Wonderful, you go out and knock them dead, tell them what Santa will put in their wage packets if they're good little girls and boys and work like good little ants.'

Carlo looked puzzled. Frank acted quickly to draw her away.

'Joy, where are the tubs for the children? Please?' His voice was urgent.

She came up close to him and he saw her eyes were not focusing properly.

'Where are the tubs?' she asked. 'The tubs are being presided over by your wife. The saintly Renata. Santa Renata.' Her face broke into a big smile. 'That would be a nice song . . . Santa Renata . . .' She sang it to the tune of 'Santa Lucia', and seemed pleased with it so sang it a little louder. Frank moved slightly away. He had to get her out. Soon.

At that very moment Renata appeared to explain that the pink wrapping paper was on the gifts for girls and the blue for boys. One year her father had given the girls horrible monsters and spiders and the boys comb and mirror sets. This time they were taking no chances.

'That's right, Renata, take no chances,' Joy said.

Renata looked at her startled. Never had she seen Joy East looking like this.

'You look . . . very smart . . . very elegant,' Renata said.

'Thank you, Renata, *grazie, grazie mille*,' Joy said, bowing flamboyantly.

'I have not seen you wear clothes like this and look so full of life before . . .' Renata spoke quietly but with a little awe in her voice. She fingered the edge of her expensive but very muted woollen jacket. It had probably cost four times as much as the striking garment that Joy was wearing but Renata looked like a bird of little plumage, dark hair, sallow skin and designer suit in lilac and pink colours with a braid of lilac-coloured suede at the edge of the jacket, nothing to catch the eye. Nothing at all.

Joy looked at Renata steadily.

'I'll tell you why I look so different, I have a man. A man in my life. That's what makes all the difference.'

Joy smiled around her, delighted with the attention from Nico Palazzo who was Carlo's brother, and from Desmond Doyle and a group of senior management who were all in the circle. Renata smiled too, but uncertainly. She didn't know quite what response she was meant to make and her eyes raked the group as if to find Frank who would know what to say.

Frank stood with the feeling that the ice in his stomach had broken and he was now awash with icy water. There was nothing he could do. It was the sense of powerlessness that made him feel almost faint.

'Was I telling you about this man, Frank?' Joy asked roguishly. 'You see me only as a career woman . . . but there's room for love and passion as well.'

'I'm sure there is.'

Frank spoke as if he were patting down a mad dog. Even if he had no connection with Joy they would have expected him to be like this. Soothing, distant, and eventually making his escape. They must all see now what condition she was in, they must have noticed. Was it only because he knew her so intimately, had traced every feature of her face and body for three years with his hands that he realized she was out of control? Everyone around seemed to be treating it all as normal Christmas high spirits. If he could stop her just now, before she said anything else, then all might not be lost.

Joy was aware she had an audience and was enjoying it. She put on a little-girl voice that he had never heard her use before. She looked very silly, he thought quite dispassionately, in her sober state she would be the first to criticize any other woman with an assumed lisping voice.

'But it's forbidden in this company to love anyone except Palazzo. Isn't that right? We all love Palazzo, we must have no other love.'

They laughed, even Nico laughed, they were taking it as good-natured banter.

'Oh yes, first love the company, then other loves,' Nico said.

'It's infidelity to love anyone else better,' Desmond Doyle said, laughing.

Frank flashed him a grateful look, poor Desmond his old pal from those long-ago days in Ireland was helping him inadvertently, he was taking the heat off. Maybe he could be encouraged to say more.

'Well, you've never been unfaithful, Desmond,' Frank said, loosening his collar. 'You're certainly a long and loyal Palazzo man.' He felt sick in his stomach after he said it, remembering suddenly the time that Desmond had been allowed to go after the rationalization and how he had to fight hard to get him reinstated. But Desmond didn't seem to see the irony. Desmond was about to answer with something cheerful when the voice of Joy East cut in again.

'No one should be married except to the company. When you join Palazzo you must marry the place, marry Palazzo. Very hard to do. Very hard. Except for you, Frank. You managed it all right, didn't you? You really *did* marry a Palazzo!'

Even Nico who was very slow must have realised by now that something was wrong. Frank had to move quickly. But he must not appear to be rattled. He must take it indulgently as anyone would take the public idiocy of a normally exemplary colleague.

'Yes, you're right, and I'm glad you reminded me because my father-in-law will be down on us all like a ton of bricks if we don't get the presents going soon. Renata, should we get the children to line up now . . . or does somebody make an announcement. Or what?'

In other years Joy East had arranged everything like clockwork. Renata had a look of relief all over her face. She had thought that there had been an insult, a jibe, but obviously since Frank didn't see one, she had been wrong.

'I think we should tell Papa that the time has come,' she said and moved away towards her father.

'I think we should all tell Papa that the time has come,' Joy said to nobody in particular.

Desmond Doyle and Nico Palazzo exchanged puzzled looks.

'Joy, you must be tired after all that busy time at the packaging conference,' Frank Quigley said loudly. 'If you like I can run you home now before it all gets too exhausting here.'

He saw the relief on a few faces around him, Mr Quigley was always the one to cope with the situation, any situation.

His smile was hard and distant as he looked at Joy. It said in very definite terms that this was her one chance to get out of what she had walked them into. There wouldn't be any other chances. His smile said that he was not afraid.

Joy looked at him for a few seconds.

'All right,' she said, 'let's say I'm tired after the packaging conference, tired and very very emotional, and that I need to be taken home.'

'Let's say that then,' Frank said easily. 'Tell Renata to save me a nice boy present from Santa Claus,' he called out. 'I'll be right back to collect it.'

They looked at him in admiration as he led Miss East who was behaving most oddly out of the big hall and towards the car park.

There was complete silence in the car, not one word spoken between them. At her door she handed him her small handbag and he took out the key. On the low glass table was a bottle of vodka with one third of it gone and some orange juice. A heap of unopened Christmas cards, and a small smart suitcase as if she was going on or had come back from a journey. With a shock he realized that she must not have unpacked her case after her trip to that conference.

'Coffee?' he asked. It was the first word spoken.

'No thanks.'

'Mineral water?'

'If you insist.'

'I don't insist, I couldn't care less what you drink, but I wouldn't give a dog any more alcohol than you've had already.'

His voice was icy cold.

Joy looked up at him from the chair where she had sat down immediately.

'You hate drink because your father was such a drunk,' she said.

'You're telling me what I told you. Have you any further insights or shall I go back to the party?'

'You'd like to hit me but you can't, because you saw your father beating your mother,' she said, a crooked smile on her face.

'Very good, Joy, well done.' His hand was clenched, and he would like to have struck something, a chair, a wall even to get rid of the tension he felt.

'I said nothing that wasn't true. Nothing at all.'

'No indeed, and you said it beautifully. I'm going now.'

'You are not going, Frank, you are going to sit down and listen to me.'

'Now that's where you're wrong. Since I did have a drunk for a father I am only too used to listening to drunks, it's a useless exercise. They don't remember anything next day. Try telephoning the speaking clock, tell it all to them, they love a good sob story from people with enough drink in them to float a navy.'

'You have to listen, Frank, you have to know.'

'Another time, a time when you can pronounce my name without stumbling over it.'

'About the conference. I wasn't there.'

'So you said, you told me. A Scotsman, well well. Don't tell me it's preying on your mind?'

'I wasn't anywhere near it, I didn't leave London.'

Her voice was odd, she seemed to have sobered up a bit.

'So?' He was still poised to go.

'I went to a nursing home.' She paused. 'To have an abortion.'

He put his car keys in his pocket, and came back into the room.

'I'm sorry,' he said, 'Very sorry.'

'You needn't be.' She didn't look at him.

'But why, how . . .?'

'The pill didn't suit me. I changed the type several times . . . but still . . .'

'You should have told me . . .' He was gentle now. Forgiving.

'No, it was my decision.'

'I know, I know. But still . . .'

'And so I went to this place . . . very nice place actually, it's a real nursing home for other things too, not just terminations as they call them . . .' Her voice shook a little.

He laid his hand over hers, the coldness was forgotten. 'And was it very bad, was it awful?' His eyes were full of concern.

'No.' Her face was bright and she smiled at him, a smile only a little lopsided. 'No it wasn't awful at all. Because when I went in there and went to my room, I sat and thought for a while, and I thought . . . Why am I doing this? Why am I getting rid of a human being? I would *like* another human being around me. I would like a son or a daughter. So I changed my mind. I told them I had decided not to go through with the termination. And I went to a hotel instead, for a couple of days, then I came back here.'

He looked at her, stricken.

'This can't be true.'

'Oh yes, it's true. So now you see why you couldn't just toddle off back to the party. You had to know. It was only fair that you should know. And know everything.'

If he lived to be an old man, something that his doctor said was highly unlikely, Frank Quigley would never forget that moment. The day he learned he was going to be a father, but not the father of Renata's child, not the father who would be congratulated and embraced by the Palazzo tribe. A father who would be ostracized and cut off the life he had built for himself for a quarter of a century. He would never forget her face as she told him, knowing that for the first time in their very equal relationship she held all the cards. Knowing that drunken and upset and having broken all their rules she was still the one in charge. Because of biology which said that the women bore the children she was winning, and that was the only reason. Frank Quigley would not have been beaten by anything except the human reproductive system.

He had played it just right, of course, at the time. He had telephoned back to base and said that Joy needed a bit of attention. He had sat down and talked to her, but his mind was in overdrive. His words were soothing and supportive, his real thoughts were taking a journey into the future.

He allowed his real reactions only a moment's indulgence while he relished the thought that he had fathered a child. If Carlo knew there would be a lot less of the chat about eating more red meat. If Carlo knew. Carlo must never know. And Renata would be hurt beyond repair. Not only at the infidelity, the knowledge that an affair had been going on under her very nose for years, but at the fact that this woman had produced a child, the one thing that Renata had failed to do.

As he stroked Joy's fevered forehead and assured her of loyalty and his great pleasure at the news and the way that things had turned out, Frank was working out logically and coldly what he must do next, what avenues were open to him.

As he urged cups of weak tea and thinly sliced bread and butter on the weeping Joy, he listed the possibilities that lay ahead and the disadvantages of each one. When he found the one that had the least dangerous minefield attached to it that was where he would head.

Joy could have the child and he would acknowledge that it was his. He would say that he did not intend to leave his marriage, but felt in fairness that the son or daughter should grow up knowing the care of a father. He considered this for seconds, only to dismiss it.

In a more liberated society this would work. But not with the Palazzos. Not for one minute.

Suppose Joy were to say that she was having the child and that the identity of the father was to remain unknown, undiscussed? Again not something beyond the imaginings in the 1980s for a liberated woman. But again this was the world of Palazzo. It would be frowned upon, it would be speculated about, and worst of all if Joy were ever to hit the bottle again it would all be revealed.

Suppose he were to deny paternity? Literally say that Joy was lying? He wondered why he had even considered this route. Joy was a woman he had intended to spend a great amount of time with, he didn't only love her for the good sex they had, he loved her mind and her reactions to things. Frank asked himself why had this possibility crossed his mind. He had never thought of stabbing Carlo in the back and taking over the company. He had not decided to woo and win Renata only for her money and position. He was not that kind of bastard. So why even entertain the idea of turning his back on the woman who had been his lover for three years, the woman who was going to bear his child? He looked at her, slack-jawed and awkward in the chair. He realized with a shudder how much he feared drink and the effects of it. He knew that whatever happened now, he would never be able to trust Joy, or trust himself to her again.

Suppose he were to persuade her to have the termination, for everyone's sake? There were still two weeks in which it would be safe. Perhaps he could persuade her.

But if he couldn't then he risked a hysterical response. And if she were to go ahead and have the child knowing that he wanted it aborted, then things would be about as bad as they could ever be.

Suppose he were to ask her to go away, to start a new life with a set of glowing references? Joy move away from London? Joy start life afresh with a small baby just to please Frank? It was unthinkable.

Suppose he were to ask her to give the child to him. Suppose that he and Renata were to adopt this baby? The child would inherit the Palazzo millions. Everyone would be pleased. Frank and Renata had done the rounds of the adoption societies, at forty-six he was too old to be an adoptive father. Not a real father as it turned out, but then Nature was never known to be a great supporter of bureaucracy.

But Joy had deliberately decided to have the child because she wanted another human being around her. She would not consider it. Or not now at any rate. Don't dismiss it utterly. She might, later on in the pregnancy. It was unlikely yet not impossible.

And then it would be adopting his own child. That would be very satisfying. In honesty he would have to tell Renata but they need not tell her family . . .

Frank stroked the forehead, administered the cups of tea and thought his own thoughts as he consoled Joy East with murmurs and sounds that would never constitute any kind of promise or contract in the unlikely event of their being recalled.

The weeks had passed somehow. The bad behaviour at the Christmas party was hardly commented upon, Frank was as usual congratulated for having as usual averted any little silliness. Joy was back at work head high in the new year, plans and ideas tripping out of her. There were no recurrences of drinking. Also there were no lazy afternoons by her fireside.

They met for a lunch early in the new year, Frank had said in front of several of the managers that the place was lacking in anything new. What it needed in these days after Christmas was some pizzazz. He would take Joy East out to lunch and have a brainstorming session, he said. Women always loved a business lunch, and he wouldn't mind one himself. They went to the best restaurant where they were bound to be seen.

She sipped her Slimline Tonic and he drained his tomato juice.

'An expense-account lunch is wasted on us.' Joy smiled at him.

'As you told me that time, I'm a drunk's son, I'm afraid of drink,' he said.

'Did I say that? I don't really remember all the things I said that day. Is that why you don't come to me in the afternoons?'

'No it's not that,' he said.

'Well why not? I mean there's no need for any precautions now, it would be like bolting the stable after the horse had fled . . . we should get value . . .' Her smile was warm and welcoming. Like the old Joy.

'It might be bad for you, they say it's not good at this stage of the pregnancy,' he said.

She smiled, pleased that he was caring. 'But you could come and talk to me anyway, couldn't you? I've waited a lot of afternoons.'

That was true, she had kept her word about not contacting him. Ever.

'We do have to talk,' he said.

'So, why are we trying to talk in a restaurant where everyone sees us? Those women over there, they're in-laws of Nico Palazzo. They haven't had their eyes off us since we came in.'

'We will be seen in public for the rest of our lives, this is exactly where we must discuss how our lives will continue. If we go to your house we slip into the old ways, we're back in the days when we only had ourselves to consider.' His voice was calm. But she seemed to sense his anxiety.

'You mean you wanted a get-away car and witnesses if I'm going to tell you anything unpalatable. Is that it?'

'Don't be silly, Joy.'

'No I'm not being silly, you're trying to get out of it, aren't you? You're actually scared to death.'

'That's not so, and stop smiling that smile that isn't a real smile. It's a paper-thin smile you put on for customers and contacts. It's not genuine.'

'And what was ever genuine about *your* smile, Frank? Did you not know, your smile never reached your eyes, never. It stopped always around the mouth.'

'Why are we talking like this?' he asked.

'Because you are full of fear, I can smell it,' she said.

'What's turned you against me, did I say anything?' He spread his hand out in wonder.

'You don't need to make those Italian gestures at me, I'm not a Palazzo. What did you say? I'll tell you what you said, you said we should sit down in a public place and make decisions about the rest of our lives. You forget that I know you, Frank, you forget that you and I know when you meet an adversary the first rule is to meet him on common ground, not your territory or his. You're doing that. We both know that if there's a danger of a row the rule is: make sure the meeting is held in a public place. It stops people making scenes.'

'Are you feeling all right, Joy? Seriously?'

'It won't necessarily work, you know, drunk or sober, at home or out I could make a scene if I wanted to.' She looked mulish.

'Of course you could, what *is* this? We're friends you and I, where's the hostility?'

'We are not friends, we are fencing with each other, we are playing games, looking for the advantage . . .'

'Well then, if that's all we are, what on earth are we having a child together for?'

'We're not having a child together,' Joy East said, 'I am having a child.'

There was a look of triumph on her face like he had only seen when she had beaten a rival, won an award or somehow got her way against all the odds.

It was then he knew that she intended him to dangle there, forever watching his step, forever in her power. It was her child, and her decision, but only for as long at it suited her. She was never going to promise him either secrecy or involvement. Her plan was that he should never know. That he would be for ever tied to her.

Frank Quigley had come across schemes like this before, the supplier who had bought up the market but hadn't told you. He would want you to advertise the produce and then suddenly could raise the price because you were committed. Frank had dealt with that one in his time. Someone had tried it on him, but only once. Frank had smiled and said there was no way he was going to pay more than the agreed price for the product. But wouldn't they look foolish, the man had said, having spent all that money advertising it and then having to admit they didn't have it? No, not at all. Frank had smiled back with easy charm. They would just take another advertisement apologizing that the suppliers had proved unreliable. Everyone would think well of Palazzo for their honesty, the suppliers would be ruined. It had been so simple. But then it had only involved fruit, it hadn't involved a child.

He had brought into play every available ounce of charm that he possessed, and limp as a wet rag at the end of the lunch he congratulated himself that they were at least speaking normally on the surface.

They talked about the company. Twice he made her laugh, real laughter, head thrown back and pealing with mirth. The two women that she had said were Nico's in-laws looked over with interest. But there was nothing for them to take home with them as gossip, this was the most innocent lunch in the history of the world. Otherwise it would not have been here and in full view of everyone.

He had told her about his Christmas and then she told him about hers. She had gone to stay with friends in Sussex. In a big family home where she had been before, full of children, she said.

'Did you tell them?' he asked. He felt the conversation must not be allowed to wander too far from what they were both thinking about lest he be labelled callous.

'Tell them what?' she asked.

'About the baby?'

'Whose baby?'

'Your baby. Our baby if you like but basically, as you said, your baby.'

Joy gave a little purr of satisfaction. It was almost as if she were saying: That's better. That's more like it.

'No,' she said. 'I'm not telling anyone until I've decided what to do.'

And then there was no more. They spoke as they always had about plans and schemes, and the inadvisability of letting Nico know anything at all that was taking place. The wisdom of Palazzo's buying the new site in that area which was meant to be coming up – Joy was afraid it was coming up too fast. The big houses were changing hands for a lot of money and then even more money needed to be spent on them to make them smart. That kind of people would shop in fancy delicatessens or even go in to Harrod's, she felt, Palazzo's would be wiser to aim for somewhere less ambitious, somewhere where you could get a huge car park. That's the way things were going now.

'We could even try to make a feature out of the car park,' Joy had said excitedly. 'You know how gloomy they look at best, and how they look like places you're going to be murdered in at worst. Perhaps it could all be brightly painted and there could be a covered terrace around it, a type of cloister effect, we could rent space to market stalls, give the place more life . . .'

She had been talking in terms of staying on, Frank had noted.

Joy East, if she were planning anything at all, planned to take three months' maternity leave and return to work once her child was born. Frank was not going to be informed about his role. That was the way she was going to play the game.

He had left that lunch white with fury. Angrier far and determined even more to regain control than he had been before Christmas. He would not be left suspended like this.

If she would not reveal her intentions like any normal person, then he was not going to respond normally.

Two could play a game of cat and mouse.

Long before Joy mentioned her pregnancy to anyone else Frank had made his contingency plan.

Based entirely on Joy's own projections about the need not to go too far upmarket for their customers, Frank Quigley commissioned surveys.

He had explained to the young men and women in the market-research bureau that they wanted confirmation of their belief that they should expand into less well-off areas. The survey was to be done nationwide but on a very small sample. It was the kind of survey which if Frank had seen cold he would have dismissed on the ground that its findings could not possibly be conclusive. But this time he wanted to let the board see from an outside agency that the way forward was to expand, and to leave North London far behind. To open up on a trial basis in the Midlands, in the North of England even. The key to it would be design and image. Palazzo was to be presented as stylish and desirable. Joy East was the one to create that image.

It would be promotion, it would be a seat on the board for Joy. He would see her once a month at board meetings, true, but he would not see her every day.

And she would not see his father-in-law every day.

And she would not be in danger of meeting his wife.

He had few weapons, he had to outwit her by cunning.

She had to think that the promotion, the move and the change were against his wishes.

The survey which Carlo Palazzo fondly believed he had commissioned himself was complete by March when Joy East broke her news with maximum drama. She announced it under the heading of Any Other Business at the weekly management meeting.

Her eyes had been suspiciously bright. Frank knew what was coming.

'Well I suppose this *is* other business in a way, I bring it up in case you should hear it elsewhere and wonder why I had said nothing of it to my colleagues. I will be seeking three months' maternity leave in July . . . Obviously I'll work around it to make sure that any promotions are well covered but I felt you should know that it was upcoming.' She smiled around sweetly, meeting the eyes of the fifteen men in the room.

Carlo was at a total loss. 'Well heavens, good Lord, I did not even know you were thinking of getting married . . . my congratulations.'

'Oh no, nothing as settled as that I'm afraid.' A tinkly laugh. 'Just a child. We don't want too much of a shock to the system like getting married as well.'

Nico's jaw dropped, the others shuffled their praise and pleasure, but looking sideways at Carlo and Frank to try to gauge the mood of the meeting.

Frank Quigley looked pleasantly surprised and admiringly amused.

'This is very exciting news, Joy,' he said evenly. 'Everyone is delighted for you. I don't know what we'll do without you for three months, but will you be able to come back to us after that?'

The inquiry was warm and courteous, nobody could have seen the way their eyes locked hard across the table.

'Oh yes indeed, I've been busy making arrangements. These things aren't done lightly, you know.'

'No indeed,' he said soothingly.

By this stage Carlo had recovered enough control to be able to murmur a few pleasantries, but he called Frank to his office.

'What are we going to do?' he asked.

'Carlo, it's 1985, it's not the middle ages. She can have thirty children if she wants to. You're not shocked, are you?'

'Yes of course I am. Who is the father, do you think? Is it anybody at Palazzo?'

Frank felt he was acting a part in a play. 'Why should it be? Joy has a full life of her own outside here.'

'But why, why on earth?'

'Perhaps she felt she is in her thirties, she is alone, she might just *want* to.'

'It's a very inconsiderate thing to do,' Carlo grumbled. 'And inconvenient too. Look at the way it will upset our plans for the North.'

Frank spoke very carefully. 'When were you hoping to get that operational, not until the new year? Its planning stages will only be coming on stream in autumn when she comes back to work . . .'

'Yes, but . . .'

'But doesn't it suit you down to the ground, not that you should *say* that to her of course. You were already worried that she might not want the move. Now that she's having a child it might be just what she'd need, new environment, fresh start, more space and room up there, away from London. . . '

'Yes. . .' Carlo was doubtful. 'I think this has thrown a big spanner in the works.'

'Then if that's where you want her, you should make it sound very very attractive for her. Put it to her in a way that it seems just the right step for her to take . . . '

'Perhaps *you* should explain it to her.'

'No, Carlo.' For the second time Frank felt that he was actually acting out a part on stage. 'No, because you see, in a way I don't want to lose her from the London side of things, even though I think in my heart you're right. It's best for the company that she should go up North and get Palazzo into a different league, a national league.'

'That's what I thought,' Carlo said, believing it.

'So I'm the wrong one to persuade her.'

'Suppose she thinks I am banishing her away?'

'She can't think that, Carlo, haven't you all the documentation and surveys and inquiries to prove you were thinking of it ages back?'

Carlo nodded. He had, of course.

Frank let the breath out slowly between his teeth. Nowhere in that whole paperwork did Frank Quigley's name appear, in fact in the files there were several letters disssenting slightly and wondering whether Miss East would be better kept in London. He couldn't be faulted now.

Frank did not have long to wait. Joy burst into his office, eyes blazing and clutching a piece of paper in her hand.

'Is this your doing?' she asked.

'I have no idea what you're talking about.' He was bland, unruffled.

'Like hell you don't, you're sending me away. By God you're not going to get away with this, Frank. I'm not going to be shunted out of your sight when things get too hot to handle.'

'Sit down,' he said.

'Don't tell me what to do.'

He walked past her and called out to his secretary in the next room, 'Diana, can we have a big pot of coffee? Miss East and I are about to have a row and we need fuel.'

'Don't think I'm bowled over by that kind of witticism,' Joy said.

'It wasn't a witticism, it was the plain unvarnished truth. Now what *is* this about? Is this Carlo's plan to put you on the board and give you responsibility for the expansion?'

'Carlo's plan, don't give me Carlo's plan. It's your plan to get rid of me.'

His eyes were cold. 'Don't let's add paranoia to everything else.'

'To what else, what else are you talking about?'

His voice was low and hard. 'I'll tell you what else. You and I loved each other, I still love you. We agreed to make love, you were the one looking after contraception. When it no longer worked for you to look after it, it would have been fair to tell me, and let me be in charge of that side. Yes, Joy, that would have been the fair thing. It was not fair to allow me to conceive a child by accident.'

'I would have thought you'd be glad to prove you were able to,' she snapped.

'No. You would have thought wrong. Then to continue your unfairness you will not let me know what your plans are for the child we conceived. I have agreed that it's your responsibility if that's what you want. You said you would let me know. You have not let me know. You have played some kind of game with me throughout. I don't know any more than I knew at Christmas time.'

She was silent.

'And now you come screaming in here with some cock and bull story that I'm banishing you off to the provinces whereas the truth is that I did everything in my power to get you to stay here. You can believe this or not as you wish but that is the case.'

There was a knock on the door and Diana came in with the coffee. She laid it on the desk between them.

'Is the row over?' she asked.

'No, it's just getting to the peak,' Frank smiled.

'I don't believe you,' Joy said when Diana had left. 'Carlo never had a thought of his own.'

Frank went to a file and showed her a letter. In black and white it said that it might be a waste of Joy East's capabilities to have her tied up away from the nerve centre of the business. He told her that there were more. He could find them if she needed proof.

'Then it's Carlo, he can't bear the shameless unmarried mother bit . . . it's he who's sending me away.'

'Joy, I warned you about the danger of paranoia. If you look through these files that survey was commissioned back in January. Months before you made your announcement.'

'That bloody survey. Who are they anyway? They seem like a Mickey Mouse outfit to me,' she grumbled.

Frank had a moment's regret, she was so sharp no complaint and bright, her thinking was exactly on the same line as his own. What a pity that it had to end in this acrimony and games-playing.

'Well, however they are Carlo believes everything they say, and they may have a point, you know. You said a lot of it yourself alrcady, long ago, before all this.'

'I know.' She had to admit that this was true.

'So what will you do?'

'I'll make up my own mind without any patronizing pats on the head from you,' she said.

'As you wish, Joy, but may I remind you, this is *my* office and it was *you* who came to see me. It's not unreasonable that I should ask since you seem determined to involve me.'

'When I've decided what I'm going to do, I'll let you know,' she said.

'You said that before.'

'But that was only about *my* child, this is about *your* company. You have a right to know.'

He sat for a long time staring ahead of him after she left, her cup of coffee undrunk. He thought she had looked frightened and a little uncertain. But perhaps he was only imagining it.

She was a clever woman and she knew that she could make him sweat it out not knowing what she was going to say next and where she was going to say it.

He thought about it again that evening in their apartment. Renata sat on one side of their big marble fireplace looking into the flames and he sat on the other. There were often long companionable silences between them. But that night he said nothing at all.

Renata eventually spoke.

'Is it boring sometimes being with me in the evenings?' There was no complaint in her voice. She was asking as she might have asked the time or whether they should turn on the news on television.

'No, it's not boring,' Frank said truthfully, 'It's restful, actually.'

'That is good,' Renata said, pleased. 'You are a very good husband to me, and sometimes I wish I had more fire and light and sparkle.'

'Oh Jesus, I get enough of that at work, it's like a Guy Fawkes bonfire. No, you're fine the way you are.'

And he nodded to himself, as if agreeing with what he had just said. He didn't want to change her for a different model, a brighter shinier brand.

The weeks passed with no further word from Joy, the plans for the expansion continued. Carlo said that Joy East was certainly giving it a lot of attention, whether she intended to go or not was anyone's guess.

'Don't force her,' Frank advised. 'She'll go, but not before she's ready.'

He hoped he had read it right. Because she was succeeding in unsettling him.

He got an ornate invitation to a silver wedding celebration for Desmond and Deirdre Doyle. He looked at it grimly. In ten years possibly he and Renata might be sending out something similar. But he wondered if it were likely.

He wondered also what Desmond had to celebrate, a wedding that everyone had assumed was shotgun even though it turned out not to have been the case. A lifetime of being snubbed by the awful O'Hagan family back in Dublin. A life's work getting nowhere fast in Palazzo. Difficult children. The eldest shacked up with some out-of-work actor, apparently, the boy hightailing it back to Mayo of all places, and Helen. A nun, a very odd, disturbed girl. Frank didn't like to think about Helen Doyle who had appeared twice in his life, both times trailing disaster behind her and around her.

No, the Doyles had little to celebrate, which was probably why they were having this party.

An unlikely outing it was going to be.

But not as unlikely as the outing that Renata told him about when he came home from work.

'Joy East has invited us to dinner, just you and me and her, she says.'

'Did she say why?'

'I did ask her, and she said she would like to have a talk to us.'

'Is it at her house?'

'No, she said that you always say when something has to be said it should be said on neutral ground.' Renata sounded puzzled.

Frank's stomach churned with fear.

'I don't know what she means by that,' he managed to say.

'Well, she said she's booking a table in this restaurant . . . and that she checked with Diana that you are free, so she telephoned me to see if I were free.'

'Yes. Well.'

'Do you not want to go?' Renata sounded disappointed.

'She's been very odd lately, this pregnancy has unhinged her a bit I think, that and the move . . . not that she's said yes or no to that, by the way. Can we get out of it do you think?'

'Not without being very rude. But I thought you liked her?' Renata looked confused.

'I do, I did, it's not that. She's a bit unbalanced. Leave it with me.'

'She said to ring her tonight.' Renata seemed withdrawn.

'Yeah, I will. I have to go out again anyway. I'll ring her while I'm out.'

He got into his car and drove to Joy's house. He rang the doorbell and knocked, but there was no reply.

He went to a public telephone and called her. She answered immediately.

'Why didn't you let me in?'

'I didn't want to.'

'You *told* me to call.'

'I told you to telephone, it's a different thing.'

'Joy, don't do this, don't have a scene in front of Renata, it's not fair on her, she's done nothing to deserve it, nothing. It's cruel.'

'Are you begging, do I hear you begging?'

'You can hear what you goddamn like, but just think, what harm has she ever done you?'

'Does this mean yes or no to my invitation?' Joy asked in a cool voice.

'Listen to me . . . '

'No, I am not going to listen any more. Yes or no?' There was a threat in the question.

'Yes.'

'I thought so,' said Joy East, and hung up.

It was the same restaurant where they had lunch last January. When Joy's stomach had been flat and when Nico's in-laws had seen them laughing. Now it was different.

Joy, still on mineral water to Frank's enormous relief, was gracious and anxious that they should be well seated and choose wisely from the menu. She did most of the talking, as Frank was edgy and Renata very reserved.

'You know the way in films they say: "You must be wondering why I asked you to come here tonight . . ." ' she tinkled.

'You said you had something to talk about.' Renata was polite.

'I do. I have come to some decisions finally after a lot of thought and I think it's fair that I should tell you about them. Frank because of work . . . and Renata, you because of Frank.'

He felt the floodgates begin to open. God damn her to the pit of hell. It wasn't even a woman scorned, it wasn't that kind of fury. He would have played straight with her. Or straightish anyway.

'Yes?' Renata's voice was anxious. Frank hadn't trusted himself to speak.

'Well, about this baby . . .' She looked from one to the other. And waited. It seemed like an age but it was probably three seconds.

Joy continued: 'I think it is going to change my life much more than I imagined. For a month or two I wondered if I'd done the right thing. Perhaps even at this late stage, I should give the child away, give it to some couple who would have a loving secure home. I might not turn out to be such a great mother figure, all on my own.'

She waited for one of them to deny this politely. Neither of them did.

'But then I thought no. I went into this knowing what it was about, so I must go through with it.' She smiled happily.

'Yes, but what has this to do with us . . . exactly . . . ?' Renata asked. Her face was fearful.

'It has this to do with you. If I were going to give the child to anyone I would most certainly have offered you the chance. You would be such good parents, this I know. But since I'm not, and since you might have harboured some hopes . . . '

'Never . . . I never thought of it,' Renata gasped.

'Hadn't you? I'm sure *you* did, Frank. After all you haven't been able to get any joy out of the adoption societies, Carlo tells me.'

'My father has no right to speak of such things,' Renata said, her face a dark red.

'No, perhaps not. But he does of course. Anyway, it was to make these matters clear that I asked you here, and to tell you that I will be going North, soon, much sooner than anyone expected. I've sold my house here, and bought a really lovely old Georgian farmhouse in need of repair, but magnificently proportioned, small and beautiful, and a perfect place for a child to grow up. If he or she is only going to have me around, then the poor love had better have a pony and somewhere to play as well!' Her smile was all-embracing.

Renata took a deep breath. 'And will the child's father be involved at all?'

'Not at all. The father is someone I met casually on a packaging conference, a ship that passed in the night.'

Renata's hand flew to her mouth in an involuntary gesture.

'Is that so shocking?' Joy asked. 'I wanted to have a child, he was as good a person as anyone else.'

'I know, I mean it was just that I thought . . .' Her voice trailed away and she looked at Frank, whose face was stony.

'What did you just think, Renata?' Joy was like honey now.

'I know this is silly.' Renata looked from one to the other. 'I suppose I was afraid that the child might have been . . . Frank's child. And that this is why you even contemplated offering it to us . . . please, I don't know what I am doing talking like this . . . please.' There were tears in her eyes.

Frank was frozen, he *still* didn't know which way Joy would jump. He couldn't put out his hand to comfort his wife.

Joy spoke deliberately and slowly: 'Oh, Renata, surely you couldn't have thought that. Frank and I? We're too alike to be a number, to be the Grand Affair of the century. Oh no. And anyway. Frank a father, that's not very likely, that wouldn't have been on the cards, would it?'

'What . . . what do you mean . . . ?'

'Oh, Carlo told me about his problems . . . I'm afraid your father is very indiscreet sometimes, but only when he knows it won't go further . . . Please don't say back to him that I ever mentioned it. But he was always so sad that Frank did not give him the grandson. . .'

Frank spoke for the first time for a long while. He thought he had managed to take the shake out of his voice.

'And your child? Shall you tell him it was a one-night stand in a hotel room?'

'No, no, of course not, something much more romantic and sad. An untraceable wonderful person, long dead. A poet maybe. Something sad and beautiful.'

Somehow they finished the meal, somehow they found other things to talk about. The hurt went a little from

Renata's eyes, and the lines of tension from Frank's face. And the serenity and bloom of pregnancy settled ever more on Joy East. She paid the bill confidently with her credit card and when Renata went to the Ladies' she sat and looked calmly across the table at Frank.

'Well, you won,' he said.

'No, you won.'

'How did I win, tell me? You frightened me to death and now you're denying me any part in the child's life. How is that winning?'

'You got what you wanted. You got me out.'

'You're not starting that again?'

'I don't need to. I investigated the market-research bureau. They told me you hired them, they even had the date, it was just after we had lunch in this restaurant. As usual it turned out the way you wanted it to. I'm out of your hair. The coast is clear for the next project. I do wonder who she'll be. But I'll never know. Any more than you'll know what it's like to play with a two-year-old, your two-year-old. Because you're not capable of fathering one. That's both your alibi and my excuse for cutting you out.'

'You never told me why. Why all this hate?'

'It's not hate, it's determination. And why? I suppose because you have cold, cold eyes, Frank. I didn't see that until lately.'

Renata was coming back across the room. They stood up, it was time to go.

'You'll be back for the meetings . . . and everything?' Frank said.

'Not all of them, I think if this operation is to be a success, we mustn't let anyone involved think that we keep running to London all the time. Major decisions should be made in the place itself. Otherwise they'll just think they're a little outpost instead of important in their own terms.'

She was right of course, as she had been so often.

He held the door of the taxi open for her. She said she was too big to fit into her little sports car any more.

For a brief moment their eyes met.

'We both won,' she said softly. 'You could put it like that.'

'Or neither of us won,' he said sadly. 'That's another way of putting it.'

And he put his arm around his wife's shoulder as they went to where the Rover was parked.

Nothing would ever be the same between them after tonight. But the world had only cracked a little for them, it hadn't blown apart as it might have. And in a way that was winning.

8
Deirdre

The article said that anyone could be truly beautiful if they would give twenty minutes a day. Deirdre settled herself with a happy little wriggle into her chair and pulled the packet of biscuits towards her. Of course she could give twenty minutes a day. Who couldn't? Lord, weren't we all up and awake for sixteen hours for heaven's sake? Twenty minutes was nothing.

She repeated the words Truly Beautiful. She could hear them being said about her when the day came. Doesn't Deirdre look truly beautiful? Who would think she was married for twenty-five years? Imagine that she's the mother of three grown children.

She sighed with pleasure and began to read. Let's see, what would she have to do? It would be her own little secret, investing this amount of time. The reward would be sensational.

First it said you must assess yourself and list your good points and weak areas. Deirdre took the little silver pen with a tassel on it from her handbag. This was fun, great fun. What a pity she had to do it on her own. Her eldest daughter Anna would say that she was fine as she was, no need to list figure flaws and dry patches in her skin. Her second daughter Helen would say it was ludicrous to be a victim and to think that looks were important, with all the suffering in the world women couldn't afford to take time analysing their blemishes and deciding whether their eyes were deep-set or too close together.

Her son Brendan, far away from her now, living in Ireland on a remote hillside in his father's part of the country . . . What would Brendan say? She found it almost impossible to imagine how Brendan would react any more. She had wept night after night when he had first left home with few explanations and less apologies. Only when he had asked her straight out on the telephone . . . When he had cut across her tears to ask, 'If you had your choice, if you had the power to choose my life what would you have me do that would be so good and so important for us all?' she hadn't been able to answer him. Because to say that she wished things were different was no answer. You couldn't wish a circle to be square or black to be white.

But according to this beauty article there were things you could wish to be different and make them different. Like the shape of your face, a little judicious use of the blusher and the lightener could do wonders. Deirdre looked at the diagrams happily, she *would* learn to do it right. There was nothing worse than people who attempted it and got it wrong, they looked like Coco the Clown.

That was something that she could imagine Maureen Barry saying in the old days. She and Maureen used to have so much fun at one time. Deirdre's mother had been bosom pals with Mrs Barry and so the girls had carte blanche to do anything they liked as long as they were with each other. Deirdre thought back on those holidays in Salthill years ago. She had called the house in Rosemary Drive 'Salthill' as a reminder, but she saw the name on the gate so often that it didn't really suggest the sea and sunshine and total freedom of their teens.

Maureen had been so entertaining those times, there was nothing that they felt they couldn't tell each other. Not until the summer they came to London, the summer that everything changed for both of them.

Deirdre wondered about the girls they had been to university with in Dublin. Did they often wonder what had happened to blonde Deirdre O'Hagan? They would all know of course that she married young, maybe she would even put an announcement of her silver wedding in the *Irish Times*. Rub their noses in it, the uppity ones who had gone on to be barristers or to marry barristers. The types who thought that Dublin was the centre of the universe and had only heard of Harrod's as a place to shop and Chelsea as a place to live. Pinner? They used to say Pinner? as if it was Kiltimagh or somewhere like that. Oh, in *north*

London. I see. It was their ignorance that they weren't travelled. But still she would put in an announcement. Or maybe it was something that the children should do . . . a little message wishing them well on the twenty-fifth anniversary. She would check the papers and see how people did things these days.

What a pity there wasn't still that closeness with Maureen Barry. If only the years could be rolled back, she could pick up the phone and ask her. Straight out. And talk to her too about face shaping, and how to shadow the jawline. But she would never ask Maureen anything like that these days. Things had changed completely as the years went by.

There were no friends around here who could share the fun of all this self-improvement. No indeed, her neighbours would think it frivolous and silly. A lot of the women went out to work, they either knew such things anyway or else they hadn't time for it. Anyway Deirdre would never dream of letting them into her business, letting them know that this was a big thing in her life, that it was her one chance to prove that a quarter of a century had added up to something. Deirdre intended to impress her neighbours rather than let them share in the fun. They weren't really important, not like people back in Dublin, but still it was good to let them see that the Doyles were people of importance, of worth.

What would Desmond say if he saw her studying this article so intently? Would he say something flowery like that she was Truly Beautiful already? Or might he just say that's nice in the curious flat way he often said things were nice without engaging in them at all? Or might he sit down and say to her that there was really no need for all this fuss and preparation. Desmond often told her not to fuss. She hated that, she didn't fuss, she just saw to it that things were done right. If somebody hadn't lit a fire under Desmond all these years where would they be now she would like to know?

Deirdre would not share her beauty secrets with her husband. Long long ago in that strange summer when it all began, Desmond would lie on a narrow bed and admire her as she brushed her long fair curls, he would say that he never knew that peaches and cream was anything except a line in a song until he saw Deirdre's lovely face. He would reach over for her and ask if he could help her rub more of that nice cold cream in, maybe down her throat a little, maybe around her neck and arms. Maybe . . . maybe. It was so hard to remember Desmond being like that. But the article in the magazine said that she could recapture all that fresh glow, it was only a matter of proper skin care.

Deirdre would follow every single step, all those upward and circular movements when massaging in the throat cream, all that avoiding the delicate tissue around the eyes. She was going to look right on this day if it killed her. She was going to show them that they had been wrong to pity her twenty-five years ago when she had married Desmond Doyle, a counter hand in a grocery shop, a boy from a poor family in the back of beyond in Mayo. A family that nobody had ever heard of.

This day would be her silvery revenge.

They had all said yes, every single person who had been expected to come. There were some of course who had been asked but knew that they were not meant to come. Like Desmond's odd brother Vincent, the man who never left his mountains and his sheep in that lonely place where Brendan had chosen to spend his life. There had been a message from her son that his uncle very much regretted but it was a bad time to get away. That was the way it should have been done. Deirdre had nodded, pleased at the correct response.

And of course the Palazzos who ran the huge company where Desmond had worked for so long. Unfortunately they couldn't come, a sweet letter from Carlo and Maria, signed personally, wishing them all kinds of happiness and full of regrets that it would coincide with their annual visit to Italy. There would be a gift and flowers. But it was right that they didn't come. They were too high up, they would cramp everyone else's style. And Deirdre's mother who felt able to talk to everyone might discuss with them too closely Desmond's career in the company. She might discover that Desmond had never risen high and had at one stage been let go. This would be at odds with the glowing picture Deirdre always painted.

Frank Quigley and his wife Renata Palazzo said they would love to come. Deirdre thought grimly that Frank, for all his vast success and his unfair advancement up the ladder even before he married the heiress to the Palazzo fortunes, was still a good man to have at a function. He always seemed to know the right thing to say, and said it. She remembered back to their wedding day, Frank had been the best man then, he had been well able to handle anything that had turned up. Including Deirdre's mother and father, with their faces like early Christian martyrs throughout the ceremony and the so-called festivities.

And Father Hurley was coming, he said it would be a marvellous chance to visit a couple whose marriage has worked out so well. Deirdre knew she could rely on kind Father Hurley to say the right thing all evening.

And of course the Irish contingent would arrive. The date had been long fixed in their minds. There had been a possibility that her brother Gerard might not be able to make it but Deirdre had telephoned with such surprise and hurt and bewilderment that somehow his plans had changed. She had told him straight out on the telephone that there was no point in *having* a silver wedding if the family couldn't be there.

'Will Desmond's family be there?' Gerard had asked.

'That's not the point,' Deirdre had said.

Mother was coming of course, and Barbara, they were going to make a long weekend out of it all, come on the Thursday, do a few shows, take in a lot of shopping. Barbara's husband Jack would combine it with a business trip of course. That's what he was always able to do.

And when they arrived they would have drinks on the lawn in Rosemary Drive in the late afternoon. Then they would all go to a special Mass where the priest would refer to blessings of the sacrament of matrimony in general and specific reference to Desmond and Deirdre in particular. Father Hurley would be called on as the priest who married them to say a few words . . . Then after photographs outside the church and everything they would gather back at Rosemary Drive, and champagne would be opened.

There had been no champagne back in 1960 but Deirdre would not let her brow furrow about that. If she were to be truly beautiful she must keep worry lines away from her face.

She told herself that there really was no need to have worry lines. Everything would go perfectly.

And even if . . . no, no, smooth out the temples, don't screw up the eyes.

The beauty plan had suggested you do a Countdown and a Chart. Nothing pleased Deirdre more, she loved making out plans and schedules like this. Anyway she already had her own Countdown to the silver wedding in terms of things to be organized.

Desmond had shaken his head sadly, but men didn't understand the way things were done. Or maybe, Deirdre thought crossly, *some* men did, and those were the ones who got on. Men like Desmond who had never risen in Palazzo, who were leaving and going into partnership in a corner shop. Those men didn't understand.

And because Deirdre was so plugged into her countdown, she knew she had exactly 110 days to go when the telephone rang and it was her mother at the other end of the line.

Mother rang only every second weekend, on Sunday evenings. Deirdre had instituted that practice years ago, they rang each other on alternate Sundays. Sometimes she felt that Mother had little to say, but that couldn't be possible. Mother wasn't good at writing letters so these conversations were Deirdre's lifeline. She remembered everything that was said, and even kept a little spiral notebook by the phone to jot down names of Mother's bridge friends, or of the party that Barbara and Jack had been to, or the concert that Gerard had taken Mother to. Sometimes Mrs O'Hagan would exclaim that Deirdre had the most extraordinary memory for little things. But Deirdre thought it was only natural that you should want to recall matters of moment in your family's life. She was always mildly put out that Mother hardly ever remembered any of her friends, and never inquired about Palazzo or about any of the outings that Deirdre had described.

It was unexpected to hear from Mother in the middle of the week, in the middle of the day.

'Is anything wrong?' Deirdre said at once.

'No, Deirdre, Lord above you sound just like your grandmother.' Kevin's mother always began every greeting by asking was anything wrong.

'I meant it's not your usual time to ring.'

Mother softened: 'No, I know, I know. But I'm in London and I thought I'd try and see could I catch you at home.'

'You're in *London*!' Deirdre cried, her hand flying to her throat. She looked around the living room, untidy and covered with Desmond's papers, plans and projections, notes that he had been discussing with the Patels, the family who ran the shop that he insisted was far more his life's dream than the great Palazzo company. Deirdre herself was dressed in a faded pinny, the place was a mess. She looked out the window fearfully as if her mother were about to come straight in the door.

'Yes, I just got in from the airport. The Underground is marvellous isn't it? Just whizzes you in, door to door almost.'

'What are you doing in London?' Deirdre's voice was almost a whisper. Had Mother come three months too early for the silver wedding, was there a crisis?

'Oh, just passing through . . . you see the tour leaves from London.'

'The tour? What tour?'

'Deirdre, I told you all about it . . . didn't I? I must have. I've told everyone else.'

'You mentioned no tour to me.' Deirdre was mutinous.

'Oh I must have, maybe I wasn't talking to you.'

'We talk every Sunday night of life, I was talking to you four days ago.'

'Deirdre, is anything wrong dear? You sound so strange. Like as if you're fighting with me or something.'

'I didn't know of any tour, where are you going?'

'Down to Italy first, and then by ship, we pick up the ship in Ancona and head off from there . . .'

'Where do you head off to?'

'Oh a variety of places . . . Corfu, Athens, Rhodes, Cyprus, and some place in Turkey . . .'

'A cruise Mother, you're going on a cruise!'

'I think that's a very grand name for it.'

'It sounds a very grand outing.'

'Yes, well let's hope it won't be too hot out in all those places, I think it's probably not the right time of year to head off . . .'

'Then why are you?'

'Because it came up, anyway enough of this, are we going to meet?'

'Meet? You're going to come here? Now?'

Mother laughed. 'Well thanks a lot, Deirdre, that sounds a great welcome, but actually I hadn't intended on going out to darkest Pinner . . . I thought you might come in and join me for a spot of lunch or coffee or whatever.'

Deirdre hated Anna calling it 'darkest Pinner', it was such an insult, as if the place was off the beaten track. And here was her own mother, who was from Dublin for heaven's sake, who didn't know where anywhere was, and whether it was on or off any track, saying the same thing.

'Where are you staying?' she asked, trying not to let the irritation show.

Mother was in a central hotel, very central she said, it had only taken her two minutes to leave the Piccadilly Line and be in her foyer. Simply remarkable. It would be easy for Deirdre to find too.

'I know how to get there.' Deirdre was white-faced.

'So will we say the bar here at one thirty, will that give you time. . . ?'

Deirdre left a note to Desmond on the table. These days she never knew whether he was going to come back or not during the day. His arrangements with Palazzo seemed to be fluid. Frank Quigley had said there would be proper arrangements made, for a manager like Desmond, setting up on his own, it wasn't a question of severance pay, redundancy, compensation, golden handshakes . . . It was all defined as Proper Arrangements. Deirdre hoped it would be finalized by the time of the silver wedding.

Grimly Deirdre went upstairs and put on her best suit. Her hair was limp and greasy-looking. She had planned to wash it later in the day, now there wasn't time. Her good handbag was being mended, the catch had worked loose. There was a grubby-looking bandage on her wrist where she had burned herself on the oven. She didn't like to open it all up and apply a fresh one, they had told her that it should be done at the hospital.

In low spirits and filled with a vague apprehension Deirdre Doyle set out to meet her mother. She felt drab and unattractive. She looked what she was, she decided, catching a reflection of herself in the window of the train that took her into Baker Street. She looked the middle-aged housewife from the suburbs, married to a not very successful man, no job to exercise her mind, not enough money to dress herself properly. Suffering badly from the empty-nest syndrome. Perhaps more than most: one daughter trying to be accepted in a convent where they wouldn't let her take her vows, another daughter who sometimes didn't come to see her parents more than once in a fortnight, and her son, her beloved son gone, fled to live at the other side of another country.

She was sure that she and Mother would fight. There had been something in the tone of the phone call that she hadn't liked. Mother had been impatient with her, and patting her down as if *she* were the difficult one.

It was extremely irritating but Deirdre would not lose her temper. Years of being reasonable and refusing to raise her voice had meant that there were few arguments in Rosemary Drive.

Deirdre had always prided herself on that. It was something to show for all those years and all that had happened.

Mother was sitting in a corner of the big-oak panelled bar as if she were a regular. She looked very well, she wore a fawn linen jacket and skirt with a cream-coloured blouse beneath, her hair had been freshly done, in fact she must have spent the hour that her daughter used to struggle in to central London sitting peacefully in a hairdressing salon.

She looked relaxed and at her ease. She was reading a newspaper and unless she was putting on an elaborate act she seemed to be reading it without the aid of glasses.

A woman of sixty-seven and she looked somehow younger and fresher than her own daughter.

Eileen O'Hagan's eyes looked up just at that moment, and she smiled broadly. Deirdre felt her movements somehow stiffen as she walked across to meet her mother. They kissed and Mother, who was already on friendly terms with the waiter, called him over.

'Just a glass of wine and soda,' Deirdre said.

'Nothing stronger to celebrate your old Mother coming to town?'

'You're never this lady's mother, seesters yes . . .' the waiter said on cue. But it had a ring that was altogether too truthful for Deirdre.

'Just wine and soda,' she snapped.

'Let me look at you . . .' her mother said.

'Don't, Mother, I look badly, I wish you'd told me . . .'

'But if I had then you'd have gone to an immense amount of fuss and worn yourself out . . .' her mother said.

'Then you admit you didn't tell me, that it didn't just slip your mind.'

'It was out of kindness, Deirdre . . . you were always one to go to such efforts, that's why I didn't tell you.'

Deirdre felt the tears sting in her eyes, she fought to keep the hurt tone out of her voice.

'Well all I can say is that it's a pity. Desmond would have loved to have had you to the house, and the girls will be very sorry they've missed their Grannie.'

'Nonsense, Deirdre, Anna's at work. Helen's at prayer . . . Desmond is up to his eyes . . . Why create a great fuss?'

There it was again, that hated word Fuss. Deirdre clenched her fists and saw her mother glance at her whitened knuckles. This was very bad, she had vowed that there would be no argument. She must keep to that.

'Right, well here we are anyway,' Deirdre said in a voice that sounded to her own ears curiously tinny. 'And Mother, you do look remarkably well.'

Her mother brightened up. 'This suit has been a godsend, you know I bought it three years ago in Maureen's shop. Maureen always had great taste, I used to wonder why some of her clothes were so expensive, but her mother always said you paid for the cut and that they never really went out of fashion . . .'

Mother patted the skirt of her outfit with pleasure.

'It should be just the thing for a cruise.' Deirdre tried to sound enthusiastic.

'Well yes, I didn't think there was any point in getting all those floral silks . . . leisurewear, cruisewear they actually call them nowadays. Better to bring something suitable, something familiar, and I have a few cotton dresses for sightseeing.' She looked animated and excited.

'And what possessed you to take off on something like this?' Even as she spoke Deirdre knew that hers sounded like the voice of an older woman remonstrating with a difficult daughter rather than the enthusiasm that there should have been for a self-sufficient parent capable of enjoying herself on her own.

'As I told you, it came up, and I have a friend who was also free at this time, so it seemed only sensible . . .'

'Oh good, someone's going with you.' Deirdre was pleased. Two old ladies on board ship would at least have each other to talk to at the time, and be able to share the memory afterwards. She tried to remember which one of her mother's bridge cronies would have been likely to be accompanying her.

'Yes, and I thought I'd seize the chance of letting you meet each other, not for lunch, we'll have that on our own, but Tony said he'd pop down and say hallo . . . Ah, there he is . . . what timing!'

And as Deirdre felt the base of her stomach fill with lead she realized that her mother was waving at a florid-looking man with a blazer and a red face who was coming across the room rubbing his hands delightedly. Mother was going on a cruise with a man.

'This is nice,' Tony said, crushing Deirdre's hot hand in his own, and telling the waiter that he'd like a large G and T, Cork and Schweppes, ice and slice.

The waiter was puzzled. Mother said affectionately that Irish gin-drinkers were fanatically partisan and only drank the home brew as far as gin was concerned.

'But we're very democratic, we drink the English tonic,' Tony said, beaming around him. 'Well Deirdre, what do you think of all this caper?'

'I've only just heard about it this moment,' she said, hardly able to find the words.

'It should be a great old jaunt altogether,' he said. 'No decisions about whether to go and see places, they come to see you instead. Perfect for the lazy man. And lazy woman.' He actually patted Mother's hand.

'Were you afraid to tell me this too in case I'd fuss?' Deirdre asked, and could have bitten off her tongue.

Tony weighed in before Mother could answer.

'Oh, there you are, Eileen, she's as jealous as the others. Barbara nearly went mad when she heard that her mother was taking me instead of her, and Gerard said that in all decency your mother should take her son instead of a toy boy like myself.' He threw back his head and laughed heartily, and Mother laughed with him.

Deirdre thought, he knows Barbara and Gerard. Why had neither of them said anything about this to her? How dare they keep quiet about something as big as this? And was he serious about Mother taking him, Mother could not possibly be paying for this loud vulgar man. Or was this a joke too?

Mother seemed to read her face. 'Don't worry about a thing, Deirdre my love, it's only his way of going on. Tony's not after the deeds of the house.'

'Fat chance I'd have if I *were* after them,' he boomed. 'Your mother will live for ever, I'll go for the chop one of these days. Hopefully not on the cruise, though a burial at sea would be something to remember, wouldn't it?'

Deirdre felt a genuine sense of nausea. This man who must be almost the same age as her mother, was a serious part of her life. And until this minute nobody had been able to tell her.

She forced the smile back on to her face, and saw her mother's approving glance. She found her mouth dry and bitter as she searched for some suitable words.

But Tony was not a man who would allow silences. He had had her glass refilled, he had commandeered a dish of olives and a bowl of crisps on the ground that one had to have all the trappings. He had assured her that he would take great care of her mother on the cruise, squeezed her hand hard again, and said he would leave the key at reception. The key. The man wasn't even pretending that they had separate rooms. Deirdre felt a sense of unreality wash over her, and she hardly noticed that he had kissed her mother goodbye on the cheek.

Mother had booked a nearby restaurant. It was small and French and expensive. The napkins were thick, the silver was heavy, and the flowers on the table were real and plentiful.

In her twenty-five years living in London Deirdre had never eaten in a place like this and here was her mother, her mother from a small country, a small city compared to this one, ordering as if she were used to it.

She was glad that Mother was making decisions, not only could she not understand the menu but she would not have been able to order, so confused and upset did she feel.

'Why didn't you tell me anything about . . . er . . . Tony?' she asked eventually.

'Well there wasn't all that much to tell until we decided to go on this cruise together, and then as soon as we set off on that I *did* tell you.' Mother spread out her hands as if it were the simplest thing in the world.

'And Gerard, and and Barbara . . . do they . . . did they . . . ?'

'Well they know Tony's a friend of mine, and naturally I told them our holiday plans.'

'And were they . . . did they . . . ?'

'Gerard drove us to the airport this morning. Tony's right, he's green with envy, he keeps saying it's just what he needs. He works too hard, he *should* take time off, and he can well afford it. Maybe this is the spur.'

'But did he say . . . what did he think . . . ?'

'He didn't say that he'd take a holiday, and you know Gerard, he probably is thinking about it.'

Could Mother really misunderstand her or was this deliberate? Deirdre was not going to be brushed aside.

'What about Barbara and Jack? What do they think of you going away with a man?'

'Dearest Deirdre, I'm not going away with a man in that sense, I am going away on holiday certainly and I am going with Tony, and yes indeed he is a man. What do you mean, what do they think? They don't think at all, I am perfectly sure.'

'But Jack's family . . .'

As long as Deirdre could remember, Jack's family had been spoken of with some kind of awe. His father was a High Court Judge, his uncle was an Ambassador. Barbara had done what the O'Hagan family had wanted by marrying such style, instead of what she, Deirdre the eldest, had done – marrying a nobody and doing it in a great hurry.

But Mother looked totally bewildered.

'Jack's family?' she repeated as if Deirdre had somehow begun to speak in a foreign language. 'What on earth connection have they with anything?'

'You know . . .'

'I don't think they ever met Tony. No, I'm sure they didn't. Why do you ask?'

Deirdre looked hard at her mother. Mother knew bloody well why she asked. She asked because the high and mighty Jack's family were always mentioned. They had been mentioned since Deirdre's young sister Barbara had started walking out with a son of the well-connected tribe. Deirdre remembered the huge wedding, given for Barbara, with the marquee, the witty speeches, the politicians and the photographers. It had been very different from her own wedding day. And now suddenly Jack's almighty clan didn't seem important any more.

Feeling a flush darken her cheek, she spoke directly to her mother.

'And do you and . . . Tony . . . have any further plans . . . like after the cruise, do you think you might get married or anything?'

'Do try to keep the surprise out of your voice,' her mother said. 'Stranger things have happened, you know. But the answer is no. No plans like that.'

'Oh?'

'And anyway, enough about me and my trip. Tell me about all your doings.' Mother smiled in anticipation.

Deirdre looked dour: 'None of them are anything nearly as interesting as your plans.'

'Come come, Desmond's setting up on his own, *and* you're going to have this whole silver wedding shindig . . .'

It was such a Tony word, shindig. Mother didn't speak like that before.

'Where did you meet him?' Deirdre asked abruptly.

'Desmond?' Now Mother was being playful. 'When you brought him home of course, and told us about the wedding. But you know that.'

'I didn't mean Desmond, and you know that.' Deirdre was cross. 'I meant Tony. How did you become involved with him?'

'We met in the golf club.'

'Tony's a member of the golf club?' The surprise and disbelief were clear in her voice.

'Yes, he plays off twelve,' Mother said proudly.

'But how did he become a member?' Years ago someone flash like Tony could not have been proposed, it would have been as simple as that. Had her Desmond known how to play golf, which he did not, he would not have been acceptable. How could someone like Tony get in?

'I've no idea, I suppose like we all became members.' Mother was vague.

'And do all your other friends know him, did Mrs Barry know him for example?' Deirdre had chosen Maureen Barry's mother, the great social barometer of their Dublin. Surely Tony had not been welcomed in her set?

'Sophie? Yes of course poor Sophie met him from time to time. Sophie Barry didn't play golf, remember, so she wouldn't have known him in that context.'

'Don't tell me Tony plays bridge?'

'No, he's frightfully dismissive of old pussy cats as he calls us, spending hour after cheery hour, day after day dealing cards.'

Mother laughed merrily and suddenly her life seemed much more fun than Deirdre's own. Desperate not to let her mother change the subject again, Deirdre tried once more.

'And Mother please, what does Gerard think? What does he say? No, not about taking holidays himself, what does he say about you and Tony?'

'I've no idea.'

'You must know.'

'No, I mean how would I know? I only know what he says to me, I've no idea what he says to anyone else. He has a rather nice girlfriend at the moment, he may talk about it with her, but I imagine not.' Mother looked supremely unconcerned.

'But he must . . . surely . . .'

'Listen, Deirdre. Everyone has their own life to lead, Gerard is probably much more worried about his career at the Bar, should he take Silk, should he stop playing the field with these little dolly birds and settle down? He probably worries about his health, he's nearly forty, he may think a lot about cholesterol and polyunsaturated fats. He might wonder whether to sell his flat and buy a house. What time on earth is there for him to spend thinking about his mother? I ask you!'

'But if you're doing something . . . if you're getting into something . . .'

'I'm sure he thinks I'm old enough to look after myself.'

'We all have to look after each other,' Deirdre said a trifle unctuously.

'That's where you are totally wrong, we all have to make very sure we don't interfere in people's lives. That's the great sin.'

The unfairness of it stung Deirdre like the lash of a whip. How *dare* Mother come out with this preachy nonsense about not interfering in people's lives. For a quarter of a century Deirdre had been trying to live up to some kind of image, some expectations for her. She was the daughter for whom there had been such hopes. The eldest of the family, very bright at university, an honours student, she might have taken the Third Sec examination and gone into the Department of External Affairs as it was called then, she might have been on the way to being an ambassador or marrying one. She might have done the Bar as her brother had done. She might have made the brilliant match that her sister Barbara had done.

Instead she had fallen in love one long hot summer, and trapped herself into a strange prison. Where since nothing was good enough for the O'Hagans and their hopes back home then everything must be made to look as if it were.

Deirdre had lived her entire life on this premise, to please the mother who was now sitting opposite her justifying her pitiable relationship with a common flashy man by saying that the main rule of living was not to interfere! It was not possible.

Deirdre spoke very slowly: 'I know what you're saying but I think it's important too not to be entirely self-centred and to take the wishes of others into account as well. I mean, did I or did I not spend all my teenage years hearing about people who were suitable, and people who were not suitable?'

'Not from me you didn't.'

'But you were always wanting to know what people's fathers did, and where they lived?'

'Out of interest.' Mother was airy about it. 'It's always nice to know who people are in case you knew them years ago or something. That's all it was about.'

'No it wasn't, Mother, you and Mrs Barry . . .'

'Oh Deirdre, Sophie Barry had nothing in her whole life except some kind of nonsensical pecking order. Nobody who knew her took a blind bit of notice of it . . .'

'Maureen did.'

'Well more fool Maureen, and anyway I don't think you're right, Maureen lived her own life, made her own way despite all poor Sophie's rubbishing on about being in trade.'

'You mean to tell me that you and Daddy were perfectly happy that I married Desmond? Don't try to tell me that. I won't believe it.'

There were tears in Deirdre's eyes, tears of rage, hurt and confusion. Suddenly the screen was falling away, the mask was being dropped, she knew she was on dangerous ground here. The polite pretence of years was being swept away.

The woman in the fawn linen suit and the cream blouse looked at her with concern. She began to speak and then stopped.

'Now, you can't deny it!' Deirdre was triumphant.

'Child, you're talking about a lifetime ago,' her mother said.

'But what I say is true, you did care, you did care that Desmond wasn't top drawer enough for us.'

'What do you mean for us? We weren't marrying him, you were, he was your choice, the words top drawer weren't even mentioned.'

'Not aloud maybe.'

'Not at all. I assure you, your father and I thought you were too young, of course we did, you hadn't taken your degree, we were afraid you would never get any qualification. In that I suppose we wished you would wait, that was all.'

Deirdre took a deep breath: 'You knew we couldn't wait.'

'I knew you wouldn't wait, that's all I knew. You were very determined. I wasn't going to oppose you.'

'You knew why.'

'I knew you loved him or thought you did, now that you've stayed with him and are dead set on having all this palaver in the autumn then you were probably right, you did love him, and he loved you.'

To Mother it seemed too simple, if you lived together for twenty-five years and were prepared to acknowledge it . . . you loved each other. Deirdre was thoughtful.

'Well isn't that what happened?' Mother was waiting for a yes or a no or an I told you so.

'More or less, but no thanks to anyone at home.' Deirdre was still mulish.

'I don't know what exactly it is you're trying to say, Deirdre. Of all my children I thought you were the most contented. You went for what you wanted, you got it. Nobody forced you to do anything, you had your freedom, you went to university, you could have worked for a living but you never did. Sophie and I used to say that you got everything on a plate, now it seems there's some grievance.'

Mother was interested but not distressed, she was concerned but not unduly curious. She tossed a salad expertly and waited for an explanation.

'Why did you let me marry Desmond if you thought I was too young?'

'I only thought, let's cause the least grief possible in the world. That's what I always think. Your father did think you might be pregnant, but I knew you weren't.'

'How did you know that?' Deirdre's voice was a whisper.

'Because nobody, not even in the far back year of 1960, would have got married to someone just for that reason if she didn't want to. And you weren't. Anna wasn't born until months and months later, quite wiped poor Sophie's eye, I think. I have a feeling she had the same thoughts as your father.'

'Yes.'

'So, Deirdre, what's the federal case as they say? What am I meant to have done? We gave our permission. Was that bad? No. We came to the wedding, that's what you wanted. You said you didn't want a huge showy number and you wanted it in England, we went along with that. We took Barbara and Gerard out of school for the ceremony.

'The house is there for you and Desmond to come over and see us but you never do, you came once and you were so touchy we didn't know what to say to you, everything upset you. We came to see you a few times and we're all heading over to see you again for your silver wedding, something it may be said that isn't at all what we're used to, and somehow still in spite of all this I am the worst in the world, and by implication your father was, and your sister and brother are.'

Eileen O'Hagan mopped up the dressing of her salad with a piece of French bread and looked at her daughter for an explanation.

Deirdre looked at her wordlessly.

The waiter came and took away their plates and discussed at length an apple tart and a burnt cream. Deirdre's mother went into the option with animation, it gave Deirdre a chance to gather her thoughts.

'I ordered one of each, I hate to be directive but I thought it best.'

'That's fine, Mother.'

'And what were we talking about before? Oh I know, Daddy and I were meant to have hated Desmond or something, isn't that it?'

'Not exactly.'

'Well not just not exactly, not at all. We both thought he was very nice, bullied within an inch of his life by you of course but then you'd be bound to be a bossy boots, you get it from me.' Eileen O'Hagan was pleased to have passed on such sterling qualities.

'What did you say about him to each other?' Deirdre's voice was small.

'Daddy and I? Hardly anything. He was providing for you all right, that was what we worried about I suppose in those days, so it was good that this side of it wasn't a problem. I think we were upset that you didn't have a career.'

'I had three children in rapid succession.' Deirdre was defensive.

'Yes, but afterwards. Anyway I suppose we thought that maybe it was a bit hierarchical in that set-up with the Italians, the Palladians . . .'

'The Palazzos, Mother.'

'Yes well, that's about the only negative thought we ever had about Desmond, so you can stop doing your outraged lioness bit about him.'

Mother laughed affectionately.

Deirdre looked at her as if she were someone never seen before.

'And Mrs Barry, was she not questioning you about us?'

'No, sweetheart. To be very honest there wasn't all that much interest at all. Nobody had. You know that yourself about Dublin, out of sight out of people's minds and immediate conversation and interest.'

'But not for you, surely you couldn't have forgotten me, your eldest daughter.' Her lip was trembling.

'Of course I don't forget you, silly thing, but not all the little bitty things that you think were never off our lips, this promotion, that remark that the Palladians passed about Desmond, the time that Anna was at the same reception as Princess Di.'

'It was Princess Michael of Kent.'

'Well you know what I mean, Deirdre, it's not some kind of score card, you know, points for this, minus points for that.'

There was a silence. A long silence.

'I'm not criticizing you, you do know that?'

'Yes, Mother.'

'And even if Kevin and I hadn't liked Desmond, which was not the case, whatever we were allowed to get to know of him we liked very much . . . But suppose we hadn't . . . what would have been the point of saying it or letting it be thought? We weren't going to live your lives for you.'

'I see.'

'When I was married to Kevin my parents were delighted, they crowed and brayed and made me very very uneasy.'

'You should have been pleased.'

'No, I was suspicious. I thought that they wanted me off their hands and I also thought they equated money with some kind of happiness or success. Your father didn't give me much of either.'

'I don't believe you!' Deirdre's mouth was wide open.

'Why shouldn't I tell you this? You and I are middle-aged women, we're talking about life and love. Your father was what they call now a chauvinist pig, in those days we called it a man's man and were meant to be grateful that he wasn't chasing the ladies. He stayed at his clubs every evening until late, you remember that growing up, don't you? I bet Desmond was at home to get to know his children.'

'He wasn't a member of any clubs.' Deirdre sounded wistful.

'And weren't you the better for it? Anyway I always thought I would neither encourage nor discourage any of my children, let them choose for themselves and go along with it.'

'Barbara's wedding . . .' Deirdre began.

'Nearly put us in the workhouse. What a bloody shower, Jack's family. They gave us a wedding list of their guests from their side of the family as long as your arm . . . we decided to do it the way the young couple wanted it. Though Barbara has often said to me she wished they had had less of a send-off, nothing ever lived up to it.'

'Barbara said that?'

'She says it every time she has a glass of sherry, it's hardly breaking a confidence to tell you. She says it in the golf club, and she tried to say it the night she was in the audience at the *Late Late Show* but apparently they didn't get a mike to her.'

For the first time Deirdre laughed a genuine laugh, and the waiter was so pleased he came running with a plate of bon bons and a refill of coffee.

'And I know you think I should be happy with my six grandchildren, your three and Barbara's three. But I never see yours. They grew up without us, and when we did meet them they were like white mice they were so afraid of us. And I was sick to death of Barbara's three when they were at the poisonous stage, we were unpaid unthanked babysitters and now that they're nice and interesting I don't see hide nor hair of them. And I don't think that Gerard is going to give us any news in that direction, but that's his business. I don't want to send him out to mate just so that I can have more people to call me Grannie.'

She looked lively and eager, she did not look like someone who wanted more people to call her Grannie, let alone someone who had grown-ups who did.

'And suppose you and . . . er Tony . . . get on well on this cruise, why don't you think there might be a chance of . . . well, something more permanent?'

Deirdre somehow felt that if he were accepted by Mother's cronies at home and by her sister and brother he couldn't be quite as common and unsuitable as she had thought at first.

'No, that's not on the cards.'

'As you said earlier, it's not such a barbarous idea.'

'Well, it is really, Deirdre. Or his wife would think so anyway.'

'He's married. Mother, I don't believe it.'

'Oh but you must, I assure you.'

'Does anyone know, is his wife sort of around, are people aware of her?' Deirdre's voice was very concerned.

Her mother was silent for the first time. She looked at Deirdre with a strange expression. It was hard to read her look. It was partly sad and partly as if she had known that things would be like this. There was a little frisson of impatience in the disappointment.

She didn't answer Deirdre's question, she never answered it. She called for the bill, and they walked together back to her hotel.

She said she had a little more shopping to do, and she sent her love to Anna, and to Helen. There was no point in sending love to Brendan, they both knew that he was only rarely in touch. No rapport of weekly phone chats had been established between Deirdre and her son on Sunday nights as there were between Deirdre and her mother.

Eileen O'Hagan said she wished Desmond well, and thought that he was quite right to have left the Palladians or the Palazzos or whatever they were called. A man had to do what a man had to do. And so had a woman.

She said she would send a postcard from somewhere that looked nice and exotic.

She said since Deirdre hadn't offered that she would be sure and give Deirdre's warm wishes to Tony and tell him that Deirdre had said Bon Voyage.

And as she left her daughter who would get the tube back to the station where the Metropolitan line would take her back to Pinner and the table full of preparations for a party 110 days away, Eileen O'Hagan reached out her hand and stroked Deirdre's cheek.

'I'm sorry,' she said.

'What for, Mother? Why are you sorry? You gave me a lovely lunch. It was really good to see you.' And Deirdre meant it.

'No, I'm sorry that I didn't give you more.'

'You gave me everything, I was only being silly, you said yourself that I was the most contented of your children. I never knew that.'

Her mother opened her mouth as if to speak but closed it again, and when Deirdre turned to wave she saw that Eileen O'Hagan's lips were moving. She thought she was just mouthing goodbye.

She was too far away to hear her mother saying, 'I'm sorry that I gave you no notion of happiness. Only how to pretend you are happy and that's no gift at all. It's a burden for your back.'

Deirdre waved again just before she went down the steps to the tube station, and she hoped her mother would stop mouthing at her. After all, here in Piccadilly Circus the whole world could be passing by, and there could be anyone, just anyone, who might see them. Someone from Pinner or someone from Dublin. The world was getting smaller and you should always behave as if you were under some kind of observation, because when it came down to it, that's what we all were most of the time. Under observation.

9
Silver Wedding

They had set the Teasmaid for seven o'clock.

Desmond had grumbled that it was too early, they would both be worn out by the time the thing began. But Deirdre said it was better far to be ahead of themselves instead of running after themselves all day. Be up and organized before the caterers came.

'They're not coming until three o'clock,' Desmond had said.

'Everything has to be cleared away for them.'

'God Almighty, Deirdre, we're not going to spend eight hours clearing the kitchen worktops. And isn't it all done already anyway?'

She took no notice of him, she poured him out a cup of tea.

For years, since they had moved into separate beds in fact, they had this morning ritual of the electric teamaker on the table between them. It somehow soothed them into the day, took the little edges off the slight sense of morning disappointment that they each seemed to feel.

'Happy anniversary,' he said and reached out for her hand.

'And to you,' she said, smiling. 'Will we give our presents now or later?'

'Whatever you like.'

'Maybe later.' She sipped her tea and ticked off in her mind all the things to be done. She had an appointment at the hairdresser, and a manicure as a special treat. Her new outfit was hanging on the wardrobe under its cellophane wrapping. She hoped it was a good choice, the woman in the shop had been very pushy, kept calling her Madam and speaking to her as if she wasn't there. Madam would look very well in pale colours, Madam doesn't want to grow old before her time. Madam could do with a little detail on the shoulder if Madam really insists that she won't wear shoulder pads.

Deirdre would like to have worn pads, almost everyone did nowadays like the women in *Dynasty* and *Dallas*, but she remembered that time years ago when she had bought a very upholstered-looking jacket and Maureen Barry had laughed at it and called it Deirdre's Marshal Bulganin outfit. She daren't risk that again. Or risk even the memory of it.

She knew that whatever Maureen wore today it would be stunning, it would take all the attention away from her, away from Deirdre whose party it was. The woman in the shop said she couldn't believe that Madam was really celebrating a silver wedding, but that was in the shop. The woman was anxious to flatter her and make a sale.

The woman hadn't seen Maureen.

She would take the limelight today as she had taken it twenty-five years ago. When the bride had looked pink and frightened and flustered, and the bridesmaid had looked dark and cool and elegant in a plain pink linen dress and a big pink flower in her hair. And Frank Quigley had never taken his eyes off her. From one end of the day to the other.

Would it be the same today? Would the great Frank Quigley remember his passion for Maureen Barry with regret as the one thing he didn't win in his life? Knowing Frank he would probably have turned it into a success rather than a failure. Look at the bigger and better prize he had won. Married to the entire Palazzo fortune. He wouldn't have had that if Maureen had accepted him all those years ago.

But she wouldn't think destructive thoughts. Not today, today was her day more than her wedding day had ever been. She had worked hard for it, put in long hours, long years. Deirdre Doyle would have today.

Desmond looked at his face in the bathroom mirror. It looked back at him, younger he thought than it had done a while ago. Or maybe he just imagined that, because he felt better. He didn't have that constant pain in the base of his stomach that he used to have going in to Palazzo. He enjoyed leaving the house now. Mornings were so much easier.

He had suggested that he and Suresh Patel start a newspaper delivery service in the area. People would like to have a paper to read in their homes if it arrived before seven. And it was a great success. It was run by the owlish boy who kept the accounts meticulously and also delivered the papers before heading off to school. He dropped the *Daily Mail* into Rosemary Drive for Desmond too, and it meant that he could read it and leave it for Deirdre.

He was annoyed with her that she had not wanted Suresh Patel and his wife to come to the silver wedding.

'It's only for people who were at the ceremony,' she had complained.

'John and Jean West weren't there,' he had countered.

'Don't be silly, Desmond, they're our next-door neighbours.'

'Well Suresh is my partner isn't he?'

'Only very recently, and anyway he won't know anyone.'

'Half of them won't know anyone.'

'Be reasonable, can't you, his wife doesn't even speak English. What am I to say to people, this is Mrs Patel, Desmond's partner's wife who can only nod and smile?'

He had left it. But it rankled. He felt sure that if Suresh Patel was having some ceremony in his house, the Doyles would have been invited. But it wasn't worth a major row, if he had won then he would have had to look after the Patels all evening. And there were so many other things to concentrate on. Like his son was coming back . . . of his own free will to be there for the celebrations. Perhaps now that he too had been able to escape from a world that had frightened him they might have more in common. Perhaps the old prickliness would have softened if not gone altogether.

And he would be glad to see Father Hurley again, he was a kind man. Even in those bad far-off days when priests were meant to be disapproving of sin and anticipating the sacrament of matrimony and everything. There had been no condemnation when he had gone and asked Father

Hurley if he could arrange to marry them as quickly as possible. Even quicker.

'Are you sure?' Father Hurley had asked.

'Oh yes, the tests were positive,' Desmond had said, fighting the panic.

'No, I meant are you both sure this is what you want to do? It's for life.'

It had been an odd question at that time. Desmond had paid little heed to it. The only important thing had been could the priest get them married in three weeks, so that their child would not be impossibly premature. The child that was never born. The child that miscarried on Christmas Eve.

He wondered had Father Hurley ever thought about it, whether the priest who had after all baptized Anna realized that she was born a full fourteen months after the shotgun wedding. And that a sister or brother had been lost before that.

Desmond sighed. Father Hurley probably had enough to think about in an Ireland which was rapidly catching up with the rest of the world in terms of godlessness. He would be unlikely to spend time speculating about what had happened in marriages made a quarter of a century ago.

Anna woke around seven in her flat in Shepherds Bush, she went straight to the window to see what kind of day it was. Good, a bright crisp autumn day. London was lovely in autumn. The parks were at their best. She had been walking last night with her friend Judy, and they had seen possibly a dozen different shades of gold and orange on the trees. Judy said that in America up in New England they had special tours and holidays for Leaf Peekers, for people who came to peek at the leaves changing colour. You could organize that in London too.

Anna was going to work for the morning. She would only be in the way in Rosemary Drive, things would be up to high doh there, the less people there were about the better. She would go there around three, the same time as the caterers, just to keep Mother out of their hair and from driving them up the walls. She had begged Helen not to turn up until five, the official time that the celebrations began. The thought of letting her sister Helen loose on any house where professional caterers were preparing a meal was enough to frighten anyone.

Helen was in very poor form at the moment, there had been some problem yet again in the convent. Apparently the rest of the Community didn't want Helen to take her vows and be a permanent member of the house. This was what Anna was reading between the lines, Helen of course was reading nothing of the sort, seeing only a series of petty irritations, confusions and obstacles.

Anna sighed. If she was in a religious community, which was possibly the last place on earth she would want to end up, then the very very last person on earth she would like with her was Helen, there was something very unsettling about Helen's very presence. On the few occasions she had come to see Anna in the bookshop it had been a matter of trying to hold on to big piles of books in displays – no other customer knocked them over but Helen would. Like she had actually swept the credit-card machine off the cash desk, breaking the glass on a display cabinet. Like her coat always caught somebody's cup of coffee. Not a restful presence anywhere. She hoped that Helen wouldn't say the wrong thing too often this evening.

What could she say that would be terrible? Well, something about Brendan, along the lines of wasn't it great we forced him to come back . . . Which wasn't the case, but Father would think it was. Or about Father having left Palazzo and working with a terribly nice Paki. Helen was the only person Anna knew who actually used words like Paki and Eyetie. Yes, she could refer to Renata Quigley as an Eyetie.

Anna padded off in bare feet to make herself a cup of instant coffee. Another pleasure and advantage of not living any more with Joe Ashe. It had to be real, the coffee, it had to be freshly ground in a machine that would split your head apart. She would not like to live for ever on her own, but she was daily finding more and more positive things about not living with Joe Ashe.

He had left as good-naturedly and easily as he had arrived. He had kissed her on the cheek and said that she was being very heavy over nothing. He had said he'd miss her, and he had taken quite a few of her records, and a very expensive rug she had bought for their bed. She had watched him fold it, and had said nothing.

'You did give me this as a present, I think?' He had smiled lightly.

'Sure, Joe,' she had said. She would not be heavy over a bedspread. Only about another woman in her bed.

Judy had been very good over the break-up.

'I'm always here, ring me if you feel a bit bleak. I'll listen. Don't ring him out of loneliness, only ring him if you could take him back.'

Friends were great, Anna thought, real pure gold. Friends understood when you got infatuated with people, and didn't mind you going mad for a while, they were still there when the infatuation was over. As it nearly was. Very very nearly.

And she wasn't going to embark on anything again for a long while. Ken Green understood that, he had said that he wanted the smell of Joe Ashe's rather sickly aftershave well gone from the place before he came round in earnest. Ken was very droll. He got on very well with her father too, which was odd, and persuaded Dad and Mr Patel to take a small selection of his paperbacks to display with the magazines, just in case there was a market, he had said . . . and of course there had been. Father and Mr Patel were going to expand. There was an opening for a bookshop in the area. Ken had even suggested that Anna might think of opening one herself, in conjunction with them.

'Too near home,' she had said.

'Maybe you're right.' Ken was agreeable but not in the way Joe Ashe agreed with people. Joe agreed for an easy life, Ken because he had thought it out. She half wished she had asked him to the silver wedding do, but it was far too public a commitment, Mother's friends would whisper, and Grandmother O'Hagan would be bound to want to know everything even though there was nothing to know.

Brendan had arrived in London early, off the boat train in Euston. It coincided with the morning rush hour. He stood watching for a quarter of an hour while the commuter population of that part of London buzzed and scuttled and darted up ramps and down stairs, down to taxi queues, in to grab a quick breakfast standing at a counter, leaping on to escalators. They looked so self-important, he thought, as if whatever petty job they were racing to was important, as if they were people of substance. And this is what his father and mother would like him to be doing, racing down from Rosemary Drive to catch a train to Baker Street, and another tube to somewhere like here. It was a preposterous way to live, and all to be able to *say* to someone that this was success.

Brendan knew he must not spoil his gesture in coming to the celebration by voicing these thoughts.

And he also remembered that Vincent had warned him to buy some proper clothes to wear for the occasion.

'You'll always be able to use a good suit, lad,' his uncle had said.

'Aw no, Vincent, not a suit, I'd never wear a suit for God's sake.'

'Well that's what we wore in my day. But then a jacket and trousers.'

'An anorak maybe?' Brendan had brightened.

'Not an anorak, you gobdaw, not for a big party in their house, a smart dark jacket, navy maybe and light blue trousers. Sure you'll have them hanging out of you at the next dance you go to here.'

His uncle had given him folding money. It was a sacred trust to buy something smart to wear. He had written to Anna, telling her how much he had to spend. He had hoped she wouldn't make fun of him, but he had wronged her even to suspect she might do such a thing.

Her letter was enthusiastic and grateful, she told him that Marks or C and A or any High Street store would have a bewildering selection, and that she was touched and pleased that he was going to so much trouble. She wrote that she herself was going to wear a dress and jacket in navy and white with awful bits of lace trimming on both, because she thought it would please Mother, it looked what Mother called dressy and Anna called yucky but it was Mother's day. Anna wrote how she had told Helen that since Vatican Two nobody expected nuns to arrive in places dressed in sackcloth and ashes, but of course Helen would suit herself, as always.

Maureen Barry came out of Selfridge's and thought she saw Desmond's and Deirdre's son Brendan walking down Oxford Street with a huge Marks and Spencer's bag as if he had bought half the shop.

But she decided that this was ridiculous. There were twelve million people in London, why should she see a member of the family she was thinking about?

And for all she knew the boy might still be in the West of Ireland, there had been some kind of coldness. Her mother had told her that not long before she died. She said that Eileen O'Hagan had said that there had been some great cover-up but the facts were that the son of Deirdre and Desmond had run away, and run of all places back to the very townland his father managed to escape from. The same place that Frank had run from. Maureen told herself to be reasonable. Even if the boy was in London, he would surely be out in Pinner helping to set up tables for the function. She must stop being fanciful and thinking she had this town down to size as she did Dublin. Only that morning at the hotel she had thought she saw Deirdre's mother, in the distance across the dining room, in fact it had been so like her she was nearly going across to say hallo but the woman had been joined by a flashy-looking man wearing a blazer with a big crest of some sort. Perhaps it was the sign that she needed glasses. She smiled, remembering how they had all told each other years ago when coming to work in London that they should get false teeth and spectacles on the National Health, it had seemed a scream to need either.

It was good to be back in London again, Maureen thought, she had a spring in her step and three credit cards in her wallet. She was merely going on a reccy as the film people called it, a little prowl examining the style in other people's boutiques and in the big fashion stores. And if she wanted to she could stop and buy herself any treat she wanted. She walked in a cloud of the expensive perfume she had just bought in Selfridge's, she had bought her father a jaunty cravat there too. He would look well in that, and he would like the fact that she had thought him a cravat man.

Helen Doyle sat in the kitchen of St Martin's with both her hands round the mug of coffee as if to get some warmth from it. It was not a cold morning but not even the bright shafts of sunlight coming in the window seemed to warm her. Across the table sat Sister Brigid, the others had gone. They must have known that the confrontation was coming, they had either gone back to their rooms or gone about their business.

A yellow cat with a broken paw looked trustingly up at Helen. She had found it and made a sort of splint which helped it to walk. The others said she should take it to the cats' home, but this would be curtains for the yellow cat, Helen said. It wouldn't eat much, they could mind it surely.

It was just one more sign of Helen around the house, and another chore. It would be impossible to expect Helen to feed or clean after the cat *all* the time. The cat began a very loud purring and arched its back to be stroked. Tenderly Sister Brigid lifted it up and carried it out to the garden. She came back and sat beside Helen. She looked straight into the troubled eyes and spoke.

'You have so much love and goodness to give,' she began. 'But this is not the place.'

She saw the lip, the lower lip that Helen had been biting nervously, begin to tremble. And the big eyes fill with tears.

'You're sending me away,' Helen began.

'We could sit here all morning, Helen, you could call it one thing, I could call it another. I could say that you must find yourself and what you are looking for in some other surroundings, you will say that I am throwing you out, turning you away from St Martin's.'

'What did I do this time?' Helen looked piteous. 'Was it the cat?'

'Of course it wasn't the cat, Helen, there's no one thing, one incident. Please know that . . . could you *try* to understand that it's not a punishment, not an exam where you pass or fail? It's a choice and this house is our life, we chose it and we have to choose how it will be shared.'

'You don't want me, you've all decided at a meeting, is that it?'

'No it's not it, there was no court passing sentence on you. When you came here in the first place it was on the understanding that . . .'

Helen interrupted hotly. 'In the old days nuns couldn't pick and choose who they had with them, if you didn't like another member of the community that was hard luck, you had to offer it up, it was part of the sacrifice . . .'

'Nobody dislikes you . . .' Sister Brigid began.

'But even if they did, in the old days it wouldn't have been a matter of a popularity contest like it is now.'

'If there were a popularity contest there are many ways you'd come out on top. And anyway looking back on the old days they were bad old days, in the very old days girls could be thrown into convents literally if they were wild or disappointed in love or something. That was a fine way to build a community.' Brigid was firm.

'That didn't happen to me, nobody forced me, in fact they tried to keep me back with them.'

'That's why I'm speaking to you today.' Brigid was gentle. 'Today no false optimism about when you will take your vows. Because you won't, Helen, not here with us. It would be unfair for me as head of this house to let you go to a family celebration in the belief that you were well on the way towards being a nun in our Order. One day you will thank me from the bottom of your heart. Today I wanted you to look at your family with different eyes, look at the other options . . .'

'You mean I'm out today. I can't come back here tonight!' Helen was stricken.

'Don't be so dramatic . . .'

'But when? If you're giving me notice, when do you want my room?' Helen was hurt and bitter.

'I thought that if you could think for a while, don't do any more work, just think, take stock of yourself, and what you might want to do . . .'

'When?' Helen repeated.

'Christmas seems a good time.' Brigid was firm. 'Say two or three months. You should know by Christmas.'

Frank and Renata Quigley planned the day ahead.

'Will I dress up or down?' Renata asked.

'Up as high as you can go,' he smiled.

'But that wouldn't be considered . . . I don't know . . . showing off a bit?' Renata was doubtful.

'Oh, you couldn't please Desmond's wife, if you're too casual you didn't make the effort, if you do make the effort you're overdressed . . .'

'So?'

'So let her have something she'll be glad to have in the photographs. The woman's a monster for snapping this and that. Every time someone farts it's recorded in that place.'

'Frank, really!'

'No, you don't know what they're like. Seriously though, their place is coming down with framed photographs. I remember a wall full of them at least.'

'That's nice in a way.'

'Yes, it would be if there was anything to remember. Anything to celebrate.'

'But you were friends, why do you talk like this?'

'I was friends with Desmond, never with Deirdre, anyway she resented me being free, she was afraid – rightly, I think – that poor old Desmond would feel tied down by comparison. Still we'll dress ourselves up to the nines and dazzle their eyes out.'

She smiled back at him. Frank was so cheerful these days, since they had come to so many decisions. There was the expansion of the business. It was going ahead up North, and it did not mean as Renata had feared that Frank would be away a lot. No, he hardly ever travelled there, her father and uncle did, and of course Mrs East had been very much part of it. Even with the baby boy, she seemed to thrive on work. Some women were able to do everything, Renata thought sadly.

Still, things were good nowadays, and this morning she was going to get injections and vaccinations, shots needed for the journey. Frank would go to work as he did almost every Saturday, he said it was so quiet in the big Palazzo building that he could dictate peacefully and get more done in an hour than he normally did in a week of ordinary days. She reminded him to get a haircut. He was looking a bit shaggy around the neck.

Frank didn't need to be reminded, he would go to Larry and have hot towels as well as a trim. He would wear his best suit, and the new shirt. If Maureen Barry was going to look at him she would admire what she saw. That was why he had asked his wife to dress up too. When Renata had the full works she looked very well. Maureen Barry would not be able to say that the man she rejected had to marry a colourless mouse with money.

Father Hurley had a great place to stay when he came to London, he always described it as a cross between a luxury hotel and a gentlemen's club. It was in fact a religious house, a simple place now where they rented most of their high-ceilinged rooms as office space. Once these had been parlours with polished tables holding copies of *Missionary Annals*. It was an oasis to come back to after a day in such a big noisy city. Father Hurley found the morning a little overtiring, it was good to know that he could come back to this house and have a rest.

His friend Daniel Hayes was Principal, a soft-spoken man who seemed to understand a great deal without having to have things explained in words. He had known last night when he asked after Father Hurley's nephew that this was not an avenue to travel any further. Diplomatically and with the polished ease of years Father Hayes slipped to another topic. Father Hayes also seemed to know that his old friend James Hurley was somehow uneasy about the silver wedding he was going to attend.

'I can tell you, Daniel, you don't know them from a hole in the ground, a nice young pair, she a real product of Dublin Four . . . though we didn't know the phrase then. He was a bit of a rough diamond from the West of Ireland without a penny to bless himself. Anyway the usual story, and she was well and truly pregnant, and I knew the family, *her* family that is, and could I marry them in a flash.'

'And you did?' Father Hayes prompted.

'Well I did of course, what else did we do in those days? Cover the shame, hide the sin, get the thing regularized as soon as possible . . .'

'And did it not work out . . . they are still together?'

'I know, Daniel, it's just that there's something odd there. Firstly they didn't have a child.'

'What?'

'Oh, they did later, three of them. But not at the time. They sort of played at being married, pretended it . . . as if they were taking parts in a play . . . Right, Desmond will play the Husband and Deirdre will play the Wife.'

'I expect a lot of people do that.'

'Yes, I expect they do, and there's ways in which we're playing at being priests. But do you know what I mean? As if the whole thing didn't ring true. Like Deirdre sending me a picture of them all on a picnic or somewhere, blinking into the light, as if she had to prove it to people.'

'Prove what?'

'Lord, I don't know, that they were a normal family or something.'

'They might be just very unhappy,' Daniel Hayes said. 'A lot of people are, seriously. They go into these marriages with such ridiculous expectations. I never thought that all the celibacy bit seemed too much of a hardship to me . . .'

'Me neither,' Father Hurley agreed. His face was sad.

'Of course when it does work, it must be the greatest thing in the world, a friendship so real and true you'd trust the other with your life . . . We never had that, James.'

'No indeed.' Father Hurley still seemed down.

'But your sister had it, didn't she? I remember your telling me that you thought she had a totally good relationship, that they seemed to know each what the other was about to say, and then smiled when they said it.'

'True, but their life hasn't been easy . . .'

Father Hayes interrupted him. 'Of course not, but it's only that kind of relationship we're talking about . . . It would surely buoy them up when things were bleak. You don't see anything like that in this wedding you're going to in Pinner.'

Father Hurley had been successfully diverted. 'No, it's going to be a lot of empty phrases, like it was a quarter of a century ago.'

'Ah, that's what we're here for, James,' laughed his friend. 'If the priests can't put a bit of conviction into meaningless comforting phrases . . . then I ask you . . . who can?'

The caterers arrived at three o'clock. It had all been arranged weeks ago. But Philippa of Philippas's Catering knew a fusser when she saw one, and Mrs Doyle had all the characteristics of someone who could raise a Class-A fuss. There were to be canapés and drinks for an hour or so then the party would proceed to a Roman Catholic church where there would be a Mass, and the Doyles would say aloud that they renewed their marriage vows. Then pink and triumphant they would return to Rosemary Drive, it would now be heading on for seven, there would be more drinks and the guests would be asked to help themselves to a cold buffet – salmon, and cold chicken in a curry mayonnaise. There would be warm herb bread with it. Philippa, having seen the size of the house and the smallness of the oven, had advised against hot food, she had convinced Mrs Doyle that people would most certainly think it was a *real* meal even if it was cold and there were no potatoes.

As Philippa unloaded crates from her van and set up her centre of operations in the Doyles' small kitchen she hoped that someone might have been detailed to distract this woman with the freshly done hair and the obviously new manicure who held her hands awkwardly as if the varnish would chip.

Mercifully a daughter arrived, a sensible-looking girl, dark and intelligent. She was carrying her own outfit on a hanger. Through the kitchen window Philippa had seen her thanking a man who had driven her. The girl had leaned back into the car and kissed him. Philippa liked to see something like that, it made a change in the highly tense homes she often found herself working in.

Still if it weren't for the weddings, the bar-mitzvahs, the silver weddings, the retirement parties, where would her business be? She thought that Mrs Doyle and her husband must both be barking mad to go back into a church and say publicly that they were still married. As if it weren't obvious. As if anyone else would have either of them! However, question it not, just keep unpacking, get the table decoration started, and maybe send in a tray of tea to the bedroom so that the mother and daughter could be kept up there.

'You look absolutely beautiful, Mother,' Anna said. 'You haven't a line on your face, did you know that? You're like a young girl.'

Deirdre was pleased. 'Oh stop it now, you're going too far.'

'I mean it. And isn't your hair great! Very elegant in all those swoops.'

Deirdre looked at her daughter's short dark shiny head of hair.

'Of course if *you* went to the hairdresser a bit . . . just now and then for a nice set . . . you'd look very much better. I know it's smart nowadays to wash your hair every day in the shower . . .' Deirdre was trying to be helpful.

I know, Mother . . . Oh look, isn't this marvellous, a pot of tea . . . brought to us on a tray! *This* is the life, isn't it?'

Deirdre frowned. 'I wish your father was back, he's going to be running late. I don't know what he had to go down to Patel's for . . .'

'It's not Patel's, it's the Rosemary Central Stores, Mother, *and* Dad is the joint owner, *and* Saturday is very busy, so obviously he's going to help Suresh *and* he'll be back in plenty of time. You know Dad.'

'What time's Brendan coming?'

'He should be here anytime. He was looking round a bit, he said he didn't want to come too early and be in the way.'

'Lord, wouldn't you think he'd come . . .'

'And of course he'll be here tomorrow and the next day and the next.'

'And why he couldn't stay in his own home . . .'

'Mother, Brendan's back now, isn't that what we all hoped? He's staying with me because it's easier, handier. He's going to be here every day seeing you.'

'His father could easily have moved all those boxes and files from his room.'

'It's not *his* room any more, no more than *my* room is mine, it'd be pointless having them waiting for us, much better letting them be offices and for filing and everything.'

'Helen's room is still there, and she's off in a convent.'

'It's always wise to give Helen somewhere to lay her head, you never know when she'll need it.' Anna sounded resigned.

'Will I change now, do you think?'

'Why don't you wait a little bit longer, Mother, we'll get hot and sweaty if we get into our finery too soon.'

'I hope it's going to be all right.'

'It's going to be magnificent. Everyone you want is coming to it . . . we don't have to raise a finger . . . they'll all be as impressed as hell.'

'Not that we're trying to impress anyone,' Deirdre said firmly to her daughter.

'No indeed, what would be the point?' Anna asked, wondering could her mother be serious. What was this about if it wasn't to wipe eyes around the place, show Grandmother O'Hagan what style they lived in, let Maureen Barry know that life in Pinner was full of sociability, point out to Frank Quigley that though Desmond hadn't married the boss's daughter he had still done well for himself. Show Father Hurley what a good strong Catholic way of life went on in what he probably thought of as Heathen England. Let the neighbours see what a team they could field, thirty people, and caterers, and speeches and a good non-vintage champagne for the toasts. What was all that if it wasn't intended to impress?

When they heard the commotion downstairs of someone beating on the side door and voices being raised they knew Helen had arrived. She didn't want to come in the front door to inconvenience people so she had been trying to push open the side door, and because boxes of wine were against it she had been having difficulties. She was handed a cup of tea very briskly by Philippa of Philippa's Caterers and pointed upstairs.

Helen came into the room, they knew by the droop of her shoulders that something was wrong. Anna hoped that they might get away without discussing it.

'Doesn't Mother look terrific, Helen?' she cried.

'Great,' Helen said dutifully and absently.

'And Brendan's going to be here any moment.'

'Is he staying here?' Helen asked.

'No, we . . . er . . . thought it would be . . . more suitable if he stayed at my place. He's there now changing, I left the key for him under a plant pot. More suitable, more central, closer to things.'

'What things?' asked Helen.

'Any things.' Anna gritted her teeth.

'So he's not sleeping here tonight?'

'No, he wouldn't even consider . . .' Deirdre was beginning.

'Anyway his room is an office for Dad now, so . . .'

'Is my room an office for Dad?' Helen asked.

'No of course not. Why do you ask?'

'I thought I might sleep here tonight,' Helen said. 'If it's no trouble, that is.'

Anna held her breath. She didn't trust herself to speak. So Helen had decided to leave her convent. And she chose now to tell everyone. *Now*, one hour before Mother's and Father's silver wedding party. Anna fixed her eyes on the two dressing gowns that hung on the back of the door. Father's had a long cord. Perhaps Anna could take this and strangle Helen, or would that in the long run mean further disruption? It was hard to know.

She was saved from having to work it out because Brendan had arrived. He ran lightly up the stairs and his mother and sisters ran to meet him. He looked tanned and well, they thought, and handsome too, in a smart navy jacket, a sparklingly white shirt and a tie with a discreet design on it.

'I got silver colours in the tie, I thought it would be suitable,' he said.

Deirdre Doyle looked at her only son with pride. There would be no need to apologize for Brendan today nor explain him away. Whatever kind of life he was leading in that backwoods, at least he had dressed up today when it mattered. And he was going to be pleasant to people, not hanging back and muttering. She would not have dared to hope for this much.

Desmond came back in plenty of time to wash and change, and at five minutes before the official starting time Philippa was able to pronounce that they all looked magnificent, and that everything was under control.

More and more in her business she felt it was a matter of calming down the hostess and family just as much as preparing a good menu and serving it well.

They stood in their sitting room. The doors to the garden were open, they were ready. With as little comment as possible Anna had found an outfit to suit Helen among their mother's clothes. It was a simple green skirt and a long cream-coloured over-blouse. It was simple enough to have been the nunnish kind of clothes she wore . . . if she wanted it to be. But also it was perfectly adequate as lay clothes too, if that was the route she chose.

Any moment now the guests would arrive. The Doyles had refused a drink from Philippa, saying that they would need to keep their heads clear.

Philippa noticed that there were no private moments between them. They didn't squeeze each other's hands and say: Fancy, a silver wedding! They didn't seem excited in themselves over the event, only that it was being marked.

The first to arrive was Grandmother O'Hagan. Deirdre's eyes raked the taxi to see if she would be followed by Tony. But mercifully Mother had decided to come unaccompanied. And just as she was being ushered in Frank's and Renata's car pulled up. The florist's van arrived with a huge floral arrangement from Carlo and Maria with many many regrets, and warmest wishes on a wonderful family occasion. It had been arranged the previous day by Frank Quigley's secretary who had also left a message with Carlo Palazzo's office noting that it had been done.

And when the Wests next door had peered out and seen the place filling up, they arrived, and they were followed by Father Hurley who had been driven there by his friend Father Hayes.

'Won't Father Hayes come in too and have a drink?' Deirdre Doyle had said. You couldn't have too many priests at something like this.

Father Hayes was tempted just to a sherry, he said it was wonderful in this world where so many people took marriage so lightly to find a couple whose love had survived for so long.

'Well yes.' Deirdre had been pleased by the compliment if somewhat startled by the way it was expressed.

At that moment Maureen Barry arrived.

She must have left her taxi at the corner of Rosemary Drive, she walked easily through the gate and up the little path to the door. The guests were both in and outside the house, it was one of those warm autumn evenings that made it not totally ridiculous to be in the open air.

Maureen seemed to expect all eyes to be on her, yet there was nothing vain or coquettish about the way she came in.

She wore a lemon-coloured silk suit, with a lemon and black scarf. She was slim and tall and her black hair shone as if it were an advertisement for shampoo. Her smile was bright and confident, as she turned with excitement from one to another.

She said all the right things and few of the things that were in mind. Yes, that was Brendan she had seen this morning struggling with a big green Marks and Spencer's bag. Obviously the outfit he was wearing now. Perfectly adequate, but think what a big handsome boy could look like if he had been dressed by a tailor.

Yes, amazingly it *had* been Deirdre's mother that she had seen that morning at breakfast with the rather over-obvious-looking man. Was it possible that the great and esteemed Eileen O'Hagan was having a relationship? How her father would enjoy hearing of that, when she went to Ascot to see him tomorrow.

She kissed her friend Deirdre and exclaimed with pleasure over the wonderful dress. In her heart she wondered how Deirdre could have fallen for the obvious-looking lilac, the matronly garment with the self-colour embroidery at the shoulder. It was a pastel Mother of the Bride outfit. Deirdre deserved better, she could have looked so well. *And* the dress had probably cost a fortune as well.

The Doyle girls didn't look smart either. Helen seemed to be wearing a blouse and skirt, perhaps that was the nearest that the Order could come to letting her wear home clothes. Anna, who was quite striking if she had just left herself alone, was wearing a very tarty-looking navy and white outfit: everywhere there could be a white frill there was one, at the neck, on the hem, at the wrists. It was like a child's party frock.

And Frank.

'How well you look, Frank, it must be years and years,' she said.

'But it's impossible that for you time has stood still,' he said, mocking her tones by imitating her, very slightly.

Her eyes hardened.

'Renata, this is Maureen Barry, she and I played bridesmaid and best man at the great occasion twenty-five years ago. Maureen, this is Renata, my wife.'

'I'm delighted to meet you.'

The two women took in each other's clothes at a glance.

Maureen saw a girl with a nondescript face and well-cut designer garments, carefully made up and wearing discreet jewellery. If that gold chain was what she thought it was Renata Quigley was wearing the price of several houses in Rosemary Drive around her neck.

'Frank tells me you are a very successful businesswoman, and you have high fashion shops.' Renata spoke as if she had learned a little speech. Her accent was attractive.

'He's building me up a bit too much, Renata, two small outlets, but I am thinking of opening up over here. Not in London, more out Berkshire way.'

'I was sorry to hear that your mother died,' Frank said. He lowered his voice suitably.

'Yes, it was sad, she was very lively and opinionated always, she could have had many more years. Like Mrs O'Hagan over there.' Maureen nodded in the direction of Deirdre's mother who was holding forth in a corner.

Renata had moved slightly away to talk to Desmond and Father Hurley.

'Of course she hated me,' Frank said, not letting his eyes leave Maureen's.

'Who? I beg your pardon?'

'Your mother. She hated me. You know that, Maureen.' His eyes were hard now. Like hers had been.

'No, I think you're quite wrong, she never hated you. She spoke very well of you always, she said you were very nice, that one time she met you. I remember her standing in the morning room at home and saying, "He's a very nice boy, Maureen."' As Maureen spoke she re-created her mother's little laugh, the unkind dismissal, the sense of amused wonder.

It was the most cruel thing she could have done.

But he was asking for it, arrogant, handsome and powerful, playing with people's lives, and planning what they would buy and where they would buy it.

'You didn't marry?' he asked. 'There wasn't anyone you could marry?'

'Not anyone I did marry, no.'

'But you were tempted, perhaps a little here and there . . .' His eyes still held hers. They hadn't faltered under her sarcasm, her reproducing her mother's deadly voice.

'Oh Frank, of course I've been tempted here and there, like all business people are. That has nothing to do with being married. I'm quite sure you have found the same in your life. I'd be *very* surprised if you didn't. But to marry and settle down, there has to be a reason for that.'

'Love maybe, or attraction even?'

'Not enough, I think. Something more prosaic like . . .' She looked round and her glance fell on Deirdre. 'Like being pregnant maybe, or else . . .' She looked round the room again and stopped when she was looking at Renata.

But she wasn't quick enough, Frank said it first.

'Like money?' he said blandly.

'Exactly,' she said.

'Not very good reasons, either of them.'

'Well, certainly not the pregnancy one. Even more specially when it turns out not to have been a real one.'

'Did you ever find out what happened?' Frank asked.

Maureen shrugged. 'Lord, I wasn't even told that there was any question of it in the first place, so I wouldn't be told that the danger had passed or whatever.'

'I think she had a miscarriage,' Frank said.

'Did Desmond tell you that?' She was surprised.

'Not a bit of it, but it was their first Christmas in London, and I was in a bit of a bad way, a bit let down and feeling very lost. I asked could I spend Christmas with them, the excuse was Deirdre wasn't well. She looked badly too. I think that's what it was.'

He sounded much more human, her eyes had softened and she felt his had too.

'What bad luck to tie themselves into all this, for nothing, over a false alarm,' she said.

'They may like it, the children could be some consolation,' Frank argued.

They were talking like friends now, old friends who hadn't seen each other for a while.

Philippa was relieved when the party began to decamp towards the church. She had no idea and didn't even want to imagine what went on there, but she knew it was some kind of important landmark for them. Not just to serve food and drink but go back to the same kind of a church where the whole thing had begun. She shrugged cheerfully as she organized the collection of glasses, the airing of the room. At least this bizarre kind of two-tier arrangement gave them a chance to clear up the hors d'oeuvres part of things and let them lay out the salads without interruption.

The church was at a nice easy walking distance, that was why it had been thought a feasible plan. If they had all to get lifts and taxis and sort out who went with whom it would have taken for ever.

They all knelt in a little group, the thirty people who formed the silver wedding party.

It was a perfectly normal Mass, many of them congratulated themselves that they didn't need to go tomorrow since a Saturday-evening attendance was sufficient in these liberated days.

Some like Anna who didn't go anyway did not see the great incidental advantage.

Brendan always found Mass a social event back home with Vincent. He didn't think his uncle believed in any kind of God, but he went to Mass on a Sunday as regularly as he would go to get petrol, or to the marts to buy sheep. It was part of the life they lived.

Helen prayed hard at the Mass so that God would tell her what was right. If Sister Brigid said that she was running away, what was it from and which was the right direction if the convent was the wrong one? If she could have some kind of sign. It wasn't much to ask.

Father Hurley asked himself why did he feel that this was all some kind of charade, almost a television version of renewal of vows? Any moment now someone would say 'Cut. Can we take that again from the top?' He didn't feel this about any other aspect of his ministry. There was just something he didn't like about a public reiteration of something that was said and meant a long time ago. Yet the faithful were always being asked to renew their baptismal vows, so why did he feel uneasy in this instance?

Frank looked at Maureen in the church and thought what a fine-looking woman she was, full of spirit, so like Joy East in many ways. He thought briefly of Joy and of his son who was called Alexander. The son he would never get to know.

It had been thought inappropriate to take pictures at the church. It wasn't as if it were a real wedding, they would look a little ancient to be photographed, Deirdre tittered, hoping that someone would disagree with her.

Maureen did, strongly.

'Come on now, Deirdre, I still have to take the plunge and when I do I'll want banks of photographers outside,' she said.

'And after all people get married at *any* age, any age at all,' Deirdre's mother said, which caused Deirdre's heart to lurch a little.

'And with the way the church is going, maybe even the clergy will get married, Mother, and Father Hurley will be coming down the aisle in a morning suit,' Helen said.

They laughed at that, particularly Father Hurley, who was rueful and said that even if he was forty years younger he wouldn't be able to take on such an undertaking.

And soon they were back in Salthill, 26 Rosemary Drive. The neighbours who had not been invited waved and called out greetings, the lights were on and soon the supper was under way.

'There's a lot of conversation, like at a real party,' Deirdre said to Desmond almost in disbelief.

Her face was flushed and anxious, her hair had fallen from its hard laquered layers and seemed softer somehow. There were beads of perspiration on her forehead and upper lip.

He felt strangely touched by her anxiety.

'Well it *is* a real party,' he said, and he touched her face gently with his hand.

It was an unfamiliar gesture but she didn't draw back, she smiled at him.

'I suppose it is,' she agreed.

'And your mother is getting on well with everyone,' he said encouragingly.

'Yes, yes she is.'

'Brendan's looking in fine shape, isn't he? He said he'd be very interested in coming down to the Rosemary Central Stores tomorrow morning to see how it operates.'

She was surprised. 'He's going to come the whole way across from Shepherd's Bush early in the morning when he could have stayed here in his own room?' She was still peeved that he wouldn't stay.

'It's not his own room, Deirdre, it's the office.'

'There'd have been room for him,' she said.

'Yes, and he will stay some time. But as a visitor.'

'As part of the family,' she corrected him.

'As a visiting part of the family,' he corrected her back.

It was gentle. But the Desmond Doyle of a few months back would not have done it. He would have been too anxious, too willing to play the parlour game of lies, backing up whatever story Deirdre told her mother and Maureen Barry about his mythical prowess at Palazzo, trying all the while to engineer these conversations out of the hearing of Frank or Renata who would know them to be untrue.

How restful it was at last for Desmond Doyle to have his own position, his own place. To be for the first time his own person, not Palazzo's person. It gave him by a grim irony the kind of confidence that his wife had always wanted to see in him, but which would have for ever escaped him in Palazzo land.

'Mother is actually talking normally to Dad,' Brendan whispered to Anna at the other side of the room. 'Does this happen often?'

'Never saw it happen before,' she said. 'I don't want to take away from your sense of wellbeing, but I do think that you have captured a very rare sighting, make the most of it.'

And indeed as they looked the little tableau broke up. One of the caterers was speaking to Mother, there was a slight problem in the kitchen.

'It's bound to be Helen,' Anna said sadly. And it was.

Helen was all for putting candles on the gateau, she had bought twenty-five of them and had rooted through the bottom of the dresser to find old cake tins holding the plastic candle holders. She could only find fourteen. She could not think why.

'Probably because that would be the age at which normal people wouldn't really want any more,' Anna said crisply. 'All right, Mother, go back to the guests. I'll cope with it.'

'It's not a question of coping with it.' Helen was hurt and angry now. 'I was just making a little gesture so that we could be festive.'

Philippa of Philippa's Caterers said that the written agreement had been a gateau with toasted almonds to be applied at the last moment to the cream topping, the toasted almonds to read: Desmond and Deirdre October 1960.

'I think it *is* better like that, Helen, don't you?' Anna spoke as she might have spoken to a dog that was foaming at the mouth or a four-year old who was severely retarded. Ken Green said he spent a lot of his life speaking to people like this, it got you a reputation for being very patient, slightly thick, and a person who could be relied on in any crisis. Anna remembered that Ken always said that the more enraged he was the more slowly he spoke.

'Don't you think we should leave the caterers to it, Helen?' Anna said, enunciating every word very clearly and slowly.

'Oh piss off, Anna, you're a pain in the arse,' Helen said.

Anna decided that they were definitely coming to the end of Helen's term of life in a religious order.

Helen had flounced out into the garden.

'Shall I go after her?' asked Philippa the caterer.

'No, she's probably safer out there, there's no one she can insult beyond reprieve, and not too much she can break.' Anna thought that Ken would be proud of her and wondered why she was thinking of him so much anyway.

Helen sat and hugged her knees in the garden where she had sat, misunderstood and thinking herself unloved, all the years of her childhood. She heard footsteps behind her. Anna no doubt asking her to come in and not to make a scene, Mother telling her not to sit on damp stone, Grandmother O'Hagan about to ask when was she ever going to be professed. She looked up. It was Frank Quigley.

A terror seized her throat and she felt a momentary light-headedness. It was of course impossible that he was going to touch her, molest her in her parents' home.

But he looked so menacing in the dark.

'I heard from your father that you're thinking of leaving St Martin's,' he said.

'Yes. They want me to go, they threw me out.'

'I'm sure that's not true.'

'Sister Brigid says the others don't want me.' She realized as she spoke that she sounded like a child of five years of age with her thumb in her mouth.

'Sister Brigid is far too fond of you to think that, let alone say it.'

'How do you know? You only saw her that night, that awful night.' Helen's eyes had become as big as dinner plates. The memory of the time she had tried to steal a baby for Frank and Renata Quigley, the night that had turned out so badly, and when the real descent had begun in St Martin's.

'No, Helen, I've met Sister Brigid many times since then,' Frank said. 'We didn't speak of you much, we had other things to talk about . . . She was giving me advice. She gave me very good helpful advice, I have you to thank for that.'

'I meant well that night, I really thought it would have suited everyone.'

'It might have, you know, but we couldn't do it that way, always running, always hiding, always pretending. That's not the way to live.'

'That's the way I've always lived.' Helen sounded rebellious and defensive.

'No, no, it isn't.'

'In this house we always pretended, we still are tonight.'

'Shush,' he said soothingly.

'How did you learn to be so upright and not to have to act like the rest of us?'

'I'm not upright. You of all people should know that.' Frank spoke seriously. 'I have done things I am ashamed of, one of them with you. I am very, very ashamed of that.'

For the first time since that day in his apartment Helen Doyle looked Frank Quigley in the eyes. For the first time for many years in any encounter she said absolutely nothing.

'I was always hoping that you would meet somebody nice and somebody young and tender, someone who would put that strange sad day into some kind of perspective for you. Show you that while it was important in one way in many others it was not important at all.'

Still Helen said nothing.

'So I supposed I was sorry when you went into St Martin's, because I always thought then that what happened might appear magnified.'

'I never thought about it again,' Helen said. She looked at him as she told him the lie, her eyes confident and her head held high.

He knew she was lying but it was important that she didn't realize.

'That is so much the right way to be, and it certainly puts me in my place.'

He smiled at her. Ruefully, admiringly. He got it just right. And he could see she was beginning to feel better.

'So what will you do when you do leave, if you're going to?'

'I'll leave. I don't know yet. Maybe I need time to think.'

'Is this the place to do your thinking?' He looked uncertainly up at Salthill, 26 Rosemary Drive.

'Maybe not.'

'Maybe you should go away, right away from London. You're good with children, Brigid tells me, very good.'

'Yes, I like them. Certainly. They don't get as upset as adults.'

'Could you mind one? For a year or two while you're thinking?'

'Do you know one?'

They seemed to talk as equals, her fear of him fell away.

'I do, his name is Alexander. I don't know him but I know his mother. However she and I had a fight and she doesn't like me, if I suggested you she would say no. If she were to advertise, and say if you were to apply . . .'

'Wouldn't it be too much of a coincidence?'

'No, we can do it through Carlo: she asks Carlo about a nanny. Carlo says the daughter of one of his ex-managers, she knew your father.'

'Is it Miss East?'

'Yes.'

'What did you fight about?'

'This and that.'

'Is Alexander nice?'

'I don't know, Helen.'

'But you'd like to know?' She seemed to have grown up in minutes.

'I'd love to know.'

'Fine,' said Helen Doyle. 'I have to do my thinking somewhere, it might as well be with Alexander East.'

The cake was produced and cut. And when everybody had a slice of rich gateau on a plate, Desmond tapped on a glass and said that Frank Quigley who had done the honours so well a quarter of a century ago was going to say a few words.

Frank stood forward, he said that it was a great happiness and a great honour to be asked to speak. He made it seem both. Those who listened felt for a moment that he was lucky to have been invited.

He said that he remembered the day when Deirdre, looking roughly the same as she did tonight, had made this commitment; she was young and beautiful, she had her life ahead of her, there were many decisions to make, many paths to choose. She had chosen Desmond Doyle. Smoothly he brought them from the marriage through the early days of Palazzo, to the joys of children, to their luck in each and all of these children, a daughter rising high in the book trade – Palazzo had tried to poach her, but with no success. Another daughter giving her entire life to looking after people, and a son with a love of the land. These were three rich rewards for Deirdre and Desmond to look at and see their hopes realized.

He himself had not been so fortunate in the early days, he hadn't met anyone he loved until later on in life. His gaze passed gently over Maureen standing cool and admiring in her lemon silk dress. But then he too had known the happiness of married life, though unfortunately unlike Desmond he had not been given the joy of fathering three fine children. But his heart was happy tonight and in no sense tinged with the envy that it might have held over the years. At the weekend he and Renata were going to Brazil, where a legal adoption had been arranged, and where they were going to take home with them and give a home to a girl called Paulette. She was eight months old. Nuns had arranged the papers. She would be very much younger than his friend Desmond's children but he hoped that the friendship would be there always, as his had been. A lifelong friendship, he said. Some things never change.

It had been masterly, there were a few tears brushed away, and the champagne glasses were raised.

Everyone was touched by Frank. Every person in the room.

Even Maureen Barry.

'My God, you are one performer,' she said to him admiringly.

'Thank you, Maureen.' He was gallant and suave.

'No, I mean it. You always were. You didn't have to try so hard, just to prove my mother wrong, to prove me wrong.'

'But your mother loved me, she said I was a very nice young man.' He put on her mother's voice. It was a good imitation.

'I'm glad about the child,' she said.

'Yes, so are we.'

'And will I see you all when I open my shop in England?'

'It will be a time before Paulette will be old enough for your clothes.'

'Oddly enough I'm having a children's boutique too.'

'Well then.' His smile was warm. But not warm enough.

Maureen thought she would discuss it with her father. The old rascal was full of advice. She wasn't going to let drop a prize like this again.

Father Hurley said he wanted to use the phone, but there appeared to be a queue. Anna was speaking to someone.

'Sure, come round,' she was saying. 'Listen to me, Ken Green, this is 1985, we are all free to make our own choices. My choice is that if you choose to be here that would be great.' There was a pause.

'And I love you too,' she said, hanging up, surprised with herself.

Deidre's mother was on the phone next.

'Yes Tony, perfectly satisfactory, no opportunity. No, no, not reneging on anything, but you know the whole art of life is knowing the right time to say things. Yes, yes. Nothing changed. Absolutely. Me too. Lots.'

Father Hurley picked up the telephone to tell Father Hayes that he was getting a mini-cab back, he would be sharing it with several others, a large car had been ordered.

Yes, he said, it had been delightful, he just felt he mustn't take up the phone, other people might be telephoning people to say they loved them.

No, he said testily to Father Hayes. He wasn't even remotely drunk, he had just been sitting listening to a woman and her granddaughter talking on the telephone. That was all.

The move to go was general now. But there was a sense of something not quite completed.

Deirdre found the camera. She had a new film in it all ready for the occasion, she ran into the kitchen where Philippa's team were busy putting polythene on the left-overs and storing them in the fridge. There would even be things for the freezer.

Deirdre explained how the camera worked and Philippa listened patiently. It was a characteristic of this kind of woman that they thought their cameras were complicated.

They gathered around the couple in a semicircle. They smiled. The camera flashed and flashed again.

Amongst the pictures in the roll of twenty-four there would be one which was bound to look good when enlarged, would look just right. There would be the picture of The Silver Wedding on the wall, for everyone to see. Everyone who came to Rosemary Drive from now on.

More books by MAEVE BINCHY available in Arrow . . .

DUBLIN 4

From the bestselling author of *Light A Penny Candle* and *Circle Of Friends* comes this vintage collection of stories set in the heart of Dublin's fashionable Southside.

* A society hostess entertains her husband's mistress to dinner . . .
* A country girl savours the delights of city life . . .
* A student faces the dilemma of unmarried pregnancy . . .
* A drink-ridden photographer tries to relaunch his shattered career . . .

Dublin 4 has all Maeve Binchy's intimate grasp of human feelings, her marvellous ear for dialogue, her subtle sense of the confusion of life. It bubbles over with fun and wit – yet sometimes leaves a taste of sadness.

LIGHT A PENNY CANDLE

'Thank heavens – a thoroughly enjoyable and readable book' – *The Times*

Evacuated from Blitz-battered London, genteel Elizabeth White is sent to stay with the boisterous Irish O'Connors. It is the beginning of an unshakeable bond between Elizabeth and Aisling O'Connor which will survive twenty turbulent years. Writing with warmth, wit and great compassion, Maeve Binchy tells a magnificent story of the lives and loves of two women, bound together in friendship.

'The most enchanting book I have read since *Gone With The Wind*' – *Irish Independent*

'A marvellous first novel which combines those rare talents of storytelling and memorable writing' – Jeffrey Archer

'Brilliant: a remarkable, panoramic and vastly entertaining novel' – Molly Keane, *Irish Press*

THE LILAC BUS

The lilac-coloured minibus belongs to Tom Fitzgerald. Each Friday night it is a meeting place for the same seven people who use it to travel home from Dublin to spend the weekend in Rathdoon. Each one has an inner life unknown to those fellow passengers . . .

There's NANCY MORRIS, a real 'Miss Mouse' who is known for her meanness. DEE BURKE – engrossed in her affair with an unfaithful hospital consultant. And KEV KENNEDY who is a bit of a mystery to everyone including his own family. Then there's CELIA RYAN who regularly returns home to Ryan's Bar to find her mother making a drunken exhibition of herself in front of half the local population. And, of course, TOM FITZGERALD himself has his own reasons for returning home so regularly.

Maeve Binchy once again has conjured up a bunch of human beings with real joys and real sadnesses, and portrayed with her unforgettable warmth.

'Touching, gossipy and as warming as a feather bed'
– *Sunday Telegraph*

'Has a lovely warm heart . . . Her prose is magnificently simple and lucid' – *London Standard*

VICTORIA LINE, CENTRAL LINE

Millions of people travel on London's tube every day yet we usually only give our fellow passengers a cursory glance. But Maeve Binchy manages to infuse these nameless people with absorbing stories to provide an engrossing cross-section of London life.

From Green Park to Brixton, from Shepherd's Bush to Chancery Lane, everyday life is not nearly as mundane as we might think! At Notting Hill, the mysterious secretary, harbouring her secrets, travels to work; at Highbury and Islington Adam has a sudden change of heart; at Holborn a disastrous reunion is about to take place.

With her characteristic mix of compassionate humour and biting realism Maeve Binchy enters the lives of these various travellers with outstanding results.

'Reading these tales is like listening to someone talking: someone you very much want to hear' – *Sunday Telegraph*

ECHOES

Growing up in a small seaside town in the 1950s, Clare O'Brien and David Power shout their hearts' desires into the echo cave, praying that their destiny will lead them far away from the town in which they live.

Years later they meet again in Dublin, where David is studying medicine and Clare has won a scholarship to University College. But eventually Castlebay will draw them back and it is against a backdrop of empty grey skies, sea-spray and wind that this drama of ambition, betrayal and love finally reaches its turbulent conclusion.

'A powerful story of love and jealousy'
SUNDAY TELEGRAPH

'Compulsive reading . . . Ms Binchy has the true story teller's knack' OBSERVER

FIREFLY SUMMER

Firefly Summer is the story of four fateful years in the life of a small, sleepy Irish town, and in particular of the family who run the local pub.

Kate and John Ryan, of Ryan's Licensed Premises, have four children, of which the eldest are Michael and Dara, twelve-year-old twins. The small town in which these children are growing up is peaceful and friendly – an unchanging background for a golden childhood and adolescence, where in long, hot summers, Dara and Michael Ryan and their friends can fish and swim in the river that winds its slow way through the town, or picnic and play in the ivy-clad ruins of Fernscourt, the great house that burned down during the Troubles.

No one in Mountfern, except possibly the lawyer Fergus Slattery, and later Kate Ryan herself, has the slightest inkling of what it will mean for their lives when the ruins are bought by an Irish American with a dream in his heart and a great deal of money in his pocket. Patrick O'Neill's dream is to return, with his two handsome children, to his roots, the village from which once his grandfather was evicted. The money is to transform Fernscourt into a hotel and a tourist attraction for Americans.

To the people of Mountfern, but especially for Dara and Michael Ryan, the O'Neill family is seductively attractive, sophisticated – and, although they don't know it, dangerous. But not until the very end of the complex drama, with its interlocking stories of loves lost and won, hopes raised and dashed, ambitions nurtured and secrets betrayed, will Patrick O'Neill understand the irony and the great significance of his great dream for Mountfern.